# WIZARD'S CREED: THE COMPLETE SERIES

## N. P. MARTIN

DARK WORLD PRESS

# CRIMSON CROW (PREQUEL)

# BACK IN THE DAY: A STRANGER CALLS

*I* had been in Blackham City a total of ten and a half hours before there was a loud knock on the door of the brownstone that I was now to call home, all thanks to my uncle back in Ireland, who bought the building years before to use as a Sanctum. The old place was now mine apparently, and I was free to stay for as long as I liked.

I'd had enough of traveling at that point, and I was tired of moving from one city to the next, whether it was in Europe, Central Asia or South America. I thought it time I put some roots down, lest I become that guy with perpetually itchy feet.

So here I am in Blackham City, a place so steeped in the desperation and misery of those who lived there, it would have made a fine backdrop for the darkest of noirs. "Give it time," Uncle Ray had said. "You'll learn to love it as much as I did."

Yeah right. Which was why dear old Uncle Ray was sitting in a grand Sanctum hidden away in the rolling hills of County Connemara in Ireland, with not a single soul or trace of sickening smog anywhere near him.

A bottle of whiskey was still in my left hand as I used my right hand to fumble with the three locks on the front door, which weren't actually locks but magical seals that I was a bit too drunk to focus on properly. "Three goddamn locks... Christ...there we go, at last."

When I opened the door I was surprised to see a woman staring there, a very gorgeous woman in a figure-hugging white skirt and jacket with large shoulder pads. "August Creed?"

I frowned slightly drunkenly at the woman for a moment. Her sparkling glamor was completely incongruous, given the neighborhood she was in. I hadn't been here long, but East Oakdale was not Upper Manhattan or Sunset Boulevard. More like Brooklyn, I'd say. Certainly not the ideal surroundings for someone who wouldn't have looked out of place on *Dynasty*. Parked on the road behind her was a black limo. A man in a dark suit and even darker stare stood by the front of the limo, hands clasped in front of him, his gaze firmly on me. Clearly, the woman had gotten the wrong address. It was the only explanation for her standing there.

*But she knows my name.*

There was that, of course. Didn't have an answer for that one, unless Uncle Ray had sent her, which I wouldn't have put past him.

*Maybe she's a hooker, one of those high-class types.*

I didn't think so. She just didn't seem the type. Her dark, chocolate-colored eyes had too much knowing in them, too much experience. *One thing is for sure*, I thought as I couldn't help but be captivated by her face, *she's no Sleepwalker*. Supernatural power was in the woman's blood. I could almost smell it on her. A sweet sort of scent, yet laced with something sharper, and with more bite.

Her eyes looked deep into mine as she seemed to size me up. I noticed her nostrils raise almost imperceptibly as she tried to get a scent of me the way a predator would nose the air at their prey. "Is there something I can do for you, Miss..."

"Crow," the woman said, offering her hand. "Angela Crow, and yes, I hope there is something you can do for me, August Creed." She smiled after she said my name as if she liked what she saw, or maybe that was just me, and she was only being polite. The whiskey haze surrounding me made it difficult to tell.

I stood waiting for her to tell me why she was here. She didn't though. Instead, she stared for a moment and then said, "Well, aren't you going to invite me in?"

That's when I realized that Miss Angela Crow was a vampire.

# THE VAMP IN WHITE

*D*espite my travels over the previous six years, I would admit to having little or no contact with vampires. They were a mysterious lot, preferring, for the most part, to keep to themselves. As part of my education as a wizard, I was required to read the lore on every supernatural creature there was, including vampires, just in case I one day ran into one of them. Before leaving Ireland, I had no first-hand experience of any of those beings. Only the information I read in books, information which was often untrue and contradictory, depending on what text you were reading.

I did end up coming across many of those supernatural beings on my travels, though, and found almost all of them to be far more complex creatures, and much more human in many cases, than the textbooks often made them out to be. Not that this made them any less dangerous.

One night while I was walking along a Paris street, early on in my travels, I came across a man in need of assistance. He was lying on the side of the road, seemingly injured, moaning in pain and asking for help. As no one else was around, I went to assist the man, at which point he sprang to his feet at frightening speed and grabbed me in a chokehold before dragging me into a side alley. It all happened so fast that I was caught completely off guard. Once in the alley, the man (who I knew was a vampire by that point) proceeded to sink his fangs into my neck and started gulping down my blood at an alarming rate like an alcoholic chugging from a bottle of spirits. For a long moment, all I could do was stand there in shock as the vamp continued to drain me. I must say, I found the whole experience to be deeply unpleasant, having a parasite attached to my neck like that. It was a gross violation of my body, and it felt like I was being raped.

Then my survival instinct kicked in, and my magic activated, sending out a blast of energy that propelled the blood-drinker across the alley where he slammed into the wall so hard he caved in a number of bricks. I was as stunned as he was as

I stared down at him, still dizzy from the blood loss and the shock of the whole situation, my adrenaline dumping like crazy.

When the vamp sprang up into a crouch, he hissed at me like a cornered animal with his fangs bared and dripping with my blood. Without even thinking about it, I formed a sphere of crackling blue energy in the palm of one hand and held it up as if to fire it at the hissing vamp, who then bared his blood stained teeth at me one final time before scurrying off on all fours like a scampering rat.

Needless to say, since that incident happened, I did my best to avoid all contact with vampires. I certainly didn't trust them. Although I should thank that vampire in a way, because he helped me realize I could protect myself, and that I could rely on my magic to do so. Suddenly, that lifelong wizard apprenticeship of mine back in Ireland started seeming useful instead of just intellectually interesting.

Understandably then, I was a little reticent about inviting Miss Angela Crow into The Sanctum. But I was drunk and a bit tired of life by that point (to be perfectly honest with you), so I didn't care all that much about letting a vampire through the door. Besides which, she had sought me out, and I was somewhat interested in finding out why exactly, even though I knew it had to have something to do with Uncle Ray. There was also the fact that she was beautiful and alluring, and for a vampire, she gave off an enticing sort of scent that I found myself unable to resist.

"Thank you," she said as she walked through the door and past me into the hallway, slowly making her way into the living room, her heels clacking on the hard wood floor as she gracefully moved along. From behind, she was a lithe sort of creature with her white skirt stretched tight over her ass, which jiggled slightly when her heels made contact with the floor. I shook my head at some of the thoughts going through my mind at that moment and walked into the living room behind her. Then I stood and watched as she strolled around the room, running her long fingers over the covers of books, smelling the potion jars, smiling at the books stuck to the ceiling. "I've always liked this place. Haven't been here in a while, though. It's usually more...full when Raymond is here."

I knew it. What are you playing at Ray, cavorting with vampires?

"He shifted most of his stuff out when he heard I was coming here," I said. "I think he's hoping I'll fill it back up with my own stuff."

Angela Crow sat down in the armchair by the fireplace and crossed her legs. Then she sat staring at me until I sat in the other armchair. "So are you going to tell me why dear old Uncle Ray sent you here? If it's a sex thing, I'm not interested." I took a swallow from the bottle of whiskey still in my hand as if to underline my disinterest. Although it was more to do with disguising the fact that I was lying. Vampire or not, the woman was goddess-level beautiful. I didn't imagine any man would turn her down given a chance.

"You look like him," she said, completely ignoring my last comment, making me feel like a fool for even saying it. "A lot younger obviously, but the features are the same. The strong chin, the high cheek bones. Your eyes are a darker shade of gray than his, though. More intense, I'd say. And that thick, dark hair, which surely must be a Celtic thing."

"Ray's hair is gray now."

She barely smiled. "Your youth is adorable."

To my ears, the only thing missing from that sentence was, "...and I vant to drink your blawd." You could say she made me a little nervous, sitting there like the apex predator that she no doubt was. Despite not looking out of her early thirties, I could still smell the centuries of age underneath her eternal youth. I also knew that the older the vampire, the more powerful they were. If I weren't half drunk, I would have been feeling more than a little uncomfortable, even threatened, under her steady gaze.

"Do I frighten you?" she asked, taking me by surprise.

I stared at her a moment, unsure of how to answer before shaking my head. "I'm just not sure why you're here. I only landed in this dump of a city about eleven hours ago. Forgive me if I seem a little put out by your visit. I was expecting to be alone so I could sit and drown my sorrows in this bottle."

"Do you want me to leave?"

"No."

The quickness of my answer didn't escape her, and she smiled that enigmatic smile again. "I intrigue you."

I smiled back. "How could you not?"

"Such charm," she hit back, leaving me unsure if she was being sarcastic or not.

As alluring as she was, I still wanted to know the reason for her visit. What could someone like me—a lost and wandering magicslinger who still hadn't gotten over seeing his whole family get massacred, and probably never would—have to offer someone like her, who likely had everything she ever wanted?

It turned out there was one thing she didn't have at that moment, though.

"I have a daughter," she said. "And she's gone missing. I want you to find her for me, August Creed."

# VAMPIRE'S KISS

*A*ngela Jordan's daughter was named Jennifer, and she was sixteen years old. After many centuries of living, Miss Angela Crow had obviously thought it high time that she had a kid, probably to carry on the bloodline. And by the way that she talked about her daughter, it was clear to me that Angela Crow considered her progeny to be not much more than a possession to be retrieved. A mere tool to be used to further her own aims, whatever those aims were. At that point, her motivations were unclear, except that she needed her flesh and blood back. There was also the fact that full-blooded vampires were quite a rarity in the world (most vampires being made, having been human once). That alone would have made Angela Crow's daughter a valuable commodity.

What was clear, though, was the fact that Miss Crow had obviously attended the same school of parenting as my father. That was the problem with having great power at your fingertips, you see. It made you selfish and completely subservient to its needs and further development. Everyone else was only around to be used in this endeavor. My mother always taught me that people came first and that whatever power I had only existed so I could help others (Miss Crow and my father apparently skipped that lesson, or more likely, completely ignored it). And despite my father trying to ingrain in me the opposite, teaching that power and its gathering mattered most above all other concerns (including people), I usually managed to live my life by my mother's credo, and not by the philosophy my father tried so hard to indoctrinate me with while I grew up under his tutelage. Of course, there was also the fact that my father was a sociopath, which handily helped him ignore the feelings of others.

I suspected Miss Crow to be of the same ilk as my father, possessing the same sociopathy, if only by virtue of being a vampire. Vamps were not known for their bleeding hearts. They preferred to bleed the hearts of others instead.

"So let me get this straight," I said to Miss Crow after taking another swig from the bottle. "Your teenage vampire daughter has gone missing, and despite your probably vast reach and influence—not to mention bottomless resources—you come to me, a lowly magicslinger with no connections in this city and even less experience in finding people, and you want me to find your missing daughter?" I shook my head. "That doesn't make any sense to me at all, even if you did used to fuck my uncle."

I probably shouldn't have said that last part. Something flashed in Miss Crow's eyes, breaking her former eerily calm demeanor, something like anger maybe.

*Great. I've just gone and pissed off a centuries old vampire. Way to go, Creed.*

"Your uncle was never this...disrespectful," she said, a hint of malice in her voice now that made her seem more dangerous than before. "Even at your young age."

*Let's see if I can claw this one back before she claws me.*

"I apologize for that last remark," I said, holding my hands up. "I'm just jet-lagged and more than a bit drunk. I meant no disrespect."

"Do you use hostility to cover your insecurities, August, is that it?"

"Hostility?" I was genuinely shocked. "Of course not. I'm not hostile. Or insecure."

"You know how long I have been alive? One thousand two hundred years. You are a mere child to me, August, and as such, I can see right through you, as I can with most humans. You would do well to remember that. There is no hiding yourself from me."

Things were getting heavy if they weren't before. She was telling me to drop the act, an act I was barely aware of at that time. A front I quickly learned to put on when I first started traveling. It was a defense mechanism, a way to cover my loneliness, a way to stop others from seeing my vulnerabilities. It wasn't who I was before I left Ireland, but it was who I became. Who I needed to be in those days so I could survive in the world.

"All right," I said seriously. "Tell me exactly why I'm your man, and I'll do my best to help you out. Hell, I got nothing better to do in this city."

"You will do more than your best. You will find my daughter."

I shifted in my seat. "Is that a threat?"

Her blood red lips parted as she smiled, and I caught a glimpse of her fangs, which she brought down just for me as vampires kept their fangs retracted usually. "I'm just trying to make you understand that you are involved in this now, whether you want to be or not. Ray said if I gave you a choice that you wouldn't do it, so I'm not giving you a choice."

"I take offense to that," I said, shaking my head. "I would have helped you."

"So if I say that you don't have to, and I get up and walk out of here, never to return. Unconditionally. You would still help me?"

I said nothing. Merely smiled and shook my head. "So why did Ray put you onto me? Did he think I would get bored and that I might need something to do? If so, it wouldn't be the first time he's stepped in on my behalf."

"Partly," she said nodding. "Your uncle wants you to stop running and start using your gifts constructively, instead of fleecing casinos and giving most of the money away to the human detritus that lives on the streets out there. Did it make you feel any better, by the way?"

"Not really. What's the other reason?"

9

"I need someone who isn't known in this city. By a twist of fate, you happen to be such a person."

*Lucky me.*

"And why would anonymity matter so much?"

Miss Crow sighed, and for a brief moment, looked more human—more vulnerable—than before. "My daughter has...run away. If she finds out I have people looking for her, she'll burrow in deeper. There's less chance of that happening if it's you looking for her. She doesn't know you. No one does. Except me now."

Again with the thinly veiled threat. She was so used to talking like that, she hardly realized she was doing it. "May I ask why she ran away?"

"No, you may not."

I shook my head. "You're giving me little enough to go on here as it is. Knowing why she ran—"

"Wouldn't help you much."

*God, she isn't making this easy.*

"Jesus," I said after considering everything in silence for a moment. "I'm not the right man for this. I don't know the city, and I'm certainly not any kind of detective."

"That's not what Ray said. He said you would be ideally suited to this job."

"Oh really? Why?"

"Because you care, he said."

I stared straight at her. "I'm not getting out of this, am I?"

"It's either that or I kill you."

"Ray said that as well?"

"No, August," she said, then crossed the floor in a flash, and I found myself trapped in my chair as she leant down on the armrests and put her face right by mine. "I'm saying that."

Then she bit me. On the lip. Hard. "Shit!" I said, tasting my own blood in my mouth.

Her face was still right by mine, her coffin-wood brown eyes looking right through me as she slowly ran her tongue over her lower lip to lick my blood. "Sebastian has a file outside, which he will give you when I leave. The file should give you enough to get started finding my daughter."

Miss Crow straightened up then and stood tall over me. I noticed a speck of my crimson blood on the collar of her white Gucci jacket, though I decided not to tell her about it (the best idea, I think). She smiled down at me, seemingly satisfied that she had accomplished what she had gone there to do, and without any bloodshed (well, hardly any). "I think you will find, August," she said as she was about to leave, "that after tonight, a whole new path will open up for you. You should be happy you decided to come to this city."

Happy wasn't the word I would have used right then.

Not that I told Angela Crow that.

# THE EYES HAVE IT

*A*fter Angela Crow left, her driver (or whatever he was, bodyguard probably), Sebastian, came to the front door with a manila folder and went to hand it to me. When I gripped the folder to take it from him, he held onto it, his piercing blue eyes intimidating as they bored into me. "Don't fuck this up, kid," he said in a calm, assured voice before letting go of the folder, smiling and walking away. And with those few words, he managed to convey quite clearly that if I did fuck things up, there would be unpleasant consequences.

*What the hell have I just got dragged into? Thanks a lot, Ray.*

Still cursing my uncle, I closed the door and walked down the hall and back into the living room where I tossed the folder on top of the mantel over the fireplace. Then I went to the phone that was hanging on the wall next to the doorway and dialed my uncle's number, knowing before I did so that the bastard wouldn't answer because he would be away on some expedition somewhere. I went through the motions of letting the phone ring several times before slamming the receiver back down. Then I stood there and considered doing a communication spell, which I had done before and which would give me a direct link to my uncle's mind. But I shook my head at the idea as it felt like too much trouble to go to so that Ray could blow off my concerns by telling me the whole situation would be character building and a good experience for me.

Like the time a couple of years ago when he underhandedly set me up to stay in an old mansion while I was traveling through the Romanian countryside, and when I got there, the place was full of ghosts. I couldn't leave the mansion until I had found a way to exorcise the ghosts from the house, which ended up taking me a week to do, by the time I figured it all out using only the knowledge I was taught growing up in Ireland, which thankfully, was quite extensive. Even armed with so much knowledge of spells and supernatural lore, however, I still struggled, and those bastard ghosts put me through the mill before I managed to get rid of them (which is to say, force them into the Astral Plane where they could move on somewhere else). Uncle Ray was like a proud mentor when I next spoke to him after that, even while I was cursing him up and down. There were many more incidents like that during the rest of my travels, of which this latest was just one.

"When the hell am I going to learn not to listen to Ray?" I said aloud, seeking out the whiskey bottle again, finding it on the floor next to the armchair I was sitting in earlier. "'Check out Blackham City, August. It's a great place. You'll have fun there. I even have a place you can stay in. Trust me, you'll love Blackham!'" I shook my head. "Yeah right. I'm here less than twelve fucking hours and already a damn vampire wants me to go all Mickey Spillane and find the daughter who probably couldn't wait to get away from her. Shit." I took a swig from the whiskey bottle, then wiped a hand across my mouth before eyeing the folder on the mantle. Sighing, I walked over to the fireplace, lifted the folder and went and sat down on the creaky leather couch.

I stared at the folder for a moment before opening it, delaying because I knew that when I opened the folder to see what was inside, there would be no turning back. The thing about me is that if I see a problem that grips me even a little bit, I won't stop until that problem is solved, no matter how long it takes. When I was younger, I spent years on certain problems, nearly all of them in some way related to magic and spellcraft. Some of those problems I still hadn't solved and those were always in the back of my mind somewhere, being mulled over unless I drowned out the noise with alcohol, which I had a habit of doing. Ray knew this about me. He knew how easily I was gripped by certain challenges, and that I ended up caring deeply over whether a problem was solved or not.

Finding a missing person was a new one on me, though. As I said, the problems I gravitated towards were mostly of the arcane variety. How to get a certain spell to work. How to control a certain form of magic. Solving the mystery of how something works. Stuff like that. Nerdy shit, if you want the truth, because that's who I am, a nerd obsessed with magic and the arcane. It was who I was raised to be by my family, by my father especially. When that all collapsed, I ran away, but I soon found I couldn't leave my interest in all things magic behind. Even on the road, I would ponder magical problems in my head (which also helped to counter the boredom and loneliness that came with traveling). In every town and city, I sought out libraries and studied books. Not just books on magic or esotericism, but books of all kinds, on every subject that tickled my interest. Learning and studying was all I knew growing up, so it's what I did when I hit the road as well.

And then there I was, in another city, about to tackle a different sort of problem than what I was used to. This one involving people. Vampires. Opening the plain folder, a tinge of excitement hit me at the prospect of what I might find inside, and at the prospect of sinking my teeth (no pun intended) into a new challenge.

"Fuck it," I said with the folder now open in my lap. "What else am I going to do?"

Forgetting about the likely dire consequences of failing the challenge before me, I instead reveled in the delicious feeling I always got upon examining a problem for the first time as I wondered what treasures, intellectual or otherwise, might lie within.

Inside the folder were two sheets of A4 paper. The top sheet was typed upon and contained information on Jennifer Crow, which I hardly looked at before examining the bottom sheet of paper, which held my interest more. It was an exquisite pencil drawing of a girl who I assumed was Jennifer Crow. What stood out most to me in that drawing was not the long mane of thick dark hair or the striking beauty of the girl herself, but the eyes. Whoever had drawn the sketch had done so with consummate skill, capturing the girl's soul in those eyes with barely a few pencil strokes. I was no stranger to an artist's pencil myself (having studied art in my own time during my apprenticeship), but I wouldn't have had half the skill of the person who drew Jennifer Crow's portrait.

Dwelling on the girl's eyes, I saw something there, something that I instantly connected with, though I wasn't sure what. Perhaps a sadness, or a yearning for something just beyond reach. Whatever it was, it made me instantly care for the girl (and almost forget about the fact she was a vampire and had probably killed innocent humans so she could feed on them).

Wherever Jennifer Crow was, I knew I had to find her. Not just because her mother would likely kill me if I didn't, but because my intuition told me the girl needed help. Help that I could give her.

Of course, my instincts about Jennifer Crow could turn out to be completely wrong and the girl could have winded up being a total brat bitch who liked to run away from Mommy (I suspected there was no Daddy on the scene, Angela Crow didn't strike me as the relationship type) just to get some attention and it was all just an oft repeated game of cat and mouse that she liked to play.

But I didn't think so. My instincts were rarely wrong, especially about people. Six years of mingling with every kind of person from all around the world saw to that (if you wanted to stay alive and unmolested on the road, you had to learn to read people).

So it was settled. I would find Jennifer Crow, wherever she was, and I would help her if I could. Hopefully, she wouldn't try to kill me when I did.

I also hoped her mother wouldn't kill me if the help I gave to her daughter weren't to her liking. Obviously, Jennifer had run away for a reason. If I found her, and those reasons turned out to be valid, was I going to just hand her straight over to be thrown back into the strife she tried to escape from in the first place?

Let's just find the girl first, I told myself. After that, we would see what's what. Although my gut was already hinting at future complications. Nothing was ever easy or straightforward in my experience, at least not for me. I had no reason to believe that particular situation would turn out to be any different, if only because of the simple fact that I was involved.

Sighing, I sat back in my chair, took a contemplative swig from the whiskey bottle and then proceeded to think about all the different ways one could kill a vampire.

# 5

# LIKE A VIRGIN

*I*'m not much of a fancy dresser. Hell, I've worn practically the same set of clothes for the last six years as I've moved around the world on my travels (I say travels as if my wanderings had some higher purpose, like self-discovery for instance, when in fact, they were just that—aimless wanderings because I didn't know what else to do with myself). Growing up in Ireland, the dress code was quite conservative, especially in the McCreedy household, where suits and waistcoats were required dress for my brother and me each day. For my sister, it was a plain, shapeless dress that hung to her ankles. On the rare days that our father was absent, we would discard the jacket and waistcoats and roll up our shirt sleeves. Roisin, my sister, would borrow one of our mother's dresses. Those days were happy and free, the days without our father.

But even after leaving all that behind, the dress code still stuck with me, if only because I was used it and try as I might, I didn't feel comfortable in anything else. So I always wore dark moleskin jeans (they last longer than trousers, as I found out on the road), a shirt made from hemp because they last a long time, and a tan colored waistcoat. No suit jacket, though. Instead, I wore a trench coat that was given to me by my Uncle Ray before I left Ireland. The coat was made out of demon skin, and as such was resistant to most things, including bullets and fire. It was a dark green color and looked like thick leather. It also had secret pockets and hiding places all over it, and a stitched-in holster for a pistol, which I didn't carry as I didn't see any need for having a gun when magic had sufficed in every threatening situation I had encountered. The coat gave me comfort, and I felt more secure wearing it, which goes a long way when you are constantly traveling to strange new locales full of unknown threats.

Like Blackham.

It was just after 9.00 a.m. and I was sitting in a local diner having breakfast while I looked over the information that Sebastian had provided me with the night before. The waitress serving me looked like that pop star Madonna, or tried to, as she was too short and plump to pull the look off properly and came across as vaguely sad instead, especially as she looked to be pushing thirty. Not that I was any expert on pop culture (I preferred the comforting heft of an old book to the flimsiness of a record, especially from someone like Madonna, who despite being the world's biggest pop star at the time, didn't interest me one bit, except for the fact that she was so successful, which to me, had to indicate dark dealings somewhere along the line because what other explanation could there be?).

Growing up, my brother and sister and I were pretty much shielded against outside influences, which meant no TV in the house, no radio (except the one my brother kept hidden, but rarely ever got the chance to play) and no newspapers either. It was all about the magic and the studying in our house. I'm sure you can imagine my sense of culture shock when I finally left Ireland. When I hit London, I was left reeling for months as I desperately tried to acclimatize myself to what was nothing short of an alien world to me. Six years later, I still struggled to understand how the world worked and why people were the way they were. Why they all acted so damn crazy most of the time. Therefore, waitress Madonna might have totally got why she was dressed like an overgrown teenager, but I certainly didn't, and I doubted I ever would.

"Pretty girl," the waitress said, smacking on that horrible chewing gum stuff with the sickly sweet smell. She was nodding down at the drawing of Jennifer Crow, which lay inside the open manila folder on the table next to my half eaten breakfast of bacon and eggs. "She your girlfriend or something?"

"My girlfriend?" I said. "A little young, don't you think?"

The waitress batted her false eyelashes and made a not so subtle show of running her gaze over me. "You don't look so old. I love that coat, is that like cyberpunk or something? You one of those? Those guys are pretty intense, though you don't look nerdy enough. Cyberpunks are just nerds really, aren't they, underneath those punk haircuts, which you don't have, and those black clothes, which you don't have either. Maybe you're not a cyberpunk. It's just the coat, I think." She stopped talking, probably because of the utter perplexity that I was looking at her with. "Oh hey, sorry, I was just talking. Sometimes I don't know when to shut up." She laughed a school girl laugh, which had to have been fake. If it wasn't, I pitied her.

"I'll call you when I need the check," I said, turning my attention back to the piece of paper in my hand, hoping the waitress would take the hint, which she did, shuffling off without saying another word. I didn't see her face, but no doubt she was offended. Offending people was like a specialty of mine, largely because I had little or no tolerance for the modern ways of most people. I couldn't help it. Everyone just seemed completely mad to me most of the time. Maybe everyone felt like that about everybody else as well. Whatever. It didn't make it any less true.

I went back to looking over the report (or whatever you wanted to call it) in my hand. In case you're wondering, the report didn't say very much. It gave a detailed physical description of Jennifer Crow, most of which I had already picked up from the sketch of her, except her height (5'8), weight (110 lbs) and eye color (sable, but I already guessed that). She also apparently had a tattoo of a dragon on her back, but as I had no plans ever to see the girl topless, I didn't focus too much on that detail.

What interested me more in the report was the list of places Jennifer liked to hang out in. I was glad to see there weren't many. A couple of bars and a club called Aquarius, which the report described as a "hangout for New Romantics and people who liked to read their desperately dire poetry on stage."

I smiled upon reading that description and wondered who wrote the document. It was cold enough in tone to be Jennifer's mother, but I suspected it was her right-hand man, Sebastian who wrote it. He seemed sneering enough of anything human, including me. He went on to mention the name of some boy (Jasper Conrad) who "was infatuated with Miss Crow" and that "Miss Crow called this miscreant her boyfriend."

Again, I smiled, but this time not at Sebastian's sneering tone, but at the fact that I now understood at least part of the reason Jennifer had run away. Like most teenage girls, there was always a boy involved somewhere, even with vampire teenage girls. Like in that movie I watched the year before in LA, *The Lost Boys*, coincidentally also about vampires. The girl in it, Star was her name, wanted to run away with a human boy. She ended up getting killed, I think. Let's hope Jennifer's story doesn't end the same way, for my sake, if not for hers.

By the time I had finished my breakfast, I had decided to start my search for Jennifer Crow in the few bars that were listed in that report. I could throw her name around, and that of Jasper Conrad's, and see what came up. If nothing else, it would give me a chance to get to know the city a bit better. And who knows, maybe I would get lucky and find Jennifer and her boyfriend smooching in the corner of some dive bar.

There was no point in going to those places yet, however. It was too early in the morning, and given that Jennifer Crow was a vampire, she wouldn't have hung out in such places during the day. So I decided to wait until early evening before I started my search. At least then, I would have been more likely to run into people who worked or hung out at night, and therefore would have a better chance of knowing Jennifer Crow. In the meantime, I decided to spend the day traveling around the city, seeing the sights and gauging exactly what kind of city Blackham was.

I left the money for the food on the table, and as I was walking out of the diner, waitress Madonna said in a girlish voice, "See ya soon, cowboy," and I left shaking my head, wondering what she meant by that in all her arrested development.

# 6

# BLACK IS THE COLOR

*F*rom the little research I had done on Blackham before I got there (a quick browse through a guide book at the airport, which made the city out to be up and coming and culturally significant at the same time), I knew that it was divided in half by the Gadsten River. At the north end of the river, you had Bankhurst, where all the money was. I hadn't seen much of that side of the city yet, except on the cab ride from the airport, which didn't reveal much, except that it was constructed mostly of glass and steel (or so it seemed), and that the people who resided there had money. People like Angela Crow, I would imagine. She was a woman—excuse me, vampire—that appeared used to the finer things in life. The lifestyle and luxuries that only considerable wealth could buy, like a limousine and a driver. No doubt her living quarters were extravagant as hell, probably with a pantry stacked full of virgin girls to feast on whenever she got peckish. It was doubtful Miss Crow did much hunting for food. She probably had lackeys for that. On the other hand, it wouldn't have surprised me if she, in fact, did do her own hunting. Going by our recent encounter, she certainly seemed to have the predatory instincts in spades.

South of the river was Freetown, where I was now based. Going by the old buildings and winding streets, the general look of age and dilapidation everywhere, it wasn't hard to work out that the most unsavory parts of Blackham were located there in Freetown. And judging by the residents I saw as I rode the subway and then started walking down the streets of a neighborhood called Treymont, Freetown had no shortage of miscreants, both human and supernatural. It didn't surprise me that the supernatural fraternity in Blackham seemed to be gathered mostly there, in the darker parts of the city. It was the same in every city I had been in. Vampires may like to play high society, but most other supernatural beings did not. Walking the streets, I saw several different establishments that were clearly hangouts for a certain brand of supernatural. The biker bar ran by werewolves, for instance. The New Age hangouts that were just fronts for covens of witches being another example. In my experience, every supernatural had their own place where they liked to hang out. The one thing each place had in common, though, was that they were invariably located on the fringes, far enough away not to be bothered by the maddening crowd, but still close enough to pick off victims from said crowd.

So it was no real surprise that Jennifer Crow apparently gravitated towards Freetown as her favorite hangout spot. It was classic teenage rebellion really, assuming that I was right about her lavish background. I doubted Jennifer Crow wanted for anything, but she still felt the need to spend her time in a place that seemed to struggle for everything she took for granted. She was basically slumming it to piss mommy dearest off.

In Treymont, I located a bar called The Dive Down Under. Yes, really. It was the first bar mentioned in the report on Jennifer. And going by my first impressions of the outside, it seemed like a Goth's paradise. Its wood paneling was painted black, and a few characters dressed mostly in dark leather hung around outside, though to be fair they looked more punkish (or should that be cyberpunk-ish?) to me thanks to their choppy haircuts and the wraparound sunglasses they were all wearing, even though it was almost dark. Whatever the case, the kids (as they seemed to be) all turned their heads to look at me as I stood staring at the front of the pub like a lost tourist.

"You lost, cowboy?" one of them said, a young guy about eighteen with long, foppish dark hair and who wore a coat that hung down to his ankles.

Cowboy? Really? That was the second time that day someone had called me that, though I didn't know why because I can't say I looked much of anything like a cowboy. Maybe it was just the coat, I didn't know.

"Nice coat," another of them said, leaving me unsure if he was serious or not. With kids, it was hard to tell.

"Thanks," I said anyway, then stopped as I went to walk into the bar. "Listen, guys. Maybe you could help me out."

"You lose your fucking horse or something," the guy in the long trench coat said, and they all snickered, except the guy who said it, who stared my way through his dark wraparound shades, which I guess was supposed to unnerve me or something.

"No, no," I said. "The horse is fine. Tied him up around the corner back there. He's probably eating hay right about now. You know horses. They love the stuff."

All of them stared at me like I was a crazy person, though it was hard to tell through the wall to wall sunglasses. "Get the fuck out of here," the trench coat kid said as he fished out a pack of cigarettes and coolly popped one into his mouth.

"I'm actually just looking for somebody," I said, unfazed by the cold shoulders and wall of cool slammed down in front of me. "Her name's Jennifer Crow. Any of you know her?"

No one answered, but the kid in the trench coat lit his cigarette and then turned towards me, blowing smoke in my general direction. "Like I said. Get the fuck out of here."

I nodded, then smiled.

*So it's going to be like that then, is it?*

I would have walked away, but there was a girl there, small in stature, wearing a black dress with red Doctor Martin boots. The whole time, she was making a show of being bored and looking around her while her friend "dealt" with me, but when I mentioned Jennifer Crow's name, her head snapped around towards me as if she knew the name. Then she quickly looked away again. That was enough for me to deduce that she knew something. If not precisely where Jennifer was, then at least Jennifer herself.

The girl wasn't going to talk to me. Not unless I made her. Ordinarily, I didn't like to make people do things against their will. Just because I knew magic didn't mean I could use it on whoever I pleased to further my own ends like some sociopath. But this was a special case. My life was literally on the line, so if that girl knew something that could help me find Jennifer Crow and save me from being drained dry by a twelve hundred-year-old platinum blond vampire, then I could put whatever qualms I had aside easily enough.

Staring over at the girl (who was still making a point of not looking at me) I inwardly repeated the words to a spell that would basically give me full control over her. She would have to obey whatever I said to her (you can see how this magic thing could get dangerous in the wrong hands, can't you?). "Excuse me," I called over to her. "The girl in the dress. Can you come here, please?"

The girl turned her head towards me, a deep frown on her face, like a subtle force was exerting itself on her, and she didn't understand what it was. Of course, a subtle force was exerting itself on her. My intent, backed by my magic, though she obviously didn't know that, which is why she looked so freaked out when she found herself walking towards me.

"What the fuck?" one of the boys said. "Donna, where the fuck are you going? Fuck that weirdo."

*They're calling me a weirdo? The nerve.*

Donna stopped right in front of me, that same look of confusion on her face as she looked up at me. "I don't want to talk to you," she said. "I don't know why I even came to you."

"That's okay, Donna," I told her reassuringly. "Why don't you just tell me what you know about Jennifer Crow and then you can go back to hanging out with your cool little gang again. Okay?"

She nodded, which caused her to scowl more deeply as she couldn't understand why she was bowing to the whims of a stranger. "Yes."

I smiled. "Good girl. Now tell me what you know."

"Tell him nothing, Donna," one of the boys said.

Pissed off at their interruptions, I gave them my best dark and menacing look, which isn't too hard for me because I tend to scowl a lot anyway as it just seems to fit most situations. The gang all turned their heads away from me after a moment, their former bravado now waned somewhat. Smiling again, I looked at Donna. "Go on, Donna. You can speak now."

Donna shook her head as if she didn't want to, but spoke anyway as she had no choice in the matter. "We hung out a few times, that's all. Sometimes we run in the same circles."

"When was the last time you saw her?"

"Two days ago. There's an old tenement building over in Astoria." She stopped and shook her head like she was fighting against the control I was putting on her.

19

To be sure she didn't break that control, I applied a smidgen more magic to it to tighten things up.

"Go on."

"It's in Amsterdam Street somewhere. A lot of artists hang out there. Jennifer runs with that crowd mostly."

"Do you know what Jennifer is, Donna?" I asked her, lowering my voice slightly. "Do you know what she is?"

"Yeah. She's just a rich girl from Bankhurst. But she's okay. I guess." She didn't seem to know what I was talking about.

"Okay. You've been very helpful, Donna. Thank you." I was about to release her from the spell I had cast upon her when her foot suddenly shot forward and she planted one of her hard, Doctor Martin boots into my balls, dropping me to my knees quicker than a silver bullet drops a werewolf. After that, little Donna of the small stature spun around and charged at her friends before wildly attacking them, screaming like a hellcat as she did so.

"Shit..." I said, wincing from the sickening pain in my testicles.

I should probably explain something here about magic. The thing is, there are a lot of paradoxes attached to magic. One of those paradoxes is this: If you use magic in front of the uninitiated (Sleepwalkers, with no knowledge that magic even exists), then there is a high probability that whatever spell you happen to cast will lead to some unfortunate consequences. The bigger the spell and the more magic being used, the more disastrous the possible consequences. Which is why you had to be careful when using magic in public. Whether or not you chose to use your magic in public was dependent on how badly you wanted results, and at that point, I needed results. I knew there was a possibility that something could go wrong, but since the spell wasn't a particularly powerful one, I had decided to take the risk.

And then the girl I used magic on turned into a hellcat. Not literally, of course, but she was doing a good approximation of one as she swiped and clawed viciously at her friends, who were doing their best to get the hell away from her as they spilled out onto the street screaming and cursing in shock. As magical side effects went, I'd had worse happen, though my throbbing testicles would likely have disagreed.

I stood up and gingerly cupped by balls as if to make sure they hadn't been driven into my body by the force of Donna's kick, which thankfully they hadn't. "Okay then," I said, hobbling away from the pub and nodding at the pile of black, wriggling clothing on the pavement as I tried to ignore the screams. "Good talk guys. Thanks."

Hey, they wanted edgy? They just got it.

7

# KNOCK KNOCK

*I* took a cab to Astoria, so I could nurse my swollen testicles in peace without a subway car full of people staring at me strangely as I made periodic faces of pain and discomfort. That girl had a kick on her, I'd give her that. She was also fearsome when she got started, as I was sure her friends would no doubt attest to when they grilled her on what the hell she was playing at attacking them like that (luckily for them and her, the spell would have worn off quickly). And she would either tell her friends that she didn't know what came over her, or that I was somehow controlling her and making her do things. Either answer would not be satisfactory or consoling to her friends, I was guessing.

You see why I don't like to use my magic too often? Or at least not directly on other people? Shit can happen. Then I end up feeling guilty for the other people involved. Like Donna. She was probably a decent kid. Now her friends would think she was mad. They might even disown her. And all because I needed information. And because my life was on the line, of course. Can't forget that. That gave me some leeway, right?

"Where you headed?" the cab driver asked when I got in.

"Astoria," I said. "Amsterdam Street."

The cabbie, a gray-haired man in his fifties with a gruff disposition, shook his head as he pulled out into traffic. "So which is it then, artist or junky?"

I made eye contact with the gravel-voiced cabbie in the rearview mirror just as another wave of sickening pain traveled up from my groin and into my lower belly. It must have looked to him like I was trying to take a shit in the back seat of his precious cab. "Excuse me?"

"Are you stringing out in the back of my fucking cab? Cause if you are—"

"No! I'm not strung out. Jesus, I'm just in a bit of...pain, that's all."

The cabbie seemed to stare at me a long time in the mirror, which made me nervous because he wasn't looking at the road. "Sorry, buddy. I thought you were a

21

junky. The only people who want to go to Amsterdam Street are junkies and artists. I'm taking it you're an artist?"

"An artist? Of sorts, yeah."

"What's your thing then? Painting? Sculpture? Not that fucking pussy performance art that's everywhere at the minute?"

Could slinging magic be construed as performance art? Possibly. "I'm just looking for somebody there."

"Let me guess. Family member?"

"Sort of."

The cabbie shook his head as he made a right turn into a market street that was full of stalls stacked with fresh food and bootleg clothing. As Halloween was a day away, pumpkins were in abundance, as was the amount of people there to buy them. "Thought so. You wouldn't believe how many kids run to that place like it's a fucking mecca, excuse my French. Who is it, your sister? Brother?"

"Sister," I said.

"She a junky?"

"Yeah. She is." Well, she was. A blood junky.

"I'm sorry, man. I hope you find her."

"So do I."

The cabbie concentrated on the road for a few minutes until we were on the freeway heading for Astoria. "I couldn't help noticing your accent," he said. "Irish, right?"

"Well spotted," I smiled, going through the motions. I'm not big on small talk. It always seems pointless to me, to talk for the sake of it to complete strangers.

"I'm Irish myself, you know. Well, third generation anyway. My great grandparents on my father's side are from Cork. What part you from?"

"Fermanagh."

"That's up north, right?"

"That's right."

"You know, my father told me once that—"

That's about as much as I heard before a sudden stabbing pain in my head made me cry out and grab my skull with both hands. "Jesus Christ..."

"Knock, knock, August."

It was a voice in my head. A voice I knew straight away. Angela Crow's voice. "How are you doing this?"

"What?" the cabbie asked, thinking I was talking to him. "I ain't doing nothing buddy."

"We exchanged fluids, remember?" Angela Crow said.

The stabbing pain finally stopped, and I let out a breathe. "A migraine," I said to the cabbie. "Just give me a minute here."

The cabbie stared at me in the mirror and nodded. "Sure, buddy. Take your time."

"You can enter my head whenever you want now?" I said silently to the vampire in my head.

"Temporarily, yes. We can arrange to make it permanent if you like." She gave a small laugh that echoed unpleasantly around the inside of my skull.

"No thanks. What do you want? I'm out looking for your daughter."

"I need her back by tonight."

"Tonight? Why? I've only just got my first lead. It mightn't pan out."

"Then find another one, August. As long as Jennifer is back in my possession by tonight."

Or what? I felt like saying but didn't. "Your possession?"

"She is my daughter. She belongs to me."

I shook my head at her cold arrogance, a trait that reminded me so much of my father I had to grit my teeth to keep my anger down. "Whatever you say. Why do you need her back so urgently?"

"Do your job, August, and you will find me a generous benefactor. I could set you up in this town, help you network. Introduce you to all the players."

"And why would I need a benefactor? I don't plan on staying here."

"Oh, you will stay, August. This town is made for you. You'll see, but only if you do as I ask of you. If you don't..." She trailed off and I shook my head.

"I don't owe you anything, you know. Not a damn thing."

"Don't be naive, August. You owed me the second you invited me into your Sanctum. The second you set foot in this city. My city."

"And that's really how you work things, is it?"

She laughed again, and I found myself wincing at the sound. "August dear, you will soon learn that this whole town works like that."

A second later, I felt her presence disappear from my head as if she had hung up the phone on me.

"You feeling better there, buddy?" the cab driver asked. "We're in Amsterdam Street now."

"Worse actually," I muttered as I looked out the window just as the cab stopped at the start of a wide street that had a mishmash of houses and tenements running up both sides, with storefronts in between. I paid the cabbie and got out onto the road.

"I hope you find your sister," the cabbie said through the open window as he pulled away again.

"So do I," I said, looking around. "So do I."

# 8

# FRANKLYN

*A*msterdam Street felt like walking into a strange sort of twilight zone. On the one hand, you had all these grimy, dilapidated pre-war houses and tenement buildings that looked like they needed pulling down before they fell by themselves. And on the other hand, you had recently constructed buildings, all shiny and new and looking like they belonged in a different part of town. Most of the new buildings were business premises that sold art supplies and books and records and fashionably used clothing. It was like the Bohemian set had decided to infringe upon a random, drug-addled neighborhood and set up shop there.

The people I saw there seemed to be mostly young, many of them emaciated whips in need of a good meal. It was hard to tell who the drug addicts were and who the so called artists were, since everyone slinking about on that street looked much the same to me, and I guessed this was because there was a lot of crossover between the junk and the art. It certainly seemed that way in similar places I'd been in the rest of the world, where often being an artist also apparently meant you had to be a junky as well. Amsterdam Street appeared no different in that respect.

Donna had said Jennifer was last seen hanging out in one of the tenements, but the problem was, she never specified which one because she didn't know. I nodded to myself, realizing I would have to pound the street until I came across someone who knew Jennifer and could hopefully point me to her or at least the building she supposedly stayed in around there.

As I worked my way up the right side of the street, I ended up trying to elicit information from half a dozen different people who barely seemed to know what day it was, never mind anything else. Thinking to myself that it might prove more fruitful to talk to someone who was on the same planet at least, I crossed the street, my interest spiked by what appeared to be a New Age/Occult type store.

Like every other such shop that I'd seen (and I'd seen many all over the world), this one had the requisite occult tomes displayed in the small window, along with small glass jars and bottles filled with God knows what, artfully placed around some black candles and witchy looking stick figures made out of twigs and twine. From experience, I knew most of those shops sold or procured little of any real occult value. Maybe a few rare books on magic if you were lucky, but that's about it. Most of the time the stores were just gateways so the owners could try to upsell the customers with psychic readings and seances. Such shops were also popular with those who liked to dabble in ritual magic. Hedge magicians as they were also known. Individuals or groups (especially cults) who sourced rituals from old books, sometimes with disastrous consequences, as when they inadvertently summoned dark spirits and got themselves killed. Most did the rituals for the thrill of it, for the taste of danger that came with it. Others took things a bit more seriously, but that didn't make them any less foolhardy.

There's a reason why it takes so long (decades or more) just to get to the point where you can start to get a handle on magic and occult practices in general. Magic as a property is immensely complex and hard to control, even for those skilled in it. Magic never stops being dangerous and foolhardy, even when you know what you're doing. Of course, that didn't stop the uninitiated from dabbling, usually to their detriment. There didn't exist the same respect for magic as their once was. Now anyone who read a book on the occult or who owned a Ouija board thought they could play around with magic.

And so it was that I entered the little occult store with a scathing disinterest in what was on display inside, crinkling my nose at the expected, sickly sweet smell of incense that tried to make me feel like I was walking into some darkly sacred place that was filled with all things strange and dangerous and enticing, when in reality, it just made me feel nauseated. My boots sunk into the plush red carpet tiles as I walked further into the shop, briefly glancing at a bookshelf and recognizing the expected titles from the likes of Crowley, Mathers, and the newest guy on the scene, the Satanist, Anton Le Fey. Such figures were always present in popular culture, having found a way to exploit people's ignorance for their own gain, which was usually money and infamy.

"May I help you, sir?"

A small man in a black suit from a different era stood at the back of the shop in front of a wooden counter, his hands clasped in front of him as he looked at me expectantly with a pleasant smile on his face that didn't mask his apparent curiosity in me, maybe because I didn't look like his usual class of customer. Which is to say I wasn't pale-skinned, sullen and dressed completely in black.

I returned the little man's pleasant smile. "Maybe," I said, fishing the sketch of Jennifer Crow out of my coat pocket and showing it to him. "You know this girl, by any chance? I was told she hangs out around here."

He looked at the sketch for a brief second, then nodded. "She comes in here with her friends sometimes. Her boyfriend usually."

*Finally, some progress.*

"Do you know which building she hangs out in around here?"

The shop owner, who I placed in his late fifties going by the lined face and white hair, looked into me for a moment with his sharp blue eyes. "I'm sensing you're no stranger to the arcane practices. No stranger at all."

I laughed as if to dismiss him. "And you can tell, right?"

He nodded and held out his hand. "My name is Peter Franklyn." I shook his hand, surprised at his firm grip. "And yes, you could say I can tell these things."

Looking harder into him, I saw that Peter Franklyn had hidden depths. Magic of a sort that he kept well concealed. "Let me guess. You're a medium, right?"

A slight smile appeared on his face as he nodded. "That is one of the gifts I am blessed with, yes."

Gifts? I never saw magic as a gift, not with the toll it extracted on the long-term user. I saw magic as more of an addiction, something you couldn't do without after a while. Something you rather wouldn't have at all half the time, as it seemed to bring more pain than pleasure, more heartache than joy. "And what of your other gifts?" I asked him.

Again, Peter Franklyn smiled. "To only be revealed to those in need of them," he said. "You don't seem to be in need of what I have, Mr..."

"Creed. August Creed. And how would you know what I need or don't need?"

That deflective smile again. "Tell me, why are you seeking the girl? You are certainly not one of her ilk. Perhaps you work for her family?"

"Something like that."

Franklyn nodded and went behind the wooden counter, producing a teapot from underneath. "Can I interest you in some tea? It's a special blend of my own. Good for opening the chakras."

"My chakras are open enough, thanks," I said as he went ahead and poured himself one into a small china cup. "You seem familiar with Jennifer. Does she talk to you when she comes in here?"

Sitting cross-legged on a stool, Franklyn sipped from his tea cup and then held it under a saucer in his other hand. "Sometimes. She comes in here after dark, obviously. I keep the shop open late most nights. Many of my customers don't come in until then. The days here are slow."

"I can imagine. What does she talk about?"

Franklyn stared at me a moment. "Do you mean her harm, Mr. Creed?"

"Harm?" I shook my head. "No, of course not."

"It's just you seem to have a deep interest in her."

"Listen," I said, holding up my hands. "Her mother asked me to find her as apparently Jennifer has done a runner from home. I have no interest in hurting her. Although I will admit, she intrigues me somewhat."

"Why?"

"The same reason she does you, I'd imagine. Someone of her background, fleeing to a place like this, no offense."

"None taken."

"It makes me wonder why. It might even make me want to help her."

"Help her?"

"If she needs help, that is."

"And if she doesn't?"

I shrugged. "Then I call mommy dearest to come pick her up."

Franklyn took a long, contemplative breath before placing his cup and saucer on the counter. "I believe your motives are genuine, Mr. Creed, which is why I might tell you where to find Jennifer."

"Might?"

"I'll be frank with you, Mr. Creed. I lost a daughter once, in a horrible accident that haunts me to this day."

"I'm sorry to hear that," I said as I thought of my own dead family members.

"Thank you," he said. "Jennifer reminds me of my dead daughter, enough for me to feel protective of her, vampire or not."

"So why are you going to tell me where to find her then?" I didn't get it.

That enigmatic little smile creased his face again. "Like I said, I have other gifts. Your motives are pure, it seems. I trust you will do the right thing by Jennifer."

"I never planned on doing anything else," I said. "Though I make no promises. There are other factors involved here."

"There always is, isn't there?"

"Look, Mr. Franklyn, it's like this. If I find her, I'll talk to her and see what she wants to do. I'll do my best to help her out. But if I don't find her soon, then her cold-blooded mother is going to flood this neighborhood with vamps, who will tear the place apart, including this shop of yours until they find Jennifer, and I don't think that's a scenario any of us wants to see go down. With me, at least she has a chance."

Franklyn maintained eye contact with me for a long time it seemed, then he nodded. "There is a tenement building at the very end of this street that sits on its own on a patch of waste ground. Jennifer squats in there with her boyfriend, who I don't care for at all, by the way. There are others in the building as well that come and go. I've never visited the place so..." He trailed off just as the phone on the counter started ringing.

"All right," I said, shaking hands with him again. "Thanks for your help, Mr. Franklyn."

"Call me Peter. And do let me know about Jennifer."

"Sure, I'll let you know. Peter."

He picked up the phone and covered the mouthpiece, his blue eyes fixing on me. "My gifts have a darker side, Mr. Creed. I hope you never have to see that side."

I stared back at him a moment, then smiled and nodded.

Franklyn gave me his enigmatic smile once more before finally turning his attention to the phone, and I left the occult shop feeling like I had made a new friend.

# 9

# FIRST CONTACT

*T*he dilapidated tenement building was at the very end of Amsterdam Street where Franklyn had said it was. It sat on its own, back from the other buildings with about twenty feet of waste ground on either side of it, the buildings that once stood there long since demolished. Graffiti, old and new, was scrawled all over the face of the building, and every window had a weathered wooden board over it. The building did appear to have a working front door, though, so I walked up the worn concrete steps and knocked on it. As I waited for an answer, I stood looking around at the neighboring houses. Most of them were in such bad shape it was difficult to tell if they were occupied or not. A few young children were playing ball in the street, so I assumed they lived in there somewhere, the last dregs of the street's longtime occupants, holding on in the face of imminent gentrification from investors looking to create the next trendy neighborhood so they could line their pockets.

There's no stopping progress, I thought to myself, turning my attention back to the front door with the few strips of peeling blue paint on it hanging on for dear life. I had knocked three times already and gotten no response. Not that I expected Jennifer Crow to open the door in the middle of the day, but I half-expected some response from whoever else lived in there with her, if indeed she was in there at all.

After banging the door with my fist a few more times, I finally heard a lock open on the other side of the door and then the door itself was cracked open. "Yeah," said a young but gruff sounding voice through the gap in the door. "What do you want? There's no dope here. Score somewhere else."

The door went to close, and I quickly jammed it with my boot, coming face to face with the person on the other side, who had long stringy dark hair hanging over most of his face. "Hey, wait a minute," I said, trying to sound non-threatening, even though jamming the door open didn't exactly make me seem so. "I'm just here to see Jennifer. Is she here?"

The boy, around nineteen or so, scowled back at me through his hair. "There's no Jennifer here, man. Get your foot away from the door. I have a fucking knife here. I'll cut you man, I mean it."

Jesus, what is this kid wired up on?

"Hey, relax," I said, wondering now if I was going to have to use magic to gain entry. "I just need to talk to Jennifer, that's all. I have something important to tell her. Is she here?"

The kid went quiet for a second as he continued to lean his weight on the door. "You don't look right to me, man."

I doubted anything looked right to him, having just glimpsed how dilated his pupils were, which probably meant he was speeding his tits off. "All right, how about I just take my boot away from the door and we can—"

The door slammed in my face the second I removed my foot from it. "Son of a bitch!"

I stood there shaking my head, looking around in annoyance as I considered what to do next. From what little I got from the kid who answered the door, it seemed that Jennifer Crow was in there. And if she wasn't, it was more than likely that someone in there knew where to find her. There was no point knocking the door again. The psycho kid from before certainly wouldn't be opening it. I could have just blasted the door off its hinges using magic, but that would have attracted too much attention. Besides, the kids playing in the street were eyeballing me, and I didn't want any more magic related injuries or unfortunate accidents to happen just because my magic use was witnessed by Sleepwalkers.

So I did the obvious thing and went around the back of the building where I found the back door to be unlocked (after I stepped through the mounds of garbage leading up to it, that is).

"Idiots," I said, shaking my head as I barged in through the door and into a back hallway that smelled dank and damp, then into a kitchen area that smelled even worse, as if there was a compost heap in the corner somewhere. The place stank to high heaven, exactly how you would expect a place occupied by a bunch of dirty kids to smell. Dusty bulbs in the kitchen and hallway bathed the place in a dull light that did little to take away from the general gloom of the place.

Indeed, it was because of this gloom that I almost didn't see the shadow figure running down the main hallway towards me, something shiny in their hand that I realized a tad too late was a knife. It was the creepy speed freak who answered the door to me a few minutes before. A screech left his mouth as he came barreling into the kitchen and charged at me with the knife pointed at my belly. Surprised by this sudden attack, I was somehow able to whip myself sideways just in time so the blade of the knife glanced off my trench coat instead (I mentioned it was made from demon skin, right? Everyone should have one).

The strung-out kid tried to push the knife through my coat, but the blade wouldn't penetrate, so I took advantage and grabbed the kid's scrawny wrist with both hands before snapping his wrist sharply to the side (after five years of traveling and quite a few violent encounters along the way, I had managed to pick up a few moves which I combined with the advice Ray had given me before I left

Ireland, which was, and I quote, Keep hitting the fuckers until they go down, then run like Billy-o!).

The kid screamed as I violently twisted his wrist, causing him to drop the knife, which clanged onto the dirty broken-tiled floor. The kid hit the floor a second later. "You broke my fucking wrist!" he yelped.

"No, I didn't," I told him, keeping the pressure on the wrist lock as I planted a boot in the center of his chest, just hard enough to keep him pinned. "You would know if I did. You would have heard the bone snap, for a start. And you would be screaming the place down right now, not complaining that I'd broken your wrist when I haven't."

"Who the fuck are you anyway, man? What do you want?"

"Those are good questions."

Questions I was about to answer when another voice sounded from down the hall, and I snapped my head around to look. A lean looking guy was walking down the hallway, dressed in blue jeans and nothing else, tribal tattoos covering most of his arms and shoulders. Long brown hair was swept back from his high forehead. He didn't seem to be particularly put out by my presence as he lingered in the doorway staring at me with intense brown eyes.

"Sorry to intrude," I said, still holding my knife-attacker down. "I'm looking for Jennifer."

"You one of them?" he asked.

"No, but going by that stake in your hand, you're obviously expecting 'one of them'."

The guy, who looked more in his early twenties than teens, fully revealed the wooden stake he had been trying to hide behind his leg. "Who are you?" he asked, pointing the stake at me.

"My names Creed," I said, finally allowing the kid on the floor to get up, which he did, scurrying out of the kitchen like an injured goblin. "I'm here to see Jennifer."

"Why?"

"I'd prefer to tell her that. Who are you?"

"Jasper. Her boyfriend."

I nodded. "Of course, yeah. Well, Jasper, I'm not leaving here until I speak to Jennifer, and since I know she's slumbering in this place somewhere for the next few hours, how about you find us some whiskey and we can go and drink and chat for a while?" I smiled. "How's that sound? And in case you're wondering, I'm not here to hurt anybody. Your paranoid, strung-out mate here attacked me, not the other way around. I'm only here to help if I can."

Jasper stared at me for a long moment as he twirled the stake around with his fingers. Then he motioned with his head. "Follow me."

"Good lad," I said smiling.

# JASPER THE GREAT

*J*asper brought me into the living room at the front of the apartment. The room was medium sized and stank of weed and incense. Thick black curtains provided extra protection from any daylight that might have penetrated the boards outside. The walls were painted a deep purple color that might as well have been black. Light came from the dozens of candles sat around the room, most of which were gathered around the large stone fireplace that still had a few logs inside smoldering away. Above the mantle, attached to the wall, was the skull of a large horned animal, a steer it looked like. Hanging from the horns were various small leather pouches and what appeared to be amulets of the kind you would expect to find in a shop like Peter Franklyn's, the leather pouches probably filled with herbs and whatever else that were supposed to have magical properties but didn't. Same for the amulets. A quick magic detection spell told me that. Nothing more than costume jewelry, although I passed no remarks about it. If people wanted to kid themselves with that stuff, that was their business.

I walked into the room and sat down on a busted leather couch, noticing that there was a magic circle drawn on the floor with red paint. A quick inspection of the symbols painted on the outside of the circle told me that enough of them were genuine to enable some magic to be generated with the right rituals and spells. It made me wonder about the kind of ritual magic being done by Jasper and his friends. In my experience, dabblers in magic only did so out of pure self-interest. They would try to use magic to increase their bank accounts, make someone fall in love with them or maybe even get revenge on someone who pissed them off. In their haste to get what they wanted, they often completely missed the dangers of what they were doing, and they would end up making deals with malevolent entities, or their spells would have disastrous side effects, often resulting in one or multiple deaths.

"So tell me," I said to Jasper as he retrieved a half empty bottle of whiskey from off the mantle, having just found two glasses in the room somewhere. "What's your interest in ritual magic?"

Jasper came and sat down on the opposite end of the couch, filling one of the dirty looking glasses with whiskey and handing it to me, which might as well have been a glass of warm piss as far as my face was concerned, though Jasper ignored my look of distaste as he filled his own glass and then put the bottle on the floor, which was in danger of being lost amongst the forest of bottles already there. "What do you know about magic?" he asked, looking over the rim of his glass at me with darkly hooded eyes.

"Enough to know that it's dangerous." I stared at the glass in my hand for several seconds before drumming up the courage to drink from it, hoping the whiskey would sterilize whatever germs and bacteria were likely crawling all over it.

"Only if you don't know what you're doing."

"You sound confident." Too confident if you'd asked me. Magic likes nothing better than to knock people off their pedestals without them even knowing there was a rope around their necks the whole time.

Jasper shrugged like some rock star with a vastly inflated opinion of himself. "Not everyone knows how to ride the lightning, you know what I'm saying. It takes a certain...talent."

Ride the lightening? Is he serious?

"What kind of rituals do you do?" I asked him.

He cocked his head to one side. "Private ones."

I nodded. "Sure. Private ones. Of course."

A frown appeared on his face as he slowly drank from his glass. "So why the hell are you here...what's your name again?"

"Creed. August Creed."

"Who says Jennifer even needs your help anyway?"

"Have you met her mother?"

"Once, when she came here looking for Jenny. Jenny wasn't here, and her mother threatened to set her guard dog on me if I didn't tell them where she was." He shook his head. "Fucking crazy bitch."

"Did you tell her where Jennifer was?"

He raised his chin. "What do you think?"

"How are you still alive then?"

"You know what an Entrapment Spell is?" He waited a second for an answer and then shook his head as if it was too much to ask that I knew what he was talking about.

If indeed Jasper didn't just run for his life when confronted by Angela Crow, frankly, I was surprised that he was able to pull off such a spell at all. He must have set the trap beforehand, then activated it later, which still would have taken a fair amount of power that for most adepts would have taken years to master. It made me wonder if Jasper was doing deals with low-level demons or other entities in exchange for power. If he was, it was foolish of him and would almost certainly end in him dying or losing his soul. Or both. Most likely both. But I wasn't his keeper and as such was under no obligation to waste my breath trying to warn him of the dangers.

"Does Jennifer play with magic also?" I asked.

"What's it to you anyway, man?" he said, suddenly sitting forward, staring at me like he was trying to scare me with his awesome power.

"Relax," I said. "I'm just doing a job here. Angela Crow asked me to find her daughter and bring her back to her."

Jasper leaped off the couch and stood with his chest pushed out. "Well that isn't fucking happening, so you might as well leave right now."

After placing my half empty glass on the floor, I held up both hands in a supplicating gesture. "I'm afraid I can't do that, Jasper."

"Oh yeah. We'll fucking see about that, then, won't we?" He took a step back and brought his arms around in a very dramatic way, holding his hands as if he was trying to conjure something from midair, at the same time beginning to mutter words that he could only have learned from a spell book, or if someone or something had taught him them.

"What are you doing?" I asked him. "I wouldn't do that, Jasper."

His face had taken on a darkly focused expression as his eyes bored into me, his spell, whatever it was, almost complete.

*Enough of this nonsense.*

Just as I felt the weakly powered magic begin to emanate from him, I held out my hand and used my own magic to block the spell he was trying to cast on me.

"What?" he said, unable to understand why his Gandalf routine had no effect on me.

"I'm blocking your spell, Jasper. You might as well stop now before you pop a blood vessel."

Jasper let out a cry of frustration and then came flying at me with his fists instead. Before his knuckles could bruise my face, however, I switched the focus of my magic and created a minor blast of energy that sent Jasper flying back a few feet before crash-landing on his ass. He got back up quickly but stayed where he was across the room, staring at me with a newfound level of wariness. "What the fuck?"

"I told you to stop."

"Where'd you learn how to do that?" he asked, most of his hostility now replaced by the excitement of witnessing and feeling the effects of a power greater than his own.

"In a place you probably wouldn't have lasted a day in before you cracked under the pressure," I said, thinking of the long hours my father used to force me to practice, and the mental and emotional torture that went along with it.

"Can you teach me?"

*Jesus. Why are people so power hungry these days?*

I hardly knew what to say to him except, "No."

He was about to plead further when a girl's voice interrupted him. "Who is this guy, Jasper?"

It was Jennifer Crow, in the flesh finally. She was standing in the doorway wearing a black lace dress that seemed to suit her more than just about any dress I'd ever seen on anybody except my mother before she died. Jennifer Crow looked even more beautiful than she came across in the sketch I had of her. Even if she wasn't a vampire and didn't have that effervescent beauty that all vamps seem to have, she would still have been beautiful. It was then that I realized why I found myself so taken in by Jennifer Crow, even though I had never met her until then.

33

She reminded me of my dead sister, Roisin. My sister had the same dark, lustrous hair, and the same bottomless eyes. Our mother's eyes.

Before Jasper could spout off any bullshit about who or what he thought I was, I stood up and introduced myself to the girl. "Hey," I said, trying to come across like I was just there to offer my help. "My name is August Creed."

Jennifer stared at me with suspicion. "Did my mother send you here?"

"She asked me to find you, bring you back to her, but—" I held up a hand as I could see she was about to go hostile on me, and as she was a pure blooded vampire (and therefore possessed of frightening speed and strength amongst other things, even at her young age), I didn't want her getting too upset by someone she probably saw as just an extension of her mother, the person she had run away from in the first place. "—I was hoping maybe we could resolve the situation to everyone's satisfaction."

"Oh really," she said. "And just how do you plan on doing that?"

I stared over at her. "Well, I guess that all depends on you, Jennifer."

# BABYLON CALLING

*J*ennifer Crow stared over at me for long moments, quite composed I thought, for one so young...and for one being so rudely awakened from her slumber. She could have been forgiven for being a tad more tetchy about things, but for whatever reason she didn't seem to view me as a threat to her. I wasn't sure if that made the girl a good judge of character, or just plain arrogant, as many vampires tend to be in their dealings with humans. For the sake of peace, and also because I found myself trusting the girl, I chose to believe she saw that I was telling the truth. More than that, it was clear she wanted away from her mother and was desperate enough to hear out a complete stranger who had practically broken into her home (home away from home at least) and assaulted two of her housemates, one of which was her boyfriend.

*Just how bad was this girl's life?* I wondered. *What made her so reluctant to go back home?*

I hoped it was something other than just good ole teen angst. If it wasn't, and Jennifer was acting out for attention so she could piss off her mother, then there would be nothing for me to do except hand her over. I was pretty certain her situation was about more than that, though, as I wouldn't have felt the need to care otherwise, even though I didn't know why exactly I cared yet. I just knew that I did and that I was justified in doing so. Call it magic. Call it intuition. They're one in the same anyhow.

"Jasper, would you leave us alone, please, babe?" Jennifer said to her boyfriend.

"What?" Jasper exclaimed. "You think I'm going to leave you alone with this guy?" He rushed over and stood beside her like some sort of tattooed guardian, even though we both knew he couldn't stop me from doing a single thing. "This fucking dude knows magic, baby. He's dangerous."

"So am I," Jennifer said throwing me a look before turning to Jasper and kissing him lightly on the lips. "I'll be fine. Wait in my room." She looked at me again. "I'm sure this won't take long."

I didn't respond to her comment. Instead, I sat back down on the couch and waited for her to finish reassuring her clueless boyfriend. I say clueless because he was dabbling in things he didn't understand, not even a little bit. If he did, he wouldn't have been doing what he was doing, which was making deals with spirits of the Underworld. Maybe not demons, as I doubt he had the skill or knowledge to conjure one, but most certainly with one of the many dark spirits that haunt the outskirts of the Underworld, souls who for whatever reason didn't quite make it into the Underworld itself and ended up lost and trapped in the fringes. Some of those spirits can be contacted if reached out to in the right way. My father, during my long training, used to make me (and my brother and sister) summon such dark spirits so that we could learn how to control them. I was twelve years old the first time I summoned one of those spirits. It was a terrifying experience and one which never got any easier the more times my father forced me to do it. Quite often, he would take over and command certain things from the spirit, things I wasn't allowed to hear. He even invented a spell to render me temporarily deaf, just to be sure. To this day, I still don't know what he demanded of the spirits. Neither do I care. The point is, Jasper was accepting power from a spirit whose only goal would be to bring him down in some unfortunate way, the endgame being death and the capture of his soul so the spirit could feed upon it (pickings in the dark fringes are meager). What Jasper was clearly enjoying now was a small taste of power that would turn sour soon enough and slowly melt his life away until there was nothing left.

Jasper finally left the room after giving me a final look that said he would be somehow watching me, which I ignored, thinking he might just deserve what was coming to him for being so bloody stupid. When he was gone, Jennifer walked to the red brick fireplace and stood facing me, her dark eyes as steady as her mothers, though not as cold. Nowhere near. "I suppose you think I'm just some spoiled, rich bloodsucker who enjoys running away from home?" she said.

"Maybe, in the beginning," I said, liking how direct she was. I was no fan of beating around bushes either. "When your mother first came to me, that's what I thought. But the longer your mother hung around, the more I understood why someone would want to get far away from her. Then I saw a sketch of you that came with a report. Something about you captured the attention of my...intuition, shall we say."

She raised her thick eyebrows and smiled a little. "Your intuition? Okay. So what did your intuition tell you, August Creed?"

"It's hard to define these types of feelings. Maybe I just sympathize with anyone who has to endure the harsh reality of being controlled by a despot parent."

She shook her head emphatically. "Not controlled. Not anymore. And what would you know about it anyway?"

"More than you think," I said, my eyes firmly on hers for long seconds.

Jennifer nodded. "So you get it."

"I do."

"Did you run away much?" she asked, sitting down on the edge of the hearth, more relaxed now, but still poised to spring if she had to.

I snorted humorlessly. "I'm still running away." That came out more blunt and honest than I expected. For a while there, I thought I had convinced myself that what I was doing wasn't running from my past, but somehow traveling into the future (or stagnating in the present). Whatever the case, I just knew then that the truth was much simpler: I was still on the run.

"I haven't really ran away, you know," she admitted, her demeanor becoming despondent. "I just needed space from my mother and her crazy fucking world. She knows that, but she enjoys the drama of trying to fetch me back home again." She paused and stared at the floor for a second. "The truth is, there's nowhere I could go where she wouldn't find me eventually."

"So you keep moving. Don't let her catch up to you."

Her dark eyes focused in on me. Her look was almost as devastating as her mother's but in a much better way. Certainly not as withering. But powerfully captivating. "Is that what you did? Is that what you're doing?"

I nodded slowly. "Maybe, yeah."

"And how is that working out for you?"

I almost didn't want to answer that. "The demons are never far away, no matter where you go."

"My point exactly."

I smiled. "For one so young, you seem...wise."

"I had to grow up pretty fast, believe me."

"I know the feeling."

She smiled then, warmly, as if she hadn't properly connected with anyone in a long time. Truth be told, it felt good to talk to someone who seemed to understand the way things were. I hadn't discussed my past with anyone but my uncle in the last six years. "So," she said. "What did my mother threaten to do to you if you didn't bring me back?"

"It was pretty clear she would drink me dry if I failed."

She smirked and shook her head. "Crazy fucking bitch. Cross Countess Bathory with Alexis from Dynasty and that would go some way to describing my mother. She didn't get the name The Crimson Crow for nothing."

I laughed. "The Crimson Crow. An apt name if there ever was one, I'd say."

"Man," Jennifer said. "It's not even fucking funny. I don't think I can take centuries more of her craziness. Seriously."

"Are you serious?" I asked her. "If you are, I can arrange for you to disappear. Not even your mother would ever find you. No one would."

She stood up slowly and stared at me hard for a moment. "You're serious."

"You ever heard of Babylon?"

"The ancient city? Yes. If my mother did nothing else for me, she at least got me a good education."

"And did that education extend as far as the arcane and the true nature of the universe?"

"Not really," she said, her brow furrowing as she probably wondered where I was going with this.

"Babylon still exists, but in another dimension. I can arrange passage for you to go there. Your mother would never know."

Jennifer's eyes widened now. "I can hear your heartbeat. You're not lying."

"No."

"Holy shit."

"So are you interested?" It was a rhetorical question as she was pacing back and forth in front of me now, probably considering all the possibilities and ramifications of what I'd just offered her. You might also be wondering at this point, why I wasn't strolling around the great architecture of Babylon myself if I was so desperate to escape my past and the simple reason for that is because I wanted to see this world first before I hightailed it to another. Now that I had seen most of this world, maybe I would consider going with Jennifer to Babylon. I could think of worse people to travel there with.

Jennifer stopped pacing to look at me. "You'd do all that for me?" she asked.

I nodded after a moment. "I would. Just you, though. No Jasper."

She shook her head dismissively. "Forget Jasper. I just hang with him sometimes. He thinks that makes us fucking boyfriend and girlfriend or something."

"All right," I said, standing. "I'll make the arrangements. You'll be going to Ireland first. The only person I know who can get you passage to Babylon is my uncle, and he lives there. In Ireland, I mean."

Jennifer gave me a nervous smile, and for the first time since entering the room, she looked vulnerable, not to mention her age. "Will you be going with me, Creed?"

I shook my head after a moment. "I don't know yet."

And that was the truth.

## 1 2

# PHOTOGRAPH

*T*he timing of everything seemed fortuitous. I had been considering going off-world for a while up until then, and now I had the perfect excuse to do so. But something was stopping me, and I wasn't sure what it was. Clarity maybe. A rare glimpse into the reality of my own existence, one which was, for a change, free from the self-deceit and delusion I had been laboring under for so long, telling myself that staying on the move was the only thing for me to do, despite the emptiness of such an existence.

A truth my Uncle Ray had seen all along. That's why he kept setting up those encounters for me wherever I went in the world, knowing they would force me to go deeper into the reality of my existence as I went about helping people and using my magic skills to do so. Ray knew I didn't have a purpose and that my existence held little of any meaning. Personally, I was mostly fine with that aimlessness, choosing not to care. But then I would end up helping someone on behalf of Ray, and however long the job lasted, I would feel different. I would feel energized, purposeful, like what I was doing held real meaning. In helping Jennifer, that sense of purpose had returned, and I felt once again like I was doing what I was meant to be doing. But I knew, as soon as the job was over, that the old sense of meaninglessness would sink in again, and my feet would start itching once more. Then I would be off on the road again until Ray would decide to maneuver me into doing another job.

As I walked around the Sanctum on Poker Street, exploring the many rooms (and hidden rooms) within—marveling at the amount of arcane material lying around still (left there on purpose, no doubt, by Ray, in his continuing effort to get me to lay down roots)—I realized that it was that sense of purpose I now had which was making me doubt my desire to keep on the move, and to head to Babylon with Jennifer. I also knew that if I did go with Jennifer, it wouldn't be long before she never saw me again because I would be off when I hit Babylon, pounding the roads that would take me to strange but familiar places, exploring cities and out of the way spaces that would ultimately serve only as marker points on my aimless, never-ending journey around the universe.

Sitting on the bare wood floor in one of the upstairs rooms (the room piled floor to ceiling with old books and wooden crates whose contents at that point were a mystery), I came across an old photograph sticking out of one of the books as if it had been left there for me to find. It was a photo I had never seen before, of my mother holding a small boy in her arms, both of them smiling for the camera. The picture was taken outside, in the grounds of the house I was brought up in. I recognized the ancient oak tree in the background (my brother Fergal had tied some old rope to one of the thick branches to make a swing one time, but my father, when he found out, cut the swing down because he said we were abusing the old tree and that it would sour our magic if we didn't stop, though we all knew he only cut that rope because he despised seeing us having anything approximating fun).

My mother looked young and beautiful in the photograph, her fiery red hair tied back, her summer tan contrasting against the white dress she was wearing. Her smile was one of love and happiness, a smile I saw less and less of the older I got. The boy in the picture was me at four or five years old. I was quite small as a child, fragile looking in my short trousers and tan T-shirt. My smile was also one of happiness. This was before my father properly sunk his claws into me and before my at times brutal (but always intensive) wizard training began.

Looking at myself in the picture, I saw a young boy who was wide-eyed with promise, someone who should have gone on to live with strength and purpose. Seeing my mother's face in that photograph—her pride and joy in bringing such potential into being—I could have cried as I imagined how disappointed she would be if she knew how I was living, how I was wasting the gifts I had been given.

And it was a gift, this way with magic that I had, despite being acquired by enduring years and years of pain, suffering, and at times torture at the hands of my main teacher, my father. Despite how it all ended (in the death of my entire family), it didn't change the fact that I possessed something that could be used to help people and that I as a person could help people. If my mother were there, she would have insisted that I take responsibility and live as she had taught me to live (despite my father's never ending stream of indoctrination).

"August, my dear boy," my mother used to say to me. "Life is pointless if you don't use what you have to help other people."

Reaching out, I gently ran my finger over the photograph as if I was touching my mother's beatific face. "I miss you," I said, and a single tear ran down my cheek, which I wiped away.

Putting the photograph into one of the pockets of my trench coat, I took a deep breath and let it out slowly as I wondered what my next move was going to be.

As it happened, I didn't have to wonder too long because the front door banged several times and someone turned up who would decide my next move for me.

# 13

## AN UNFRIENDLY VISIT

*A*s soon as I heard the door bang, I knew it had to be someone from Angela Crow's brood as no one else knew where I lived (at least I didn't think so, though you wouldn't know with my uncle, who could have informed half the city I was around for all I knew). And indeed, upon opening the door, I wasn't surprised to see the wolfish face of Sebastian staring back at me. The vampire was wearing motorcycle leathers and cradled a black helmet in his hand. Outside, dusk had just fallen, the street now bathed in twilight. Sebastian's blue eyes were intense, even though he was smiling at me. "Hello, Creed," he said. "Are you going to invite me in?"

Every word that came out of his mouth sounded threatening to my ears. "No limo tonight?" I asked, looking past him to the red motorbike parked on the street.

"Just me. Can I come in?"

"That depends."

He kept his smile up, but it didn't distract me enough not to notice the flash of irritation in his eyes. "Depends on what?"

"Are you here to threaten or hurt me?"

The vampire shook his head. "That depends," he said, his smile widening. "Have you done something to warrant me threatening or hurting you?"

I smiled back. "Not that you know of."

Another flash of irritation in his eyes. "Well then, I think it's safe for you to let me in, wouldn't you say?"

Staring at him, I eventually stepped to one side and told him to come in. The way I saw it, there was no point delaying the inevitable.

"Thank you." He stepped past me and waited for me to close the door, then followed me as I walked into the living room. I stood by the fireplace as he spent a minute looking around the room with a slight look of distaste on his face like the place was a hovel compared to the grandeur he was probably used to.

"So," I said, eager to get rid of the vampire as soon as possible. "What brings you here? I said I would bring Miss Crow her daughter by tonight when she rudely jacked my head earlier."

Sebastian sat down in one of the armchairs, but not before he had wiped the cushion over first with his hand. His stare was unnerving, I have to say. Eyes like orbs of pure ice. Cold. Emotionless. I couldn't help wondering how many people Sebastian had killed over the course of his lifetime, murdering them in horrible ways before drinking every drop of their blood. Maybe he didn't drink all of them. Maybe he just killed some of them for the sake of it. For the sheer pleasure. Whatever the case, I felt like immediately rescinding his invitation into the Sanctum, just to get him away from me. As it was, I held back, unwilling to come across as hostile or uncooperative, which probably wouldn't have worked out well for me. Or Jennifer, for that matter. "I'm just here to see how things are going," the vampire said, his unsettling grin appearing permanent on his face. "Have you located the girl yet?"

Do I tell him? I wondered. Probably best not to lie. Something told me he would know. Mind reading was not uncommon amongst older vampires, and Sebastian came across like he had been around for a while. "Yes," I told him. "I found her."

He didn't seem especially surprised or pleased that I had managed to track down Jennifer. "Good. Did you speak with her?"

"Yes."

"What did you talk about?"

"Not much."

"Not much?"

"She told me she didn't want to go home."

"Did she say why?"

I shook my head. "No, not really. Mommy issues from what I can gather."

He stared at me for an uncomfortably long time before speaking again. "Mr. Creed, I hope you are not thinking about helping the girl in any way. I hope you know what the consequences would be if you did."

*Shit. Did he just read my fucking mind? Careless. I should have shielded myself when I had the chance.*

I wondered how much he uncovered from digging around in my noggin. "I'm well aware of the consequences."

"Are you?" He stood up slowly, his grin now a predatory sneer. "I don't think you are."

"Look," I said, raising my hands. "Why don't I just tell you where she is and you can go get her yourself? At least then—"

"I already know where she is."

I frowned. "So why—"

"Why send you to look for her?" He took a few steps toward me. "Don't be fooled by the girl's seeming innocence. She can still be formidable when she wants to be. And slippery. Last time I tried to bring her back, she almost killed me. Then she went to ground and wasn't seen again for weeks."

Was he talking about the same girl? Vampire or not, Jennifer didn't strike me as the type of person who could nearly kill a psychopath like Sebastian. But then again, who knew? She was a full-blooded vampire, a direct descendant of a powerful vampire queen. Someone like Sebastian was probably turned at some point, and therefore wouldn't possess the same inherent power. Made vampires were the watered-down versions of the real thing, which made them no less dangerous to most people, myself included. "So you think she'll come quietly with me, is that it?"

"She'd better, Mr. Creed," the vampire said, taking another step forward. The bastard was too close for comfort now. Was he trying to intimidate me? If so, it was working. "Jennifer is royalty, and therefore a future leader of our species. If she were to disappear again, perhaps to somewhere off-world like Babylon maybe…" He paused to watch my reaction, my eyes giving away my surprise, and probably, fear. "You can rest assured that her mother will get mad, and when Angela gets mad, blood is usually shed. A lot of blood. They call her The Crimson Crow. Did you know that?"

"I may have heard it mentioned."

"Do you know why?"

"Not really."

"It's because she plucks the eyes out of her victims, preferably before she kills them. Then she eats their eyeballs."

I nodded, doing a pretty good job (I hoped) of not appearing too rattled by the fact that he had read my mind and saw that I was planning to help Jennifer Crow flee to Babylon. I was still cursing myself for that one. "Look, I get it," I said. "Your queen will kill me."

He snorted. "Not just kill you. She'll make you suffer in ways you could never imagine."

I could imagine actually. Very well. "Shouldn't the choice be down to Jennifer?"

Sebastian shook his head at what he saw as my naïveté for asking such a question. "You don't live in our world, Mr. Creed. Believe me when I say, Jennifer doesn't have a choice in any of this. She knows that already, she just isn't ready to accept it yet. But she will. In the meantime, we put up with her occasional bouts of rebellion."

I felt like telling him that Jennifer seemed to have made up her mind already about her future, but I knew he wouldn't want to hear it. Instead, I told him what I thought he wanted to hear, just to get rid of him. "Fine. I'll bring the girl to you. She'll be here, before midnight. Trust me."

Sebastian stared at me once more, clearly trying to read my intentions, but I didn't let him this time, walling off my mind with magic. When he felt the resistance I was offering, he backed off. "Don't get involved, Mr. Creed," he said, just before he left. "Just do your job, and all will be well."

Somehow, I didn't believe him.

14

POINT OF NO RETURN

*A*fter Sebastian had left, I sat in the living room, staring into the cold grate of the fire as I considered my options. According to Sebastian, I had no options, but that was bullshit. There were always options. Years of growing up solving what amounted to magical puzzles had taught me that there was nearly always a solution to even the most difficult of problems. You just had to figure out the best approach to the problem and then keep prodding at it until a solution revealed itself.

The situation I was currently in was no different. A solution existed that might just resolve things, but not necessarily to everyone's satisfaction, and certainly not without significant risk to myself. The question was, did I want to put myself at risk for the sake of a sixteen-year-old vampire girl that I barely knew?

I could have just ran, of course. I could have fled the city, never to return. Forget I was ever there and continue on with my aimless traveling, maybe to Babylon with the aforementioned vampire girl, or maybe alone, which seemed a safer bet. Thinking about it, though, I didn't fancy looking over my shoulder the rest of my life, waiting for some vampire to trek me down and kill me. Besides which, I didn't feel like going on the road again. I was sick and tired of constantly moving around at that point. My soul was suffering, demanding that I put down roots somewhere. And maybe also, I wanted to become a valid member of society, so I could use my gifts to contribute, to help people. Blackham was starting to seem as good a place as any to do that. It was certainly a place where I could thrive if I wanted to, doing the job my uncle had intended for me all those years, whatever title you wanted to give that job (Magicslinger? Arcane fixer? Occult detective maybe?As in magic He Wrote? You see what I did there?).

The more I thought about it, the more staying in Blackham seemed like a good idea. The only thing was, if I was going to stay, I would have to deal with the

44

vampire situation first, which also meant deciding what I was going to do about Jennifer Crow.

It was time to pay the girl another visit.

* * *

After I had taken a cab to Amsterdam Street (with a thankfully much less chatty driver this time, and one who spent the entire journey listening to a Richard Prior live recording on tape, laughing hard even as he took my money), Jennifer Crow let me into the tenement once I banged on the front door. This time, she ushered me up a flight of stairs and into a bedroom that had a single mattress covered with a few scratchy looking sheets, and candles in bottles placed on the floor amongst scattered items of mostly black clothing, all of which I half expected to see before going in. What I didn't expect was the art that covered every grubby wall in the room. Charcoal drawings mostly, with a few oil paintings in between.

"You did all these?" I asked as I examined the art pinned to the grubby walls. Many of the charcoal drawings were of people, some obviously of those who shared the building with her, others that looked like vampires. The few oil paintings looked surrealist in nature, depicting Daliesque dream images of dark, stick-like figures stalking nightmarish landscapes.

Jennifer looked around for a moment as she stood next to me. "All my own work."

I nodded approvingly. "You have talent."

She smiled, but it was a plaintive smile. "Mother doesn't approve, thinks I'm wasting my time when I should be learning how to become a ruthless bitch like her. Needless to say, I don't get to practice my art much at home. It's why I like coming here, so I can indulge my creativity. Creating these pictures makes me feel like I have an actual soul, you know?"

"Who says you don't have a soul? Your mother?"

"She said vampires don't have souls."

*Cruel bitch.*

"Vampires have souls, Jennifer," I said. "Including you."

She shrugged. "Doesn't feel like it sometimes."

I nodded. "I know."

We stared at each other for a moment, her because she saw some depth of understanding in my eyes, me because I was looking deep into her like I was trying to see the soul she thought she didn't have. Which I was in a way, using every sensory power I had to gauge her essential nature so I could make up my mind about what to do about her. "What?" she asked after my stare went on a little too long for her liking.

"Tell me, Jennifer." I firmly took hold of her strong shoulders. "Are things really that bad for you? Do you really want to disappear? For good?"

She frowned. "You think I'm lying?"

I shook my head. "Of course not. I'm just making sure before going down a dangerous path."

Jennifer took a step forward so that she was standing right up close to me, her dark eyes effortlessly drawing me in. "I may have been born a vampire, but I don't have to live like one. I take no pleasure in cruelty and spilling blood. Innocent blood. I have as much right to live my life as anyone else does."

"Your mother would likely disagree. So would Sebastian."

"Sebastian," she spat, anger showing in her perfectly unblemished face. "That fucking toad. I hate him. He's my mother's lapdog. Nothing more."

"He says you nearly killed him once."

She nodded. "I regret not finishing the job."

"You're not a killer."

"How do you know?"

"Because if you were, I wouldn't be about to help you."

The almost innocent light came back into her eyes. "You'll help me disappear?"

"If that's what you really want."

"It is," she said. "Believe me."

"All right," I said. "Do me a favor then. Get me that bottle of whiskey out of the living room. That's if Jasper the Great hasn't drunk it all in my absence."

Jennifer tittered at that. "Anything else?"

"Yeah," I said. "Sharpen your teeth and polish your claws. I have a feeling you might have to use them before the night is out."

No sooner had the words come out of my mouth when there was loud crashing noise from downstairs.

Like someone had just kicked in the front door.

# TOOTH AND NAIL

*J*ennifer and I looked at each other for a second when we heard the noise from downstairs, both of us knowing that something was up and what that something was.

"Sebastian," Jennifer snarled, opening her mouth just as her fangs came down.

"Shit," I said, my adrenaline spiking as I heard a loud scream from downstairs, a sick feeling forming in the pit of my stomach as I realized one of Jennifer's friends had just met an untimely death.

Jennifer stood listening for a moment, her previously placid face changing with the anger and aggression building up in her. Eyes darkening to a near pitch black, fingernails lengthening, Jennifer looked dangerous now like a panther about to strike. "This ends now," she growled in a low voice, her eyes still on me.

Saying nothing, I barely nodded back at her as I prepared myself for what was to come. I had been expecting to meet some violence at some point that night, but not so soon. Clearly, Sebastian didn't believe me when I told him I would bring Jennifer back to the fold. He must have known I would try to help her, which was why he was chancing confronting Jennifer himself, even though she had nearly killed him when he tried to bring her back before.

Running to the window, I looked out into the semi-darkness and wasn't surprised to see at least a dozen burly looking vampires outside, all gathered around the steps leading up to the building we were in. "There's more outside," I said, wondering how I could best defend myself against that merciless looking lot.

Then I spun around upon sensing movement in the room, and my adrenaline spiked again when I saw a massive bald man dressed in dark clothes standing in the doorway. Opening his mouth, he bared fangs at me and then glowered at Jennifer, who had backed into the middle of the room. The vampire looked around for a second with a look of total distaste on his face. "We've come to escort you home and out of this shithole, Princess Crow" he said in a deep voice.

It was the first time I had heard Jennifer's official title being used by anyone, and it somehow underscored the importance of who she was, at least to her own kin. I also found it interesting to note the differences between the two vampires. As a full-blooded vampire, Jennifer was an evolutionary machine. When her fangs came down they did so to a length not seen in made vampires. Jennifer's fangs where a good inch longer than the vampire before her (who came about through infection, not evolution), and her claws were much longer as well. To me they seemed sharper too. More deadly.

Jennifer's antagonist didn't stand a chance against her, which he surely must have known. I could only conclude he had his orders and that he would die anyway if he disobeyed them. Which made him and the many others like him in the employ of The Crimson Crow nothing more than cannon fodder.

"I don't think so," Jennifer said back, crouched down slightly, both arms out, her lengthy claws ready to strike.

Another scream sounded from the floor above. A girl this time.

"You don't have to kill them!" I shouted, coming forward slightly, my magic already crackling within me as I thought about blasting the vamp in the doorway with it.

But before I could do anything, Jennifer leaped at the vampire in front of her, who was almost twice her size. She became a blur of movement as she went about slashing the bigger vampire with her claws and biting him with her fangs. The other vampire tried to fight back, but he was much slower than Jennifer was and she easily evaded every one of his blows, finally latching herself onto his back and grabbing hold of his enormous bald head. Then, with a shrieking sound, she pulled hard and ripped the vampire's head right off his shoulders, immediately tossing it away like it was mere trash. The head bounced off the filthy carpet and landed somewhere around my feet. I couldn't help fixating on the still open eyes, disgusted by what lay before me, but even more shocked by how awesomely lethal Jennifer had been. Suddenly, I didn't feel as insecure about the situation. I could also fully understand Sebastian's reticence about going after Jennifer himself.

Jennifer stood looking at me for a second, hardly out of breath after her whirl-wind assault on the bald vampire. "I hope you're ready to fight, Creed," she said, before licking a spot of blood from her lower lip.

I nodded at her, realizing fully then that I had chosen the path that I was now on. I could have been moving in the opposite direction by then, avoiding what was about to happen. But even as the fear I was facing rose in me, I was somehow still confident I had made the right decision. No one said putting down roots in a place like Blackham was going to be easy after all. "I'm ready to fight," I told her.

As it turned out, I didn't have to wait long in order to prove my intentions, for a second later, two more vampires burst into the room, the female of the duo locking horns with Jennifer, the other male vampire rushing at me with one hand out ready to grab my throat and rip it out.

Luckily, I was ready. As the vampire came arrogantly forward, plainly seeing me as no threat at all, I shot out the palm of my right hand, so it was level with the vampire's face. Then out of my hand came a beam of almost pure white light that immediately made the vampire stop dead and scream in pain as he covered his face with his arms. As I continued to beam the magical light down on the vampire, I was aware of Jennifer and the other vampire fighting furiously beside me, sounding like two feral cats going at it. As distracting as the tussle beside me was, though, I kept my attention on the vampire in front of me, who was still screaming as the light from my hand caused his skin to sizzle as if it was being exposed to direct sunlight. The light from my hand would not kill the vampire. His pain would ease the second I stopped beaming it onto him, at which point he would try to kill me again, probably just as Sebastian had ordered him to do.

So with my left hand, I reached inside my coat and pulled out the knife that was sheathed inside. The blade on the knife was twelve inches long, curved at the end, as razor sharp as the fangs of the vampire in front of me. Normally, it would take a wooden stake to end a vampire for good, but the knife in my hand was no ordinary knife. It was over a thousand years old and forged by Druids to help kill their many enemies at the time. The Druids wanted a tool that would kill anything they stabbed or cut with it, so they used their magic and alchemy skills to make what became known simply as a Death Knife, for that was its only purpose. To cause death. And on that front, the knife did a very thorough job.

Of course, when I plunged the knife into the chest of the vampire, he didn't know his life was about to end. Staring at me with the same supremely arrogant look on his face even while his skin continued to bubble under the light from my hand, he thought I had stabbed him with an ordinary knife and was about to come forward so he could attack me again. But when he went to move, his face changed as he realized something was wrong. He looked down at the knife still in his chest, then up at me again, his eyes full of shock. That's the thing when you think you're immortal. When someone kills you, it's like the biggest kick in the balls ever as you realize you aren't going to be around forever after all.

When I pulled the knife from the vampire's chest, he staggered back a step and fell to his knees. Then as I watched, the once immortal being seemed to fall apart all at once as if whatever dark force had held him together previously had now vanished, taking with it every ounce of the life it once gave, right down to the very last cell. What remained after the vamp had fallen apart was just a pile of gray dust on the carpet.

"You've done this before." Jennifer stood over the dusty remains of the other vampire whose heart she had ripped out of her chest, and which she still held in her hand as blood dripped from it onto the floor. Two seconds later, the heart turned to dust like the rest of the vampire, the tiny grains flowing through Jennifer's hand like sand in an hourglass.

"No, actually," I said, staring now at the remains of vampire I had killed, then at the bloodless knife in my hand, unsure of how to feel. In the past, I had killed a few full-blown monsters and had banished or obliterated several spirit entities. But never a vampire. It was hard to shake the feeling that I had just killed a person of sorts, a human being, albeit one who was already dead.

"Hey," Jennifer said so I turned my head to look at her. "Process later. We gotta go. Babylon, remember?"

I nodded, bringing my focus back to the whole reason I was there in the first place, which was to help Jennifer escape the evil constraints of her mother. "We have to get out of here then."

As I said it, a voice called from downstairs. "Princess Crow." It was Sebastian. "I have your boyfriend here, Princess. If you don't come down, I'll snap his neck."

Jennifer snarled, showing her fangs. Then she went to the door and shouted down, "If you hurt him, I'll kill you, Sebastian. You know I can."

"It won't come to that if you just come back with me," Sebastian shouted back. "Your mother just wants you home, where you belong."

"I don't belong there! How many times do I have to tell you and her? You're evil, both of you!"

"Fine. I'll snap the boy's neck then."

"No!" Jennifer flew down the landing to the stairs, and I ran after her. As I reached the top, she was already at the bottom, standing in the downstairs hallway. I went down the stairs, pausing halfway when I saw Sebastian standing in the dimly lit hallway, holding a terrified Jasper tight to him, one arm wrapped around Jasper's neck. Behind Sebastian stood two dark-suited men, and behind them, more out on the street.

"Don't let him kill me, Jennifer," Jasper pleaded in a frightened voice. "Please..."

"Let him go, Sebastian," Jennifer said, her tone less aggressive now as if she didn't want to antagonize the older vampire any further.

But Sebastian wasn't even looking at her. He was staring up at me. "Mr. Creed," he said. "I assumed you were dead already."

"You thought wrong."

"That's a nice knife," he said, smiling.

"Why don't you let the boy go, Sebastian," I said. "He has nothing to do with this."

"Neither do you, Mr. Creed. You were only supposed to retrieve the girl, not help her run."

"I didn't ask to be involved in the first place. You and your mistress forced my hand. Now I'm just helping the right person."

Sebastian shook his head. "I knew you'd be the wrong choice for the job. But then, no one listens to me, do they, Jennifer?"

Jasper made a choking noise as Sebastian's forearm tightened further around his throat.

"Don't!" Jennifer shouted. "Wait! I'll go with you. Just let him go, Sebastian."

"I'm not a fool, Princess," Sebastian said scowling at her. "The second I let him go, you'll attack. Which is why Jasper here is coming with us."

Just as Sebastian's smile returned, something happened that I didn't expect. Despite only being half conscious, Jasper's hand flew up as if he was attempting to slap Sebastian in the face. But out of his hand came a weak sort of magic blast that was barely visible such was its lack of potency, though it was strong enough to shock Sebastian into releasing his arm from around Jasper's throat so that Jasper fell to the floor in a heap.

If I'd had time, I would have smiled at Jasper's tenaciousness and his daring use of magic. For a hedge magician, he didn't do too badly. But I didn't have time to think about any of that because I knew I had to act so that Jennifer and I could take full advantage of the opening Jasper had just given us.

Knowing that Jennifer would immediately go for Sebastian, I sent a double magic blast at the two large vampires standing by the front door. A bright sphere of amber energy hit each of the vampires on the chest, sending them flying back through the front door and out onto the steps. Then I telekinetically slammed the front door shut before any more vampires could come pouring into the house (no doubt Sebastian had already issued them all invitations, after one of Jennifer's friends had unwittingly invited Sebastian himself in).

Just as Jennifer predictably flew towards Sebastian, I rushed down the rest of the stairs, stepping over Jasper (who was gasping on the floor) and past the whirlwind of violent motion that was Jennifer and Sebastian. Then I put a ward on the front door by placing my hand on the wood and uttering a few words that would prevent any of the vampires getting through it. If they tried, a blast of energy would come from the door and knock them back.

When I turned around again, Jennifer was on top of Sebastian, lashing her razor sharp claws across his face, back and forth at incredible speed so that the flesh on the other vampire's face became a shredded mess. Nothing that wouldn't heal in time, if Jennifer let him live, that is.

As much as I disliked Sebastian and his cold-blooded ways, I had seen and caused enough bloodshed for one day. There was no need for Jennifer to kill Sebastian as long as she followed the plan I had worked out for her. "Jennifer!" I shouted to get her attention.

Jennifer stopped hitting the unmoving Sebastian and snapped her head around like some carnivore that had been disturbed during feeding time. She stared at me with pure violence and bloodlust in her eyes, and at that moment, I couldn't help but be amazed, and more than a little unsettled, by her complete transformation into a lethal predator, her carnivorous vampire nature at once awesome and truly frightening. The longer she looked at me, though, the more her feral mask began to slip, until eventually the innocent girl's face I was used to seeing came through once more. "What?" she said, her face flecked with Sebastian's blood.

"You don't have to kill him. We should just go."

She shook her head just as Sebastian groaned underneath her. "I made the mistake of not killing him last time. He will keep hunting me."

"It doesn't matter," I said, coming towards her. "Where you're going, no one will find you. I'll make sure of that. Trust me."

Staring hard at me, she considered for a moment. Then she got off Sebastian. "I trust you," she said.

"Good. We need to leave then."

"You're leaving?" Jasper said, sitting up on the floor now, nearly recovered from almost being choked out.

Jennifer looked down at him. "I have to, baby. I'm sorry."

"I'm coming with you," Jasper said, standing up.

"No," I said. "You can't."

"Fuck you!" Jasper snapped. "Who the fuck are you anyway?"

Jennifer went to Jasper then, putting her arms around his neck and focusing her dark eyes on his, her voice taking on a low, soothing quality as she spoke. "Jasper, baby, you're going to forget you ever knew me. You're going to forget everything that happened here tonight. After I kiss you, you're going to go out the back door and go home to your parent's house, and you won't remember any of this. In fact, you will realize how much you've missed your parents, and you will make it up with them. Okay?"

Jasper nodded in a dazed sort of way. "Okay," he said.

Smiling, Jennifer leaned in and kissed Jasper softly on the lips, then she took her arms from around his neck and stood back. "Now go."

Nodding once more, Jasper turned and made his way to the back door before leaving the building. And that was that. He was gone.

"Nicely done," I said. "Not your first time, I'm sure."

"It was the kindest thing to do," she said.

"Yes, it was. You ready to get out of here?"

"How? My mother's goons are outside. They'll bust in here soon enough, once they realize Sebastian isn't coming out."

I went forward and placed my hand on her shoulder. "A new method of transportation I've been working on," I said. "Teleportation."

# 16

# TRAVEL ARRANGEMENTS

*T*eleportation is something that takes a long time to master. You have to manipulate a lot of different strings at once to pull it off successfully. I mean, it involves splintering yourself into a gazillion tiny pieces and then transporting those pieces across space and time so you can reassemble them all afterward. Imagine if you threw a handful of sand as far as you could, and then tried to rearrange that handful of sand into the exact same formation as it was in before you threw it. Every single grain. Does that sound hard? Impossible even? Well, that's the level of difficulty you're up against when you attempt teleportation.

Fortunately, magic is on hand to help out. With magic, one can achieve the impossible after all, but you still need to know what the hell you're doing, and you still need to manipulate the magic correctly, so it does what you want it to do. So it follows your intentions to the letter. That in itself is hard enough to do, never mind anything else.

But enough of my yakking. The point is, I did manage to teleport both Jennifer and me away from the tenement in Amsterdam Street, landing us both seemingly intact just a few blocks away, next to a dumpster in some alley. A drunken homeless guy at the end of the alley sat up and stared for a moment, then lay back down again as he probably thought he was seeing things.

"Holy shit!" Jennifer said. "I thought moving fast was a rush. That was like...I don't know what that was like. I feel like I was blown up and then put back together again." She checked herself over as if to make sure everything was still intact.

"This is as far as I could manage," I said, looking around. "Any further and I think we would have come out of it like mutants."

"Mutants?"

"Yeah, as if a child had reassembled their doll in the wrong way. Something like that. Not pretty anyway."

"So what now?" Jennifer asked, seemingly enjoying the experience of her getaway.

"Now we grab a cab and get you to the airport. My uncle passed along a contact of his who owns a private jet, should I ever need to get somewhere in a hurry. I'll make the necessary arrangements so you can fly to Ireland. My Uncle Ray will take care of you once you're there. He'll arrange your passage to Babylon."

Jennifer frowned. "You're not coming with me?"

I was mildly touched that she seemed somewhat disappointed that I wasn't going to Ireland with her. "I've decided to stay here," I told her.

"But you can't. My mother will kill you."

I shrugged. "That's a chance I'll have to take. I'm tired of running, and there's something about this city that's making me want to stay."

"This city is dangerous."

"I know. Maybe that's why I'm staying."

She shook her head. "You must be mad. You'll be committing suicide if you stay here, trust me."

Her words weren't lost on me. "It doesn't feel that way to me. And besides, you might have noticed I'm not completely powerless."

"My mother is a bloodthirsty demon, seriously."

"Let me worry about your mother," I said, directing her down the alley now towards the street. "Right now, we need to get you to the airport before the wrong eyes see us."

* * *

After taking a cab to the airport, I left Jennifer in a dark corner inside one of the bars while I found a phone so I could begin making her travel arrangements. The one thing I was worried about was not being able to contact my uncle, who was often out of the country on wizard business. If he didn't answer his phone at home, I would have to try and establish a psychic link with him. And depending on where in the world he was, that could take some time. Plus I needed quiet and privacy to do it, which wouldn't have been easy to find in a noisy airport.

My luck was in, however, as Uncle Ray answered the phone when I called his house in Ireland. "Ray, it's August," I said, my eyes flitting around the airport in search of vampires, thankfully seeing none.

"August, my boy!" Ray said. "It's good to hear from you. Where are you?"

"You know full well I'm in Blackham City, Ray. You directed me here in your not so subtle way, remember?"

Ray laughed like he laughed at everything. It was like he'd been around for so long that he had now dispensed with the need to take anything seriously as if everything was just one big cosmic joke to him now. "I do remember."

"And before we go any further here, thanks for sending that The Crimson Crow to my door. I'm in fucking deep shit with that bitch now."

"Who said I sent anyone to you?"

"She did, so don't even try and deny it, Ray. Like you try to deny all of these little tests that you somehow arrange for me no matter where I am in the world." Ray laughed again, and I shook my head at him. "I'm glad you think it's funny."

"Oh, August, everything is funny, lad. You'll see that one day. But in the meantime, why don't you explain to me the nature of the deep shit you're in?

I went on to explain everything to him, about Jennifer, about the plan to send her to Babylon and about the almighty bitch-fit her mother would take when she found out about it all. "She'll make me suffer, of that I've no doubt," I said, referring to The Crimson Crow.

"Can you handle a vampire like that?" Ray asked casually as if asking if I could handle doing my own tax returns (if I actually paid tax, that was).

"She's over a thousand years old."

Ray went silent for a moment. "Tell me, August. Why aren't you getting on that plane with the girl? Why are you choosing to stay?"

I almost didn't want to tell him, so that I didn't have to hear his satisfied laughter. "I'm tired of traveling, and I want to help people. Your plan worked, Ray. It's the only purpose in life I can find."

"And a damn good one, my boy," he said seriously. "Your mother would be proud."

I closed my eyes for a second when he mentioned my mother, emotion welling up in me out of nowhere. "Yeah," I said quietly. "I'm sure she would be."

"Get the girl on the plane. I'll take care of the rest." He paused. "As for that other problem."

"The one where I might die?"

"That's the one. Just remember, a vampire like The Crimson Crow only cares about power, even above her own daughter or someone betraying her. Show her the way to more power, and she should leave you alone."

"Should?"

"One never knows with these situations."

"That's reassuring."

Ray laughed. "I have faith in you, boy. I've always had faith in you."

I nodded. "I know you have, Ray."

"And August?" he said before he hung up.

"What?"

"I'm proud of you as well. Always have been."

I couldn't help smiling. "Thanks, Ray."

## 17

FAREWELLS

*A*s I was about to walk Jennifer Crow out onto the runway where the private jet awaited, the young vampire girl stopped and turned to me. Her normally confident demeanor was now riddled with anxiety it seemed, and I knew why before she even said anything. I had a very similar moment with my Uncle Ray before I left Ireland six years ago. Despite the fact that my family was dead and all I had was an empty house and an obscene amount of money that I didn't want or need, there still felt like there was something in me that didn't want to let go of everything I had ever known. Yes, my life up until that point had been filled with sacrifice and pain, and also tragedy at the end, but it was all still hard to walk away from. It felt like if I did walk, I would have been committing some huge act of betrayal that I would never be able to come back from. A betrayal against who or what, I wasn't really sure. But as Ray soon explained, what I felt was fear. Fear of the unknown, of what lay ahead of me. And the pain of separation also, from the roots that ran deep in the place of my birth.

"It's all about you now, boy," Ray had said, placing his hands on my shoulders and smiling like a father whose son was about to leave and make his way in the world. There was pride in his smile, something I never saw in father's smile, even if the bastard had smiled at all. "Go out into the world and find your place in it. It's your right to do so. Never forget that."

Now, with Jennifer looking at me with her lost puppy eyes, I placed my hands gently on her shoulders and told her what my uncle had told me. "You're doing the right thing," I said, smiling. "It's your life. You can live it how you want."

Jennifer smiled back. "My mother would disagree with you. She gave birth to me, provided me with everything."

"Maybe, but that doesn't give her the right to mentally abuse you. Or treat you like a possession."

"Is that what happened to you?"

I nodded after a fashion. "You could say that."

"And you're happy now that you left it all behind?"

I laughed without much humor. "Happy? I'm not sure what that is. You just make choices and hope they work out, don't you?"

She stared at me a moment with searching eyes. "Yeah, I guess you do."

"Anyway," I said, letting go of her shoulders. "Your jet is waiting. You'll fly to Belfast. My uncle will meet you there."

"How am I supposed to know who he is?"

I couldn't help laughing. "Trust me. He'll find you right away. And if you happen to get peckish on the flight, I'm sure one of the crew will oblige you."

Jennifer nodded, looking nervous again. "I'll take your word for it." She stepped forward then and planted a kiss on my mouth with her soft lips, which I had to admit, felt kinda nice. "Thank you, August. I won't forget this."

"I know I won't."

She laughed. "Seriously, though. Thank you. I don't why but I see things clearly when I'm around you. You should help more people. I think that might be your purpose, the reason for all your pain."

"I'm starting to think so," I said. "I guess I'll see what happens. I still have to deal with your mother first."

Jennifer shook her head, still unable to believe I wasn't getting on the plane with her to escape her mother's inevitable wrath. "How are you going to stop her from killing you?"

It was a pertinent question, and one I didn't have an answer to yet. At least not a complete one. "Let me worry about that. You go now. Enjoy your new life in Babylon."

She opened the door to step out onto the runway, then stopped to look at me. "Will we ever meet again, do you think?"

I gave her the warmest smile I could and nodded. "I'll be pissed if we don't."

She smiled back. "So will I."

# 18

# NOCTURNUS

*R*ather than wait around for any of Angela Crow's goons to ambush and kill me, I thought it best if I went straight to the vampire's abode in The Highlands. Jennifer had already given me the address, so I took a cab to the building where the Crows had made residence, which happened to be a heavily guarded fortress a quarter mile outside of Green Street where the city's financial traders gathered every day. It didn't surprise me that Angela Crow lived so close to the action, so to speak. From what I could see on the cab ride over, The Highlands was where all the movers and shakers of the city had chosen to make their base. Grand government buildings were sandwiched in between massively tall skyscrapers of steel and glass, many of which were interconnected by walkways. It was a place of money and politics, a place from which to control the masses. I had no doubt that Angela Crow had made herself one of those controllers, albeit a more shadowy one than most.

When I stepped out of the cab, I was greeted immediately by four guards all dressed in black, shiny suits, automatic weapons barely concealed under their expensive looking jackets. As the guards rushed forward to the road, recognizing me straight away, I raised my hands just as the cab drove off. "I'd like to talk to Angela," I said. "My name is—"

That was as far as I got before one of the vampire guards slammed the butt of his gun into my forehead, knocking me unconscious.

\* \* \*

When I came to, I opened my eyes to a darkened room, unsure for a second of where I was. Then I sat straight up in a mild state of panic when I remembered what had happened and I quickly scanned the room I was in for any sign of threats. As it turned out, there was only one threat in the room, and she happened to be the most dangerous one.

The Crimson Crow.

"You must have a death wish coming here," she said as she stood by a large old-fashioned brick fireplace with nothing but ashes in the grate.

I had been laid out on a red velvet chaise lounge which I now sat on the edge off, my heart beating faster than I would have liked. Although given the circumstances, I couldn't blame the old ticker for sweating bullets.

There was also the girl hanging from a rope that was tied to a hook in the ceiling. A naked girl, hanging by her wrists, blood running out of various twin puncture marks in her body. The girl appeared motionless, and I couldn't tell if she was still alive or if Angela Crow had drained her dry. Regardless, there wasn't much to be done about her. It wasn't like Angela Crow was going to let me cut the poor girl down, was it?

So I focused on Angela herself, who was dressed in a white pantsuit with wide shoulders. Her platinum blond hair was neatly tied back in a ponytail, and her rouged lips seemed to stand out like a warning sign against all that white. The way she was looking at me, I could tell I had about ten seconds before she made her move on me and I was dead. Sure, I could have tried a few spells on her, but why delay the inevitable?

"I'm not mad," I told her, keeping my voice level. "I simply have a proposition for you. One I know you will like."

She stared back at me, her eyes seething. "The only thing I want from you is the location of my daughter. Tell me that, and I will kill you quick. If you don't tell me, I will torture you until you do, and believe me, I can make your suffering last for an eternity." As if to demonstrate her intentions, she walked over to the girl hanging from the ceiling and ran her fingers over the girl's belly, glancing at me as she did so. Then, in a movement I barely seen, she slashed her long fingernails across the girl's stomach, and I watched in horror as the girl's intestines spilled out onto the dark wood floor with a wet slapping sound. If the girl wasn't dead before, she certainly was now.

Swallowing, I thought to myself that I was mad for thinking this ploy of mine would work. That I was about to suffer greatly for betraying this psychopathic vampire. But I managed to keep those thoughts in check before they spilled over into full-blown panic. "I can help you walk in the daylight."

I just threw it out there, seeing no point in holding back. Either she went for it, or she didn't.

Again she stared at me as blood dripped from her already red fingernails. The cold look of murder had at least gone from her eyes now, replaced with what appeared to be a mixture of surprise, curiosity and an unmistakable desire. Which was understandable, because the ability to walk in pure sunlight was the equivalent of turning lead into gold for a vampire. Vampires had never managed to solve the problem of being fatally allergic to UV light. Scientists and spellcasters alike had worked on the problem, but for some reason, nothing they tried ever worked.

But let me tell you a story. My mother was a witch, a distinguished one as it happened. She was also a lover of botany, knowing everything there was to know about plants and herbs, their individual properties and applications. But there was one particular plant that my mother could never figure out. A rare plant that was only to be found on the island of Madagascar. The plant was called Nocturnus, and as the name suggests, it only came out at night so it could bloom its single black rose-like flower before closing up again and shrinking back into the earth at dawn every morning. Somehow or other, my mother had gotten a hold of one of these specimens, which she kept in the huge greenhouse at the back of the main house in Fermanagh. She became fascinated with the little plant and spent months trying to unlock its secrets. Most of all, she tried to find out why the plant was unable to survive in sunlight, why it withered and died in a matter of minutes. It became something of an obsession for my mother, trying to figure this out. She kept many clones of the plant, just so she could experiment, trying to keep the plant alive in the daylight. Failing with science, she finally turned to magic, until one day, one of the spells she had designed actually worked and she managed to keep Nocturnus alive in the daylight without any ill effects. She was so ecstatic that she brought me to the greenhouse to show me what she had done, explaining every single step in detail because she knew I would appreciate the delicate intricacy of her work. And her work was amazing. The spell she crafted was one of the most ingenious I had ever come across, and also the most intuitive, because no one else would ever have thought to put the things together she did, combining various forms of magic and fusing them with science in a way that was inspiring, to say the least, to a young student of spellcraft like myself back then.

I still remembered the entire procedure and everything needed for the spell to work. What I didn't know was if the spell would work on a vampire. Making a little plant impervious to sunlight was one thing, but a much more complex organism such as a vampire? I wasn't sure at all. The only thing I was sure of was that the spell was my only shot at staving off The Crimson Crow.

Luckily for me, Angela Crow was like every other vampire her age. Despite her obvious love of the dark, she still yearned to walk in the light. It was a possibility no vampire would ever turn down, for any vampire who could walk in both day and night was going to become more powerful than the rest. And if I've established anything about Angela Crow, it's that she lives for power.

"Only I can do this," I said, encouraged by her apparent interest, but still wary of her blatant mistrust. "I can make you more powerful than the rest." I spoke deliberately, making sure she knew the implications of what I was saying.

When Angela Crow finally smiled, I knew I had her.

# 19

# DEALING WITH THE DEVIL

"Why should I trust you?"

It was an expected question from the vampire queen. How did she know I wouldn't just try to kill her, or banish her to some far off dimension forever?

Still inside her art deco room, the dead girl hanging from the ceiling, the stench of her spilled guts drifting unpleasantly into my nostrils, I stood up and walked towards Angela Crow, stopping just in front of her and looking into her hardened eyes. "Your daughter trusted me," I said. "So should you."

It was a bold thing to say when I had just helped her daughter run away for good. Indeed, after I said the words to her, I immediately regretted them, knowing she wouldn't be able to see past my betrayal of her.

Before I knew it, she had gripped my head in both hands, holding me firm while she flashed her fangs at me. "You have some nerve saying that to me," she said, her lips peeled back like a predator. "You betrayed me!"

I held her gaze, despite the fact that her eyes were now a deep red color and full of murderous rage. "I betrayed no one. I did what was best for the girl."

She hissed again and snapped her jaws at me, her teeth mere centimeters away from my firmly held face. "It was not up to you to decide what was best for my daughter! Nor was it up to her. It was up to me and me alone!"

I said nothing, knowing there wasn't much I could say to justify my perceived betrayal.

The vampire glared at me with her red eyes for long moments as she seemed to be on the verge of killing me. It was all I could do not to try a spell on her, but I knew whatever spell I came up with would only be a temporary fix. Angela Crow was too old to be held back for long by mere magic, or at least not the kind of magic I had available to me at the time. A true master wizard could have perhaps taken her down long enough to destroy her heart, but my skills were not at that level yet. Far from it, in fact. The only thing I could bank on was that her desire to walk in the daylight was stronger than her desire to kill me.

As I continued to hold her hypnotic gaze, it quickly became apparent that she was rooting around inside my head. She was much more skilled at it than Sebastian was. I didn't even feel her initial entry, and the only way I could tell what she was doing was from the look in her eyes, which had intensified as if she was looking past me and into my mind. Too late, I tried to defend against her intrusion, but she batted away my psychic defenses without even blinking an eye.

Then finally, she let go of my head, and I took a step back, exhaling sharply as I regained my movement.

Angela Crow never moved. She just smiled and stared at me. "I know where my daughter is going," she said, sounding satisfied that she had got what she wanted from me.

Sighing, I shook my head. "You're going to go after her, no doubt?"

"That depends on you, August Creed."

A frown crossed my face. "What do you mean?"

Her eyes went back to blue again, and she seemed to relax, which didn't relax me any. "Here's the deal. You make it so I can walk in the daylight and I won't go after Jennifer. She can stay in Babylon if she wants. But, if you can't deliver what I want for any reason, or if you try to trick me in any way, I will go after my darling Jennifer, and I will enslave her for the rest of her days, which as you know, for us vampires, is a long time. I know you care for her, Creed. You see yourself in her. If you want her to stay free, you will deliver on what you promised."

What a cold, conniving bitch, I thought. Using her own daughter like that. Jennifer was truly better off away from her.

"All right," I said. "But how do I know you won't kill me and go after Jennifer anyway, once I give you what you want?"

She smiled and licked her lips. "You don't. I'm afraid you will just have to trust me, as my daughter put her trust in you."

Nice, throwing that back at me. "Looks like I don't have a choice then, do I?"

"One always has a choice, Creed. It's what you chose that matters."

"Fine," I said after a moment. "We'll have to do the spell at my Sanctum. I'm sure Sebastian can drive us, assuming he's recovered from the flaying your daughter gave him."

"He's still healing. It will take some time."

I smiled inwardly, glad to hear it. "Not to worry. I have a quicker mode of transportation anyhow."

# 20

# ENTER THE CHAOSPHERE

*I* teleported Angela Crow and myself to the brownstone on Poker Street, which I had already decided to make my Sanctum in Blackham. Assuming of course that I managed to pull off the spell that would allow the Crimson Crow to walk in daylight. The truth of the matter was that I wasn't entirely confident that I could pull it off. Don't get me wrong, by any standards, I'm a skilled wizard. Given my upbringing and my teachers over those years, there was no way that I could be anything other than good.

But the fact was, in wizard terms, I was still a fledgling with many more years of practice and study needed to reach the heights of a master wizard like my Uncle Ray, or even my dead father for that matter. So while it was certainly possible that I could properly execute the Nocturnus Spell, it was also possible that I might just fuck it up completely. My mother had been a spellcaster of rare talent and only a talent like hers could have created something as intricate and sophisticated as the Nocturnus Spell. It was one thing having the recipe to bake a cake, but quite another to actually bake it so that the cake came out the way it was supposed to. It was much the same thing with spells. So all in all, you could say I was more than a little nervous when I landed in the Sanctum with Angela Crow. At that point, I knew there was no turning back. It was either find my game or die.

"I take it you have never done this spell before?" Angela Crow said, standing in the living room as I slipped my trench coat off and placed it over the back of a chair. "I take it no one has, otherwise I would have heard of it by now."

I nodded. "You are correct," I said reluctantly.

Her eyes narrowed. "Then how do you know it will work if no one has tried it?"

It was a fair question. The Nocturnus Spell had only ever been used on a single plant species. After my mother had cracked the code so to speak, she had no interest in trying to apply the spell to anything else, least of all vampires. For her, it was just an intellectual puzzle that she had now solved and so she moved onto

63

other things. So you may now be forgiven for thinking the same thing as Angela Crow. Why do I think the spell will work on a vampire?

The only answer I have to that question is faith. I have faith that the spell created by my loving mother will work as I want it to. Sometimes, faith in something is all you have to go on. In this case, that was especially true.

The vampire Crow got edgy as she waited for my answer, which I finally gave her. "My mother created the spell. I have faith in my mother that the mechanics of the spell are sound. Besides, it has been tested before. Just not on a vampire like yourself."

Angela Crow frowned. "On what then?"

"A plant."

She seemed to stifle a laugh before looking at me seriously again. "A plant?"

"Yes. A special plant that could only survive at night. My mother made it so the plant could survive in the daytime also."

The vampire seemed to think about that for a moment. "Once again, Creed, let me remind you of our deal. And let me also tell you that if you are fucking with me, I will hunt down every person you have ever met and tear them into tiny pieces."

I held my hands up. "Hey, I'm not stupid. I get it. I promise I'm not fucking with you."

"No," she said, coming towards me, which always made me nervous. "Maybe not, but you are winging it here, aren't you?" She stopped in front of me and gave a slight smile. "I don't know whether to admire you for that or just kill you right now."

Holding her gaze, I kept my cool. "The spell will work. I'll make sure of it."

"Yes, you will."

And with that, I went to work on getting things organized and preparing for the spell, while Angela Crow waited impatiently in the living room, sometimes appearing behind me in the basement while I was down there, scaring the shit out of me, seeming to enjoy doing so. After the third time she did it, I just ignored her, brushing past her as I continued my search for the right ingredients needed to do the spell. Which was a lot, by the way. Like I said, my mother threw everything she had at the problem, which ended up being a long list of rare ingredients. Things like Wolfsbane, the eyes of a Scarlet-Backed spider, the claws of a Singing Bat, Belladonna, petals from a black rose, anus of newt (yes really), toad sweat, wizard's eyelashes and a whole slew of other ingredients. As spells went, it was more complicated than any I had ever tried before, and believe me, I'd slung many a spell that would make even Einstein weep at their complexity.

Luckily for me, Ray kept the basement of the Sanctum fully stocked with every ingredient a magicslinger could ever need, and then some. It was almost as if the old bastard knew I would need access to all those ingredients at some point. Sometimes I wondered if he had found a way to see into the future. Given the circumstances, the thought brought me some comfort, because if Ray knew what shit was going to go down before I did, then that meant he must have thought I could handle whatever was going to happen next. Or maybe I was just making shit up to make myself feel better, I don't know. Either way, it didn't change anything. It was still do or die.

Hours later, I had finally managed to assemble everything I needed for the

Nocturnus Spell. I had also managed to mix or combine whatever ingredients needed doing so, the whole time working under the pressure of not only Angela Crow's stalking presence, but also trying to recall from memory everything that I had to do. One missed step and the entire spell would fall flat, or worse, drastically misfire.

"Kindly fill that with your blood," I said to Angela Crow as I handed her a wide brimmed wooden cup that dated back to medieval times and which had become darkly stained by all manner of liquids (magical and otherwise) over the centuries.

The Crimson Crow gave me a suspicious look, but she took the cup after slicing open a vein in her wrist with one of her long, sharp fingernails, allowing her blood to spill into the cup until it was almost full. Then she handed it back to me, and as I took it carefully, I noticed the deep slice in her wrist heal over in a matter of seconds. "A useful ability," I said, placing the cup on the floor of the living room, next to the array of bottles, jars and vials I had gathered around me.

"Yes," she said, looking straight at me. "It makes me hard to kill."

I glanced only briefly up at her as I caught the emphasis in her voice. "I've no doubt."

After that exchange, I worked in focused silence for the next while as I carefully added all of the ingredients around me into the cup containing the vampire's blood, fittingly using the foot of a crow to gently stir the mixture around.

Once that was done, it was time for the real work to begin. I now had to infuse the blood mixture with magic--magic that had to be perfectly conjured and processed in a certain way, and all done without mistake. It was the part of the spell I was most worried about as it was going to take a phenomenal amount of focus and concentration on my part, not to mention an expert handling of the magic itself once it was fully conjured and shaped to perfection. It was akin to trying to solve a puzzle with just your mind, moving pieces around whose properties could drastically shift in any given moment as you tried to put them together in a way that made no sense at all, but which you knew to be right anyway. And if that sounds hard and confusing, that's because working with magic was exactly like that most of the time. Working with magic was more about feel and intuition which could only be cultivated so far with training. You still needed to have a certain connection with the magic itself, and often that was achieved through pure faith.

Which was all I had to go on as I requested that Angela Crow remain quiet and not disturb me in any way until I had completed what I had to do. Then I knelt by the cup of blood on the floor, closed my eyes and went to work.

Within moments, I was somewhere else. Not physically, of course, but in my mind, I was literally somewhere else. A giant open space filled with the buzzing, crackling energy of pure magic. It wasn't a real place. It was simply a place I created long ago, a place where I could access and work with the magic I had learned how to cultivate and channel inside me. Every magic practitioner had their own version of this place. I called mine the Chaosphere because that's what it resembled. A giant sphere of pure energy that was completely chaotic in nature and which required my skills as a wizard to tame and channel it so it could do my will. I stood in the center of this Chaosphere, like standing in the center of a hollowed-out sun, the energy buzzing around me at once terrifying and exhilarating as I began to pull strands of that energy towards me, twisting them this way and that, melding them together, twisting them again, forging them into new forms and shapes, the whole time allowing my intent to infuse every single strand of magical energy to ensure each strand would bend in the direction of my will.

I don't know how long I was in the Chaosphere for. In there, the constructs of time and space ceased to exist. I could have been in there minutes or days at a time, and I wouldn't have known either way.

When I finally opened my eyes, Angela Crow was kneeling in front of me, her eyes full of fascination as she watched what I was doing, almost like she wished she could see inside me to observe me working the magic. I barely registered her, however, as I placed my hands just above the cup of blood and began to direct the magic I had conjured and shaped in the Chaosphere into the blood mixture. A yellowish-green energy released itself from my hands and infused with the blood mixture in the cup, causing it to go from a dark crimson to a deep yellow color with streaks of purplish-red in it. At the same time, I began to recite the incantation that was part of the spell. It was an awkward incantation because it was formed with over a dozen different languages, none of those languages having been spoken in this world for centuries. The only saving grace was that the incantation was relatively short and basically helped to focus the effects of the spell on a certain subject, which in this case, was Angela Crow.

After finishing the incantation, I finally lifted the cup and held it out towards the vampire Crow. "Drink," I said simply, sweat running in rivulets down my face, my shirt stuck to my back.

Angela Crow took the cup and stared at me as if she was going to voice some doubt, but whatever she saw on my face made her think otherwise, and she finally drank down every drop of the blood in the cup, licking her lips afterward as she placed the empty cup on the floor. "Is that it?" she asked, hardly able to keep her excitement from her voice.

Nodding, I said, "That's it."

The vampire stood up. "How do we know if it worked?"

I nodded to the rays of light coming through a crack in the living room curtains. "Only one way to find out, isn't there?"

Swallowing hard, I watched as the vampire walked to the window and stood there for a moment. Then she flung open the curtains and the morning light swallowed her whole.

# SUNSHINE GIRL

*S*tanding in the pure morning sunlight streaming through the living room window, Angela Crow made a noise that I at first interpreted as pain, and my heart sank as I fully expected to see the vampire erupt in flames before me. But then I realized that the vampire wasn't expressing pain, but joy. I could only stare in wonder and gratitude as The Crimson Crow appeared to be resistant to the incendiary effects of the UV rays bathing every inch of her. "Yes," she said as she probably realized that she was now the most powerful vampire in the city, in the world even. Walking in the daylight would not necessarily make her invincible or even any more powerful than she already was, but it would certainly make her special, and more often than not, that's all it took to dominate those who were less special. Which of course, Angela Crow knew all too well. To the rest of vampirekind, she would be held up as god, as The Daywalker perhaps (it remained to be seen what catchy titles were assigned to her).

Eventually, she turned to me and smiled, looking more powerful than ever as the sunlight lit her up, giving her an angelic appearance that belied the darkness in her soul. "It appears you have succeeded," she said to me as I continued kneeling on the floor, exhausted now from the long hours of concentration.

"So it seems," I said. "Thankfully."

"One final test."

Angela Crow left the living room and went to the front door. A moment later, I heard the door open as she must have stepped outside. I stayed where I was, having no wish to witness her day-walking firsthand. All I wanted to do was get rid of the bitch, so I could have a drink before going to bed. It was all I could do to hold myself up.

From outside, I heard joyous laughter, and I imagined Angela Crow standing in the middle of the street, her arms extended as she welcomed the rays of the sun on her milky white skin. No doubt it was a rush. Overwhelming even.

She didn't seem too overwhelmed when she came back in, however. She seemed as calm and composed as always in fact, apart from the grin on her face and the unashamed delight in her normally cold eyes. Her smile widened as she came and stood over me. "Creed," she said. "You are truly a talented boy. Your uncle's faith in you is well placed. So was my own it seems."

"Are we even now?" I asked, only wanting to be rid of her.

She breathed in deeply as a conciliatory look came over her face, a look I didn't welcome seeing because I knew what was coming next. "Not quite, I'm afraid."

I shook my head. "Why am I not surprised."

"Come on, Creed. You must have known I couldn't let you live after this. I can't risk you giving this precious gift to any other vampire. Surely you can understand that?"

With the little energy I had left, I got off my knees so I could stand and face her. "I do understand," I told her, my voice dulled from fatigue, but also blunt so she would feel what I was about to tell her. "That's why I built a failsafe into the spell I just did."

The girlish delight left her eyes and became replaced with cold suspicion. "What did you do?"

"I put the magic equivalent of a bomb right next to your heart. The bomb is linked to me, so that if I die, the bomb goes off and your heart is destroyed. I'm sure you can guess what happens next."

Angela Crow's scarlet lips slowly peeled back to reveal her fangs. Her eyes burned red as she seethed from within, her body tensing as if preparing to attack and kill me. I held her murderous gaze so she'd know I was deadly serious. "You fucking rat," she seethed, extending her hand towards my throat, but stopping herself at the last second. "I should—"

"What?" I said, unafraid. "You'll kill me? If you do, you'll also kill yourself. You got what you wanted, Miss Crow, which is power. But like all power, it comes at a price. You of all people should know that."

She stared at me a moment longer before shaking her head and turning away, after which I allowed myself to breathe normally again. When she next turned around, the cold smile was back on her face. "How do I know you're not bluffing?"

"You don't, not unless you kill me and find out..."

She shook her head again frustratedly. "Damn you, Creed."

"Relax," I said. "As long as nothing happens to me, you'll be fine."

"And what if someone else kills you?"

"That's a chance you'll have to take."

"And when you eventually die from old age?"

"I'll deactivate the bomb before that happens."

"Very considerate of you."

I smiled without humor. "You can go now, Miss Crow. Our business is concluded. I rescind your invitation here."

Upon saying those words, it was like the vampire got pulled back by a rope wrapped around her as she was dragged against her will by an invisible force, out of the living room, down the hallway and out the front door where she came to a stop on the front step. Rejuvenated slightly by my victory over The Crimson Crow, I walked to the front door to see her off for good.

"I'll find a way around this," she said. "And when I do, I will make you suffer, Creed. Mark my words."

"Mark my words also," I told her. "If you do anything to Jennifer, if you hurt her in any way, I will activate that bomb around your heart and obliterate you out of existence. Are we clear on that?"

Angela Crow nodded reluctantly. "We're clear."

"Good," I said. "Bye Miss Crow. Enjoy the sunshine. Maybe some of it will even penetrate that black heart of yours, who knows?"

And with that, I closed the door on The Crimson Crow.

# SLAINTE

*A*fter spending the next few hours sleeping and recuperating, I called my uncle to check on Jennifer. I wanted to know if she had landed in Ireland safely, and as it turned out she had. I had a brief conversation with her on the phone as I explained what had happened with her mother and how I had managed to sort things out with her. I also told Jennifer that her mother would not be bothering her again anytime soon, although I did warn the girl that her mother knew of her travel plans, so I told Jennifer to keep an eye out when she was in Babylon. Jennifer thanked me once more, her gratitude creating a sense of contentedness and satisfaction in me that went a long way towards strengthening my motivation to not only stay in Blackham City but to also use my particular skills to help more people, supernatural or otherwise.

I told Ray as much when I spoke to him on the phone again. He was happy to hear I had found the right path at last.

"A path," I told him. "Time will tell if it's the right one."

"It is," Ray said before he hung up the phone. "Trust me, my boy. It is."

After the phone call, I took a walk around The Sanctum. It was the first real physical Sanctum I'd ever had (the Sanctum I kept in the Astral Plane not counting). For as long as I needed it, the Sanctum in Blackham City was mine. More than that, it was a permanent base. A place to call home at long last.

Throughout all those years of traveling, I thought I didn't need anything permanent in my life, apart from magic. But walking around the Sanctum, feeling the history and magic steeped in its walls, I realized that permanency (as much as such a concept exists) was what I craved all along. For some reason, I had spent the last six years convinced otherwise, perhaps because (I was now realizing) I was scared of stopping anywhere for too long for fear of what would catch up with me.

That fear was still there in the background, but the difference now was that I was prepared to face whatever came along, from my past or from the present. And Blackham City was as good a place as any to do that.

Of course, now that I was there, I wasn't sure exactly how to proceed. I knew I had to set up shop, but I wasn't sure what kind of shop or even how to go about it. But that was okay because these things had a way of sorting themselves out when you decided on a particular path in life. In the meantime, I would make The Sanctum my own while also getting to know the lay of the land in Blackham City. Something told me that the more I knew about the place and its inhabitants, the easier my job (whatever job that was...magicslinger for hire, I guess) would be.

Standing now by the fireplace in the living room, I poured myself a glass of whiskey and looked around the room for a moment with a contented grin on my face. Then I raised my glass to the empty room and my new Sanctum. My new life. "Sláinte," I said, before knocking back the whiskey. And I don't mind telling you, it was the nicest glass of whiskey I'd ever had.

Oh, and you're probably wondering about that magic bomb I put next to Angela Crow's heart. Did I really do that, or was I bluffing, as The Crimson Crow had tried to say I was?

Well, all I'm going to say on that is this:

A wizard has to have his secrets, doesn't he?

Sláinte!

# BLOOD MAGIC (WIZARD'S CREED BOOK 1)

AN URBAN FANTASY NOVEL

# THE WIZARD'S CREED SERIES

CRIMSON CROW (PREQUEL)
BLOOD MAGIC
BLOOD DEBT
BLOOD CULT
BLOOD DEMON

*MORE TO COME*

Be sure to sign up to my Reader Group and be the first to hear about new releases, cover reveals and special promos. Plus get access to my private fans only Facebook group.

http://www.npmartin.com/n-p-martin-reader-group/

## 1

# SPELL BLASTED

*T*he sheer force of the magical energy that crackled through the air was so powerful it slammed me against a brick wall as surely as being punched in the chest by the Devil's fist. I slid down the wall to the stinking floor like I'd just taken a hard right hook to the jaw. The invasive magic took hold within me, initiating a chain reaction that I couldn't stop. The spell blew through my every defense: the talisman around my neck, the protective tattoos on my body, and the Druidic runes etched into my trench coat. I might as well have been a goddamn Sleepwalker with no protection at all.

*What am I even doing here? Where am I?*

The faint smell of decayed flesh mixed with sulfur hung thick in the air, signifying that black magic had just been used, which is never good. It's like turning up at a children's party to find Beelzebub tying balloon animals with a shit-eating grin on his face, from which nothing good can surely come. It's the same with black magic; nothing good ever comes of it.

I sat dazed on the floor, blinking around me for a moment. My mind was fuzzy and partially frozen, the way it would be if I'd just woke from a nightmare. It appeared I was inside an abandoned office space, the expansive rectangular room lined with grimy, broken windows that let cold air in to draw me out of my daze somewhat. It was night, so darkness coated the room, the only real light coming from the moon outside as it beamed its pale, silvery light through the smashed skylights.

Confused and more than a little uneasy, I struggled back to my feet and blindly reached for the pistol inside my dark green trench coat, frowning when I realized the gun wasn't there. Then I remembered it had gone flying out of my hand when the spell had hit. Looking around for a moment, I soon located the pistol lying on the floor several feet away, and I lurched over and grabbed it, slightly more secure now that the gun's reassuring weight was back in my hand.

There were disturbing holes in my memory also. I vaguely recalled confronting someone after tracking them to where I was. But who?

Try as I might, I couldn't get a clear image. The person was no more than a shadow figure in my mind. I didn't even have a clue as to why I was following the mysterious person in the first place. Obviously, they had done something to get on my radar. The question was what, though?

The answer came a few seconds later when my eyes fell upon the dark shape in the middle of the room, and a deep sense of dread filled me immediately; a dread that was both familiar and sickening at the same time. Swallowing, I stared hard at the shape lying prone in the gloom. Then, over the sharp scent of rats piss and pigeon shit, a different smell hit my nostrils—the heavy, festering stench of blood.

When I gingerly crossed to the center of the room, my worst fears were confirmed when I saw that it was a dead body lying on the floor. A young woman with her throat slit. Glyphs were carved into the naked flesh of her spreadeagled body, with ropes leading from her wrists and ankles to rusty metal spikes hammered into the floor. I marveled at the force required to drive the nails into the concrete, a feat that surely could only have been achieved through magic.

Along the circumference of a magic circle painted around the victim was what looked like blood-drawn glyphs. The sheer detail of them unnerved me as I took in a quality that could've only come from a well-practiced hand. The tingling in my spine from all these factors combined with a vague recognition, one inhibited by whatever spell I'd absorbed.

I breathed out slowly as I reluctantly took in the callous butchery on display. The dead woman looked to be in her early thirties, though it was difficult to tell because both her eyes were missing; cut out with the knife used to slice her throat, no doubt. I shook my head as I looked around for a few seconds in an effort to locate the dead woman's eyeballs. Not finding them, I surmised the killer probably took them; or worse, used them in some way. Sick bastard.

Staring down at the woman again, I noticed she looked underweight for her size. She was around the same height as me at six feet, but there was very little meat on her bones, as if she were a stranger to regular meals. I also noted the needle marks on her feet, and the bruises around her thighs. This, coupled with how she had been dressed—in a leather mini skirt and short top, both items discarded on the floor nearby—made me almost certain the woman had been a prostitute. A convenient, easy victim for whoever had killed her.

If the symbols carved into her pale flesh were anything to go by, it would seem the woman wasn't so much murdered as ritually sacrificed. At a guess, I would have said she was an offering to one of the Dimension Lords, which the glyphs seemed to point to. The glyphs themselves were not only complex, but also carved with surgical precision. The clarity of the symbols against the woman's pale flesh made it possible for me to make out certain ones that I recognized as being signifiers to alternate dimensions, though which dimension exactly, I couldn't be sure, at least not until I had studied the glyphs further. Glyphs such as the ones I was looking at were always uniquely different in some way. No two people drew glyphs the same, with each person etching their own personality into every one, which can often make it hard to work out their precise meanings. One thing I could be certain of, however, was that the glyphs carved into the woman's body resonated only evil intent; an intent so strong, I felt it in my gut, gnawing at me like a parasite seeking access to my insides, as if drawn to my magic power. Not a pleasant feeling, but I was used to it, having been exposed to enough dark magic in my time.

After taking in the scene as a whole, I soon came to the conclusion that the woman wasn't the killer's first victim; not by a long stretch, given the precision and clear competency of the work on display.

"Son of a bitch," I said, annoyed now that I couldn't recall any details about the case I had so obviously been working on. It was no coincidence that I had ended up where I was, a place that happened to reek of black magic, and which housed a murder that had occult written all over it...quite literally, in the victim's case. I had been on the hunt, and I had gotten close to the killer, which was the likeliest reason for the dark magic booby trap I happened to carelessly spring like some bloody rookie.

Whoever the killer was, they wielded profoundly powerful magic. A spell that managed to wipe all my memories of the person in question wouldn't have been an easy spell to cast, or even to come by for that matter. The killer was also an adept of some kind, of that that there was no doubt. And given the depth of power to their magic, it also felt to me like they had channeled magic from some other source, most likely from whatever Dimension Lord they were sacrificing to.

Whatever the case, the killer's spell had worked. Getting back the memories they had stolen from me wasn't going to be easy, and that's if I could get them back at all, which depressingly, I feared might just be the case.

After shaking my head at how messed up the situation was, I suddenly froze upon hearing a commanding voice booming in the room like thunder.

"Don't move, motherfucker!"

2

---

# BADASS

*I* JUMPED AT the sound of the deep, but unmistakably feminine, voice coming from behind me. The reason I jumped wasn't so much out of fear or fright, as it was out of sudden recognition. The voice projected an effortless authority, containing a husky quality that would have been sexy if the woman's blatant aggression wasn't so overpowering.

I stood slowly whilst turning around, all the while assuming the woman would recognize me, as I did her. A booming echo and chipped concrete flooring just inches from my feet quickly put a hole in that reasoning. The volume of sound and the chips of concrete kicked high enough for random pieces to sting my eyes, which made it seem as though a grenade instead of a bullet had gone off. "Jesus!" I shouted as I jumped back in shock, my ears ringing from the gunshot. "What the fuck are you doing? It's *me*, for Christ's sake!"

"Drop that pistol...or the next one goes in your chest!"

"What?" What was she playing at? Didn't she know who I was? "Leona, it's me. It's Creed."

Leona Lawson cut a dark, imposing figure as she stepped out of the shadows. She was tall and athletically lean, her black hair short and brushed over to one side of her forehead. I couldn't see her eyes very well in the gloom, but I knew they would look like focused blue chips of ice set into that delectable porcelain skin of hers. She was dressed as she usually was, in tight fitting black leather trousers and a top that clung to the mounds of her perfectly sized breasts. A long, black leather coat that hung down almost level with the top of her heavy combat boots made her look streamlined and dominant, which I already knew her to be.

The hugely intimidating gun she held looked almost too big for her hand, but she didn't struggle even slightly with the gun's heft, and looked entirely comfortable holding it. It was one of two custom Berettas with laser sights that she carried in leg holsters, each fully loaded with 9mm hollow-point rounds that would put a hole in just about anything. A case in point being the sheer damage done to the cement flooring.

"I said drop the pistol." There was no doubting her seriousness.

I shook my head and concealed my frown by looking down to obey her command. I could now also take in the laser's red dot on my chest as I placed my old custom made Smith and Wesson on the floor. I'd known her long enough to know that Leona's words were more than bravado. Her word was her bond. I'd also been present when perps made the mistake of believing her incapable of pulling the trigger.

Maybe it was because of the pressure of having to look down the barrel of her gun, but it now dawned on me that I'd called her and asked her to meet me at this very location. Why else would she be standing in front of me now?

Yet she was treating me like a stranger; like she didn't know who I was, which was bullshit, because she knew me better than almost anyone. We slept together, for Christ's sake! She was, although she would never freely admit it, my girlfriend. And yet there she was, pointing one of her cannons at me, ready to put a hole in my chest big enough to fit her fist through. There could only be one explanation for her lack of recognition. The goddamn spell. "Are you saying you don't...*know* me?" I shook my head, then smiled. "Wait, is this some new kinky sex game you've devised? Are you going to make me strip all my clothes off right now, so you can have your way with me...at the scene of a murder..."

Her face said I was all wrong about that as she came forward, her boots thudding loudly on the floor, her leather coat swishing against her legs. "Firstly, you're sick. Secondly, I don't know you from Adam, motherfucker. As far as I can tell you're the lunatic who killed that woman right there, and for that crime I'm going to put a bullet in your skull. That way you won't be able to ever kill anyone else."

My heart missed several beats when she pulled back the hammer on the Beretta. "Wait!" I said. "Jesus...how would I know your name is Leona Lawson, and that you work for a secret government division that investigates occult affairs, huh? I called *you*, for Christ's sake, told you to meet me here." I thought of something. "Check the call records on your phone. You have me listed as Creed. Do it."

Leona shook her head as she said, "There's no one named Creed in my contacts, and neither did anyone call and tell me to come to this shithole."

"Then how did you know to come in the first place?"

Her stare turned a frown. "I..."

"You don't remember, do you? That's because your memory has been wiped, along with my name off your phone it seems. Does it not seem strange that you don't know why you came here?"

She stepped closer, frighteningly imposing, her face an impassive mask as always, though I still sensed the confusion underneath. "You think I don't know you're trying to trick me like the dirty hedge witch you are?"

"Wait, hedge witch? That's a bit low, even for you, Le—"

She stepped forward and stuck the gun in my face, the barrel looming large and dangerous in my sight line. "Why'd you kill the woman? Some fucked up ritual is it? A sacrifice to one of your messed up gods?"

My hands were up as I leaned my head back slightly away from the huge gun. "Look, Leona, I called you, remember?"

"Stop using my name. How the hell do you even know my name?"

Oh Christ, this was worse than I thought. She didn't seem to know me at all, even after more than three years of friendship; if you could call what we had a friendship. Leona didn't do friends particularly, or relationships for that matter. Not normal ones, anyway. If you asked her to describe our relationship she probably would have said, "Working."

"Listen," I told her, knowing I was wasting my breath, but stumbling ahead anyway. "My name is August Creed. We're friends. We work together sometimes. We even, you know..."

"What?"

"Sleep together."

A snort of derision burst through her thin lips. "First of all, I would never sleep with someone like you—"

"What? That's just—"

"—And second of all...I have no idea who the fuck you are, except that you're a killer and I'm taking you in. Although I'd prefer just to shoot you in the head right now, since that's what you obviously deserve. My boss, however, will want to talk to you, to see what kind of psycho you really are first."

This wasn't good. I was only now starting to understand the full extent of the spell that I was under; or curse, rather, which is more like how it felt. It had been designed by the killer to make people forget that he (assuming it was a he) ever existed. But in the process, I got caught in the blast; though by accident or design, I still wasn't sure. In any case, I had arrived at the sickening conclusion that no one remembered me anymore either. All memory of me had been wiped from people's minds, and I was now a stranger to my closest friend in the world. To my goddamn girlfriend!

I shook my head. What a disaster. "All right," I said in a vain attempt to explain things. "I can see how this all looks. I know it sounds crazy and everything, but Leona, you have to believe me. I came here to confront the real killer, the person who murdered that poor woman right there. I called you to tell you to meet me here as well. Only when I got here, the killer set off a spell that erased all memory of him from existence...and I got caught in the blast. So now, all memory of *me* has been wiped out of existence as well." I paused to see if she believed me or not. It didn't appear that she did, going by the look of disdain on her face. I couldn't say I blamed her. It was a lot to take on faith. "Don't look at me with that face...I know that face. You think I'm some crackpot trying to lie my way out of this...I'm not, I swear."

She sighed and shook her head. "Turn around and put your hands on your head. I've heard enough of this bullshit."

She didn't believe me. It was Leona after all, so I should have known. She didn't care about the sob stories that spewed out of the mouths of those she hunted. She only cared about catching them and bringing them in. The rest she left up to Brentwood, her boss at Division.

I couldn't let her take me to Division HQ as a total stranger, for they would send me to the "Containment Unit" and I would just be another powerless inmate among dozens of others. I had to do something, and quick, before she handcuffed me. Not that I couldn't slip the cuffs if I wanted to, but why make things harder for myself?

"I know you, Leona," I said in a last ditch attempt to get through to her. "I know you have a birthmark in the shape of a star on the inside of your left thigh, and a scorpion tattoo on your back. I know you work out every day and that your favorite exercise is barbell squats, simply because you know so many people hate doing them, which motivates you to do them. I know your favorite food is Chinese and you like to eat at the little restaurant near where you live, which is in Worthington, by the way. And I also know that you love oral sex and that when we sleep together, you hold my head down there so long sometimes that when I come up, it feels like I've been deep sea diving."

A snorting laugh involuntarily left her mouth when I said that, but she quickly caught it and shook her head, resetting her stony expression.

"You also have a hell of a grip," I continued, fully aware I was now at serious risk of pissing her off beyond the point of no return. She had a habit of shooting people when that happened. "Which is why you favor big guns over small ones, like that Beretta you're pointing at me right now, which you had custom made two years ago by a gunsmith called Tony Brasco over in Pinehurst. I could go on, but we both know I'm telling the truth here. And given the crazy magical world we live in, is it so beyond the realms of possibility that this shit could happen? You've encountered stranger, Leona. I know you have."

Doubt was creeping up on her, I was glad to note, causing her normal stone cold expression to falter somewhat. She never lowered the gun though, despite the fact that she was clearly having doubts. "Either you've read my file or you're using magic somehow," she said, though her voice wasn't as certain as it was before.

Building upon her growing uncertainty, I said, "We both know your military and government records are completely sealed. It would take a top level hacker or a highly skilled Technomancer to get a hold of your files, and I wasn't aware that *'loves oral sex'* is on your file anyway." I gave a small chuckle when she didn't respond, and she just kept staring at me with those cold blue eyes that always seem to lock on like magnets. I shook my head. "All right, you know what I'm saying. I've never seen your files. And I'm also not working any magic either. Don't forget, you're wearing that talisman around your neck, underneath your top. The talisman I gave you shortly after we met. It's Alexian crystal, bright blue, imperfectly cut, and it wards you against most magical attacks. I have a similar one around my own neck."

Her eyes narrowed, and she tilted her head to the side slightly. "All right. Let's say I believe you—"

"Yes, let's do that. Good idea. Then you can finally lower that cannon from out of my face."

"Are you always this annoying?"

"Only when guns get pointed at me."

She shook her head. "So let's say I believe you. Maybe you did know me, though I can't believe I'd ever sleep with you. I mean..." She snorted as she trailed off, leaving her supposed lack of interest in me as a fuck buddy (we were more than that, but whatever) hanging in the air for me to notice.

I started shaking my head at her. "You see, you say that now, but you actually couldn't resist my charms, and if you'd just lower the gun, then you—"

Leona pressed the gun to my forehead. "You talk too much."

"Only when—"

"Yeah, I know. Only when you have a gun pointed at you."

"Something like that."

"Fact is, whether you knew me or not, it doesn't matter. You still could have killed that woman there."

"True," I said.

"So then I wouldn't be doing my job if I just let you go, would I?"

I couldn't argue with her logic. Leona had a habit of doing that, mentally or physically maneuvering people into corners they couldn't escape from. It was a special skill of hers, honed to perfection when she was an interrogator in Iraq. "No, you wouldn't."

Which is why, the whole time I'd been talking to her, I'd been inwardly reciting a spell, and charging up my magic. A spell that I knew would bypass the defensive capabilities of the talisman I had given her.

But just as I was about to unleash the spell, something dark and screechy whooshed over our heads, causing us both to flinch and duck.

"What the fuck was that?" she asked, looking around her, the gun still on me.

"That," I said, "is something that might be trouble if you don't take that gun away and let me deal with it."

She seemed to consider hard for a moment as the dark entity continued to rush around the room, still making that awful screeching noise as it went. Then she finally shook her head and lowered the gun. "Goddamn it. Sometimes I hate this fucking job."

"I know you do, love," I said, breathing easy once more. "But you're also the best I know at it, so let's kick this thing's ass before it kicks ours, shall we?"

# 3

# SPECTER

*T*HE SCREECHING ENTITY whooshing about above our heads was called an Atavism, which is distinct from a Trauma Ghost. A Trauma Ghost is, as the name implies, the spirit of someone who has died in generally traumatic circumstances, and who refuses to move on until they correct their unfinished business as it were. The thing flying around above our heads was not so much a ghost as a specter. It was the ectoplasmic leftovers of the dead girl's soul. While the girl's soul had by now probably risen into the Astral Plane and beyond to the River of Souls, the extreme emotions she gave out just before her violent death remained behind in the form of the ghostly specter that was swooping and darting around the room like a trapped bird, as it made an unholy noise that was part terror and part fury. A noise that sounded like scores of long fingernails being scraped along a blackboard. Both Leona and I had our faces screwed up as we flinched away from the noise.

Leona was trying to draw a bead on the specter as it rushed blindly overhead.

"Don't bother," I said, speaking loudly to be heard over the constant wailing and screeching. "Your bullets won't do any good. Haven't you come across one of these things before?"

"I've seen ghosts," she said, still eyeing me suspiciously, almost like I had called the specter here myself as part of some elaborate escape plan. "Not quite like this, though."

We both ducked when a plastic chair came flying toward us, which sailed over our heads and crashed into the wall behind us. Then the specter itself—somewhat approximating the previous physical form of the dead woman, only more stretched and translucent, its face twisted and grotesque—barreled right at me at speed. Before I could move, the specter hit me like a gust of screaming, Arctic wind, passing right through me as it took my breath away and filled me with a psychic pain that manifested as deep fear and dread. For a long moment, I was all but crippled by the emotions the specter had elicited. I doubled over as my body tensed with such debilitating fear that my chest became so tight I couldn't breathe properly. It was like the specter had left behind enough of itself, in passing through me that is, to ensure that I would feel everything she had before her death. I found myself unable to move as the woman did, then felt the stabbing pain in my eye sockets as if someone was carving out my eyes with a blunt knife. Then over various parts of my body, I felt a sharp, burning pain as if my flesh was being carved. And finally, the quick but shocking pain across my throat as if someone had just slit it open. The pain only lasted a few seconds, but it was some of the most intense I had ever felt, especially with the feelings of sheer terror that underlined it all.

I jumped when I felt Leona's strong grip on my arm as she tried to pull me up. "Come on!" she shouted. "We're getting out of here!"

"No!" I said, my paralysis easing a bit so I could at least stand up again. "We can't let that thing roam free. It'll just get more powerful, and then it will cause real damage somewhere else. I have to take care of it."

"Take care of it? How?"

The specter turned at the end of the room and began to fly toward us—toward *me*—again. Leona raised her Beretta and fired twice at the atavism. The specter seemed to disintegrate for a second as the bullets passed right through it and hit the far wall. Then it reformed as it started doing circles in the center of the room, creating a whirlwind of energy that began to pull whatever was lying around on the floor—chairs, bottles, dead rats and pigeons, even the pools of water on the floor caused by the leaky roof, as well as the dead woman's blood—into itself. For a specter, its power was unusually strong. Normally, such entities didn't exhibit such poltergeist abilities, the extent of their influence usually being no more than a faint spirit manifestation and perhaps the transference of whatever emotions it held on to. In this case, the girl's death had obviously been so horrifically traumatic that the accompanying emotions were among the strongest I've encountered. It made me wonder what kind of monster the killer was, if they could inspire such terror in their victims.

Free now from the negative emotions put in me by the specter, I stood up straight and started to gather myself, beginning to shape and form the magical energy that was already crackling inside me. The only option was to destroy the specter. The dead girl's soul had already moved on, so obliterating her insane and translucent ectoplasmic leftover wouldn't cause the girl's soul any harm. Unless of course the girl's soul was still in the Astral Plane and she was actually manifesting and controlling this spectral thing herself, using it to lash out at the world she had been so cruelly snatched away from. The only way to tell is to travel to the Astral Plane to find and confront the girl's spirit whilst there, but I didn't have time to do so myself. If the specter was being controlled, the worst that would happen to the girl's spirit when I killed the specter was that she would experience little more than a bit of psychic pain. She was already dead after all.

"Are you going to do something or not?" Leona asked me. "Before this thing gets any stronger."

Yes, I was going to do something. I was already sub-vocalizing the appropriate spell to deal with the specter, a Disintegration Spell, and it was almost ready to go. First though...

"That depends," I shouted above the noise and the wind now howling throughout the room. "Do you believe me yet?"

"What?" Leona shouted back. She was still pointing the gun at the specter, not because she thought she could hurt it by shooting it, but because it made her feel better when she pointed her gun at things, less insecure about situations she couldn't always control due to the magical forces involved.

"Do you believe I didn't kill the girl and that we are friends?"

She shook her head at me in angry frustration. "Just get rid of this fucking thing, will you?"

I knew that was as much as I was going to get by way of agreement so I turned my full attention to the crazy specter busy tearing up the room around us. My magic crackled just below the surface of my skin like electrical energy begging to be released. Magic didn't like to be held in too long once conjured. It always wanted to be out there, bending and shaping reality to whatever form intended by the user. In this case, I intended for the magic to wipe the specter out of existence, which the magic would happily do as long as my control over it was strong enough. You still had to be careful though. The spells that conjured and propelled the magic had to be exact, and your control and belief had to be spot on, otherwise things could go awry.

Fortunately for all concerned, I'd had a lot of practice at that stuff.

Muttering a few last words in a language which wasn't well known to anyone outside of wizard circles, I directed the magical energy I had inwardly conjured so that a sphere of amberish light the size of a soccer ball formed in my right hand. The ball of energy turned bright yellow in the center as I charged it up further, and the air around the ball crackled and sparkled with animated light particles.

The specter stopped in the center of its whirlwind and gave an ear piercing screech that would have cracked the windows in the room if they weren't already broken. It was reacting to the magical energy in my hand, even though it didn't know what it was. The specter was just having a primal reaction to something it didn't understand. Everything it came across was a threat to it. Everything was worthy of being lashed out at.

Then, just as the specter burst from out of the center of the maelstrom it had created, I launched the ball of energy in my hand at it. The magic blast cut through the air at the speed of a cannon ball and slammed into the specter, spreading its blue colored energy throughout the ghostly entity until the specter gave one last screech as it exploded in a ball of blinding light, its form completely disintegrating in the air. The wind it had created stopped instantly and the objects it had swept up fell to the floor all at once. Then all was silent, and nothing remained of the specter apart from a few cobalt sparks floating in the air like fire-flies, eventually fading out a moment later.

"Fuck yeah!" I said, still buzzing from the magic flowing through me, turning to Leona for a high-five, only to see she was pointing her gun at me again. "Oh, for gods sake! Seriously? I just saved us from a malignant specter."

"That thing seemed pretty pissed at you," she said. "Why would that be?"

"Because specters like that often fixate on the type of person who traumatized and killed them. It could just be that the girl was murdered by a man. They don't have much of mind, as you seen. They run on raw emotion, nothing more."

"You seem to have an answer for everything, don't you?"

I nodded. "I normally do, yes. It's kinda my job to sort situations like this out. You would know that if you remembered me."

"Which I don't."

"Ah!" I said. "So you admit it is possible you do know me?"

"I'm not admitting anything," she said, finally lowering the gun. "As far as I'm concerned this is just another fucked up situation that I find myself in. Sometimes I wonder—"

"Why you ever took the job at Division? Yeah, you say that a lot."

A slight smile creased her thin, but perfectly formed, lips. "All right. So maybe you didn't kill the girl. What now?"

"Now, I try to find a way to reverse the spell I got caught up in. Then you'll remember me, and we can get back to being best buddies again."

"You're kidding, right? Best buddies?" She shook her head as if the idea didn't compute. "I just don't see it."

I smiled back. "As much as this spell I'm under is a pain in the ass, it's still going to be fun breaking down your barriers again to get to the soft center that I know lies underneath all that armor."

"I don't have a soft center," she said, almost in disgust. "Fucking chocolates have soft centers. Not me."

As Leona put her gun back in her holster, I went and picked mine up off the floor, sliding it inside my trench coat. "So this is where we part ways for now," I told her. "I'll call you when I find anything out. I have your personal cell number."

"Of course you do," she said with characteristic sarcasm. "Because we were such good friends, right?"

I grinned at her. "You go it."

She stepped in front of me. "I don't think I should be letting you go anywhere. I should keep you here until Brentwood arrives."

"Look," I said sighing. "I know you have your protocol and everything, but that would be a waste of time. Brentwood would have me taken into Division HQ and I don't have time for that. It would be better if you let me go so I can start looking into this mess and maybe find a way to fix it so we can catch this killer."

"We?" she said, raising her eyebrows.

I smiled at her as I began to walk away, glad when she didn't try to stop me. "The two of us work well together. You'll see."

"That's what I'm worried about. And Creed?"

I stopped and turned around. "Yes?"

"Don't make me regret letting you go. If I find out you tricked me, or had anything to do with that woman's murder, I'll hunt you down and kill you. You can bank on that."

My smile widened. "I wouldn't want it any other way."

4

# FORGOTTEN

AT DROPLETS OF rain fell from the night sky and made a faint crackling sound on the roof of the 1967 Cadillac Eldorado I was driving through the congested streets of Blackham City. The windshield wipers squeaked loudly over the glass as they worked in vain to clear the water pouring down the windshield, and the exhaust occasionally blew out as I drove, making it sound like gun shots going off.

It was October, so it wasn't that cold yet in the city, which was just as well, for the heating system in the car was busted. Come December, driving for me would feel like sitting in a fridge with wheels on, since I'd probably just keep forgetting to get the heating fixed as I always seemed to. Someday the old beast would break down altogether, hating me for neglecting it so much. Cars have feelings thanks to the psychic energy pumped out by their owners, turning the hunk of metal from a thing into an entity of sorts. You ever seen the movie *Christine*? It's kinda like that.

It's not just cars which are given life by their owners. When an object is exposed for a long enough period to strong emotions, such as love or hatred, it can obtain sentience. I once had to save a woman from her favorite vibrator when her Rampant Rabbit got a little *too* rampant and wanted to insert itself into any orifice it could find, no matter whose orifice it was. The priest that was called before me had a bit of a shock when he walked into the room where the vibrator was kept locked up. The rubbery thing came flying at the poor priest like a vibrating missile, earnestly trying to insert itself up his ass. I dare say it wasn't the first time that the Randy Bishop had something poking rampantly at his rear orifice. Whilst not a Bishop, his nickname was given by parishioners who knew of his fetishistic ways. Ultimately, Randy's fetishes were no match for Rampant's, and the two separated ways, the former in horror, the latter with a vibrating chuckle.

When I turned up, the sentient vibrator propelled itself at my ass as well. This happened several times before I finally got a hold of the squirming length of rubber to perform and exorcism. Yes, that's right. I performed an exorcism on a dildo. One of the joys of being a wizard for hire. You frequently end up in the most unusual and bizarre situations. I can only imagine the amount of time that woman must have spent with her Rampant Rabbit in order for it to become so animated and so singularly driven by blind lust. She must have *really* loved that thing.

I finally pulled the car up outside the brownstone building I lived in on Poker Street, a not quite affluent part of East Oakdale, but respectable nonetheless. The brownstone (or the Sanctum as I preferred to call it, since that is what it was) actually belonged to my Uncle Raymond, who bought the place over fifty years ago. I've been living in it, on and off, for quite a while. Rent free of course. Family rates and all that. My uncle spent most of his time in Ireland these days anyway, which is where I'm originally from.

The rain was still pelting down as I bounced out of the car and bounded up the steps to the front door of the Sanctum. Then I said a few words under my breath and concentrated my magic toward the heavy, reinforced door. A few seconds later, three different locks clicked one after the other from top to bottom and then the door thunked open. No front door keys for this wizard. I'd probably lose them anyway, as I had a habit of doing with keys, and much else besides. Today, for instance, I appeared to have lost my entire worldly identity, which took things to new heights, even for me.

Stepping inside the Sanctum, I closed the door behind me and each of the three locks reengaged by themselves. Security was important to me, as you can probably tell. There are just way too many dangerous things in the house, and given the break-ins that always occurred in my neighborhood, I refused to take any chances. Besides opportunistic burglars who might help themselves if given the chance, Blackham's full of people who grew up around magic (other wizard's, occult practitioners and Seekers), who therefore think nothing of breaking into a known wizard's house to steal their stuff for personal gain. Certain items contained within the Sanctum's various rooms have the power to cause major chaos and damage in the wrong hands, so you can't blame me for being so security conscious; besides which, no self-respecting wizard fails to employ wards throughout their domains to both keep certain things out, and others in.

Besides the warded front door, the Sanctum's also equipped with an alarm system of sorts. If anyone but me entered the house, I got hit with a vision in my head of the offending person or persons, no matter where I was.

For extra insurance, the Sanctum also has a backup security system in the form of Blaze, a Garra Wolf who I rescued from the clutches of a slave trader in the great city of Babylon in the Axius Dimension. The slave trader—an odious buffoon by the name of Toadious Brigstock—was someone I was chasing at the time, for he was abducting people from Earth and then taking them to Babylon to sell as slaves. A client's daughter was taken, so I went after Brigstock to get the girl back. In the process, I found Blaze chained up in the back of the slave trader's house. Brigstock used to use the wolf to round up his slaves and keep them in line like some sort of sick sheep herder, but at some point, Blaze refused to cooperate anymore (perhaps sensing the wrongness of what he was being asked to do) and so Brigstock chained the poor animal up. Being a sucker for animals (and people for that matter) in need, I broke Blaze free and he followed me and the girl I rescued back to Earth. That was over ten years ago. Blaze has been my faithful companion ever since.

Walking down the hallway and into the living room, I dropped my coat over the back of a chair piled high with fairly new books, most of them on some aspect of the occult because I liked to see if there was much truth in them. Which there often wasn't, but I read them anyway to reassure myself that real magic isn't making it too far into the world of the Sleepwalkers.

I found Blaze lying in the corner of the large room in his usual spot when I wasn't around. It was like he was waiting vigilantly for some intruder to pounce on, which he had done in the past, almost killing the first poor sod who ever tried to break in. Afterward, I had words with Blaze and told him to tone down his response next time. Now, if Blaze has cause to confront any intruders or unwelcome guests, he mostly just scares them away, perhaps gifting them an amorous love bite in his efforts to convince them into never coming back.

The big Garra Wolf (named after Garra, the Babylonian Goddess of Fire) stood up and came padding over to me as I crouched down to pet his thick black mane. Blaze was slightly bigger than your average Earth wolf. A magnificent beast and my most faithful companion (next to Leona, of course, but we won't go there at the moment). "Glad to see *you* still know who I am," I said to Blaze as he rubbed his big head against mine, his fiery yellow eyes—containing an intelligence and depth of understanding that never ceased to amaze me—looking deep into mine as he pushed his snout into my face, rubbing it affectionately against me as he made small but friendly growling noises in the back of his throat.

Obviously, the spell I was blasted with (indirectly it now seemed) didn't extend to the animals in my life, just the people. Although in saying that, I still had no idea of the spells full extent. Many spells have delayed effects that are often unknown until it's too late. So I reminded myself to do some knowledge gathering at my earliest convenience, lest I be taken surprise by some horrible latent effect.

I headed into the kitchen and asked Blaze, who'd followed me into the spacious room, if he was hungry. Dishes were piled up around the sink I hadn't a chance to clean up yet, and the place still smelled of Freddy Wong's Chinese food, that I'd ordered in the night before, Freddy being my favorite Pixiu slash chef in the whole of Blackham.

I opened the fridge and took out a plate with a large T-bone steak on it. The steak looked good, I have to say, but it did nothing to stimulate my own appetite. All I wanted was a drink. So after putting the plate on the floor so Blaze could have his dinner, I went to one of the kitchen cupboards and took out a bottle of Glenfiddich and a relatively clean glass, taking both back into the living room and sitting down in an old antique armchair that I often found myself sleeping in instead of my bed upstairs.

As I relaxed into the familiar contours of the chair, I poured myself a measure of the whiskey and sat drinking for a while, staring around the room at nothing, the rain outside pelting off the big bay window to the side of me. It was hard to relax or enjoy my drink with thoughts of my predicament dominating my mind. The worst part was the not knowing. How far did the spell extend? Did everyone I ever knew now see me as a complete stranger?

In an attempt to find out, I got up and retrieved a small leather-bound book from the mantelpiece above the fireplace. The scruffy black book was my book of contacts, gathered up over many years of being in Blackham. I did have a smart phone, of course, and a laptop, but I was, and always would be, decidedly old school. I therefore preferred to keep my most important information on paper or in my head. Magic was usually all the technology I needed.

There were hundreds of names in the contact book, but I picked out the number for the person who had known me the second longest. My mentor, Mitsuo Sanaka. Even though I had a physic link with the man, I decided to call him instead. If I'm now a complete stranger to him and he finds my presence in his mind, things will very promptly get quite ugly for me.

"Hello?" said a quietly deep voice after a few rings. "Who is this?"

"It's me," I said, awaiting his response to see if he recognized my voice.

"Me?"

I sighed, knowing where things were going. "August Creed? Your long time student?"

The silence on the other end of the phone extended for what felt like an age but in all likelihood was only a score of seconds, so much so that my hope grew to the level where his denial felt like a swift kick to the balls when it indelibly arrived. "I don't know any August Creed," in his at times infuriatingly calm voice. "Don't call me again, please."

"He hung up on me. Goddamn it." I looked at Blaze who was now lying in the middle of the living room floor on an old Persian style rug, next to a pile of old vinyl records (only a few of which have magical properties, the rest only there for my enjoyment). "If Sanaka doesn't bloody know me anymore, then who does?"

Blaze stared back at me with his deep yellow eyes as a mewling sort of noise came from deep within his throat.

"Exactly, Blaze. Let's try a few more people before I go all in with the despair, shall we?"

I chose another contact from the black book. The infamous John Constantine. Maybe the old dog still remembered me. "Constantine," I said when he answered, using the tone of someone who knew the irascible wizard well. "How you doing?"

"Who the 'ell is this?" Constantine asked.

"It's Creed. August Creed. We—"

"Creed? I don't know any *Creed*, mate."

I cursed silently. "We met in London years ago, John. The kid from Ireland, dark hair, good looking." I gave a chuckle. "You warned me to forget about magic, have a normal life. I didn't listen. You introduced me to the Astral Plane, gave me exorcism tips, showed me the best bars in London."

Constantine went silent for a moment, during which I heard the unmistakable chatter of a pub in the background. For a moment, I got my hopes up, thinking he finally recognized me, but alas, that wasn't the case. "Nah, sorry mate," Constantine said eventually. "Don't know ya. Now, if you don't mind, I'm kinda in the middle of something 'ere, so piss off and leave me alone, will ya."

Sighing again, I said, "Sure, John. Bye."

After that, I tried a few more contacts from the book. Every person I called had never heard of me. Frustrated, I tossed the phone away where it landed with a clacking sound on the floor (I'm a chronic phone abuser). Then I got up and went to the large dresser in the room, pulled open one of the drawers and lifted out a stack of photographs. Family stuff mostly, pictures of my parents, my sister and brother when they were all still alive. I should have been in those photos as well. I wasn't. I rifled through more drawers, looking for identity papers and a passport that should have been there, but weren't. Exasperated, I eventually stopped rifling, taking the hint.

"Well, Blaze," I said, leaning against the dresser with my arms folded. "Its official. I've been erased." I shook my head. "Question is, how the hell do I get *un*erased?"

The mewling noise from Blaze's mouth said he didn't know.

# 5

# A FRIENDLY CALL

 AYBE YOU HAVEN'T guessed yet, but I'm older than I look. A fair bit older, in fact. I'll not tell you exactly *how* old, for I'm sure you will work that out for yourself at some point. Despite my age, however, I still don't look a day over twenty-nine, maybe thirty if I have a particularly nasty hangover, which can be all too often. Thanks to the wonders of magic, I don't age the way most people do, which is one of the few benefits of being a wizard (I wish I could say pussy was one, but it isn't).

That's not to say my life was all sparkly stars and rainbows. Far from it. I mean, look at the situation I was in. No one in the world bloody knew who I was anymore, and for someone who had been around for as long as I had been, that was a lot of people.

So when I woke up the day after being hexed, I did so with a heavy sense of existential loneliness. It was a cold feeling, knowing that I was all alone in the world, with nary a fucking soul to comfort me.

Except maybe Leona. Despite being a stranger to her as much as I was to everyone else, thanks to our run-in the day before, Leona now knew me better than anyone else on the planet. It remained to be seen whether that meant she would give me the time of day next time we spoke.

To test the waters, I decided to call her up after making myself coffee in the kitchen, noticing as I did so that Blaze wasn't around. This probably meant the wolf had turned himself invisible and had gone strolling around the city as he liked to do sometimes. Either that, or he was lying in some other part of the house somewhere. No doubt he would turn up again in his own time.

"Leona," I said when she answered my call, my voice groggy after the whiskey the night before. "How are you this fine morning?"

"You," she said, sounding like she had been up for hours, as I knew she had

been. She worked out every day before breakfast. Kettlebells and heavy bag training, followed by stretching. "How'd you get my number?"

"I told you I already had it, didn't I?"

"Yeah, you did. What do you want?"

"What's your progress on the case?" I asked

"None of your damn business," she replied.

Normally she wasn't quite so curt with me when I asked her about Division
business, which the murdered girl had no doubt become. At that point, she didn't
know or trust me enough to be so forthcoming with such information, however.
Which was also exactly how she was when we first met a few years before. She was
hostile and guarded, as was her nature when it came to people she didn't know or
trust. "Come on, Leona. Don't be like that. I'm going need your help on this."

"On this? You say that like it's your case or something. It isn't."

"Oh, yes it is, don't even go there. I've been made into God's lonely man here.
No one fucking knows me anymore. Not a single soul, apart from Blaze that is."

"Blaze?"

"My Garra Wolf. You two get on. You both have the same predatory instincts
and intolerance for fools."

"Fools like you, you mean?"

"Yeah, very funny. And harsh, I gotta say. This is no joke, you know."

"I didn't say it was."

"So why are you refusing to help me then?"

"Because despite what you say, I could never see us being friends, or, God
forbid, sleeping together."

"Well, we were friends, Leona, and more," I said, getting a little cranky now. I
needed more coffee. "What can I say, I grew on you like moss on a stone."

"Moss on a stone? You're so weird."

"Yeah, and so are you. Trust me, sweetheart, we were pretty good together,
considering. And I know you have no other friends. You need me."

"Firstly, I don't need *anyone*. And secondly, don't *ever* call me sweetheart again."

"Or let me guess, you'll cut my balls off?"

"Yeah," she said, after a moment's hesitation.

"You know why you hesitated there? Because you were actually going to say
that. You said the same thing to me the first time I ever called you sweetheart. It's
like I said, I know you, Leona Lawson."

"Why would I tolerate a pain in the ass like you anyhow?"

"Because," I told her, "you have affection for me. We get on. It might not seem
that way now, but we do, trust me. What if I name your favorite film, will that help?"

"That would just be a cheap parlor trick, but go on."

"It's *The Matrix*. You have the hots for Keanu Reeves."

"Un-uh."

"Don't un-uh me. This isn't a game show. Admit it."

"I'm going now."

I sighed, defeated. I'd forgotten what a brick wall she was. "Fine. Enjoy your
morning Cappuccino-to-go at Barney's."

"How did...you're beginning to creep me out now. You better not be fucking
stalking me."

"Just call me if you find anything out, will you? I'll do the same. We'll keep each other in the loop like we used to."

"Goodbye, Creed." She hung up the phone.

"At least she used my name," I said hopefully to Blaze, who had just walked into the kitchen. "That's progress, right?"

The big wolf stared at me, then walked over, his claws clacking on the hardwood floor. Then he pressed his head against my leg and made a growling noise. Crouching down, I put my arms around his thick neck and gave him a squeeze. "At least I have you, Blaze, eh?" Blaze pulled away then and wandered off into the living room where he would most likely lie for the rest of the day before prowling the streets in invisibility mode when darkness fell that evening. "I'll take that as a yes, then. Good boy."

Shaking my head and pouring myself another coffee with lots of sugar, I idled in the kitchen for another while, staring at the floor while I figured out my next move. My chief concern was reversing the spell I was under, which I wasn't even sure could be done. In general, the more powerful the spell, the less likelihood there was of ever reversing it, and the spell I was under was a fucking powerhouse. Certainly one of the most potent and expert uses of magic I had seen in a long while. I mean, think about it, the power it would take to erase the world's memory of anyone affected by it and anyone else standing close enough to it. Like me, for instance. There weren't many who had access to that kind of power and those that did probably channeled it from an entity much more commanding than themselves.

All of which meant only one thing. If I had any chance of reversing the spell put on me, I had to find out exactly what kind of power I was dealing with.

It was time to hit the books.

6

---

# A WELCOME DISTRACTION

$\mathcal{T}$HE BASEMENT OF the Sanctum was where the majority of the spell books were kept, or at least, the ones that held real power. Make no mistake, some books are dangerous. Some books will kill you just for opening them up. With books like that, you need to make sure you're fully suited up before you even think about approaching them. And by suited up, I mean charged up with defensive magic.

There are two books in the Sanctum—*The Babylonian Book Of Black Magic* and *The Book Of Deathly Shadows*—that are virtually unapproachable. My Uncle Ray warned me not to go near either of them when I first moved into the Sanctum, not unless I wanted to be sucked into a dimension that wasn't anywhere near as much fun as Earth. Only a master wizard like Ray could have handled those books, and only when he absolutely had to. Luckily, I had no need for either of the books. I was hoping to find what I needed in one of the less dangerous tomes. Assuming the spell was documented anywhere at all. There is always a high probability that a spell won't be documented anywhere except in the mind of its creator, especially if said spell had only recently being crafted. Time would tell on that front.

The basement itself was long and narrow, with a low ceiling and a perpetual smell of damp mixed with the strange odors of the books themselves. An entire wall was filled floor to ceiling with hefty, dusty tomes that buckled the wooden shelves under their weight. And despite there being thousands of books, each one was unique in both appearance and content, and I knew them all intimately. If there was a spell that erased the world's memory of a person (and I was living proof there was), I hoped to find it in one of those books.

In the center of the basement floor, there was a large wooden table with stout, intricately carved legs. Scattered over the surface of the table were a whole collection of glass funnels, flasks, beakers, cylinders and other stuff that I used for my alchemical experiments. The wall opposite the bookshelves was where I kept all the potions, elixirs, magical compounds and a plethora of other ingredients that I used for spells (not every spell required props, of course, but many of them did).

Also on that side of the room was an old record player and a stack of vinyl from the sixties through to the eighties (anything after that I didn't much care for). After sorting through the pile, I selected the 12" extended version of *Blue Monday* by New Order, a tune that always helped me think. And when the soothingly familiar synth hook of the track kicked in, I began to walk slowly by the book-shelves, running my eyes over each title.

The first book I took out was a centuries old Grimoire that had been bound in dark red leather and which smelled faintly of decayed vegetable matter. I dropped the heavy book on the table next to all the alchemy stuff and opened it up, a cloud of dust blowing up to greet me as I did so, causing me to sneeze.

For the next twenty minutes, I turned each waxy page in the book, quickly scanning the spells in there to see if any of them resembled the one I was looking for. When I came up empty, I slammed the book closed and moved on to the next one. And the next one. And the next one after that. Until before I knew it, I'd spent half the day down there, pouring over dusty tomes (which was nothing new for me as I'd lost weeks at a time studying old books, time that I barely noticed go by, such was the depth of my fascination and concentration).

Eventually, I halted my search and poured myself yet another whiskey, half filling one of the glass beakers on the table and plunking myself down in a rickety chair, the sounds of Crimson Glory now filling the stuffy basement.

*What the hell am I going to do?* I wondered.

Already I felt the dark corners of my mind begin to stretch out as they threatened to consume my sanity, driving me toward a madness that I might never escape from. For the first time in a long while, I felt genuinely scared about my prospects. The thoughts of going out into the world and starting afresh, although it might appeal to some people, didn't much appeal to me. The weight of loneliness was crushing.

*You only think that now*, I thought, drinking more whiskey and trying to keep my mind focused on finding solutions instead of highlighting the problem. *You'll find a way.*

I hoped I was right as I finished the whiskey in the beaker and went to leave the room, intending to go upstairs and start in on the books up there. As I went to leave, however, my phone rang. The caller ID said LEONA. A smile crossed my face when I saw her name. Thank God for Leona. She was the only thing making my nightmare more tolerable. "Hey, sweetheart," I said, tipsy from the whiskey. "I told you I would grow on you, didn't I?"

Leona made a tutting sound. "Get over yourself," she said sternly. "And didn't I tell you not to call me that?" She sounded agitated.

"What's wrong? And what's all that noise in the background? It sounds like explosions."

"It *is* explosions. There's some fucking nutjob in Harlington blowing the place to shit, using fireballs that come out of his hands."

*A Pyromancer*, I thought straight away. Probably one of the aforementioned breed of practitioners whose obsession with magic has gotten the better of them.

"So shoot him. That's what you always do with these out of control types, is it not?"

"You think I haven't tried to already, genius? He has some sort of forcefield around him. Nothing is getting through, and no one can go near him without instantly bursting into flames. People are fucking dying here, Creed."

I made my way hurriedly out of the basement to the living room where I grabbed my trench coat and pulled it on. "Don't worry. I can help you. I'll be there in a minute."

"You're in Harlington?"

"No, East Oakdale."

"Then how—"

"Hang tight. I'm coming."

I tossed the phone on the armchair and looked over at Blaze, who was lying on the floor, his head now raised as his yellow eyes sparked with interest. "This sounds like a job I could use your help on, Blaze. Come on."

Blaze jumped immediately to its feet and quickly crossed the room before standing at heel beside me, making excited rumbling noises in his throat. One thing about Blaze, he was always up for some action.

"Ready?" I said to him.

I placed a hand on Blaze's back, closed my eyes for a few seconds and then we disappeared out of the room like we never even there to begin with.

# 7

## PYROMANCER

*T*eleportation is something that takes a long time to master. You have to manipulate a lot of different strings at once to pull it off successfully. I mean, it involves splintering yourself into a gazillion tiny pieces and then transporting those pieces across space and time so you can reassemble them all afterward. Imagine if you threw a handful of sand as far as you could, and then tried to rearrange that handful of sand into the exact same formation as it was in before you threw it. Every single grain. Does that sound hard? Impossible even? Well, that's the level of difficulty you're up against when you attempt teleportation.

It's a skill that took me nearly thirty years to master, and one which I didn't use very often, mainly because it put a significant drain on my magic reserves. The farther I had to teleport, the more of a drain I experienced. I could also only teleport to within about a five hundred mile radius at that point. Which was okay, because Harlington was well within that radius, being about ten miles away from East Oakdale.

After fully visualizing where wanted to go, I landed with Blaze in a dark alley in Harlington, which was intentional. Onlookers tend not to take too well to people just appearing on the street out of thin air. Plus, there was also another reason for my secrecy that I haven't yet mentioned. Due to the paradoxical nature of magic, if any non-adept (Sleepwalker) happened to witness magic in action, the magic itself would become skewed (how skewed would depend on how many people saw it). The consequences of misaligned magic could often be disastrous, as I found out to my detriment enough times in the past. To a certain extent you could offset this unwelcome side effect by concocting a spell and casting it on certain individuals, so their presence would have no negative effects on any other spells that were cast. As with Leona for instance (I neutralized her influence shortly after we met since I would often have to perform magic around her). So bottom line, I gotta be careful about who sees me do my thing.

I couldn't say the same for the maniac who was burning up the place in Harlington. From the alley, I saw flames and smoke rising half a block away, past the rundown tenement buildings and near the local Taco Box. There was also a gas station nearby, and I wondered how long it would be before the whole place went boom. "Not looking good," I said to Blaze, who was standing beside me with his ears pricked up, his tail held straight out as if he was waiting for a signal to go charging in. "Not yet, Blaze. Let's see what we're dealing with first."

Blaze looked at me and then turned invisible as we headed out of the alley, although he was still clearly visible to me. He could show himself to whomever he wanted, which was usually only me.

We ran across the street and hurried the half block to where all the chaos was originating. Not surprisingly, there was only one firetruck that I could see, four firefighters attempting to put out a number of burning cars in the street and not succeeding because the flames were so fierce. I couldn't see any cops or media yet, nor did I expect to. Harlington wasn't far off being a slum town, so the city authorities tended to avoid it as much as possible. Cops and other badge carriers were not welcome in Harlington, and given what was happening at present, that was probably for the best. The last thing I wanted to see was some out of control Pyromancer all over the damn news and social media.

"Creed!" Leona came running across the street in her usual getup, her long black coat billowing behind her as she ran on powerful legs. She gripped one of her custom Berettas in one hand. "How'd you get here so fast? And is that a damn wolf with you?" She stayed back a few feet as she eyed the huge wolf with fearful suspicion, raising her gun slightly, so it pointed toward Blaze.

"You can see him?" I asked.

"Of course I can see it. It's a huge fucking wolf. How can I not see it?"

Leona and Blaze knew each other well. But as Blaze was attached to my memories, that meant Leona's memory of the wolf had been erased along with everything else about me. The spell was thorough, I'd say that much. "He's here to help. Don't worry."

"How'd you get here so fast?"

"I teleported of course. Now where is this firestarter at?"

Leona gave me a queer look like she didn't quite take in what I said. Then she just shook her head and pointed toward the Taco Box across the street. "Behind there, currently blowing up cars." As if to confirm what she said, there was a loud explosion from behind the Taco Box and a cloud of black smoke billowed up into the night sky.

*Goddamn amateurs*, I thought as I shook my head. They don't know how to keep it in their pants. "Let me guess. A kid, early twenties at most? Looks like a crazed obsessive?"

"He has that look," Leona said, eying me up at the same time like she saw the same look in me. "Why? You know him?"

"Not him specifically, but I know his type. A member of this new Occult Underground that has sprung up in the last ten years or so. You've heard of them, no doubt?" I had told her all about the new breed of adepts before, but of course, she wouldn't have remembered a single word of it, only the information given to her by The Division. "I've heard of them." She shook her head dismissively. "But listen, they're all fucking hedge magicians to me. I don't care what they call themselves. When they do shit like this, that's when I care. You gotta plan, you and...your wolf?"

"I hadn't thought about it," I said, beginning to head across the street toward the Taco Box. "Hey, maybe it's just a guy who had too much chili on his taco earlier."

"Did you really just say that to me?" she asked, striding purposefully beside me.

"Humor. Don't worry. I know it isn't your strong suit."

She threw me a look. "Like this is a really fucking funny situation. Three people have burnt to death so far."

"Just trying to lighten things up. Why have you no backup here?"

"Because we're stretched kinda thin right now, that's why. So much shit is happening in this city these days that we can hardly keep up. Every day, some new freak like this guy comes crawling out of the woodwork."

"I hope you don't include me in that summation."

"We got incidents all over tonight," she went on, ignoring me. "Crazies everywhere for some damn reason."

We were at the corner of the Taco Box. I had to stop and stare in astonishment at the post-apocalyptic scene of destruction in the small lot. There were about a dozen cars in the parking lot, and about half of them were on fire, creating a fierce heat that you could feel searing your face. The cause of all the fiery destruction was a young looking dude standing in the center of the parking lot. From what I could see of him he was completely naked, either from his clothes being consumed by the flames and heat surrounding him, or because he'd presumably wanted to save that very thing from happening and thus came out without them. Either way, I didn't care. I just wanted to stop the guy before he decided to hit the gas station down the street and caused even more damage. Getting to the guy would be the first challenge. Getting to the guy was going to prove difficult, however, and not just because he was shooting jets of flame like napalm from his hands, but because he was surrounded by some sort of crackling, fiery force field that shimmered around him, sealing him in an orangey translucent cocoon.

Leona stood beside me, her gun aimed at the naked hedge magician in the parking lot. "So what do we do, Mr. warlock?" she said. "Any bright ideas?"

"I'll excuse your pun there," I said back. "And I'm not a warlock. warlocks are drama queens. Do I seem like a drama queen to you? Don't answer that." I stood and thought for a moment, then nodded to myself. "I might be able to work something here."

"Well, do it quick because he just saw us."

I snapped my head toward the wannabe adept in the parking lot, who was now staring straight at us. Through the veneer of his defensive energy cocoon, I noticed the sneering grin on his face as he was quite literally drunk with power.

*He thinks he's unstoppable.*

In my mind I was rapidly sorting through an index of spells that I could use on the guy. It had to be something that would bring down his defenses, so that Leona could then shoot him. No sense thinking she was going to detain the guy, not after he killed people.

Standing just ahead of me, and showing no fear of the crazed fire conjurer, was Blaze. Wisps of dark smoke were beginning to rise out of his hackles, and along his head and body, deep veins of fire began to split open and spew small but intense flames. The Garra Wolf in Blaze was coming to the fore, his elemental power reacting to the Pyromancer before him. "Wait, Blaze," I barked at him. There was no way Blaze would get through the force field surrounding the guy in the lot, and I didn't want to take the chance that it would somehow cause him injury. You never knew with crazed, uncontrolled magic.

Just as the naked Pyromancer raised both hands in our direction, gearing up for another infernal blast, my mind hit upon a spell that might just take care of the dude's defensive shield. It was a simple enough elemental spell that would counter the fiery energy protecting the guy. But just as I was about to quickly utter the words that would focus the magic for the spell, the novice Pyromancer's hands lit up with flames and then erupted like volcanoes, spewing twin jets of fire right at us. It felt like we were being attacked by an angry dragon who wanted only to anni-hilate us from the face of the Earth.

Now having no alternative due to the immediate reduction of my reaction time, I opted for the only option that matters; which is to say, I grabbed Leona to tuck her tightly against me whilst completing a 180° turn, and raising my trench coat to protect us from the approaching conflagration (despite what you might be thinking, that is the exact priority order I'll always opt for, that which protects Leona first and foremost). You see, a crucial piece of information pertinent to this scenario that I've not yet mentioned, is that my coveted trench coat is actually the cultivated hide of some unfortunate demon. Born of skin capable of withstanding the infernal flames that scourge the Underworld clean of creatures too weak to survive there, meant that I was comfortably sure that it could handle the abuse of some manic earthly Pyromancer. Fortunately my faith in my trusty clothing item was paid in full. Besides which, having a sneaky spooner moment with my gal' did wonders for my morale.

A split second later, I felt the hot pressure on my back as the jets of fire hit like two high-pressure hoses, forcing me to pitch forward into Leona as the two of us fell to the ground. The flames continued for another few seconds, my trench coat beginning to heat up to a temperature that was going way past comfortable.

But despite the vicious heat, I forced myself to focus on the spell I was about to cast a moment ago. By the time the flames had stopped ravaging my back, I had the spell charged up and ready to go.

Spinning around quickly, I forced out one hand to direct the spell's magic toward the Pyromancer. A blast of ice blue energy left my hand and poured over the defensive shield surrounding him. The guy smiled at first, thinking his shield had withstood my attack. But his smile soon faded when the fiery energy around him began to freeze up, and a thick frost spread rapidly over it until the guy inside was no longer visible. There was now just a huge ball of ice there in the center of the parking lot.

As Leona detached herself from me, she looked to where the Pyromancer had been and seemed stunned for a second by what she was seeing. "Nice," she said, bouncing to her feet.

"We won't have long before—"

My words were interrupted when the icy cocoon surrounding the Pyro in the parking lot exploded in a ball of flame, bits of thick ice propelled in all directions, melted before they hit the ground.

"You were saying?" Leona had her gun pointed at the guy again.

"Shoot him while his shield is down!" I said, taking out my own pistol and pulling back the hammer as I aimed at the Pyro, fired and missed. "Shit!"

Leona got three shots off, one of which hit the Pyro in the leg, but which did nothing to slow him down.

*Too jacked up on power and adrenaline to even feel it.*

Then the Pyro directed a fireball at Leona as she was shooting. I dived and pushed her out of the way, taking the fireball in the back, the force of it lifting me off my feet and sending me flying forward to the hard ground. It was like getting hit with a hot ball of lead and having it drop on you as you got smacked to the ground. More than that, it hurt like a motherfucker.

Despite the pain, I groaned and managed to flip myself around so I could direct another attack at the Pyro. But then I saw Blaze go charging in, and I stopped with my attack. He was majestically ablaze, lines of fiery elemental energy all over his body like thin trenches of magma. The flames which erupted from these power lines were intense, surrounding Blaze. The Pyro didn't even notice the wolf coming at him until the last second, and when he did notice, his mouth dropped open as he realized that he couldn't counter fire with fire, at least not fire with sharp teeth and claws.

Blaze growled with guttural aggression and launched himself at the Pyro from over ten feet away, his fiery black body bolting through the air, his massive jaws wide open and aimed squarely at the Pyro's throat. The Pyro all but screamed as he tried to backtrack, but he didn't stand a chance. Blaze hit the guy in the chest like ten tons of steel, his jaws clamped over the Pyro's throat as he flattened him to the ground.

"Halt!" I shouted at Blaze as I scrambled to my feet. "Halt, Blaze!"

Blaze's eyes found mine, his powerful jaws still wrapped around the Pyro's throat. I knew by the look on the wolf's face that Blaze wanted nothing more than to crush the Pyro's neck and rip the dude's head off, which he absolutely could do, but I didn't want him to go that far.

Leona joined me as I ran into the parking lot and commanded Blaze to back away from the downed Pyro, whose fire magic had all but burnt out by then. Without all that fiery energy, the guy was just a skinny, naked cretin who no longer inspired even an ounce of fear. When Blaze finally let go of his target, he left behind a number of puncture wounds in the guy's skinny neck, blood oozing from the shallow holes.

"Don't let it kill me!" the guy screeched.

"Don't worry," Leona said. "The wolf isn't going to kill you. I am."

She aimed her gun at his head and fired.

# 8

# A VISITOR

"YOU DIDN'T SEEM too put out by me shooting that guy."

We were sitting outside the Sanctum in Leona's black, government issue SUV. Blaze was in the back, lying stretched across the leather seat. "Put out?" I said. "I stopped being put out by things a long time ago. Besides, I've known you for three years. I know how you operate. I know the protocol you've been given."

Leona stared across at me for a moment, her expression softer now than it was before, but still guarded. "Three years, huh?"

"Three years, and in that time I've seen you shoot more than a few people."

"Like who?"

I thought for a second. "Most recently, that vampire who was raping and feeding on girls in Mansfield Park. You inflicted massive physical damage with eight hollow points before bringing the body back to Division HQ for his Final Death."

"I remember that," Leona said, shaking her head slightly. "But you weren't there. I was alone on that."

"I was standing right beside you. You shot him with a Desert Eagle, took half his head off. You complained about the mess in the back there, about his brains spilling out on the carpet."

Staring straight ahead, Leona asked, "So what are you going to do about this curse you're under, Creed? How are you going to fix it?"

"I'm still working on that," I replied, a by now familiar feeling of impending doom coming over me.

"Any progress?"

"Nope, unfortunately not."

"Well, you look like a guy who has ways." Her ice blue eyes reflected the yellowish light of the street lamps outside, making her eyes look almost preternatural and damn sexy, I have to say.

I laughed. "Oh, I have ways all right..."

"I'll bet," she said, laughing herself as she started the engine. "I gotta go and make my report."

"Any information yet on the dead girl?" I asked her.

"They're still running forensics. The investigation is just getting started. I'll let you know if anything comes up."

"All right, thanks," I said, happy to hear she was finally co-operative toward me, and even civil it seemed. Despite nearly getting scorched to death by a nerdy Pyromancer, I was glad that I had gotten the chance to earn Leona's trust by saving her life. As a soldier, she wouldn't forget that.

I opened the passenger door and then looked around at her. "You know there's going to be more bodies, right? Whoever killed that girl isn't going to stop. God knows how many he killed before casting that spell."

"There's always more bodies," Leona said sighing. "We'll deal with whatever comes up like we always do."

"And by we, you mean The Division, or me and you?"

She shook her head and kept her gaze straight ahead. "I'll see ya, Creed."

I opened the back door for Blaze and he jumped out to the pavement, invisible once again. I was about to close the door when Leona said, "Hey, Creed?"

"Yeah?" I said.

"Thanks for earlier. You saved my life."

I smiled, happy to hear her say it, consoled that I had at least some connection left in the world with someone. "It's what I do."

She smiled before gunning the SUV and taking off down the street, tires screeching as she turned the corner at the end of the block and disappeared from view.

When I went inside the brownstone and closed the door behind me, Blaze stopped dead in the middle of the hallway and started growling, his heckles up. Without thinking I took out my pistol, pondering as I did that I needed to kick my own arse for only picking up on what Blaze was sensing after his reaction pointed to that conclusion first. Someone was in the Sanctum.

Walking past Blaze, I stepped inside the living room, pistol aimed in front of me as I looked around the room, unsure of what I would find. Then, in the chair by the window, I saw a figure sitting cloaked in shadow. Aiming the pistol, I cocked the hammer back. "Who are you?" I said, wondering how the hell anyone managed to get past my security measures. Why didn't I get a vision that someone was in the house? Unless I did, but I was too busy with the Pyro to notice, though I doubted it. More like the intruder somehow blocked the vision in my head.

"I think the real question," said a deep, steady voice that I recognized straight away. "Is who are you?"

And that's when it felt like a vice had been clamped over my head and my brains were about to be squeezed out of any orifice they could find in order to reduce the pressure inside my head, beginning with my ears.

9

---

# BAD NEWS

*T*HE CRUSHING PRESSURE in my head was caused by Mitsuo Sanaka as he mentally forced his way into my mind, pulling apart the very fabric of my consciousness as easily as pulling back a pair of curtains. Normally my mind wasn't so easily broken into, protected as it was by various warding spells that would repel most attempts at forced entry by hostile adepts. But this was no mere adept breaking into my mind, and I couldn't help wincing at the pain Sanaka's psychic foraging was causing. I could only wince as Sanaka's barrage indiscriminately carved up the grey matter inside my skull. His reckless rummaging mimicking what I imagine it might feel like to have a starving rat be given free rein to consume at will whatever morsels are left over from such foraging. Sanaka was opening and slamming doors in my mind, searching through my memories. But the curse I was under was such that it made it impossible for anyone to know me through my own memories. *I* was still conscious of those memories, but for Sanaka, the memories were closed off. For him, it would have been like moving through a black fog that obscured almost everything from view.

After several long and drawn out moments of that painfully invasive probing, I could tolerate it no longer, so I started to force him back out of my mind. But this was no mere wizard I was pushing against, this was a master wizard, the person who had taught me in the first place how to enter someone's mind and how to force out anyone who invaded my own.

"If you were really my student," Sanaka said. "You would eject me from your mind."

My face screwed up with the extreme effort it was taking to fight back against him. It was like trying to push a stubborn bull out of a field, so firmly planted in my mind was he. And it wasn't just that. Part of his cunning was that he didn't direct all his energy in one big block. He instead would allow his psychic energy to branch off like tentacles that reached around your defenses from all angles, making it impossible to block them all. But Sanaka had also taught me how to mount multiple defenses at once that would allow me to counter his splintered attacks. My eyes scrunched closed as I concentrated harder, my hands and arms tense with the effort, until I eventually managed to throw Sanaka out of my mind.

He could've increased the depth and ferocity of his attack to leave me in a vegetative state whilst he accessed my mind at will. But the point of the test that arose once he'd found whatever he was looking for, shifted to assessing whether my defenses handled his efforts in a manner akin to any he'd have taught me if I were telling the truth about being his student.

"Jesus," I said, relaxing a little and turning on the light, although my head was still thumping from the pressure put on it. "Sanaka. What are you even doing here? You said you didn't know me when I called you earlier." I didn't need to ask how he got past my security measures. That would have been child's play to him.

The old wizard stood up from his chair. Of Japanese descent, Sanaka wasn't a particularly tall man, nor was he what you would call physically imposing. He did, however, exude a calm composure that frankly, could be a little unnerving at times. In the two decades I had known him, I had seen him lose his composure exactly three times, and two of those times were down entirely to me. Things could get a little heated between us sometimes, although I haven't seen Sanaka for the past few months, as he was always off on some clandestine mission doing God knows what. For someone who was over three hundred years old at that point though, he looked good in his black slacks and dark pullover, although his gray-streaked dark hair and beard were slightly longer than they were last time I saw him.

As always, Sanaka was not without his sword, which rested against the front of the chair. The sword was a Japanese Katana and was made by Sanaka over two centuries ago in Japan so he could protect himself against a brutal band of Ronin who were out for his blood at the time. Sanaka served as a wizard of sorts to the Emperor at the time. The Ronin once served as Samurai to the Emperor, until one day Sanaka realized the Samurai had sold their souls to a demon in return for greater fighting and healing abilities. As far as Sanaka was concerned, anyone who sold their soul to a demon could no longer be trusted because they could be made to be a puppet of the demon at any time, and thus the Samurai posed a threat to the Emperor, who banished the Samurai immediately. None of the sixteen Samurai took kindly to being banished. Revenge was promised. Inevitably, the Samurai returned and managed to overrun the palace, killing the Emperor in the process. The Samurai had become so preternaturally strong that no one could stop them. Sanaka managed to escape the palace, which is when he decided he would need the right weapon if he was going to avenge the Emperor's death and restore justice in the palace, which he was honor bound to do. So he forged himself a sword from steel and magic, a sword so powerful it would be able to strike down anything it cut. I'm sure you can guess what happened next. Sanaka used his sword to kill every one of the sixteen Samurai, including the demon they sold their souls to. The sword had hardly left his side since. To Sleepwalkers, the sword was invisible. To the magically initiated however, the polished, blood-red scabbard stood out against Sanaka's customary dark clothing—serving as a warning not to fuck with the man carrying it.

Blaze had stopped growling and was now padding over to Sanaka like he was an old friend, rubbing his head against the master wizard's waist. Despite not remembering the Blaze, Sanaka didn't seem uncomfortable at all in his presence as he stroked the wolf's head. "That's Blaze," I said, taking off my coat and examining the back of it. Apart from a few scorch marks, it seemed fine. Demon skin. Every high street should stock it. "You two were friends, in fact."

"That doesn't surprise me," Sanaka said. "A magnificent animal."

I poured myself a glass of whiskey and sat on the arm of one of the chairs after moving the books that were stacked there. "I'll not offer you one. I know you don't drink anything you haven't made yourself."

He looked at me with his usual cryptic smile and deep, knowing brown eyes that never gave anything away. Ever. "It appears you do know me."

"You've been my mentor for the last twenty years after my Uncle Raymond put me on to you. Raymond McCreedy?"

Sanaka nodded. "A wizard of great distinction."

"What brings you here, Sanaka? I'm just a stranger to you, after all, as I am to everyone else now."

"Your phone call stirred something in me."

"As long as it wasn't your loins. We might have a problem then."

Sanaka gave me a dismissive smile and shook his head before sitting down again, his left hand automatically going for his sword, which he held in a loose grip. Blaze sat on the floor, at Sanaka's feet. "I felt a faint connection when I heard your voice. You also mentioned the spell you were under. It's a type of spell that I have encountered before."

I straightened up in interest. "Really? Great. You can tell me how to break it then."

"There is no breaking it," Sanaka said, shaking his head. "If you were really my apprentice, then you would know such spells can't be reversed."

I sighed and slumped my shoulders again. "I do know that, unfortunately. I've been trying to find some reference to the spell itself, but so far I've come up empty. I thought maybe if I knew what kind of spell it was, then I could try to find a way to counter it somehow."

Reaching inside my coat, I took out my phone to bring up the crime scene photos for Sanaka to hopefully provide feedback on the symbolic details of the gruesome sacrifice, perhaps something in the details that I've thus far been unable to discern. Sanaka took the phone and flicked through the photos, his face impassive as he did so, giving nothing away. Eventually, he handed the phone back and I waited expectantly on his input. I knew better than to rush him. Sanaka was never in any rush to speak and sometimes sat in contemplative silence for a long time, to the point where you thought he was just ignoring you. But then sometime later he would speak again as if the conversation had just started. On this occasion, his lapsed silence only lasted a few moments while he seemed to consider the photos he had just looked at. "These symbols point toward a power only found outside of this dimension, a place of continual chaos and horrors that I can't even begin to describe, a place known as the Kiroth Dimension."

Dimensions are as infinite in number as the universe is infinite in size. Each one represents an entire world that has sprung up or been deliberately created within a pocket of space and time. Dimensions can be accessed through portals if you have the power and expertise to open one, plus the knowledge of how to navigate once inside the portal. Safe to say, inter-dimensional travel is a bit more complicated than traveling on the subway system and if you don't know what you are doing you could end up trapped between dimensions forever.

"The Kiroth Dimension?" I thought for a second. "Yes, Kiroth. Ruled over by Rloth, if my memory serves. Which by the way, is a bit shaky now, thanks to your breaking and entering earlier."

Sanaka smiled humorlessly. "Rloth originated from the Outer Dimensions. The darkness it brought with it to Kiroth was all encompassing. Kiroth is a vicious dimension of chaos and disorder. The spell affecting you goes by a language even I can barely speak, but in rough translation, it is called the Memory Shredder."

I snorted. "The Memory Shredder? It's certainly an apt name, considering what it did to me. And before you say it, I wasn't careless with my defenses. The spell's power blew right through them."

"I would have expected nothing less. Any magic originating from the Kiroth Dimension would be unstoppable here."

"Good to know," I said, draining my glass of whiskey before pouring another one. "So you're saying I'm fucked, that I won't be able to counter the effects of this spell?"

"Yes and no," Sanaka said, resting his elbows on the chair and interlocking his fingers in front of him. "Neither of our magics could undo the spell. Rlothian magic is much too dark and powerful. In fact, I'm surprised that any mortal was able to channel such magic without having their soul obliterated in the process. One can only conclude that whoever did the ritual is not mortal at all, or they have found a way to counter the negative effects of the Rlothian magic, chiefly through the symbols used on the victim I would imagine. Most of the Glyphs are protective in nature."

I shook my head. "So not much hope then?"

"There are always ways," Sanaka said. "I must have taught you that, at least."

"You did, yeah. So what's the way?"

Sanaka shook his head like he expected me to have already discovered the answer. "To counter such dark magic, you need an entity that is just as dark to do it."

"Like a demon, for instance?"

Sanaka nodded.

"Yeah, about that," I said, getting up and standing over by the fireplace. "I don't really do demon summonings."

"You are a wizard, how could you not do summonings?"

"Oh, I do, but mostly low-level spirits, not demons."

Sanaka looked confused. "Why not? Are you afraid of them?" He laughed, the way a parent would laugh at their kid when the kid expressed his fear at the monster in the closet (which by the way, existed more than people realized).

"Look, long story short," I told him. "I lost my entire family to a demon after my father summoned one and lost control. I've tended to avoid demons ever since."

"Why did you survive then?"

I sighed and shook my head. "I'm still trying to work that out."

"Well," Sanaka said, having about as much sympathy for me as he did the first time I told him about the incident from my past. "You must get over your fear if you want the world to remember you again." He stared at me a moment. "Why do you even want the world to remember you? It doesn't matter. All that matters is that you are here now. That should be enough."

"It matters to me."

"Why?"

"Because unlike you, Sanaka, sometimes I'm a fucking human being underneath all the wizard shit. I have friends, relationships that I want back. I'm not even in any of my old family photographs anymore. You know what that feels like? It feels like you never even mattered and that you might as well have not have been born."

Sanaka took a deep breath then let it out. "Well," he said standing, holding his sword loosely by his side. "Confronting what scares you the most is the only thing that is going to get you out of this predicament you are in. There is no other way around it." He looked at me gravely then. "There is one more thing."

*Great*, I thought. "I know that voice, Sanaka. You only have that voice when you're about to impart bad news. Like the time you told me I'd have to sleep with a corpse for three days straight to enhance my Necromancy skills." I sighed. "What is it?"

He seemed amused for a second by that bit of information like it was proof that I really was his student for the last twenty years. His smile of amusement disappeared when he spoke, however. "There is another side effect of the spell that I didn't tell you about."

"Christ, am I going to die now?"

"Not quite. The power of the spell is such that I'm afraid even your own soul no longer recognizes you as it gets transformed into a blank slate that no longer holds the essential essence of who you are. Eventually, your soul will will leave your body and go off into the Astral Plane, where it will remain, lost forever. No doubt the killer protected themselves against this particular aspect of the spell."

I shook my head. "I knew there was something else wrong. I felt it after the spell hit, like a light dimming inside me, though I couldn't explain it at the time. Fuck. How long?"

"Before your soul abandons you forever? Three days at most. Maybe four. It's hard to know for certain."

"Bloody hell! Things just can't get any worse, can they?"

Sanaka shrugged. "I don't make the rules." Another one of his frequent sayings, usually when I was being forced to do something horrible, like lying with a damn corpse. "I suggest you get moving. Find me if you need my help."

Sanaka gave Blaze a final pet, stared at me a moment and then vanished into thin air as he teleported out of the room.

I looked down at Blaze and sighed. "How the fuck do I always end up in these situations, Blaze?"

Blaze stared silently back at me, his yellow eyes seemingly indifferent to my pain.

# 10

## DO OR DIE

*I*F I'M HONEST, I knew there was something else wrong with me after I got blasted by that spell—the Memory Shredder as Sanaka had called it. I felt it soon after the spell hit, like something dying inside me, or a vital part of me that was slowly beginning to pull away and detach itself from the rest of me. Somewhere in my mind, I knew it was my soul pulling away, but I hadn't wanted to acknowledge that to myself (the rest was painful enough).

The thing is, if the light of my being departed, I would become a soulless ghoul that's literally dead on the inside and no longer capable of emotion or any real human contact. I'd end up wandering aimlessly around the city like the rest of the ghouls—like the walking fucking dead—only I wouldn't feast on flesh, not living flesh anyway. Dead meat is what my diet would soon consist off. If you need to find yourself a ghoul, check the graveyards, or the bins outside the back of a butcher's shop, or an abattoir. Anywhere there was dead meat, you could find a ghoul nearby, dispassionately munching on maggot-infested flesh, its mouth moving as lazily as a cow chewing the cud, clothes ragged and dirty, face and body emaciated, flesh pale and waxy. That was going to be me in three days if I didn't find a way to counter the effects of that goddamn spell. And even my own magic wouldn't do much good without a soul or the proper mind to wield it. Most of my magic was based on the fact that I had a soul. Soulless magic is black magic, reserved only for monsters and psychopaths, of which I am neither.

Speaking of souls, I was on the roof of the building where I lived, drinking coffee this time instead of whiskey. Above me, the sky was clear and black, and the stars were out in force. As a chill wind surrounded me, I looked ahead, past the few blocks of buildings to the winding Gadsden River that cut a slow path through the middle of the city, effectively cutting Blackham City into two halves. You had the old town where I lived (known as Freetown), with its dark and winding streets that sometimes went nowhere and ended abruptly in odd places. Then you had the other side (known as Bankhurst) where Gadsden Park was, as well as all the financial and government buildings and streets that were arranged in perfectly symmetrical blocks. As I looked East toward Red Hill, I spotted an orb of bluish light rising into the night sky. Like a mini comet, the orb had a wispy trail behind it as it shot up higher into the sky. Another soul heading for the Astral Plane before making its way to the Realm of the Dead for sorting in the Afterlife. If it even made it through the Astral Plane first that is, which was full of predators who delighted in preying upon fresh souls, picking them off the way predators pick off newly emerged turtles on a beach. An innocent soul could soon enough be pulled into the Underworld, or devoured completely by one of the many malevolent entities that haunted the Astral Plane. As in life, death and the afterlife was never easy.

I could make out the silvery ephemeral edge of the Astral Plane, much like Earth's surrounding thin blue line, as the soul passed through both and then disappeared. You could stand up here most nights and see at least a few souls make their departure from the Earthly Plane. Watching them has seen me pondering my existential future with some sadness for those making the trip. But my own soul would eventually leave to do the same in as little as three days, despite my previous expectations about some far off future date.

"Shit," I said, shaking my head, trying to think of ways out of my situation and continually coming up empty on ideas, or at least ideas that would work. It was becoming more apparent that Sanaka's suggestion of asking a demon for help was my only option. "Fucking demons. I hate them."

"Don't we all," said a voice behind me.

I didn't turn around. "Hey, Arthur."

Arthur's ghostly form saddled up beside me. The old man used to own the building we were standing on until he died of natural causes several years ago. He was so attached to the building, however, that he refused to move on from it, and now remained there like some ephemeral caretaker. He was a short but stout black man, with a thick white beard and a surprisingly dense white afro on his head. He was seventy-three when he died of a heart attack. His son-in-law now owned the building, which Arthur wasn't happy about, but there wasn't much he could do about that as a ghost. "August, my boy," Arthur said. "How's business going?"

"Not too good," I replied, glancing at him. "An unexpected shitstorm has happened."

Arthur chuckled. "Ain't that always the way with business." He shook his head. "God, I miss doing business."

Arthur was something of a property mogul in his time, owning several other properties besides the one I lived in. "Your soul is up there waiting for you somewhere. I could take you to it. You could move on somewhere else. Babylon maybe. With your acumen, you'd thrive there." I knew I was wasting my breath. I'd made the offer dozens of times over the years, and every time he turned me down, though I still wasn't sure why.

As expected he shook his head. "No thanks. My place is here."

"But you're dead, Arthur."

"Don't you think I know that?" he snapped. "I can't let that good for nothing son-in-law fuck up my business. Not after all the work it took to build it up."

Whatever, I thought. If the old man wanted to stay a ghost, that was his prerogative. I had enough problems of my own. "Maybe you can help me then."

"If I can. What's the problem? Your magic get you in trouble again?"

"Not my magic. Someone else's."

"Shit. You can always rely on other people to fuck things up." He shook his head, probably thinking of his son-in-law, who had recently managed to lose one of the buildings he was supposed to be looking after. Word is he lost it in a card game. The dude was an inveterate gambler, much to Arthur's distaste. "Can you fix things?" He chuckled again. "What am I talking about, of course you can. That's what you do, isn't it? Fix problems."

"Other people's usually. My own, not so much."

Arthur's ghost walked right through me to the other side, and I shivered. I wished he wouldn't do that. "I'll give you the advice my father gave to me when I was starting out," the old ghost said. "He said to me, Arthur, son, the hardest solution is usually the right one. You just have to bite the bullet and get it done. Are you prepared to bite the bullet, son?"

"At this point, I could probably *take* a bullet quicker."

"That bad, huh?"

"That bad."

"Well shit, son, I don't know what to say to you. Sometimes its do or die, but that don't mean you can't still be smart about things."

"Thanks, Arthur," I said, distractedly gazing at another soul rising nearby, his words not making me feel any better. "I'll bear that in mind."

"Why you so scared anyway? I've never known you to be this afraid of anything."

I turned my head to look into his partly transparent face. "Because I'd be damn stupid not to be afraid, that's why."

He tried to pat me on the back, but his hand went right through me, emerging out of my chest. "What will be, will be, son. Now, that shithead son-in-law of mine is gambling with my money in some back alley card game over in Milford. I'm gonna go there now so I can go all poltergeist on his ass. I think he's starting to realize that I'm haunting him now. Hopefully, he'll soon take the hint and stop gambling my fucking legacy away."

"I could force him to see you, you know. You could speak directly to him."

"Nah," Arthur said, walking away. "I'm having way too much fun haunting his skinny ass. I'll see ya, August. And remember, do or die."

"Sure," I muttered back. "Do or die."

# THE MCCREEDY FAMILY MASSACRE

*I* COULDN'T HELP feeling that fate had a hand in all the bad shit that was happening to me. When you avoid something for so long like I did, it was inevitable that it would one day rear up and bite you in the ass when you least expected it. Some things you just couldn't run from, like the massacre of your whole family.

It happened back in Ireland, at the old family home in County Fermanagh, in my late teens. My family lineage was steeped in magic and occult practices. Many of my ancient ancestors were Druids and wizard's. My father was a master wizard, my mother, a witch (nothing to do with gender, only the specifics of their magic). My siblings and I, my brother and sister both, were all adepts at the time. It was the McCreedy family tradition. Magic was in our blood. My father, Christopher McCreedy, besides being a ruthless father, wizard and businessman, was also a member of various cabals and occult organizations, all of which helped him amass a large fortune. He often used the status and leverage of those groups to further his ends while having no emotional ties, as he was essentially a loner in life. Money was a form of power for my father, and he would do many morally dubious things to further his lust for power to assuage his often rampant ego. Summoning a high-level demon to gain more power was one of those morally dubious things.

He got us all involved in the summoning, the whole family. He said if we all stuck together, we would be able to force it to grant my father access to its power. In spite of my mother's reservations about the high level of risk involved, we all took part, having no real choice in the matter.

So the summoning took place in a windowless room for a safer containment environment, absent of any furniture that might get in the way if summonings went south, which had we known what the night would herald, then furniture would be the least important thing to get in the way. The only light was from the five candles involved in the ritual. In true summoning fashion there was one placed

117

at each of the four cardinal points of the outer summoning circle, with the fifth and final candle aligned with the aether star point on the inner circle that encompassed the containment pentagram. When the demon appeared in its true form, our collective eyes beheld the impenetrable darkness of hell, an indescribably grotesque monster that could only have been born of the Underworld.

With the help of the rest of my family, all of whom were terrified of the truly most frightening thing we'd ever seen, my father was able to contain the demon at first.

But then something went wrong. To this day, I'm still not sure what. Somehow, my father lost his control over the demon, probably because the demon itself was too powerful to be contained by any Earthly adept, no matter how skilled that adept was. Some powers just cannot be contained, and to try would have been folly, not to mention supremely arrogant, which my father unfortunately was.

The demon—a huge black skinned thing with strange appendages all over its weirdly misshapen body and dozens of eyes on its nasty looking face—broke free from the demon trap and proceeded to fly around the room at terrific speed, a trail of thick darkness behind it as it went about massacring everyone in the room. My mother was killed first, followed by my dear brother and sister and then finally my father. As carnage so horrific that I could barely keep my eyes open to play witness to the preternatural theft of their lives did play out, the screams of my family were an unbearable litany of echoes that will haunt my dreams and nightmares to the end of my days. The demon ripped them each apart, spraying blood and guts all over the room, an unearthly roar never ending from its mouth as it went about its wanton destruction. In a matter of seconds (or at least that's how it seemed to me) my entire family was dead. I was left sitting on the floor, cowering and shaking, hardly able to take in what was happening around me, the smell of blood causing me to vomit over myself.

Then the demon came hurtling toward me, its supremely terrifying face hovering right over me, so petrifying that I couldn't even look at it without wanting to go insane. I shut my eyes and waited for the inevitable. And waited. When nothing appeared to be happening, I finally got the balls to crack open my eyes and saw that the demon was gone. All that was left was a room full of carnage, the remains of my family.

To this day, I have no idea why the demon left me alive. But whatever the reason, I left Ireland for good a short time later, after burying what was left of my family in the plot on the grounds of the house. I went to London first, changing my name from McCreedy to Creed, partly to try and forget that I ever had a family at all, partly because it was the seventies and the Troubles (the understated title for the civil war playing out in Northern Ireland at the time) were in full swing and Irish people in London were looked on with suspicion back then. A year later I left London and spent the next five years traveling the world before landing in America. And here I still am, thirty years later, the memory of my family's massacre as fresh in my head as the night it happened. Even more so now that I had to consider summoning a demon myself.

I was sitting cross-legged on the floor of one of the bedrooms upstairs, surrounded by books on demonology when I got a call from Leona. "Hey," she said when I answered. "Forensics came back on our victim."

"Yeah?" I said, my voice distant. "You find anything?"

"You all right there, Creed? You sound strange. Something wrong?"

"Is that supposed to be a joke?"

"No need to be so sharp. I'll call back if it's a bad time."

I sighed. "No, don't. You want to meet for a drink? I know a quiet bar nearby if you're about."

"It's barely noon, Creed."

"So what? I'm Irish. There are no bad drinking times."

"Fine. Where?"

I told her the name of the bar and she said she would be there soon. Closing up the book I was reading, I gladly left the bedroom, having had enough of demon lore and summoning practices. The more I read, the more of a bad idea a summoning seemed, but it was either that or eat rotten flesh for the rest of my days. Seeing Leona might make things better, but I doubted it. When you're on death row, nothing makes you feel better unless you got off death row, and that wasn't likely to happen anytime soon, not without considerable personal risk anyhow.

Downstairs, I grabbed my coat and left the Sanctum, wondering as I went out the door if death by demon was going to hurt much.

# QUICK DRINK

$\mathcal{T}$HE PUB I met Leona in was called Master McGrath's (named after a champion greyhound that became something of a racing legend in Ireland back in the day). It's a small family run bar that's suited to intimate meetings and close quarters contact between regulars, friends, and even colleagues; those whom all see it as their own personal watering hole, a mood encouraged by the McCafferys, who originally built it. In true druid fashion its aged dark wood paneling is adorned with various Celtic knots and crosses, and familial photos spanning its past generations, and lightly glowing runic wards visible only to patrons with magical heritages of their own. The ancient Nordic alphabet has been used to ward off physical aggression in its patrons and external harm from most sources such as fire, vandalism or even magical attack. In essence, it's a small oasis where the magical races and even Sleepwalkers (unknowingly) can congregate in relative safety, to while away the hours in communal relaxation.

Gerard McCaffery, a tall, well-built man in his fifties with a lined face and a stare that would give any hardened werewolf biker a run for their money, was head of the family. Gerard was serving behind the bar when I went in, as he usually was. So was his daughter, the lovely Sinead, ringlets of fiery red hair dangling down past her slender shoulders, her magic blue eyes smiling at me even though she didn't know me from Adam. I did sleep with her once, though, a few years back. Luckily her father didn't find out, or he wouldn't have taken kindly to it. Gerard was very protective of his daughter. Even now, when he saw Sinead eying me up, he stepped in front of her and scowled at me. "What can I get you, friend?"

Gerard and I were friends, but he obviously didn't remember that, nor Sinead for that matter. Normally we would have exchanged a bit of banter when I came into the pub. But as he didn't now know me anymore, all he saw was some scruffy dude whose eyes lingered a little too long on his precious daughter.

After giving my order to Gerard (not bothering with small talk because I knew he wouldn't respond) I looked around the pub for Leona and saw only a couple of old men at separate tables, betting pages spread out in front of them, eyes on the widescreen TV on the back wall watching horse racing. When the drinks arrived, I gave Sinead a knowing look that I think freaked her out slightly as she didn't know whether to smile or be creeped out it seemed. Then I moved to the back of the pub and sat at one of the small tables there while I awaited Leona's arrival. A few minutes later, Leona came striding through the doors of the pub like someone out of a Western movie entering a saloon, pausing for a second while her eyes scanned the place. Knowing Leona, she was scoping out the exits, just in case she had to get out quickly, not to mention scanning the patrons for potential threats.

Did I mention Leona is an ex-Army Ranger? Well, she is. An Army Ranger, highly trained and highly skilled as you'd expect. She is the toughest woman I know. Have ever known. It's part of her appeal. Her toughness brings out the teenager in me, the one who used to fantasize about warrior women and their dark and dangerous sexuality. Leona is certainly one of those women (see kids, never give up on your dreams). Her boots clunked on the pub floor as she strode across it toward me, Sinead giving her a look of death that many women seemed to reserve for Leona. Her absolute confidence and impressive mental and physical presence often made other women intimated by such elements, jealous and hostile. They hated her but wanted to be her at the same time.

"Creed," she greeted me as she pushed her leather coat out behind her before sitting in the chair opposite. "What gives? This mine?" She lifted the orange juice and drank half of it in one go before placing the glass on the table.

"What gives?" I asked. "I thought you had information for *me*?"

"I do. Jesus, what's wrong with you? You always this tetchy?"

"Tetchy?" I barely laughed and shook my head. "No. Things have just taken a turn for the worse, that's all."

Her blue eyes regarded me with a detached sort of interest. "Why, what's happened?"

"You first."

"I don't have much."

I tried to mask my disappointment by sipping my pint. "Tell me anyway."

"Well, forensics came back on the girl's body," she began, looking toward the front door as if someone was going to come in and hear what she had to say. "The girl died from having her throat cut, which was obvious anyway. The symbols carved into her were all done before she died. We're still trying to match the symbols in the database but so far we've come up empty. As for DNA of the killer, there was none."

"It wouldn't matter, you wouldn't be able to match it to anyone. That's all you got?"

"Pretty much."

"Jesus, you weren't kidding when you said you didn't have much."

"We're still working on it, like I said. Brentwood isn't happy that the media have picked up on the story somehow and that they're stressing the 'Satanic' elements of it. He thinks we have a leak somewhere. This isn't the first case where details have been leaked to the press."

"He ask about me?"

"I didn't tell him about you. He'd only have you taken in for questioning."

I nodded. "I know how he is. He interrogated me for two days straight a few years ago if you...I was going to say remember, but you obviously don't."

"No."

"He doesn't like me all that much, considers me a rogue element."

Leona laughed. "Sounds like something he'd say. So what do you have?"

"More than I'd damn well like."

"Okay," Leona said, frowning.

"Turns out the spell I was hit with was powered by some very dark magic. The girl I found was a sacrifice to a Dimension Lord called Rloth. I haven't checked yet, but the symbols carved into the girl will most likely all point to Rloth in some way. The reason they were carved was not only to do with ritual magic. They were done to cause suffering to the girl before she died. Without suffering, a being like Rloth wouldn't accept the sacrifice."

"So this nutjob is making sacrifices to a Dimension Lord in return for, what? Power?"

"It would seem that way, and going by the power of the spell that was cast, he seems to be doing quite well. Makes me wonder what he has planned next."

Leona shook her head and took a sip from her orange juice. "Dimension Lords. Jesus. Sometimes I just can't fathom this universe. Things were easier when I lived as a Sleepwalker, and all that existed was normal shit. These days it's fucking magic and monsters and beings from other dimensions. My brain still struggles to process it sometimes."

"I know. But that's why the Sleepwalkers are kept in ignorance. It's easier that way."

"Can you imagine if the whole world woke up to the supernatural? What would happen?"

"The Sleeping Tiger would turn on the rest of us, that's what. It's happened before in Ancient Egypt. Why do you think the whole civilization crumbled? Then there was Rome..."

"That's why Rome fell? I never knew."

"There's a lot you don't know. Probably safer for your sanity that way."

"What about yours?"

"My sanity?" I laughed. "My sanity crumbled a long time ago." She probably thought I was joking. I wasn't. Being a wizard, chasing and slinging magic for decades, that carry-on takes you to the brink of madness. Shit, it demands it.

"You don't seem too bad," Leona said, moving her fringe from her face.

I smiled. "Is that a compliment?"

"Fuck no."

We both laughed, and for a moment, it felt like we knew each other again, which made me feel slightly better, glad that I had decided to meet her. "This is what it's normally like between us, you know," I said. "You enjoy jesting with me in your own barbed way."

"I do, huh?" Her eyes focused on me a moment, her guard down for once. "You miss that?"

"You've no idea."

"Well then, we need to reverse that curse you're under, don't we?"

"That might not be so easy."

"Why?"

I explained to her the nature of the spell, the effect it was having on my soul, and about the demon I needed to summon to try and counter the dark magic whose influence I was under. "There's a great likelihood that I could die at the hands of any demon I summon."

"And that's the only way?"

"Yup." I took a large swallow of my whiskey like it was going to make things better. "But since I barely have three days before my soul departs, I have no choice but to risk it. It's either that or become a goddamn ghoul for the rest of my days."

"Shit," she said.

"Yup."

Her phone rang, and she answered it. "Yeah, got it. On my way now." She sighed as she put her phone back in her pocket.

"Trouble?"

"Yeah, reports of some teenager running around Gadsden Park biting people in the neck."

I rolled my eyes. "Newly turned vampire it sounds like."

"We get them all the time. Fucking vamps, they're like rats, I swear, the way they multiply." She drank the rest of her orange juice and stood up to go. "Thanks for the drink, Creed."

The thought of being alone after she left filled me dread and loneliness, so I stood up as well. "Fuck it, I'm coming with. Newly formed vamps are dangerous, like wild animals. You might need my help."

"This isn't my first rodeo, you know," she said, somewhat rhetorically. She knew I knew that.

"I could use the distraction."

She nodded. "All right. Let's go catch us a stinking vampire then."

Sinead was behind the bar cleaning glasses and smiling at me as we passed by, that is until her eyes met Leona's scowl, and her smile was replaced by a look of mild hostility. As they proceeded to momentarily scowl at each other, I secretly hoped it was because they both considered each other as rivals in the same game, the one where I was the prize. After all, if my days are limited to three, then you couldn't blame a guy for taking the small victories where he could, could you? It's possible that to my chagrin they just didn't like each other. But in self-flattery, I chose to believe the former as we left the pub.

# DARKNESS CALLING

$\mathcal{G}$ADSDEN PARK WAS across the river in Bankhurst. We took the Monaghan Bridge in Leona's SUV, her driving as aggressive and erratic as ever as she weaved in and out of traffic, cursing and gesticulating at other drivers for not getting out of her way. As usual, I gripped the handle above the door to stop myself from crashing into the dash or flying across into Leona's lap, which wouldn't have been the first time...or entirely undesirable, except for the high-speed accident thingy. "I've mentioned this to you more than once over the years," I said to her, raising my voice over the loud metal music pumping out of the car speakers. "Not that you listened before, but I'll get it out there now anyhow, just so you know. You maybe want to think about slowing down occasionally."

She gunned the SUV harder to overtake a truck as we came off the bridge, as if to prove that she didn't care what I had to say about her driving. "I have advanced driving skills," she said. "I know what I'm doing. I've been driving since I was seven."

"That doesn't make me feel any safer, but thanks for letting me know."

"You already knew."

"I did, but same answer as before."

A smile crossed her face as she barreled on down the expressway, still weaving in and out of traffic like she was playing some crazy video game. "The Army taught me to drive like this. I also grew up with four brothers who loved cars."

I knew all this already, as I did most things about her, but I was happy to let her talk as if I didn't know anything. Honestly, it was cool having her tell me things as if for the first time. Sure, the glee of hearing new information wasn't present, but I was enjoying the feeling of us getting to know one another as though we've just met for the first time again. It helped me take my mind off the impending doom on the horizon. "You still see your brothers?"

"Sure," she said, mercifully slowing down as she screeched off the expressway into 20th Avenue before heading for the nearest park entrance in the distance. For some reason, it always seemed sunnier when you got to Bankhurst, partly because Freetown always seemed dark and dingy, and partly because Bankhurst was populated by relatively young buildings, most of them grand steel and glass structures that reflected the light onto the pristine streets. "Three of my brothers are still in the military, posted in Iraq. One of them is in a cemetery back home in West Virginia."

"I'm sorry."

"You knew that already, right?"

I nodded. "I know you were close with your younger brother. Jessie, right?"

She looked at me surprised like she didn't expect me to know that. "Yeah, Jessie. It's been three years, and I still miss him every damn day."

Leona's younger brother Jessie was killed in Iraq while they were both on assignment together, part of a four-man reconnaissance team that was sent into the desert to try and find a suspected mountain hideout for terrorists. What they found instead, once they stepped inside the mountain cave system, was an old man who proceeded to pick off the team one by one. The old man, who Leona described to me as being like Yoda in a turban, was able to walk through walls, conjure fire in his hands and get inside the minds of the soldiers. He then forced Jessie Lawson to shoot his Sergeant and best friend in the head before turning the gun on himself. The other member of Leona's team was lit up by a fireball hurled at him by the old man, who also tried to bring the cave roof down on top of Leona shortly after. Leona moved just in time and evaded the collapsing boulders, sprinting from the cave and making her way back to camp, distraught at her brother's untimely death, her mind reeling at the impossible abilities of the old man in the cave. There was just no way an ordinary human being could have done such feats, defying the laws of physics completely. She didn't want to believe it, but it could only have been...magic. There was no other word to describe the power wielded by the frail old man. Leona said as much in her debriefing, and that's when Division stepped in, the secret government organization she came to work for shortly after.

Division, and its leader, General Brentwood, offered Leona a chance to do right by her brother. If she wasn't able to prevent his death at the hands of someone with powers she didn't understand, then she could at least prevent other deaths at the hands of people with powers she would hopefully *come* to understand. That's why she stuck at the job and continued doing the dirty work that Division demanded of her. She did it all for the brother that she couldn't save, as if saving others from similar fates, would somehow alleviate her guilt over what happened in those caves. For despite everything, she blamed herself for what happened. Some would call that survivors guilt. Leona called it a reminder of her failure as a soldier. Either way, it was mostly what drove her, and also what made her such a formidable agent in the field. There was rage in her, and by the time you saw it, it would be too late. She would already be putting a bullet in you by then.

"It's not easy," I said. "I lost my whole family over thirty years ago, and I still think about them every day."

"Shit." She looked shocked, possibly more so than the first time I told her. "That must have been hard."

I smiled plaintively. "You could say that."

Leona was silent for a moment as we passed by the Blackham City Historical Museum with its green copper roof and huge pillars along the front entrance. Then she said, "Wait, you said thirty years ago you lost your family. You only look thirty now."

"I know," I said. "The wonders of magic."

"So what age are you then?"

"A gentleman never reveals his age."

She shook her head at me. "So what, you're immortal, is that it?"

"Not exactly, but I can stay in this body a long time if I want. I'm kinda under the gun for the next few days, though, so living a long and happy life is looking less and less likely at this point."

"You'll find a way."

I wished I had the same faith in myself as she seemed to have. "This is strange, you know."

We had arrived at the park entrance. Leona steered the car through the main gates, taking note of the ambulance parked up near Cedar Lake. "What is?" she asked, as we passed the tennis courts.

"You being so...friendly toward me. I remember you being a lot more hostile when we first met. It took you a while to warm to me."

"Who says I've warmed to you now?" She flashed me a wicked smile.

"I guess you were going through a lot when we first met, what with your brother and everything."

"Probably," she said, stopping the SUV behind a Park Police car. "Can we just focus on the job now, if that's okay? Or do you need a hug first?"

"A hug would be real nice actually."

She shook her head. "Let's go."

Smiling to myself, I jumped out of the SUV and followed Leona to the Park Police squad car where two uniforms were standing, looking out of their depth. One of the uniforms, a middle-aged guy with a gut like an orangutan and the same color hair to match, came saddling toward us. "Sorry, but—"

Leona flashed her ID at him, shutting him up mid sentence. "Homeland Security," she said. "You can go now."

"What?" the park cop said. "We didn't call you."

"You didn't have to," Leona said.

The cop looked at me as if for an explanation. "Hey," I said with a shrug. "Count yourself lucky the professionals are here."

"Screw you," the cop said. "We got it under control."

"Oh really," Leona said, pushing past him, throwing the other cop—a young guy with curly dark hair who looked like it was his first day on the job—a look that made him avert his gaze immediately. "I don't see the suspect in the back of your squad car, so that must mean he's still out there hurting people."

"Actually," said the younger cop, almost apologetic for interrupting. "He's down by the lake there, feeding on...someone's dog."

"A dog?" I said. "He hasn't hurt anyone then?"

"Yeah, he has," the fat older cop said. "He's attacked three people so far. Luckily they all managed to get away. He took a chunk outta one, though. A jogger. She's in the back of that ambulance over there."

"So why haven't you stopped him?" Leona asked.

"Because the kid's a fucking animal, that's why," the older cop said. "I ain't risking going near him. We don't get paid enough, right?" He looked to his partner for confirmation, who just nodded weakly.

"You called anyone else?" Leona asked.

"Yeah, of course. Local precinct said they'd send someone out. That was a while ago."

"Okay. Call back and tell them everything is fine. Also, get the fuck out of here and let us handle this."

"You gotta a real attitude, lady, you know that?" the cop said, looking Leona up and down.

Leona stepped toward the cop, towering over him. "Are we going to have a problem here?"

The cop dropped his head slightly. "No problem." He headed back to his squad car. "Come on, Jimmy. Let's leave this to the professionals." He threw Leona another look before plopping his weight into the car and driving off.

"You learn your diplomacy skills in the Army too?" I asked her. "They could use some work."

"I don't have time for diplomacy," she said, striding across the grass toward the fledgling vamp currently sucking on a dog by the lake.

"Yeah, you're right," I said, catching up with her. "Who needs diplomacy when you've got guns and a badge, right?"

"Exactly."

"So how you going to handle this kid?"

"That depends on him." She already had one of her Berettas in hand.

"He probably has no control over himself," I said, alluding to the fact that newly turned vamps are always consumed by their hunger for blood. "They usually have other vamps around to help them through the initial turning process, and to help them control their hunger."

"I know that. So where are they?"

I couldn't see anybody else around, either people or other vamps. That didn't mean the vamps wouldn't turn up at some point, though. Vamps in general thought of themselves as a separate species to humans, and also superior to the human race itself, which meant they liked to handle their business themselves. They didn't like people like Leona or myself getting involved.

The newly minted vamp was by the lakeside, hunched over the body of a large Golden Retriever, his head buried in the dog's neck while he sucked the blood from its body. The vamp looked about thirteen years old. He was dressed all in black, and his filthy long hair hung down over the dog's bloodstained coat. Tendrils of smoke also rose off the kid's body. At that early stage, the fledgling vamp still maintained a tolerance to sunlight. Soon enough, though, he would lose that tolerance and the UV rays of the sun would fry him. If he weren't careful, his whole body would explode into flames like a Tibetan monk at a war rally.

"Disgusting," Leona said as she eyed the kid vampire. "Disgusting and infuriating that he's killed that beautiful dog. I ought to stake the fucking thing on principle alone, which I'd do in a blink if there weren't extraneous variables involved. This is just one of many reasons I wish we could simply eradicate them."

"We could just do nothing, you know," I told her. "If he keeps absorbing the sunlight he'll explode soon enough."

"I have stake rounds loaded." She pointed her gun at the kid just as he looked up at us and snarled, fresh blood dripping copiously from his open mouth, which was full of small, pointed teeth, along with two longer incisors that were a good inch in length. "I can just take care of him now." The stake rounds were, as the name suggested, bullets made from weighted wood. A precisely aimed shot to the heart could instantly induce the Final Death, but only in the case of younger vamps.

You didn't want to fuck with older vamps. Not much could stop them, and you had to get close enough first, which wasn't always easy. Not that I was any kind of vamp hunter. I'd had cause on occasion to take a few out, but mostly I did business with them, sometimes mediating between different groups to prevent a street war that would inevitably cause collateral damage. Other times I did favors in return for information or magical knowledge. For the most part, though, I avoided vampires because they tended to be too sneaky, and thus hard to trust.

"Or we could take the kid to his own kind," I said, knowing it wasn't the kid's fault he was behaving like an animal. He obviously hadn't been turned on purpose. If he had been, his Maker would be with him, looking after him. He was probably jumped somewhere and left for dead, waking up with an unquenchable thirst for blood, as often happened.

Leona looked at me like I was as bad in her eyes as the dog drinker before us. "They're vermin, Creed. Why would you want to save it just so it can kill people in the future?"

"They don't all kill, you know. Some of them have other means of quenching their thirst."

She shook her head. "I don't care. I'm following protocol and protocol says I put this thing down now."

*Sorry kid*, I thought. *Nothing I can do for you.*

Leona aimed her gun at the kid again, but as she did, something happened. The kid's reddish eyes turned completely black, which is something I'd never seen before. Then his head snapped toward me like some force had pulled it that way. "Creed," he snarled in a voice that was too deep—too evil—to be his own. "The darkness is coming, Creed, and you can't stop it. Soon all of you will be consumed by it." The vamp—or whoever or whatever had taken him over—grinned lasciviously at me with sharp, bloody teeth. Then it began to laugh like it knew what it was saying was true and that everyone in the world was fucked, and there was nothing I, or anyone else, could do about it.

"Who are you?" I demanded in a voice that probably sounded less disturbed than I actually was.

The entity in the vamp didn't answer me, just kept laughing, grinning and staring at me with those eightball eyes. Then I heard a shot and the kid vampire in front of me exploded in a burst of blood and guts, bits of it showering down into the water, staining the green grass around it. I looked at Leona, who was staring at the mess she had just made, the gun still in her hand. She turned her head to look at me. "He talked too much."

Saying nothing, I looked over at the rippling lake. The fish were coming to the surface, nipping at the bits of gore floating on the cloudy, crimson water.

A chill went through me, causing a shiver in its wake, along with an innate understanding of the implications by some subconscious element of my soul.

# PLAYING WITH FIRE

*I* DIDN'T SAY much on the journey back to Freetown. Neither did Leona. It was like we were both trying to process what had just happened at the park. It wasn't every day that a dark entity took over the body of a fledgling vamp and spoke to you direct, underscoring your impending doom. Needless to say, the experience had disturbed me. It seemed to disturb Leona equally as much, but as her army training taught her and as she did with everything that hinders her functionality, she seemed to readily and habitually compartmentalize in order to both be ready and able to focus on the tasks at hand. In this case, driving me home to the Sanctum in East Oakdale. After that, she would be on to another case. There's always another case for Division and thus Leona, just as there'd usually been for me as well. That is until the curse heralded by this blasted spell brought an immediacy unavoidable, taking with it the important cathartic release that having something to keep you busy and from thinking provides. Now I had just one case: *The Case Of Saving August Creed's Ass...And His Soul.*

After telling Leona I would call her, and after her telling me she'd be there if I needed her (with a hint of rare sympathy in her eyes as she did so), I went inside the Sanctum to find Blaze sitting on the floor in front of the fireplace. The wolf got up to greet me, and I crouched down, so his big head was level with my face as he nuzzled his snout into me. Things weren't always so relaxed between me and Blaze. It took the wolf a few years to get to the stage where he didn't feel like attacking me out of innate aggression and general suspicion of humans. A few times in the beginning, he did jump me and pin me to the floor, even putting his jaws around my throat once. It was a timely reminder that Blaze was a wild animal —and an elemental creature—and wouldn't be domesticated like a dog. Eventually we reached an understanding that entailed me not trying to tame his wilder instincts, and in return, he would put those instincts to good use when I needed them. Based on that understanding, our bond grew, as did our friendship.

Putting my arms around his thick neck, I gave Blaze a hug for a moment. "Someone's messing with me, Blaze," I said. "And I intend to find out who." The wolf pulled away and fixed me with his yellow eyes, letting me know he was there for me, as he always had been since I rescued him from Babylon all those years ago. "Thanks, Blaze. I know I can always count on you."

And Leona, of course, who had been surprisingly supportive so far, given that she didn't even remember who I was. On some level, she seemed to trust me, and for that I was grateful. It was difficult sometimes, not showing her how I really felt about her. And while a woman like Leona wasn't exactly into relationships, the relationship I had with her previously was the closest I'd ever had to one. Living your life pursuing magic and sorting out other people's problems didn't leave much room for romantic entanglements. There had been a few women over the years (one of them a vampire) who I had shared a closeness with, but none as deep as with Leona. She seemed to get me, and I got her. That in itself was a rare thing, and it enabled us to be close, but not too close. Enough to give each other what we needed while still giving each other the space to do what we each needed to do. It worked out pretty well before my life went sideways.

I flopped down into the well-worn armchair by the fireplace. Logs were stacked on top of the grate, but the fire wasn't lit. Staring at the logs for a moment, I mumbled a few words and directed a small dose of magic at them. Flames appeared instantly in the grate, licking at the logs until they caught and started crackling in the heat.

Every time I lit the fire and stared into it, I was reminded of the huge fire that was always burning in the family Sanctum back in Ireland. My father would often sit in one of the two chairs by that fire with some ancient book in his lap, sipping at brandy and smoking cannabis as he read. Sometimes I would join him, sitting in the other chair with my own book, and he would look over at me occasionally as if I was distracting him.

My father was hard on me and my siblings growing up, forcing us to spend hours every day studying and practicing. Even when he left on some business trip or expedition to some far-flung corner of the realms, my mother would oversee our studies in order to avoid backlash against all of us, should he return to find we'd made no perceived progress. Although thankfully, her oversight was in a much more relaxed manner. I loved those times spent with my family when my father was absent. We loved and protected each other, until that is, my father—with his ego that could never get enough—overestimated the limits of his power and fucked it all up for everyone. Something I still haven't forgiven him for over three decades later.

But now I was about to do the same thing, wasn't I? I was planning on summoning forces that were very likely beyond the limits of my control. But I wasn't about to do so out of ego or some selfish grab for more power. I was about to do so out of necessity, for survival. I also wasn't planning on putting anyone else at risk in doing so.

That didn't make it any easier, though.

I was getting ready to play with fire, and how burnt I got depended only on the whim of whatever demon happened to respond to my call.

And going from experience, I feared I might just end up incinerated, soul and all.

# 15

# THE LIBRARY OF DARK MAGIC

*I* SPENT THE next several hours inside a room in the Sanctum that didn't exist on the plans of the brownstone (one of many hidden rooms in the place). The hideaway was subbasement, accessed via a magically sealed and hidden trapdoor in the corner of the main basement, a trapdoor only visible via a Reveal Spell I spoke whilst waving my hand over the blank floor, which then gave access to the Sanctum's Library of Dark Magic.

As the name suggests, it is where the most dangerous and outright evil books are kept. Books that are full of spells and instructions for accessing the darker regions of the universe like the Myriad Hells and all kinds of other dark and sinister dimensions that most sane people would have no need or desire to access or travel to. These dark pockets of the universe were filled with entities and things that could only be described as monsters, beings that would rip a person apart and devour their very souls on the spot if you made yourself known to them.

The kind of dark magic contained in the books that lined the wonky shelves is just the sort being practiced by the bastard who killed that girl and put the curse on me. To access a dimension like Kiroth and the dark lord Rloth, one would have to be very familiar with the practices outlined in the books I was now about to look through myself. And unfortunately, the only way I was going to counter the black magic spell I was under was to use black magic myself.

A rusty ladder led down from the basement into the library. Therein a maze of narrow corridors has been created through its endless rows of bookshelves all exuding their own kind of dark energy that never fails to raise my heckles, and to cause occasional times when I recoil in fear. I didn't exactly make it a habit to go down there. When I took over the brownstone, my uncle warned me not to enter the dark library unless I really had to, telling me that there were books and artifacts down there that would try to seduce me into touching them; into opening them up and using the dark magic inside.

As I now stood in its stifling atmosphere, the narrow walkways instilling a regularly occurring sense of claustrophobia, I once again resolved myself into getting in and out as fast as possible. Already I could feel the strange pull of some of the more powerful books, their tendrils of dark influence trying to probe inside my mind, begging me to open their pages as they tried to lure me to them the way a Venus Flytrap lures a fly with the promise of sweet rewards before springing its deadly trap.

The book I was looking for was a centuries-old tome written in an arcane language that very few could read (not without a Translation Spell) and still fewer could even handle without going mad or being dragged down into total darkness forever. The book's title roughly translated into *The Book Of Many Hells And Demons*. It was kept at the back end of the library, locked up inside a large trunk along with the other more dangerous books in the library.

The trunk at the back of the library was nestled underneath a shelf of books. One of those old time trunks with a rounded lid, the kind you might expect to be filled with priceless treasure gathered up by bloodthirsty pirates. The books and artifacts inside were as invaluable as it gets, but only to the right people and to those who knew how to use them.

Taking a breath, I undid the Locking Spell originally designed by my uncle years ago. The spell required my blood on the lock, so I took a small penknife out of my back pocket and winced as I drew the four-inch blade across my left palm. As the blood welled up in my hand, I smeared it over the locking mechanism. A few seconds later there was a clicking sound that felt loud and ominous in the narrow confines of the sub-basement library.

Before opening the lid on the trunk, I wrapped a handkerchief around the cut in my hand. You did not want to drip blood on to any of the books in the trunk, which would be like dripping blood into the mouth of a hungry animal. It would make it ravenous, and it would hunger for more. Same thing with the books. Blood would ignite the dark magic inside, and the books would get overexcited. Things would get out of control quickly, to say the least.

I popped open the lid on the trunk and was hit with the stench of what can only be described as flesh rotting from the inside out: the stench of bindings made from human flesh and text from human blood. In a nutshell, from the essence of death and decay itself. The stench was down to the human skin that bound the books and the blood on many of their pages. It was also down to the rotten essence of the books themselves. I gagged a few times as I quickly sorted through the books until I found the one I was looking for, taking it out of the trunk and immediately shutting the lid, the locking mechanism engaging again by itself. Relieved to have sealed the trunk and its sickening smell, I took a few deep breaths, as much to steady my nerves as anything else.

The binding of stretched leather made from waxy and bumpy human skin, like that which feels as though it were cut directly from the worst patches of a leper's skin, to give a visceral experience that's cold and horrible to behold. Filled with a large number of thick parchment pages, the binding struggled to enclose its necessary volume required for the vast amount of information it contains. It was also heavy, much heavier than your average Bible. The pages were thick parchment and there were many of them. There needed to be, to hold the vast amount of information inside.

"All right," I said. "Time to put on my big girl's pants and get out of this cursed place."

I moved quickly back through the maze of walkways, ignoring the books that psychically tried to reach out and grab my attention like vines coming alive in a thick jungle. It seemed to take forever, but I finally got back to the ladder and climbed up it into the main basement, hurriedly slamming the trapdoor shut behind me. After that, I stood for a moment, taking deep breaths of air that was much fresher than the stale air down in the dark library. I hoped I wouldn't have to go down there again anytime soon until I realized I would have to return the book I was then holding in my hands. My heart sank at the thought, but I forced myself to forget about it. I had more important things to worry about at the time.

Blaze had wandered down into the basement by then and was sitting on the floor near the big table in the center of the room. "Fuck that shit," I said to him. "I hate going down there. Come to think of it, I hate black magic altogether." I went and placed the book I was carrying on the table, glad to get it out of my hands. I could already feel its dark energy begin to seep into me and I reminded myself to exercise caution when handling the book. Too much direct contact could result in my soul being corrupted, and I didn't want that. It was bad enough my soul was preparing to leave me for good. I didn't need to corrupt it with evil as well.

On the floor, Blaze growled up at the book.

"Hey," I said. "I don't like it any more than you do, but it has to be done. Otherwise, you're going to end up with a soulless ghoul as a master, and I don't think you'd want that. I might try to eat you."

Blaze growled again as if to say, *Yeah like I'd even let you try to eat me. I'd eat you first.*

Warily, I stared at the book as if waiting for it to come alive and attack me, keeping a respectful distance from it until I told myself just to get on with it, that the book wouldn't read itself. I was right, of course. There was no point delaying any more. I needed to read the book so I could put together a summoning ritual. After that, it was up to fate what happened.

*Fuck fate. That's what magic is for.*

It was a bold thought, and one which I tried to get behind as much as possible, which was difficult because it felt then like I was slipping ever deeper into a dark hole that I would never be able to escape from.

Shaking my head, I went and grabbed a bottle of whiskey. Because hey, if you can't have a good drink before your possibly untimely demise, then when can you?

# 16

## BLACK MAGIC

*E*VER SINCE I lost my family to that demon, I have done my best to avoid the darker forms of magic at all costs. Before that, I dabbled a little, as did my brother and sister. We were young, wanting to rebel, naturally attracted to the darker forces that existed in the universe. Our mother always warned us not to meddle with black magic, however, often citing the story of our great uncle, Patrick.

Patrick was from our father's side of the family. He was also a wizard, as were most of the men in the McCreedy family. Patrick McCreedy was always known as the black sheep of the fold, my mother said. Always liked to go his own way, never wanting to tow the family line when it came to anything, including the practice of magic. The family philosophy being to stay the fuck away from dark magic in all its malicious forms. That was the official line anyway. Unofficially, things were clearly different.

Hence, Patrick didn't listen (neither did my father for that matter, but more on that later), and being a bit of a rebel, he dived headlong into the world of black magic, summoning demons and using the power he gained from them to further his own ends, whether financially or sexually. Patrick accrued a vast fortune in a short period. He also became a serial killer, which no one knew until after he had butchered nearly a hundred people. By that point, Patrick's soul was as black as it gets and all he thought about was how much evil he could unleash on the world.

In the end, Uncle Patrick was consumed by the darkness he had created in himself, to the point where he lost his humanity and became a demon. He now resides in the Underworld, in one of its many hells, wallowing in a pit of filth that is so foul it is beyond human comprehension. So the story went anyway.

Needless to say, that wasn't enough to put me or my brother and sister off toying with black magic. We summoned low-level spirits to make them do cruel things to people, like appearing above the bed of an old woman who lived nearby, and thus giving the poor dear a heart attack in the process. It was never our intention to kill her, only to scare her because we thought she was weird and deserved it, which is awful, I know, but we were kids playing with black magic, so what do you expect? We also communed with dark entities who lived in the Astral Plane, and these entities would try to fill our heads with dark thoughts. Their aim was to get us to do nasty things to other people and each other. After my sister stabbed my brother in the leg at their beckoning, we put an end to the meddling in all things black magic; or rather, our parents did. My mother went crazy over the incident, of course, and remained furious at us for days afterward. Our father, although he gave us a cursory telling off in the form of a lecture warning against the dangers of dark magic, also seemed secretly pleased by our foray into the darkness, though that could just be my mind twisting things to suit what I know about him now.

Besides, our father then went and summoned a goddamn demon, breaking the cardinal rule he had forced us to live by our whole lives (even though he rarely stuck to this rule himself, always playing with the darker forms of magic behind the scenes).

So you can see why I'm more than a little uneasy about the whole demon summoning thing. Dark magic twists your soul, turns it grotesque and eventually monstrous. It eats you up from the inside, and the worst part is, you are happy enough to let it do so.

Of course, dark forces can never be completely avoided, especially in my line of work. I had dalliances with them all the time, but I never got in so deep that I ended up losing myself to them. What I was about to do—summon a high-level demon—amounted to slightly more than a mere dalliance, however. This was diving into the darkness head fucking first. I would either lose my mind, my body or my soul. Possibly all three.

The things we have to do sometimes.

* * *

I SPENT A WHILE IN THE LIVING ROOM, STUDYING THE SUMMONING RITUAL AS outlined in *The Book Of Many Hells And Demons*. As I sat turning the pages, my mind translating the ancient words for me thanks to the Translation Spell I had cast beforehand, I grew steadily more uncomfortable, shifting awkwardly in my chair, feeling like the room was getting hotter, cold sweat running down my face and body. I felt the tug of black magic in the air. Felt the way it ripped through the quantum fabric around me, slicing and dicing it like a kid with a razor blade swiping at a sheet of newspaper. It was destructive energy, but it was also seductive as it beckoned me in further. Then after a while, I ended up lost in a kind of trance as dark thoughts swirled around my mind like malevolent spirits. It was only Blaze's insistent growling that shook me out of it. "It's okay, Blaze," I said in a distant voice like I had just woken from a dream. "It's all right."

Blaze stopped growling but kept his yellow eyes on me as he sensed the darkness that probably surrounded me like a black fog. I finally snapped the book closed then and placed it on the arm of the chair I was sitting in. It was time to prepare for the ritual, and I had many items to collect for it.

But first I had to go to the city morgue to steal a dead body.

# 17

# THE MORGUE

$\mathcal{T}$O PROCURE A cadaver, I had to go to Blackham City Police Headquarters, which was located in Bankhurst. Courthouse Plaza in the Highlands to be exact, where the city's movers and shakers gathered in their shiny skyscrapers, government facilities and business parks. Thanks to the name, the politicians and corporate crones who resided there were known as "The Clans". Needless to say, the local journalists often made reference to this, comparing the day to day political and financial moving and shaking as the "Highland Games".

I didn't give a shit about any of that, though. I just needed a dead body.

\* \* \*

THE BLACKHAM CITY POLICE HEADQUARTERS IS A HUGE STONE BUILDING THAT reaches ten stories, with a further few below ground level that includes three basements plus an underground car park. The Medical Examiners office and the morgue were in one of the subbasements. Needless to say, the whole building was crawling with cops (quite a few of whom I used to have working relationships with before, you know...) and just walking in there and stealing a dead body wasn't going to happen. Obtaining a cadaver by simply driving down to the underground car park to steal and load a body in the trunk without being caught and arrested during the act is next to impossible, though. The last thing I needed was to end up in police custody. Leona would probably have gotten me out, but still, I didn't need the inconvenience.

I also needed a body pronto, which the cops obviously wouldn't just let me collect along with my personal belongings on the way out. "*Yes, sir, here's your keys, your belt, your wallet...and the dead body you took from the morgue. Have a good day now. You need someone to help you carry that corpse? Tony, give this guy a hand, will you?*"

Yeah, not too likely to happen, was it?

The best way for me to enter the building clandestinely was to simply teleport in. I knew the layout of the building pretty well, having been in the morgue with Leona a few times, so I knew exactly where to go. All I needed was enough time to locate a suitable corpse, and then I could teleport straight out of there with it.

Except these things are never that easy, as I was about to find out. I teleported directly into the morgue, only to find the Chief Medical Examiner and two detectives standing around an autopsy table while another young pathologist was in the process of cracking open the sternum of the corpse on the table. All four of them froze as they stared at me a moment, probably wondering how I was able to appear out of thin air in front of them. "What the fuck?" said one of the detectives, frowning in confusion as he instinctively went for his gun.

"How the hell?" the other detective said, going for his gun as well.

The ME and the pathologist stopped what they were doing and stared open mouthed at me, probably as much for my decidedly non-city official appearance as much as for the fact that I had seemingly appeared out of nowhere.

"Hey guys," I said, giving everyone a small wave. "Sorry to interrupt and all, but..." I started sub-vocalizing the words to a spell that would make all four of them forget about the fact that I was even in the room. The magic crackled in my fingertips as I directed it toward them. All four men flinched at the same time as if they had been hit with a bucket of ice water. This was followed by expressions of extreme confusion as they all started to look around like they didn't know where they were anymore.

*Oh shit*, I thought. I should have remembered the cameras in the room, which to all intents and purposes, were witness to my magic use. Remember I said that if a Sleepwalker witnesses magic that the magic would not always work as expected? Well, the four men in the room didn't just forget I was there, they forgot everything—where they were, who they were, what they were supposed to be doing. Everything.

"What...where am I?" mumbled one of the detectives as he looked around him like everything was now strange and unknown, just as the other three men were also doing.

The taller detective seemed more panicked than the rest, though, and he took out his gun, even though he probably no longer knew how to use it. "Who the fuck are you people? What are you doing here?"

The pathologist held up a bone saw. "Stay away from me all of you!"

The ME screamed at the dead body on the autopsy table, causing the others to get frightened as well. Next thing I knew, the two detectives were pointing their guns at each other, screaming that they were both going to kill each other.

*Jesus, what a disaster.*

Quickly, I sent a magical charge into both security cameras, short-circuiting them both, along with the drive they were connected to. That took care of the whole farce being on record. Now I just had to stop the two cops from killing each other.

I blasted them both at once with a mild charge of magic. It was enough to rattle their brains and render them unconscious. When the two cops hit the floor, both the ME and the pathologist screamed and they each ran to separate corners of the room where they cowered in fear like frightened children. "Don't worry," I told them as if they were even listening. "You'll be back to normal soon. In the meantime, I'm just gonna get what I came here for."

Wasting no more time, I started checking along the wall of steel drawers, looking at the names printed on the front of each one. I was looking for a John Doe, someone who wouldn't be missed all that much as I wouldn't have felt right taking somebody's loved one from them. Thankfully, the city was full of John Doe's, and after a moment, I found what I was looking for and pulled the drawer open to reveal a ravaged looking corpse on a steel slab. It looked like a homeless guy. The corpse had long straggly hair and a grayish beard, the body itself emaciated, the ribs showing through under thin, mottled skin that was full of sores and bruises. "You'll do," I said to the bum's corpse. What the hell, it was only old flesh and blood. The guy's soul would already have departed somewhere else.

I was just starting to gather my energy for the teleport when I heard a frightened, screaming sound, and when I looked, I saw the ME with a scalpel in his hand as he charged toward me, a look of murder in his gaunt face. "Monster!" he screamed at me. "Monster must die!"

*Shit.*

My magic had clearly driven the poor guy insane. Whoever said that magic was always reliable was full of shit and had obviously never wielded a single goddamn strand of it. "Sorry, man," I said apologetically as I laid my hands on the cold meat of the corpse beside me. "But I gotta go now."

The mad ME with the scalpel kept rushing toward me, and when he was two feet away, I said, "Bye now," and teleported myself and John Doe out of the morgue and back to the Sanctum, hoping as I did so that the ME wouldn't kill anybody before the spell wore off.

# JOHN DOE

*I* REMATERIALIZED ALONG with John Doe in the basement of the brownstone, the corpse appearing in mid-air before falling four feet to the floor like a sack of gone off meat. "Sorry, dude," I said, slightly out of breath after all the excitement in the morgue. "You were on a slab when I took you."

John Doe lay dead as dead can be on the floor, eyes shut, looking even more like a corpse now than he did in the morgue for some reason. Maybe it was just the dim lighting in the basement, making his skin that flat chalky grayness and more like dead flesh. The guy's soul must have been cursing me right then, wherever it was. It wasn't unheard of for a soul to come rushing through into this world again just to protect the physical body it used to inhabit. I hoped that wouldn't happen, however. The last thing I needed was John Doe's vengeful soul out to get me. The Sanctum was warded against forced entries by unknown entities, but even still, defenses didn't always work. Like I said, magic can be wholly unreliable at times, almost like it enjoys fucking with people who think they have a handle on it. The odd fuck up or outright disaster serves to remind cocky magicslingers like me that they are just conduits for a force they will never fully control.

Blaze came down into the basement, pausing at the bottom of the stairs to have a look at what fresh madness his loyal friend had brought back to the Sanctum, his nose raised high as he sniffed the air. The corpse had been refrigerated back in the morgue. Soon enough, though, John Doe's flesh would begin to warm up, and the accompanying smell would be overwhelming, something I wasn't looking forward to. The near fruity tones of death and decay would permeate the whole Sanctum. From experience, I can tell you that it takes days to get fully rid of the stench. "Yes, Blaze, I know," I said as he looked at me like I never ceased to amaze him. "It has to be done, though. But hey, you can eat him afterward if you like. No? Too rotten? Okay then."

As I stood looking down at the body on the floor, I wondered what kind of man John Doe had been and if he ever thought his dead body would end being used as an avatar to be possessed by a summoned demon. Probably not. Not even at the height of his delirium tremens, which he surely must have had given how much his body had been so obviously ravaged by alcohol. "I just want to let you know that I appreciate this," I told John Doe. "As a demon will be summoned to temporarily possess your body, I'll do everything in my power to ensure it is ejected as soon as I'm able to perform the closing of the circle, and that regardless of the state your body could be left in, that I'll make good on a proper cremation so your eternal soul can rest knowing no further abuse of it can take place."

Just as I was shaking my head at the fact that I was talking to a dead body in my basement, I heard a faint knock at the front door upstairs. Frowning over at Blaze, I waited and another knock came. "Goddamn it," I said. "Who the hell could that be?" I decided not to answer the door, thinking it would just be a sales call or the like, but then there was another knock, this one louder and more insistent. "Shit."

Stomping up the stairs, I made my way to the front door and looked through the spy hole to see the face of Leona looking back at me from the other side of the door. "Shit."

*What to do, what to do...*

Leona knocked again. She wasn't going away. *Just open the door*, I thought. *See what she wants.*

I opened the door, trying not to look too put out by the unexpected visit. "Leona. What brings you here?"

She stared at me a moment with her penetrating blue eyes. "Just checking if you're still alive." Her eyes drifted past me into the hallway, a frown crossing her face as she took in the strange art on the walls, the boxes of books that I still hadn't gotten around to sorting out yet. I saw her breathe in through her nose like she was smelling something weird. Not the body, surely. Probably the strange, burnt almond smell of magic that permeated the whole house. Whatever, her interest was sparked, and before I could stop her, she had brushed past me and strode into the hallway like a cop entering a suspects house.

"Now is not really a good time," I told her.

"Did I used to come here much?" she asked, completely ignoring me as she moved further into the house toward the living room.

Sighing, I closed the front door and followed her into the living room. "Quite a lot, yeah."

Leona was now standing in the center of the living room, looking around in near wonder. "How do you live with all this...clutter? It would drive me insane."

"I know. You got used to it."

"And why are there books stuck to the ceiling?"

"They rise up there by themselves. Some magic can be...buoyant."

"Buoyant books?" She shook her head. "Every day is something new."

I cleared my throat as I hovered casually by the living room door. "So what brings you here again?"

"I told you, I just came to see if you were still alive after your demon summoning."

"Oh, right. I haven't done it yet."

"Why not? I thought you wanted this shit sorted."

"I do. I just have a few more preparations left to do."

She nodded, still looking around the room at what I knew she saw as a state of chaos. If you've ever been inside Leona's Worthington apartment, you would know what I mean. She takes her minimalism very seriously, as she does her cleaning. "Okay. I was kind of hoping you'd done it already. I'm...intrigued as to what my memories are of you."

Given how we ended our last meeting before I got cursed, I thought, she'll probably sock me in the face first chance she gets. At least I have that to look forward to.

"Really?" I said despite myself. "So you find me intriguing? I'll take that."

"I'm intrigued as to the content of those memories, not intrigued by you necessarily." She smiled, almost wickedly. "Not the same thing."

"That's okay. I already know how you feel about me. Felt about me, I mean."

"And how did I feel about you?" she asked.

"See, I have you intrigued now."

She shook her head. "How did I feel about you?"

"You loved me."

She snorted, then laughed. "Seriously?"

"I'm glad that amuses you."

"Fuck off, Creed. That can't be true."

"And why not? Is it because you think you could never love anyone? That there's something wrong with you that you can't love properly?"

The usual scowl on her face disappeared for a moment as she took on a look of vulnerability, then discomfort. She didn't need to ask how I knew all that, but she asked anyway. "What the fuck would you know?"

I held my hands up. "Maybe a little soon to be going that deep. I'm sorry. It's still true, though. We had a good thing going, you and I. I miss it."

Leona stared at me for a long moment, like she was trying to detect some deep connection between us. Then she frowned and shook her head slightly as she looked away.

As he usually does whenever he detects Leona's presence, Blaze chose that point to appear in the kitchen, having presumably climbed the stairs after recognizing her stop was more than a passing message. His ears went down when he saw Leona, and he went padding over to her, rubbing his head against her thigh. Leona gingerly stroked Blaze's head like she was still unsure about the wolf.

"You two were close," I said, glad to feel some of the tension dissipating from the room.

"Seems like it," she said. "You have a basement, I see."

"Eh, yeah." I moved across the room to the kitchen entrance and tried to lean casually against the wall. Jesus, I thought to myself. Could I make it any more obvious?

Leona's eyes narrowed as she stopped stroking Blaze. "What you got down there?"

"Oh, not much. Junk mostly. Nothing you'd want to see."

She walked forward. "You know, normally when people say that it means they have something to hide. You have any dead bodies down there, Creed?"

"Dead bodies," I guffawed a bit too theatrically. "Wise up, will you? You think

I'm Dr. Frankenstein or something?" I laughed again as I shifted nervously around like a suspect under questioning.

Leona stared at me, a hint of knowing in her eyes. "You can cut the act now, Creed. I smelled it as soon as I came in."

"Smelled what exactly?"

She shook her head. "The dead body, Creed. You know how many bodies I've smelled over the years? Course you do. That wolf of yours would have nothing on me when it came to sniffing out death." She glanced back at Blaze. "No offense, Blaze."

I sighed. "Damn you and your keen senses."

She smiled and made her way past me into the kitchen, then down into the basement. I didn't even try to stop her. There would have been no point. "Jesus," she said when I got down into the basement to find her standing over John Doe. "You could have picked a better-looking corpse."

"I didn't have the luxury of time," I said. "Plus I didn't pick him for his looks."

"Clearly."

"The corpse is just a tool."

She raised her eyebrows. "A tool?"

"For the summoning, of course. The demon needs an offering before it will appear. Sometimes they like to have a human body to possess as well."

"You'd think they'd prefer a live one, wouldn't you?" She prodded John Doe's ribs with her boot as if she expected him to wake up any second.

"They sometimes do, but I'm not about to make a live offering, am I?"

Leona turned to face me. "I suppose not." She kept staring at me.

"What?" I asked, a little uncomfortable under her gaze.

Taking a short breath, Leona came toward me and stopped with her face close to mine. It took me by surprise to have her willingly move so near. To smell her delicious scent and to take in the fine beauty of her facial features. Even the small scar on her right cheek that only added character, which she'd gotten from the fine edge of a knife slash whilst on special assignment in an undisclosed location with the Army Rangers. How perfectly shaped her mouth was, her lips having just the right amount of fullness to them. The specks of hazel in her ice blue eyes. And of course, how incredibly deadly she seemed up close, like a Jaguar eying up its prey.

"You know," I said. "I don't think I've ever asked you exactly what country you were in when you got that scar. I only know it was in South—"

That was as far as I got before she leaned in and kissed me on the mouth, her tongue gently probing my lips for precious seconds. Then she pulled her head back and stared at me again, this time with a slight smile on her face.

"I was curious to see how that would feel," she said, the croak to her voice sending shivers of excitement through me. "Or if it would trigger a memory or something."

"Did it?" I asked, unable to take my eyes off her, wanting nothing more than to pull her close so we could kiss again, but knowing that if I did that, I probably wouldn't like how she reacted.

She shook her head. "No. Didn't feel a thing."

"Oh." I tried to conceal my crushing disappointment. "I thought maybe...you know...that there was something there..."

Her head shook again. "Not for me."

There was a slight twinkle in her eye this time as she gazed back at me.

"Are you...messing with me?"

She snorted in my face. "Yes, Creed, I'm fucking with you. Jesus, are you always this easy?"

I at least allowed myself to laugh. "When it comes to you, yes, I am."

"Does that mean you're my bitch then?"

"Eh, not quite."

"I bet you're my bitch. Admit it. You bow down to me, don't you?"

I laughed again. "All right, my esteem has taken enough of a battering. Time for you to go. I have a demon to summon."

"I should stay then. Help you out."

I looked at her like she was mad. "No way. Not happening. Absolutely not."

"You're seriously gonna do this alone?"

"I have to. If I get killed then hey, fair enough. If you get killed, my soul would never be able to live with itself."

Leona stared at me for a long moment, and I could tell from her face that she was somewhat taken aback by the genuine feelings I clearly had for her. "Okay," she said eventually. "I get you. My soul would probably hunt and kill your soul for killing me anyhow."

"I don't doubt it."

She walked to the side of me and then stopped, her breath soft on my cheek. "Be careful, Creed," she said, then added as she was walking out of the room, "Oh, and by the way. The country? It was Paraguay."

19

# THE SUMMONING

*A*FTER MAKING Blaze go upstairs so he was safely out of the way, I locked the basement door and began the process of summoning a demon. Needless to say, I was scared shitless, and I couldn't stop thinking about the night my family was torn apart. But I was also determined to go ahead with things, determined not to cave into my own doubts and fears. For my own safety, I needed to go into the ritual with an open heart and clear mind, otherwise the ritual could fall apart.

I wanted the curse lifted, I wanted people to remember who I was (Leona especially) and I wanted not to turn into a damn ghoul. I also wanted to find out who it was that put me in that situation in the first place. That person was still out there, most likely getting ready to kill again if they hadn't already done so. And given that they were communing with Dimension Lords, who knew what sinister magic they were going to work next. They had to be stopped before any more people got hurt.

The first thing I did in the basement was clear space in the middle of the floor, pushing the large table and stacks of books to one side of the room, giving myself half the floor space to work with. Then I went about drawing a magic circle on the concrete floor, using red chalk that partly contained the dried blood of a lesser angel to draw the design I was copying from *The Book Of Many Hells And Demons*. It was a complicated design that contained a number of geometric shapes and characters from a language that had long since died out. The circle was mostly for my protection, so I spent nearly two hours trying to get the design as perfect as I could. Of course, the thing about protective magic circles is that they didn't always work as they should. Some of the more powerful demons could not be bound by such things, no matter how strong the circle was. It would hold them back for a while, but if the demon was determined to get at you, it would, and there was nothing you could do about it. That was another thing about summoning demons:

144

wizards liked to feel as if their power and knowledge gave them control over such beings, but in many cases, they were only kidding themselves, and often to their detriment.

Which meant I needed a backup plan if the demon managed to break the circle. That backup plan came in the form of the Sword Of Rishanti, which was forged many centuries ago by an old Hindu wizard for the express purpose of killing demons. The sword—with its short, curved blade made from a metal not found here on Earth—was part of my uncle's collection, handed to me like everything else in the Sanctum. It remained to be seen if the sword did as it was supposed to. I also hoped I wouldn't have to use it to find out.

After I had finished drawing the magic circle, I went about lighting black incense candles that were made mostly from the dung of creatures found in the underworld. The candles reeked and filled the basement with a heavy, ammonia type odor that felt cloying and thick in my nostrils. I used six of the thick candles, all set around the outside of the circle.

The next thing I did was prepare the body of John Doe. On him, I had to cut a number of symbols into his softening and reeking flesh. The air of putrefaction John Doe was putting out was stomach churning, to say the least, and I didn't exactly enjoy desecrating the poor guy's body either, but it had to be done. I then dragged his body toward the magic circle, lifting the corpse in so I didn't break the circle.

The ritual also demanded that I leave a cup of my own blood for the demon inside the circle, so I used the Sword Of Rishanti to make a cut on my right arm and allowed my blood to fill a small bronze bowl that was covered in engravings and precious stones, an artifact I found myself while traveling in Tibet one time.

And that was it. All I had to do then (after healing the cut on my arm) was to strip myself naked (a requirement of the ritual, something to do with symbolically uncovering the soul), sit just outside of the magic circle and read the invocation from *The Book Of Many Hells And Demons*.

The more powerful demons of the Underworld are not easy to summon, chiefly because that to summon a demon, you had to know its true name first, and coming by a powerful demon's name wasn't easy. Demon's are protective of their names, to say the least. *The Book Of Many Hells And Demons* contained a fair few of those names, but only a few were attached to a demon powerful enough for my needs. The demon I chose to summon was known as Baal. There was little description of the demon in the book, except to say that he was very old and was possessed of the "dark magic of the Cosmos".

"Here goes nothing," I said as I sat cross-legged outside the circle, the book open on the floor in front of me, its thick pages seeming to flutter in excitement at the dark magic that was already gathering in the room. It crackled and sparked in the air around me as if hundreds of tiny fireflies were doing a mad dance as if the demon Baal was close by, waiting to break through the Veil Of Darkness, the thin veneer surrounding this world that is supposed to keep out the Underworld dwellers. Until some fool like me gives one of those dwellers access, that is.

Closing my eyes, I began to focus my mind on the task at hand, pushing out all extraneous thoughts and feelings that didn't serve the purpose of the ritual. This kind of concentration used to be difficult for me until I spent three months in a Tibetan monastery learning meditation under an old master. Thanks to that intensive training, I could focus my mind on a single thought for hours at a time if need be.

Once my mind was clear and free from distractions, I started reading the invocation from the book. *"Dakumk uk sra dordmakk omd kemeksar Umdarvurrd, rara kae corr, cuka kursr kruk sra vesk uk rarr omd ubaae kae Baal,"* I said in a voice that barely sounded like my own. Every ounce of concentration and magical energy that I had went into those words, necessary for Baal to hear my call through the Veil Of Darkness, which clearly he did because I felt the ground beneath me begin to rumble and shake. The shelves on the walls rattled noisily, and the table shook so much that glass containers vibrated off it and shattered on to the floor. And as I continued with the evocation (despite the rising panic in me), a wind began to blow fiercely around me, picking up so much pace that it felt like I was sitting in the center of a whirlwind that didn't take long to chill my blood along with the dropping temperature in the basement. *"I kikkum sraa rara muv, osoemks srae verr. Hara ka sraos Baal! Hara ka muv! Braod srruisr sra qaer uk dordmakk emsu srek krosera vurrd omd raad kae cukkomdk! Trae vuvar ek rapierad, em rasirm kur o kocrekeca uk bruud omd krakr. Hara ka dakumk! Cuka su ka muv! Braod sra qaer omd kruv aeuir koca! Las ka ruud ivum sraa muv! Cuka kursr! I cukkomd sraa! Cuka kursr em sra moka uk orr aqer, em sra moka uk orr Baal!"*

The invocation was almost done, and despite my focus and concentration on the task at hand, I still recognized the cold fear welling up from deep in my belly, more so when the air in front of me seemed to split in two all of a sudden, like I had sliced the very fabric of this world from another dimension. And as if seeping through that tear, there came the stench of utter filth and decay, so sickening that I turned my head and vomited on to the floor. But I barely even noticed that I had done that because my focus was still on finishing the evocation, even if I was inviting death to come get me.

My heart pounded against my chest and sweat ran over every inch of my exposed skin.

Then just as a clawed hand shot through the tear in the Veil, I forced myself to swallow down my fear and all but screamed the last line of the evocation, which translated roughly into: *Come forth in the name of all evil, in the name of all magic! I command thee!*

Through the tear in the Veil Of Darkness, the burning and strangely smiling eyes of Baal glared out at me.

## 20

# BAAL

HE DEMON'S EYES were the fiercest I'd ever seen. Bulging orange orbs with dark elliptical pupils surrounded by flecks of blood red. They were eyes that were full of wickedness and diabolical intent as they glared at me through the torn Veil Of Darkness like a monster peeking through the curtains at a scared kid, enjoying every second of the fear it was inducing. Then one of the demon's enormous clawed hands burst through the tear in the Veil, joining its other hand as it then began to force back the Veil further, exposing its face and the rest of its body. It was all I could do to keep myself together as that monster began to climb forth from the depths of the Underworld on the other side of the Veil. My whole body was tense with fear, every vein in me bulging, every pore sweating. The dark power that poured through was overwhelming as it flooded through me to tear at my insides as though it contained a thousand tiny claws, turning my blood to acid in a manner akin to liquid fire circulating where my blood had before. The pain was so great, and so unexpected that I soon started screaming like a torture victim in some dark enclave of the Underworld.

While I was lying on my back outside the magic circle, screaming for my very life, the demon Baal was busy climbing all the way through the fabric of the Veil. And the more the demon stepped into this world, the more I felt its dark and brooding presence.

Then the pain just stopped as if it were never there to begin with, my screams cutting off only after the agony had blessedly ceased. I caught my breath and sat bolt upright on the floor, my body now dumping relief in the form of adrenaline and endorphins by the boatload. Even so, I had to force myself to look upon the wicked thing I had summoned forth from the unfathomably dark depths of the Underworld. This thing was no spirit. Baal was flesh and blood. He also looked more unsettlingly human-like than I expected, given the monstrous, indescribable horror of the demon that had killed my family back in Ireland. The demon Baal

147

had a human-shaped head if you discounted the pointed lumps of bone that pushed upward out of its skull like the tips of spears. He also had four sets of black horns, two smaller pairs near the center of his skull and a larger pair that curled up and back over his head. The demon also had two slits that flared in the center of its face where a nose should have been. His mouth had so many teeth of different lengths—all of them pointed in some way—that I couldn't even count.

*Oh Jesus, what have I done*, I thought as I stared in horror at the beast before me. *It's going to rip me apart just like that other demon did to my family.*

Baal reared up to his full height of six and a half feet or so. Like his head, Baal's ghastly and thickly muscled body was bipedal in a humanoid fashion, the skin a greenish-black hue with bright orange markings running its full length (perhaps revealing some Underworld characteristic at the core of our own tribal tattoo practices). Baal's glowing amber eyes—set deep into hollow sockets—glowered down at me. "Who dares to summon me?" it roared in a voice so deep and resonant, and so full of absolute authority, that I felt my bowels loosen to the point where I almost shat myself, which would have been a fitting response to that question. Somehow or other, though, my sphincter retained more dignity than the rest of me.

I opened my mouth to speak, but all that came out were unintelligible croaks as my throat was so stricken by fear. This was mostly down to the fact that the demon hadn't possessed the body of John Doe like I thought he would. Instead, he appeared in his true form, which made him a much bigger threat to me. *Another fuck up*, I thought. I didn't have the time however, to ponder what went wrong.

"Speak!" the demon commanded as I felt the heat radiate off it, the smell of something foul and otherworldly creeping over me like a noxious gas, turning my stomach.

*Come on. Get a grip of yourself, Creed. Take control of this thing before it fucking kills you!*

"I am...August Creed," I said, somehow managing to stand up on shaky legs, the demon seeming even more fierce and frightening as I came face to face with it. "I...I summoned you here to do my bidding, Baal."

I put as much command and authority into my voice as I could, thinking it would be enough to take control of the demon, but it wasn't. So I wasn't expecting what happened next.

The demon stepped forth out of the magic circle like it wasn't even there and gripped me around the throat with one of his enormous hands, his skin like sandpaper around my neck, his grip crushing. Then he lifted me off the ground and held me up, turning my head this way and that like he was inspecting a half-dead animal found on the side of the road. When he pulled me close so my face was just inches from his own, his fetid breath—like the worst fart you've ever smelled in your life—blasted into my open mouth. I'd have vomited if Baal's grip hadn't been so constraining. I could also barely look the demon in the eye as he continued to breathe his foul stench, such were the tears flowing freely to blur any image I might've otherwise been able to make out.

"You think you have power over me, human?" Baal said, not as loud this time, but his voice still boomed in my ears. "You think you can command me?" I looked into the demon's eyes long enough to see the black heart of evil in them before Baal casually tossed me against the nearest wall, slamming into a stack of shelves. When I crashed to the floor again, heavy books and glass jars rained down on top of me. It was as if a giant had casually swiped me aside and I could only lay there in shock, struggling to recover the air from nearly being choked to death, and that final bit which had been whooshed from my lungs when my body contacted the wall. There was also pain, but adrenaline and endorphins still being dumped by my brain and other related systems masked most of it.

Then the demon was on me again in a flash, his rough hand around my throat again, lifting me up and pinning me against the wall, holding me there as his eyes bored into me.

"Wait!" I managed to croak out before the pressure around my neck got too great. "I...left you...an offering."

The demon's huge maw stretched into some rictus grin, and it pressed me harder into the wall until I felt the darkness starting to pull me under, blackening out my vision until only a small tunnel existed in its centre. "That rotten sack of dead meat? You insult me!"

Just as I started to black out, Baal let go of me so I crashed to the floor while it crossed the room in a blur of motion. Blood rushed into my head along with my returning consciousness, and I watched the demon pick up the body of John Doe like it was nothing and begin to rip it apart. In a matter of seconds, John Doe's body had been torn to pieces and thrown all over the basement. Chunks of flesh slapped into my naked body, splattering blood all over me. When the demon was finished, John Doe had been reduced to a thousand tiny pieces.

*It's going to do that to me next if I don't do something*, I thought in a panic.

The Sword Of Rashanti still lay inside the magic circle a few feet away. Quickly, I focused my magic and thrust out one hand as I concentrated on the sword, which rattled for a second and then skidded across the floor toward me. I grabbed it immediately and struggled to my feet, thinking what a stupid idea it was to fight a demon who could rip apart a body in seconds. But stupid or not, I knew it was necessary.

"All right, motherfucker," I said, holding the sword high, sounding a hell of a lot more confident than I felt. "Let's fucking do this!"

Baal, covered in blood and gore, laughed and came barreling toward me.

# 21

# FIGHT

*B*EFORE THE SUMMONING, I dared have in my head a little movie featuring Baal and me, the two of us talking and working things out, and certainly not fighting. I knew it was foolhardy to even consider that such far-fetched notions could be possible, but all I can really say is that my idealism and optimism sometimes get the better of me, especially in such otherwise unfathomable situations.

Baal got to within three feet of me before I thrust my hand out and stopped him dead with my magic. To be honest, I was as shocked as Baal to find it could even work against a powerful demon such as he. It was also just this kind of plaintive consideration that led to the conclusion staring me in the face, but which had otherwise been missed in the heat of the moment: my magic was working differently! Due to all the dark energy in the room—what with the demon, the still open book on the floor, and all the bad intent in the air—my magic had shifted into darker territory. It felt different inside me. Not cool and flowing the way it normally did, but hot and burning, like a hundred snakes slithering around inside me, their bodies covered in tiny razors that cut my flesh as they moved along. The pain was dreadful, I have to say, but it was also somehow sweet at the same time, maybe because I felt the increase in power I was getting in return for all that pain and darkness. As I held a surprised Baal in place, I added a bit of pain into the mix, and that's when I really felt the difference in power, when my magic became fueled by sheer bad intent that seemed to materialize unbidden from within me, serving as explosive fuel for my magic.

Baal growled in anger at first as he felt the pain in his chest, then he smiled and stretched his arms out, as if to say, "Bring it on, motherfucker. Do your worst."

So I did.

I channeled as much pain and murderous intent as I could muster into the demon (and I seemed to be able to muster a *lot*), driving the beast back toward the wall, my features twisted by effort and the sinister feel of the black magic I was wielding. Even the color of the magic itself, normally bright blue or white, sometimes green or yellow depending on the spell, had darkened into tones of purple, deep orange and red, even black. A perfect reflection of the intent that fueled it.

And I loved it. It was like I had been injected with a massive cocktail of drugs that were now taking me on the ride of my life, the rush as strong and impressionable as any heroin junkies first ever hit.

The force of the darker magic coursing through me had now driven the great demon down to his knees. Even so, there was a look of defiance on Baal's face and something else that seemed to suggest he was somehow pleased that I was doing what I was doing. "Can you feel it, warlock?" Baal asked me. "Can you feel the darkness coursing through you?" His laugh was deep and sinister.

The evil intent in me had built up to a point where all I wanted to do was destroy the very demon that I had gone to so much trouble to summon in the first place. I wanted to wipe it out of existence, tear it into a million tiny pieces and incinerate each one. Through sheer force of will, I channeled more of the black magic through myself and into the demon. Baal roared at the increased intensity of the magical assault on him, his roar one of genuine pain this time. I still gripped the Sword Of Rishanti tight in my hand, and I raised my arm back in preparation for a decapitation. Rage and a burning desire for vengeance against demonkind fueled my will to kill as I brought the sword down toward the demon's neck in a wide arc.

*Stop!*

The swords killing arc was cut short by a tiny, far away voice coming from somewhere inside my head, telling me to stop what I was doing, and that if I killed the demon, I would be killing the power needed to break the curse on me. It took a monumental force of will for me to listen to that tiny voice. Other, far more sinister voices were begging me to carry on, to let the darkness take over and kill the demon.

With a scream of effort, I managed to cut my magical assault short and stepped away from the still kneeling demon. "No!" I bellowed as I tried to fight against the darkness taking hold of me.

"Don't fight it!" Baal shouted. "Accept it!"

And there it was, the final clue telling the wary what the darkness and its agent wanted, likely the thing my father neither had the desire or conscious mind to care what road he was heading down in pursuit of his sole care, more power and consequences be damned, including those he was meant to love and protect, those who'd proven they'd do anything for him, a sentiment denied in return.

Every muscle and sinew in me were twisting against the darkness as I tried to cleanse it out of my system, while at the same time calling back up the lighter magic that I had spent decades cultivating. Closing my eyes, I compelled myself to relax and focus on drawing up my own magic again. It took a few moments, but I was able to flush most of the poisonous black magic out of my system. Then I turned and looked at the demon, who was back on his feet again. "You knew this would happen," I said, aware that I was back in danger now that I didn't have the darker magic to increase my powers. "You *wanted* this to happen."

Baal reared up, looking down at the scorching hole that went halfway into his chest like he had just been hit by a burning meteor. Then he fixed his fierce gaze on me. "You are more powerful than I thought you were, human." He grunted. "You have proven yourself to me." Another grunt left his mouth, low and guttural as he took a few steps toward me. "That doesn't mean I am at your service."

"What does it mean then?" I asked, feeling like the games were just beginning.

"It means I will help you, but only if you do something in return."

*And there it is*, I thought. *Always a condition*. Did I expect any less? Of course not. "What do you want?"

The demon came closer to me, and I tried not to step back away from him. The fighting was over, and strictly speaking there should have been no need to fear Baal anymore, but I would have been foolish not to. "You've been marked."

I frowned, not understanding. "What?"

"Another demon has marked you."

Another demon? Does he mean the one who killed my family? "You know the demon?"

"I know it."

"What's its name?"

"That isn't why you summoned me here."

"How do you know why I summoned you?"

"I see your retreating soul. I see the energy of the spell you are under. You want me to reverse it."

"And can you?" I asked, really hoping the demon would say yes, otherwise the entire summoning would have been a waste of time.

Thankfully, Baal nodded. "I can help you reverse the spell."

I exhaled in relief. "All right. Tell me what you want. I don't have much time left to fix this."

Baal grinned hungrily, exposing his glistening, pointed teeth. "I want souls who will serve as my slaves. Get me one hundred souls, and I will lift your curse for you."

"One hundred souls?" I shook my head in disbelief. "How the hell am I going to get one hundred souls? That's too many." It would be bloody near impossible to gather up so many souls. Plus, I wasn't in the business of stealing people's souls, especially a hundred of them.

Baal glowered at me for a moment, infernal fires seeming to burn deep in his amber eyes. Then he grunted dismissively. "Find another demon to summon."

Panic rose in me as Baal's body began to turn to smoke and fire before my eyes. He was about to vanish, and I would be back to square one again. *Shit.* What did I expect anyway? That Baal would be happy with a case of beer and a carton of Lucky Strikes as payment? "All right!" I shouted as the smoky vapors became nearly completely transparent. "I'll get you your souls!"

"Summon me again when you are done," Baal said, no more than a fiery outline in the dark of the basement now.

I watched for another moment as the demon finally disappeared, leaving only a trail of smoke and a sulfurous smell behind as evidence he was ever there in the first place (and the scattered remains of John Doe, of course). My body dropped in relief, now that the demon was gone. I thought for sure I was going to lose myself earlier as all that black magic was flowing through me. So powerful. So addictive.

Sighing, I noticed Blaze standing on the stairs leading down from the kitchen, smoke rising out of his pelt, his dark yellow eyes smoldering. I had no doubt he had heard and understood everything from upstairs.

I looked back at Blaze. "I'm sorry, buddy," I said. "I don't like this shit anymore than you do, but it had to be done."

Blaze made a slight mewling noise as the heat died down on his body. Then he came down the stairs and pressed himself against me, a gesture which at least made me feel like I wasn't completely alone, and which at that point, I highly appreciated.

# 2 2

## SANAKA'S SANCTUM

*T*HE FIRST THING I did after I left the basement was take a long, hot shower. I felt soiled by the infernally dark magic that had run through me, and I wanted to be cleansed of it, although I knew it would take more than a hot shower to do so. A Purification Ritual would have to be done to rid myself of all traces, but to be honest, I didn't see the point. Not yet anyway. A heavy feeling in my gut told me that I probably wasn't done with black magic just yet (or it wasn't done with me more like). And given what I now had to do to pay Baal, I would have been wasting my time with a Purification Ritual. A hot shower would have to do.

In the living room after the shower, I called Leona. "Hey," I said when she answered. "Its Creed."

"Creed," she said, sounding sleepy. "You know what time it is?"

"Three a.m."

"Exactly."

I smiled, despite her annoyance. "I thought you might want to know that I'm like, you know, still alive and all, so..."

"All right. Thanks for letting me know, Creed. Now if you don't mind, some of us have to get up at dawn..."

"Sure," I said as if I was there with her (wishing I was). "Go back to sleep."

She had hung up even before I finished speaking. Then as I stood holding the phone, a weird sort of cold feeling came over me, followed by an uncontrollable shaking in both my hands. Shivering, I made a fist with both hands in an effort to control the tremors, and after a moment, they subsided and my body returned to its normal temperature.

What the hell was that about? I wondered as I leaned against the wall.

Though I knew what it was about. It was my soul getting restless within me, being made to leave the person it no longer recognized.

Ghoulship was getting closer all the time.

* * *

A WHILE LATER, I SLIPPED ON MY TRENCH COAT AND TELEPORTED TO MY mentor Sanaka's house a few miles west in Little Tokyo, one of four Asian sub-neighborhoods located in Chinatown. Little Tokyo was a weird place, the buildings being an eclectic mix of Japanese and Western architecture that some found to be quirky and pleasing, others to be hideous. I quite liked the place myself as it was the closest you would ever get to experiencing the culture of the real Tokyo without actually going there (although not the otherworldliness of the place itself).

Sanaka's Sanctum was a small Pagoda style house set in a patch of forest on the edge of a small parkland. Unless you were looking for it, you would hardly know the house was there; and if you did see it, you would probably think it was some decorative feature of the park, in keeping with the Japanese fantasy theme of the park itself. Sanaka's house was a two story, each floor having its own little curved roof that wing-tipped at the ends. The whole structure looked like it had been thrown together by a drunken wizard and a carpenter who'd eaten too many magic mushrooms. The symmetry was all off, and there were odd protuberances here and there, like things were pushing through from inside the house and buckling the wood, which somehow made the house seem more natural than the trees surrounding it. In all, it was like something only a wild eccentric would live in, which fits Sanaka to a tee.

Even though it was almost 4 a.m., it was highly unlikely that the old wizard would be sleeping. Sanaka only slept once a week, which had been enough to keep him going for the last century or so. If he were at home, he would sense me immediately.

True to form, the front door opened wide by itself to admit me entrance into the outwardly ramshackle Sanctum. Inside told a different story, though. It was like walking into a completely different house. The layout didn't seem to match the outside for a start, which didn't faze me as it wasn't the first time I'd been there. I practically lived there at one stage while he put me through hellishly intensive training. My memories of the house were somewhat tainted by the daily anguish and pain I went through in order to push my magical abilities to their limits. Most experiences of pain and anguish were psychological aspects of both, notwithstanding frequent physical occurrences too, and even infrequent spiritual ones. The mysteries of the universe painstakingly unravel with more than a little spiritual malaise, that which results from coming to grips with a more complete impression of the myriad worlds and dimensions of your own and other universes, a seemingly infinite magical nature of the knowledge being a conduit for your learning. Sanaka as a teacher was particularly ruthless anyhow. He cushioned none of my pain or discomforts, believing I had to feel everything so that I could learn and know things properly. Maybe he was right, but I often hated the bastard for his intermittently sadistic leanings. That had been over a decade ago, however, when my tutelage under him ended, and I went my own way. Sanaka would always still be my mentor though, along with Uncle Ray, of course. We had a connection (or at least we did have before I was cursed) that went pretty deep. Plus he knew more about magic than anyone I knew.

The inside of the house was all polished wood floors and sliding screens that led into many more rooms than there had a right to be in such a small house. The normal laws of physics did not exist in Sanaka's Sanctum, as they didn't in most wizard's Sanctums. It was so big inside that you could easily get lost for days if you didn't know where you were going. You would end up like I did more than once, wandering the corridors, frustratedly opening door after door, only to find some strange room filled with even stranger things. Sometimes you would open the door to a seemingly small room and find yourself stepping inside a huge library containing thousands upon thousands of books. Other rooms would expose some weird outside space, like a meticulously kept garden, or a forest or a river. The rooms were like portals to other lands. If you weren't careful, you could lose your way forever.

Sanaka appeared out of thin air in the center of the wide front hallway. Lit candles in small wooden holders adorned the walls, casting a pleasantly soft light that relaxed me. The entire house was lit only by candles. Sanaka had no use for electricity. The candles also never went out as they magically renewed themselves when they burnt down. "You summoned the demon," Sanaka said. He was wearing the dark robes he liked to wear while at home. Sort of like wizard lounge wear. I never went in for the whole robes thing myself. They made me feel too much like a monk or some misguided Satanist, neither of which I wanted to be.

"Yes," I replied, walking slowly toward him after first removing my shoes and leaving them by the front door.

"And now the demon wants payment in return for his power."

His habit of seeming to know everything was annoying when I first met him. After twenty years, though, I was used to it. "Yes."

Sanaka nodded in that sagely way of his. "So why aren't you out securing this payment?"

I stopped a few feet from him. Sanaka liked his personal space. "Because securing payment means stealing a hundred souls, that's why."

Sanaka said nothing for a moment as he stared at me. "You have the stench of black magic on you."

I dropped my head almost in shame. "I do."

"Would you like to bathe in the pool? I'm sure you know what that is."

"I do," I said. "And no thank you. I'm afraid I may once again have to use magic that isn't clean before I'm done with this curse. If the stench offends you, I can go. I know you hate it."

Sanaka more than hated the blacker forms of magic. Long ago, Sanaka allowed himself to become enamored by the darker forms of magic, to the point where he became completely obsessed and the dark magic nearly consumed him, soul and all. Only the intervention of a benevolent Dimension Lord saved Sanaka from an eternity of tortured madness. Sometimes it helps to have friends in the right places, even in—especially in—the magical universe. "Come," Sanaka said. "Let us have tea. I will be interested in seeing your execution of the ritual, which you must surely know."

Christ, was the old man still testing me? Probably. Sanaka made everything into a test, something else I used to hate him for.

I followed the old wizard down a few faceless corridors into a smallish room that was used only for the ancient Japanese ritual of the Tea Ceremony. As Sanaka knelt on the floor by a small wooden table, I went about the tea making ritual. I won't bore you with the details, except to say that the whole process is complex and sophisticated and took nearly half an hour to complete. Back in the day, when Sanaka insisted I learn the tea ritual, it used to take me hours to complete, and the whole ritual felt insufferably tedious, at least at first before I realized the value of it. Doing it now, the ritual felt reassuringly calming to me as I went about it, helping me to forget about my troubles for a short time. When the tea was ready, I brought the cups to the table, arranged them in the manner the ritual dictated, then knelt down at the other side of the table. The tea tasted good. Sanaka seemed satisfied. At least he didn't put his cup down and wordlessly walk away like he used to when the tea wasn't to his liking. Although I always suspected his walking away was more to do with mistakes I had made during the ceremony than the quality of the tea.

"So tell me," I said in a slightly subdued voice that respected the peacefulness in the room. "How does one go about stealing a hundred souls? I have no intention of taking them by force from random people. I was thinking of maybe visiting the Astral Plane, gathering up strays there. What do you think?"

"Most of those strays are still innocent souls. You would condemn them to an eternity of enslavement under a demon in the worst of hells?"

I shook my head. "I suppose not."

Sanaka sipped his tea, then carefully put the cup down on the table. "I know of a place where you can collect your souls, a place where only the darkest of souls gather. You might say that such souls are even deserving of the punishment you would be sending them to."

"What place?" I asked, not liking the sound of it already.

"The Devil's Playground," he said, regarding me with his deep brown eyes.

"The Devil's Playground?" I thought for a moment, coming up empty. "I don't recall ever hearing about such a place."

"Not many have. And for good reason. It is a secret place, an island off the coast of Morgan County. Officially, the island is known as Red Tail Island. Unofficially, it is called the Devil's Playground. It is a place where the very wealthy go to indulge their darker desires. Innocent victims are brought there to be hunted like animals. Many of them are also tortured and abused in ways that defy the imagination. Nothing on Devil's Island—not a single taboo—is off limits. Men can go there and do as they please to whomever they please. For the right price, of course."

"How long has this been going on?"

"Since the island was purchased in the late 1880's by a wealthy German businessman called Hans Belger, who is also a powerful warlock."

"Is?"

"He still owns the island. He lives there, in fact, in a tower at the very center where he can see all that goes on there. Belger encourages his followers to indulge their worst sides. For many of them, their worst sides are all they have now, their souls are so stained and blackened by their heinous acts of cruelty toward others. Belger himself is known in his home country as the Black Forest Butcher. He used to steal local children for use in his black magic rituals and experiments. Given his power, stealing his soul would be like stealing one thousand souls. Your demon would be more than sated."

"I'm sure it would, but by the sounds of it, I'd have more chance of getting killed or worse before I managed to steal this Belger character's soul. How does he even still have a soul, given his penchant for black magic?"

"He has a soul," Sanaka said. "It is as black as his heart. A terrible, hideous thing."

"And you expect me to go and steal this terrible, hideous thing that sounds like it shouldn't be touched by anyone?"

"I do not expect you to do anything. You came to me for help, remember?"

In my mind, I began to wonder if becoming a ghoul wasn't going to be so bad after all. I mean, no soul, no attachments, dead inside, eating rotten meat to sustain myself. Not so bad, right?

I shook my head. "Looks like I'm going to the Devil's Playground."

## 23

# BITCHCRAFT

$\mathcal{A}$FTER LEAVING SANAKA'S, I decided I would walk the few miles back to The Sanctum. Dawn was just starting to break over the city, muted light coming through the clouds to signify the start of the new day. Although for me, the dawn only meant the beginning of day two in my countdown. One day left to sort everything out and get the demon what it wanted, if things worked out that is. Stealing the soul of a darkly powerful warlock like Hans Belger wasn't going to be easy. It might even prove to be impossible, but as ever in these sorts of situations, it wasn't like I had much of a choice.

On the plus side, Sanaka had given me a parting gift in the form of a small wooden box that looked and smelled like it might have once contained herbs or compounds of some sort. As boxes went it was unassuming, with just a few basic carvings of leaves on the lid and around the sides. It wasn't very big either, the whole box fitting easily into the front pocket of my trench coat. According to Sanaka, though, the bland wooden box was a powerful wee number, as it had the ability to trap and contain any soul it was asked to. All I had to do was get close enough to Belger to use it and hope that he didn't banish me to the asshole of the universe (where the Titans dwelled in the dark depths) before I got the box to work.

Walking through the park in Little Tokyo as a dawn chorus of bird song began to sound from the cherry blossom trees, I began to get the sense that someone was following me. Keeping my demeanor casual, I carried on walking, past the ornamental fountain with the koi in it, then past the kids play area. At the same time, I cast my awareness out behind me in search of whoever was following me. After a moment, I sensed another aura at around a hundred yards behind. The aura was human with a low-level magical signature running through it. I shook my head. Probably some bloody hedge magician out to—

A sudden force stopped me in my tracks, a force that also attempted to rip my

159

magic from me. The attack was clumsily made, a factor no doubt attributable to the aforementioned signature making it easily repelled. On turning around to face my attacker, I could make out a figure at roughly half the previously estimated distance since making my scan. They now thus now stood at around fifty yards back, sheltered under a large cherry blossom tree I'd not long since passed. "Son of a bitch," I said, raising my hand and sending out a blast of magic toward the person who was trying to steal it from me. The magic blast hit the dude in the chest and sent him slamming back against the tree he was standing near. I held him there against the tree as I walked over.

"What the hell do you think you're doing?" I asked. "I'm taking my possibly last pleasant walk in the park, when you attack without provocation, and with the intent to steal my goddamn magic." I increased the pressure of my hold. "You could say I'm a little pissed off here."

The guy I was holding against the tree looked to be some sad, wannabe wizard. He was small and bald and wore something that resembled a plastic cape with stars on it, like something a kid would wear, or a magician at a children's party. Underneath the cape, he appeared to be wearing a dark robe that was pushed out by his rotund form. His face was like a fat weasel grimacing. "Please, let me go. You're hurting me."

These fucking people, I thought. They attack you, they try to steal your most valuable commodity and then they have the nerve to complain when you don't take too kindly to their despicable actions. "Oh, am I? I'm sorry. Wait. There. Is that better?"

The grimace the pathetic wannabe wore on his face worsened. "That's *worse*..."

"I know, it is, isn't it? It can get much worse than that, believe me."

"Please, I'm sorry...*ahhhhhh*..."

I sighed and let him go, and he fell forward on the ground to his hands and knees, seeming even more pathetic now. "Why did you try to steal from me? And why are you wearing that ridiculous cape? Is there something wrong with you? Wait, forget I asked that."

The little man started to cry suddenly, softly weeping to himself. "I'm sorry..."

"Shit." I shook my head. "I was only kidding about the cape, you know. It's lovely, really, very...sparkly."

"It belonged to my daughter," the man said, looking up at me with a red face wet with tears. "She died...she's dead..."

"Oh. I'm sorry to hear that."

*Shit.*

"I'm trying to get her back. I just need the power to do it. I don't have enough yet."

"Enough for what?"

"A Resurrection Spell."

"I don't think a Resurrection Spell is the way to go. Why would you want to bring your daughter back as a zombie?"

The little dude burst into tears again. "I just want her back! It was my fault she died!"

Jesus. Things were getting a little heavy for that time of the morning. I looked around uncomfortably as if others were watching, then I asked Sam how his daughter had died and he told me Leukemia. "How is that your fault?"

The little dude in the shiny cape stood up and looked at me, his height reaching to just below my chest, so he had to crane his neck at me. "I should have saved her," he said like he was stating the obvious. "Except my minuscule magic wasn't enough."

"Look," I told him. "I know what it's like to lose someone. I know you don't want to accept this, but your daughter is gone from this world now, and there's nothing you can do. Bringing her back as a shell is not the answer. Neither is trying to steal magic from people. Do yourself a favor and forget about the bitchcraft. In fact, if I were you, I'd forget about magic altogether. It causes more pain than it alleviates."

"But I have nothing else. My wife left me when our daughter died. Magic is all I have."

I nodded. He was clearly all alone in the world, or else he wouldn't have been running around in a kids cape trying to steal magic. I knew what it was like to be alone in the world, with no one to turn to. Magic was all I had at one point as well. Sure, magic took my whole family, but it also got me through when that happened. Maybe it would get this guy through as well.

"All right. Take it seriously then. Stop with the bitchcraft and learn it properly. Dedicate your life to it, it's the only way. And maybe not wear that cape in public. I know it makes you feel close to your daughter, but you know..."

"It's like she's with me when I wear it." His face lit up a little, probably thinking of his daughter. He thrust his hand out. "I'm Sam."

"Creed," I said, shaking his hand. "I need to be getting off now, Sam..."

Sam nodded. "Will you teach me magic?"

I almost laughed, but didn't want to upset him any further. So I lied instead. "I already have an apprentice. Sorry."

"Oh. That's okay. Just thought I'd ask. Well, bye then." He turned and walked toward the trees, his cape flapping behind him in the morning breeze.

"Sam?"

Sam stopped and turned around. "Yes?"

"Here." I handed him a card with a number on it that I fished out of my coat pocket. The card was blank until I used magic to imprint the details I wanted on it, which in that case, was the number for a small school of magic run by someone I had helped quite a bit in the past. "Ring the number, tell whoever answers that August Creed told you to call. They'll take the rest from there. Although you might want to wait a few days before calling...they won't know me at this point, but anyway..."

Sam took the card like it was some rare magical item, which it was in a way. Admittance into the school I was referring him to was difficult unless you had good references. My reference was solid and would almost certainly get Sam into the school, unless he did something on his own to fuck it up, which I doubted he would. He seemed like he wanted it. Time would tell. "What is this?"

"It's what you want. Your path starts here."

His face lit up in excitement. "I don't know how to thank you."

I flashed him a smile and started to walk away. "Stop the bitchcraft. It isn't becoming of a wizard-in-training."

# 24

## APPARITION

*D*ESPITE LEAVING SAM the cape-wearing wannabe back in the park in Little Tokyo, for some reason, I still had the feeling that I was being followed, and that this someone was watching me from afar. When I cast out my awareness again, I sensed nothing out of the ordinary, almost as if whoever was tailing me disappeared somehow when they sensed me scanning for their presence. But despite not seeing anyone, I couldn't ignore the tingling sensation in the back of my neck. By the time I got to East Oakland, I was constantly stopping and looking around, staring at the people commuting to work, thinking one of them might be following me, but knowing they weren't because by then I was convinced that a dark spirit was at my six. The only way to be sure, though, was to cast a Reveal Spell and force the spirit (if indeed that's what it was) to show itself. But there were too many Sleepwalkers around, and I couldn't risk a public display of magic. So I walked on as I headed for home, intending to call Leona when I got there to see if she would accompany me to the Devil's Playground (something told me I was going to need her skills to back me up).

When I turned on to Comptonville Street, a block away from the Sanctum, I walked into an underpass where the morning light had yet to penetrate properly. I had barely set foot inside when the gloom of the underpass turned to full darkness, and the light at the openings disappeared as if the tunnel I was in had become sealed off to the outside world. The question was, who sealed it?

Whoever or whatever sealed me inside the tunnel had a dark presence to it, that much was certain. The air around me became thick with the smell of black magic as if there were a hundred animal carcasses in there with me. But rather than be repulsed by the smell, a large part of me welcomed it. Or rather, welcomed the dark magic it was emanating from.

For a few elongated seconds I wanted nothing more than to drink that malignant magic in, to take it deep inside so I could indulge the twisted, dark places of my mind and psyche. Before the dark magic could get its hooks into me, however, I managed to fortify myself against it with my own magic, creating a forcefield of sorts around myself that manifested as a kind of glowing blue bubble. The light from my magic penetrated the darkness by only a few feet, and I could see nothing beyond that perimeter. Although I didn't need my sight to know that there was an unmistakably evil presence in the tunnel with me.

"Show yourself!" I shouted whilst projecting a fierce sense of fearlessness, a necessity lest dark spirits turn your emotions against you, to take advantage of momentary weakness to bridge the gaps in their strength that will enable them to defeat you. "Why are you following me, spirit?"

Something flew overhead, like a large bat in the darkness. Then again, back and forth like the thing was trying to taunt me or make me afraid of it, which to be honest, it was doing a good job of, at least with the taunting part. When you only have a day or so left before your life as you now it gets decimated forever, you tend to be a little tetchy and a bit intolerant of annoyances like that, no matter how malevolent they were.

A raspy, whispering voice sounded throughout the tunnel, the voice seeming to bounce off the brick walls in every direction. *"Creeeeeed..."* the voice rasped. *"Creeeeeeddddd!"*

"Is that supposed to scare me?" I made a point of laughing at the thing overhead. "You obviously don't know who you're dealing with here. If you don't fuck off right now, I'll take great pleasure in banishing you to the Abyss where you will toil in your own insanity for eternity."

I was about to open my mouth to spit more threats at the apparition when it felt like a freight train plowed into me. A great force broke through my protective shield like it was nothing, slamming me against the brick wall, the shock and heavy impact knocking the wind clean out of me as surely as a fist to the solar plexus.

And then right in front of me, there appeared a face. A terrible looking face with a malignant, twisted smile. The face was unmistakably human, perhaps even familiar, though it was too distorted for me to tell. I soon realized, though, that the face belonged no ordinary apparition. I was looking at the deliberate manifestation of someone's twisted soul, someone who existed in solid physical form somewhere else. The eyes that stared back at me were light green but swirled with darkness and malevolent intent mixed with sadistic enjoyment. It was difficult not to feel rattled by those eyes, by the depth of evil in them. But despite the cold fear those eyes inspired, I still tried to summon my magic to launch some sort of counter attack. My magic was blocked, however, by the much stronger magic flowing from the apparition, which put me entirely at the mercy of the thing that glowed faintly but clearly in front of me. "How do you know my name?" I asked in an attempt to buy more time to crack through its defenses.

"I know much about you, August Creed," the dark spirit said. "You used to know me also..." It trailed off and smiled grotesquely while it waited for the penny to drop.

"You killed that girl," I said. "You're who I was chasing. *You* cast the spell. *You* put this curse on me."

I tried to push back against the power that was holding me, but neither my magic or my physical strength moved me an inch. It was like a thousand nails had pinned me to the wall. "Why are you doing this? What have I ever done to you?"

The apparition's face came closer. Its eyes, full of strange and unfathomable darkness, bored into me. "You wouldn't leave me alone to complete my work," it spat, pushing with yet more force again, crushing my chest ever more painfully still as it mimicked the freight train it bestowed. "You had to keep pursuing me. The spell was my way of getting rid of you and myself in the process. With no one remembering me or what I did, now I can carry on my work in peace, without busy bodies like you meddling in things that don't concern them."

Son of a bitch. This was the motherfucker that cursed me, who put a ticking time bomb inside me. I stared into that face, trying to recognize it, but it was so twisted up and constantly shifting that it was difficult to make out properly. "Fuck you and your spell. I'll have it lifted soon enough."

"Ah yes, the demon." It laughed when it saw how much of a surprise it must've been for me that I could still show it on my face, despite the concrete scowl caused by being in so much pain. "You will never pay the demon what it wants. We both know you're too moral for that, Creed."

Despite the spell, this apparition—this person—still seemed to know things about me. No point asking how. He cast the spell in the first place, so he could control who it affected, choosing to keep his memories intact, to give him an edge I was sorely lacking. I wondered how long I was chasing him for before he cast that spell. Weeks? Months? Years even? "Hide behind your apparition if you want," I said. "I'll still find you. I'll stop you."

The pressure increased in my chest until it felt like my sternum was going to cave in. Then I felt icy fingers push up under my ribs. "Then perhaps," the apparition said in that raspy whisper. "I should just rip out your soul now, devour it whole..." The cold fingers pushed further inside me as they grasped at my soul. My teeth gritted against the scream that wanted to come out of my mouth. He was going to do it, whoever he was. He was going to rip my soul right out of me, finish me there and then.

As I felt the fingers tighten, images of my family flashed through my mind. Scenes of walking through green fields of tall grass with my brother and sister as we tried to take possession of and control the birds in the sky, quickly followed by images of them all dead and then of Leona, of her blue eyes and the soft smile she reserved only for me, and then my father's face, cold and stern, his gray eyes beaming his disapproval as always.

And that's when it hit me. There was only one way to fight back against the apparition, and that was to channel its dark power into me. The channels were already open thanks to the demon summoning, and the apparition's hands were inside me, which meant they could act as a conduit. So with the last of my concentration, I focused on tapping into the vile black magic that powered the apparition, taking the darkness in before the apparition, and the killer behind it, even knew what I was doing. Its face flared up in rage when it felt me draw on its power, but by then it was too late. The balance had tipped in my favor. With the scales now evenly weighted, I had enough to push back against it, and a deeply pitched scream of rage exploded from me as I blasted the apparition with its own power, sending it reeling back.

And my, what dark power it was. Darker even than the power I experienced at the demon summoning. This was another level, despite there only being a minuscule amount of it nonetheless raging through me. With that kind of power, and with enough of it, I got the sense that it would be possible to destroy entire worlds if one so desired. I also got the sense that whoever the person was manifesting as that grotesque spirit, they planned to do just that. They planned on plunging the world into eternal darkness.

"You yet surprise me, Creed," the apparition said as it floated around me, maintaining a respectable distance this time as I followed it, tendrils of black magic trailing from my fingertips like snakes. "You willingly taint yourself with the foul stench of my magic." It moved hypnotically like a cobra in the darkness as it spoke. "Do you like it, Creed? Does it eclipse your weaker light magic? Does it fill your body with pleasure and your mind with dark desires that you even now grow impatient to fulfill? Do you want to give yourself to it, Creed?"

The blacker magic was seeping deeper into me, almost like the apparition was somehow coaxing it to do so. And as much as I wanted that to happen right then —as much as I wanted to give myself, as the apparition said, over completely to a much darker power—I still had that voice inside me somewhere, faintly but insistently reminding me of who I was and what I still had left to do.

"Fuck you," I snarled at the apparition, forcefully compelling the black magic out of me. Which goddamn hurt like hell I can tell you, like thousands of tiny barbs pulling at my skin, shredding my flesh internally.

"Coward!" the apparition screamed at me.

When I expelled the last of the black magic from my body, I quickly uttered a spell that a split second later filled the entire tunnel with a blinding white light that even I had to close my eyes against. Then I heard a high pitched scream from the apparition. A second later, I opened my eyes, the bright light in the tunnel now giving way to natural daylight.

And no apparition.

# 25

# MR. BLACK

*B*ACK INSIDE THE Sanctum, I made myself a coffee and sat at the kitchen table just as the morning sun streamed through the grimy window, the bright but cool rays feeling good on my skin. The light was a welcome contrast to the darkness I had just faced in the underpass...and the darkness that was still inside me.

*I can't keep letting dark magic inside me like that*, I told myself. It wasn't good for me, especially the way it always left me feeling like all I wanted to do was plot out some nefarious plan to bring darkness to the world.

Speaking of which, whoever was behind that apparition in the tunnel (Mr. Black, as I had just now decided to name him) also wanted darkness to descend on the world. Quite how Mr. Black planned on doing that, I wasn't sure yet. Obviously, rituals involving human sacrifice were a big part of the plan in order to channel power from a Dimension Lord, which appeared to be working for the guy because his power was like none I had ever encountered before. It was blacker than black. And as to the motives of that headcase...well I wouldn't have liked to speculate. Who cared anyway? He was clearly just insane, consumed completely by his own lust for the darkest of powers, and by the power itself.

One thing was certain, though. I would hunt Mr. Black down, just like I did before. Once I got out from under the spell he had cast on me that is. I would be more careful about my pursuit than I was before, however. Maybe I didn't fully know who I was dealing with last time, which is why I wasn't prepared enough when I finally caught up with him. I wouldn't make the same mistake again, that was for sure.

My phone rang, pulling me out of my thoughts. "Where are you?" said Leona Lawson.

"Home. Why?"

"You might want to meet me. There's been more murders. Same MO as the last girl."

I sat forward in my chair. "Did you say murders plural?"

"That's what I said."

"Son of a bitch."

"What?" Leona asked.

I shook my head. "Nothing. Tell me where you are."

Leona gave me the address of the crime scene.

"On my way," I told her.

* * *

I pulled the Cadillac up outside the address Leona had given me. An abandoned warehouse in Bayside, across the bridge in Bankhurst. The warehouse was one of many that were due for development along the edge of the shipyards. A fleet of black SUVs and Sedans were parked outside the crumbling warehouse, with men in dark suits and ear pieces guarding the entrance to the building.

*It looks like Division has the place locked down tight*, I thought. I saw no sign of the city cops or even the FBI, which meant that Division was keeping this one tight under wraps, as they always did with magic related murder and mayhem.

As I got out of the car, two tall men in black suits came walking over, their guns visible under their jackets. "You can't be here," one of them said as he moved to force me back into the car again. "Get the hell out of here now." His hand went to his gun as he stopped two feet from me.

"Relax, will you?" I said, holding my hands up. "I'm here by request. Lawson sent for me."

The guy took his gun out and aimed it at me, as did his partner. "Get back in the car before I shoo—"

"Let him in, Martinez." It was Leona, standing in the doorway that led into the warehouse. "He's with me."

Martinez, a heavy set guy with dark, gelled hair, lowered his gun, but still held it in his hand as he looked at me as if I was the cause of the murders inside. "Can I go now?" I said to him. "Unless you want to shoot me. You look like you really want to shoot me."

With tightly clamped lips on his shaking head, this Martinez fellow grudgingly stepped aside, clearly having already decided in a mere ten seconds that he hated everything about me. Sometimes on mostly military trained personnel who're incapable or reluctant of looking past a superficial impression—in my case the weird front of an unruly cowboy without his Stetson—I could be known to have this affect on them. I shook my head at him as I walked toward the warehouse.

Leona held the door open for me. "This way," she said, her face grimmer than usual, which told me the scene inside wasn't going to be pretty (not that murder was ever pretty). For her part she looked gorgeous in her pant suit, attire she didn't wear nearly often enough if you were to ask me, her preference being the utilitarian practicality and comfort of her fatigues and coat. She wore it well, though, the trousers tight around her muscular thighs and curvy ass. Women in power suits were always a turn on for me. I thought about telling her that but decided against it when her face told me it would be inappropriate. Still, she looked sexy as hell.

"You're all very serious, you know that?" I said as I went inside. "That dude wanted to shoot me. Wanted to."

Leona shook her head. "Stop exaggerating, Creed. You're lucky you're even here. Brentwood didn't want any unauthorized personnel on the scene. He doesn't want this getting out and causing a panic."

"Brentwood? He's here?"

She pointed toward the center of the large warehouse where Division personnel stood around what appeared to be an arrangement of dead bodies with small piles of something beside each one. "He thinks you might be useful in this particular case. Don't give him any reason to think otherwise."

I made a tutting sound. "As if I would do that."

Brentwood spotted us walking across the floor. He excused himself from the conversation he was having with two other dark-suited personnel. Then he started toward us before we could get to the murder scene. From a distance, and through the crowd of people, I saw a number of bodies on the floor, maybe five or six, arranged into a circle of sorts. I also saw a lot of blood and what disturbingly looked like piles of guts on the debris-strewn floor. Brentwood loomed into view before I could take anything else in.

"You must be Creed," he said, not bothering to offer his hand. Brentwood was a tall, well-built black man with a perfectly smooth bald head and wide eyes that seemed to bore right into you. Like most of his team, Brentwood also had a special forces background, moving on to the CIA after the military. His back was always poker straight, his chest and shoulders always pushing out his unwavering self-confidence. Like everyone else there, he was dressed in a dark spook suit.

"Yes," I said, a stupid smile on my face. "That's me."

The head of The Division gave me a hard look. "Is something funny?"

"Funny?" I shook my head. "No, it's just—"

"We know each other already, I know. Lawson already filled me in. Did I like you?"

"Not really."

"Thought as much." He looked me up and down for a second. "Anyway, you're saying the sick son of a bitch who did this has done it before? Only no one remembers, is that it?"

"Pretty much," I said.

Brentwood sighed and shook his head. "This job gets stranger every goddamn day."

"You say that a lot," I said as I pondered if he's who Leona adopted it from. "Just something I know about you."

There was a moment of awkwardness, at least for me, as Brentwood glared. Then he said, "Come on, I'll show you the scene."

When Brentwood turned to walk away, Leona looked at me and shook her head. Before I could even ask what, she strutted after Brentwood.

It was as I said to her. Division personnel was deadly serious about everything.

## 26

# SYNCHRONIZED SWIMMING

*B*RENTWOOD DISMISSED ALL personnel at the murder scene by telling them all to go and get coffee. By the time I approached the scene, it was just him and Leona standing there, Brentwood staring expectantly at me as I rushed to take everything in. "Have you ever seen anything like this before?" he asked. "Because I sure as shit haven't."

Looking at the bodies and the shocking amount of blood around the scene, I doubted if anyone had ever borne witness to such horror before. Seven different bodies lay on the floor with a summoning boundary circle drawn around them, although there was so much blood, you could hardly see the circle anymore. Judging from the symbols I could make out around the circle, I would have said they were the same symbols that were present at the last murder site. But like I said, there was so much blood it was hard to tell.

*Son of a bitch*, I thought. *Mr. Black must have done this before his apparition cornered me in that underpass.*

And by the looks of things, the killer was stepping things up. A single victim was one thing. Seven at once was quite another. "Seven sacrifices," I muttered to myself.

"Sacrifices?" Brentwood said. "That's what these are?"

I nodded. "I know they are."

"Sacrifices to whom?"

"Rloth, Lord of the Kiroth Dimension."

Brentwood huffed once. "The Kiroth Dimension? What is this, Star Trek?" He looked at me dead serious.

"I've had this discussion with you before," I told him, glancing back at the bodies. All their stomachs were cut open, the insides excavated like valuable minerals and placed in careful piles. "There are many dimensions in the universe, more than anyone can count. Rloth, as Dimension Lords go, is as dark and scary as it gets."

"I don't really care about some fucking Dark Lord in another dimension," Brentwood snapped. "I care about the motherfucker who is piling bodies up in *this* dimension."

*That's it*, I thought as anger suddenly rose in me. *I've had enough of this man's stupid fucking ignorance.*

"Listen to me, Brentwood," I said, turning to face him with a deep scowl on my face. "Let me just explain to you a few home truths about this fucking situation. Firstly, you had better start caring about fucking Dark Lord's from other dimensions, because if you don't, one of those fucking Dark Lords is going to destroy this fucking planet and every goddamn soul on it. That's *every* soul, Brentwood. Every last fucking one, including you and your loved ones, and their goddamn pet guinea pigs."

Brentwood glared at me with barely contained anger in his eyes, but I didn't care. I'd had enough of being treated like a second class citizen by these fucking government types. Leona told me to calm down, but I pretended not to hear her.

"And just to set the record straight," I continued. "You'd be hard pressed to find an adept not only as capable and as experienced as me, but one who fucking cares more than I do. Believe you me, Brentwood, if the shit hits the fucking fan and Rloth invades this world, you can guarantee that every adept capable of doing so will save their own skin by moving elsewhere in the multiverse, leaving every Sleepwalker behind to suffer in agony at the hands of Rloth. They won't give a shit, but *I* do. That's why I'm here, so you'd better start fucking appreciating just what it is I do for you, or I'll be joining my brethren setting up shop in some other world that is far from away from this one."

Brentwood stared at me after I'd finished balling him out. As a general in the Army, he was more used to dishing out the verbal than taking it. His face said it all. He was seething.

"Okay," Leona said as she awkwardly intervened while throwing me a look. "Now that we're all on the same page, why don't we get back to work."

"That depends," I said. "*Are* we on the same page now, Brentwood?"

Brentwood nodded slowly. "I guess we are."

"Well, that's great," Leona said. "I'm glad to hear it. Why don't you tell us what you know, Creed?"

There was another moment of awkward silence before I turned back to the scene of bloody carnage beside me. All seven bodies laid out in spreadeagled postures carried the same demographics as the only other 'remembered' victim, that being young women in their twenties with symbolic carvings from their flesh, the only visible difference being the aforementioned depositing of innards by each of the bodies. Had there been coptic jars present, you'd be forgiven for thinking that the horror before you had some form of ties to the immensely detailed and varied practices of the ancient Egyptian culture of this realm; given the exception of tattooed symbols in lieu of actual carvings from the flesh, and the obviously large difference between respective purposes. The heads of the bodies met in the middle to form a circle, and with their feet touching as well, they reminded me of synchronized swimmers in a pool of blood. The outlay of the blood had increased the size of the summoning circle from the typical size of such circles which usually measure nine feet in diameter. The killer had obviously cut the throats of the women first. Then he had arranged their bodies to his liking post mortem. All the victims' intestines were also removed and placed on the floor between the women's legs. The smell was as awful as you'd imagine it to be. From somewhere high in the rafters of the warehouse, a pigeon shat and the whitish gray mess landed on the head of one of the victims. A final insult after death.

"Creed?" Brentwood said, a new level of respect in his voice now, I was glad to hear.

With great effort, I managed to turn my head away from the repulsive, yet strangely hypnotizing scene so that I could address Brentwood. "I met the guy earlier."

Both Brentwood and Leona looked at each other. "He made contact?" Brentwood asked.

"In a way," I said. "His apparition appeared to me. Did more than appear actually. It tried to snatch my soul."

"Did you recognize the man, or his ghost or whatever you saw?"

"His apparition was like a more twisted and grotesque version of the man," I said. "Obviously I didn't recognize him because he didn't want me to. I'm calling him Mr. Black for now. Seems apt."

"So what did this Mr. Black say then?"

"Not much," I said, looking down to see that I'd stepped in blood. With a small sigh, I wiped my boot across the floor, leaving a red streak behind. "He said I'd caught up to him before, which I knew anyway. He also said he wouldn't be stopped."

"What's his endgame? All these crazy fucks have an endgame. What's his?"

"Not sure," I said. "But I got the sense that he wanted to somehow plunge the world into darkness."

"Don't they all?" Brentwood huffed.

"Yeah, but this guy could actually do it. He has the power. My guess is that he's trying to bring Rloth here, probably by opening up a portal."

"Jesus Christ," Brentwood said, sounding like he could have done without hearing that. But tough shit because it was the truth.

"How are we going to stop this maniac?" Leona asked.

"By finding out exactly who he is first," I said, glancing over at the bodies again. "And as he seems to have stepped things up, he's probably nearing whatever endgame he's got going. Which means..."

"We don't have much time," Brentwood finished.

I nodded. "Exactly."

Brentwood sighed and thought for a moment, during which time my eyes drifted to Leona and her tight fitting trousers, the perfect curve of her buttocks and her—

"Creed." Leona was throwing me sideways glances.

"Yes?"

"Stop."

"I—"

"All right, Creed," Brentwood said in his frighteningly deep voice, startling me slightly, and for a second I thought he was going to admonish me for eying up

Leona, but he didn't. "Lawson tells me you helped us with cases in the past. Is that true?"

"It's true," I said, smiling over at Leona, causing her to look away in near embarrassment. "I've offered you my services before."

Brentwood nodded. "Fine. Since you seem to have a connection to this case, you can work it with Lawson here."

"Sir," Leona said. "I don't think—"

"You have a problem with that order, Lawson?" Brentwood demanded.

"No, sir."

"Good. Find this motherfucker before he kills anyone else."

"Yes, sir."

"I need some time first," I said, just as Brentwood was about to walk away.

"Time?" Brentwood said, confused and clearly irritated that I wasn't playing ball the way he would have liked, which is to say that I didn't immediately jump to it. "What for?"

"I have something important to take care of first."

"What the hell is more important than this?"

"My soul," I told him.

Brentwood shook his head. "What do you mean?"

I sighed. "Long story short, I'm going to lose my soul very soon thanks to the curse Mr. Black put on me. I'll spur you the details of what happens when my soul departs forever, but it ain't pretty. Bottom line, I need to do this before I can work on stopping our serial killer."

Brentwood had that frown on his face that he sometimes got when I explained things of an esoteric nature to him, like everything I was saying was in an alien language that he couldn't fathom or understand. "All right," he said eventually. "If doing this thing of yours means getting you back on this case, then I'm all for it." He turned to Leona then. "Go with him. Make sure he doesn't get killed. As Creed so eloquently argued earlier, we need him on this."

I nodded, a slight smile of victory on my face. "You do indeed."

# PARTNERS

*L*EONA AND I left Brentwood and his team of suits at the scene of the latest murders and went outside, but only after Brentwood had pulled Leona aside for a quiet word, probably telling her to keep a close eye on the weird magic guy; which if you're wondering, would be me. I mean, how many other weird magic guys are out there? Yeah, you're right...too fucking many.

"What did Sergeant Major want?" I asked Leona as we walked to the Cadillac, the agent who almost shot me earlier giving me the hard man stare as I walked away, as if I'd actually done something on the guy. I tell you, those ex-military types, they have chips on their shoulders the size of Mount Everest. The ones I keep meeting do anyway. All that action they see in foreign lands, it fucks with their heads. At least that's what Leona told me in one of her more vulnerable moments (vulnerability being like a disease to Leona--something to be avoided at all costs, but sometimes it leaks out no matter how good your defenses).

"He told me to keep an eye on you," Leona said, wearing her mirror sunglasses against the bright sun, looking like a sexy secret service agent. "But you knew that."

"Of course. I've known Brentwood longer than I've known you. He could never bring himself to trust me, or even like me for that matter. I think he views me as part of the problem he thinks he's fighting against."

"And what problem is that?"

"Magic of course, even though magic is not the problem."

"What is then?"

"People. The problem is always people."

"You're saying there's not bad magic out there?"

I shook my head. "It's all just energy at the end of the day. It's what you do with it, and what you use it for."

When we reached the car, I leant lazily on the roof, like I hadn't a care in the world. Leona tended to have that effect on me, her very presence making me forget about my worries. She was so damn beautiful and poised, so confident and self-assured, that all I wanted to do was bask in her magnificence. Leona had her faults, of course. She could be cold at times, uncaring if she were in a dark enough mood. She also had the annoying habit of removing cups and plates before I had finished the contents. Like if she was finished eating or drinking, then so was I. It was the clean freak in her.

Leona opened the passenger side door, hovered there as she looked across at me, her face unreadable with those shades on, which I'm sure was the point. "All right, Creed," she said like she'd been waiting to ask this since we left the warehouse. "What were you talking about in there? What is it you have to do? Something to do with getting that curse lifted?"

"Precisely," I said. "And as we're partners now and everything, I thought you could help me."

Her head cocked to one side like it did when she was about to put me straight on something, which she often did. "Let's get one thing straight, Creed. We're not partners. You're just helping out on this case. I don't do partners."

I nodded. "I know, you don't like the idea of being responsible for anyone else, not since Iraq."

She stared across at me, and I stared back into her black mirrors. "I hate it when you do that."

"What?"

"Pull stuff like that out. It's like you're reaching inside my head. I don't like it, and it's really fucking weird not being able to remember you."

"How do you think I feel? No one remembers me, except the psychopath who cursed me in the first place, and trust me, I wish to hell he *didn't* know me."

Leona looked away for a second as if she knew the situation was weird and unprecedented, but also knew that she would just have to live with it for a while longer. "All right, Creed. So what is it you have to do? I thought the demon you summoned was supposed to fix this?"

"It wants payment in return. Souls, to be precise."

"Souls? How many?"

"A hundred, but I'm just going after one."

"One?"

I nodded. "One dark soul that's worth a thousand souls to a demon. I'm hoping anyway."

"Belonging to whom?"

"A psychopathic warlock with a soul as black as this car."

"Another psychopathic warlock?" She shook her head. "Are you attracted to these fucking freaks or something?"

"Attracted? No, definitely not. But unfortunately, my path crosses with many undesirable people. Magic is like any power. It corrupts absolutely."

"Are you corrupt, Creed?"

I looked away for a second, felt the magic in me pulse and swirl. It was a feeling so familiar to me, and it felt as essential to my system as the blood that coursed through my veins. As far as answering Leona's question, I could have said something like, "*Sometimes I wield the magic, sometimes the magic wields me,*" or, "*My moral code is shifty, like most people's,*" but neither of those answers would satisfy Leona, who wasn't really one for ambiguities. So I decided to ignore her question completely and hope she accepted that as some sort of answer. "Hans Belger is the name of the warlock whose soul I will try to steal. He lives on an island off Morgan County. The plan is to go in there, to get what I need to give the demon what it wants, and thus to fix this mess I'm in as soon as possible. I can't do it alone, though."

"You want me to go to this island with you?"

I nodded. "Yes."

She gave a short sigh but nodded back. "Fine, Creed. I'll go with you, make sure you don't get killed, if only because Brentwood wants this killer caught and I happen to think you're the only one who can do that."

Thanking her, glad she was going to be with me on the mission (but also worried now in case something happened to her), we got inside the Cadillac. "And FYI," I said, starting the engine.

"Who says FYI anymore?"

"FYI," I said again, ignoring her. "We are actually partners, though not in any official capacity. We've worked a fair few cases together, you and I."

"And that makes us partners does it?"

"In a way, yes."

"You can't tell me that I sanctioned any such partnership. I would never do that."

"You didn't," I said, now driving off through blocks of warehouses and shipping containers, heading for Leona's Worthington apartment because I knew she would want to gear up before breaching the island with me.

"I don't do partners."

"You said."

She threw me a look, her sunglasses still on, even though the sun had now disappeared behind gray clouds. "What's this island called?"

"The Devil's Playground."

She couldn't help herself and gave a small chortle. "The Devil's Playground. Are you serious?"

"Deadly," I said. "Though not nearly as fun as it sounds. Let me fill you in..."

# GEARING UP

"SO," LEONA SAID as we entered her spotlessly clean apartment, which I was in just a week before for a mind-blowingly hot sex session before she tossed me out afterward, claiming she needed sleep even if I didn't. Not that she would remember that now. "You're telling me we are going to this island run by fucking Sauron and we have no clue as to what we're walking into?"

"Sounds about right," I said, enjoying the familiar smell of Jasmine in the air. Leona's apartment always smelled agreeable, unlike the sometimes offensive mixture of scents in my Sanctum (like the scent of a dead body, for instance).

She stopped in the middle of the living room, next to one of the only pieces of furniture in there, which was a nondescript black leather sofa. Also in the room was a TV I knew she barely watched and a large book case, every shelf stuffed with paperback novels and personal development books. "That's crazy, Creed. I don't like going into situations blind, especially where magic is concerned." Something flashed in her eyes, and I wondered if she was thinking about the cave in Iraq where her brother died.

"I get it," I said. "Look, you don't have to come with me—"

"I'm going with you. I'm just saying I don't like surprises."

I nodded. "Let's hope there are none." Wishful thinking, I knew.

"I'm going to get changed."

Leona walked into the bedroom, not bothering to close the door behind her. I went to the bookcase and stared at all the books, most of which would have been purchased new from Amazon as Leona didn't like to read used books. She said you never knew whose fingers had been on the pages and that she couldn't bear the thought of holding a book that some guy had held straight after masturbating or while he was wiping his ass on the toilet. Consequently, nearly all of the books on the shelves were shiny and new, the spines unbroken on some of them where they hadn't been read yet. Leona was a big fan of Jack Reacher, and she had all of Lee

Childs' novels in a row on the top shelf, the spines well broken from multiple readings. She also read detective novels, techno-thrillers and the occasional noir novel. Mixed in with these were self-development books and books on martial arts and fitness, both of which Leona was heavily into, as well as books on guns and general combat tactics.

Almost out of habit, I walked to the still open bedroom door and leant casually on the doorframe, the way I often did when Leona was changing, so that I could chat with her. She was standing over by a teak open wardrobe that was filled with mostly dark clothes, her back to me as she stood in nothing but her black underwear, the kind she preferred, the kind that looked like shorts and which perfectly accentuated the shape of her ass, which quivered not an inch when you were mounting her doggy, due to the manicured tightness from all the pelvic floor exercises that she did. Despite the fact that I had last seen her naked only a week ago, I still found myself struck by her angelic form and by her long, lithe body. By the muscle tone in her back and arms, and the way her thighs were built up (though not too much) on her smooth-skinned legs. As I stood gazing at her, my belly tingled, and there was an uncontrollable stirring in my groin. Then she turned around and noticed me standing there, instinctively putting one arm across her firm breasts. There was also a fleeting flash of something in her eyes, like a deep connection she was hardly aware off, perhaps a recognition of how things used to be between us. But it was only fleeting and her hard stare soon returned. "What the fuck, Creed?" she exclaimed. "Are you perving on me?"

"You make it sound so dirty," I said, unable to keep the smile off my face. "We used to do this all the time."

"In your reality, maybe. Not in mine. Get the fuck out and let me finish changing."

To take my mind off the sudden desire to fuck Leona until she made that high-pitched squealing noise she always made right before she was going to come, I went and sat on the sofa and tried to focus on the mission ahead. Tactically speaking, I didn't have much of a plan. So far, it was just to go to the island and see what happened. But even I had to admit that as far as plans went, that one sucked big fat hairy donkey balls. If I wasn't to get myself or Leona killed, I would have to come up with something better than that.

When Leona finally emerged from the bedroom ten minutes later, she was dressed in full tactical gear, black from head to toe as if prepped for some special forces mission. I was going to tell her the plan I had just come up with (such as it was), but instead, I said, "You look awesome. Badass, as always."

She threw me a sarcastic smile, still put out by my spying on her earlier, even though that wasn't what I was doing (all right, I was spying on her, but so what? It may have been the last time I got to see that perfect body in all its glory). "You come up with a plan yet?" she asked as she tightened the velcro straps on her body armor.

"Yes, actually. We're going in stealthy."

She couldn't help laughing at me. "Seriously Creed. You crack me up, you really do."

"No really. I have a spell that will make us invisible."

Her head tilted to one side as she raised her thin eyebrows. "Invisible?"

I nodded. "We can sneak on the island and move around without being seen. It's the best option, believe me."

"I'm still taking guns."

"Of course. Everything on your person will be invisible under the spell."

She walked over to the corner of the living room to a large steel cabinet. That's where she kept her guns. I got up and followed her over, hovered conspicuously beside her. "I'm going to be honest here," I said. "I seriously want you right now. Sorry if that makes you uncomfortable, but I can't help it."

Leona stopped just as she was opening the doors of the cabinet, staring straight ahead a moment like she was afraid even to look at me, which I should've known because saying what I just said probably wasn't the best thing to say to a person who I knew would have walls on top of walls around herself. I knew that because I spent the last three years doing my best to dismantle those walls, with some success, I might add. "Look, Creed," she said, finally looking at me. "We may have had some relationship going before, but the fact is, I barely know you. I have no memory of you. We haven't long met, for Christ's sake—"

Propelled by some force or latent desire, I quickly leant in and kissed her, a kiss which lasted exactly one second before I found myself gripped and slammed against the hard metal gun cabinet, Leona's forearm like an iron bar pressing against my throat, though thankfully with not much pressure. Under her steely glare, feeling like a cornered criminal, I waited on the inevitable tongue lashing. Which is why she surprised me by smiling instead. "You always this pushy?"

"Hey, you kissed me the other day, remember?"

She nodded. "I remember."

"So..."

"What? You think that gives you permission to go full steam ahead?"

"No...yeah...maybe..."

"It doesn't. Things are weird enough right now without this." She leant in closer so her soft lips barely brushed against mine. "Patience. At least wait until I remember who you are again."

"But you know who I am." I sounded like a love sick teenager begging his first crush to go out with him. Not very dignified, I know, but I just wanted her so badly.

"No, I don't. I just know you're a magicslinger with a smart Irish mouth and a big fucking wolf for a pet. You probably drink too much as well."

"See, you know me so well."

She smiled, shook her head, let me go. "Outta the way. I need my guns."

A cheeky smirk appeared on my face. "I know you do."

Roughly pushing me aside, Leona opened the doors of the cabinet to reveal an impressive array of weapons inside, mostly guns, but also a few scary looking knives, a Katana and a black truncheon with a steel ball on the end of it. She put a custom Beretta in her leg holster and one underneath her body armor. Then she looked for a minute at the rack of automatic weapons before selecting a high tech looking rifle. I'm not big into guns (owning only one, which I had on me) but the rifle looked military grade. She checked the weapon with the swiftness and assurance of one who has done so countless times before. As marksmen went, Leona was easily in the top ten percent in the country. A two thousand yard shot wouldn't have been a stretch for her.

As she set the rifle against the wall and began to lock up the gun cabinet again, I felt a rush of gratitude that Leona was backing me up on this crazy mission to steal a soul. She might not have known magic in the conventional sense, but she sure knew how to create her own form of magic when it came to fighting, either armed or unarmed. God help any of Belger's acolytes should they try to accost us on the island, that's all I could say.

"So," Leona said, locked and loaded, anxious now to get going. "How are we getting on to this island?"

"First we drive to the coast, then I teleport us over to the island itself."

"Teleport?" She shook her head like the idea of teleportation disagreed with her. "I've seen *The Fly* you know. What's to say we won't end up a conjoined mess when we land?"

"Get a grip," I said laughing. "This is magic, not technology."

"Yeah, I know," Leona said as we hauled ass out of the apartment. "That's always what worries me."

# THE LEAP

*I*T HAD BEEN a while since I was outside of the city, so it was a pleasant change to see green fields and rolling hills set against an expansive sky, instead of buildings like skeletal fingers reaching up into the gloomy Blackham skyline. It was late afternoon by the time I drove the Cadillac off the expressway and started taking the back roads that headed toward the coast. On the two hour journey from Blackham to Morgan County, Leona and I discussed, amongst other things, our impending clandestine assault on the Devil's Playground, the gist of which was: get in, get out as quickly as possible. I also heard her opinions on her boss, Brentwood , who she saw as a good soldier, but as a pain in the ass boss. Her hatred for modern pop music, which I shared, also came up, and the fact that she was hungry by the time we got off the expressway. So we ended up stopping at a roadside diner so she could munch on a burger while I watched and drank coffee. Then we were off again, driving along winding roads, the smell of the sea air creating an air freshener scent inside the car as we got closer to the coast, one you'd make millions from if you could actually delineate the artificial components needed to mimic its scent and its effects.

Then finally, we made it to Birkenhead Cliffs, driving the car over the wide stretch of grass to within several feet of the cliff edge.

When we got out of the car and walked to the edge of the cliffs, the wind was brisk and had a sharp bite to it thanks to the cold air blowing off the sea. "It's beautiful, isn't it?" I said as I gazed out over the vast expanse of dark, choppy water a few hundred feet below, the sun just starting to sink toward the horizon. "These cliffs are known as Maggie's Leap, did you know that?"

"No," Leona said, as she stared hard at the island in the distance. "No doubt you've told me that before though, right?"

I suppressed a smile. "I might have. About a hundred years ago, a woman named Maggie Gilpenstein threw herself off the top of here, falling to the rocks below."

Leona looked down at the waves crashing against the rocks. "Some fall. Why'd she do it then?"

"She was an infamous child murderer. Apparently kidnapped and killed scores of local children before people realized it was her."

"What was she? A witch or something?"

"Some say she was. She was apparently obsessed with the story of Countess Bathory, thought it a good idea to follow in the Countess's footsteps and bathe in the blood of virgins to keep herself looking young. When the local townspeople found out, a lynch mob marched to Gilpenstein's house so they could burn her as a witch."

"But she did a runner before they got to her."

"Yes. Killed herself rather than give the people the satisfaction of burning her at the stake. Henceforth, these cliffs have come to be known as Maggie's Leap. Her ghost apparently still haunts the town."

We fell silent for a moment as if listening for signs of ghostly activity, then Leona said, "Was there a reason for that story, Creed?"

I shook my head. "No. Just thought you might be interested in a little local lore."

"Okay, well thanks for the history lesson. Are we going to start the mission now?"

I looked across the water to the island about six or seven miles in the distance. Near to dusk lighting made it hard to distinguish much about the island, except perhaps that it isn't very big (a few square miles maybe) and that most of the island seemed to be covered by thick forest. That is at least from what we could see of its perimeter. Who knew what lay beyond the dark trees?

"Sure," I said, vacillating over the increasing coldness and emptiness of my soul shrinking still further, making me think of a cancerous growth or an empty husk needing to be cast off. My situation was now shifting to a constant impression of there being a pure light source at the centre of this diseased vessel, seeking as soon as possible to leave the virtual stranger it now considered my body to be. That way it could make its way to the next evolutionary plane of its existence. Whatever else happens from here, I knew my life as I know it was down to a matter of hours and minutes instead of days. Barely holding back my despair, I said, "Let's get this done."

I popped the trunk on the Cadillac to reveal a large wooden box. Leona asked me if I'd brought a picnic. "Not exactly," I told her. "More like a tool kit." I opened the lid and the whole thing opened out like a fishing tackle box, segmented with various drawers and compartments filled with a variety of supplies: this includes but isn't limited to a bunch of glass phials, small plastic bags, and other miniature boxes, all of them filled with an array of necessities for the well-prepared wizard. "We'll need a few ingredients out of here for the Cloaking Spell."

"I always wondered what it would feel like to be invisible," Leona said. "Ever since I saw that Kevin Bacon movie, *Hollow Man*." Leona wasn't big into movies, but she had a thing for Kevin Bacon, almost crying when his TV show, The Following, was canceled. She even threatened to go after the executive who made the decision to cancel the show. If I hadn't of been there at the time to calm her down,

I think she might have followed through on her threat to take out the Hollywood exec. I certainly wouldn't have put it past her.

"So you can lurk in people's apartments unseen, watching their every private move?" I said salaciously.

"You're such a perv, Creed. Have you done that? Wait, don't answer that. I don't want to know." Then she shook her head and drew back from me slightly. "And while we're on the topic of being a perv, don't think I didn't notice you checking out my ass and other bits back at the last murder scene. Apart from being grossly inappropriate given the macabre setting, it's still weird as fuck when you get that look of knowing what's beneath the layers, and totally fucking lecherous when you do it."

I chuckled to myself as I selected a phial of dark blue liquid from the box, along with a little jar of greenish-black ointment. I held up the phial of blue liquid. "We need to drink this first. Just a drop will do."

"What is it?"

"You really want to know?"

"Yes," she said, seeming unsure now.

"It's the blood of a very rare fish that can only be found in the River Troyden, which runs through Babylon. The blood is then mixed with pure dream essence found in pools on the Astral Plane."

"That's it?"

"And semen from a sewer rat."

Her mouth dropped in disgust. "That's gross. You're just kidding about that, right?"

"Sure." I held up the little round jar of ointment for her to see. "This is mostly plant matter, from various plants."

"And what else? Piles from a demon's asshole?"

I stared at her a moment then shook my head. "That's disgusting. Nothing so foul. Just the crushed up scrotum of a recently deceased man and the armpit hair of a three hundred pound Russian weightlifter."

"Now you're just taking the piss."

"I know I am," I said, removing the cork from the glass phial of blue liquid. "At least about the armpit hair. The crushed ballsack is still in there."

"Jesus," she said. "magic is disgusting."

"Can be." With Leona watching with a sheer grimace, I put the phial to my mouth and supped a small amount, unable to keep a similar grimace from rearranging my facial expression over its bitter, acrid taste. "Hmm, lemony."

"I'm sure it's more than that." Leona took the phial from me and immediately put it to her mouth, her face soon twisting against the sharp and bitter taste. "Jesus, that's worse than the piss we used to drink in Iraq."

"You used to drink piss? I hear it's good for the skin."

She shook her head. "Not actual piss, obviously. I mean the alcohol we used to drink tasted like piss. Although I have actually drank my own piss. We were made to do it in training. We were made to do a lot of things in training."

"I'm sure you were." With a sardonic smile on my face, I took the phial from her and put it back in the box. Then I opened up the jar of ointment and scooped a small amount out with my fingers before applying the waxy lotion to both my cheeks.

"This may seem like a stupid question," Leona said. "But if we're both invisible, how are we supposed to see each other?"

"That's what the accompanying spell is for. I can tailor it how I want. Magic can be pretty flexible in that way."

She nodded as she took the jar from me and made a face as she put some of the contents on her fingers and did as I did, rubbing it into the skin of her cheeks. "This shit smells awful. All I can think about is that I'm rubbing some old guy's scrotum on my face."

"Not for the first time, eh?" I laughed. Leona wasn't amused as she threw the jar back at me. "I just mean that I'm fairly old by normal standards, and we have slept together and my balls—"

"Yes, Creed, all right. Enough. I get it. I'm going to get my rifle from the car now. Don't be surprised if I shoot you with it."

I chuckled again as she walked away and I put the jar back in the box, closing the lid before slamming the trunk closed. "Get everything you need before I do the spell."

After attaching a suppressor to the end of her rifle, Leona attached the rifle to a strap on the front of her. "Shouldn't you be wearing armor as well? I'm sure there's going to be guns on that island. Invisible or not, you still might get shot."

"I have my fetching trench coat, don't forget. Demon skin is as good as any armor you could give me."

Daylight was beginning to fade, and the sky was taking on an ominous appearance as dark clouds gathered, making the water look almost black. As I looked out at the island barely visible now in the distance, I thought about Hans Belger. Did the old warlock know we were coming? He certainly would when we landed on the island, that was for sure. It remained to be seen what his response to our trespassing would be, though. Something told me he wouldn't be waiting for us with tea and biscuits.

I called Leona over and put my hand on the back of her neck, pulling her close, so our foreheads were touching, our eyes looking into the others for a moment before I closed mine and started reciting the spell that would make us invisible, at least for the next few hours or so. After that, the spell would fade, and we would be exposed to the world again. Hopefully, we would have completed our mission before that happened. "That's it," I said, stepping away from her. "It's done."

Leona looked down at herself like she half expected her body to have disappeared. "I don't feel any different."

"You won't, except when other people look right through you." I grabbed her arm then, after I'd grabbed the Soul Box. "Ready?"

She nodded once. "Ready."

"Devil's Playground, here we come..."

# THE DEVIL'S PLAYGROUND

*W*E TELEPORTED TO a stretch of sandy beach on the north shore of the island, our boots sinking into the soft, wet sand as we landed, the stiff breeze coming off the choppy water biting our skin. Leona still held on to me as she tried to get her bearings again. "That was a rush," she said as if we had parachuted out of a plane thousands of feet up.

"It takes a bit of getting used to," I said, as I looked around for signs of life, seeing nothing but rocks, trees and sand. "The dizziness will stop shortly. It's just your brain readjusting and trying to make sense of the fact that it was somewhere else a second ago. But it's fun, right?"

Leona let go of my arm and shouldered her rifle, keeping the barrel pointed downward as she surveyed her surroundings, looking every inch the professional soldier. "Seems quiet."

"So far. No doubt that will change when we move further inland." No doubt at all. I was pretty certain that Belger knew we were there on his private island. Any warlock or wizard worth their salt would have been able to detect intruders immediately, even if said intruders happened to be invisible to everyone but themselves.

Leona seemed concerned as she stared toward the dark woods about ten yards away. There was something ominous about those woods like an evil presence lurked there. "Something isn't right about this place."

"Your instincts are spot on as always." I stared down the beach toward a rocky outcrop that jutted into the water like a huge demon mouth. "There's a lot of darkness here."

"Darkness?"

"Evil."

We exchanged glances like we were crazy even to come to the island in the first place. Which we were, of course. Batshit crazy, although Leona didn't know the full danger. How could she? If she knew magic like I did—if she knew the full

184

extent of its dark potential in the hands of someone like Hans Belger—I doubt she would have come with me. Or maybe she would have. One thing about Leona was that she was loyal, and despite only knowing me for a few days, she seemed more than willing to help. When I first met her three years before, it took her nearly a year before she displayed the kind of loyalty toward me that she was exhibiting now. I guess I should have been grateful, but I still wondered what was different. Was it because on some level she knew I was telling the truth, or because deep down she still remembered me, even if it were only on a subconscious level that her being or soul still recognized what her conscious ego could not? As curious as I was, it wasn't the time for indulgence. It was a time for focused action so we both could stay alive.

"All right," Leona said, her slender fingers curling around the stock of her rifle. "Are we going to do this? I want off this island as soon as possible."

I didn't blame her for wanting to leave. So did I. The presence of dark magic on the island was palpable, more so to me because I still bore the stain of it inside me, and that stain was acting like a magnet to the black magic that permeated every square inch of the island. Drawing the magic to me, which demanded access so it could fill me up and consume me once more, we moved off toward the interior of the island. Leona threw me a look and asked if I was all right. "The magic here is corrosive," I said. "I can feel it burning my skin."

"I don't know about magic, but this place gives me the damn creeps."

"We'd better get a move on then, before—"

"Before what?"

"Before someone or...something, comes looking for us."

"Very fucking reassuring, Creed."

Smiling despite myself, I fell into step beside her as she strode across the sand and headed for the trees. The wind on the island was blustery, and it whistled as it blew through the branches, rustling the dry leaves. What daylight there was got swallowed up the second we entered the woods. The trees were thick and gnarly, their branches twisted in a grotesque way that didn't seem natural, like sinewy arms with spidery fingers that looked like they might try to grab you if you got too close. The terrain included patches of grass and dirt that occasionally became swampy. We moved around the swampy parts, knowing we would disappear as surely as if it were quicksand we were trying to traverse.

There was also a smell in the air that I can only describe as the lingering smell of death. On my travels in Europe years before, I once visited the Auschwitz concentration camp because I wanted to see for myself the large scale horror and brutality that man was capable of, and because I was curious about how strong the magic would be in the place. As it turned out, the black magic in Auschwitz was as strong as I expected it to be. Maybe not as potent as it once was when the camp was fully operational, but I still felt burned by it as soon as I walked through those gates. Needless to say, Auschwitz was also full of ghosts, mostly the lingering essence of those who had died at the camp, and also at least one vengeful spirit that I saw haunting one of the gas chambers. The ghost of one of the Nazis who ran the camp. Aside from that, though, my overwhelming impression of Auschwitz was summed up by the toxic stench of death that poisoned the air around the place. You didn't need to know magic to smell it. Everyone could smell it, could feel it seeping into their skins as they toured the death houses. The Devil's Playground had that same sickening scent of death to it, like thousands of people had died there over the years.

Then as if to prove my assertion, we came across a sight that caused us both to stop and shake our heads in sheer disgust. At least ten corpses in various states of decay were nailed through the chest to an unnaturally thick-trunked tree. A few were nothing more than skeletal remains with bits of ragged skin and rags still clinging to them. The rest spanned states of decay from fresh kills to the afore-mentioned; men, women, and even a child too. The trees used as though they'd become a systematic part of the evil effigy or trophy cabinets, seemed to reflect the greatest degree of deformities that astonishingly still somehow managed to separate them from their diseased brethren, perhaps as though being used to reflect such evil could be further mutated from just the air of darkness that was likely to have mutated their brethren. The spikes in their chests were thick like railway spikes. As the flashlight on Leona's rifle moved over the bodies, the extent of their wounds also became apparent. Each one had died a violent death. Some had bullet holes in them, others slashes and gaping wounds made by sharp blades. Still others twisted around in a way that didn't seem possible, as if a great force had twisted them so.

"What the fuck?" Leona said.

"I mentioned they hunt people on this island, didn't I? I'm assuming these people were the hunted."

That wasn't the full extent of it either. As we moved further through the trees, it became apparent that there were bodies everywhere. Some strewn across the ground, others hanging from the branches of trees, ropes around their necks, their bodies in horrific states of degradation. At one point my boot kicked something heavy on the ground, and when I looked down, I saw it was a disembodied head. The head of a young woman to be precise, her lower jaw ripped off by someone or something. Everywhere we looked there were signs of death and decay, extreme violence and bloodshed.

And something else.

Some of the bodies looked eaten as if something with a huge mouth had taken chunks out of them, after and possibly before death. I decided not to mention it to Leona. She seemed spooked enough already.

"I've never seen so much death in one place."

For Leona to say that, I knew the island must have been bad because Leona had seen her fair share of death over the years, serving in some of the most war-torn places on Earth. She was no stranger to horror, but the kind of horror on display on the island, the sheer malevolence behind it, was enough to turn even the hardest of stomachs.

We carried on through the woods, doing our best to ignore the human remains that came into view with every step we took. Then after walking in silence for more than twenty minutes, the dark woods seeming to go on and on, we came to a clearing, on the edge of which was a large mound of rock jutting out of the ground. We both shone the beams of our flashlights over the rock and noticed there was a hole in the center, like a cave entrance. To the side of the cave entrance was an iron gate. Some warning signal sounded in me as I moved the beam of my flash-light from the cave entrance to a trail in the grass that led off into the trees like something going in and out of the cave had worn away the grass underfoot.

"What is it?" Leona asked. "A secret entrance to somewhere?"

I shook my head just as I caught a strong, musky smell coming from the cave. "More like a pen."

"A pen?"

"Yeah, like a dog pen."

"A dog pen?"

I closed my eyes for a moment as I cast my awareness out around us, reaching into the woods in different directions, not sure exactly what I was looking for, but knowing there had to be something out there. Then I sensed it a couple of hundred yards to the west of us, something alive and predatory. Something closing in. When I opened my eyes again, I said, "We should go. Now."

"What is it, Creed?" Leona asked as I started jogging into the woods again.

"I don't know. A werewolf maybe. I'm not sure."

"A fucking werewolf?" Leona was running alongside me now as we tried to avoid the bodies scattered over the woodland floor. "Those things are hard to stop. They just keep fucking coming. Are you sure?"

"You couldn't smell it?"

"Maybe, I'm not sure. Where are we running to?"

A howling noise cut through the night air behind us, sealing with it the debate over what I'd sensed, and we both stopped dead. "Shit. That's not far away."

Leona shouldered her rifle. "Fuck it. Let it come. I'll kill it. It can't see us anyway, right?"

"No, but it can still smell us, whatever it is."

Something crashed through the trees about a hundred yards away, splintering branches, churning up the earth with heavy sounding paws or feet. Without thinking, I formed a sphere of blue energy in my right hand, ready to blast whatever came through the trees at us. Leona stood near me, her rifle shouldered as she sighted into the trees beyond.

Snarling noises sounded as the creature got closer. Then there was more noise from the east side of the woods, the snapping of branches underfoot. Loud, menacing snarling. "Oh, shit," I said. "There's more than one. It's coming up my side."

"Take it," Leona said. "I'll take the one in front."

Leona was more at ease than I was with the fact that we were about to be flanked by unknown enemy combatants. Her training was kicking in, whereas fear was the only thing kicking in on me. Over the years, I'd come across numerous entities that could be described as monsters—werewolves, wendigos, vampires, pissed off ghouls and goblins, various other creatures that most people never see or hear off but which are still out there—and some of those monsters I had to face down in battle, sometimes successfully, sometimes not. It wouldn't have been the first time I got bit by a werewolf or thrown across a room by a vampire. I would face those things if I had to, but I certainly didn't get pleasure from doing so (as Leona sometimes seemed to). The rush of battle has never really been my thing, even if in said examples I've been forced to fight. In terms of a flight or fight response, I'm more the flight kind of guy, one who'd rather read a good book.

Cold sweat ran down the back of my neck as the creature nearest me forced its way through the trees and undergrowth. As it drew closer there was no mistaking the hard and loud rhythm of its breathing, gut instincts screaming that regardless of what caused it, there was a madly salivating predator anticipating the rarity of still living human meat and an opportunity to make a kill of it. The creatures were no doubt responsible for the half-eaten bodies lying around. Belger's pets, probably used in the hunts. Bastard must have let them out, which meant he knew we were here on his island.

We waited, but nothing came. The noise stopped as well.

"What are they doing?" whispered Leona.

As I kept staring at the trees, a pair of glowing red eyes made my heart stop for a second. "Playing with their meat," I replied.

No sooner had I said it when the red-eyed creature came bounding out of the trees toward me. In my peripheral vision, I saw the blur of movement as the other creature charged at Leona.

Adrenaline dumped into my system.

Then the fight was on.

# PIT BULLS ON STEROIDS

*M*Y FOCUS LOCKED on to the animal that was charging at speed toward me just as gunfire sounded from behind me, telling me that Leona had her own fight on her hands. With my adrenaline pumping, I tried not to panic when I saw the creature coming, its red eyes fierce in the dark of the night. The full moon still beamed overhead, casting its pale silvery light over the hell-hound-like creature that burst through the undergrowth. The thing was moving so fast, I only got a snapshot of what it looked like. It was bigger and bulkier than your average wolf of comparable size. Excess musculature warped its look grossly, as though it were a pit bull on steroids, bred purely for fighting and killing things much larger in size and weight. At first, I thought it was a werewolf, but then I noticed the long spikes sticking out of its back along its spine like thick porcupine quills. Then, as the creature got nearer and opened its mouth to snarl, I caught sight of the long incisors curving down from the top of its mouth. Not quite as long as a saber-toothed tiger's, but long enough to make me shutter. Certainly not something you would expect to see on a wolf, but very much so on a hellhound, which I'd encountered before. This creature, however, seemed more like a hybrid that some twisted mind had dreamed up in a lab. *Like the fucking Island Of Dr Moreau this is,* I thought.

I didn't have time to think about the Razor Wolf's origins, which is what I'd decided to call it, regardless of any other impressions I may have had. It leapt at me from ten feet away, getting scary height and velocity thanks to the rippling muscles beneath its gray pelt. With a sharp intake of breath, I drew back my hand, which still held the sphere of crackling blue magic. As I released the magic blast from my hand, I was vaguely aware of more gunfire from Leona's automatic coming from behind me, then a scream of pain which undoubtedly came from Leona. This knowledge was reinforced by her shouting, "You fucking stinking mutt!"

I wanted to run to Leona so I could help her, but my focus had to be on the beast cutting through the air toward me, its jaws wide open, globs of saliva dripping from its stained teeth. The magic blast caught the creature in the belly, halting it in mid air like it had just slammed into an invisible brick wall. It was thrown back several feet before it thumped to the ground and skidded back into the trees.

While the Razor Wolf was down, I chanced a look over my shoulder, calling Leona's name and getting no answer. I couldn't see her anywhere, nor the Razor Wolf that had attacked her. "Leona!"

A blast of gunfire resounded through the trees, loud in the night. Hard to tell exactly from which direction it came from.

*She's out there somewhere with that thing*, I thought. *I have to help her.*

For the moment, though, I turned my attention back to the Razor Wolf I had just put down. It was now rolling to its feet, snarling at me, its red eyes never leaving me (or at least where it sensed me to be) as it shook its head as if to clear it so it could ready itself for another charge.

There was no time to mess about. Leona was out there facing off against the other Razor Wolf. If the creatures were creations of Belger's, the warlock would have made them hard to kill. It was doubtful if bullets would stop them.

*No ordinary bullets anyway.*

Sticking my hand inside my coat, I found the pistol in its holster and pulled it out. It's a rare occasion when I have to get the pistol out, normally reserving it for hard to kill beasts like werewolves, vampires or Fae (or genetically engineered wolves with foot long incisors and spikes in their backs). Unsure of what I would end up facing on the island, before I left, I made sure the pistol was loaded with heavy duty ammo. In this case, that ammo was hollow point rounds infused with chaos magic. The hollow points by themselves would inflict enough damage on most creatures. The chaos magic gave the rounds an extra kick, though it was hard to anticipate the effect of the magic itself. It being chaos magic, it sometimes had a surprising effect on whatever creature it infused. Sometimes they exploded. Sometimes they would be reduced to a puddle of goo on the ground. The last time I used the bullets was on a goblin serial killer (if you can imagine that). Nasty little fucker was taking victims from my neighborhood, so I tracked it and shot it in its ugly head with one of the chaos bullets. Imagine my surprise when the goblin mutated into something even uglier, and twice the size, nearly killing me before I managed to take it down.

As I pointed the pistol at the Razor Wolf, I prayed that the pit bull on steroids wouldn't get any bigger after I shot it. It was scary enough as it is.

The Razor Wolf made a barking noise that any hellhound would kill for, so bone-rattlingly scary was it. Then it dug its huge paws into the earth, its muscles tensed and rippling as it took off toward me again.

I thumbed back the hammer on the pistol and tried not to panic too much as I got the beast in my sights. When the creature got to within six feet of me, I pulled the trigger, the heavy recoil slamming it against the palm of my hand.

The bullet was on target, catching the wolf in the upper chest just as it reared up to launch itself at me. The power of the shot forced the wolf back down again, and it made a high pitched yelping sound as the hollow point ripped through its chest. I pulled the hammer back on the pistol, ready to fire again, but after a moment, I realized I wouldn't have to. The wolf was down, blood pumping from the fist-sized hole in its chest, tendrils of chaos magic crackling inside the exit wound, already racing around the body of the wolf, doing God knows what to it.

I stood back as the creature thrashed around on the ground like it was full of deadly poison, arcs of chaos magic (dark blue mixed with flecks of cobalt) breaking out all over its body, which was beginning to bubble in places as if its very molecular structure was changing.

*More like its fucking insides are turning to mush, and it's about to explode like a goddamn blood volcano*, I thought.

I'd seen it happen before. Trust me, you don't want to be standing within a ten foot radius when it did happen, not unless you wanted to look like one of those game show contestants after they got dunked in a tank of offal.

As an unearthly howl of pain and fear sounded from the creature's mouth, its skin still bubbling all over like hot mud now, I decided not to stay for the big finale and turned and ran off into the trees, in the direction I'd heard the gunfire coming from a few moments ago. "Leona!" I called, as I tried not to run into any trees or trip over any human detritus on the ground.

I stopped to listen for a moment. Then I heard a scream coming from not far away. Cursing, panicking in case Leona had been hurt by the other Razor Wolf, I bounded as fast as visual conditions would allow in the direction of the scream. Then, under the pale moonlight, I caught sight of the Razor Wolf up ahead, partly shielded by a gigantic, gnarled tree. All I could see was its head twisting violently, its jaws snapping at Leona, who was underneath it, the beast having pinned her down. "Leona!"

Running toward her and the beast, I aimed the pistol as best I could at the wolf on top of Leona, but the creature was moving too erratically and I didn't want to fire in case I hit Leona. Stopping a few feet away, I thrust out my hand, ready to use my magic. Before I got the chance however, the beast on top of Leona gave a shrill cry as it suddenly fell to the side. And that's when I saw the huge knife in Leona's hand glinting in the moonlight, dark blood running down the blade. As the creature fell, Leona rolled herself over on top of it, straddling the beast, raising the knife again and again as she stabbed the creature multiple times, over and over, thick jets of blood arcing up in the silver moonlight, the creature squealing uncontrollably before suddenly going silent.

The Razor Wolf was clearly dead, but Leona didn't stop stabbing. She kept thrusting the knife into the Razor Wolf until the beast was just a mess of blood and guts.

"Leona," I said, stepping toward her. "I think it's dead now. It stopped moving ages ago."

Leona pulled the knife out of the creature's body one final time and then looked at me, rage still in her eyes, flecks of blood all over her face and neck. "Motherfucker bit me," she gasped.

"Where?"

She looked down. "My damn leg." She tried to stand up, but couldn't. "Shit..."

"Wait." I put the pistol back in its holster under my coat. "Let me help you."

Wrapping my arms under hers, I helped her stand up. "I don't think I can walk, Creed. The bone..." She winced in pain as I helped her hobble over to a nearby tree.

"Sit," I told her, helping her down to the ground.

"What are you going to do?"

"Heal your wound."

"Seriously? You can do that?"

"I can do a lot of stuff." I smiled at her as I knelt down in front of her.

"What about that other mutt? Did you kill it?"

I nodded. "It's even deader than yours, and that's saying something."

"I was mad at that fucker."

"No shit."

She smiled, and I put both my hands over the blood-soaked wound in her left thigh, causing her to wince slightly, which didn't surprise me because the damage was severe; at least one incisor having hit and scraped off the bone. If it were me, I would have been screaming the damn forest down by then. Leona was made of sterner stuff than I, however, and merely gritted her teeth as I poured a phial of yellow ointment over the wound, the greasy substance mixing with the crimson blood to form a dark orange color.

"What is that shit?" she asked. "Not some old guy's scrotum again, I hope."

I couldn't help chuckling. "No, everything in here has special healing properties. Backed up with magic, it should at least mend the bone and close the wound."

"Handy stuff."

"I never leave home without it."

"Lucky for me, eh?"

"You mightn't think so in a second."

"It's gonna hurt, isn't it?"

"Yep." Closing my eyes, I said a few words to activate the magic in the ointment. When I opened my eyes again, I saw a yellowish glow bathing the wound in Leona's leg. "Get ready."

"For what?" No sooner had she said it when her head slammed back against the tree she was sitting against, and her blood-flecked face screwed up in pain, her teeth gritting as she grabbed her leg with both hands. Then, just a few seconds later, she seemed to relax, taking a few deep breaths to calm herself. "That hurt more than the fucking bite did."

"It's the damaged bone and tissue regenerating so fast. It can pack a punch."

Leona stood up and tested her weight on her leg. "That's amazing." She bounced all her weight on her left leg as if testing a loose board on the ground. "Thanks, Creed."

"No problem...only the best for my girl!" The redness of Leona's cheeks would most likely have been derived from either the previous pain, or her anger at my comment, but either way I still chose to believe it was a blush. "Now, let's get the hell out of these woods before any more of those things turn up."

## 3 2

# A SOUL WITH ITCHY FEET

E EVENTUALLY MADE it out of the dark woods without encountering anymore Razor Wolves, or anything else with teeth and claws, thank God. However, that didn't mean the danger was over. On the contrary, it was just beginning.

Before us, rising into the night sky like an ominous monolith built by some unknown race, was a giant wizards tower. The tower appeared to be made from massive stone blocks, and it seemed to stretch on forever into the inky sky above, making it hard to tell just how tall the tower was. There also appeared to be something covering many of the stone blocks. Or rather *growing* on the stone blocks. Something black and viscous looking that seemed to glisten like a giant slug in the moonlight.

"Jesus Christ," Leona breathed. "That's the most sinister thing I've ever seen. You can't even see the top. I take it our target is in there?"

I nodded. "That's Belger's Sanctum."

"Figures. You warlocks and your weird-ass hangouts."

"My place isn't weird. I live in a brownstone."

"Yes, it is. You have books on the ceiling, not to mention a wolf, and last time I was there, I recall seeing a dead body in your basement."

"John Doe."

"What?"

"John Doe. That's what I named him."

"Not very original, Creed. If you're going to steal and use someone's dead body in a satanic ritual, at least give them a better name."

"What, so calling the corpse Fergus O'Hanlon would have made the whole thing more acceptable?"

"Who's Fergus O'Hanlon?"

"No one. And by the way, I don't do satanic rituals. Only hedge magicians who don't know any better and death metal bands make reference to such things...and David Icke. It was just a summoning."

"Whatever," Leona said, slamming a fresh magazine into her rifle. "We can discuss naming corpses and satanic rituals—"

"Summonings."

"—later over a drink."

"For real?" If my smile was any wider, my face would split.

"If we get through this."

"We will. You'd really have a drink with me? I've tried to get you to drink loads of times in the past, and you always refused. You fear losing control."

She shrugged. "Maybe that's what I need to do."

I smiled again and shook my head at her. "I think you're still in shock after the Razor Wolf attack, but still, I'm holding you to that drink. I have the perfect bottle of whiskey—" A wave of dizziness stopped me from speaking any further, and I fell forward onto my knees as a great pain shot through my chest, as though someone was trying to pull my heart out with their bare hands. Clutching my chest, I collapsed onto the ground, barely hearing Leona call my name as she tried to hold me up but couldn't. It felt like I were having a heart attack, although I knew that wasn't the case, not a natural one in any case. It was possible Belger had his dark reach inside me somehow, but I didn't think so. This was something much worse.

This was my soul trying to make a run for it, the bastard.

*No, not yet...*

The pain and pressure in my chest increased as my soul pushed against me, trying to break free, and if it kept up the pressure, it soon would be. I had to do something before ghoul status was thrust upon me and I lost everything. I doubted Leona would have any interest in dating a ghoul either. So throughout the pain, I focused on a spell that would fortify my body from the inside, preventing my desperate soul from pushing its way out. It took all of my concentration and enduring a further few minutes of pain before my soul got the message and settled back inside me again. "Well, that was pleasant," I said, getting slowly to my feet.

"What the hell happened?" Leona asked. "You looked like you were having a heart attack."

"Felt like it too. My soul was trying to escape. Safe to say it no longer recognizes me. Only my magic—which is fading, by the way, thanks to the curse—is keeping it in. I don't know how much time I have before the spell wears off and my soul makes a break for it again."

Leona stared at me, concerned. "You sure you're up for the rest of this mission, Creed?"

I took a deep breath and nodded. "Don't have a choice, do I?"

We both looked toward the glistening black tower again. There was nothing surrounding it but dead grass and trees, interspersed with the occasional head on a spike. Neither of us batted an eyelid at the heads, though, having seen much worse already.

"I expected to see people here," Leona said. "Why are there no people?"

Walking toward Belger's tower, I held my hands out to my sides, palms down, trying to sense something. Then I stopped and looked at Leona. "It's because they're underneath us."

"Like an underground base?" Leona scanned the ground. "I can't see any entrance."

"It's here." I started searching the ground again, then stopped about ten feet from the tower, having sensed something hidden, not by the ground, but by magic. Crouching down, I put both hands on the slightly damp earth and closed my eyes as I tried to make the entrance reveal itself. It was a bit like picking a lock. The entrance was locked and made unseen by magic, so it was a matter of picking my way through the magical layers until I could use my own magic to crack the lock. Which took longer than it should have due to my magic's diminished potency.

After much wrangling on my part, an entrance finally revealed itself in the ground in the form of a large set of double doors, which thankfully were unlocked. Crouching down next to the doors, I closed my eyes for a moment, trying to contain my despondency at my sudden loss of power. Considering I still had to face Belger—who was undoubtedly running at full magical capacity—and somehow steal his soul, things were not looking good.

"You all right, Creed?" Leona asked, standing beside me.

I took a deep breath and stood up, doing my best to come across as calm and assured, despite not feeling that way at all. "I'll be all right," I replied, turning to her. "Listen, you don't have to go in here with me. This Belger guy is dangerous. I don't want you getting hurt, or..." I trailed off, unable to say it.

"Hey, I'm a soldier, remember? This isn't my first rodeo and considering how weak you seem, you're going to need me."

"I just don't want anything to happen to you, that's all. This is my mess, after all."

"Don't worry, you're going to owe me after this."

"Owe you?" I said with a slight smile.

"What, you think I was doing this out of the goodness of my heart?"

"Well, yeah."

She took a step toward me, her eyes firmly on mine. "Given the craziness of my job these days, I need someone just as crazy to help me make sense of it. I've decided you'll be that person, Creed."

"I thought I *was* that person."

"Either way, you definitely are now." She leant her face close to me, our noses almost touching. "We both stay alive, we both get off this cursed island. Got it?"

Arguing with her at that moment would have been like trying to argue with a Drill Sergeant. Pointless. "I got it."

"Good. Now open those doors so we can get this guy."

## 33

FRANK AND JOHN

*L*EONA AIMED HER automatic rifle at the doors as I pulled one of them open to reveal a set of concrete steps leading underground to a dimly lit corridor. As I let the door fall to the side, Leona, still shouldering her rifle, headed cautiously down the stairs, ready to fire at anyone or anything she saw as a threat. I closed the door behind us and followed.

The first thing I noticed as I walked down the stairs was the smell. Quite simply, it was awful. It was as if we had just broken into a tomb filled with bodies, their combined stench so strong it immediately turned my stomach. And it wasn't just the smell of human offal, it was also the combined putrid stench of urine and excrement, thickening the air so it felt like you were breathing ammonia instead of oxygen. Add to that the cloying stench of disinfectant, and your nostrils didn't know what hit them.

"Jesus Christ," Leona said in a harsh whisper.

I stood beside her, facing a long corridor that was lit with the occasional fluorescent light on the ceiling, one or two of them blinking on and off, making a high-pitched buzzing sound as they did so. There were also doors on either side of the corridor, dozens of them the whole way down. And people, coming and going in and out of rooms. Most of the people were men, but I noticed one or two women. Some of them were naked. Others wore blue butcher's aprons and overalls. Every one of them had blood on them somewhere. A lot of blood in most cases. "What the hell is going on here?" I said, although I already knew what was going on. I was just too sickened to admit what it was.

Leona shook her head, her rifle lowered only slightly. She said nothing.

Then a door opened not far from where we were standing, and a torrent of screams came gushing out. A second later, a man wearing a blue butcher's apron and nothing else walked out of the room and closed the door behind him, shutting out the screaming coming from inside.

*Soundproofed rooms. To keep the screams inside.*

Leona had her rifle aimed at the guy in the corridor, perhaps forgetting that we were invisible and he couldn't see us. I placed a hand on the barrel of her rifle and pushed it downward. As I did, Leona relaxed a little, though knowing Leona, she wanted nothing more than to put a bullet in the man's head.

We watched as the man (late forties, longish gray hair and lined face) in the butcher's apron leant against the wall and slid a hand into some hidden pouch on his apron, pulling out a pack of cigarettes and a disposable lighter with a hand that still dripped blood. Blood ran off him from everywhere in fact, as if he had literally been bathing in it.

One of the door's opposite opened then, and another man walked out into the corridor. No screams issued from the room he came from as he closed the door behind him. This man was likely in his sixties, with dark hair seemingly impossible for such an age. He wore white overalls that were stained everywhere with blood, and he smiled when he noticed the other man standing across the corridor. "Hey, Frank," he said. "Looks like I'm just in time. Gimme one of those, will you?"

"Hey, John," Frank said. "You having fun in there?"

They both smiled at each other as John came and stood beside Frank, taking the cigarette he was offered. "What do you think?"

They both laughed and Frank lit their cigarettes. "You got the girl, right?"

John nodded. "Oh yeah. How's the mother? I bet that bitch can scream."

"Fuck yeah. You should have heard her when I used the acid on her tits. *Damn*, that stuff can melt a fucking hole. What's the daughter like? A screamer as well?"

"Silent type mostly. Terrific pain tolerance for a kid. I'm enjoying breaking her. She's almost there. You know when they just seem to give in?"

"Mine's long past that stage. She's accepted her fate."

Leona aimed her rifle as if she was going to shoot them both. Once again I stopped her, shaking my head wordlessly at her as she glared at me. My eyes told her to wait.

"Hey," John said. "You wanna swap for a while? You can have a go at the kid. I'd like to finish the mother off. Got some stuff planned in my head."

"Oh yeah? Tell me more. What stuff?"

Smiling, John said, "Next level stuff. If it works as good as it seems in my head, maybe I'll tell you later."

"You're a sick bastard, John," Frank said, almost laughing, hyped up from whatever buzz he was on.

"That's why we're here, though, right?"

"You fucking know it." They both did a little buddy shake with bloodstained hands. "All right, John. You can take the mother. I'll finish breaking the kid for you."

"My man."

"Hey, there's plenty to go around, right? Belger always keeps us happy."

"That he does," said John. "That he does."

They both finished their cigarettes and disappeared once more into each other's rooms.

"Fucking sick bastards," Leona growled as soon as the two men were gone. "Every one of those rooms..." She trailed off as she shook her head. "We can't let these sick fucks get away with this, Creed."

"That's not why we came here," I said.

"So we're just going to ignore this? Let them get away with it? Fuck that." She shifted her disapproving glare from me to the door down the corridor that John had just gone through. Then she let her rifle hang loose while she took out one of her Berettas.

*Goddamn it.*

The look on Leona's face is one I'd come to know well in the three years I'd known her. She wanted blood and justice in that exact order.

Before I knew it, Leona had stomped over to the room occupied by John and his current female victim. With the gun in her right hand, she pushed down on the handle of the sturdy looking steel door. "Unlock this door, Creed," she demanded. "I know you can."

I stared at her a moment, saw the look on her face that said she wouldn't be swayed from doing what she thought was right. Sighing, I walked over to her. "Don't forget this is my mission, Lieutenant Colonel."

Her lips pursed, and her eyes narrowed in response to me using the authority card. On this mission at least, she knew I outranked her. "Just open the door, Creed."

Seeing that she wasn't going to back down, I went for a compromise instead. "All right, I'll open the door. But only this one. When we get off the island, we contact Brentwood, and we let Division handle the rest. Deal?"

She stared hard at me for another moment, then said, "Fine. But I want the bastard in that other room as well."

Jesus, she had a real hard on for those two. Not that I blamed her. "Just make it quick. I don't have time for this."

Using my magic, I had the door unlocked in a few seconds. Then I stood aside to let Leona do her thing. She opened the door and stepped into the room just as the woman inside issued a loud scream. A second later, a shot rang out from inside the room. I stood outside, unwilling to see whatever horrors the room contained.

Another shot rang out.

Then Leona emerged from the room a few seconds later, the porcelain skin of her face now an ashen gray color. She looked at me with eyes that had seen too much horror to bare. "Open the other door," she said in a flat voice.

I didn't argue with her, crossing the corridor and unlocking the door to the room in which the man named Frank resided with his torture victim. Once again, I stepped aside to allow her access and Leona wordlessly entered the room, a kind of dead focus in her eyes. Then I heard her say, "Oh...my God..." to herself as if she was witnessing some unimaginable horror in there.

Then Frank's voice: "Who said that? Who's there?"

*Bang! Bang-bang-bang-bang-bang!*

Frank was dead.

Gunpowder smoke escaped from the room, the acrid scent assailing my nostrils along with the smell of human offal.

A final shot sounded.

*Bang!*

Leona all but staggered out of the room, the color completely drained from her face now. In the corridor, she leant over and vomited onto the floor.

*Jesus Christ. How bad is it in there?*

Not that I wanted to look, but a morbid need-to-know got the better of me. Before I knew it, I had made the grave mistake of standing in the doorway so I could see into the room. Almost immediately, my mind was overloaded with images that were just too horrific to even comprehend at first. In the brightly lit room with the dark walls, my mind struggled to take in the scene. There was something like a dentist's chair in the middle of the room, and strapped to the chair was a small body that had been tortured and mutilated in ways that I couldn't even begin to describe. The girl's body was barely recognizable as human anymore. It just looked like a twisted mound of flesh sitting there, but even so, I still made out the features of the girl underneath all the blood and mutilation. There was other stuff in the room as well—a gurney loaded with tools, nasty looking torture implements racked on the walls (a chainsaw, a weed whacker, a huge drill)—but I hardly took those things in. Before I finally turned away, my eyes fell on the body on the floor. The man called Frank, full of bullet holes, blood pooling rapidly around his body and joining with the girl's blood already over the floor.

Moving quickly away from the door, I pressed my back flat against the cool concrete wall and closed my eyes for a second while I tried to keep my gorge down. I opened my eyes again to the sight of Leona still retching in the corridor, a small pool of vomit on the floor by her feet. "You all right?" I asked her.

Leona threw me a sharp look after wiping her mouth with her sleeve. "I just put a bullet in a little girl's head because she begged me to kill her," she snapped. "What do you think?"

It was then, in her eyes and the medley of torrential emotions tainting the color of her soul, that I knew in my bones that if there was ever any doubt about the decision to obtain assistance from Leona in this mission, then it was gone and only an apocalyptic failure of good judgement was left in its wake. The only doubt now being whether I could've walked away from this episode if I had kept her and Division in the dark about what I had to do before getting back on track with stopping Mr. Black? That is, if I actually do manage to walk away now that the element of surprise is gone. Although, given Belger's magical and bestial protections, the element was likely well and truly gone to begin with. Well, at least that is what I'd tell myself, as it's a far better option than to go away thinking the love of my life cost us our lives.

Turning away from her gaze as guilt stung me, I gave her another moment before softly suggesting we push on. She barely nodded in response.

As we went to walk down the corridor, all the lights began to flicker on and off, and a sudden chill froze the air around us. I put an arm out to stop Leona as I became aware of a malevolent presence in the corridor. In the gloom an intimidating and hooded figure then emerged, blinking in and out of view as it walked toward us, seeming on and off to merge with the shadows so they appeared to be dragging along behind it.

It was him, I knew.

It was Belger.

Belger stopped half way down the corridor, still cloaked in shadow, and spoke in a low, deep voice that was chillingly casual in tone. "I hope you came here to die, for die you shall. Slowly."

I swallowed hard and prepared myself for battle.

# 34

# SOUL RIPPER

*B*ESIDE ME, LEONA took aim at the hooded figure standing not twenty feet from us. Belger had his head bowed slightly, but even so, I could still see the bright greenish glow to his eyes under the hood. It was doubtful if the old warlock had any humanity left in him at this stage. He was probably controlled completely by the black magic he had undoubtedly given everything to over the millennial timespan of his lifetime. It felt like I was in the presence of a dark demigod, or a lower Dimension Lord.

"Why did you come here?" Belger asked in that voice which seemed to go directly into your head, invading your mind like a parasite, and attempting to penetrate your psychic defenses.

I didn't answer him. What was I going to say? That I was there to steal his soul? That we fancied a tour of his sick facility? No, this was only going to go one way—with Belger trying to kill us. And given the warlock's power, it would take little effort for him to break down my weakened defenses. Our only option was to stick to the plan and to try and take him by surprise. For all his power, he didn't seem to know why we were really there. Not yet anyhow.

"Get ready," I said quietly to Leona just before I stepped forward to address Belger. "We're here to put you down, Belger. This island is an abomination. So are you and your sick followers."

Belger gave a gravelly chuckle and raised his head slightly, his bright green eyes fixing on me in the gloom. "You think you have the power to kill me, wizard?" He laughed. "No one has that power in this dimension."

"Yeah, well." I started to summon whatever magic I had left in me, which wasn't much at this stage. "We'll see, old man." After reminding myself never to try and write witty comebacks for any fantasy novels (hey, I wasn't exactly in top form at that point), I took a few steps forward and made a show of conjuring up my magic by forming a sphere of bluish-white energy in each hand.

Belger laughed once again, a sound that only served to highlight, in my mind, the woeful inadequacy of my magic right then. It was shocking how much of my power had seemingly drained into the ether, leaving nothing behind but cold, empty channels that were becoming more and more barren and lifeless. And as if sensing the danger, my soul was deciding to make another break for it as well, this time with renewed vigor. If we were going to capture Belger's soul, we would have to do it fast, before Belger killed us in the slowest way imaginable. I certainly expected that our failure would lead to an agonizingly long death; perhaps even one that involved repeated catastrophic torture that he proceeded to heal before starting out over and over and over and... well you get the point I'm sure.

Hans Belger stepped forward under one of the flickering lights, raising his head to reveal his grotesque mask of a face from within his hood. The way his sunken face was nothing more than dark, leathery skin attached to a misshapen skull, it was like his human essence had been somehow sucked out of him, leaving behind nothing but a shell through which the blackest of magic flowed. I thought that if you drained Belger of his magic, his body would probably cease to exist at all.

Belger was turning his head from side to side as if he was trying to see something. Which he was. He was trying to see into me. I felt his invasive presence poking around inside me, slithering through me like razor-backed snakes. "There is something not right with you," the old warlock said.

"You're not the first person to ever tell me that," I said back, using the time to try and increase the strength of my magic, which wasn't happening at all.

Belger stretched out his arm then, his long, bony fingers moving like he was trying to grab something. "I see now. It's your soul. I can feel it trying to escape your body. Here, let me help it along. It seems to be struggling." He made a fist with his outstretched hand and drew his arm back sharply.

At the same time, a massive pain went through my chest. The same sharp, cutting pain like last time, only far greater. "NO!" I shouted, fighting to keep from falling to my knees. I gritted my teeth against the hellish pain, as it felt like the fucking Alien was about explode from my chest. I then managed to raise my right hand enough to launch the already conjured energy blast, my aim thankfully proving true even under such harsh conditions.

Not unsurprisingly, though, Belger simply took the blast in the center of his mass with barely a flinch or a pause. Straightaway, I conjured another blast and fired it at him. This time, Belger stopped the sphere of blue magic mid-air before redirecting it at Leona. The blast hit her in the chest, and she cried out in shock as it took her off her feet and sent her flying back down the corridor behind me.

"Leona!" I shouted...or tried to. The pain of having my soul ripped out of me was becoming unbearable. All I could do was fall to my knees like a puppet with severed strings.

Then I screamed shrilly like a pig having its throat cut as my soul finally burst free from my body, a luminescent white orb with a wavy tail behind it making it look like a little comet. It was so beautiful I wanted to cry. My soul then drifted upward in a languid sort of fashion before slowly passing through the ceiling, on the way to wherever it was going. I could only stare upwards in dismay, a terrible sense of emptiness quickly filling the space left behind by my departed soul. Any sense of emotion or humanity that I may once have had, drained away just as fast.

"There now," Belger said, unmistakable glee at his own sadism in his voice.

"Does that feel better? I'm sure you were glad to get such a weight of your chest." He laughed loudly, his cackling voice echoing horribly off the walls and through my ears.

Then I remembered Leona. I called her name as I looked behind me, but saw no sign of her.

*Where did she go?*

The magic blast should have knocked her out, although it was possible that Division had discovered a way to partially neutralize the effects of the magic. Brentwood had a whole team behind him researching ways to counter magic and balance the scales a bit for field agents like Leona. Whatever the case, Leona appeared to be gone, probably having seen the futility of what we were trying to do and thus saved her own ass. If I still had a soul, I would have felt desperately sad and alone at that moment, not to mention shitty for believing Leona capable of leaving any man behind, but all I felt was nothing.

Leona was gone. I was going to die. That's all there was to it.

"Go on, Belger, you Nazi fuck," I said. "Just kill me."

"I will," Belger replied, coming closer. "After you tell me why you are here."

"I came to steal your rotten soul."

The warlock stopped a few feet from me, his burning green eyes fixed on my own. "Only a fool or a desperate man would attempt that. Which are you?"

"Both, it looks like."

"Why would you need my soul?"

"To give to a demon so it could save my own soul."

"Too late for that now, isn't it?" His lipless mouth formed a rictus grin.

"Fuck you."

Belger stretched out a hand that exerted invisible pressure around my neck, hauling me up to my feet and holding me there. He'd obviously attended the same Dark Lord University as Darth Vader. "What if I don't kill you? I could always use another ghoul to do my bidding. What do you think? Would you like that? Lots of foul meat around here for you to feast on."

I said nothing as I stared back at him, hardly even caring what he decided to do to me. Keep me or kill me. It was all the same to me without a soul at that moment.

Then out of nowhere, ear shattering gunfire explosively echoed through the narrow confines of the corridor, and despite the difficulty in situating its origin it was still possible to deduce it having come from behind the warlock. His body bucked as at least two rounds went right through him, one of which whistled past my head on the exit, the other ricocheting off the wall and exploding the bricks out, the shards like glass that cut into my face. Belger roared as he released his invisible grip on me so he could spin around to confront whoever was shooting at him. He shot out one hand and formed a shield of magical energy in front of himself to stop any more bullets from hitting him.

Surprisingly calm and indifferent to the fact that I almost got shot in the head, I backed over toward the wall and looked down the corridor to see Leona standing, Beretta in hand, emptying her clip into Belger. A voice then sounded in my head:

*Now would be a good time to do something.*

Yes, of course! With Leona now distracting him, Belger now had his back to me. Whipping out my pistol from under my coat, I took aim at Belger's back, pulled back the hammer and fired, hitting the warlock between the shoulder blades. Belger cried out and staggered forward, though he still maintained his shield against Leona's continuing stream of rounds. As he half turned toward me, I fired again and shot him in the neck, forcing him back against the wall.

"Leona!" I shouted. "The box!"

I didn't know if she heard me or not, for at that same moment, Belger's magic slammed me into the wall like a cannonball to the gut. As I fell forward, it was all I could do to remain conscious. My head hit the floor as I was looking up at Belger, who was still not too far away, and who was screaming in agony whilst his bullet-proof shield dropped away. He appeared to be bathed in a mass of dark, undulating shadow, and it took me a second to realize the swirling blackness was coming from the box that Sanaka had given me. Leona had somehow managed to open the small container and get it in front of Belger. The box was now ripping out Belger's soul, a feeling I knew all too well. To hear him scream, you would think it was ripping him apart in the process.

When the Warlock's soul finally emerged from his body, it was a twisted black thing that writhed and screeched as it got pulled along. No matter how powerful Belger was, or had been, his soul couldn't resist the pull of the box, and seconds later, riding on a final scream from Belger, the black soul was sucked into the box, and the lid got closed on it.

As I slipped toward oblivion, I saw Belger's robes fall to the floor as if he had simply disappeared from existence.

## 35

# GHOUL STATUS

*W*HEN I CAME to it was to the sound of the world's loudest sewing machine, or so my befuddled brain thought at the time. There was a sense of motion underneath me, and I soon realized I was in some sort of transport. A helicopter maybe, judging by the chopping sound that the engine made. Then a figure was leaning over me. It was Leona. "Creed," she shouted over the engine noise. "Creed, are you all right?"

I tried to tell her I was, but for some reason, my mouth didn't seem to work. It was like I had lost the connection between my mind and body. Then as Leona stared down at me, I looked into her eyes and the memory of what had happened hit me all at once. The confrontation with Belger. Losing my soul.

*My soul is gone.*

A pained mewling noise escaped my lips.

"Hang in there, Creed," Leona said. "We're getting you home."

We?

I focused past her and saw Brentwood, his dark face staring back at me, impassive as always, as if he was totally indifferent to my condition. Which knowing Brentwood, he probably was.

He wasn't the only one to feel like that either. I felt dead inside. Scraped out. The only emotion that seemed to be left in me was the misery that came with knowing I was no longer a human being. That I was just an empty shell, not even a shadow of my former self. My magic, all that I had ever known, had been snatched away from me; and with it, the whole of my humanity. How ironic that I went to Belger's island as part of a plan to get my soul back, only to have it ripped it out of me while I was there. Soon, I would be a sad, shuffling thing, roaming around aimlessly, all memory of my former life gone.

Dead, but not dead.

In my gut, I felt a powerful appetite begin to grow, one that I knew quite soon that I wouldn't be able to ignore. An appetite for rotten meat. Any meat, the more decayed, the better to match the sense of decay I already felt seeping through me.

"Everything's going to be all right, Creed," Leona said.

*No, it wasn't. Nothing was going to be all right anymore.*

After that comforting thought, I passed out again, grateful for oblivion.

* * *

THE HELICOPTER HAD LANDED WHEN I NEXT AWOKE. BRENTWOOD WAS PULLING the door open, and cold air came rushing into the inside of the chopper, bringing me round slightly, enough that I could sit up. "Where are we?" I asked, my voice flat and emotionless.

"Back in Blackham," Brentwood answered after he had exited the helicopter. "We'll get you to a hospital, Creed."

I shook my head. "No."

Leona stood over me. "You need to get seen to, Creed," she said.

Getting to my feet, I climbed unsteadily out of the helicopter, the light outside hurting my eyes. Photosensitivity to light was another ghoul trait, the progression now seeming to move at full steam. It wouldn't be long before I couldn't stand the light at all, and I became a creature of the night only. A human rat, holed up all day, coming out at night to feed. "Just take me home," I said to no one in particular, not even sure why I wanted to go home at all. What was left for me there but a house full of useless books and artifacts, and a Garra Wolf that wouldn't want to know me anymore when it realized the person it once knew to be me no longer existed?

Still, for the time being at least, where else was I going to go?

* * *

SITTING IN THE FRONT PASSENGER SEAT OF THE BLACK SUV LEONA WAS driving, I barely listened as she tried to tell me about what happened after I lost consciousness. Leona's debriefing voice filled the vehicle's cab with a flat and level monotone, going over the way Belger's husk reduced to ash of its own accord, and which was followed up by her radioing in the reinforcements Brentwood was on standby to receive. With Division's arrival, an outbreak of followers resisting arrest resulted in many being killed, the small number remaining were thus couriered to the mainland for processing. Brentwood was happy apparently, as it was a huge bust for him and would surely go a long way to securing the next year's budget, which according to Leona, is all he really cared about. I didn't react to anything she said as I stared out the window in a semi-catatonic state. After a while, she gave up on trying to talk to me, and she lapsed into silence until we got to the Sanctum in East Oakdale.

Robotically, I got out of the car and walked up the steps, then stopped when I saw that someone was standing there. It was Sanaka, though I barely acknowledged him as I stopped at the front door and realized I wouldn't be able to open it on account of... you know... the whole having no magic thingy. "Damn," I said.

"I sensed what happened to you," Sanaka said, his hands plunged into his black trench coat, his long hair blowing in the gusty wind. "I thought you might need my help."

Leona came up behind us. "Who are you?" she asked, addressing Sanaka with suspicion as she eyed up the sword he held in his hand.

Sanaka gave her a small, respectful bow. "My name is Mitsuo Sanaka. I am a friend of Creed's. I'm here to help if I can."

Leona shook her head like she didn't have time to wonder at my relationship to Sanaka. "*Can* you help him?"

Smiling patiently, Sanaka said, "Unfortunately, when a soul is gone, it is gone."

"He's right," I said, staring at the door, wondering why Sanaka hadn't opened it yet.

"So what do we do then?" Leona asked. "Leave him like this?"

Sanaka didn't answer as he waved his hand by the front door. A second later, the locks disengaged, and I pushed the door open, going inside, wondering vaguely as I did so why I was even there in the first place. I should have just got dropped off by a nice, comfortable dumpster and waited for nightfall so I could begin my new life as a ghoul.

"Look at him, for Christ's sakes," Leona was saying to Sanaka, her frustration and concern for me getting the better of her now. "He's like a goddamn zombie. Are we just going to leave him like this?"

Sanaka stood in the center of the living room just as Blaze entered from the kitchen. Blaze stopped and stared at me as he growled slightly, knowing I wasn't the person who had saved him from imprisonment. He looked at Sanaka as if for an explanation. "His soul is traveling through the Astral Plane as we speak," Sanaka said for Blaze's benefit, as I sat down in one of the armchairs to stare dead-eyed at the floor. "Soon it will merge with the River Of Souls before being sent to the Realm of the Dead."

Blaze made a small mewling noise in his throat before padding cautiously up to me and rubbing his head lightly against my leg. Then he licked my hand, making another mewling noise before walking away again. I just about understood his sadness, but I was largely unaffected by it.

"Can't you just get his soul back?" Leona asked, standing by the side of my chair.

"It is not that simple," Sanaka said. "There are millions of souls in the Astral Plane. It would take too long to locate Creed's. He only has a short time left before his physical form atrophies, shutting out the possibility of his soul being able to return and enter his body ever again."

Leona sighed sharply. "What fucking good is magic if you can't use it in times like these? So that's it? Creed is just a fucking zombie now for the rest of his life?"

"A ghoul," Sanaka said, as infuriatingly composed as ever.

"A fucking ghoul then," Leona spat. I could feel her anger and frustration building beside me. Not that I was flattered by her concern or anything. I was busily slipping fast into a twilight world where normal human beings (ones with souls, that is) were becoming like ghosts to me, as if they weren't there at all—as if *I* weren't there at all. Whatever the case, the effect was the same: complete alienation.

"There is someone who may be able to help," Sanaka said. "Some*thing*. The demon that Creed summoned. It will have the power to get Creed's soul back. Whether it will do so or not all depends on Creed."

"How?" Leona asked.

Sanaka smiled patiently. "On what Creed is prepared to offer it in return."

# 36

# RETURN OF THE DEMON

$S$ANAKA PREPARED EVERYTHING for the summoning ritual in the basement, electing not to procure any John Doe's for the ritual, figuring Baal wouldn't be expecting any offering this time around. Except, of course, what had been required as payment versus the actual payment I have. It remained to be seen whether or not the demon would be happy with the one soul I had stolen for him.

While Sanaka was down in the basement, I sat in the living room, staring at the floor like a zombie in between meals. Leona sat in one of the other armchairs, saying nothing, occasionally checking her phone as she got updates from Brentwood on the island siege. By that point, I didn't even care if I got my soul back or not. I was that far gone, feeling nothing but the hunger growing inside me. A hunger for meat. A hunger that would soon become all consuming and insatiable, becoming my only raison d'etre. I still wasn't sure if ghouls were partial to live meat in the form of people. They've been known to attack animals, such as cattle and horses, leaving most people to believe that the animals were the victims of Satanists or aliens. In reality, it was just ghouls having a munch. Whatever the case, Leona was looking more tasty to me by the minute, her firm, pale flesh causing me to salivate like a dog that hadn't eaten in days.

"You all right there, Creed?" Leona asked as she looked at me strangely. "You don't look so good."

I growled at her then. Yes, growled, like a fucking animal.

Leona stood and told me she was going to check on Sanaka. As she went to walk past me, I grabbed her arm and pulled it toward my salivating mouth. "Creed!" she screamed, then punched me hard in the face, causing me to let go of her arm. "What the fuck?" She backed away from me, her hand going to one of her Berettas, ready to draw on me if she had to.

I growled at her again, and snapped my jaws at her.

"Stop it!" Leona shouted angrily. "Settle to fuck down, Creed, or I swear I will shoot you!"

Her words somehow cut through the foggy haze in my mind, connecting with the semblance of humanity I still had in me somewhere, but which was fast diminishing like a candle in the darkness only seconds away from burning out completely. Another small growl left my mouth before I settled back in the chair and began staring at the floor again.

"I'll be back in a minute," Leona said, her voice at a normal level again. "Don't try to eat the damn wolf while I'm gone."

No chance of that. Blaze was staying well away from me, lying in the kitchen somewhere, I think. The wolf wasn't afraid of me exactly, but it was afraid it would have to hurt me if I tried to attack it in any way. Ghoul or not, I was still Blaze's master and thankfully the wolf respected that.

Leona returned a while later with Sanaka and they both took hold of me and led me down into the basement, which I let them do without protest. Lucky for them, I was going through another semi-catatonic phase, the hunger in me subdued for the time being. In the basement, they pressed me down to the floor, and I sat there in silence while they discussed what to do. Sanaka eventually came to the decision that he would summon the demon as I wouldn't be able to do it. It could have been done without magic of course, but given the state I was in, I would have been lucky to be able to utter a single word; never mind an entire evocation in an ancient language.

So Leona (electing to stick around for the ritual this time) stood over me, guarding me, while Sanaka sat just outside the magic circle and went through the ritual. Sometime later, the room began to shake like a minor earthquake was happening. The temperature in the room dropped, and then I heard Leona take a sharp intake of breath before saying, "Jesus Christ."

"What is this?" Baal's voice seemed to cut through the fog in my mind, and I looked up to see the monstrous figure standing inside the summoning circle.

Sanaka kept his voice respectful, his head slightly bowed as he addressed the smoldering demon, its orange eyes blazing. "I summoned you on Creed's behalf," Sanaka said, gesturing to me. "He has done what you asked."

Baal growled at Sanaka, then looked at me, his head moving from side to side as he did so. "You are soulless, Human," he said.

I stared back at Baal like he wasn't even there, the fear I felt in his presence once before now a distant memory. Baal growled and then turned his attention to Leona. In a flash, the demon crossed the room and wrapped one massive clawed hand around Leona's throat. She half screamed in fright as the demon's face came close to hers. "A delectable specimen," Baal said, almost to himself. Then he made a noise that was halfway between a growl and a moan of pleasure as he thrust a long, pointed tongue out of his sharp-toothed mouth and licked Leona's face, leaving a trail of slimy saliva on her skin. All credit to her, she hardly flinched, even though she must have been terrified.

When Baal released Leona, he turned and crouched down beside me. "There is nothing left of you, wizard," he said, looking at me like I was just a useless piece of meat, which I kind of was.

The demon stood up and walked slowly toward Sanaka. "I want the souls I was promised. Or I take yours instead, wizard, as well as the girl's." Baal looked around at Leona and did something that could have been a smile or a sneer. "I might just take it anyway."

Sanaka asked Leona for the box, which she warily handed over to him so he could give it to Baal, which he did. Baal held the box for a moment, which looked no bigger than a matchbox in his enormous hand. "Not the one hundred souls I asked for."

"No," Sanaka said. "Just one soul, but worth much more in terms of currency."

Baal growled but seemed satisfied nonetheless. "The curse will be lifted."

"There's one other thing," Sanaka said.

"You want me to get his soul back."

Sanaka nodded. "Yes."

Baal stared over at me while he considered Sanaka's request. "If I do so, you will be in my debt, Creed, and it will be a large debt, I warn you."

"Very well," Sanaka said on my behalf, as I was obviously unable to respond myself. "He doesn't have a choice."

The demon vanished from the room then. Leona started rubbing at her face like it was covered in some diseased substance. "It fucking licked me," she said. "Can you believe that? It was disgust—"

Baal reappeared in the basement again with a glowing ball of light in one of its four hands.

*My soul.*

That semblance of light left in me seemed to react to the presence of my soul in the room, reaching for it, pulling me to my feet like it were the puppet-master and I the lowly puppet. The demon came up to me, held the soul in front of my face, its luminescent beauty contrasted against the clawed hand of the monster who held it. Then without warning, Baal shoved my soul back into my body, his hard hand impossibly entering my chest, sending me staggering backwards into the arms of Leona, who caught me before I fell. It was the closest I had ever come to experiencing rapture.

As soon as my soul was back inside me where it belonged, a warmth began to spread through me as the light of my soul filled me up again, bringing with it an orgasmic sense of relieve as my humanity was finally restored. Then to add to this influx of joy even further, my magickal powers returned as well, like a cascade of water coming off the top of a mountain to replenish a dried out river bed. It was glorious.

A smile spread across my face, and I breathed a huge sigh of relief, knowing I would never feel the likes of that again, basking in it until I remembered there was a massive demon still standing in front of me. "Thank you," I said, standing on my own now. "I am in your debt."

"Yes, you are, wizard," Baal said. "And don't forget it." The demon flashed his sharp teeth at Leona before backing into the center of the room.

"Before you go," I said, knowing I was pushing my luck, but in for a penny, right? "I could use a lead on the person who started all this."

Baal shook his head. "Humans," he said. "Nothing is ever enough."

"I'm in your debt already. A little information can't hurt, can it? Besides, you hardly want this world coming under new management, do you? What would happen to your playground then, with no souls left to torture? Surely it's in your best interests to help me stop what's about to happen..."

"Leave it, Creed," I heard Leona mutter behind me.

"I don't need you telling me what my best interests are," Baal said. "But there is no denying you have a point. I'll see what I can do. But in return, I want this person's soul. Or I will take yours instead, wizard."

"You drive a hard bargain, but it's a deal. So when—"

The demon vanished before I could finish.

"Jesus, Creed," Leona said, coming around to face me. "You really know how to push your damn luck, don't you? Oh, and by the way."

"What?" I asked.

She punched me in the face then, and I fell over.

# MINDFUCK

"*W*HAT THE HELL was that for?" I asked, one hand clamped over my smarting nose.

Leona stood with her hands on her hips staring at me, a different look in her eyes now. Before when she looked at me, she would often come across as guarded, like she didn't want to fully reveal herself. But as she looked at me then, her blue eyes seemed more naked now, her true self revealed in them. Clearly, her memories of me had returned now that my curse had been lifted. "You know what that's for," she replied casually, her tone suggesting that I fully deserved the violence she just wrought.

"I don't—" Then I remembered. "The restaurant. The night before all this happened."

"I told you never to stand me up, Creed. You left me hanging."

"In my defense, I was working. I just forgot to call to let you know."

She stepped forward and kissed me, more passionately than how she kissed me the other day. "This is very weird, by the way."

"What?" I asked, so glad to be back to normal. So glad to have my girlfriend back, even though I did enjoy the time I spent with her when she didn't know me as well.

"It's like I've been hanging around with a different person the last few days, or like someone pretending to be you."

"I imagine it's a bit of a mindfuck."

"Mindfuck. Yes, that's exactly what it is."

"I must agree," Sanaka said from behind Leona. He was stood patiently looking over at us. "A strange sensation indeed."

"Well, it sure is good that you both remember me again. Think about how weird it was for me, knowing everything while you two didn't even remember me. *That* was a mindfuck."

"Yeah, yeah," Leona said. "You always get it harder than everyone else, don't you?" She was smiling as she said it.

Before I could reply, Sanaka said, "I must go now. I have my own business to take care off."

"Anything I can help with?" I asked.

He shook his head, a more knowing look in his eyes than before. "You have a killer to catch."

"Yeah, thanks for reminding me."

Sanaka smiled once more then vanished as he teleported out of the room.

"So what now, Creed?" Leona asked. "I seem to remember a guy I met a few days ago at a murder scene who compared going down on me to deep sea diving, something about being unable to come up for air. You want to go diving now, Creed?"

My jaw went slack. "Now? I mean if you want, I don't really...I'm not—"

Her sudden laughter cut me off my fumbling reply. "You should see your face. You look like a terrified virgin whose girlfriend just asked if he minded her bringing a friend around to play."

I shook my head. "You're a cruel woman, Lawson. At least give me a chance to get back on form before you mention the dirty deed again."

"All right," she said, having finished laughing at my expense. "What do we do now then?"

"Well," I said, still shaking my head at her. "The other me, the one who brought up the deep sea diving at a murder scene a few days ago, has already been assigned to you by Brentwood. I'm sure that still stands unless Brentwood has suddenly remembered that he hates me, in which case I'll get a phone call soon telling me to stay away."

"He thinks you're unpredictable and he doesn't like that."

"I know."

"Though I think he'll keep you on this. He wants this killer caught."

"I think we all do."

"You think that disgusting demon will come through with a lead?"

"It licked your face," I said, unable to keep from smiling.

"Screw you."

"How was it? Was it long, hot and wet, you know... just how you like it?"

Leona punched me in the shoulder and was about utter a stream of expletives when my phone rang. The caller ID said, Forsyth. I answered, still smiling at Leona while rubbing my sore shoulder. "Forsyth. What can I do for you?"

Forsyth was a vampire lieutenant who ran the neighborhood in which I lived. He was one of the few vamps I have any real dealings with. By their nature, vamps liked to keep their business in-house, and as such, rarely required the services of a wizard like myself. As I lived in Forsyth's neighborhood, however, our paths often crossed, usually when trouble of some sort brewed.

"I just had the strangest experience," Forsyth said. "You suddenly popped into my head for no reason, like I just remembered who you are. It's hard to explain... and weird. Did something happen to you?"

"You could say that. It's sorted now, though."

"Well, that's good. So tell me, Creed, when are you planning on doing that job I asked you to do...last week, was it? See, there it is again, the weirdness. How come

I completely forgot that I asked you to do that? It's like some freaky mind trick. I don't like it."

"I didn't either," I said, looking at Leona, who was texting on her own phone now. "Listen, I'll find your man, vampire, whatever for you. There's just someone else I have to find first. You heard of the recent murders that were more like sacrifices?"

"I heard something," Forsyth said in his overly theatrical voice. "I heard they were strange and brutal. I don't know much else, though, before you ask. If you want I could look further into it, but you must promise to soon come over and have a drink. That way I can also admire that tremendous ass of yours. And who knows, with the right amount of social lubricant we might also be able to do a little coming ourselves?"

I shook my head, used to Forsyth's shamelessly flirtatious behavior by now. "Sure. I'll wear my tightest jeans." I raised my eyebrows at Leona who shook her head as she threw me a look.

"Super. See you soon, Creed. I'm still weirded out, you know, by the fact that I feel like I'd forgotten you. I could never forget you, Creed, that's what's so weird. Hardly a day goes by when I don't—"

"Bye, Forsyth. If I ever need an ego boost or start batting for the other team, you'll be the first person I call." I hung up the phone, knowing he was tittering to himself right then.

"You finished your flirting now?" Leona asked.

"Forsyth. You've met him. You know how he is."

"Yeah. We gotta go."

"Go where?"

"Take a wild guess."

"More murders?"

Leona nodded. "In Lafayette. It's worse this time apparently."

She began to move out of the basement, and I followed behind her. Blaze stared at me from the living room as I came out. "It's okay, Blaze," I told him. "I'm back." I crouched down as Blaze approached, ruffling his dark fur. Then I looked up at Leona. "How many victims this time?"

She gave me a grave look. "Too many to count."

## 38

# THE ROUNDHOUSE

*I* WAS QUIET on the drive from the Sanctum to the crime scene, which was over on Lafayette. Now that I'd gotten my mojo back (mostly anyway...my magic power was still in the process of replenishing itself) it was time to concentrate all of my energies on tracking down Mr. Black. The evil son of a bitch was stepping things up with every murder (although he wouldn't have seen his heinous acts as murder, but as sacrifices, a means to a nefarious end). He was getting close to whatever endgame he had planned, which meant we had to go at him with everything we had. The only problem was that I didn't have a single goddamn lead on the guy. Aside from the spectral form that ambushed me a couple of days ago, I had no clue as to the killer's real identity. It was even more frustrating that just a few days ago I knew exactly who Mr. Black was. But thanks to the spell cast by the killer, all former traces of his identity had been wiped out.

*Maybe the demon will come across with a lead.*

Something else I wasn't comfortable with. Did I really want to be in debt to a demon?

*Yes, if it helps to catch this killer, not to mention stop Rloth's planned apocalypse...which is no small thing in itself.*

Looks like I don't have a choice then.

A small sigh escaped my lips, and I looked at Leona, who was driving as erratically as ever as she headed for the expressway exit up ahead. "You all right?" I asked, settling back into my relationship with her, enjoying the deeper connection between us again.

"I just want to catch this creep before he kills any more people," she said, yanking hard on the steering wheel to overtake the car in front. "This is my town, and I don't like motherfucker's painting it with innocent blood."

"I get you."

Leona hated Blackham City when she first arrived. Coming from West

Virginia, she was used to wide open spaces and expansive skylines. City life got to her. In case you haven't guessed, Leona is not a people person. Although she could interact quite expertly with others when she needed to, she preferred her own company. So being around so many people in a packed city like Blackham was a struggle for her, as it was for me at first as well. You get used to it, though, and if you hung around the city long enough, you even grew attached to the place; as both Leona and I had done. Despite our backgrounds, Blackham is where we call home, for better or worse. Most people are wont to protect the places they call home, we two being no different, and especially Leona who has a sense of self-determined responsibility to keep it safe from the creatures that call the night their own; say nothing for my particular peers and brethren who are susceptible to allowing the magic to control them instead of their own self's.

"Thanks, by the way," I said to her. "For helping me. For trusting me when you didn't even know who I was. Knowing you as I do, I can fully comprehend how out of the ordinary that was and is for you."

"It wasn't."

"Yet you did. Why?"

She turned the SUV off the main road and into the Lafayette neighborhood. Lafayette is a shithole. That's about the only way to describe the place. A sprawling rats nest of low rent housing and rundown tenement buildings that spilt over into nearby Little Haiti. Not a place I had visited very often in the past. Not too many magical goings on there. Gang-related activity was the only thing that happened in Lafayette. Once upon a time the place was up and coming, but something happened during its development, and most of the investment got pulled. Of the businesses that were built in that development stage, only a few survived, mainly just essential services like corner stores and a gas station. And a cinema, believe it or not. Which is exactly where we were heading to.

"You seemed to be telling the truth," Leona said. "You knew things. That was enough for me."

"Admit it," I said smiling. "You just couldn't resist my Irish charm again, could you?"

A smirk creased her lips. "Wise up."

"That's what I thought."

As Leona negotiated the narrow streets while we headed for our destination, I stared out the window at the dilapidation all around us and the human detritus in the form of gangs, bums and drug addicts that littered every street. I used to think that parts of Ireland were bad until I came to the States and saw what real poverty and degradation looked like.

"Can you believe there's a cinema in this dump?" Leona said. "Why would this place need a cinema of all things?"

"It's a relic from times past that shows mostly classic movies. Even these people need a bit of escapism, you know."

"I thought that's what the drugs were for."

I shook my head. "You have a dim view of people sometimes."

"Hey, I just think people need to help themselves, because sure as shit, no one else is going to do it for them. If they want to remain in their filthy origins, then I have no sympathy for them."

"Not everyone wants to join the military," I said, well aware of Leona's convictions when it came to personal development, which the Army only strengthened.

"I get that, but look at them." She gestured out the window at the people lining the streets, nearly all of them staring hard at us as we drove by. "They don't even try."

"Maybe they're happy where they are. You ever think of that?"

"I doubt it, but more fool them if they are."

I shook my head as we came upon the roadblock that cut off the street near the cinema. Leona put her window down and flashed her ID at one of the uniformed cops manning the barriers. The cop nodded at her and signaled for the barriers to be moved so we could drive through. Down the street was the cinema, flanked on either side by empty tenements and a corner store across the street. As expected, the street was full of dark-suited government agents and parked SUVs. I also noticed the black trucks, three of them, which I knew were meat wagons there to transport the dead to Division HQ in the Highlands. Leona parked the SUV in the first free spot she found, and we both got out, heading grimly toward the cinema building.

The Roundhouse Cinema was an incongruous looking building made out of white stone, with two thick pillars manning the steps to the entrance. When it was first built, I was sure the Roundhouse was a grand building, but after years of abuse by the Lafayette residents, it looked more like something that might be used as a drug den, with nearly every inch of stone covered in old and new graffiti. Chunks were missing from some of the stone blocks as well, almost as if bullets had struck off them, which, to be honest, was probably the case. It amazed me that a place such as the Roundhouse had stayed open for so long and I couldn't imagine how hard it must have been for the owners to have maintained the place in such a hostile environment over the years.

Leona flashed her ID at a couple of dark suits who tried to stop us on the way into the cinema (which as always it came down to me and the way I appear). Once inside, we stood for a moment and looked around as the intense activity of the crime scene agents continued around us, with forensics teams and investigators scurrying back and forth or hovering to talk in small groups. A few of them gave me dirty looks, as our paths had crossed before, and not in a good way. There were no cops inside the building, only Brentwood's people. As always, Brentwood was keeping the scene locked down tight.

The foyer was an open square space with marble floors. Tattered red curtains hung down the whitewashed walls. To our left was the ticket booth, the owners having learned from experience to protect the booth with bulletproof glass. Above the circular hole at the bottom of the glass was another less symmetrical hole at about head height, the impact clearly caused by a bullet. I shook my head at the surreality of the place and headed toward the door to the central screen up ahead, Leona falling in beside me. The two agents guarding the door moved aside as Leona showed them her ID. "He in there?" she asked one of the guards, a tall man with a goatee.

"Yep," the agent said. "I should warn you. It's rough in there."

Leona shook her head. "Is it ever anything else?"

# GREEN FIRE

*T*HE FIRST THING that hit me as I walked into the screening room was the smell. On closer inspection, the putrid stench of blood, offal, and urine mixed with the excrement of loosened bowels could be identified as the primary sources; secondaries being the underlying layers of smoke, dust, mold and christ only knows what other smells associated with a cinema of its age and location. Something you might get if you put the worst toilet in the world inside an abattoir. As horrible as the smell was, though, I was used to it, having come across too many dead bodies over the years. What disturbed me more was the acrid smell underneath all the death. The smell of black magic had become so thick and cloying in the stuffy air of the cinema, making it feel like you could reach out and grab a handful of molasses or treacle, such was the thickness of the permeated essence.

And speaking of treacle, black stuff slowly oozed down the red walls like they were bleeding, only with a much thicker substance like that of tar. A forensics guy was going around scraping samples of the stuff into Petri dishes. Which horrified me slightly, because if he knew exactly what he was dealing with, the technician wouldn't be going anywhere it.

"Mr. Black," I uttered to myself.

"What?" Leona asked, too preoccupied with trying to process the carnage all around her to pay me much attention.

"Mr. Black was here."

"No shit." She pointed to the dirty white cinema screen and the words written there in blood in large letters: RLOTH, EATER OF WORLDS, IS COMING.

"At least he bothered with punctuation. Most serial killers don't, I find. Usually too worked up and in too much of a rush to even think about it."

Leona gave me a hard look. "Are you fucking kidding me right now? All these bodies and you're talking about fucking punctuation?"

A scowl came over my face as anger set in. "Now hold on a damn minute there. Remember it's me who you asked assistance from, and who'll be the poor suicidal bastard who inevitably goes up against this insanely powerful crackpot. Remember, I could just portal to Babylon and leave all your disrespectful asses here. Next to me you have diddly squat chances of stopping this guy, and might as well all go home this minute to spend your last remaining hours with your loved ones. So why don't you all just step aside and allow me to point out what you're not seeing because you're to consumed with the obvious. I'd suggest you all back-the-fuck-off and remember that without me you're all dead inside of a few days."

Leona looked shocked by my outburst for a moment, then she nodded as if she understood. "I'm sorry, Creed, I didn't mean..."

"Forget it," I said, only wanting to get on with examining the scene. "What I said before about the punctuation...I just mean the killer was calm and collected enough to use it. He was in no hurry. It also obviously mattered to him, otherwise, why bother?"

Shaking her head, Leona stared around the room at the dead bodies that seemed to be in every seat. "Well, he's hurrying up his body count, that's for sure. How many would you say are in here?"

"Sixty-seven."

I turned to catch the owner of the spoken answer that'd come from over my shoulder, to catch an even grimmer-faced than usual Brentwood, who now stood beside Leona, having finished his approach from the top of the centre aisle.

"Jesus," Leona said like she had a foul taste in her mouth, sickened by the extent of the horror in the room. And she wasn't the only one. Everyone that was here—the forensics people and the investigators—all had the same grave looks on their faces like they were being forced to drink their own piss. Clearly they were overwhelmed by the sheer number of bodies they had to deal with. I couldn't blame them. Sixty-seven bodies was a lot to process. It was mind-boggling, in fact, that someone could kill so many people. And for what? So some fucking Dimension Lord with a barely pronounceable name could come along and eat the fucking world up? I swear these nutjobs confound me sometimes.

"What's up with you, Creed?" Brentwood asked though he didn't wait for an answer. "A while ago I had a sudden recollection of our history. I can't tell you what an unpleasant experience that was."

"I'm sure," I said, unsurprised by Brentwood's sudden frostiness toward me. It's as Leona said, Brentwood considered me something of a liability and a downright pain in the ass, mainly because I did what I did alone and I rarely informed him about anything. He seemed to think that since I worked magic-related cases that I should, therefore, be working under him. And while our paths did often cross (largely due to Leona), he knew I would never consider working for him or any other government agency, just so they could control what I did and how I did it, which more often than not, wasn't exactly in line with how *they* did things. Brentwood and those like him were all about containment and coverup. That was their main priority. They didn't care who they railroaded or hurt in the process, and they certainly didn't care about helping people. That was the difference between Brentwood and me. I used my power to help people (whenever possible anyway), whereas he used the power he had (which wasn't inconsiderable) to shut people up and bring people down; at least those involved in nefarious occult and supernatural activities. Of course, I found myself having to bring people down as well from time to time, but it wasn't policy for me. To do the right thing, sometimes you had to do the wrong thing, a fact I was less comfortable with than Brentwood was. Or Leona for that matter, who shared Brentwood's military callousness, though to a lesser degree.

"Now that you're burned back into in my memory again," Brentwood said. "It doesn't surprise me that you ended up involved in this, Creed. Or that you ended up on that island. Wherever there's trouble, you always seem to be in the thick of it."

"You would never have known about that island if I hadn't led you there," I pointed out, tearing my eyes away from the body of a middle-aged man whose face was frozen in terror, his throat slit to the bone. "And by the way, I wouldn't always have to be in the thick of things, as you put it, if official policing were different."

Brentwood tutted and shook his head. It was an old argument he obviously had no wish to revisit, even if I did. "Think what you like. And we *did* know about that place."

"So why didn't you do anything about it?"

"Because there was no one crazy enough to take on Hans Belger. Until you, that is."

"I did you a favor then."

"That remains to be seen. A lot of powerful people were connected to that island, some of whom run the damn government."

I nodded with sickening understanding. "Which is the real reason why you never tackled Belger. Why he's been so protected all these years." I shook my head in disgust. "That puts the blood of all those people on your hands as much as Belger's. You should be ashamed."

Brentwood looked away for a second. "I just follow orders. The government is what it is and no one's going to change that. Not even you, Creed, with your self-righteous bullshit."

"Christ, all right!" Leona said agitatedly. "Now is not the time for a pissing contest. I mean, take a look around, will you?"

Brentwood and I looked at each other as we silently agreed to put our mutual hostility aside, for the sake of the dead people in the room. All sixty-seven of them. "All right, Brentwood," I said. "Fill us in."

Nodding, Brentwood began to reel off what he knew so far. "All of these people here sat down around 8:30 p.m. to watch a screening of *Evil Dead 2*."

"Groovy," I said.

"What?" Brentwood asked, scowling at the fact that I had interrupted him.

"Nothing. Carry on."

Leona threw me a look, and I shrugged. I mean, if you see an opportunity for an *Evil Dead* reference, you gotta go for it, right?

"Anyway," Brentwood continued. "The current owner, a Mrs. Duvall, closed the doors once the film began. Then at around 9:00 p.m she heard screaming coming from the screening room. She ignored it, thinking people were screaming because of the movie. Then a few minutes later, she seen a flash of orange light around the screening room door and then heard more screaming. When she went to investigate, she couldn't open the door. That's when she rang the local cops, who got here about half an hour later."

"Good response time for Lafayette," I said. "It's usually hours...or never."

"We picked up the call," Brentwood said. "Got here at the same time as the cops."

Brentwood's Division kept a constant monitor on the emergency channels in the city, always on the lookout for any calls that concerned odd or supernatural goings-on. I was convinced that the Division's reach extended further into every phone and internet cable in the city, but they would never admit that, of course.

"Let me guess," Leona said. "They were all dead when you got here."

"Correct," Brentwood said. "All sixty-seven had their throats cut. So far, it also seems they were all marked with the same symbols as before. We're still checking bodies, though. We've a lot to get through."

"How was he able to do this?" Leona asked. "It doesn't even look like any of them put up a struggle. It's like they just sat there and waited to be killed. And why sixty-seven people? Did he really need that many for the ritual?"

"Magic," I said in answer to her first question. "He cast a spell on them. A Paralysis Spell would be my guess. They wouldn't have been able to move. Our Mr. Black would then have just gone from person to person with his blade like these people were no more than cattle lined up for slaughter. As for numbers, I'm not sure. My guess is that if there were a hundred people in here he would have killed them all just the same. Which raises another question."

"What?" Leona said.

"The time it took him to do all this. The time it would've taken to cut all those throats."

"Are you thinking he had accomplices?" Brentwood asked.

"It's a possibility. He could've brainwashed a few helpless fools into helping him, but I seriously doubt that. Mr. Black is a loner. He hates people, and probably thinks he doesn't need them either. No, he did this on his own. I'd say with the use of additional magic to speed things top somehow."

"What about that shit on the walls?" Brentwood said. "What is it?"

"A residue from the use of black magic. A bit like ectoplasm. I'd tell your techs to be careful with it. It's been known to put bad thoughts into people's heads if handled too much. Violent thoughts."

"My guys know what they're doing."

"You find anything else?" I asked him.

"Yes, actually. A video of Mr. Black."

"A video?" Leona said. "How?"

"This place still uses old fashioned projectors and film reels," Brentwood said. "The projector room is up there." He pointed to a small window above the seats at the back of the cinema. "The projectionist was in there when Mr. Black showed up. He managed to get a three-second video on his phone through the window before he was killed. Had his neck twisted completely around. Never seen anything like it."

"Can we see the video?" I asked.

"The phone has been taken away for testing, but I had the file sent to my phone."

Just as Brentwood reached into his jacket pocket to get his phone, there was a loud whummfing sound. The sound you get when flames ignite. Then there was an even louder scream. Everyone looked to the back of the cinema to see a forensics tech covered in flames, waving his arms around wildly and screaming continuously as the fire melted his flesh. The body he had been examining was ablaze also. It was no ordinary fire either. The flames burned a bright green color and seemed to burn hotter than ordinary fire. In seconds, the forensics tech had stopped screaming and had dropped to the floor.

Before I could even say holy shit, another corpse ignited not far from the first one, then another and another in a chain reaction at different places around the cinema, spraying out green flames like human blowtorch's and giving off a fierce heat in the process.

"Booby traps!" I shouted.

"Get those flames out!" Brentwood yelled.

"No!" I told him. "That's not just any fire—it's hellfire! Everyone in here will burn if we don't get out now!"

"But the scene—"

"Now!"

"Damn!" Brentwood turned and yelled for everyone to exit the room. People rushed to the door, trying not to panic as the flames spread at a rapid rate, filling the room with the acrid smell of burning flesh.

The three of us ran back up the aisle toward the door, only to be blocked halfway by one of Brentwood's agents who was currently on fire and burning to a crisp in front of us. Without hesitation, Leona took out her gun and put a bullet into the burning agent, who immediately stopped moving and fell to the floor as the flames continued to burn his body. As brutal an act as it might have seemed, Leona did the guy a favor, putting him down like that.

"We're trapped!" Brentwood shouted.

My thought was to grab Brentwood and Leona and teleport them out of the building. But after casting a quick spell that showed up the glowing lines of the magical wards painted all around the room, I realized that Mr. Black didn't want me leaving here, knowing full well I would have to try and deal with the fire first if I wanted out. Which in Mr. Black's mind, would probably be the end of me anyway.

"Move!" I said, stepping past him and holding both hands out in front of me, tapping my magic so I could use an ice blast on the flames. But the spell had no effect on the roaring hellfire, which refused to succumb to the effects of the freezing ice.

"Creed," Leona said. "Whatever you're doing, do it fast. The fire is coming behind us too!"

I looked over my shoulder to see a frightening wall of green flame advancing toward us, almost like the flames were sentient and were actively seeking people to burn.

Turning my attention back in front of me, I refocused and tried a different tact. This time I tried to force the flames down enough so that at least Leona and Brentwood could jump over them and get out the door. It wasn't easy as the hellfire was intimidatingly strong, but I dampened the flames down by a few feet, then shouted for Leona and Brentwood to move, which they both did, leaping over the lowered wall of flames.

Leona turned around as she landed. "Creed!" she said, her face twisted with worry.

"Go! I'll be right behind you. Go now!"

Leona took a few steps back, looking like she didn't want to leave me, but she had to, or she would have burned to death. She turned and bolted to the door as the flames seemed to chase her up the aisle. When I saw her get safely through the door after Brentwood, I released the spell and the flames in front of me leapt up to the ceiling and spread across it, intensifying the heat in the room to blistering proportions.

Surrounded on all sides by advancing green flames that sounded like they were screeching in delight at the prospect of incinerating me, all I could do was put my head down, pull my demon skin trench coat over me and run in the direction of the door.

# UNLEASH THE MAGIC

*I* BURST THROUGH what was left of the cinema door to find the flames had already spread to the foyer, and were burning everything in their path at such a rapid rate, it was as if all they wanted was to keep burning until the whole city had been consumed. I couldn't help but wonder how anyone was going to stop the growing conflagration.

"Creed!" Leona was standing by the front exit, waving frantically for me to get moving. From outside, the sound of sirens roared. It looked like the firefighters had arrived, although I had a horrible feeling that water wasn't going to stop those supernatural flames. I wasn't sure that anything would.

"Come on, Creed!" Leona shouted again. "Before you fucking burn to death!"

Just as she said it, I felt a searing heat on my back as the wall of flames from the cinema caught up with me. Running toward the exit, I began struggling out of my coat at the same time, hardly able to touch the thick material it was so hot. When I burst outside, Leona helped me remove the smoldering coat, and I let it fall to the ground. Despite the great heat it had to endure, the trench coat seemed largely unaffected, if a little blackened.

Leona looked at me with a mixture of concern and relief. "I didn't think you were going to make it out of there."

"For a minute there, neither did I," I said, gazing as the firefighters' hoses released their payload on the green flames devouring the smoking building. "Are you all right?"

"I'm okay." She came up close to me and took my hand, squeezing it for a moment before letting go. Leona didn't normally do public displays of affection, especially around this crowd, so she must have been worried. "You saved our lives."

I shrugged. "You would have made it out okay."

"No, we wouldn't have," Brentwood said, walking up to us, his jacket off, probably having been burned by the fire. "Lawson's right. You saved our lives, Creed. Thank you."

I nodded my thanks, unused to hearing such genuine gratitude from him. Normally he was scathing in his passive aggressiveness. "Let's hope we can stop these flames from spreading any further."

The firefighters had several hoses pointed at The Roundhouse building as they tried to douse the green flames, but unsurprisingly to me, the water didn't seem to be having any effect. The flames burned like thermite, melting through even the large blocks of stone like they were Lego bricks. Everyone stood back and watched as the firefighters hit the flames with everything they had, but the green fire just kept advancing, melting everything in its path, including the foundations of the building itself, causing it to sink as the flames burnt into the ground.

"Nothing is stopping it," Brentwood said.

"And nothing will," I said. "That fire is supernatural. Only magic can stop it."

"You're the wizard, Creed. Can't you do anything?"

"You want me to use magic in front of all these people?"

"You can go around the back of the building," Leona said. "There's an alley. No one will see you."

"All right," I said, turning to Brentwood. "I'll do my best. Get all these people out of here, though, in case I can't stop it."

Brentwood focused hard on me. "You *will* stop it, Creed."

"Sure, no pressure."

"I'll go with you," Leona said. "We can go through one of the empty houses. Come on, before the whole damn street burns down."

*It will be more than the street that burns if I don't manage to get things under control.*

Leona ran to one of the empty houses a few doors down from the burning cinema. Then she raised one of her long legs and forcefully slammed her heavy boot into the door left of center. The door splintered slightly, but didn't open. She cursed as she kicked at it again. This time the door flew open to reveal a dark hallway. Leona rushed inside like she was about to arrest someone and I ran in behind her. The house was stinking, the smell of mold and decay heavy in the dank air. Claws of some sort scraped the floors upstairs; probably vermin nesting. I followed Leona down a hallway and into a kitchen where you could hardly see anything. She tried the door, and it opened, but there was a plywood board nailed over the frame. "Allow me," I said as Leona stood aside and I fired a blast of magic at the sheet of plywood. The board got wrenched from its nails as it flew back several feet, into a wide and vacant alley, just as Leona had stated.

"All right, Creed," Leona said, looking up and down the alley. "There's no one there. Go do your thing."

Using magic in full view of the public could've been disastrous. With so many Sleepwalkers looking on it probably would only have ended up making things worse. I had the feeling that Mr. Black knew that when he set the booby traps. He knew the hellfire could only be dealt with magically.

*Son of a bitch. What the hell was his beef with me anyway?*

I wished I could remember what it was that lead to me knowing where Mr. Black's then next sacrifice was going to occur, or whom it might've been who tipped me off, or even how I might've known who the next victim was going to be. So in essence, I wish I knew how it was that I managed to arrive at the crime scene seconds or minutes too late, so I could once again use whatever info I had to seek out the next place he'd strike—just like I did last time, only better. Now it felt like I was back to square one. God knows how long I had been chasing him the last time, or how many people he killed before I caught up with him.

No time to dwell, however. My main priority had to be figuring out a way to put out the hellfire. The flames seemed resistant to anything that might extinguish them, so any water or ice based spells were out. Like any fire, though, this one needed oxygen to flourish and spread. All I had to do was to cast a spell containing two individual facets, assuming indeed that hellfire requires oxygen to breathe like the way any other fire does. Yes, I know it's a bit iffy, but hey, you can't blame a man for hoping. So first, my spell had to contain the flames by creating a vacuum space over which all areas it had already spread to were covered. Then, the secondary aspect would be like a syphon that promptly sucked out all the air contained within the vacuum. I say promptly because by now the area involved had tripled in size from the time Leona and I left Brentwood to clear bystanders. It should smother the hellfire in one fell swoop, without suffocating any poor fire-fighters still looking on from just inside the area Brentwood had cordoned off.

"Any time you're ready," Leona said.

"Step off, Leona," I snapped, a bit more harshly than I meant to, but she knew not to rush me when it came to magic. It didn't matter how many times I tried to explain to her the intricate processes that have to be set in motion when casting any spell—the deep focus and conviction required—it never seemed to sink in with her. Leona viewed magic as a skill like any other, like shooting for instance, and as such it could be done at speed under pressure if practiced enough. Which it could in expert hands such as my own, but you still had to be careful you didn't forget something or fuck up the delicate internal processes involved. Otherwise, the results could be less than impressive, and often dangerous.

I got as close as I could without the heat scorching my face off, thinking to that I was going to enjoy killing this Mr. Black when I finally found the fucker {i.e. found him *again*}. There was no other option. Letting such a monster live would not be doing the world any favors, nor the victims or their loved ones.

Centering myself as best as I could under the pressure, I dug as deep as I could go and gathered up every ounce of magic in me, drawing it into the center of my body before beginning to infuse it with intent, all backed by the unwavering conviction that the spell I was about to cast would work. Any self-doubt or uncertainty would only weaken the magic.

When I was about to cast big spells like that, I always entered the Chaosphere first. The Chaosphere is a giant open space inside my mind that is filled with the buzzing, crackling energy of pure magic. It is a place I created long ago, a place where I could access and work with the magic I had learned how to cultivate and channel inside me. Every magic practitioner has their own version of this place. I call mine the Chaosphere because that's what it resembles: a giant sphere of pure and completely chaotic energy requiring the sorts of skills and knowledge only gained by years of experience and research.

I stood in the center of that Chaosphere as if standing in the center of a hollowed-out sun, the energy that flowed around me at once terrifying and exhilarating as I began to pull strands of energy toward me, twisting them this way and that, melding them together, twisting them again, forging them into new forms and shapes, the whole time allowing my intent to infuse every single strand of magical energy to ensure each one would bend in the direction of my will.

I don't know how long I was inside the Chaosphere. In there, the constructs of time and space ceased to exist. I could have been in there minutes or days at a time, and I wouldn't have known either way. When I was ready, the real world would open up again, and the magic would go rushing out to wherever I needed it to go.

In this case, it was aimed toward the green inferno before me. I cast the magic out like a net, and a bluish-white bubble began to form around the entire Roundhouse building, sealing in the flames that still raged within it. Once I was sure I had covered every lick of green flame, I began to shrink the bubble so that it beat down the flames, suffocating the fire and sealing it in. The expanse I had to cover was so great that it took everything I had to keep the entire area constantly covered, painfully aware that if only one flame escaped, then in a flash the whole thing could start all over again.

With both arms out in front of me, I drew them together as if I was physically shrinking the bubble around the fire (which I was in a way, as magicslinging always felt physical). The rippling magic drew ever tighter around the flames, until finally, the green fire became no bigger than a tennis ball in the center of the ruined Roundhouse building. Not that you would have been able to see that small green ball of flame through those thick blocks of stone. I could see fine, however, but on a different field of vision thanks to the connection I had with my magic (my magic and I were separated by nothing, and if I needed to see it, I could, no matter what was in the way).

On that alternate field of vision, I saw a small orb of fiercely hot green energy. It resisted my magic every step of the way, and for a moment, I didn't think I would be able to fully extinguish it. But finally, the green flames died out for good, leaving nothing but smokey devastation behind.

Completely drained, I fell to my knees, glad the magic had done its job, but gladder still that the whole ordeal was finally over.

Or so I thought, for only a few seconds later the world around me was pitched into complete darkness.

## 41

# REVELATIONS

*T*HE DARKNESS DIDN'T last long before it gave way to a sickly yellowish-green light that seemed to seep in around me like a creeping fungus. My previous surroundings had all but faded to a ghostly outline in the background. As I looked around me, I could make out nothing but endless space. I didn't even appear to be standing on solid ground. It was like I was suspended in the weird greenish light, like a specimen in a jar.

*Mr. Black. It has to be.*

"How right you are," a voice said, a deep, almost silky voice that seemed to come from all directions as it echoed around me. Although sounding less distorted this time, I still recognized the voice as being the same as the apparition's.

"You again," I said, my own voice echoing weirdly around me within whatever dimension I was suspended in. "What do you want?"

Mr. Black laughed. "That's the burning question, isn't it, August? Excuse the pun."

No one had called me August in a long, long time. Almost everyone knew me as Creed. A few called me Gus. No one used my first name of August. Only my family ever used my first name. At that moment, a chill ran down my spine as it felt like someone had walked on my grave. "Why do you use that name?"

"Is August not your name?"

"I prefer Creed."

"Yes, but that isn't your proper name either, is it?"

Again, only a few people knew that I had changed my name long ago. Leona was one. Sanaka and my uncle were the others. "How would you know?"

"I know everything about you, August McCreedy."

It was jarring to hear him say my first name, and once again a horrible chill went through me, but I didn't let it show. "Is that supposed to impress me? That you used your formidable dark power to do a background check? Well done."

A lightening bolt of pain stabbed through my chest. It only lasted a few seconds, but it felt like a dragon's claw had punctured my sternum and was rooting around inside me. Needless to say, I screamed like a bitch. "Mind your manners, boy," Mr. Black said, his voice now reminding me of someone, but I was in too much pain to figure out who exactly.

Only when the pain had subsided did I manage to speak again. "What is it you want with me?"

"With you? At first, nothing. Then you started chasing me, interrupting my work."

"Your work?" A bitter laugh escaped me. "You kill people."

"Mere sacrifices. Pawns in a much bigger game. You had it all figured out once, Creed. You knew everything."

"Which is why you erased my memories of you."

"Yes. I didn't need you breathing down my neck in these crucial final stages."

"Final stages? You mean allowing a Dimension Lord to come to this world and destroy it?"

"You always did have trouble seeing the bigger picture, August."

"What?" What did he mean by that? There was something in his voice, something familiar, a note of authority that I knew I recognized but couldn't quite place. "Who are you? Tell me."

"Those who restrain desire, do so because theirs is weak enough to be restrained," Mr. Black said, his words heavy in the thick air around me, bringing with them a memory of someone who used to say those exact words to me whenever I dared to question his motives.

"William Blake," I said in a low voice. "From *The Marriage Of Heaven And Hell*. My...father used to say..." I shook my head, not liking where things were going, but also desperately wanting to know who I was dealing with, even though, deep down, I already knew. I just didn't want to believe it. "Who are you? Tell me now!"

"Wake up, August!" Mr. Black shouted. "You know full well who I am."

"But it can't be..."

"Did you think I was gone forever, August? That my soul could be kept down? A man of my power?"

"No...no...you're...you're *dead*..."

A wind blew around my head as if a spirit form was on the move. "You know better than that, boy. Death is for Sleepwalkers, not the Enlightened. There is no death for people like us, only change. Didn't I teach you that?"

I grabbed my head with both hands like I was trying to stop it from exploding. "Stop it," I said. "Just stop it. You're lying, you're not him. You can't be."

"Why not, August? You know in your bones it's me. You've always known. You just didn't want to admit it."

"Know what? What are you talking about?"

"That it was me, August. That I killed them, your mother and brother and sister. That I sacrificed them all to the demon!"

"Shut up! Shut the fuck up!"

"It's time to face the truth of your past, August—"

"No--"

"I let you live, August. You were supposed to join me, be by my side—"

"NO!"

"LOOK AT ME!" The voice boomed inside my head, rattling me to the core. I froze in fear just as a figure materialized in front of me. A tall figure of a man in a dark suit, with broad shoulders and thick, graying hair. I didn't have to look into those intense and frightening gray eyes to know it was him.

My father.

Christopher McCreedy.

His ephemeral form floated right up to me and placed both hands on my shoulders. Then suddenly I was a kid again, staring up at my impossibly tall father, scared to even look into his stern face. "Leave me alone," I said, my voice now sounding childish and afraid. "Please..."

"Look at me, son," my father commanded, leaving me with no choice but to obey his command like I did when I was a kid. "I am your father, and you will obey me. Is that clear?"

I found myself nodding, unable to resist him. "Yes."

"You have hidden from the truth for too long, August. It's time you remembered."

He placed one of his large hands on my head then, and that's when the memories were unleashed in me, like a pack of wild dogs who had been locked away in my mind before now, snarling and slavering as they ripped my mind to pieces.

And I had no choice but to let them.

# 42

# GROWING UP

*I* PROBABLY GAVE you the impression before that I had an idyllic, privileged upbringing in Ireland, what with the big house by the lake and all my father's wealth to keep us pampered; and that because there was all that cool magic around, the family home was like Hogwarts, with spells and fun times had by all. Well, there was spells and magic, and occasionally my siblings and I managed to have some fun, but mainly my memories of that house and my upbringing were not what I would call happy ones, and this was mostly due to my father's constant overbearing authority and strict discipline. He made our home into a bootcamp where the priority was always exercising discipline and studiously learning how to channel and wield magic without causing a disaster.

Most of my memories start around age four or five. I don't remember much before that. I had the sense that I was a loved child, and this was only down to my mother and older brother and sister, who always had a smile and a hug for me (or a punch to the shoulder in my brother's case).

My father remained aloof for the most part. When I did spend time with him as a child, it was never to play, but to be exposed to the concept of magic.

The first time I saw any kind of magic was when my father conjured a small sphere of dark blue energy in one of his large, long-fingered hands. The swirling blue energy was the most beautiful thing I had ever seen at the time. When I went to touch it with a curious but tentative finger, my father slapped my hand away, the sting of the slap bringing tears to my eyes (in hindsight I suppose this could've been the first sign of what was to come). "Not yet," I remember him admonishing me. "Only when you're ready."

"When father?" I would say back.

He would stand over me, tall and domineering. "When I say you are."

As things went, he thought I was ready by age five, and I joined the regime my older brother and sister were already on. My brother, Fergal, was eight years old and my sister, Roisin, was seven. They were both experts in magic already, or so it seemed to me at the time. They could do things with magic that I couldn't do yet. I barely knew what magic was at that point. That all changed, however, when I had to start getting up every morning at 5:30 a.m. If my father were around (which he usually was), he would lead us around the grounds of the house and through the neighboring forest on a long run, believing as he did that a good wizard needed to look after their physical body because it was the conduit through which their magic flowed. The morning runs were hateful and grueling for the first couple of months. Though because I was so young, my father allowed me to walk whenever I got tired, while he and my brother and sister carried on running. This usually meant that it took me a long time to make it home for breakfast. It didn't matter how wet or cold it was outside. We never missed a run. If I was late getting back for breakfast, I had to go without (although Roisin always saved me a piece of bacon or sausage, just one of the many exemplary reasons why I always loved her). Needless to say, I soon learned to keep up.

The rest of the day was structured around various classes and tutorials, as we were home schooled at my father's insistence, because that's always the way it had been in the "McCreedy household". My mother Brenda, a beautiful woman with long, curly red hair and kind blue eyes, handled the standard education that most kids get, teaching us literacy and numeracy and a whole host of other subjects; including art, which I always loved (and still do to this day). My mother's classes were usually relaxed. She tried to make learning fun for us, and even though we were all at different levels, she did a great job of educating us.

My father's tutelage was a lot less relaxed, and he was always dominant with us, explaining that magic had to be taken seriously, and was not to be messed around with. His teaching sessions were grueling on every level. He usually started with magic theory, forcing us to memorize huge chunks from antiquated books that most of the time, were written in some obscure language that was difficult to get your tongue (or your brain) around. If you messed up your recital, you got a slap on the back of the hand with the thin willow stick my father always carried in the classroom. If you really fucked things up, you got the stick across the back of the legs, and let me tell you, my father didn't hold back. Your tears and pain meant nothing to him. In his eyes, that was how you learned not to fuck things up again. My brother and sister were used to this kind of brutal instruction, but I wasn't. I don't think I ever got used to it. My father's stern and often aggressive behavior had me constantly on edge, which meant I fucked up a lot. The only way I could advance in my studies was to spend what little free time I had trying to learn or master whatever I was supposed to have learned in class. On my own, I picked things up pretty quickly without the overbearing presence of my father there to fluster me.

That was my life for nearly eighteen years. We were allowed weekends off unless my father had arranged for us to study under a different teacher, which he often had, bringing in his wizard friends and acquaintances to teach us specific magic techniques. Some guest speakers had quite a fun approach to teaching, but for the most part they were simply a reflection of his own dark views, and his approach to teaching. I often thought if becoming a wizard made you so damn serious and joyless, what the hell was the point?

Thank God for my mother, who always made a point of taking us places on our weekends off, where we at least got to mingle with other kids our age. My favorite place was always the cinema. Now that was true magic, and over the years, those films were the only real window I had into the rest of the world. Sad, I know, but when you're a kid, you need some sort of escapism. Needless to say, my father knew nothing of these cinema visits. Otherwise he probably would have banned them, like he did most things that involved fun.

That was my life, pretty much, right up until the night my father performed the demon summoning that changed everything.

The day before that happened, my father called me into his study, a memory that I had forgotten for a long time. My father sat behind his imposing oak desk and had me stand (as always) opposite him, hands clasped behind my back, head up, staring straight ahead like a soldier standing in front of their superior officer. "What I'm about to tell you, August, must go no further than this room. Are we clear?"

Of course we were clear. I wouldn't have dared to disobey him. "Yes, sir."

My father interlocked his fingers atop his desk, a gesture that always preceded him saying something important. "Things will change around here soon. I need you to be ready for those changes."

"Changes, sir?" I asked, confused. Nothing ever changed in the McCreedy house. Everything was always depressingly the same, so what was going on?

"What is the only thing that matters?"

It was a question we had been asked a thousand times over the years. "The pursuit of greatness, Father."

"And at what cost?"

"At all cost, sir."

My father nodded. "That is correct. At all cost. Do you believe in that doctrine, August?"

Of course I didn't. Neither did Fergal or Roisin. But what was I going to say, no? "I do, sir."

His intense gray eyes stared into me, and as always, it felt like he was reading my soul for the truth. "Good, because you know, out of the three of you, you have the most potential, August."

It was the first kind of praise I had ever heard come out of his mouth. My eyes met his for a brief moment before looking away again. "Thank you, Father."

"Don't thank me, boy. It is a matter of not wasting that potential. I intend to see to it that you don't."

"What do you mean?"

"Those who restrain desire, do so because theirs is weak enough to be restrained. I taught you that, didn't I?"

I nodded. "Yes, sir."

"My own desire has been shamefully weak of late," he said, adjusting the cuffs on his dark suit. "Progression is called for."

"Progression?"

"Yes. Advancing to the next level of power. You understand?"

"Yes." I didn't though. The desire he saw in me was merely the desire for greater learning, as, by that point, I had developed a deep and genuine appreciation of the arcane arts. Granted, I never had a choice in the matter, but like it or not, magic was in my blood. It was a part of me. Sure, I was always striving to

increase my skills and the potency of my magic, but that striving was never motivated by some all-consuming lust for power or the desire to rule the damn world. I
hardly knew the world at that time anyway, having spent most of my life within the
walls of the house. The desire my father was talking about was merely the desire
for raw power, or power for power's sake. It was a level of ambition I couldn't
relate to, but I wasn't about to tell him that either, which would have been like
telling Adolf Hitler he was taking things a bit far.

"Good," he said, nodding. "Because sacrifice will be required. You understand
the need for sacrifice, don't you, boy?"

I was no stranger to sacrifice, but sacrifice had limits. There were things I
would never think of doing in the pursuit of power. That especially included not
hurting other people. For my father though, I knew there were no limits as to
what he would do for more power. The constant glaring ambition in his eyes said it
all, an ambition that was much too strong for me to even think about arguing with,
so I simply said, "I understand."

My father looked at me for a long time, as he liked to do from time to time.
Under his glare, I felt naked and vulnerable, sometimes shameful. "We shall see,"
he said, finally taking his eyes off me.

The next night, the summoning took place, and I saw firsthand just how much
my father was willing to sacrifice in pursuit of his goals.

# 43

## FATHERLY LOVE

"*Y*OU KILLED THEM!"

The memories of that night came rushing back into my head like an out of control freight train. All too vivid images flashed painfully in my mind: the violence inflicted by the demon on my poor mother, and on my brother and sister; all the blood and screaming.

And my father's face. His face as he watched his family get torn apart by a monster he had summoned. He knew what was going to happen, had planned it all, in fact. He had watched his own family get killed with hardly a look of remorse on his face. And when I screamed his name, begging him to help, he merely looked at me as if to say that it had to be done.

My father's look from that night was now seared into my brain, and I screamed and attacked him, swinging my fists at his face, wanting only to pummel him to death, to rip him apart the way the demon had ripped my family apart. But my fists went straight through him like I was punching only air.

"You have no physical body here," he said like he was talking to a child having a temper tantrum. "You might as well stop."

Fuck him. I wasn't going to stop swinging just because he said so, though eventually, I did give up on trying to hurt him when I lost the energy to do so. I backed my spirit form away and glared at him. "I'm going to kill you."

My father shook his head impatiently. "August, you need to stop with this childish nonsense. You need to face the truth of things. Magic and power are all that matters. How can you not see that by now?"

"The only truth here is that you're a monster," I spat, staring hard at him, making sure he could see the hatred and murderous intent in my eyes. "You took them from me. You left me all alone in the world." I lashed out at him again, only because I didn't know what else to do. And despite only being in spirit form, I still felt the hurt in my belly as it twisted my guts. A hurt that seemed like it was there to stay forever, like a cancerous cyst that couldn't be excised in case its poison spilt into my bloodstream.

Which is why I blocked out the truth of what happened that night in the first place. Some memories are just too painful to bear.

"Your childish spats are becoming tiresome, boy."

"Fuck you. I'm not your fucking boy. I never was."

My father averted his eyes from me for a moment, perhaps hurt by that statement, though I doubted it. A man who would willingly sacrifice the lives of his family in return for power, wasn't going to be hurt by anything so inconsequential as his youngest son disowning him. *Despising* him. "It's not too late, August. You can still join me. It's what I planned all along, to have you by my side."

I shook my head in disbelief. "Why would you ever think I would stand by you after you had my family slaughtered like animals? You're fucking insane. You've always been insane..."

"I thought you would come to understand eventually. Clearly, I misjudged you."

*Well, thank fuck for that...*

"Understand? Understand what?"

"If you have to ask, then you will never know."

"Oh, I know, father. I know that you're just a power-mad psychopath like all the rest. I know that your soul is corrupt and blackened by your selfish lust for power."

"Selfish?" My father's face twisted up in a fury. "I gave you everything!"

"Yes, and then you took it all away like the tyrant you are! You should have had me killed that night along with Mother and Fergal and Roisin." Just saying their names filled me with sadness. "Why did you let me live? You should have just let that demon kill me instead of leaving me all alone."

"I was supposed to be with you, August. The demon betrayed me, kept me prisoner in his filthy domain in the Underworld."

"It was less than you deserved. And did you actually believe that I would want to stay with you after what you did?"

"It didn't matter what you believed."

"Why not?"

He stared straight at me. "Because I was going to steal your physical body. I was getting old, and my body was becoming frail. I needed a new one. Yours, August."

If I weren't a mere spirit, I would have thrown up right then.

*Just when I thought this pretender couldn't get any more despicable...*

Anger and pain coursed through me like twin streams of acid. "You want my body? Fucking take it then, you despicable *cunt*! Take it, and I'll rip myself apart just to kill you."

My father didn't seem at all fazed by my outburst. He merely made a dismissive gesture with his hand. "I have no need for anyone's body now. I can take whatever physical form I want. Besides which, when Rloth comes here and grants me the power he has promised me, any physical form will be beneath me. I will exist in a place of *pure* power. A place where I can manifest whole worlds if I so desire. Or destroy them entirely."

I had heard enough of his insanity. "Release me from this cage. Now!"

"As you wish," my father said. "But I wanted you to know the truth, and now you do." *Sadistic bastard*. He drifted close to me, and it was all I could do not to turn away in disgust. "But you should know. If you continue with this pursuit of yours, I will destroy you."

Despite everything, it still hurt like hell to hear him say that. "You might as well kill me now then because I won't stop hunting you until you're dead, *old man*."

He nodded and something of a smile came across his ghostly face. "I expected nothing less. You are my son after all."

Then he waved his hand and disappeared along with the void we were floating in.

"Creed?"

I was still standing in the alley, Leona's voice and the noise from the street at the front of the cinema welcoming me back to reality. Leona was standing a few feet away, looking unsure if I was back with her or not. "Yes?" I said to her in a distant voice.

She looked relieved as she came up and put a hand on my shoulder. "Where did you go?" she asked. "You've been standing in a trance the last twenty minutes. It was like you were frozen or something."

Shaking my head, I sighed deeply and said nothing. I was so gutted, I couldn't even bring myself to speak, least of all try to explain what had just happened.

Leona gently squeezed my shoulder. "Come on. I'm taking you to my place."

It was the first good thing I had heard all day.

# 44

# SCORPION

*C/M*Y MIND WAS still reeling when we got to Leona's place. Actually, that's an understatement. It felt like a bomb had exploded inside my head, in the process dislodging and scattering memories and thoughts that I had kept safely locked away until now. And with my father's unveiling of his evil self and the revelations he chose to impart, it was too much for me to handle. Leona didn't seem too sure about how to be around me, considering I hadn't said a single word to her on the drive back. When we got inside the apartment, she told me to sit down on the sofa. Then she went to the kitchen and came back with a bottle of Glenfiddich and an empty glass which she filled with the whiskey. "Drink," she said, holding the glass out to me as if it contained some magical medicine that would cure all the bad in me. I looked at her blankly before taking the whiskey and downing it in one, handing her the glass back straightaway. "Okay, its like that then, is it?"

I nodded. "Its like that."

"I'm going to make tea for myself. When I come back, you're going to tell me what happened."

I said nothing as she walked away and I sank into the sofa, cradling my glass of whiskey in both hands, the alcohol doing little to alleviate how I was feeling; which was betrayed mostly, and sickened. Sickened that my own father could do such unspeakable things, that he was *still* doing them. This despite the fact that I thought he had been dead and gone for so long now, along with the rest of my family.

The family that *he* had killed.

My fingers wrapped around the glass so tightly I thought it would shatter in my hands. "Fucking bastard," I said, my face twisting up in anger and pain. Tears were streaming down my face by the time Leona came back in and sat beside me.

"Creed," she said as if talking to a victim of abuse, placing her cup of green tea on the coffee table next to us. "Talk to me, Creed."

"He killed them," I blurted out. "He killed them...*all* of them..."

"Who are you talking about?"

"My family! He killed my family...oh God..." I clamped a hand over my mouth, thinking I was going to be sick.

Leona put a hand on the back of my neck. "It's okay, Creed. Who killed them? Mr. Black?"

My head turned slowly to look at her. "My father," I said. "My father is Mr. Black."

Needless to say, she looked shocked and then confused. "But you told me your father was dead. That he died with the rest of your family when the demon killed them."

"He did die." I forced myself to drink more of the whiskey to try and stop myself from becoming a jibbering wreck, which wasn't my style, mainly thanks to my father, who was all about beating into me the importance of self-control at all times. I almost let go of myself just to spite him (I certainly fucking felt like it), but decided to spare Leona the song and dance, who didn't do so well with people falling apart in front of her (I remember she once slapped me across the face when I cried while watching an episode of *Ray Donovan*, telling me to get a grip). "Now he's back."

"Why?"

"It hardly even matters why."

Leona shook her head. "You're being cryptic. I can't help you if you're being cryptic. So Mr. Black is your father?"

"Yes."

"That's...fucked up. That's some real *Star Wars* shit, right there. What did he say to you?"

I took a breath before answering her. "That he deliberately sacrificed my family...my mother and brother and sister...to that demon he summoned."

"Jesus, Creed. I'm sorry."

"He watched them die, Leona. I saw his face as that demon was—" I had to pause for a second. "He planned the whole thing, the destruction of his whole family. And for what? More power."

"But the demon killed him as well."

"It betrayed him. He got what he deserved."

"So how is he back?"

"He crawled his way back from the Underworld like some disgusting worm."

"And what did he want with you?"

I shook my head. "To remind me of what happened, of what he did. To hit me with some half-assed notion of me joining him. As if I ever fucking would. I mean, how deranged do you have to be? And that's not even the worst thing he told me."

"Really? What's worse than killing your whole family?"

"He was going to let me live. You know why?" Leona shook her head, her face saying she was dreading hearing why. "Because he needed my body. His was getting old, and he was going to steal mine." A bitter laugh left my mouth. "You couldn't make this fucking shit up."

239

Leona sighed and rubbed the back of my neck, her touch the only good thing I was feeling right then. "I'm sorry, Creed. You don't deserve any this."

"Obviously the universe thinks differently."

"Fuck the universe," she said, moving closer, taking my drink off me and placing it on the coffee table before kissing me, gently at first as I tried to decide if it was really the time to make love, before deciding that it was exactly the right time. What better way (so it felt) to get back at my father than to make love, despite the evil shit he had filled my head with, and despite his lifelong attempt to quash whatever love was in me?

*Fuck you, father.*

I pressed my lips harder against Leona's, and she responded in kind. It wasn't long before we were both in that blissful bubble where only the two of us existed and all the horrible things that had and were happening were forgotten about for a short time at least.

\* \* \*

I WOKE UP LATER IN LEONA'S QUEEN-SIZED BED AFTER A BRIEF, FITFUL SLEEP that followed the intense, almost desperate sex we had. Hard dawn light seeped through the cracks in the blinds, spilling over Leona's slender, naked form lying beside me. She was still asleep as I sat up and stared at her for a while, getting lost in the beauty of her curves and her athletic but still feminine musculature. Then there was the all black scorpion tattoo on her back, the claws extending over both shoulder blades, the thick tail unfolding down her spine, the stinger itself at the side of her fourth lumbar. It was a bold image, and a little unsettling the first few times you saw it. But when you got to know Leona like I did, you soon realized that the tattoo was entirely symbolic of who she is. Leona was a survivor, a fighter, a cunning hunter when she had to be, with a sting that hurt like hell and often killed if it had to. Yet despite all that ferocity, even scorpions had a caring side, and I considered myself lucky to be one of the few people she revealed that side of herself to. She was also funny in her own blunt, abrasive way. It still amazed me that she had a sense of humor at all, given the things she had seen.

Leaning over, I kissed her gently on the back and then slipped out of bed. In the living room, I gathered up my clothes which were scattered around everywhere, after Leona had hurriedly pulled them off me. After getting dressed, I went to the kitchen and made coffee with Leona's ridiculously expensive coffee machine, one of the few luxuries (maybe the only one) that she had in the apartment. Whatever she paid was worth it, given the brew it served up. I carried the mug into the living room, and opened the sliding door to step out onto the balcony. The cold morning air that was like a slap to the face at first, but invigorating once you got used to it.

From Leona's swanky apartment building, I looked down to the street below and watched a road sweeper move along like a ladybug on a leaf, the vehicle stopping once so the driver could wind the window down and toss out a cigarette butt into the street he was supposed to be cleaning. Across the way in the tenement buildings, lights began to come on, and curtains were drawn open as the occupants rose to meet another day in Blackham. And rising behind the tenements were the skyscrapers made of steel and glass. Huge structures that almost made you feel like you were in some other futuristic city somewhere. Through the gaps in the skyscrapers, you could also see Blackham State University, the Gothic-style building that churned out the city's best and brightest (allegedly).

As I gazed out over the north of the city, my thoughts inevitably turned to Mr. Black. I refused even to think of him as my father. My father was bad enough when he was alive but however bad or manipulative he was while I was growing up, he was still my father, and I was loyal to him. I had no reason to be loyal to him anymore, though. The man who forced a meeting with me a while ago in Lafayette was not my father. My father was dead and gone as far as I was concerned, and good riddance. Mr. Black was just the evil shadow that endured after the demon tore my father apart, turning him into the monster that I had been hunting before I got hexed, and still hunted. That much hadn't changed, despite Mr. Black's true origins. I was still going to bring him down.

The question was though, how was I going to do it?

# BAD COFFEE BLUES

*I* HAD JUST sat down in the living room when Leona came walking in, looking effortlessly sexy in her white silk dressing gown that just about came down to the top of her thighs. "How long have you been up?" she asked, sliding herself onto my lap and languidly kissing me.

"Not long," I replied, gazing like a lost puppy into her blue eyes, which always seemed lighter in the mornings. "But in that silk offering I'd say it was getting shorter by the second, depending on which 'up' you meant, if the difference isn't something you can feel between your thighs at this very second!"

Leona sniggered and shook her head. "Bad boy..."

"I try," I said after I'd finished kissing her, then my anxiety hit again and I went back to being despondent.

She smoothed my longish hair for a moment before hugging me. "Don't worry. We'll figure it all out."

I nodded as she pulled away. "I know." I didn't, though. So far, I had no idea of how I was going to stop Mr. Black, and his insane plan to bring forth an ancient, unimaginably monstrous being to eat the fucking world up. No idea at all.

"I'm making coffee. You want one?" Leona asked me.

"I'll get it."

She put a hand out to stop me. "No. Your coffee sucks, Creed."

"I don't make the stuff. The machine does."

"There's still a knack to it, which you don't have."

"What, like place the cup in the machine and press the button? Where's the knack in that?"

She was already off me, heading for the kitchen. "I'm glad you don't approach sex the same way."

"What do you mean?" I said in a serious voice. "Of course I do. Insert penis and turn on machine. What other way is there?"

Shaking her head, Leona laughed as she walked into the kitchen. "You are not wise."

"Owls and old men are wise. I don't want to be either."

"Given your age, you're not far off the latter."

"Careful, Lawson. You're no spring chicken yourself, you know."

"I'm thirty-two years old," she said, throwing me a look from the kitchen while she waited on the machine to fill her cup up.

I nodded. "I know. That's nearly middle age."

Shaking her head, she carried two cups of coffee back into the living room, handing me one. "Shut up and drink your coffee."

Smiling, I tasted the dark brew, then smacked my lips. "You're right. Your coffee does taste better than mine."

"You'd think with all that magic, that you'd be able to make a decent cup of coffee." She lifted the remote control off the table and turned on the TV to the local news station.

I shook my head at her comment as I turned my attention to the news. Unsurprisingly, the conflagration at the Roundhouse Cinema was the top story. The news showed images of the building, now reduced to a pile of blackened, molten ash, as if the building had melted (which it had in a way). The onsite reporter mentioned the strange color of the flames but reported that it was due to a methane gas leak from the sewers underneath. There was no mention of any murders. "Brentwood's done his job then," I said. "Covering up the murders."

"Are you surprised?"

"No." Brentwood was good at his job, I'd give him that. It sometimes amazed me the things he managed to cover up from the media and the public at large. I often wondered if he was bumping off witnesses, because some of the events he was involved in were quite public, with lots of witnesses. "People believe what they want to believe, I suppose. An accidental fire is easier to process than sixty-seven people all having their throats cut by a mad..."

"A mad what?"

"I don't even know what he is. A dark stain on the world."

Leona said nothing and we sat and watched the rest of the news in silence, the only other noteworthy event being one of the city's biggest porn stars (Wendy Gush) dying on the job. I was acquainted with Miss Gush through another mutual acquaintance. I also knew the porn star practiced sex magic. The circumstances surrounding her death sounded a little suspicious to me. When (if) I dealt with Mr. Black, I would look into Miss Gush's death. For a porn star, she was quite an accomplished adept, surprising me with her command and knowledge when we'd last met a couple of years ago. I doubted the cops would look too deep into her case, so I would.

"Freak," Leona said, shaking her head at the picture of Wendy Gush on the TV. "I don't know how they could do it to themselves." Despite not holding back during sex (with me anyhow), Leona was still something of a prude. It could have been her overly-religious upbringing, but I suspected it had more to do with her dignity and integrity at all costs way of thinking. Not that I thought there was anything particularly undignified or dishonest about what Wendy Gush did for a living, especially when she was using the sex to channel her magic. But standards of integrity were relative, especially in the occult world. I and every other adept could attest to that. I didn't bother offering any of this blinding insight to Leona because I knew she wouldn't want to hear it. Her attention was on her phone anyway, having just received a text.

"Let me guess," I said. "Brentwood?"

She nodded. "I have to go to work. He wants updates on the Mr. Black case."

"What are you going to tell him?"

"What do you want me to tell him?"

"Not the truth. He already blames me for enough." Just being involved with magic was enough for anyone to make it on to Brentwood's shitlist. "Tell him I'm still chasing down leads. Not that I answer to him anyway."

Leona shook her head. She thought my problem with authority figures was juvenile. You'd think after hearing all about my father's domineering parental style, that it would've made her more sympathetic, but Leona's nothing if not stubborn and set in her ways. For the most part you either got on board, or out the way. She was military to the core. She would never understand my aversion to authority figures. "He could make your life difficult, you know. He could have you locked up in the Pen."

"With the rest of the 'freaks', you mean?"

"Come on, Creed. You know I don't think of you like that."

"I know you don't. He does, though. Not that I care."

"He's just trying to help. Same as you are. Same as I am."

"Just different methods." I'd heard it all before. The fact was, I would never be comfortable with Brentwood's brute force tactics. He didn't care who he hurt in the process of carrying out his directives. I did, though.

"Right, well this big bad government agent has to shower before going to work." She stood up, leant down and kissed me quick. "You can stay here if you want."

"No thanks," I said, swallowing the last of my coffee. "I need to get back to the Sanctum and figure out what I'm going to do about....*Mr. Black*. Maybe your demon friend left me a clue."

"That brutish abomination is not and never will be my friend."

"Oh, I don't know. You two seemed to hit it off. And with that tongue of his..."

"You're disgusting, Creed. Get out of my apartment. I'm rescinding my invitation for you to stay."

I laughed. "All right, I'll go. Tell Brentwood I said hi."

"I'll be sure to do that. Now get your magic ass in gear and get the hell out of here."

"I love it when you get bossy."

She turned and walked toward the bathroom. "Bye, Creed."

"I love you too."

She didn't answer as she disappeared into the bathroom. I stood for another minute, until I heard the shower being turned on, and I realized I didn't want to leave because then I would have to go home and face the awful truth that had been hanging over me since yesterday.

Which was that my father, in his post-death madness, was about to end the world.

# 46

## STANDING TALL

*I* didn't go straight back to the Sanctum after leaving Leona's because I knew that going there, meant I'd have to fully face the dire and fucked up nature of my situation, if not the whole world's too. So I teleported to the roof of the highest building in Blackham City, which was the Moreland Building, named after Reginald Moreland, the city's billionaire real estate mogul who wanted to leave a little something for people to remember him by when he died three decades ago. That little something became one hundred and twenty-six story's tall with a gold tipped pyramid on top. A gridiron walkway went right around the whole building at the base of the pyramid. Apparently people used to make a big deal that he liked to sit out on that walkway to meditate every morning, made easy by his penthouse suite access, suggested as one of his many supposed secrets to his incredible financial success. There was also talk that old man Moreland was an Illuminati general, which he may have been, I don't know (I take no interest in those self-serving war mongers). I do know that he practiced magic though, and that he was good at it, even if he did mostly use it to amass a fortune. Whatever kind of man he was, I was grateful to him for constructing the Moreland Building, and especially the walkway I was standing on. I have been teleporting to this walkway for the last twenty years or so. It's a place I like to go to clear my head. All the way up there with the wind rushing around you, it's hard to dwell too much on your problems, and I could see why old man Moreland used to go there every morning.

Needless to say, the view is also spectacular. If you wanted, you could have a full three-sixty view of the whole city and beyond if you walked right around the building. From that height, the city looked vast. A huge conclave of stone and brick and steel and glass, criss-crossed with streets and pulsing with the life of the people inside. I stood facing east because I liked to look past all the modern skyscrapers in the Highlands, and out toward the vast expanse of sea beyond, my gaze finally settling on the horizon; that point in the distance that always seemed to promise great things, if you only made your way toward it. The promise of a place where dreams could come true and potential could be fulfilled. Or maybe that was just me. Whatever the case, as soon as I focused on that horizon with the sun rising up over the sea, my mind seemed to expand as I felt a certain release from the pressure in my head. Which didn't make things any less dire, but it at least enabled me to escape from the quagmire of dark emotions I had been previously drowning in.

I spent a while up there before I decided to make a call that I hadn't been looking forward to making since my meeting with my father. That's if I even got a hold of the person I wanted to speak to, who was notoriously hard to contact. This is because he is usually away in some far flung corner of the multiverse in search of some artifact or rare text.

As it turned out, it took me six attempts to finally get through to my uncle, Raymond McCreedy. "August, my boy," he said when he answered, the line sounding clear and not full of static the way it usually was when I called him. "It's good to hear from my favorite nephew again. How long has it been?" His accent was still strongly Irish, despite all his traveling.

"A few days ago actually," I said, shouting slightly to hear myself over the wind noise. "You didn't recognize me though."

"Yes, very strange. What was that about?"

"Long story, but that's not why I'm phoning. Well, actually it is." I shook my head suddenly in anger. "Fuck it, you know why I'm calling, Ray. You can't not fucking know." The line went silent. "Hello? Ray, you there?"

"Yes, August, I'm here."

"Then answer me. Did you know?"

"Know what? I've been off-world for over year. I just got back here to Ireland a few days ago. What's been happening?"

I took a deep breath to calm myself. "Did you know about my father, Ray? About what he did? About what he really did that night of the summoning?"

"August, why you bringing that up for?"

"You knew, didn't you? You knew he meant for the demon to kill my family, didn't you?"

"August, I—"

"Why didn't you tell me? I had a right to know the kind of monster my father was."

"I thought if you knew what he really did, that you would—"

"What Ray? I already blamed him for summoning the demon in the first place."

"I know that. I was afraid the truth would—"

"Push me over the edge? I was already there."

"How did you find out? What has happened?"

I never answered for a moment as I stared down at the city below, feeling raw and exposed. "Just tell me if you knew, Ray."

Ray sighed before answering. "I didn't know what your father was going to do, August. Don't you think if I did that I would have tried to stop him? It's my greatest regret that I didn't keep a close enough eye on you all, then maybe..." He trailed off into silence, a silence which lasted for close to a minute before I spoke.

"I'm not blaming you, Ray. I just wanted to know..."

"You have every right to blame me, son. I should've been there when you most needed me."

"But you weren't," I felt like saying, but didn't. As much as it hurt that Ray wasn't there when I needed him most, he is my only remaining family, and I wasn't going to push him away over something that wasn't really his fault at the end of the day.

I therefore proceeded to tell him everything about Mr. Black, who Mr. Black really was, the murders he had committed and his crazy plan to create a portal so Rloth could come to Earth and eat it.

"Sweet Christmas," Ray said after I'd finished. "I knew there was something going on. The Tapestry has been unsettled of late and I couldn't figure out why. I can't believe that bastard brother of mine managed to crawl out of the Underworld. Well, actually, I can. He was always slippery, was your father."

"He's not my father," I corrected him. "He's a monster, plain and simple."

"I'm sorry, August. I should have told you the truth long ago. You had a right to know."

"I did have a right to know, but I understand why you kept it from me."

"I was trying to protect you. Your whole family had just been wiped out and—"

"When did you know the truth, Ray?"

"Not soon enough, I'm sorry to say. Shortly after, when an Underworld contact informed me. I was trying to make sure Christopher stayed down there and never got out after what he did to you's all. Now it seems, my numerous bribes weren't enough to keep him locked up."

"Unfortunately not." I paused for a moment as I watched a Kestrel land on a nearby building. "I always knew the truth anyway."

"You did?"

"I saw his face, Ray, which told me that he had planned to sacrifice us all. I must have buried the memory."

"I don't blame you for that."

"He was going to steal my body, you know? But the demon betrayed him. I've still no idea why the demon didn't kill me as well though."

"You know demons, unpredictable bastards at times. Count yourself lucky, my boy."

"I need to know how to stop him, Ray."

"That won't be easy, not if he's been getting power from a Dimension Lord."

"But it *can* be done, right?"

"With the right magic, anything can be done. It's finding the right magic though. You want me over there with you?"

"No. This is my fight, no one else's."

"He'll kill you, August."

I squinted out toward the horizon again and steeled myself against the rushing wind. "Only if I let him."

"No, I'm coming over there. This is as much my responsibility as yours, August, probably more so."

I shook my head. "No, Ray—"

"Yes!" he shouted. "You're my nephew, the son I never had. I'll be on a plane within the hour. I'll teleport off it as soon as I can. Somewhere over the Atlantic probably."

I sighed, knowing there would be no talking him out of it. Not that it mattered anyway. By the time he got here, it would most likely all be over and either Mr. Black or I would be dead.

"All right, Ray," I said. "I'll see you when you get here."

I hoped.

47

# ABANDON ALL HOPE

*I* teleported down off the top of the Moreland Building to an alley down below. I then hailed a taxi, not wanting to waste any magical resources by teleporting. From here on out I'd do well to conserve and build on them. A twenties-something Asian driver stopped at the curb, the car's interior being pelted by Hindu drum-and-bass he so obviously enjoyed. "Hey man," he said cheerfully as he pulled out into traffic, causing the car behind to sound its horn, which the cab driver completely ignored. "Hope you don't mind the music. It gets me through the day, you know?"

The hectic music seemed to pummel at my skull, and I winced. "Maybe just drop the volume a little."

"Oh sure, man." The driver turned the music to half volume and looked at me in his rearview mirror. "That okay?"

I could have done with no volume at all but decided not to argue the point. Instead, I just nodded and stared out the window at the passing traffic and the scores of people walking around in business suits. We were heading through the heart of the financial sector, where all the big banks and stock brokers resided in their intimidating skyscrapers. Everyone seemed to be engaged in animated conversations, either on the phone or with other people. I imagined they were all making deals, hammering out conditions, issuing demands, all with the sole aim of making more money, and in doing so, increasing their power and prestige.

*Like any of that will matter if Mr. Black gets his way. Nothing will be around to matter if that happens.*

It was a depressing thought that the world could be devoured by an ancient being so insatiable in its appetite, that it could consume every living thing until nothing was left but a barren husk of a planet that once supported life in such vast abundance. It was also frightening to think that a person's insanity could allow them to permit billions of souls and a living planet to be wiped out in the first place, to obtain more power. And what was Mr. Black intending to do with all this power when he got it? Use it to wipe out more worlds in the universe, continually chasing power for power's sake? Or did he have some other plan in mind? I didn't know. The only thing I knew was that I couldn't give Mr. Black the chance to make good on those plans. Even if it meant my own annihilation, I had to stop him.

"So hey, man, what you make of this big storm coming, huh? It's scary shit. They say it's the biggest storm to ever come out of the sky. You see that shit on the news yet?"

In my reverie, I had barely noticed that we were now on the expressway, heading toward Freetown. "What?"

"The storm that's coming, man." The cab driver stared at me in the mirror like he fully expected me to know what he was talking about.

"Storm? What storm?"

The cab driver shook his head. "Seriously, guy? It's all over the news."

"I saw the news earlier. There was no mention of any storm."

"That's because it just appeared, like an hour ago."

"Appeared? Appeared where?"

"That's the weird part. They say it came from space and it's coming down right on top of us, man. Right on fucking top of us! You believe that? As if this city hasn't got enough problems. How am I going to drive cab in a storm?" He was gesticulating madly with his hands over the wheel, barely looking at the road ahead, the drum and bass still pumping in the background. "I can't drive cab, I can't feed my family. It's that simple."

After a quick check of the news media on my phone, I found out the cab driver was telling the truth about the storm, though I was left wondering about the precise nature of the storm itself. Storms didn't come from space. They were born in the Earth's atmosphere. Which meant whatever was coming down over the top of us, it was no storm, but something else entirely.

Like a portal forming.

"Son a bitch," I said, shaking my head, realizing with near certainty that Mr. Black was a lot further on in his plans than I thought. If the portal was forming above the Earth already, that meant it could open at any time, and Rloth could enter this world. And once the Dimension Lord got through, that would be it. There would be no stopping an ancient, primordial being such as Rloth. The powers of such beings were insurmountable, and no mere mortal (or wizard) could ever hope to stand up against one. Unless, like Mr. Black, you offered up human sacrifices.

Taking out my phone, I called Leona. "Creed," she said upon answering. "I take it you're calling about the storm."

"It's not a storm," I said, aware that the cab driver was listening in.

"Well, no one knows what else to call it here. No one has seen anything like it."

"That's because it's a portal, created by you know who."

"Shit."

"How about we're fucked if we don't find a way to close it?"

"And how do we do that, Creed?"

"I don't know. I've never had to close a portal like this before. No one's been fucking insane enough to open one before."

"Creed?" It was Brentwood.

"Brentwood," I said, sighing.

"What are you doing to resolve this situation?"

"I'm doing my best, is what I'm doing."

"You know what this gathering mass is?"

"Gathering mass? It's a portal, but you can think of it as the end of times because that's what's gonna come through that portal once it's fully formed and open."

"What do you need to stop this, Creed?" Brentwood asked. For the first time since I'd known him, he sounded desperate. I couldn't blame him.

"Probably the one thing I don't have. Time."

"Then you'd better find time, Creed, or—" He stopped short.

"You do realize I don't work for you, right?"

"I'm just making sure you know what's at stake here."

"The entire human race," I said, almost laughing, the words underscoring how unbelievably dire the situation had become. The cab driver was frowning at me in the mirror, probably thinking I was mad the way I was talking, or that he had stumbled upon a player in a giant conspiracy.

"That's right," Brentwood said, sounding like the enormity of the situation had just hit him full force as well. "Whatever you need, Creed."

*How about a different father? You got one of those handy?*

"Sure. I'll keep you informed."

"I know you will. In the meantime, I have no choice but to declare a state of emergency in this city. The brass are breathing down my neck, asking how I'm going to fix this. You're the only one I know who can do that, Creed."

"Thanks for the vote of confidence, but—"

"But nothing. The city is already in a panic and it's spreading fast across the whole country. Just tell me what you need and it's yours, Creed."

"Okay, Brentwood. I'll call you when I need you."

"Make sure you do."

Brentwood disconnected us, which pissed me off slightly because I wanted to talk to Leona again. What with the end of the world coming fast, I felt the need to hear her voice in case I never got the chance to again. At the very least, if all became lost, I wanted to be with her at the end.

"That some crazy shit you talking there, man," the cab driver said. "Portals and shit? What you on about, man? It's fucking aliens, ain't it?" He slammed the steering wheel with both hands. "I knew it! It's those gray motherfuckers, right? The ones with the big eyes? What they want, man? You think I'll still be able to drive a cab when they take over? Hey, maybe they let me drive one of their space ships instead, huh? Long as they pay well, who cares, right?"

I shook my head at the cab driver, wondering if everyone was going insane and if the portal had something to do with it. "Yeah, right."

The cab driver shook his head as we finally made it into Freetown. "Fucking aliens, man."

As we drove down a nearly deserted street in East Oakdale, my gaze out the window went to the gable of a building. Spray-painted on the bricks in red were the words: ABANDON ALL HOPE.

Outside the cab, the sky seemed to have darkened dramatically in the last five minutes.

When he dropped me off, the cab driver looked over his shoulder at me and said, "Hey, man. What do you think the aliens eat?"

"Us," I said, staring back at him.

The driver gulped and drove off.

# 4 8

# DEALING WITH THE DEVIL

𝒶 SURPRISE AWAITED me when I got inside in the Sanctum, and not the good kind either. When I walked into the dark living room, I looked left into the kitchen to see Blaze sitting, staring intently at something in the living room, his hackles raised as if in response to a threat. "What's up, Blaze?" I asked him as I wondered what had his attention. His yellow eyes glanced at me briefly and he growled slightly as if to warn me of something. Frowning, I turned to see what Blaze was trying to warn me about, and I caught the outline of someone sitting in the armchair by the window. Assuming it was Sanaka again (as he was the only one who could bypass the locks), I flipped the light switch on the wall and nearly cried out in shock when I saw who was sitting there.

It was a man in a tattered and torn suit, and he looked like he had just been in some sort of accident. He was covered in blood, and his neck was twisted at an odd angle as if it had been broken. I was also horrified to see a jagged length of bone sticking out of one of the man's thighs. Blood dripped down his leg as it pooled around his bare foot. The other foot still had a scuffed black shoe on it. And to top it all off (as if he wasn't gruesome enough looking), one of his eyeballs was hanging out of its socket, resting grotesquely against his blood stained cheek. Hard to guess an age due to the damage to his face, but I put him in his late fifties. The balding head seemed to suggest so anyway.

All I could do was stand there and stare at the broken figure currently staining my armchair and floor with his blood. In a situation like that, it was hard to know what to say. "Who the hell are you?" just didn't seem to cut it, especially when I wasn't even that surprised that a man who looked like a walking corpse was sitting in my living room. Such was my life.

I was glad when he finally spoke first, although his voice didn't seem to match, as it was deep and gravelly like a lid grating on a stone coffin.

"August Creed," the man said, smiling and showing me a mouth full of broken and bloody teeth. "I've been waiting for you."

"I can see that. Who are you?"

The man smiled again, blood spilling out of his mouth as he did so. "Don't you recognize me?"

I didn't until his eyes glowed a deep orange color and then, for just a second, the man was replaced by the demon I had summoned. Baal. "You," I said, not knowing whether to feel relieved or keep feeling worried. "Why are you in that body?"

"It was the first hunk of meat I could find," Baal said. "This man was killed by one of your metal machines. I will find a better hunk of meat when I leave here."

I crossed the room to the drinks cabinet and poured myself a whiskey (and no, I didn't even entertain the ridiculous notion of offering the demon one). "Why do you even need a human vessel?"

"It's been a long time since I played here. Your summoning reminded me of the fun to be had here."

"The fun? I can only imagine."

The demon gave a throaty laugh. "Yes, you can."

I sat down in the other armchair next to the fireplace and gratefully drank some of the whiskey. "There may not even be a world left to play in soon. I take it you know this."

Baal nodded in his meat suit, or tried to, given the state of the man's broken neck. "I am well aware."

"Have you come to honor our deal then? Do you have a lead for me?"

*Careful, Creed. Not so demanding. Remember who you're dealing with.*

"It's not a deal yet," the demon said, his eyes amber again, that unmistakable fire in them. "It becomes a deal when you submit to my terms."

"Which are?" I asked, sipping from my glass, trying to play things cool, which was difficult. The mere presence of the demon in the room was intimidating, to say the least. It could have dragged me right then to the Underworld if it wanted and there wouldn't have been a thing I could do about it. Plus there was that poor man's broken body. His soul was likely trapped around the scene of his accident, a rampaging ball of frustration in the knowledge that a demon had commandeered his body.

Baal rose suddenly but stiffly, horrible cracking sounds and limbs moving at odd angles accompanying that movement, these sights and sounds of rigor mortis telling me the actual owner died between two to six hours ago. Then he rushed toward me at a speed that shouldn't have been possible, zig-zagging across the floor in the blink of an eye. "What do you suppose I want, human?" Baal asked, looming over me as I continued to sit in my chair. When seated he hadn't seemed so tall, but his angry amber eyes now staring down at my still seated ass, reflected a greater accuracy with an intimidating form.

I shook my head, trying to stay calm. "Apart from my soul, I really wouldn't know."

*Please don't ask for my soul. I just got it back.*

"Souls are plentiful. I don't need your soul."

Relief washed over me, though I didn't show it. "What then?"

"I will need you to find something for me."

I frowned. "What, like an object?"

The demon forced its neck forward with a horrible snapping sound. "A human."

"Okay. You want me to find someone. Who?"

"I will let you know." He continued to stare down at me as he licked his bloody lips.

"So the lead then?" I said, wishing the demon would step back away from me, which it didn't. "I don't mean to press you, but finding your human won't even be possible if either I'm dead or there's none of them left to look for, so you know... time is kind of running out here."

"I can tell you where your daddy is at this moment. Will that suffice?"

"You knew all along, didn't you? You knew it was my father."

"Yes."

I didn't ask Baal why he didn't think to tell me before. His tone made it clear that no justification would be forthcoming. "Where is the bastard?"

The demon leant over slowly, snapped his neck down another bit, so his eyes were level with mine, that busted face and dangling eyeball too close for comfort. Then he chuckled, a sound that made my stomach tense. "Your daddy dearest has been right under your nose all along, August Creed."

"Where?" I asked, and he told me where my father was supposedly holed up. My stomach turned over when I realized I now had a location for Mr. Black, which meant there was only one thing left to do, and that was to finally confront the bane of my existence.

"You will hear from me again, August Creed," Baal said as he limped out of the living room and into the hallway, leaving a trail of blood on the floor behind him.

"If I'm still alive," I said, though I don't think he heard me. A moment later, I heard the front door open and then shut again, the demon off to find a new body to have its fun in.

Blaze padded into the living room after Baal had left. He stopped by a large pool of blood on the floor, sniffed it, looked at me and then started lapping it up.

"Nice, Blaze," I said, shaking my head at the wolf. "Real fucking nice."

49
<br>
# FINAL GOODBYE

**A**CCORDING TO BAAL, Mr. Black was just a short distance away from the Sanctum, holed up in an abandoned building. He would no doubt be waiting on the source of most of his power, Rloth, to make an appearance, providing of course that he had done everything he had to in order to get Rloth here in the first place.

I stood in the living room for another few minutes after Baal had left. While Blaze continued licking up blood from the floor, I considered my next move, soon realizing that there was only one move left to make: to battle Mr. Black. There would be no use taking weapons with me as they would all be useless against him, as would any fancy spells. Mr. Black would block them all. He would be using raw black magic against me, unfiltered by any spell, directed by his will alone. That's what it was going to come down to, I knew.

A battle of wills.

His against mine, a battle of dark versus light.

Only Mr. Black was more powerful than me, and I wasn't even sure if my magic would be light enough to counter the darkness in his, especially because I allowed black magic into myself only a few days before. I could still feel it deep in my core like a dormant monster, wanting to feed and grow irrespective of whether I wanted to feed it. I could have gone to Sanaka's and had him do a Purification Ritual, but there simply wasn't time for that. The only thing to do was to trust in my magic and hope it was enough to defeat Mr. Black.

Blaze was staring up at me, having finished with the blood on the floor, an expectant look in his eyes as if he knew something was about to go down. "No point telling you to stay here," I said. "World's going to end anyway if I can't stop you know who." Blaze raised his head and barked once as if to say there was never any doubt that he was going with me. "Gimme a minute. There's a call I have to make."

It was a call I wasn't looking forward to making either. To Leona.

"Hello?" she said upon answering.

"You sound stressed," I said.

"It's chaos here. Brentwood has put the city on lockdown and people are going crazy trying to get out. Plus the President is breathing down his neck, demanding that he find a solution to what's happening. The National Guard are here as well to try and maintain order in the city. You find out anything yet?"

"Eh, no, not yet." I hated lying to her, but I knew how she would react if I told her the truth. She would only gather a small army and rush to back me up, getting everybody killed in the process.

"What about that demon?"

"Nothing, I'm afraid."

"Goddamn it. The portal is getting bigger. We have to close it, Creed, or..."

"I know, or we're all doomed. You don't have to tell me."

"Sorry, it's just..."

"Scary shit?"

"I don't scare easily, but this..."

"You'd be mad not to be afraid," I said, wishing I could be there to see her, to hold her, one final time.

"What are we going to do, Creed?" She sounded like a little girl, and I closed my eyes for a second, trying not to let my emotions get to me. I had to stay strong, for her and everyone else.

"I'm about to look into something that might put an end to this whole thing. I'll have to see."

"What?" she asked hopefully.

"If it pans out, you'll know. If it doesn't—" I paused for a second. "If it doesn't, you'll also know."

"You know where he is, don't you?"

"I—"

"Creed, you have to tell me so we can help you. You can't fucking do this alone."

"I have to go. I love you, Leona. More than you'll ever know."

"Creed—"

I pressed the button to end the call and then turned off the phone completely, tossing it away onto the sofa, my chest heaving with the swell of emotion that had arisen in me. Screwing my eyes shut, I stood for a moment and took a few deep breaths, doing my best to refocus on what I had to do. My eyes opened again when I felt Blaze push his head against my leg. Crouching down, I smoothed the fur around his head and hugged him to me for a minute as he made small empathetic mewling noises. "Looks like its just you and me now, Blaze."

I stood up, straightened my trench coat and placed a hand on top of Blaze's head in preparation for teleporting us to Mr. Black's location. "All right," I said. "Let's go get this bastard, Blaze."

Blaze barked loudly in response, and then we were gone.

# THE LAIR OF MR. BLACK

*T*HE DEMON WASN'T lying when he said that Mr. Black had been right under my nose all along. My father (I really have to stop calling him that...) was using an old, abandoned factory building as his base, which was just a few blocks from where I lived. I teleported Blaze and I to the expanse of waste ground on which the factory stood. In the unnaturally dark sky above the warehouse, a massive hole was forming and growing like a huge tornado might, swirling around and swallowing the sky as it sucked everything into it.

With horror, I watched a gigantic black tentacle extend its way out of the center of the maelstrom, dropping down like a giant worm. Then there was a massive roaring sound which came out of the portal, a sound that chilled me to the bone and made me feel insignificantly small and afraid like a child happening upon an angry giant. It was the sound of coming doom, the sound of Rloth's approach; and contained within that roar was the promise of the unimaginable power that would soon be unleashed. A form of darkness so deep and all-consuming that no one who witnessed it ever lived to tell about it. Rloth is a being of pure destruction, spawned in a place that no mortal mind could ever fully conceive without utterly going mad in the process.

Mad like Mr. Black.

"Dear God," I said, staring up into the churning black sky. Even Blaze whimpered when he heard Rloth's unearthly roar.

Suddenly my mission to stop all this from happening seemed utterly pointless. In the face of such monumentally insane odds, I felt like sitting on the nearest pile of bricks and waiting for the world to end, along with everyone else. I couldn't conceive of anything stopping that thing from coming through to this world, not even if I managed to stop Mr. Black first.

As if to emphasize that doomed feeling in the pit of my stomach, Rloth bellowed that petrifying sound again, rattling me to my very bones. As the roar went on longer this time, it froze me to the spot, and all I could do was gaze up in horror at that gargantuan black tentacle slithering further out of the portal. The thing was mesmerizing in its size and otherworldly darkness. I had seen plenty of things in my lifetime that made me freeze with fear or sick with horror, but this thing above me was beyond comprehension, and thus it scrambled my brain just looking at it. God knows what everyone else was thinking as they saw it.

Speaking of everyone else, I had no doubt the city was in a state of terror as electrical energy got discharged from the portal and arced across the sky in thick reddish forks, striking some of the taller buildings in the city, exploding bricks and shattering glass. At the same time it seemed to knock out most of the power in the city, bringing on a total blackout just to add to the devastation. Also, while this was happening, a constant chorus of screaming could be heard as the city's inhabitants no doubt ran around in a blind panic, probably thinking they were all going to die horribly. Which they most assuredly would, if I didn't manage to stop Mr. Black.

It was only Blaze barking beside me that pulled me out of my trance-like state. He was standing just in front of me, looking toward the old factory in the center of the waste ground. When I followed Blaze's line of sight, I saw a dark form that seemed to be hovering over the top of the factory. As I looked harder, I saw the form wasn't hovering, but growing from within the factory itself. A huge, black mass on which stood a tall figure that could have been the silhouette of a demon with horns pointing out the side of its head. Only I knew it wasn't a demon, but Mr. Black. He had transformed himself, become the physical representation of the darkness that lay within his soul.

*That bastard is the cause of everything*, I thought, as anger surged through me. Even if there was no stopping Rloth, I could still try to put an end to Mr. Black once and for all.

What did I have to lose anyhow?

Nothing, at that point.

Placing a hand on Blaze's head, I teleported us both inside the lair of Mr. Black.

# 51

# GRASPING HANDS

*T*HE INSIDE OF the factory was warm and sickening in its suffocating humidity, which was entirely down to the thick, pitch black tar like substance that covered every wall and ceiling. The stinking, glistening residue of Mr. Black's dark magic, the same residue that covered Hans Belger's tower at the Devil's Playground. The continually undulating, shifting substance also gave off a stink that was stomach churning in its intensity. As soon as I entered the broken front doors of the old factory, the stench from inside seemed to jump straight down my throat to make a grab for my guts, churning them up until I had no choice but to vomit.

"Jesus Christ," I said, in between choking and fighting every instinct I had to turn and run back outside. It was like entering the foulest of sewers, and a place you would only go into if you had no choice. Beside me, Blaze sneezed once. That was the height of his reaction (well, what do you expect from an animal that laps the blood of corpses off the floor?).

As much as I wanted to flee that place of pure evil, I forced myself to cross what was once the reception area of the factory. I then started walking down a corridor that I hoped would take me to Mr. Black. It was difficult even to see where I was going thanks to the light-sucking black magic residue. Luckily Blaze was walking just in front of me though, his head and body now veined with red fire that gave off enough light to just about see by. I had never been so glad to have him with me as we walked together into the heart of darkness, the possibility of death for the both us seeming more and more likely the closer we got to Mr. Black.

Every now and again, a mighty roar would sound from outside as Rloth continued to announce his presence and our coming destruction, the roar shaking the very foundations of the old factory. If it wasn't for the residue covering all the walls, the factory would have likely collapsed under the sheer reverberating force of his guttural roar.

With Blaze lighting the way, I continued to edge my way further down the corridor. Or at least I did, until the wall in front of me stretched the way it would if a face and head were seeking to push their way out through the black vinyl appearance of the wall, from the inside out. I stared at the face as it turned toward me, its mouth opening to issue a tortured moaning sound like it was trapped in the worst place imaginable and knew it was never escaping—much like how I felt at that moment. Then another face stretched out of the opposite wall, along with a hand that tried to grab me. In seconds, there were faces pushing out everywhere, hands grasping at me, making it impossible to move any further.

*What the hell are these things?*

Then I realized, as much as I wished I hadn't: they were the souls of the people murdered by Mr. Black. Scores of them all around me, their desperate cries and moans coming from all directions. Before I knew it, I was being held tight by numerous pairs of hands stretching from the walls and ceiling. Fingers dug into me, clawed at my face, caused me to cry out in panic.

Blaze was in front of me and snapping at any hands daring enough to reach for him, his alighting coat and snapping jaws making quick work of them, often turning the wallow of despair to the cry of a more painful tune. Any hands that did manage to touch him got immediately burned, which again caused the grasping appendages to pull away from him. Then he rushed forward and started biting at the arms and hands that had a hold of me, but there were too many for him to deal with, and for every one he removed another was ready to take its place. When I felt one of those hands clamp over my face, covering my mouth and nose, I knew I had to do something. I'd been refraining from using my magic thus far because I knew I'd need as much as I could get when I found Mr. Black, but desperate times and all that.

Focusing on my magic, I pulled back on it like an archer pulling on a bow, and then I let it go, releasing a blast of blue energy that cleared away all the hands, and which also sent Blaze skidding across the floor. He recovered quickly, though, and I urgently beckoned him to rush down the corridor with me. He recovered quickly, though, and I urgently beckoned him to hurry as I rushed down the corridor before any more grasping souls could get a hold of me.

When we finally got to the end of the corridor, we turned up another hallway that looked like it might lead to the center of the factory, but the hallway was already criss-crossed with scores of arms and hands and wailing heads. There was no way I would make it down there, not without getting stuck again. It would take a long blast of magic to cut back all those limbs. But I was reluctant to use any more magic than I already had, because I knew I'd need every ounce I had for the coming battle ahead.

Thankfully, Blaze lived up to his name and moved in front of me as he cranked up the length and intensity of the flames spurting out of the red veins on his body, until he was completely covered by scorching fire. I stayed as close as I could to him as he moved up the long corridor, burning back the limbs and faces that stretched out of the walls, the souls wailing as they got burnt by his elemental fire.

Minutes later, Blaze burst through a set of double doors, and we crashed through into a massive open space containing mangled machinery pushed against all the walls as if it had been swept aside by a powerful force.

Which of course it had. That powerful force was currently in the middle of the room, raised high upon a dais of what looked to be black tentacles or miniaturized versions of Rloth's own, those currently pulling him inexorably toward our destruction. Standing upon the dais, however, with tentacles moving it along the floor as if at his will, was the nightmare instigating that terror: none other than Mr. Black.

Or at least it used to be, because the figure standing atop that undulating black mass didn't look like any version of Mr. Black that I had yet seen. The evil bastard had now triumphantly transformed into a demon-like figure that was as black as his magic excretion, with two long, twisting horns. There was barely even a recognizable face there anymore, just two glowing green eyes set against a faceless black mask. He seemed also to have acquired a trident from somewhere, to complete the whole demonic look. There was no doubt the bastard was intimidating, raised so high off the ground, the roof blown apart to reveal the swirling portal, and the ever lengthening black tentacle belonging to Rloth: Eater Of Worlds.

When he spotted me standing there, Demon Black moved his dais forward, spreading his arms out in greeting, or as if to say, "Look at all I've achieved!"

"August!" he bellowed above the noise of the maelstrom outside, and the continued deafening roar of Rloth. "You have come to witness the end. Welcome!" The voice of the black demon was deep and guttural, but I still heard my father's voice in there. It was still him underneath everything.

To say I was afraid would have been an understatement. The coming of Rloth was terrifying enough, but having to face Mr. Black in his new demonic form was a terrifying prospect. Especially when he spoke with my father's brutal authority, that somehow only made me feel like a child again, completely dominated by his father's will. It was only Blaze's loud barking that shook me out of my fearful state.

*Don't let him intimidate you!* I thought. *He's nothing more than a bully, always has been!*

Which was true, but that didn't make him any less scary...or dangerous.

"Stop this!" I shouted, the apparent confidence in my own voice giving me strength. "Or I will!"

*Demon* Black laughed, a sound that seemed to echo all the way from my childhood, making me feel small and insignificant. "Oh, August," he said, aiming his trident at me. "When will you ever learn that your father knows best?"

He blasted me with dark red energy then, which shot out of the tip of his trident and hit me hard in the chest, lifting me off my feet and bouncing me off the wall behind.

As I lay there groaning, only a single thought crossed my mind: This shit is going to hurt.

# 52

# DARK MAGIC RISING

*A*S I PICKED myself up off the ground, supporting my chest just to be able to breathe and move through the pain, Demon Black scuttled toward me atop his viscous mass of darkness; that self-satisfied bellowing once again originating from his throat. "You are weak, August," he said. "I thought I made you stronger than that. Obviously, I was wrong."

Anger rose in me, and I straightened up. "Firstly you megalomaniacal madman," I shot back. "My name's Creed to you, you fucking sociopath...and secondly you old bastard, the only fucking thing you ever gave any of us, was unadulterated misery. We all hated you, even Mother."

A growl issued from him and he jabbed his trident at me again. "I gave you power! All of you! You would be nothing now without me!"

"They *are* nothing thanks to you!" I strode forward, my rage trampling down whatever fear I felt before. "They're all dead!"

His burning red eyes glared at me. "Don't worry, August. You will be joining them soon." He laughed as he looked up towards the sky just as Rloth gave another rumbling roar, which sounded much closer now, vibrating the very ground I stood on. "Everyone will!"

Blaze stood a few feet from me, his whole body a mass of flame as he growled at the demon. As I conjured a swirling ball of blue energy in my right hand, Blaze turned his head towards me, and I nodded at him. Then, as Demon Black stared in awe at his master breaking through the portal, I fired the ball of energy at him, catching him off-guard and just below the chest, knocking him back a few feet; but not much more, and not nearly enough for there to be any current impression that I would win this battle on a toe-to-toe basis of my own magical repertoire versus his own.

At the same time, Blaze cranked his elemental heat and sprinted right into the twisting mass of tentacles beneath our quarry. With Demon Black's glare steady on me, preparing to retaliate in kind, Blaze penetrated the ectoplasmic mass and burnt right through it like acid through metal, causing Demon Black to cry out in shock, and what sounded promisingly like pain to me.

As Blaze continued boring his way, Demon Black vented a cry of angry frustration as he shifted backwards at speed, exposing Blaze as he continued to destroy the mass. With trident in hand, he used telekinesis to trap and raise Blaez, so that he bucked and swished at nothing but air as he sought to escape the force holding him in place.

To try and save Blaze, I fired another blast of magic at Demon Black, but he merely held out his free hand and stopped it midair before launching it back at me. As the blast sphere was made up off my own magic, I was able to catch it in my hand without much trouble, intending to fire it straight back.

But Demon Black was a step ahead as he suddenly swung his trident in my direction. The next thing I knew, a massive fireball in the form of Blaze was hurtling towards me, moving so fast that I barely had time to get an energy shield up to protect myself. A howling Blaze slammed right into me, knocking me down onto the floor, his flames scalding my face and neck. I screamed in pain and managed to push Blaze off me, my demon skin trench coat thankfully absorbing most of the wolf's fierce heat.

It was then that I saw the trident come screaming through the air like a deadly missile, before piercing Blaze's body right through and pinning him to the ground. Blaze howled in pain as sparks and flames flew up around him, so much so that there was no way I could get near him to even try and pull out the trident. Blaze was stuck there to the floor, blood that was orange like lava seeping out of him as he gradually stopped moving and finally lay still.

"No!" I screamed, turning in a rage to glare at Demon Black, who had now detached himself from the ectoplasmic mass. He then came striding towards me, dark, leather-like clothing covering his even darker form, his eyes seeming to burn ever fiercer as he fixed me in his sights. Clearly, he was done with messing around.

But so was I.

Shooting an arm out in his direction, I used it to focus a spell I was inwardly reciting, channeling the growing magic down my arm and into my hand where it formed into a yellowed mass of bright energy.

"Your spells will not work on me," Demon Black said, stopping several feet away. "Your power is pitiful compared to mine."

*Always with the arrogance. Son of a bitch.*

The spell I was crafting as quickly as I could was a Medusa Spell that would hopefully paralyze the demon completely, long enough for me to use a Destruction Spell on his rotten soul.

Uttering the final few words of the spell, I cast it at Demon Black, focusing every ounce of conviction I had into it, causing Demon Black to suddenly begin to tense up on the spot. He tried to move his arms out from himself but couldn't. His legs no longer worked either as I slowly came towards him, forcing the spell to do its work.

"No!" Demon Black growled as his whole body froze up and went still like he was made out of stone.

When I saw that he couldn't even open his mouth to speak anymore, I halted the spell, satisfied that it had done its job.

Another mighty roar came from up above, and a large section of the roof got ripped off in the violent maelstrom. Soon, the portal would give off so much energy that it would rip up anything that was beneath it, sucking it into that black hole, including me.

"Time to end this," I said, standing close to the paralyzed Demon Black. "Time to erase you from existence completely. Time for you to pay for your sins, *Father*." I practically spat that last word in his face, hating him so much at that moment that it all but consumed me, and in the process, stirred up the residual black magic that still lay deep within me. I could see in his eyes that he could see what was happening to me, and if he could have smiled, he probably would have.

As I stared at him with hatred and malice in my eyes, I felt the dark magic grow within me, spreading through my body, demanding to be set free.

It *would* be set free, because I was going to use it to destroy Demon Black, once and for all!

# 53

# SUFFERING DEFEAT

THE POWER FLOWING through me was terrific in its intensity, even more consuming than it was the last time I allowed it to come forth. It was like it was reacting to the other forms of dark magic around me, that which came from Rloth and Demon Black. Somehow it was feeding off those influences, wanting nothing more than to merge with them, and thus become stronger.

As the black magic coursing through me filled every pore, I found myself conjuring a spell without even thinking about it, without ever having known the spell. It just seemed to come from nowhere, a force of intent fueled by hatred and rage which I began to direct at Demon Black, who was still paralyzed and couldn't do a thing about it. Utterly consumed now by the dark power flowing through me, I stepped right up to him and plunged my hands into his chest, gripping and pulling at the darkness contained within as I searched for his soul, intending to rip it out and obliterate it when I found where it was hiding.

Then Demon Black did something I wasn't expecting.

He laughed, before grabbing both my arms and pulling my hands out of his chest with little effort, his green eyes gleefully staring at me the whole time, enjoying the look of shock on my face. "Did you really think you could beat me that easily, boy?" he said, forcing my hands down and holding them there, his horned head almost touching mine as he spoke. "You thought you could beat me with darkness? Boy, I *am* the darkness!"

As Rloth seemed to roar in agreement, Demon Black's hands shot up and wrapped themselves around my throat. Then he lifted me off the ground and dangled me there—like a freshly caught rabbit—as he began to squeeze, his chitin hands cutting off the oxygen supply to my brain. I struggled against his grip, but with my legs kicking uselessly above the floor, there was nothing I could do except look at his demonic face as he squeezed the life out of me, knowing that I had failed and that he had won. Even the black magic still coursing through me seemed to laugh at my predicament, as if it had gleefully misled me, edging me toward the life threatening situation the whole time; which of course it had, as its desire for death never excludes its wielder entirely.

Then, as I was seconds away from losing consciousness, a strange thing happened. A memory popped into my head, unbidden in the closing blackness. Not exactly a life flashing before my eyes moment, this was like someone had reached in from somewhere and purposefully planted that memory there for me to see.

The memory itself was a long forgotten conversation I had with my mother when I was a teenager. She had come into my room one day and saw that I was reading a book on black magic, a book that my father demanded I read to get a more balanced view of magic. When my mother came and sat down—her long, wavy red hair spilling over the summer dress she was wearing, a placid smile on her face as usual—she said I had to be careful of such books because they had a habit of drawing you in with the promise of power, but at the expense of your soul.

"But the spells seem to be so much more powerful, the magic stronger than the magic we practice," I said.

My mother smiled patiently. "It only seems that way, August. Light magic will always defeat darker magic."

"Always?" I was skeptical, as I was about a lot of things.

"If done right, yes, always."

"But wouldn't it be better to fight dark magic with the same?"

She took hold of my hand, and her blue eyes went serious. "You cannot fight hatred with hatred, or stand up against rage with rage. Darkness does not extinguish darkness, August, it begets it. Only light can banish the darkness. Always remember that."

My mother's kind face faded from view as the memory dispersed. But that was okay because I knew what to do now. Or something inside me knew what to do the whole time, some kernel of light in the very core of my being that seemed to activate, like it had been waiting on me to connect with it, to trust in its light.

Despite being nearly dead a moment ago, my consciousness returned all at once. At the same time, a warm light spread fast around my body, infiltrating my entire being as it canceled out every bit of the black magic that had overcome me.

My mother was right. You can't fight hatred with hatred, and you can't fight darkness with darkness.

When this realization sunk in, my body relaxed all at once. All tension was banished and a comforting lightness of being took over.

I opened my eyes and looked calmly at the demon who was once my father. Demon Black looked shocked for a moment when he saw into my eyes, which must have been a window to the pure light magic that filled every part of me. His next reaction was to squeeze his hands harder, but no matter how hard he squeezed, he didn't seem able to apply any pressure. Smiling, I took hold of his cold fingers and pried them from around my neck, my feet touching the ground again a second later.

"No," he growled, staring at me with increased hate and rage in his face before letting fly with a punch at my chest.

"*Yes*," I said back, catching his fist in my hand as easily as if I was catching a child's fist. "I'm done with hating you. I'm done with allowing you to shroud me in darkness...*Father.*"

I pushed his arm back toward him, and before he knew what was happening, I rushed forward and jammed my other hand right inside his chest. There was no malice or aggression in my actions, just a calm sense of purpose and the certain knowledge of what needed to be done.

Demon Black howled as my hand dug around inside him, in search of his black soul. He grabbed my arm with both hands and tried to pull my hand out, but I was able to resist him without much trouble, as if he had lost all his dark power and was now just a frail old man again.

Above us, Rloth let out a mighty roar that sounded different to the previous ones. I doubted a timeless being like Rloth felt anything approximating an emotion, but his roar sounded to me like one of anger, and perhaps even fear, for the monster undoubtedly knew that if Demon Black's soul was annihilated, so too would his connection to the portal.

Still staring calmly into the increasingly worried face of Demon Black as he kept struggling to break free of me, I continued to search around inside him for his soul. I should explain that I wasn't rummaging through his guts, as you might think. I was searching instead within his spiritual essence, the realm of pure energy that the soul puts out, also known as the metaphysical realm. Depending on the person, such inner realms could be vast, or they could be shrunken if the outlook of the person was narrow and unenlightened enough. Demon Black's inner realm was as vast as any I've encountered before. It was also made up almost totally of darkness, which made it difficult for me to feel out his soul.

"You think you can defeat me, boy?" Demon Black bellowed, his eyes burning madly in their dark sockets, spilling over in rage. "*YOU WILL NOT DEFEAT ME!*"

A massive blast of energy then issued from Demon Black, so powerful it pushed me out of him and right across the warehouse floor, before landing on the concrete floor to wonder in a confused daze about what the hell just happened. Before I could even get a groan out of my mouth, or try to sit up, a searing pain hit my entire body all at once. My body bucked up off the floor like ten thousand volts of electricity was going through me, and through the pain, I glimpsed my father's outstretched hands as red, crackling energy shot from them. I screamed as the unbearable burning pain continued, and after long seconds, it felt like my insides were beginning to melt.

Then, blessedly, the pain stopped as suddenly as it had started.

Demon Black stood over me. "You almost had me," he said. "I'll give you that. But like I said, you will never defeat me, boy. For all your light magic, you're still a shadow under me. Everyone is." His dark form came closer, eclipsing my entire vision. "I'm not going to kill you, boy. I'll just let the great Rloth consume you along with everyone else on this pathetic planet."

Demon Black then walked away whilst laughing in his triumph, and all I could do was close my eyes in defeat and agony, and wait for the world to end.

# SOMETIMES THEY COME BACK

"*A*UGUST."

IT WAS the third time the voice had spoke. My eyes were still closed, but I vaguely recognized the soft Irish accent. My mother's voice, which must have been some auditory hallucination, as I lay barely conscious with the darkness coming down steadily upon me...and the rest of the world.

"Open your eyes, August. The world needs you."

My mother's voice sounded clearer this time, and something in me said, *Hey, what the hell. Might as well.*

I opened my eyes, and there was a shimmering, transparent figure standing over me. After blinking a few times to clear my vision, I saw the figure was indeed my mother. "Mother," I said with a smile. "You've come to help me on my way."

"No, August," a different voice said, and I turned my head to see the translucent figure of my beautiful sister, Roisin standing there, wearing one of her pretty summer dresses that she used to wear, her long, dark locks flowing down over it.

"Roisin?" I said, confused, but delighted to see her, even if she was ephemeral.

"You have to get up, Gus. You have to stand up to him."

I shook my head. "But I can't. He's too powerful."

"Gus!" Standing directly in front of me now was my older brother, Fergal, wearing the shirt, trousers and waistcoat combo we grew up having to wear every day. His swarthy features were as dashing as I remembered. "Stop pissing about, will ya? Get yourself up!"

"Fergal," I said in wonder, finally sitting up (albeit painfully). "You're here as well."

"Jesus Christ," Fergal said. "Did you get hit on the head or something?"

"No. Maybe," I said as I looked at all three of them, from one to the other, with sheer joy. "You're all here. I've missed you all so much..." Tears rolled down my cheeks, and they all looked at each other like it was painful for them to be there. "How are you all here?"

"That doesn't matter, August," my mother said. "But you have to listen to us."

"You have to stop him, Gus," Roisin said. "He's going to end the world."

I couldn't help but be pissed off they were even mentioning the monster who was currently hovering near the hole in the roof, singing his deranged praises to his coming master of darkness. "Why are you talking about him? Are you not here to take me with you to wherever you've been all this time? Is it some sort of Heaven? A different dimension? I've tried so many times over the years to locate all your souls, but I couldn't—"

"Enough, Gus!" Fergal shouted, floating his shimmering, silvery head right close to mine. "Your place is still here. You aren't going anywhere yet, you here me? Instead, you're going to get back up, and then you're going to finish that bastard off. You got that, little brother?"

"But how, Fergal?" I asked him.

He pulled back, and Roisin's head was suddenly there in front of me now. "You find that light again, Gus."

"I tried that."

"No," she said, shaking her head. "Find the light that kept us together, Gus. The light that helped us survive that tyrant for so many years."

"But you didn't," I said.

"We're still here, aren't we?" Fergal said. "We're just in a different place now, that's all."

"Where? I want to go there with you."

"Stop being daft, Gus, and bloody listen," Fergal said in that big brother way I missed so much. "This battle is not about how much power you have, but the *kind* of power you have. You have a kind of power he could never have because it would destroy him."

"Love," Roisin said.

"*Our* love, son" my mother said.

"It's what used to hold us together," Fergal said. "It still does. Use it, Gus. Use it to defeat him."

I shook my head. "How?"

Rloth bellowed an almighty roar just then, and it seemed to ripple right through my family's ephemeral forms

"You'll find a way, August," my mother said, just as all three of them started to fade from view, as if someone was turning down a dimmer switch on them.

"Wait, don't go!" I said, springing to my feet.

But a second later, they had disappeared back to wherever they came from. I stared sadly at the empty air for a moment, crushed that my family had gone from my life once more.

Then, in my head, I heard my big brother's voice as if he was still there. "Stop your whining, Gus," he said, "and get the hell on with it. We love you."

"I love you too..."

## 55

# CONSUMED

*W*HILE I WAS speaking to my family (or their Astral forms—I still hadn't had time to process what had just occurred), Demon Black was still hovering up by the hole in the roof, using his dark magic to rapidly accelerate Rloth's entry into the world. Pure black energy belted out from his hands as he channeled it into the portal, ensuring the portal expanded and tore the sky further, so the great Rloth could fit through. Rloth's giant tentacle protruded from the mouth of the portal, looking like it belonged to some monstrous Kraken. However monstrous it was, I knew it wouldn't be anywhere near as monstrous as the rest of Rloth. Few people had ever laid eyes on a being like Rloth and lived to tell about it. Beings such as Rloth tended to live in the deepest, most primordial parts of the universe, unless, like Rloth, they created their own dimension for whatever reason. One of the oldest grimoires in my Sanctum, contains pages that hold a few rough sketches of beings like Rloth, and I can tell you right now that none of them are pretty to look at. If you want to know the kind of creature about to spill through that portal like a defective birth, then go and read Lovecraft, a fellow magicslinger. His descriptions of Cthulhu and the rest are based on fact.

So this was it, the last stand before the world ended: me against my demon father and an ancient being with power beyond imagination. You gotta love those odds.

I wasn't even sure at the time what I was going to do to stop Demon Black. There was no real plan in my head, so I decided just to go with the flow and see what happened. Although it did occur to me that fighting against Demon Black and his dark power wouldn't get me anywhere, and indeed, would only exacerbate the problem. The more I fought against him, the stronger he seemed to get. So now it was time to go all Gandhi on his ass and see where that got me.

The words of my family were still fresh in my head, telling me to tap into the love and compassion that kept us all together. The more I focused on this, the more I remembered the terrific strength and bond that came with those feelings we had for each other, especially in the face of my father's tyrannical and abusive behavior.

"Father!" I shouted, refusing to let any fear arise in me. Even when Demon Black spun around to glare at me, I focused on maintaining that sense of love and inner calm that I felt in the presence of my family. I knew above all else, that I had to trust in them the same way I did as a kid, trusting the light would always be there for me to turn to; even when darkness was all around.

Demon Black's leather smock billowed underneath him in the tornado-like winds that were gathering pace outside. His face changed when he realized there was something different about me. Which there was.

I was no longer afraid of him.

"Boy!" he shouted, his face twisting in anger. "Why do you never learn?"

I smiled at him then. "See, that's always been your problem, father," I said. "You always thought I didn't learn anything. But I did learn. I learned exactly what kind of man you were. I learned about everything you are doing now. But most of all father, I have learned how to finally defeat you."

Demon Black glared at me for another few seconds, then let out a scream of pure rage as he came barreling down through the air toward me, his hands thrust out so he could direct his dark energy right into me. When it infiltrated my body, I made no move to fight or to counter the attack with one of my own. A part of me wanted to, of course, the part of me that wanted to react only out of fear, but I wouldn't let it. The only thing I focused on was the light inside me, the light that grew from my love for my family, and from my joy at seeing them again after all those years. My father could never break that love when he was still human, even when he sacrificed them all to that demon. He may have destroyed their bodies, but their love remained.

Inside of me.

A black mass of undulating energy was beginning to build up around me as Demon Black continued to fuel it with his rage. A dark, wet mass that spread up over my body like a rapidly growing fungus. "May the darkness consume you...*son*," Demon Black said with a sneer on his face. A sneer that almost disappeared once I smiled calmly back at him.

"Creed!"

The shout came from behind me, and I recognized the voice instantly. It was Leona. Somehow she had found me.

I quickly turned around to see where she was before the dark mass running up my whole body prevented me from doing so.

There she was, standing just past the doors, her two Berettas pointed out in front of her, her face constantly changing as she tried to take in what was happening to me. When she realized I would soon be overcome by the dark mass enveloping me, her face relayed her devastation as she realized I was going to die.

Then, before I knew it, the creeping blackness had reached my face, and I was trapped in that twisted position as I looked around at the woman I loved more than anyone else in the world. I took that love, and I added it to the beacon of light within me, making it stronger, brighter.

"Creed," Leona mouthed again, tears streaming down her face, at which point her expression changed quickly to one of pure anger, as she then rushed forward, rapidly firing both of her Berettas at Demon Black, all the while screaming as if doing so would make the bullets hit harder. It was a magnificent sight, seeing the woman I love in full badass mode, firing those guns like the incredible soldier she was. She had never looked sexier as she kept advancing forward, no doubt every one of her bullets hitting Demon Black, but undoubtedly having no effect on him whatsoever.

Immensely proud, I continued to smile at Leona and her heroic actions, right up until I became engulfed completely by the black, suffocating mass, and I could see no more.

# 56

# LIGHT AGAINST DARK

*T*rapped in that thick mass of undulating darkness, I felt it worm its way into my every pore as it tried to consume every part of me, including my immortal soul.

And I let it. I let the darkness seep into me. Resisting it would have made it stronger while also weakening the light magic that continued to grow with it.

So I merely relaxed (which wasn't so easy, given that I was trapped in a suffocating cocoon) and trusted that the light magic would save me.

The whole time, I focused on, a mental picture of those family members in whom I love, and the love I have for Leona. All the people that I loved the most in the world (I think even Uncle Ray was in that mental picture somewhere, skulking reluctantly in the background with Sanaka, like reluctant subjects in a family photo).

Then I felt it. A steady vibration that seemed to emanate from my core, as the light finally opened itself up, and began to break down the darkness all around me, as it extinguished it all with its divine illumination.

The dark magic resisted, screeching and squirming all around me, but the more it resisted, the deeper the light magic penetrated into it, eventually neutralizing and consuming it like it had never been brought forth in the first place.

At some point, I opened my eyes to find myself standing within a sphere of utterly beautiful bright light that had all sorts of colors (cobalt blues, sparkling reds, deep yellows and purples and oranges), swirling and crackling through it. It was like I was standing within the source of all creation, the source of all love in the universe. My soul cried out in joy as the light seemed to heal me on every level.

And then my eyes fell upon Leona, who was still standing by the doors, crying, a look of disbelief on her face, but also unmistakable joy and relief that I was alive. More than alive. *Illuminated.* A conduit for the divine, and no doubt the closest she's ever seen and been to divine angelic grace, the sort of light present at the humblest beginnings of creation in this realm.

Then I turned around to face the biggest source of darkness and pain I had ever known.

My father.

Demon Black.

He was no longer in his demon form. Instead, he had taken on his old form of Christopher McCreedy; the tall, gray-haired man in the dark suit that I always remembered him to be. His face was full of fear. "My boy," he said, flabbergasted by what was happening, by the power of the light issuing from me. It killed him even to look at me as the darkness in him was so repulsed by the light. Even Rloth increased the frequency and pitch of his ear-splitting roars. The ancient being of darkness could sense the light below it, and it was afraid of its power.

I held my hands out. "Come to me, father," I said with only love in my voice. "Come to me, and we can end this darkness."

My father shook his head. "No! Never! Rloth will come! The world will end! I shall ascend as a higher power!"

The placid smile on my face widened. "No, father. You won't."

Tendrils of arcing light suddenly sprang forth from me like vines from a tree, attaching themselves to the body of my father, who screamed and struggled and tried to bring forth his dark magic again. But whenever he did, the magic was immediately snuffed out by the greater force of mine. The tendrils of light then pulled my father toward me, holding him at arm's length.

"Please, August," he said, genuinely afraid now. "I'm your father. Please don't do this."

Reaching out a hand, I gently stroked his cheek. "I should probably thank you. If it weren't for you, I wouldn't have gotten a visit from Mother and Fergal and Roisin."

His eyes widened, and I thought I saw a hint of guilt, something I had never seen in them before. "You saw them?"

I nodded. "They convinced me I could defeat you. And I have."

Before he even realized what I was doing, my hand had slipped gently inside his chest, emerging a few seconds later with a hard ball of darkness in the palm of my hand.

My father's blackened soul.

He looked aghast when he saw his own soul held up before his eyes, and he started shaking his head, even tried to grab it back. But a tendril of light entwined around his wrist and stopped him.

"What goes around, comes around, father," I said. "With all your power and knowledge, you would think you would know that."

"August, please!" It was the first time I had ever seen him truly afraid. His normal psychopathic confidence had been shattered, and it rattled him to the core to see that I held his very life and soul in the palm of my hand. He had been on the cusp of gaining unimaginable power, and now it was all about to be taken away from him.

A terrifically bright white light began to beam from the palm of my hand so it could engulf the blackened thing I held. My father screamed as the light began to eat at his soul. "I do this out of love, father," I said. "Not for you, but for Mother, Fergal, Roisin and all the other innocent souls you murdered since."

"NO!" Rays of bright white light began to shoot out of my father's body. The more of his soul that disappeared, the more light erupted from him, until all at once, his entire body exploded in a massive flash of blinding brightness, just as his soul did the same in my hand as it was finally reduced to nothingness.

I could hardly believe it, but my father and his rancid soul were now wiped out of existence.

Forever.

# 5 7

# RESURRECTION

*N*EEDLESS TO SAY, the great Rloth roared out his dissent (to put it mildly) as soon as the monster realized its portal to Earth would be snuffed out of existence along with the power that was keeping it open in the first place. And as I stared up through the huge hole in the roof at the tumultuous sky and the swirling portal directly above me, I couldn't help but breathe a sigh of relief when I saw that gigantic black tentacle begin to retract back inside the portal as the portal itself started to shrink in size.

*Better luck next time, Rloth.*

"Creed!" Leona ran up and threw her arms around me, and I hugged her tight as I shut my eyes, so glad to have her in my embrace again. Something that, for a while there, I thought I would never do again.

When she finally broke our embrace, Leona stared up into the sky through the gaping hole in the roof, a look of near wonder on her face as she tried to comprehend the otherworldliness of what she was seeing. "Is it going back to where it came from?"

"Yes," I said. "Without He Who Shall Not Be Named around anymore, the portal can't stay open. Thankfully, for us."

She smiled and then suddenly pounded me on the chest with both fists. "That's for going in here alone and not even telling me where you were going."

"He would have killed you, Leona. You know that."

She shook her head. "When we get out of here, I'm having a drink with you."

"A real one?"

She nodded. "I think I've earned it after surviving this shitstorm."

I went to smile, but a sudden thought kept the smile from my face. "Blaze!" I said, suddenly remembering the Garra Wolf.

Before I could run to find my loyal companion, however, Leona grabbed my arm. "Creed." She shook her head. "I don't think he's—"

"*No.*" I emphatically shook my head. "Not Blaze. He's stronger than that. No way."

Pulling out of her grip, I hurriedly crossed the factory floor to the far end of the room where Blaze still lay motionless, the trident that had stabbed him now gone along with all other traces of Demon Black (except for the devastation the bastard left behind).

Tendrils of smoke still rose off Blaze's lifeless body. Blood that was a dark orange color pooled around the floor, seeping out of the three large holes on either side of his ribs. Staring down at the wolf, it felt like my guts had spilt onto the floor when I realized with sickening certainty that Blaze was dead.

"I'm sorry, Creed," Leona said, her hand on my shoulder. "I know how much he meant to you."

"How much he means to me," I said, steadfastly refusing to accept the fact that there wasn't something I could do to bring Blaze back. It was my fault he was dead, and he died protecting and serving me, the person who was supposed to keep him safe. "I'm not letting him go. Not like this. He deserved better."

"He died defending you."

"Exactly." I stared down at Blaze's unmoving body as a sense of stubborn determination began to fill me. "Leona, go check on the portal, see if it's still closing."

"What are you going to do?"

"I'm going to bring my friend back to life."

Leona said nothing as she nodded and walked away, though I knew she thought I was being overoptimistic out of grief. Maybe so, but I couldn't just let Blaze die without at least trying to bring him back. I owed the wolf that much.

Kneeling on the floor, I reached out and gently stroked Blaze's still warm body, unable to keep from sighing when I felt how lifeless he was. "Don't worry, Blaze," I whispered. "I'm gonna bring you back, buddy. It's just you and me against the world, remember? I need you back here with me, buddy...okay?"

I wiped away the tears streaming down my cheeks as I forced myself to focus on the magic still flowing through me, the same light magic I had used to defeat Demon Black earlier. If I could channel some of that same magic into Blaze before it dissipated altogether (as it surely would, for such powerful magic does not hang around for long), I thought there might be a good chance of saving my once faithful companion. Bringing a body back to life again was not something I had ever done. It wasn't the same thing as reanimating a corpse after the soul had departed the body, as with Necromancy. That was just like turning on a machine. Restoring life to a body in which the soul still resided was a different matter. Too much could go wrong (changes in the mind of the recipient usually, and not good ones), which is why I had always refrained from trying it.

Closing my eyes, I entered the Chaosphere and quickly went about channeling and shaping the magic into the form I needed it to be in. At the same time, I began chanting the words to the spell. The spell itself was Japanese in origin, so that's the language I spoke it in while I continued to focus everything I had on shaping the remaining light magic that still resided in me. Then, when I was ready, and the magic was formed, I allowed it to course out through my hands and directly into Blaze's dead body.

The magic itself was invigorating, so full of life and brimming with the possibilities of creation. A blissful smile appeared on my face, despite the grief I was trying to keep down. When such powerful light magic flowed freely through you, it felt like you were channeling the source of all creation and that there was nothing you couldn't do with it. Even bring life back to the dead.

When I had said the last few words of the spell, I opened my eyes and concentrated further on the bluish-white energy coursing out of my hands, and which now surrounded Blaze's body, contrasting sharply with the deep orange blood still on the floor.

Then after a moment, I felt something.

Blaze's body bucked slightly as if I had just given him a jolt of electricity. Then it bucked again, more violently this time, so hard that I had to hold him down. "Come on, Blaze! You can do this! Come back to me, buddy!"

I watched in joyful wonder as the wounds in his side started to close over until they disappeared like they were never there in the first place, and I thought to myself, *Yes, he's alive again, he's come back to me!*

But then Blaze's body went suddenly still again. "NO!"

"Did it work?" Leona asked, now standing behind me.

I shook my head in confusion as I took my hands off Blaze's body, the last of the light magic now gone from me. It didn't make sense. The spell should have worked. The magic should have worked! It was working, so what happened? I clamped both hands over my mouth and nose, unable to understand why I had failed.

Then, just as tears stung at my eyes again, Blaze moved, his ribs rising almost imperceptibly at first, then more noticeably as air began to fill his lungs. "Blaze!" I put my head down next to his just as the wolf opened its eyes. "Yes, Blaze, you're alive, buddy, you came back to me, Oh God, you came back..."

A huge smile appeared on my face as joy flooded into me. The big bastard rolled over and then stood up as if it hadn't just been dead a moment ago and was now looking at us wondering what all the fuss was about. As Blaze came forward, he put his head on my shoulder, rubbing his fur against my face in a gesture of gratitude. Throwing my arms around the wolf, I hugged it tight for a moment. "Welcome back, old friend," I said. "I thought I'd lost you there for a while."

"You might like to know that the portal is almost closed," Leona said, smiling down at the two of us.

I looked up at her. "Is that a tear there in your eye, Lawson?"

She laughed and the tear rolled down her cheek, which she quickly wiped away. "Come on," she said, vaguely embarrassed. "Let's get out of this fucking place. It gives me the creeps."

I stood up with Blaze by my side once more and nodded. "That's the best goddamn idea I've heard all day."

# AFTERMATH

*a*S SOON AS I walked out of the factory with Leona (and Blaze, who turned himself invisible and tagged along behind us), we were met by men in tactical gear holding automatic weapons who immediately fell in at either side of us as if they were about to escort us somewhere. The waste ground was swarming with people in dark suits, others in full tactical dress, still others running around in hazmat suits as if such a suit would have guarded against the dark magic and the once imminent apocalypse. I glanced up at the still dark sky where the gigantic swirling portal had once been, glad to see the tear in the sky fully closed again and with no sign of any monstrous black tentacles pushing through it.

"What's going on?" I asked Leona as the armed agents continued to escort us toward a black van that was parked up on the road. From a distance, I could see Brentwood standing there, giving orders to various personnel while also talking into his phone.

"Brentwood told me if I made it out with you that he wants to see you," Leona said.

"What for, to give me a gold star?"

"Probably just a debriefing."

I let out a long sigh, exhaustion suddenly taking its toll on me as my body went heavy. "I could do without this. I was all for taking us to a bar that still had the apocalypse happy hour on. Getting drunk with you for the first time ever is not something I want to pass up."

"Don't worry, Creed," Leona smiled. "I'm still getting drunk with you."

I slipped my arm around her waist. "And then what?"

An elbow poked me hard in the ribs. "Just because you saved the world doesn't mean you can manhandle me at work."

"You're still working right now?"

"What do you think? I still have to debrief."

"Then we can go?" I said like a kid badgering a recalcitrant parent to take him to his favorite place, which in my case, was the pub.

"You know what you sound like?"

"Like someone who nearly died saving the world and now just wants to sit and get quietly shit-faced drunk with his awesome girlfriend?"

She smiled. "Get a grip."

"Creed," Brentwood said in greeting as we stopped by the back of the black van, the two agents escorting us dropping back. Brentwood was in his usual dark suit, and his wide shoulders were pushed right back as he stood in front of me and held out his hand. "The world owes you a debt."

Well, this was new. Brentwood being civil for a change. I took his proffered hand and shook it. "Just doing my job," I said.

"I don't know how you did it, but you damn well did it," Brentwood said. "I know we've had our differences over the years, Creed, but I'd like to think we're still on the same side and that we can work together from now on."

"I'm not coming to work with you," I told him. "We've been over this."

"I don't mean work *for* me, Creed. I mean work *with* me. There's plenty of Mr. Black types out there who need neutralizing."

*Neutralizing? One way to put it.*

"I hope not," I said. "One Mr. Black was enough."

*One insane father was enough.*

"Unfortunately Creed, there's always some power or other out there looking to cause murder and mayhem. In fact—" He paused for a second while he looked from me to Leona and back to me again, and I thought, Shit, here we go. "—right now there's a group of them out there, a cult actually, who—"

I held up a hand. "I'll stop you right there, Brentwood. No offense, but I've had my fill for one night. I'm knackered, and I just want to go sit in a bar with Leona here and do something normal for a while. Then I might sleep for a day or so. After that, we can talk."

Brentwood wasn't the kind of man who liked being interrupted. Normally when I would do that to him, he would take a step toward me and give me his battlefield death stare to let me know he didn't appreciate my insubordination, as he saw it. This time, though, he didn't do that, and after a moment, he nodded and even cracked a smile. "All right. Get out of here then." He looked at Leona. "Both of you."

As we walked away, Blaze tagging along by my side, Brentwood called to me. "Creed?"

Rolling my eyes, I stopped and turned around. "Yes?"

"That thing I just mentioned. It's serious."

Shaking my head, I said, "When is it ever anything else?"

"I expect to hear from you, Creed."

"You will," I said, already walking away.

# HAPPY HOUR

OR SOMEONE WHO didn't drink anymore, Leona could hold her whiskey. We were sitting in a little Irish pub called The Wonky Shamrock, which was only a block away from the Sanctum. Initially, it had been packed with people who thought the best place to go when the world was ending was the pub. Then, when they all realized that the world wasn't going to end after all, most of them shuffled home as if it was just another strange day in Blackham. A few stragglers remained, along with Leona and I, who sat in one of the secluded booths in the back of the pub, the two of us firing back shots of whiskey like they were going out of style. Even though we had matched each other drink for drink, I was feeling the effects a lot more than she was.

"I'm disappointed in you, Creed," she said, a relaxed grin on her face after she had downed another shot. "I thought that you could at least hold your drink against a woman, especially since you're Irish."

"My dalliance with Mr. Black has taken it out of me," I replied, slurring my words slightly, slumped back in the cushioned seat like I had no intention of moving anywhere ever again. "Besides, you're a soldier. Holding your drink is as much a requirement as being able to shoot."

She chuckled and shook her head. "Light-weight. That's all you are, Creed."

I laughed back, too drunk and too exhausted to argue with her.

The big screen TV on the wall across from us was showing the local news. The top story was obviously the mysterious "storm" that threatened to engulf the whole city at one point, but which then inexplicably went away as if it were never there in the first place. The storm itself, however, was secondary to what came out of it. The giant black tentacle that scores of people had filmed on their phones and posted to social media—so the images of that writhing, monstrous thing were on screens all over the world right now—was naturally attracting much attention.

Many people were saying it proved the existence of aliens and that we just averted an alien invasion. Some talked about a new military weapon being tested, a weapon built using advanced biotechnology. A lot of other people believed that Satan had tried to break into this world from Hell.

"You think people will forget about this eventually?" Leona asked, slumped in beside me, her head on my shoulder.

"It was a giant black tentacle poking out of the sky," I said. "What do you think?"

"I think Sleepwalkers are Sleepwalkers. For the sake of their own sanity, they'll forget, or put it down to something else."

I nodded sagely, my eyes half closed. "I think you're right. What do you think, Blaze?"

Blaze lay on the floor, visible only to Leona and I. He opened one eye to look at me for a second before going back to sleep again. Clearly, getting speared by a trident and dying had taken it out of him.

"He's exhausted," Leona said.

"He's not the only one," I said. "We can't all have your endless energy."

"Hey," Leona said, pressing her head into my neck. "I'm tired, believe me. I just don't show it the way you do."

"Military grit?"

"Something like that."

The curly haired waitress who'd been serving us since we arrived (Jenna was her name), came to our table and lifted our empties. "One more round for the road," I said to her.

"By the looks of you, Creed," Jenna said. "One more round is all it's going to take before you end up on the road."

Leona chuckled beside me, and I made some stupid face at Jenna before she smiled and walked off. Then I lapsed into drunken silence as I found myself thinking about my mother, and about Fergal and Roisin. It was good to know that their souls were not in some hellish part of the Underworld, although I was annoyed they didn't tell me where they resided now. If they had, I could have taken steps to contact them again. As it was, they could have been anywhere in the damn universe, which made trying to pinpoint them like trying to find a particular needle in a huge stack of needles.

"You've gone quiet," Leona said.

"Just thinking about my family."

"You should be grateful you got to see them again. I'd give anything to see my brother again."

I put my arm around her and squeezed her gently. "I know. I am grateful. Course I am. I just wish they could have stuck around a bit longer."

"Doesn't work that way, Creed. You know that better than anyone."

"It's a cruel world at times."

Leona said nothing as she pulled away and reached into her pocket to get her ringing phone. "God..." she said when she looked at the screen.

I didn't need to ask who it was. "Jesus, the man is incorrigible. I don't know how you put up with him. If it was me—"

Raising a hand in front of my face, Leona cut me off before I could say anymore, which was probably just as well given the stream of drunken nonsense that was about to spew from my mouth. "Yes?" she said into the phone, unable to conceal her weariness, bless her. Even hardened soldier badasses like Leona got tired sometimes.

While Leona talked on the phone (or rather listened, as it seemed Brentwood was the one doing all the talking), my eyes drifted to the front of the pub when the double doors opened, and an unusually tall man wearing dark brown corduroys, and a beige shirt with the sleeves rolled up, walked in. There was a slightly strange, placid smile on the man's face as he went and stood at the bar to be served. As I continued staring at the guy, I couldn't shake the feeling that there was something about him, but I just couldn't put my finger on what it was; the drink wasn't helping in that regard. He looked normal enough in a bookish sort of way. With his light beard and short, mousy hair, he reminded me of an English Lit teacher or a book store owner, someone who didn't look remotely threatening, and yet, there was still something about him that made a tight knot form in the pit of my stomach. When he had given the barman his order, the tall man started casually looking around the pub until his eyes finally stopped on me for a second. A slight smirk creased his still placid face as he stared at me as if he knew me.

*Who the hell is this guy?* I kept wondering, unsettled now by the fact that he appeared to recognize me from somewhere.

Before I could think about it more, however, I felt Leona nudge me with her elbow. "What are you staring at?" she asked.

I shook my head. "Nothing. What did Brentwood want?"

Leona gave a small sigh before answering. "He wants me to go to New York."

"New York? When?"

"Now."

I stared at her in amazement. "Are you fucking kidding me?"

"Unfortunately not."

"What's so urgent?"

"He never said much. A few bodies have turned up, and The Division thinks it might be something to do with an out of control Adept. That's all I know."

I slumped back into my seat like a huffy child. "Can't someone else handle it? You deserve a rest at least."

She laid her warm hand on my cheek and kissed me softly on the lips, which only made me feel worse, because it's a rare and nearly absent occasion in our history, where Special Agent Leona Lawson is willing to show tenderness. So, it goes without saying that not only would I be unable to capitalize on such a development, I would also be missing it once she left. "I'm sorry," she said in a low, husky voice that stirred up feelings of desire in me, a desire which I knew would go unfulfilled. "You know the job. It never stops."

"Then maybe we should stop."

She kissed me again, longer this time, then said, "You couldn't if you tried."

"And neither could you. Yeah, I know. Just saying, though."

"I tell you what. When I get back, we'll go somewhere. How about that cabin of yours, in the mountains? We had fun there last time, right?" She smiled and kissed me again.

"I'm holding you to that."

"I know you will." She got up, and I grabbed her hand to stop her from going, giving her the doe eyes in the vain hope that she would forget about going to New York and stay with me instead. But no suck luck.

"I love you," I said as she walked away.

Leona looked over her shoulder and gave me another smile, but she didn't say I love you back.

She never did.

# NO REST FOR THE WICKED

*M*ILDLY DEPRESSED NOW by Leona's unexpected departure, I drained what was left in my glass and slammed it back on the table, a little too hard perhaps, but I was pissed off. Not at Leona so much as with Brentwood. The stern-assed son of a bitch thought he owned Leona sometimes, the way he expected her to follow his every order like they were both still in the Army. It wasn't fair on Leona as far as I was concerned, even though it didn't seem to bother her much. The idea of her leaving The Division and partnering up with me properly had come up before, but she never seemed keen on the idea, despite my enthusiasm. Maybe it was time to broach the subject again? When she got back from New York that is, whenever that would be.

*She can't even tell me she loves me. Why would I think she would leave the Division to come work with me?*

Honestly, I didn't.

"You look like you could use a drink," a voice said, startling me out of my drunken reverie.

When I looked up, the tall man from the bar was standing there, his weirdly serene face looking down at me as he held a shot of whiskey in each hand. "Do I know you, Mister?" I asked him, taken aback slightly by the aggression coming through in my voice.

The tall man smiled, appearing not to be put out in the slightest by my hostility toward him. "May I?" He didn't wait for an answer as he came and sat beside me, placing the two shot glasses carefully on the table, like they contained nitroglycerin instead of whiskey.

Shifting away slightly, I stared hard at the guy. "Why do you seem familiar?"

The man turned his head slowly, and I saw that his eyes were now a deep orange color, as if infernal hellfires burned within them. "Maybe because I *am* familiar to you."

"*Baal*," I said, suddenly realizing who he was. I would have been more put out by the demon's presence if I hadn't of been so drunk. As it was, I was too drunk to care, and besides, I'd been expecting him anyway. Just not so soon. "You found yourself another body then?"

The demon nodded. "I did. This man stopped to help me as I lay on the ground in that necrotic hunk of meat you last saw me in."

"And for being a good Samaritan, you stole the dude's body?"

He nodded. "Yes."

"No good deed ever goes unpunished, eh Baal?"

"Thankfully not." The demon grinned broadly at me, the hellfire gone from his dark blue eyes, his complete lack of goodness showing all the more in his new face. Behind his new gaunt features and unwavering calm, his delight in his evil nature and casual sadism bubbled just below the surface, but nonetheless it still came through in his weird and particular mannerisms; such as which words he emphasized and paused at, no doubt a relic of his ancient status as one of the Old Ones, those creatures who've been around since before we homo sapiens walked among this realm of ours. Baal was scarier now than he had been as a full-fledged monster. If I weren't so drunk, I would have been a lot more nervous about the fact that he was sitting comfortably beside me, like we were just a couple of friends having a drink together.

"By the way," Baal said. "Do not call me by my true name again. If you do I'll be forced to rip your tongue out." He smiled at me then, all too casually like a father gently correcting their child. "You can call me Gabriel."

"Gabriel?"

He nodded. "For my own amusement. The real Gabriel has no sense of humor whatever. None of those winged automatons do."

"You're referring to angels?"

"Angels, yes. Narrow-minded automatons that they are."

"I've never met one, so I couldn't comment."

"Thank yourself lucky you have yet to put up with their insufferable presence."

"Yet not so lucky as to escape your presence."

Baal, or Gabriel, made a slight growling noise in the back of his throat. "You summoned me here."

I couldn't argue with him there, so I let it go. "So let me guess," I said, aware that Blaze was wide awake now, his eyes firmly on the demon. "You're here to call in your debt, right?"

"Correctamundo," the demon said, grinning again.

"I didn't know they spoke dude in the Underworld."

"It was a favorite expression of this man."

"Before you pitched his soul into the Underworld like you were tossing away a piece of rubbish, you mean?"

"Speaking of souls. I believe you owe me your father's."

"About that," I said shifting uncomfortably in my seat. "His soul was destroyed. I couldn't save it." Not that I would have saved my father's soul, even if I could have, though I wasn't about to tell Baal, or bloody Gabriel that.

As it was, the demon didn't seem too concerned at my lack of offering. "That's okay. If you find who I'm looking for, that will more than make up for your empty hands."

"This person must be pretty important to you."

Gabriel focused his stare in front of him for a moment, as if deep in thought. "They are."

He reached down then and lifted the shots of whiskey off the table, handing one to me, which I took resignedly, knowing I didn't have a choice. Then he grinned at me as he held his glass up, waiting for me to do the same. With a sigh, I clinked my glass against his. "To your success in finding who I'm looking for," he said. "I sincerely hope you do not disappoint."

I downed my whiskey as I wondered what fresh hell awaited me around the next corner.

Gabriel lifted his own glass slowly to his mouth and poured in the whiskey in a weirdly deliberate manner, closing his eyes for a second as he swallowed and then stared right at me.

All I could think of was that it might as well have been my soul in the demon's glass. For he owned me now, at least until I managed to get him what he wanted.

*If* I managed to get him what he wanted.

Either way, I knew I would come to regret ever dealing with the demon in the first place.

Of that, I had no doubt.

# BLOOD DEBT (WIZARD'S CREED BOOK 2)

# FAMILY REUNION

*S*taggering through the streets after being turfed out of the Wonky Shamrock at closing time, I could hardly stand up I was so inebriated from the copious amounts of whiskey I drank after Baal or Gabriel or whatever his fucking name was--the demon, the latest thorn in my side, the infernal pile attached to my rectum, the...fuck it, whatever--vanished from the pub after making sure I knew he had his claws firmly in me.

In the words of Rudyard Kipling, I was as drunk as Davey's sow on a frosty night. I was doing my best to walk in a straight line, but it seemed like people kept getting in my way. And just when I thought I had the whole walking thing figured out, some other street walker would cause me to swerve, and the next thing I knew, I would be falling across the sidewalk in a dangerously uncoordinated fashion, having about as much control of myself as an alcoholic toddler. I was vaguely aware of being shouted at by a few people who I may have inadvertently bumped into. Someone might have pushed me into a line of trashcans. Or I might have fallen into them myself. I wasn't sure which.

Not that it mattered. All that seemed to matter on my excruciatingly slow and labored journey home (it never occurred to me to get a cab, or to teleport, which was just as well for God knows where I would have ended up) was that I killed my own father. That and the fact that the rest of my family resided somewhere else in the universe and I was stuck here on shitty Earth all alone. Even Leona, the supposed love of my life, had abandoned me (I was sure *she* didn't think of it like that, but *I* did, melodramatic fool that I am).

At some point, I came across a bag lady pushing a shopping cart full of junk up the street. I grabbed the startled woman's cart as her scraggly face blurred in and out of focus. "Why me?" I demanded to know from the old woman. "Why does everything happen to me, huh? Tell me!"

"You take it!" the old woman screamed back (or at least I think she did... with the world spinning at hyper speed around me, it was hard to tell who was saying what). "Right in the ass you fucking scumbag cocksucker!"

Now lying on the cold sidewalk, I thought the old lady was quoting Gordon Geko at me, and I thought, *What a strange thing for the old lady to do.* Except when my focus came back for a mere second, I saw the old woman was just staring down at me with a blank expression on her face as if she had said nothing at all. I think I quoted Gordon Geko at myself. Either way, the words seemed painfully apt for someone who hadn't long killed--fucking *destroyed*--his own father. It didn't matter that my father--good old Mr Black--had been trying to obliterate the Earth for his own gain. It only seemed to matter that I had killed him. I should have been jubilant that I took down a true monster, but all I felt was shame.

Something cold pressed into my ear, and I cried out as I flinched away from a bulky shape that was now looming over me like an escaped shadow demon. For a second I thought it was Mr Black, impossibly having returned from utter annihilation to wreak revenge on me. But it was only Blaze. The Garra Wolf had been walking behind me the whole time, keeping a respectful distance as if knowing I needed the space. Either that or he was just ashamed to have such a waste of space for a master.

I could feel oblivion reaching out to grab me, and I let it, wishing for nothing more than a reprieve from the cruel world I was in. But before I fell into unconsciousness, I became aware of another, taller figure standing over me, and then a voice. "August," the voice said. "Let's get you home, my boy."

The voice barely registered in me, but I still knew who it belonged to.

Uncle Ray.

* * *

I CAME TO IN THE LIVING ROOM OF THE SANCTUM, SLUMPED INTO ONE OF THE chairs. Peeling my eyes open, I became aware of a dull ache in my skull as if my heart had shifted locations and was now beating hard in the place where my brain used to be. A long sigh escaped me, and I rubbed at my head. "Jesus Christ," I muttered, then looked up to see where the person who had brought me home was.

Uncle Ray had probably teleported us both back to the Sanctum unless the old man had thrown me over his shoulder and carried me home, which I doubted. It wasn't that Ray didn't have the strength to lift me, it was because I knew he didn't stress himself if he didn't have to. Ray tended to use his Blaze for everything, even going so far as to compel the toilet tissue to wipe his ass for him (true story). "I have better things to do on the bog than wipe my own ass," he told me once. "I'm always in deep study with a book on my lap."

Where was the old bastard anyway?

It felt weird to know Ray was in the Sanctum somewhere. We hadn't seen each other in over ten years. We stayed in touch over the phone, or through the occasional psychic link, but we never met up. Partly because I had no interest in going back to Ireland, partly because Ray was always off on some adventure somewhere.

"There you are." I turned my head to see Ray enter the living room. There was a reason I never heard him walk down the stairs. That's because he didn't walk down them, he floated down them. Even walking was too much trouble for Ray these days as he preferred to hover off the ground a few inches and float around everywhere. Not in public, of course, only when he was alone, or with those of an enlightened mindset like myself.

Ray glided into the living room and floated just in front of me, a happy go lucky smile on his face as always. "You're a bit late," I told him, feeling grumpy from the hangover and the mess of thoughts and emotions still festering in me. Still, I shouldn't have been so curt with him. He was my only family after all. "I'm sorry, I didn't mean..."

"That's quite all right," Ray said. "You've been through the mill. I understand."

"That's one way to put it."

"Sorry I didn't make it in time for the big showdown. It seems you had everything in hand anyhow. Which of course, I knew you would."

I raised my eyebrows. "Did you?"

"No," Ray said. "I thought that bastard brother of mine would have destroyed everything by now, including you."

"He almost did."

"But you defeated him, and that's all that matters. Now stand up and give your old Uncle a hug. I haven't seen you in ten bloody years!"

Smiling despite myself, I wrenched myself out of the chair and stood to give Ray the hug he was so eager for. When I spread my arms, Ray wrapped his own burly arms around me and pulled me in tight, half knocking the wind out of me. I'd forgotten how bloody strong he was. A strength that only seemed to increase with age. "You're crushing me," I winced.

He let go but kept his hands on my shoulders as he looked up at me. Ray was a few inches shorter than me and apparently the shortest in the McCreedy family. "It's wonderful to see you again, my boy. I've missed you." His thick fingers squeezed my shoulders, and I tried not to wince again.

"I've missed you too, Ray."

He didn't look any older than he did the last time I had seen him. If anything, he looked younger and still as exuberant as ever. His light gray hair, still thick and longish, was swept back across his head as if a gust of wind had blown it that way. He still wore the goatee beard I had always known him to wear, but it was slightly longer now as it seemed to spill down into his open shirt collar.

Ray smiled, his blue-gray eyes sparkling as he gave my shoulders another shake, and then began walking around the living room. "Good to see you're maintaining the old Sanctum," he said. "I have many fond memories of this place."

"I'm sure you do." A weakness washed over me, and I half fell, half sat back in the chair again.

"You all right? The hangover should go soon. I used a Sobering Spell on you as you were completely out of it by the time I got you home. I found you screaming at some old lady in your drunken state."

"Rough night."

Ray extended one arm and a second later the bottle of whiskey on the fireplace mantle came flying through the air and into his hand. "Hair of the dog?"

My stomach rolled at the thought. "I'm fine, thanks."

Shrugging, Ray opened the bottle and took a mouthful of the whiskey. Then he left the bottle hanging in midair as the top screwed itself back on. As he sat down in one of the other chairs not far from me, Ray made a small finger movement and the whiskey bottle floated over and placed itself down on the mantle again. Then, reaching into the pocket of his brown trench coat--a coat that was probably older than he was and which was scuffed and marked everywhere, having been worn on countless adventures--he pulled out a curved pipe and a pouch of tobacco. "So tell me," Ray said as he began filling the bowl of his pipe with the sweet smelling tobacco. "How did you defeat your old man in the end? I'm eager to know."

*God, do I have to talk about this now?*

To be honest with you, all I wanted to do was sleep so I could block out the world for a while. If Ray hadn't of been there, I would have made myself a potent sleeping potion and knocked myself out for several hours. My mind seemed to be conspiring against me, throwing up dark thoughts and expressions of woe and despair. I needed to shut that shit down for a while so I could then get some much-needed perspective on the state of things at present. But since Ray was there, I couldn't just fuck off to bed and leave him, so I would have to suffer the pain of dredging everything up again for his benefit. But regardless of how I felt, he had a right to know what happened. "My family helped me defeat him," I said, now eyeing up the whiskey bottle on the mantle, wondering if I should start drinking again, then looking away and deciding against it.

"Your family?" Ray said, pausing his pipe loading for a moment to look at me. "What do you mean?"

"I mean they appeared to me somehow. My mother, Fergal, and Roisin. They all came to me just when I thought all was lost."

"Really? Well, that must have been a wonderful thing."

"It was. I loved seeing them again. It was their strength--the bond between us-- that made it possible for me to defeat Mr. Black."

"Mr. Black?"

"My father. It's what I called him before I knew who he was when he was just a psycho going around murdering people."

Ray nodded. "I see." He popped the pipe in his mouth and gave a small laugh. "Mr. Black. How very apt." A flame suddenly appeared on the end of his right forefinger, and he used the flame to ignite the tobacco inside the pipe. Although, once I caught a whiff of the thick smoke, I knew there was more than just tobacco in there.

"Still mixing up the weeds, I see."

After blowing out a long stream of smoke, Ray held the pipe out towards me. "Take it. It will relax you. You look like you need relaxing."

I used my magic to pull the pipe through the air and into my hand. "It's been a while since I've smoked anything."

"That's a special blend of mine. You'll like it."

I drew on the pipe and inhaled the smoke, which was surprisingly smooth as it expanded out in my lungs before I blew it out again into the room, which by that point smelled like an exotic herb garden. "Nicely cured." I took another draw on the pipe and propelled it back into Ray's waiting hand. The smoke hit me straight away, enveloping me in a warm blanket of calm that caused me to sink further into my chair.

"Told you," Ray said, smiling.

I smiled back as my head began to buzz pleasantly from the smoke. "They never told me where they were."

"Who?"

"My family. They never told me what part of the universe they were in now. I could have traveled to see them."

"They didn't tell you for a reason, August. They're in the afterlife now, and the afterlife is no place for the living. You'll see them again. Of that I'm sure."

I sat there stoned wondering if he knew more than he was letting on, but I knew better than to question him on it. Ray always knew much more than he let on, but the point was that he firmly believed in allowing others to find their own way. Even if he did know where my family resided these days, he wouldn't tell me. "Anyway," I said, a heavy body stone coming over me. "I managed to tap into some powerful magic that Mr Black--my father, your brother--couldn't counter or stop. It was amazing really. I've never felt anything like it."

Ray kept puffing on his pipe as his eyes smiled over at me. "You tapped that magic because you're a master wizard, August, whether you believe that or not. Your family just steered you in the right direction." He paused for a second before continuing. "I could have made it over here in time to help you with Christopher. You know why I didn't?"

I shook my head as I puffed my cheeks out. "No."

He pointed his pipe at me. "Because I knew you could do what needed to be done. I've always had faith in you, August. Even when you didn't."

"And what if you had been wrong? The whole world would have ended."

"Then it would have ended. There's an infinite number of other worlds out there. Earth isn't that special."

"And the seven billion people who live here? What about them?"

"Same answer as before. Nothing and no one are special. Everything just is. That's all."

"I think I need another puff if you're going to go all Nietzsche on me."

Ray chuckled and propelled the pipe towards me. "I'll spur you."

"Thank Christ," I said smiling.

"Watch it, boy. I may be an old man, but I'm still fit enough to run rings around you."

"I know you are." I took two more hits from the pipe and passed it back to him. Then we sat in stoned silence for a while. My headache had cleared up by that point, and I was starting to feel slightly better, physically anyway. Mentally, I had a ways to go before I felt like releasing the worry and anxiety that still strongly gripped my mind.

"What's up, August?" Ray asked. "There's something you aren't telling me."

Of course. I could never keep anything hidden for long from Ray. Not that I was hiding anything anyway. I just didn't feel like talking about the latest cluster-fuck I was embroiled in. Out of respect for my uncle, however, I spilled my guts. "When Mr Black spelled me--"

"It's odd that you call your father that," Ray interrupted.

"Mr Black is a much more fitting name for the bastion of evil I went up against. If you'd seen him, you would understand."

Ray nodded. "Of course. Carry on then."

"Like I say, he spelled me. An effect of the spell was that my soul no longer recognized me and I had about three days before I became a ghoul."

"Distasteful creatures, ghouls." Ray made a face as if he was thinking about a hunk of maggot infested meat.

"Yes, I know. Which is why I didn't want to become one. But I did anyway, as it happened, though not for long. I made a deal with a demon, initially to break the spell. But payment was late and my soul had departed by then. Thankfully the demon was able to retrieve it."

"But know you owe this demon. Again."

I nodded. "Correct."

"And what does the demon want from you?"

"All I know so far is that he wants me to find someone for him. I'm awaiting further instructions."

Ray snorted as he drew on his pipe. "I'll tell you this much. Whatever he asks of you, it will be more than simply finding someone. I know demons. They always have a hidden agenda. What's the demon's name?"

"He calls himself Gabriel since he possessed a human body, but his real name is Baal."

Ray almost choked on his pipe as he stopped mid-puff. "Did you say, Baal?"

"I take it that's not good. I figured as much."

"Not good?" Ray sat forward in his chair. "That's an understatement. Do you know who you're dealing with?"

"I'm not sure I want to know, but tell me anyway."

"Baal is the demon that other demons fear." The look on Ray's face was serious. When Ray had his serious face on, you knew things were bad. "He is the spawn of two very ancient primordial beings, the Things That Should Not Be as they are known. A dark experiment between two monsters to see what would happen."

"And Baal happened," I said, not liking anything I was hearing. The demon was evidently much worse than I thought.

"The creature was cast to the Underworld like a disused plaything by the Things That Should Not Be. Baal predates most of the beings in the Underworld, including the Fallen Ones. He rules that place from the shadows. How did you even learn his name?"

"*The Book Of Many Hells And Demons*." I felt very stupid now like a clueless boy caught playing around with magic he didn't understand.

Ray shook his head. "I told you to stay away from those books under the basement, especially the ones in the trunk. They were put there for a reason, boy."

"It was an emergency, Ray. Do you think I would have gone near the book if I didn't have to? It doesn't matter now anyway. Baal already has his claws in me."

Sitting back in his chair again, Ray regarded me as he resumed puffing on his pipe, a cloud of thick smoke surrounding him. "Well then, you don't have a choice, do you? You have to do as the demon says and hope he spurs your soul."

"We have a deal," I said. "As long as I do what he asks."

"Oh, August," Ray said. "How long have you been in this game? You've never known a demon to break a deal?"

I shook my head, thinking of the demon that massacred my family. "Goddamn it." I thrust a hand out and caught the whiskey bottle that came flying off the mantle. Unscrewing the cap, I took a large mouthful of the amber liquid, wincing as it burned its way down my gullet and pooled in my sour stomach.

Then I looked at Ray and said sardonically, "What were you saying earlier about me being a master wizard? Maybe strike that one from the record."

# HANGING AROUND

*R*ay stayed for another hour or so as we passed the whiskey bottle back and forth, and occasionally that pipe of his, which he refilled more than once. By the time I walked him to the front door, I was half drunk again, not to mention stoned out of my head on whatever herbs Ray had in his pipe. Everything seemed brighter to my smoke soaked brain, and I'm pretty sure I was tripping slightly as well because sometimes when I looked at Ray, I saw the face of Mr. Black. This despite the fact that Ray and my father shared little in the way of physical similarities. Ray often joked that his brother Christopher was left on the doorstep one morning by the milkman. By a demon more like, I'd say.

"So how long are you going to be in town?" I asked him as we stood in the hallway with the front door open, darkness and cold air still present outside.

Ray made one of his smiley faces and said, "Maybe a while. Maybe less. I have some business to take care off, some people to see."

"Like the Crimson Crow?"

A guffawing sound came out of Ray's mouth. "Please. That old bag?"

"Old bag? Last I checked she still looked like a supermodel. And she walks around in the daylight now."

"Yes. Thanks to you."

I shrugged, seeing dancing lights out on the street, unsure if I was hallucinating or if it was something else. When I blinked, the lights disappeared. "You do what you have to to stay alive," I said in a slightly distant voice.

"That you do, my boy. That you do. Now give your old uncle a hug before he whisks off into the night."

Smiling, I stepped forward and hugged my uncle for a long moment, glad that he was there. At that moment at least, I still had family, and I wasn't alone. "Thanks for coming here, Ray."

Ray patted my cheek with his surprisingly soft hand. "Anything for you, August. You know that."

* * *

AFTER RAY HAD LEFT, I SHUFFLED AROUND THE SANCTUM FOR A WHILE looking for Blaze, wondering where he had gone. When I failed to find him, I gave up and went downstairs again, too fucked up on whiskey and psychoactive herbs to worry that much. Blaze was probably huddled away in some corner somewhere anyway, recovering after being dead. No doubt it took a lot out of him.

I sat in the living room for a while, staring at the walls as they seemed to move and shift under my wavering gaze. Eventually, the moving walls started to make me feel sick, so I made an effort to get up and move around the room for a bit. This seemed to clear my head slightly, enough that I felt like grabbing my phone from my trench coat hanging over the chair so I could call Leona. She would be in New York by now if she traveled by helicopter. She answered after several rings that seemed to go on for a long time. "Hey," she said. "Kind of a bad time. I'm about to go into a briefing."

"Oh, right, sorry," I said, hearing a gaggle of other voices in the background, gruff voices mostly, belonging to men in uniform and dark suits probably. "I was just calling to see how things were going."

"I don't know much yet. Just that there's been a string of murders here. Pretty bizarre by all accounts. Definitely magic involved."

"Sounds like my kind of case. I wish I could be there to help you." As distasteful as sifting through murder scenes was, it seemed more appealing than having to stay where I was to deal with Baal, especially after everything Ray had told me about the demon.

"I think Brentwood wants your help on a different case. Expect a call from him s--yeah, I'm coming. Creed, I gotta go. The briefing is about to start. Are you okay? You sound slightly weird. Weirder than normal anyway." She laughed, sort of.

"I'm okay. Just tired, I guess."

"I'm sure. Get some rest, Creed. I'll call you later."

"Sure," I said, but she had already hung up. "Bye."

I stood with the phone in my hand for a second, looking at it like I was expecting answers from it as if it would tell me what I was doing with a woman like Leona. A woman who was married to her job--to her way of life--and probably would never have the time for me that I felt like I needed from her. It was frustrating at times, how brief our irregular encounters often were because one or both of us had other business to take care off. It was a three-year relationship that hadn't moved much beyond casual, which seemed to suit Leona more than me.

*Wise up, Creed,* I thought to myself. *Look at the life you lead. The life she leads. There's no room for deep and meaningful relationships. This is as good as you are going to get.*

As depressing as that was, I knew I was right. I wasn't a normal person. Neither was Leona. The fact that we had sustained at least some sort of relationship for the last three years was a miracle in itself. Surely that was special enough? Anyway, what was I going to do, marry her?

A small laugh of amusement escaped my lips at the thought. I shook my head. Time to get back to planet Earth again. To reality.

"Fuck it," I said. "I'm not hanging around here feeling fucking sorry for myself any longer," I said it aloud because I was trying to rouse myself into action. It was either that or continue to sit around waiting for Baal to make an appearance, and God knows when that would be. Whatever the demon had in store for me, I would deal with it at the time. Until then, I grabbed my trench coat and did the only thing that still made some sense to me.

I went out to work.

# FORSYTH

*A* short while later I found myself standing in a large, spacious room with oak paneled walls and an elaborately carved wood paneled ceiling. The rectangular room had no windows and was lit with low lighting from the lamps attached to the walls. The carpet was a deep red shag pile. The color of blood. Easier to hide the stains that way. The room also had a fully stocked bar along half of one wall. Large cushions and bean bags were scattered all over the place, and at the very back of the room, there was a huge fabric corner suite, on which lay a vampire named Forsyth. Beside him lay two naked girls, one on either side of him. Both of them beautiful, one blonde, the other brunette. They didn't look much older than seventeen, and they each had blood trails running down their arms were Forsyth had evidently been feeding on them. Not that either of the girls seemed to mind as one rubbed at his exposed chest, the other his flaccid cock flopping out of his trousers.

The girls smiled over at me, and I smiled politely back. Normally, Forsyth tended towards boys for his sexual pleasure, but on occasion he entertained girls, just to remind himself how much he loved the boys better. So he told me once.

"Creed!" Forsyth said, waving a wine glass at me that contained either wine or blood, I wasn't sure. "What a wonderful surprise. Would you care to join us? These two are delectable. I'm sure they wouldn't mind you joining us, would you girls?"

"The more, the merrier," the blonde one said, and both girls giggled, as did Forsyth (somewhat more ironically), who knew full well I would never join in his depravity.

I shook my head. "No thanks," I said. "I'm here on business."

Forsyth sighed dramatically, his long wavy fringe bouncing off his forehead. "Always business with you, isn't it, Creed? Lighten up and come have some fun, if only so I can see what you're packing inside those scruffy but still sexy trousers."

"You couldn't handle what I'm packing," I retorted, wondering why I keep getting into these mock flirtations with the vampire, especially since Forsyth didn't see those little moments as mock anything. He wanted into my pants, and he made no secret of it.

"Is that a challenge?" he said with a smirk, his dark brown eyes staring mischievously at me.

"Not at all," I said, my eyes going to the bar now and the bottle of outrageously expensive whiskey sitting on one of the under-lit glass shelves. "Just a fact."

Forsyth gave a throaty laugh. "You don't how horny that makes me."

I glanced over at him as I crossed to the bar. "I can see how horny it makes you. Put it away, for fuck's sake."

"Does it make you uncomfortable?" Forsyth asked.

"I just feel sorry for you, having a dick so small."

Forsyth laughed. "Whatever Mr Straight Magic Man."

"Oh," squealed one of the girls, the brunette I think. I was too busy savoring the smell of the whiskey in my hand to notice which one. "You do magic?"

I said nothing as I poured the whiskey into a crystal glass.

"Oh, he does magic all right," Forsyth said. "*Real* magic."

"What's that?" one of the girls asked.

"How about I show you?" I said after sipping from the whiskey glass.

"Oh please!" both girls said in unison, sitting to attention like a couple of kids about to see a magic show.

"You ready?" I asked, putting down the whiskey glass.

"Yes!" they screamed, a little too loudly, probably from the coke Forsyth undoubtedly fed them.

"All right," I said, cracking my knuckles. "Here we go." I started to move my hands around like I was conjuring some wondrous and mysterious magic from the air.

The two girls were on the edge of their seats now in rapt attention as if they expected to see me pull a white rabbit out of thin air. Even Forsyth looked captivated as he waited to see what I was going to do.

"And..." I clicked my fingers, and both girls disappeared as if they had never even been there. "Vanish." I picked up my whiskey again and downed it one.

Forsyth seemed shocked for a moment as he looked from side to side. Then he laughed uproariously and started clapping his hands. "Bravo!" he shouted.

I bowed my head slightly as I poured another whiskey. "Thank you."

"So where are they? What did you do with them? Did you send them somewhere horrible like a werewolf bar?"

"No, you cruel bastard. They should be in one of the other rooms in this mansion of yours."

"There's over forty rooms in here."

"I'm sure they'll find their way."

"Or someone else will find their way to *them*. There are other vampires in this house, not all of them as soft as I."

I chuckled. "Soft? Give me a break."

Forsyth flashed a devilish grin at me, his erect cock still standing proud. "I know, right?"

"Put that fucking thing away will you before I make it disappear as well."

Forsyth looked vaguely horrified by the thought of his cock suddenly disappearing. "Please don't"

"Zip it up then."

He sighed. "If I must."

I was glad to see him put his bulging cock away and stand up. As usual, he was dressed flamboyantly in a frilly shirt, a glittering waistcoat and tailored tweed trousers. He carried himself with cocky aplomb as he came to the bar and started making himself a gin and tonic. "So what brings you here anyway, Creed? I thought you'd be resting up after saving the world from that thing that tried to come through that portal."

"How'd you know it was me?"

"I could think of no one else who could stop such a monster. Plus I have spies who placed you at the scene."

"Of course you did."

Forsyth finished making his gin and tonic and took a large gulp from the glass. "It's my job to know what goes on around here. You know that."

"Well," I said. "You can thank me for saving your ass by telling me about this vampire you want me to be find."

Forsyth cocked his head to one side for a moment as he stared at me. "Why are you here, Creed? You just saved the fucking world. You should be at your Sanctum shagging that military hardbody of yours. What's her name? Leona? Where is she tonight?"

"New York, on a job." I downed what was left in my glass and poured another.

Forsyth stared for another moment, making me uncomfortable. He had a habit of seeming to look right into you when he stared. "I see now. You're pissed at her, aren't you? For not being here."

I shook my head. "That's none of your business, Forsyth. I'm here because you asked me to come here a while ago. Now I'm here, tell me who you need me to find."

"All right," Forsyth said, seeming happy enough to drop the subject thankfully. "Only I don't need you to find anyone now. More like retrieve something for me."

"Retrieve what exactly?"

"A flash drive containing all of my business accounts. I've been robbed, Creed."

"Who the hell would be dumb enough to rob you, Forsyth?"

"A werewolf gang from Red Hill. They kidnapped Marcus a while back. You remember Marcus? He did all my accounts."

I nodded. "If I recall he did you on occasion too," I said, remembering walking in on the two vampires one time as they were having sex.

Forsyth smiled. "Yes," he said. "Marcus and I got down and dirty sometimes. God, I'll miss that humongous cock of his." He seemed to drift off for a second, then he shook his head and gulped down the rest of his gin and tonic before making another. "Anyway. I did some digging and was finally able to attribute poor Marcus' death to the stinking werewolf gang. Luckily for me, the drive is encrypted, and those dumb animals are probably too stupid to ever get past the encryption. Still, I'd like my property back."

"I don't understand why you need me. Why don't you just send a load of soldiers in to wipe them out and get the drive back?"

"As much as I'd like to tear every one of those stinking mutts apart with my bare hands, the Crimson Crow has forbidden it. She's trying to get elected to the city council, and she doesn't want a war breaking out in the city and making her look bad. And God forbid the delectable Miss Crow should ever look bad. I still hate you for fixing it so she can walk in the light. Why won't you do it for me, Creed?"

"You know why," I said, pouring another whiskey, thinking to myself that maybe I should slow down on the drink, especially since I might soon have to deal with a bunch of irascible werewolves soon. "The Crow would kill me if I gave the ability to any other vampires." Not strictly true, but it's what I told other vamps like Forsyth to keep them off my back. As far as Angela Crow is concerned, she can't kill me without killing herself in the process. If I die, she dies. That's how I rigged the spell I did on her a long time ago now. Not that anyone but her and me knew it.

"No one would have to know. I'd stay under the radar."

I laughed. "You wouldn't know how. Staying under the radar is not your style, Forsyth."

Forsyth laughed back. "No, it isn't, is it? Oh well, a nightwalker I shall remain."

I leaned my elbows on the bar. "The daylight wouldn't suit you anyway."

"Perhaps," Forsyth said, slightly forlornly. "Still, to bask in the sunlight, just once..." He trailed off for a moment, then shook his head. "Fuck it. We can't have everything, can we Creed?"

"No."

We both went silent for a bit as we sipped on our drinks, during which time my thoughts turned to Baal. I wondered when he was going to show up again. He said it would be soon when we last spoke in The Wonky Shamrock. Despite being under the demon's thumb, I thought at the time the business I had with him would be fairly straightforward. Find whoever he wanted me to find and that would be it. Now I wasn't sure, not after what Ray said about the demon always having a hidden agenda. Which I should have known, of course. Nothing was ever straightforward when it came to demons. But I had been through the mill going up against Mr Black, and I allowed myself to believe that things would be easy with the demon. Now I was almost certain they wouldn't be.

"Things on your mind, Creed?" Forsyth asked me. "You're even more broody than usual. Anything I can help you with?"

Sighing, I said, "I'm just in one of those tricky situations I can't get out of."

"I know a bit about tricky situations. I've been in many over the centuries." He smiled somewhat salaciously.

"I bet you have."

Forsyth smiled, showing his fangs slightly. "Point is, I might be able to help you if you tell me what kind of trouble you're in."

I sipped on the whiskey and put the glass down again. "At this point, there isn't much you can do for me. Maybe down the line, though. I'll have to see how things pan out."

"Anything you need, my friend." Forsyth raised his glass and nodded at me.

"Thanks, Forsyth. I appreciate it."

Leaning off the bar, I stood up straight and inhaled deeply, deciding I shouldn't drink anymore if I were going to be dealing with a bunch of werewolves soon. "all right. How do you want me to handle the werewolves? I could just steal the drive back from them. An Invisibility Spell and a bit of time and I'm sure I could find the drive. Unless you want a message sent. Which I hope not. I'm not an enforcer, as you know."

Forsyth nodded. "I know you like to remain neutral in these matters, Creed. But I don't need neutrality in this situation. I need someone to remind those mutts that they can't steal from me and get away with it."

"What do you want me to do, wipe them all out? Not my style, Forsyth. There's plenty of independent contractors out there willing to shed as much blood as you want."

"I know that, but I can't trust anyone else with that drive. I need you to get it. And I hate to say it, but you sort of owe me for that scroll I managed to get for you a while back."

"Yeah, I know." I went silent as I thought about what Forsyth was asking of me. He was expecting to walk into a club full of werewolves, demand to see the leader and then tell the leader that the vampire Adrian Forsyth wants his property back. Something told me things wouldn't go without a hitch. A violent one perhaps.

But hey, fuck it. I needed something to do to take my mind off things, to distract me from the image of my father's face as he screamed for mercy just before I destroyed his soul. "all right, Forsyth," I said. "I'll get your flash drive back for you."

Forsyth smiled, more genuine than his usual insouciant grins. "Creed, my friend, I won't forget it."

I focused my gaze on him. "I know you won't."

# 4

## THE RED HILL GANG

*O*ver the years, I'd had dealings with a few different werewolf gangs in the city. I found most of them to be quite brutish in their ways, intensely loyal to their pack and prone to frequent outbursts of violence. Individuals within the packs varied of course, but in the main, werewolf gangs behaved as most other supernaturals expected them to behave. They liked to party, which is why all of the gangs had their own bar or club to hang out in while they drank until it was time to fight someone. Vampires did the same thing, but more quietly, and they liked to bite instead of fight.

The Red Hill Gang as they were known resided in, well, Red Hill. The place itself was a mix of apartments and old brownstones, interspersed with small business and numerous bars. These gave way to crumbling warehouses and a small industrial estate the closer you got to the docks. The people there were an insular sort of folk, most of them having been born and bred in the area, rarely leaving it unless they really had to. There was a backwoods feel to the place, despite the urban setting, which was strengthened by the overabundance of gun shops and army surplus stores.

It was mid-morning by the time I drove to Red Hill in my black 1967 Cadillac Eldorado, which I think I already told you is a temperamental bitch at the best of times. That morning, though, despite the freezing temperatures overnight, the old beast seemed to run fine for a change. I wasn't overly familiar with the Red Hill area, so I had to drive around for a bit until I found the place I was looking for, which was Big Joe's Custom Bike Shop. Despite never having any dealings with the Red Hill werewolf gang, I still knew them by reputation and where they liked to hang out. The gang's reputation preceded them, and they were known throughout the city as a vicious bunch of mostly petty criminals, specializing in grand theft auto and the occasional armed robbery. Aside from their criminal activities, the gang mostly kept to themselves.

That's why I was surprised to hear that the pack (or members of it) had kidnapped and killed a top-ranking vampire in the city. Did they really think they would get away with it? It was tantamount to an act of war. A war the Red Hill Gang would never survive, despite their fearsome reputation for violence. There may have been fewer vampires than werewolves in the city, but the vampires were better organized, were much cleverer, and had nearly infinite resources at their disposal which they could use to level any foe without much trouble. That was also why vampires ruled the roost in Blackham City, as they did in most other cities around the world.

When I finally located Big Joe's garage, I parked the Cadillac across the street and sat there for a moment as I stared through the window at the muddy-blue colored building across the way. It looked like an old apartment building that had been gutted to create space. In the front of the building was a large rectangular opening with a steel shudder hanging part way down it. On the shutter, I could just make out a faded image of a spark plug, underneath which were the words, BLOOD SWEAT GEARS. A battered looking jeep was parked on the sidewalk in front of the garage, as were two motorcycles.

There didn't seem to be much activity around the garage, which I guessed was a good thing. The less angry werewolves I had to deal with the better, although I was prepared with a spell in case things went pear-shaped.

I got out into the cold morning air, the stiff breeze making me pull my trench coat tighter around myself. As I crossed the road, I heard rock music coming from inside the garage, and the clanging of metal as tools and parts were dropped to the floor. The smell of grease and motor oil hit me as I paused at the garage entrance to have a look a round. Needless to say, the place was filled with motorcycles, mostly of the chopper variety. I noticed a couple of guys working away on their respective bikes. At the back of the garage was a small office with a dirty window, through which I could see someone else seated at a desk. Big Joe, I was guessing.

"Can I help you, friend?" One of the mechanics addressed me as he stood up and started wiping his hands on an oily rag. The guy was short and stocky, in his fifties, powerfully built, wearing a grubby white T-shirt and even grubbier blue jeans. His bare forearms were covered in tattoos, and his hair was tied back in a ponytail. He and the other guy (who had stood up as well now) were looking at me with a mixture of bemusement and suspicion as if I was some city dweller who'd just wandered into their backwoods garage.

"Yeah," I said, stepping inside the garage. "I'm looking for Big Joe. He here?"

The older mechanic with the ponytail narrowed his eyes at me as he stuffed his oily rag into the back pocket of his dirty jeans. "Who's asking?"

"Name's Creed. I'm here on behalf of Adrian Forsyth. You know, the vampire you guys robbed a while ago?"

The ponytailed mechanic exchanged glances with his younger co-worker, who nodded and headed to the back of the garage, then disappeared through a doorway.

*Of to get reinforcements, no doubt. Shit. Maybe that opening introduction wasn't the best idea. Now they think I'm here to cause trouble.*

Which I wasn't, not really. If trouble started (and it was looking likely at that point), it would be on them. I was hoping for a peaceful settlement, but then again, I was dealing with werewolves, so who was I kidding?

"I tell you what, friend," Ponytail said. "Why don't you just walk on out of here, get back in your car and go back to wherever you came from."

"East Oakdale. It's not *that* far away out there in the big bad world."

Ponytail's eyes smoldered as he made a small growling noise at me. Werewolves. No sense of humor. "I warned you, smart mouth."

From behind me, I heard footsteps and looked around to see three big guys come walking into the garage. Then the other mechanic who had left came back in with two more of his buddies. Every one of them were typical biker types with leather cut-offs, except one who wore a sleeveless T-shirt.

*Where the hell where all these guys hiding? Christ, were they waiting on me or something?*

Either that or the clubhouse wasn't too far away.

I was now surrounded by seven large men who looked like they wanted nothing better than to shift into their wolf form so they could tear me apart. "Listen, guys," I said, holding my hands out. "I'm just here to talk, that's all. I don't want no trouble."

"Oh yeah," one of the biggest guys said. "Well, you got it now, motherfucker."

Ponytail stepped forward from the rest. "You think you can come in here and threaten us? You're no vampire. Who are you?"

I didn't answer the guy, but stood there with my gaze slightly down, avoiding direct eye contact as I quickly fired up the spell I knew I would need before I went there. Ponytail's questions were just a formality, a prelude to the blood feast they were all about to have. I felt like a stuffed pig with an apple in its mouth being eyed up by hungry diners.

But as I was about to cast my battle magic, another voice made itself heard. This voice was deeper than the others, and it seemed to command fear and authority from the rest of the pack. "His name is August Creed."

I looked past the men surrounding me towards the office to see that the man inside--who I was now certain was the pack leader, Big Joe--had stepped out and was now walking towards me and the rest of his gang. The man was massive, easily six and a half feet tall, which put him five inches over me. He was also hugely built, slabs of muscle barely contained within his tight black T-shirt and leather cut-off. His eyes were as dark as his thick mane of hair and shadow on his face, and if I had to guess, I would have put the guy in his late thirties.

"You must be Big Joe," I said, not bothering to seem surprised that he knew my name. Blackham may have been a big city, but in many respects, it was still a small town, especially when it came to the supernatural community and the occult underground. Everybody knew everybody else. "I can see why they call you that." I gave a small laugh, sounding more nervous than I felt. The truth was, I wasn't nervous at all, partly because I was still raw and emotional inside (and therefore didn't care much for anything at the time, including my own well-being), and partly because I had the situation in hand. Or at least I would when I used my magic.

Big Joe remained unamused at my little quip as he stood next to Ponytail in the rough circle of men surrounding me. It was disconcerting to see that most of them had by now half shifted into their werewolf forms. Not fully of course. They could only do that on full moons. But the rest of the time, they could still summon their brute strength, heightened speed and senses, as well as the fangs that were bared at me. "What are you doing here, wizard?" Big Joe asked.

Ponytail answered for me. "He says he's here on behalf of Forsyth."

Big Joe's face darkened. Clearly, he must have thought he had gotten away with his little indiscretion. His jaw muscles bulged as he clamped his teeth together and stared hard at me, which was just a front, I knew. Underneath the mask was the real face of someone who had just been caught with their hand in the cookie jar. I could practically see him debating with himself over whether he should have his pack tear me apart right then and there, every one of whom seeming to be only too pleased to do so.

Then one of the pack edged forward a couple of feet, a massive barrel-chested guy who looked barely out of his teens, his eyes now glowing yellow, his jaw hanging open to reveal his fangs. That was close enough for me. It was time to activate my defenses. With a sharp movement, I pushed both my hands out either side of me and inwardly said a few select words. A second later and I was surrounded by long, pointed shards of pure silver that hung in the air, quivering slightly as the sharp ends pointed towards the men surrounding me.

The young werewolf who had started towards me now stopped and looked confused. "What the fuck?"

"These are shards of pure silver," I said, looking around at the pack members. "You try to touch me, and I'll pierce you with silver."

The pack seemed to growl in unison, and then one of them shot forward in an attacking motion, trying to be the hero in front of his pack members. Immediately, I used my mind to project one of the floating shards of silver at the attacking werewolf. The shard embedded itself into the werewolf's thigh, causing him to scream and fall to the ground. Then I sensed movement behind me, and I sent another shard in that direction without looking. Another loud cry of pain sounded out.

I should probably explain that werewolves don't like silver, but then you probably knew that already. If silver pierces the head or heart of a werewolf, it will kill them. Everywhere else it just causes them a huge amount of pain. The wound left behind would also take several days to heal, as opposed to most other wounds that would heal almost straight away on a werewolf.

"Anyone else?" I said, figuring it was time I showed a bit of authority.

When no one else came forward, I looked at Big Joe. "Look, I can riddle your pack with these silver shards, even kill you all with them if I wanted to. Or, you and I can go into your office and have ourselves a chat. I'd much prefer the latter option. How about you?"

Big Joe growled at me before shaking his head. "Stand down," he commanded the pack.

The werewolves surrounding me growled in unison as they snapped their jaws at me, but none moved.

"Tell them all to leave," I said to Big Joe, who clearly didn't like being told what to do, but he nonetheless told his men to clear out. Ponytail protested, demanding to stay, but Big Joe gave him a withering look and Ponytail soon left with the rest of the pack, out the front door. As soon as they were gone, I made all the silver shards disappear. All except one, which I kept trained on Big Joe.

"Really?" he said. "You're going to keep a gun to my head?"

"That depends on you."

"You're safe, wizard. Don't worry."

After a moment, I made the shard disappear from the air. "As long as you know I can summon that back up in an instant. You try to make a move on me it will end up in your skull before you can even say, *Teen Wolf*."

Big Joe looked disgusted by the reference. "*Teen Wolf*? Really?"

I shrugged. "The Michael J. Fox movie of course."

"Oh, well that's all right then. For a minute there, I thought you were talking about the TV show. Silly me." The big man shook his head and turned to walk off into his office. Smiling to myself, I followed him in.

The small office consisted of a desk and two chairs at either side. Big Joe sat behind the desk, and after looking through the window to make sure his pack hadn't snuck back into the garage again, I took the seat opposite him. The office smelled vaguely of musk or sex, and I wondered if Big Joe had his way with some wolf chick recently. Or wolf man maybe. "You can't be too surprised to see me," I said. "You didn't think you would get away with ripping off a vampire like Forsyth, did you?"

"Hey," Big Joe snarled, seeming even huger as he sat behind the tiny desk. "I didn't rip off anybody. That's not what happened."

"Well, Forsyth thinks you did. You killed one of his own. Conveniently the one who handled all his accounts."

Big Joe took a breath as if to calm himself. Why did all these guys seem so full of rage all the time? Maybe it was the wolf hormones driving them all crazy, I thought. "Look, some of my guys got into a fight with Marcus one night at a club in the city. I don't know what it was over exactly. Marcus was off his head on coke, my guys were all drunk. One thing led to another and the next thing a fight broke out in the club. Everyone was thrown outside, but the fight continued. Marcus was outnumbered, and he got himself killed. Nothing was planned. It just happened."

"Okay. So how did you know about the flash drive?" I asked him.

"I didn't. I wasn't even there that night. One of my guys searched Marcus's pockets after they tore his heart out. They found the flash drive and a load of cash. They gave the drive to me. I still don't know what's on it because of the encryption."

"Count yourself lucky you don't know what's on it. Forsyth wants me to send a message, a bloody one, but I'm not going to because it's not my style. Just give me the drive, and we'll call it quits. I'll explain to Forsyth what happened."

Big Joe reached into the breast pocket of his cut-off and took out the small flash drive, holding it between his thick fingers as he seemed to consider it for a moment. "So all Forsyth's accounts are on this, huh?"

"Don't be stupid. Even if you managed to find someone who could break the encryption, you would never get away with it."

"But I'd have access to all his money." His dark eyes lit up at the thought.

"Yes, you would. Then you'd be dead."

Big Joe's massive chest expanded as he inhaled deeply and then slowly let out a long breath. "This is too valuable just to hand over," he said eventually. "What do I get in return?"

"You get to live," I told him, wondering how he could be so stupid as to think he could go up against Forsyth and win. His own greed and constant need for a score were getting the better of him. "Be smart. There's no way you'd win a war against the vampires. The only reason you and all of your pack aren't dead already is because the Crimson Crow is moving into politics and she doesn't want anything to distract from that."

Big Joe snorted. "The Crow is going into politics? She already runs most of the city."

"Maybe she wants to run the rest from City Hall. I wouldn't pretend to know the Crow's motivations. So are you going to hand that drive over or what?"

Pursing his lips, Big Joe nodded. "I'll give you the drive if you do something for me."

*Jesus, this guy. Always hustling.*

"I don't owe you anything. I'm just the mediator here."

"So your buddy Forsyth won't be pissed off if you return empty handed and he has to come here himself? Whatever you're getting for doing this, I doubt you would get it then."

He was right, in a way. Depending on how things panned out with Baal, there was a chance I might need Forsyth's help. If I didn't bring him the flash drive, that help wouldn't be too forthcoming. Sighing, I said, "Fine. What is it you want?"

Big Joe smiled. "I have a cousin who thinks he was hexed by a witch."

"Thinks?"

"He's been having a lot of bad luck lately."

I couldn't help but snort at that. "Story of my life. Shit happens."

"Not exactly. The other day he was working on his bike when the engine blew up in his face. The engine wasn't even on. Lucky he's a wolf, or he would have no face left."

"Like I said, shit happens. Just give me the drive."

Big Joe pressed his lips together and shook his head. "The day before his bike blew up, my cousin got run over by a car going the wrong way down the street. Day before that, a manhole cover gave way when he was walking down the street, and he fell into the sewers, breaking a leg. And just this morning, a tree fell on top of his house. A tree that had stood for years, withstanding every storm that passed by. There was no wind this morning. At least none strong enough to blow a tree into a house."

"All right," I said nodding. "There's a possibility your cousin could be hexed. Did he piss off any witches lately."

"My cousin likes his women. Women of all kinds, including witches. Unfortunately, most of them don't like it when he gets a little rough with them from time to time."

I rolled my eyes as I shook my head. "I wonder why that is."

Big Joe ignored my sarcasm. "My guess, some witch chick he banged is getting a little payback."

"So go and find this witch, make her lift the hex."

"That's what I said, but apparently the bitch in question was Scandinavian or some shit. She was just blowing through town on her way to somewhere else. She's gone."

"All right, fine. I'll look into it for you. Although you may tell your cousin to wrap himself in bubble wrap for a few days. I won't be able to help him until then. I got other stuff going on."

Big Joe considered me for a moment with his darkly hooded eyes. "You better not be playing me. I'll come find you if you are."

"Sure thing, Big Joe. Just give me the drive now."

After a moment's hesitation, during which time I thought I was going to have to forcefully take the drive myself, the werewolf handed it to me and then sat back as if he held all the cards. "Don't keep me waiting, Creed."

"I'll try not to," I said as I walked out the door.

## 5

## A DARK BRIEFING

*I* landed back in Forsyth's Riverside Hill's mansion about an hour after I left Big Joe's garage with the flash drive in hand. Forsyth was still in the same room I had left him in, working behind his desk, shuffling through papers. "Creed," he said expectantly as I walked in. "Did you get it?"

Nodding as I approached his desk, I said, "I got it. Don't you ever sleep? It's the middle of the day."

Forsyth looked relieved as he refilled his wine glass with a bottle that sat on his desk. "I'll sleep when I'm dead. Oh, wait..." He giggled sarcastically. "Did you send those mutts a message? Did you spill some blood?"

Taking the drive out of my coat pocket, I placed it on the vampire's desk. "Don't worry. They got the message. And according to Big Joe, this was all a big misunderstanding. They didn't try to rob you."

"Oh really?" Forsyth said, waving his wine glass about. "So they didn't *mean* to kill Marcus and *steal* the drive? Lying mutts."

"Apparently a few pack members got into a fight with Marcus and Marcus lost. They were after cash when they discovered the drive in Marcus's pocket." I sat down in the leather chair opposite Forsyth, still feeling weary and more than a bit drained on every level. "Needless to say, they never broke the encryption."

"Too dumb that's why." Forsyth shook his head. "And they just handed the drive over without quarrel?"

I didn't tell Forsyth about the deal I made with Big Joe. "I had to hurt a couple of them first. Big Joe was eager to co-operate once I explained the situation."

Forsyth looked doubtful. "Eager?"

"I said you would kill him and his whole pack if he didn't give the drive back."

"I still *am* going to kill them."

I shook my head. Vampires. Always had to be the alpha. "There's no need for

312

that. It was a misunderstanding. You got the drive back. What's the point in killing them?"

"You're defending the werewolves now? Who's side are you on here, Creed?"

"No ones, as you well know, Forsyth. I just get the job done whatever way I can."

Smiling, Forsyth said, "And that's why you're the best, Creed. You always find a way, don't you?"

*I hope that remains true*, I thought as I stood up, thinking about Baal again. "I have to go."

"It was nice seeing you, Creed," Forsyth said as he twirled his wine glass around with his long fingers. "Don't leave it so long next time."

"I'll be in touch if I need you."

"You can always count on me, Creed."

"Thanks Forsyth."

As I was leaving the room, he called out to me again. "By the way, those two girls you vanished earlier?" There was a grave look on his face as he paused. "Both dead."

I couldn't keep the shock from my face. "What? How?"

"You somehow moved them into the dog pens. Not much left of them now, I'm afraid."

"Jesus Christ." The guilt was already welling in up me as I wondered how I could have done such a thing.

But then, Forsyth laughed. "Relax, Creed, I was just kidding. Jesus, you should see your face."

*Bastard.*

"Funny, Forsyth. Fuck you."

"I'm sorry, I couldn't help myself. Both girls are fine, sleeping in one of the guest rooms."

Shaking my head in disgust, I walked out of the room without saying another word and slammed the door behind me.

Forsyth was still laughing to himself as I walked down the hall.

\* \* \*

On the way back to the Sanctum, I stopped in my neighborhood butcher shop and picked up half a dozen T-bone steaks, figuring Blaze would be hungry when he finally came around. I couldn't remember the last time I'd eaten something myself, and when I saw the steaks in the butcher shop, I was hit with a sudden hunger and couldn't wait to get home to throw one on the frying pan.

Only I didn't get the chance to eat when I got back home because there was somebody there waiting on me. It was Baal, or Gabriel as he had christened his new human form (not that I would be humanizing him with that name because in my mind, I was still dealing with a demon, and I preferred to keep that in mind at all times, so Baal it was).

Baal was sitting in the living room in one of the armchairs, his long legs crossed as he sat reading from one of my books. The demon looked up and smiled his creepy smile at me, casually, as if we were housemates. "*The Book Of Many Hells And*

*Demons*," he announced, holding the book up slightly. "Surprisingly accurate about most things, although this picture of me...not a very good likeness."

I said nothing for a moment as I stood staring at the demon in my living room. He still wore the same brown slacks and beige shirt he was wearing when I last saw him, although he had since added a tweed coat to the ensemble. He looked even more like an English Lit professor than he did before. I wasn't sure whether to be worried at Baal's presence or relieved that he had finally shown up again, hopefully, to tell me who he wanted me to find so I could just get on with it and get it over with (if indeed it would ever be over). I decided to be both worried and relieved at the same time. It seemed fitting. "That book needs locking up again," I said. With everything that had been happening recently, I had neglected to return the book to the trunk in the Library Of Dark magic down below.

Closing the book, Baal smoothed his hand over the dark cover. "Why would you lock such an exquisitely beautiful thing away? It deserves to be on display."

"So it can infect people's minds with its darkness?"

Baal smiled, his large hooded eyes full of composed evil. "Yes."

I stared back at him a moment as he continued to smile, then I walked off into the kitchen and placed the steaks in the fridge, pausing for a moment afterward to compose myself before walking back into the living room and taking a seat opposite Baal.

The demon placed the book he was holding gently on the floor as if he feared to hurt it. The book itself seemed to come alive in the presence of such ancient evil, the skin on its cover pulsing like blood was pumping through it, the pages jumping and flickering with apparent excitement. As soon as I felt the book's dark power try to invade my mind, I stood up and went to lift it, intending to through it down into the basement for the time being, but Baal stopped me, an amused smile on his face. "Leave it," he said.

"It's distracting me."

"I know."

I stood for another moment, inwardly sighing before sitting back down. *What a dick*, I thought as I strengthened my psychic defenses against the dark magic that tried to claw its way into my mind. It was difficult enough dealing with a monster like Baal at the best of times. I could have done without the book and its power distracting me. But I suppose that was the whole point for Baal. Maybe he wanted me to feel uncomfortable, unsure of myself and the situation, which would have made it easier for him to wrong-foot me if he had wanted to. Or maybe, as I thought in the first place, the demon was just being a dick.

"All right, Baal," I said. "Are you going to tell me who you want me to find now?"

"Gabriel, please," he responded with a tight smile. "Didn't I warn you about using my true name? I don't want to have to cut your tongue out."

I couldn't help swallowing. "Gabriel, then."

He kept staring at me, the faint hint of a fire burning deep in his eyes. "You seem troubled, Mage. What is it?"

I was surprised by the question. Why did he care if I was troubled or not? Or was this another one of his attempts to rattle me? "I don't see--"

"I'm asking, that's why." Baal leaned forward in his seat. "You will answer."

At that point, I felt something penetrate through my psychic defenses. A small amount of dark energy, but enough to trigger in me a range of dark emotions that I hadn't felt since facing off against Mr Black. I shifted in my seat and tried not to let my emotional turmoil show. Clearly, Baal wanted some measure of truth to spill forth from me. Lying to him in any way would only serve to piss him off. I had to remind myself then that the demon could snuff me from existence with the click of his fingers, or worse, plunge my soul into the bottomless depths of the Underworld. Neither fate was very appealing. If the demon wanted to play shrink, then I'd let him.

"I killed my father," I told him. "A thing like that has an effect on you."

Baal shook his head and smiled like he was pitying a clueless child. "You humans and your emotional ties. You would prosper far better without them."

"Then we wouldn't be human anymore, would be? We'd be like..." I trailed off, unwilling to finish the sentence out loud.

"Like me, you mean?"

"Monsters come in all shades."

"Monsters, demons...just labels. There is only power. That's it. Only power matters."

The dark magic was still rapping on the door of my mind, demanding to be let in. Damned if I was going to let it corrupt me again, so I hardened my defenses against it. "Are you here for a philosophical discussion? I thought you were here on business."

"I am," the demon said, resting back into his seat again. "I was merely curious. A greater man might use those conflicting emotions inside of him. You have such dark potential, Creed. I saw that when you embraced the dark magic at my summoning. Who knows what terrible things you may achieve if you just let the darkness consume you completely."

"Is that what you want? To see my soul irreparably corrupted?"

"It is in my nature to turn light into dark. I was born of the darkness, a greater darkness than you could ever to hope to imagine in a thousand lifetimes. And ever since, I have wallowed in the darkness of my own making."

"Always?"

I expected a resolute yes answer to that question, but instead, the demon hesitated for a split second. Long enough for me to sense that he was hiding something. "Always, Mr Creed."

"You never get tempted to try on a different suit from time to time? Does the light never tempt you the way the darkness tempts some?"

Baal stared back at me, his gaunt face darkening slightly, the infernal fire in his eyes burning that tiny bit brighter. "Temptation haunts every being in the universe. The temptation to grasp for more, the temptation to experience more. But it is only temptation, and it can it be controlled."

"Not always," I said. "That's the nature of temptation. At some point, for however long, you always give in."

Crossing his legs and interlocking his fingers, Baal took a long, deliberate breath as he kept his eyes on me. The intensity of his stare made it difficult for me not to look away. His stare was the most withering I had ever come across. You just couldn't help feeling small and insignificant in his presence. It was humbling and terrifying at the same time. "I like you, Creed. You aren't afraid of me."

I would have begged to differ, but I could see what he was getting at. "We're just doing business, right? You have no reason to hurt me." Even as I said it, I realized how ridiculous that was, to think myself safe from the demon's malevolence just because we had some deal together.

"Just business. Yes..." The sinister way he said that didn't exactly fill with me confidence, but it was the only reassurance I was going to get from a heartless, soulless bastard like Baal.

"Anyway," I said, breaking the long silence that crept up between us, during which time it felt like it was just me and Baal in the whole universe and nothing else. I can't tell you how deeply unsettling that was. "This person. Who is he?"

"She," Baal said. "Who is *she*."

There was an odd note in his voice when he emphasized that last word. Something like rage or betrayal. Not business, but personal. Again, I was surprised he cared enough about anything or anyone to take things personally. Perhaps there was some hint of a soul inside all of that evil, buried so deep it was barely anything, but yet still managed to send out a signal of its existence now and again as if crying out defiantly, "*I am here, and you will pay attention to me!*"

I could have been overstating things, of course. Maybe I was just misreading Baal, which wouldn't have surprised me, given the amount of attention and mental energy I was giving to keeping the dark magic from finding its way inside of my mind. But I didn't think so. There was something there, I was sure of it. "Okay. Who is *she*, then?"

"A witch." The anger in his eyes was plain to see. For a being that supposedly didn't deal in emotions, the demon sure was showing his fair share. This witch he was talking about had undoubtedly pissed him off in some way. Clearly, she was on his shitlist. And neither could he find the witch himself. Otherwise, he wouldn't be asking me to.

But then, Ray did say that Baal was known to be a master manipulator, always having a hidden agenda. Who's to say he wasn't playing me right then? Dropping faint hints of emotion into the mix to make me think it was all personal for him? But to what to end? Already my head was hurting thinking about it. It was impossible to tell if I was being conned or not. The only way to tell was to let it play out. It wasn't like I could just get up and walk away, was it? I had no choice but to see it through and hope that I was just paranoid. But how the hell could you not be paranoid around a demon? It was the only safe way to be.

"So what did this witch do that you want her found?" I asked. "I'm assuming she betrayed you in some way."

Baal nodded his head slightly. "Your assumption is correct. Her soul belongs to me. I want it back."

"I have to ask. How did you...lose it in the first place?"

The brown in Baal's eyes got overtaken by the intensity of the burning orange-red that usually was no more than a fleck in his dark retinas. His lips peeled back as he made a snarling sound, and for a second, I thought he was going to pounce on me for asking the question. I stiffened up out of fear as I heard his claws pierce the fabric of the chair he was sitting in. "That," he said, the rage simmering just beneath the surface in his face, "does not concern you."

I held my palms out towards him. "I thought it was a fair question. I'm sorry."

"It wasn't."

I said nothing more as I was forced to wait on Baal as he simmered back down and regained his previous composure. *Jesus*, I thought, *what the hell did this witch do to him?*

Whatever it was, it must have been bad. Which made me wonder at the type of person this witch was. I didn't know whether to fear her for what she had plainly done to Baal or respect her. For the time being, and until I found out more, I thought doing both would be wise.

When Baal had calmed down, he went on to tell me a little bit about the witch. He gave me a description of her but warned me that she could change her appearance and hide in plain sight. Baal also said the witch was somewhere in Blackham or one of the surrounding counties. He didn't tell me why he couldn't locate her himself, and I didn't ask. I assumed it was because the witch was using magic to hide from the demon. If so, it hinted at the power she held if she was able to hide from someone as powerful as Baal.

"What do you want me to do if--when--I find her? I asked him.

"Hand her over to me, of course."

I nodded, but said nothing.

As if taking my silence for doubt, Baal said, "That is your only course of action. I hope you are very clear on that, Creed."

"I'm clear, don't worry."

"Good." The demon got to his feet, looked like he was about to leave, which I couldn't wait for him to do if only to get out from under the suffocating influence of the dark magic book which still lay on the floor.

"What's this witch's name?"

Baal's lips pursed as if he was struggling even to say the name, and when he did, his teeth were almost clenched. "Margot Celeste."

I nodded. "all right. I'll get to finding her right away. If she's here, I'll find her."

Baal smiled his creepy smile. "I hope so, for your sake. Oh, and just to give you a little extra motivation, if you fail or try to go up against me in any way, I will take the soul of that pretty girlfriend of yours. She will suffer for eternity alongside you."

I could only stare back at him, speechless, devastated that he had brought Leona into this. I knew it would be useless to argue with him. As far as Baal was concerned, his word was law, and unfortunately, it was law for me too.

My heart sank in my chest.

Leona's life--her eternal soul--was now in my hands.

Baal vanished on the spot, teleporting off to God knows where. Probably to torment some other unfortunate soul. Either way, I was glad he was gone, and I exhaled a huge sigh of relief, then swallowed hard and gritted my teeth at the fact that I had allowed Leona to be brought into this.

*If she dies...*

Christ, it didn't bear thinking about.

I leaped out of my chair then and grabbed *The Book Of Many Hells And Demons* that still lay on the floor, the dark festering magic within its pages still emanating from it. As soon as I touched it, the book's attacks on my psyche became magnified to the point where I thought my head was going to explode through the tension of mounting my continuing defense. I practically ran with the foul text into the kitchen where I flung open the door to the basement and immediately threw the book down the stairs, quickly slamming the door closed again. The book could stay down there until I felt up to locking it back up in the Library Of Dark magic where it belonged.

"Jesus," I said, leaning against the basement door, breathing like I'd just run a three-minute mile. "I need a fucking drink."

# 6

# SINGED EYEBROWS

*W*hile I was standing in the kitchen drinking whiskey straight from the bottle (you know things are bad when you're drinking straight from the bottle), Blaze finally emerged from whatever dark enclave of the Sanctum he had been recuperating in. The big Garra Wolf paused in the kitchen doorway to look at me as if asking if the demon had gone yet. Despite being off somewhere else in the Sanctum, Blaze would still have sensed the presence of the demon in the place. If I were Blaze, I would have taken one sniff and said, "Fuck that noise. I've had my fill of dangerous demons for a while. I'm going back to sleep."

Evidently, that's what Blaze did. I didn't blame him for avoiding Baal. The wolf was only getting over dying at the hands of another demon in the form of Mr. Black. Why would he want to be around another who was probably more powerful and more devious than Mr Black ever was?

"Hey buddy," I said, tilting my unshaven chin at him. "You just missed our guest. No blood left behind this time for you to lick up, but I have steaks in the fridge. You must be starving."

Blaze padded into the kitchen as I went to the fridge, his claws clacking off the wood floor. I took two large steaks out of the greaseproof paper in the fridge and placed the meat on a dinner plate. Blaze made a noise in the back of his throat that indicated he couldn't wait to get his teeth into the raw meat. While he nearly devoured the first steak whole, I considered preparing a steak for myself as well, but after a moment's consideration, I decided I wasn't hungry. My mind was in too much of a spin to think about eating, and now that I had a case to get to work on, I was starting to feel jacked up. It happened every time I committed myself to a case, even though in this particular case I didn't have a choice in the matter. It was commit or die. But whatever my motivations, I was still committed, and that commitment kicked off an internal process in me that I still didn't quite understand. The effect of which meant that I wouldn't stop until I had closed the case. It didn't matter how, as long as I brought things to a very definite (but not necessarily satisfying) conclusion.

In this particular case, that meant locating the witch known as Margot Celeste and handing her over to Baal. And by handing her over, I mean signing the woman's death warrant. In some part of myself, I was well aware of the callousness of such an act. Clearly, Baal carried a serious grudge towards the witch in question, which meant the witch's eventual torment and suffering would be great. Probably fucking monumental, to be honest. And I was going help force the woman towards all that pain.

I had no idea what the witch had done to Baal to piss him off so much, but my initial instinct was to feel sorry for Margot Celeste, whoever she was. Whatever she had done, it was likely done out of desperation or just plain foolishness (like most human behavior). No one would try to cross a demon like Baal unless they didn't have a choice. But then, what did I know? I just knew that power (especially magical power) corrupts and that people will do anything to get more of it, including crossing demons who shouldn't be crossed.

But those were issues were incidental at that point. The most pressing matter was to find the woman first. Regardless of what she had done or how she did it--regardless of how innocent or guilty the woman was--the only thing that mattered to me at that point was preventing Leona from getting killed because of me and losing her soul to that that monster. There was just no way I was going to let that happen.

*Well, you'd better get fucking cracking then, eh?* I thought.

I left Blaze to his meal and headed into the Room Of Operations.

* * *

THE ROOM OF OPERATIONS COULD BE ACCESSED VIA A HIDDEN DOOR IN THE fireplace wall of the living room. I waved my hand over the wall, uttering a few words to reveal the door that was previously hidden with a Cloaking Spell. Then opening the door, I went inside the room.

The room itself was large and square, and it didn't exist on the original plans of the brownstone. There were a lot of rooms inside the Sanctum that shouldn't have been there. In fact, if the hidden rooms existed in physical reality (instead of on a magical plane as they did), the Sanctum would have taken up near half a block. Luckily, with magic, it was easy to keep things a little more contained and compact.

The Room Of Operations was one of the few extra rooms in the Sanctum that I created myself, most of the rest having been created by Ray when he bought the place decades ago. When I began hiring out my services as a magicslinger back in the day, I decided I needed a place where I could go to work on my cases, and also store my case files. After every case, I wrote up a report and filed it in the Op Room. It was a practice I had maintained since my first case many years ago (when I was hired by the Crimson Crow to find her daughter). I figured the case reports would come in handy for future cases, plus I wanted to maintain some semblance of professionalism. Just because I dealt with magic and the supernatural, that didn't mean I couldn't be organized about things.

The Op Room had white walls, most of them being covered by photographs, crumpled documents, and endless post-it notes, many of which were interconnected by string held in place by thumb tacks. One entire wall was taken up by shelves that were densely filled with folders containing case reports. Even though I did my reports on the computer, I always printed a hard copy as there was no substitute for reading words on real paper.

Dominating the room was a large mahogany table that sat in the middle of the wood floor. Just about every inch of the huge table was covered by something, be it old case reports, maps, photographs, grimoires, potion bottles and various magical instruments such as the Quill of Nostradamus, which had the power to predict the future if you wrote with it. Not always accurate, but it came in handy from time to time.

Also on the table was a MacBook, which I mostly used to type up reports and access the internet. Despite my magic, I still had cause to go online from time to time, if only to access some of the resource sites that were tucked away deep in the Dark Web. Resources such as the Blackham City Online Grimoire, which not only listed every kind of supernatural being and magical adept in the city but also their names and who they were. No one knew who maintained the site, and many of the names on it were not happy that they were listed, despite the fact that the site was only accessible to a handful of people, of which I was one. Access to the site could not be requested by anyone. Instead, it was granted to those who were deemed worthy or in need of it by whoever ran the site itself. I just happened to log into my computer one day to find a message saying I had been granted access to the site. My guess was that the site was run by some Cybermancer as the passwords had to be backed up with magic sent through your fingers and into the computer so your identity could be verified.

Most of the time when I was tasked with finding someone who belonged to the occult and supernatural underground, the Online Grimoire was the first place I checked. Almost always, the person I was looking for would be listed there, and if I were lucky, there would also be other information about them, such as last known address or a history of the person. It was quite unbelievable the extent of the information to be found on the site. In many cases, there were pages and pages of background information attached to the names. Entire histories in some cases. I was listed on the site as well needless to say, but thankfully my background info didn't run too personal. It was just standard stuff like place of birth, family tree, current address and details about my job and some of the more notable cases I had worked on.

As much as I found the Online Grimoire a useful resource to have at my disposal, there were many individuals and groups who were not happy about being listed. Most of the protestors didn't even have access. They had just heard they were included on the site. It pained most of them that they were unable to erase themselves from it. Although as far as I knew, no one had used the site for malicious purposes. It was like the webmaster behind it all knew exactly who they could trust with access. No one had a clue who ran the site, which made it nearly impossible to take it down. Many had tried (including some skilled Cybermancers and human hackers), but most couldn't even find their way to the load screen. Just when they thought they had pinpointed the site's location, it would suddenly shift and disappear again into the depths of the Dark Web. And as a final security measure, approved users of the site would only be granted access if they were alone. If any non-approved users were present, you would find you had forgotten the address of the site, and it would simply be unreachable.

Standing at the table and clearing some space for the MacBook, I logged onto the Dark Web via the Tor browser and keyed in the address of the site from memory. A moment later, a login screen opened up that asked for a sixteen digit password, which I typed in, again from memory. As I typed in the password, I allowed a small amount of magic to flow from my fingers into the keyboard so the site could verify my identity. It did this by scanning my magic the same way you would scan a fingerprint. Every adept's magic was unique to them in some way, so it served as a unique identifier so you could access the site. If you didn't have magic, then your blood would do.

The screen flashed a few times before finally granting me access to the site. The site was a simple design with just a few functions. You could search directly for someone if you knew their name, or you could browse the list of names that were stored in alphabetical order (which I sometimes did just out of sheer interest, and also to familiarize myself with any new players in town).

In the search box, I typed the name of the witch I had to find: MARGOT CELESTE. When I hit enter, one search result was returned. "Well," I said. "At least she's on here."

Clicking on the search result, I was brought to a black screen containing green text (very old school aesthetic, which I liked...no fucking annoying ads anyway!). "Right, Margot Celeste, let's see who you are..."

Disappointingly, there wasn't much information on our witch. Certainly not as much as I hoped for, but I also wasn't surprised either. From what I could gather, Margot Celeste was a master at hiding herself from the world, which meant she would not be easy to find.

She was listed on the Online Grimoire as a witch. And also as a known murderer. A multiple murderer no less. I looked away from the screen while I let that information sink in for a second. She had killed people. Her murders were verified, or she wouldn't have been listed on the site as a murderer in the first place. It was hard not to start thinking of the witch as being a bad or evil person having read that, but I knew there could be many reasons for committing murder, not all of them bad. But again, did I really care what kind of person Margot Celeste was? No, I didn't, not at that point anyway. I only cared about removing the gun Baal had at Leona's head (a gun she didn't even know was there). Everything else had to be secondary to that, including saving my own skin. So I moved past the murderer thing and went back to looking at the screen

Her overall power was scored as a surprising and very impressive 8 out of 10 (mine was an 8.2 if you are interested, Sanaka's a 9.6) and her last known address was the French Quarter in New Orleans, which was...ten years ago. "Bastard," I cursed under my breath. Now I was going to have to find Margot Celeste the harder way. Through magic. Or good old fashioned detective work. Likely a combination of both.

Underneath the scant background information (which just listed a few different previous addresses and some verified spells of note) there was a link entitled "Associations". I clicked the link and was taken to a different screen that had

Margot Celeste's name in the center. Branching out from her name was a host of other names, people that the witch had associated herself with over the years. Predictably, many of the names belonged to other witches. The rest were a mixture of adepts and supernatural entities (Sleepwalkers were not listed in the Grimoire). I recognized a few of the names on the screen and wrote them down on a post-it note as possible leads. If I failed to find her directly, I could always contact those associates and pump them for information.

In the meantime, I closed up the MacBook and put it one side before unfurling a large map of Blackham City that was rolled up on the desk, using some paperweights to hold the corners down. The map not only detailed the geography of the city but also the surrounding areas. With no luck on the Online Grimoire, it was time to try a Location Spell.

Location Spells could be hit and miss. In general, the accuracy of the spell depended on how much you knew about the person you were trying to find. Even better to have a personal item of some kind that belonged to that person. Unfortunately, though, all I knew about the witch was her name and not much else. That didn't give me much to go on, but it would have to do. Besides, I didn't hold out much hope that a Location Spell would work, no matter how much information I had on the target. If the witch could shield herself from a demon like Baal, it was unlikely her presence would be picked up by a mere Location Spell. Still, I had to try, if only for the sake of elimination.

I held both hands over the map and shut my eyes while I conjured up the spell, entering the Chaosphere just long enough to direct the required amount of magic needed to fuel the spell. When I opened my eyes again, I lifted a small knife with a very sharp blade of the table and used the knife to make a thin cut in the palm of my left hand. Then I made a fist with my bloody hand and held it over the center of the map while I completed the words to the spell, emphasizing the name of Margot Celeste as I did so. Drops of blood soon flowed from out of my loose fist and splashed onto the map. After a few drops had landed, I took my hand away from the map, wrapping a grubby handkerchief around the still bleeding cut. Then I waited.

As I had done the spell countless times before, I knew exactly what was supposed to happen if the spell was doing its job. The blood on the map was supposed to run across it and eventually stop at whatever location the target was at. At the very least, you would have a rough idea of where your target was at. Then you would go there and resume the detective work, but that bit closer to your mark.

But in this case, nothing happened. Or at least not for a few moments, when the blood in the center of the map suddenly spread out in all directions at once and spiderwebbed over the entire surface. I shook my head. "Damn it," I said, not surprised at all that the spell was going awry since it was being fucked with by the magic of Margot Celeste. Her influence and reach were indeed substantial. Impressive.

So was what happened next.

The map exploded suddenly into flames as if the blood covering it was highly flammable. The flames were explosive and burst upwards past my face, singing my eyebrows and beard in the process. "Shit!" I exclaimed, jumping back.

Then the flames died down just as suddenly, finally vanishing as if some hidden force had extinguished them. In the wake of the flames, there was a pile of blackened ash on the table. The remains of the map.

After a moment, I couldn't help but smile. "Touché," I said as I smoothed over my singed eyebrows.

# 7

# DRUNKEN BASTARDS

$\mathcal{A}$s I wasn't able to locate the witch using my own magic, I thought perhaps that the magic from a more powerful wizard might be able to. My first instinct was to call Uncle Ray since his magic was powerful and he was in town. When I tried to call him, however, his phone went straight to voicemail, and I knew right then that my uncle didn't want to be contacted.

Probably too busy shagging the Crimson Crow or some other supernatural sexpot that he shouldn't really be with.

Bearing in mind that Ray was over one hundred and fifty years old. He was no spring chicken as they say, but that didn't stop him from having his fun when he wanted to. He had always been one for the women, which was probably why he never married. That and his fondness for constant adventure made Ray bad husband material, but a hell of wizard and a fascinating storyteller.

*And hard to bloody contact.*

Ray could have his fun. I decided to seek help from Tetsuo Sanaka instead. The man was still my mentor after all. If I should have been going to anyone for help, it was him. Sanaka would likely disagree, mind. He liked to be left alone, and for the most part shared the same philosophy as my uncle, which was that every man should beat down his own path and make his own mistakes. Even if that meant getting hurt or dying in the process. In fact, as far as those two were concerned (Ray more than Sanaka, it had to be said), the greater the risk, the greater the potential for learning. "August, my boy," Ray once told me. "A man will learn the most the closer he is to death's door."

"That's not much if you end up dying anyway, is it?" I responded at the time.

And it was true. Dying, or nearly dying, to learn a lesson (not matter what the lesson was), struck me as being foolish, to say the least. Why take risks if you don't have to? I learn more from avoiding death than running towards it, even though I run towards death on a regular basis. I'm all for accepting help and giving help when I can. It just makes more sense than going it alone all the time, which might be character building, but isn't always fun. In fact, it's not fun at all being alone most of the time. That's one lesson I've learned at least.

I drove from the Sanctum to the park in Little Tokyo where Sanaka's own Sanctum was located, hidden away at the edge of the park in a small woodland, shielded by magic against prying eyes. The only way into the grounds of Sanaka's quirky little Sanctum was to teleport in, or else to know the correct magic sequence to create an entrance. I chose to teleport in as it was easier.

As always when I landed in the place, I got that immediate sense of familiarity and the many painful memories that were associated with it. My live-in mentorship with Sanaka was like a season spent in Hell. I've mentioned the man's sadistic teaching methods before. Let's not dwell on them now.

I didn't need to knock on the arched front door of the pagoda style Sanctum. Nearly a decade spent living there had at least earned me the right to return as I pleased, and to enter when I pleased. That's how I saw it anyway. Sanaka may have had a different view on the matter, though he hadn't turned me away yet. There was always a first time, however.

After making a few complicated movements with my hands held just in front of the door, the door itself opened.

Well, at least he hasn't changed the Locking Spell since the last time I was here.

Before stepping inside, I wrenched off my boots and left them outside, walking inside the Sanctum in socks that were long overdue for a change. I had expected to see Sanaka standing in the hallway, having sensed my arrival as he always did. But he was nowhere to be seen. Which was strange. For Sanaka, greeting a visitor at the door wasn't optional, it was mandatory. The honorable thing to do.

Frowning, I traipsed across the polished wood floor in the wide hallway, glancing around for signs of my mentor. "Sanaka?" I called out but got no reply.

But then I heard voices coming from a room down the hallway to the left. I stood and listened for a moment, surprised that anyone else was there. Virtually no one visited Sanaka, except me, and that's exactly how he liked things to be. Yet going by the noise he was clearly entertaining someone.

Then I heard a laugh. A deep, rollicking laughter, allowed to come forth with carefree abandon like the person it was coming from had not a worry in the world. There was only one person I knew who laughed like that.

"Ray? What the fuck?" I shook my head as I walked down the hallway towards the room where Ray and Sanaka where. The sound of Sanaka laughing made me stop and freeze on the spot.

*What dark magic is this?* I thought to myself. *Sanaka never laughs. Unless...*

"You're *drunk*?" I said to Sanaka as I walked into the room to find both him and my uncle lying on the floor on top of a pile of cushions like a couple of drunken teenagers. "And Ray? What the hell are you doing here?"

Ray finished drinking from a clear glass bottle full of clearer liquid that I assumed was sake. "Why, I've come to visit my old friend, Sanaka," he said waving the bottle around and nodding his head, Sanaka nodding his as well as if to back up what he was saying. "And I think the better question is, what the hell are *you* doing here? Don't you have a demon to appease or something?"

They both burst into laughter, and I stood there shaking my head at them, feeling like a father come home to find his two teenage sons drunk as skunks. "I'm glad you both find my misfortune funny," I said, which promoted more uproarious laughter.

"Other people's misfortune and pain are always funny," Sanaka said. "Why do you think I was so hard on you when you lived under this roof? You kept me entertained."

I pursed my lips and stood staring at Sanaka. *Take a breath, Creed,* I thought. *He's drunk. They both are.*

And stoned as well, going by the presence of Ray's pipe on the floor and the thick layer of smoke stratifying the air in the room. "I'm just going to go ahead and pretend you didn't say that."

"He's just messing with you, boy," Ray said. "Here. Come and have a drink with us. You could probably use one. Being a demon's bitch is thirsty work I hear."

More raucous laughter filled the room as Sanaka leaned over and slapped Ray on the knee. "Real mature, guys," I said. "Why don't you's high five each other while you's are at it."

And of course, that's what they did, nearly collapsing into each other as they slapped palms, sparks of wayward magic leaking out of their hands.

*Jesus,* I thought. *So much for getting help. These two look like they couldn't even stand up never mind perform a damn Location Spell.*

Still, I couldn't help but smile at them both. Sanaka especially, who I had seen drunk exactly two times since I had known him. Trust Ray to lead the old wizard astray.

"So tell us, apprentice of mine," Sanaka said as he did his best to focus on me with his dark brown eyes, his long grayish hair falling into his face, which he made a half-assed attempt to brush aside. "Why do you need our help? Have you lost your soul again?" He laughed once more, and Ray tittered away beside him as he drank more of the Saki from the bottle.

I shook my head. "Firstly, I'm technically not your apprentice anymore. I stopped being that some time ago."

"Ohhhhhhhhh," Ray said. "Backtalk. I like it."

"He thinks he is a master wizard now," Sanaka said to Ray as if I wasn't in the room. "Yet, he still needs my help."

*God, this is impossible,* I thought. I might as well come back later when hopefully one or both of them had sobered up enough to help me. "I'll come back later," I said. "When you've stopped being a couple of teenagers."

"Oh, God," Ray said exasperatedly. "Get a grip, August. Just because we've been drinking this superbly smooth and potent sake all day, doesn't mean we won't be able to help you. The old guy's are just having a little fun, that's all. I don't come around often. Here." He held out the bottle. "Have a drink and tell us what's up."

Sighing, I took the bottle from Ray and took a drink. The sake was like firewater, and it burned the hell out of my throat. "Jesus," I said. "You's have been drinking *this* all day? This shit would burn a hole in your stomach."

"Or put some hairs on that chest of yours," Ray said.

"I have enough hairs on my chest," I said, drinking again despite feeling like my tongue was melting like chewing gum in hot sunlight.

"Needs some on his balls, though," Sanaka said, bursting into laughter at the same time as Ray.

I couldn't help smiling this time. "You two...Jesus..."

"Look at him, Tetsuo," Ray said with a lop-sided grin on his face. "Look at the fine specimen he has become. Aren't you proud of your former student, Tetsuo?"

I stood shaking my head, vaguely embarrassed now as I took another swig from the bottle, the sake like lit fuel trailing down into my stomach. I was aware of Sanaka staring at me as he tried to keep his head still but couldn't.

"Best student I ever had," the old Japanese Mage said.

"The *only* student you've ever had," Ray pointed out.

"I know," Sanaka said.

They started laughing again.

"That's because no one else was mad enough to apprentice under you," I said, refusing to take the slagging lying down.

"No!" Sanaka barked, suddenly very serious as he held up a finger. "The only one *worthy* of my time."

Our eyes met for a second, and he nodded, then he stuck his hand out for the bottle, which I passed over to him. "Thanks," I said. "I guess."

"Take the compliment, August," Ray said. "They don't come around often."

They didn't come around at all actually. Maybe Sanaka should have gotten drunk more often. Although looking at the state of him, I thought, *Maybe not.*

"Right," my uncle said, grabbing Sanaka's arm. "Let's get up and help the boy. Show him how real magic is done, eh?"

Sanaka nodded and put the bottle down on the floor. They both tried to get up at the same time, leaning on each there as they did. They got barely halfway up before collapsing back down into the cushions again, falling into fits of laughter as they did so.

Once again, I shook my head.

*This might take a while*, I thought.

* * *

It took some time, but I finally managed to wrangle Ray and Sanaka to their feet and move them out of the room and into a different room at the other side of the Sanctum. Along the way, I had to wrestle with Ray to stop him from entering rooms that were doorways to different dimensions. "I want to go to the Amazonian Dimension," he said loudly. "Tetsuo, you need to see the women there. Statuesque goddesses all of them..."

"I know," Sanaka said.

Ray elbowed him. "You dirty dog..."

They both started laughing, holding onto each other as I moved them along.

Ten minutes later (yes, ten) I finally ushered the two drunks into the Map Room. It was a huge room, every wall lined with wooden shelves and pigeon holes containing thousands of rolled up maps that not only charted Earth but also many other worlds and dimensions in the known universe. Ray let go of Sanaka as they entered the room, my uncle's eyes lighting up as he gazed at all the maps, then went to the large table in the center of the room, holding onto it as if to keep himself from falling over. "The Avexus Nebula," he proclaimed as he looked over the map that was opened out on the table. "A wondrous place indeed. I've been there many times. They make the most amazing wine--"

"And medicine," Sanaka said.

"Medicine?" I said frowning.

Sanaka nodded. "I need more than magic to maintain this body."

"Aye, indeed," Ray said. "Give it another few decades, August. You'll see what we mean."

"I'm sure I will," I said, already searching for a map of Blackham, finding it a moment later rolled up on one of the shelves. I removed the map of the Nebulas Dimension that was on the table and unrolled the Blackham map instead. "Right. Baal wants me to find a witch named Margot Celeste. She's apparently in or around Blackham somewhere. When I tried my own Location Spell, I was blocked by her magic. The map I was using burnt to a crisp in fact."

Ray raised his bushy eyebrows. "Really? She's got chops this witch. You might have your hands full with her."

"He hopes," Sanaka said, sniggering like a naughty schoolboy.

"Nonsense," Ray said, coming over and putting his arm around me. "He's committed this one. Foolish boy."

I sighed and shook my head. "So are we going to do this spell or not? I'd like to honor my deal with Baal as soon as possible so that I can get back to my life again. If that's all right with you two, that is."

"You worry too much, August," Ray said going back to the table, with Sanaka joining him a moment later. "You should learn to let go and go with the flow."

"Right. Maybe I'll get sloshed on sake and see how it goes."

Ray shook his head at my sarcasm but said nothing.

Standing by the long table, still unsteady on his feet, Sanaka rubbed his hands together as if warming up for the spell. Ray joined him, a small penknife in his hand now, which he used to make a slice in the palm of his right hand. He passed the knife to Sanaka who made a cut on his own palm. Then the two of them hovered their fists over the center of the map and allowed a few drops of blood to drip down onto the paper. When they both opened their palms again, their cuts had healed.

"Do you need me?" I asked.

"Just watch and learn, son," Ray replied. "Watch and learn."

Shaking my head, I stood at one end of the table and watched as Ray and Sanaka held their hands over the small pool of blood on the map as they both repeated the words to the Location Spell. Hopefully, their combined power would get a result. I doubted the witch's magic was that strong that it could resist the magic of two Master Mages (or even one of them for that matter). If the witch's magic did resist, I'd be screwed because there would be no way to find her otherwise.

As before when I did the spell myself, the blood on the map tried to spread out in all directions, but Sanaka and Ray managed to contain it, not letting the witch's magic mess up the spell. Ray closed his eyes for a moment as he poured more concentration into the spell. When he opened his eyes again, a smile appeared on his face, and he looked at Sanaka, who smiled back.

I smiled as well when I saw the thin line of blood begin to trickle its way from the center of the map, running in a rivulet in a westerly direction. It was exciting watching the line of blood wind its way across the map as I wondered where it was going to end up. My guess was outside the city, but we would see. A few times, the line of blood tried to double back, but the combined magic of the two master wizard's held it in check and prevented the witch's magic from leading us astray.

This battle of wills and magic went on for a few minutes until the line of blood entered into Morgan County on the map and eventually stopped altogether. "There's your witch," Ray said, finally relaxing along with Sanaka. "Red Branch Falls, Morgan County."

"Red Branch Falls," I said, relieved to have finally pinpointed the witch's location. "That's hundreds of acres of woodland."

"She's in there somewhere," Ray said, retrieving the bottle of sake from one of the shelves behind him. "I'm sure you can work your magic when you get there."

I nodded, wondering how I was going to find the witch in all that woodland. A whole army could hide out there and not be found. "all right, I suppose I'd better get cracking then. Thanks you two."

"Good luck," Sanaka said. "You might need it."

Frowning I said, "Why? Did you sense something?"

"Only that the witch's magic is strong. As is her resolve not to be found. She will have sensed us searching for her. Now she knows someone will be coming."

"Yes," Ray said. "Be careful, August. Not all witches are as nice as your mother was. I find most of them to have chips the size of Everest on their shoulders. Great in bed, though. Wildcats. I could tell you some stories..."

I held a hand up to stop him. "Don't bother. Save the stories for when I'm gone."

Ray chuckled to himself, and Sanaka smiled knowingly. "I hope you have more of this delicious sake, Tetsuo."

"Plenty," Sanaka said, although he looked like he had had enough already. He didn't have the capacity for it that Ray had. No one did, in fact.

After enduring a few more drunken jibes from Ray, I left them to it. "Try not to fall into any dangerous dimensions after I go," I told them. "One wild goose chase is enough."

And with that, I left to prepare for my trip to the wilds of Morgan County.

# 8

# DIVISION

*A* black SUV was parked on the street outside the Sanctum. The windows were all blacked out, so it was impossible to see who was inside. Though as I parked the Cadillac behind the SUV, I noticed the government plates on the vehicle and deducted that I was getting a visit from a member or members of the Division, the secret government department charged with policing and investigating the occult underground and supernatural community. Before I had even got out of the car, the doors of the SUV opened, and two men got out, both dressed in dark suits, both with guns in their hands. One of the men then opened the back door on the passenger side and out stepped another, taller man. I shook my head when I saw who it was.

*Bloody Brentwood*, I thought. *I don't have time to deal with him right now.*

I had a witch to track down after all, and a demon to appease.

*And a girlfriend to save, don't forget.*

How could I forget?

"Brentwood," I said as I got out of the car, in a tone that I hoped would make clear to the Division boss that I didn't have time to stop and chat.

"Creed," Brentwood said, standing military straight in his suit and dark overcoat, looking every inch the government agent that he was. "I need to speak with you. It's urgent."

"Isn't it always?" I breezed past him and walked up the steps to the Sanctum, making a few hand movements by the front door to open it.

"I wouldn't be here if it weren't," he shot back, still offended by my lack of concern for his problems, not to mention the little respect I had for his authority. As I said before, I didn't always agree with Brentwood's methods, and I found his incessant pushiness annoying. His rules and regulations didn't apply to me, nor did I live by his military code, so that tended to make him view me as some dangerous outlaw that had to be watched carefully. In my darker moments, I sometimes wondered if Leona wasn't just a plant, that she was just pretending to be my girl-friend in order to keep a close eye on me at her bosses behest. Not that I believed that (although I wouldn't have put it past Brentwood to do such a thing), but the thought did cross my mind occasionally. Usually when Leona refused me sex on the grounds of needing her sleep, or sometimes when she didn't laugh at my jokes or other times when she and Brentwood would talk from a distance and look over at me as they did so as if Leona was briefing him on what I had been up to. Moments of fleeting insecurity. Nothing more.

"All right," I said. "Come inside. Tell me what's so urgent. Although I'll warn you now, whatever it is, it will have to wait. I have more urgent matters to take care of."

I didn't wait for his response and went inside the Sanctum to the living room where I stood waiting on him. Blaze was lying in the corner of the room by the bookshelves, sniffing the air as if to identify the person coming in behind me. Blaze already knew who Brentwood was, so once the wolf got the scent, he settled back down again and idly stared in my direction as if he couldn't wait to see me squirm in Brentwood's presence.

Brentwood himself entered the living room like a tall, dark shadow, his mahogany skin starkly contrasted against his white collar. As always, he wore his usual expression of mild disdain as if everything offended him all of the time. Including me. Of course. "This place is still as creepy as the last time I was in it," he said, looking around the room, his eyes going to the ceiling and the books which floated up there like giant moths.

"I hope you didn't come here just to slag off my Sanctum, Brentwood." I folded my arms across my chest and stood like I wasn't in the mood for any shit. Which I wasn't. "Does this little list have anything to do with the case Leona is working on in New York?" I almost threw a sarcastic thanks at him for sending Leona there in the first place, but he just would have retaliated with one of his fuck you stares, so I didn't bother.

"No, it isn't." He jammed his hands into his coat pockets. "A few days ago, the Division got word that a certain book had fallen into the hands of a fringe group, a cult almost, called the Scientists of the Arcane. You ever heard of them?"

I nodded. "I think so. A bunch of alchemist types, right? Like to run experiments that combine magic with science?"

"Yes. Harmless experiments up until now mostly. We had an eye on them, as we do on all of the fringe groups in this city."

"So what's changed?"

"The Scientists have managed to get their hands on a book called the Dark Codex, which I'm sure you've heard of."

I had. The book was famous in the occult underground because it supposedly allowed whoever read it to untangle the mysteries of the universe, and to tap into powers that no one should be able to tap into, powers that would be a handful even for a god. There was talk of a few such books in existence, but they were mostly a myth, born of people's desire to gain control over the universe itself and to tap into knowledge that would make the bearer of such knowledge a god. It was the highest form of magic, but no more than a lofty ideal for the most part. In all of my time spent searching for books and ancient arcane texts, I had never come across a book like the Dark Codex, which handily contained instructions to wield the ultimate form of magic in one convenient place. "Are you saying a bunch of scientists has managed to get their hands on the Dark Codex? How do you know this? That book is just a myth."

"We thought so too," Brentwood said. "Until we got word that the group had invented a machine that would allow anyone access to the Astral Plane whenever they wanted. To make matters worse, they put the plans for the machine online and encouraged people to build their own. They believe magic and the technology they build should be available to all. I don't need to tell you, I strongly disagree with that notion."

A machine to access the Astral Plane? Without using magic? Very inventive. I could just picture people lining up to try it out and then never making it back because they had been attacked by one of the Astral predators that stalked the Plane. I was curious, though, as to how the inventors managed to make it so the body didn't have to be left behind before entering the Astral Plane itself. Did the machine render the physical body ephemeral somehow? "So why don't you just send a team to retrieve the book if you think the Scientists have it? Why are you telling me?"

Brentwood sighed as if his hands were tied. "We would if we could find them. The group has used the book to create their own plane of existence. All of their work is done within that plane. And even if we could get to them, they aren't just going to give up the book. These people are radicals, Creed. Anarchists. They want to put so much power in the hands of the people that society will blow itself up."

"Sounds like you got a serious problem on your hands."

"Fucking right. And I need your help to fix it, Creed."

It was my turn to sigh. "And by fixing it you mean what?"

"Infiltrating the group and retrieving the Dark Codex."

"You want me to go undercover."

"Precisely. You're the only man for the job, Creed."

"You're staring at me like I don't have a choice. I hate it when you do that."

"Look, Creed," Brentwood said as he took a few steps towards me. "I don't pretend to like your methods, but there's no denying you get results. I'll give you whatever you need to get the job done. There's a lot of very nervous people above me who want that book found, including the President."

"And what do you plan to do with the book once you get it? I'd say the military would be very interested in a book like that."

Brentwood looked away for a second. "What happens to the book is out of my hands, Creed."

"I'm sure," I said, having heard enough now. "Look Brentwood, I'll *maybe* take the job on, but not right away. I have a more pressing matter to take care off first."

His jaw clenched for a second as he once again struggled with the fact that he didn't have the authority to command me into doing as he said right away. He knew he would have to wait. "How long?"

I shrugged, shook my head. "Not sure. A few days maybe."

*Hopefully anyway.*

"Fine. Contact me when you're ready." He turned to walk out of the living room. I didn't follow him.

"Sure," I said wearily.

When Brentwood was in the hallway, he called out, "Don't leave it too long, Creed. People are waiting."

After the front door had closed, tension filled my body, and I gave Brentwood the middle finger, even though he had gone.

Blaze made a small barking noise form the corner of the room, and I looked over at him. "It never ends, Blaze," I said. "It never fucking ends."

* * *

An hour or so later, as I was gathering everything I needed for the trip to Red Branch Falls, my phone rang and I answered it, glad to hear Leona's voice on the other end. "Hey," I said, taking a seat in the living room. "How's it going there?"

"Okay," Leona said. "Same old shit, different madman. You know the score."

"You sound tired."

"I'm leading the field team on this. A lot of running around. I came back to my hotel to grab an hours sleep before we have to run down another lead."

"So who's the madman you're chasing?" I asked, settling into the chair, just glad to be able to listen to her sultry voice as she spoke.

"We don't know yet. He's killed eight people so far, uses magic to grotesquely deform the bodies before leaving them in public like sick sculptures. He's been taunting the local PD with letters as well. We'll catch the son of a bitch, though."

"You always do."

She went silent for a moment. "I miss you, Creed." She said it quietly like it was hard for her to say, which I knew it was.

I swallowed. "I miss you too. You've no idea how fucking much, in fact."

"Are you okay? You sound tired and stressed."

"I'm both. I'm getting ready to go and find a witch on behalf of Baal."

"That's who he wants you to find? Why?"

"I don't know. Neither do I care. I'm just going to find her and turn her over to Baal. After that, I'm done."

"You think that demon will let you walk?"

I said nothing for a moment. It was a possibility I didn't want to consider much, the fact that Baal may just keep me on retainer after I did that one thing for him. The last thing I wanted was to remain in the demon's service in perpetuity. Fuck that. "I hope so," was all I could say.

Silence fell between us again, a silence that for me was filled with a longing to be with the woman I loved right then, in person. "We should run away," I said eventually. "Just the two of us. Maybe off-world. Forever. What do you think?"

She gave a small laugh. "Right now, that idea doesn't sound too bad."

"Really?" Normally she would have dismissed such notions as silly and not worth thinking about.

"Really."

I smiled. "There's hope for you yet, Lawson."

"Don't get too excited, Creed," she jested. "I could do with some time off, though. With you."

"We'll make it happen. I promise."

Fuck Brentwood. Fuck everything else. I was going to spend some quality time with the woman I loved, no matter what.

In the background, it sounded like someone knocking Leona's hotel room door. "Shit," she said. "I gotta go."

"All right," I said. "So do I."

"Be careful of that witch. Them bitches are crazy."

"Don't sweat it. I'll be fine." Not that I was sure if I believed that.

Another knock sounded on her hotel room door, more insistent this time, followed by a male voice calling her name. "Creed?" she said, ignoring the other voice.

"Yeah?"

There was a pregnant silence while I waited on her saying something, but eventually, all she said was, "Nothing. Forget it. We'll talk later."

Then she hung up.

# 9

# DARK PASSENGER

*I* left the Sanctum just before dawn the next morning, driving through the mostly empty streets of the city on my way to Morgan County. I didn't sleep much the night before, my mind turning over everything that had happened recently. While I watched the sky turn from dark gray to a pale lilac color as the sun came up, I began to wonder if I hadn't lost something of myself when I destroyed my father's soul. Before it happened, I never stopped to consider how taking him down would make me feel. I had been so angry at him, despising his bloodlust and thirst for power, that it never even occurred to me that I might feel bad for killing him. I just wanted to stop the son of a bitch at any cost.

Of course, my father was, to all intents and purposes, dead anyway. He had died a long time ago at the hands of a demon with the rest of my family. What I faced off against in that abandoned factory wasn't my father, but Mr Black, a purely evil entity that was created in the Underworld. I should not have been feeling bad for destroying such a malevolent creation.

*And yet...*

I shook my head as I barreled down the expressway in the Cadillac, forcing myself not to think about Mr Black or my father any longer. They had taken enough from me, I decided, and they were both gone now anyway.

"What's done is done," I said as if to try and convince myself. "Fuck him. Fuck *them*. Time to move on."

Leaning forward, I turned on the radio. "Sympathy For The Devil" was just beginning, and I shook my head, considered changing the station and thought, *Fuck it.*

*"Please allow me to introduce myself, I'm a man of wealth and taste..."*

I looked out the side window at the dark expanse of the lake I was passing by, framed by the mountains at the far side. The cold morning light made the lake look gunmetal gray, and the wind made the surface choppy. Altogether, it was quite an ominous landscape at that time of year.

*"I've been around for a long, long year. Stole many a man's soul to waste..."*

"I like this song."

I cried out in shocked surprise when I heard the voice beside me and lost control of the wheel for a moment, the Cadillac veering off towards the lake as I wrestled the car back to the center of the road again. "Jesus *Christ!*" I shouted at the person who now sat in the passenger seat beside me.

Or rather a demon.

Baal was wearing his creepy smile and overly calm demeanor as he stared over at me. "Careful," he said. "You might cause an accident. I wouldn't want to damage this perfectly good flesh suit, now would I?"

Resisting the urge to pull over and punch the living shit out of Baal (not that he would have let me, but it was how I felt), I sat fuming as I gripped the steering wheel hard with both hands. "In what world is it ever a good idea to just appear beside someone like that when they're driving? You're lucky there's hardly any traffic at this time of the morning, or else you would have had to find yourself another suit to wear. Maybe you could have scraped mine up off the roadside and wore it."

Baal just sat staring at me as I vented, his face as unexpressive as a Buddhist monk's. Under other circumstances, I probably wouldn't have dared shout at him like that since he could snap my neck with barely a twitch of his finger if he wanted to. But in that case, I thought my outburst was justified. "Have you finished now?" he asked.

I shook my head. "What the hell is so urgent that you had to teleport into my car while I was driving? We use phones here. You should get one."

Frowning slightly, Baal reached into his corduroy jacket pocket and pulled out a phone. "Is this the device you are talking about?"

"Yes. You want my number?"

Baal smiled as he wound down the window and dropped the phone to the blacktop where it probably shattered into pieces. Then he sat staring at me once again, those eyes of his causing me so much discomfort it was almost unbearable. "Rest assured, Creed. If I want to contact you, I will do so in person. Always."

I nodded uncomfortably. "Awesome. I'll bear that in mind."

Baal smiled and seemed to relax a little in his seat as if we had come to some understanding, one which I wasn't aware of, but he seemed satisfied nonetheless. His head even started to bob upon and down gently as the Stones continued to play on the radio. He seemed even more scary and weird when he was relaxed. Suddenly, it felt hard to breathe inside the car, even with the windows open. I just wanted him gone. For good would have been nice, but I knew there was no way that was going to happen. Not until I had handed over the witch he so desperately sought. "I like this music," he said. "Nowhere near as torturous as the music to be found in the Underworld, but still...catchy."

"Wait till you hear Justin Bieber," I said. "You'll feel right at home then."

"I don't know this Justin Beaver. Is he from the Underworld?"

"There are many who think so. Including me."

"Is he a demon?"

"Of a sorts, yes. Definitely. Justin Bieber is a demon. Without a doubt."

Baal nodded. "I must look him up. He sounds like he could be useful."

I didn't dare ask for what. "Yeah, do that. I'm sure he'd be glad to have you around."

The demon went back to smiling out the window again and sat that way for what seemed like an hour, but really, was only for a few moments. Still long enough for me to crack under the silence and ask him again what he was doing inside my car. "How'd you even know where I was?"

He gave me a look as if to say, *Please, do you know who you're talking to?* "I thought I would join you for the ride. I'd like to see where the witch is hiding out."

*Shit. He's coming along for the whole damn ride? Just great.*

"I thought you were letting me handle this," I said.

"I am. You will still secure the witch for me."

I wasn't sure if that was because he was forcing me to fulfill my debt to him, or if it was because he somehow couldn't handle the witch by himself. If the latter were true, that didn't hold out much hope for me. Who the hell was this witch anyway? Why did Baal seem afraid of her? Or was that just my imagination? I didn't think so. There was something there in the demon like the witch had hurt him badly at one time, and he had come to fear her on some level ever since. As strange as it may sound for a demon, but he took the witch's betrayal or whatever it was that hurt him very personally. Demons were not supposed to take anything personally. They were demons, for God's sake. They weren't supposed to have such emotional responses.

*Unless he was in love with her.*

I very nearly dismissed the notion out loud but held it in as Baal glanced at me suspiciously. I also made sure my psychic defenses were well and truly secure in that moment. The last thing I wanted was for Baal to rape my mind. Even if I was right about him being in love with the witch, I didn't want him knowing that I knew. I doubted he would have taken that too well.

"I've tracked your witch to Red Branch Falls," I said, bringing things back to business. "It's a massive expanse of woodland. She could be anywhere in it."

"So how do you plan on finding her?" Baal asked.

"I have a device that can detect sources of magic and the supernatural. It's sort of like a Giger counter, only instead of radiation it detects--"

"Magic."

I nodded. "magic can be concealed, but it can't be truly hidden. It will always show itself if you know how to look."

Baal smiled like he was pleased. "See. I knew I chose wisely when I chose you to find Mar--" He stopped himself short before he said her name, swallowed it back down like he was swallowing a pebble. "The witch. To find the witch."

I pretended not to be embarrassed by his obvious emotion and decided to change the subject. There was still an hours driving left. I thought I might as well get some answers while I had the chance. But as I looked over at him, I caught him glancing into the wing mirror at a black pickup truck that was coming up behind us. When he saw me looking at him, he smiled and stared straight ahead as the pickup overtook us, the windows blacked out so I couldn't see the driver inside. Weird, I thought as the truck sped off up the road, eventually disappearing up some side road. I could have just been paranoid, but it almost seemed like Baal had been expecting the pickup truck. I was going to ask the demon about it but decided not to when I realized Baal would just deny knowing anything. Shaking my head, I asked him something else instead. "Back when I summoned you," I said. "You mentioned I was marked somehow by the demon who killed my family. What did you mean by that?"

Baal cleared his throat and grasped the opportunity I had given him to stop thinking about the witch. "Ah yes, that's right," he said. "You do indeed bear the mark of the demon."

"What mark? Where? I don't have any such marks on me anywhere. I've checked."

"The mark is not visible to human eyes. It is only visible to demons."

I was starting to get freaked out now as I glanced between the road ahead and Baal. It creeped me out to know that there was some sort of mark on my body somewhere. The vile stamp of some demon. "So what does it mean, this mark? Is it like a brand? Was I branded like fucking livestock?"

"In a way," Baal said, nodding casually, looking every inch the poor professor whose body he had stolen as he began to patiently explain to me the meaning of the mark like I was his student in class. "To put it simply, you were marked for possession."

"Excuse me?" Did he just say possession? I nearly veered off the narrow road we were on, the very word possession like a slap in the face right then.

An amused smile appeared on Baal's face. "The demon who slaughtered your family can possess your body whenever it wants. And there is nothing you can do to stop it."

"Are you...are you fucking kidding me?" It was a redundant question. I knew the demon was telling the truth. "Why me?"

"The demon must have thought you would make an interesting ride in this amusement park one day. Rest assured there are lots of other humans out there just like you, all marked by some demon or other. I used to do it myself, but I stopped because I didn't often venture up here much. Anyway, the mark is permanent. I doubt even your magic could remove it." He smiled again, amused by my discomfort over these revelations.

I wish I had never asked about the mark in the first place. Now it felt like a great fat Albatross had landed around my neck, or as if someone was now beside me at all times with a gun to my head, smiling all the while, letting me know it would just be a matter of time. And the very thought of that demon jumping inside my body, taking over and forcing me to take a back seat while it runs riot doing God knows what terrible and horrific things, maybe as it tore another poor family limb from limb while I had to watch...

*Jesus.*

My stomach turned over at the thought, and I slammed on the brakes. Then I fumbled open the door and vomited out onto the road. Passing cars beeped their horns at me, but I ignored them. When I'd finished being sick, I pulled the door closed again.

"Not feeling well?" Baal asked with a wicked smile.

I wiped my sleeve across my mouth. "I'm just going to drive," I said in a flat voice as I pushed down on the gas pedal again. "I don't think we should talk anymore until we get to the woods."

Baal still held his smile as he reached out and turned up the radio a notch, filling the car with the sound of The Police's "Every Breath You Take."

# 10

## WARDED

*I* was never as glad to arrive anywhere than when I finally parked the Cadillac on a back road that ran alongside the sprawling forest in Red Branch Falls. About half a mile back was the small town of Red Branch Falls itself, a place that prompted Baal to make some remark about humans being like ants because they would build a nest anywhere. I barely listened to him, however. The revelation he had hit me with earlier was still seriously stuck in my craw like a diseased tumor. Between that and the presence of the demon in the car, I felt sick and as if I needed oxygen or I would soon pass out.

I practically abandoned the Cadillac on a grassy verge next to the tall trees and jumped out immediately to try and shake the feeling of claustrophobia that clung to me like a suffocating blanket. Walking away from the car a bit, I took in deep lungfuls of air to clear the mess of bad feelings that had built up in me since Baal's sudden appearance in the car. The cold, fresh air went some way towards making me feel slightly better. The rest I had to do myself, beginning with focusing on what I had to do next. The fact that I was marked for future possession by the very demon that had slaughtered my family would have to be pushed aside if I was to have any hope of finding the witch in that sprawling hiding place of hers. My mind had to be clear for my senses to be at their keenest, and for my magic to work as it should.

So I stood for a few moments with my eyes closed as I forced myself to focus. Then, when I was ready, I turned and went back to the car.

Baal was leaning on the hood with his arms folded like some nerdy professor version of James Dean, looking like he was enjoying the fact that he was now in the great outdoors.

*More like enjoying the fact that he's here busting my balls.*

I sincerely hoped that he wouldn't follow me into the forest. Aside from the fact that I work best alone, the last thing I needed was some fucking demon tagging along like a monkey on my back who delighted in making little barbed comments in my ear now and then. No fucking thanks. But at the same time, it wasn't like I could stop him, was it?

"You feeling okay, Creed?" Baal asked. "You look a little peaky there. Perhaps a touch of car sickness, eh?" The smile on his face widened.

"I'm fine," I said, strolling past him to the back of the car where I popped the trunk to get what I needed for the trek ahead. Given the fact that the forest covered hundreds of square miles, I was well aware that it might take days to locate the witch, assuming, of course, she was in there at all. Not that I didn't have faith in Sanaka's and my uncle's abilities, but they were both blind drunk when they did the Location Spell. There was a chance they could have messed up somehow. Still, with no other leads to go on, it was a chance I had to take.

Besides, I was no stranger to the woods. I grew up next to a massive woodland near the family home in Ireland. With not much else to do with our irregular free time, my brother and sister and I would often venture into the woods and go exploring for several hours at a time. Sometimes we took camping equipment and stayed overnight. Once, just to test ourselves (and with our father's permission of course), the three of us spent three whole days deep in the woods with no equipment. All we had was the clothes we wore and our magic abilities. Over those three days, we hunted our own food, made our own shelters and also conversed with the many nature spirits in the woods, sometimes taking over the animals with our own spirits so we could run or fly through the forest in the body of whatever animal we had chosen. It was a fun few days, and intensely freeing to be away from everything. And despite the gravity of the mission I was now on, I was still looking forward to entering the deep woods and experiencing that sense of wild freedom once more.

Preferably without the demon professor beside me.

Speaking of which, I looked up when I heard a loud crack of energy to see Baal being thrown back several feet into the air before landing hard on his back in the middle of the road. Shocked, I bit my cheeks so I wouldn't laugh at Baal's misfortune.

"That bitch!" the demon roared.

I frowned over at him, doing my best to conceal my amusement. "What is it?" I asked, knowing full well what the problem was. The shimmering blue light that stretched around the woods--turned temporarily visible thanks to Baal's contact--made it very clear what the problem was (although for me, it was less a problem and more of a welcome solution).

Baal looked none too happy. "She has warded the forest. I cannot enter."

I had to fight to keep a smile of gratitude from appearing on my face. "Really? That's...what a bitch, eh?"

At that point, I found myself feeling grateful towards the witch for having the foresight to ward the forest against demons. But surely she wasn't that powerful that she could ward an entire forest, was she?

"Like I said before," Baal said walking back towards the car. "The woman is as devious as they come."

"She's just protecting herself," I said. "She knew you would make it here at some point."

Baal glared at me with eyes that now burned a deep orange. He thrust a hand out then, and the next thing I knew I was being lifted into the air without him even touching me. Then with a sickening speed, I was turned and slammed down hard onto the ground. With the wind knocked out of me, I lay choking in the dirt, my vision blurred and my head was spinning from the sudden impact. "What...the hell?" I managed to choke out.

The demon stood over me, his eyes filled with cold rage. "Do not make the very grave mistake of defending that woman," he spat out.

"I was...just saying..."

"Remember, Creed, the terms of our agreement." He leaned down closer to me, his eyes now demoned out completely. "You find the witch and hand her over to me. If you sympathize with her or try to help her in any way, I will devour your bitch girlfriend's soul. She will suffer greatly for your actions, Creed."

Nodding, I held my hands up slightly. "Okay, I understand."

Baal nodded back with a sneer on his face. "We will see," he said. "We will see."

Then he vanished, and I let my head roll to the side, partly in relief that the demon was gone, partly in despair at my situation. "Somebody fucking kill me now," I said.

# 11

# INTO THE WOODS

$\mathcal{I}$t had been a while since I had done any hiking outdoors. Almost all of my business was conducted in Blackham City and its decayed underbelly (and believe me, there was enough business there to keep me going for the next one hundred lifetimes). So when I finally set off into the woods, a sense of relief and even freedom gradually built up in me, a feeling like I was leaving everything behind as I headed into some new world. Such feelings were familiar to me from when I was traveling the world a long time ago. It was that sense of walking away and leaving the past behind—of entering a new future in a different place—that kept me on the move for over six years. Maybe that's why I felt so relaxed as I made my way up the incline, picking my way through the tall trees and often dense undergrowth. In the height of summer, when the undergrowth would have been at its densest, I imagined trekking through the woods would have been tough going indeed, especially since the forest was on the slope of a mountain. After an hour of walking my legs had begun to tire somewhat, my muscles burning as if they were struggling to keep up the pace.

"Jesus," I said as I paused to lean against a tree while I took a long swig from a bottle of water I had in my trench coat pocket. Rivulets of sweat ran down my face and soaked my back. Suddenly, the thought of spending perhaps days trekking through the thick woods didn't seem quite so romantic as it did earlier. It was bloody hard work! I just hoped I wouldn't have to walk for too long before I picked up the witch's trail. Wherever she was, I guessed she wasn't that deep into the woods. She had already warded the place against Baal and his supernatural ilk, so she had no need to go all the way to the top of the mountain or deep into the heart of the woods. I was also pretty sure the witch would be surrounded by some sort of Glamouring Spell, something that would cloak her residence and keep everything hidden from view. Most likely her abode would look like just another part of the woods. It's what I would have done. If you had the magic, it was the only sensible and safe thing to do if your intention was to stay hidden from everyone.

Just in case the trip lasted longer than I anticipated it would, I had a small backpack with me that contained enough food items to last for a few days. Also in the pack was more bottled water (I could refill in the stream that ran down the mountainside if need be), a few healing ointments in case I took any damage (a distinct possibility if the witch turned out to be hostile, which let's face it, was a distinct possibility) and finally (and arguably the most important item for the trip) a flask of whiskey. At the very least, if I managed to subdue the witch and hand her over safely to Baal, I could have myself a well earned drink. That wasn't to say I couldn't drink any before that happened, of course. That would just be crazy talk.

I was also packing my pistol (loaded with Chaos Bullets) and the Killing Knife that would, well, kill most things stone dead. Supernatural creatures mostly. Magic-slingers such as the witch I was searching for, not so much (at least not the ones who knew their shit).

In my left hand, I also held an old fashioned compass that used to be in the possession of George Washington. The compass was a gift from a grateful client many moons ago. It was said that Washington used to use the compass to detect the presence of powerful magic. The compass arrow, instead of pointing north, would point in the direction of a whatever magical presence was nearest. The closer you got to the magic, the faster the compass needle would spin until it was just a blur when you were right upon the magic source. The compass didn't work so well when I got it, so over time, I made some alterations using my own magic and recalibrated it as I went along. The compass was now able to detect any strong magic source from a considerable distance away. Not so useful if you are in a place were magic and the supernatural are everywhere (like many of the clubs and hangouts in Blackham), but very useful if you are in a large space where you know only one source of magic existed. It was doubtful if anyone but the witch lived in the woods. If anyone else did live there, they would just be a tribe of hillbillies, not adepts.

The compass had yet to pick up on any sign of magic as the needle hadn't locked into place yet. Instead, it was gently swinging back and forth on its bearings as it searched for sources of power. When it found one, the needle would lock in place, pointing in the direction I needed to go, eventually spinning constantly the closer I got.

The compass was more for backup than anything else. First and foremost, I was relying on my senses to help me find the witch. Senses that had been finely honed to a very accurate degree thanks to all the bounty hunting cases I had taken on over the years (I hated that term, by the way, bounty hunter...I just found people, that's all there was to it).

After rehydrating, I started walking again, trudging through the undergrowth and the trees as I continued to climb the slope I was on. Which wasn't getting any less steep, I had to say.

Then, after ten minutes of walking, I heard a noise behind me, and I spun around to see what it was, thinking it might be a deer or some other animal. Imagine my surprise when I saw a little girl standing there. She was no older than eight or nine, scruffy in appearance, her light brown hair long and braided, her face grubby like she hadn't washed in a while. Her clothes also looked handmade, stitched together from some dark material that I didn't recognize. "Hello there," I said to the girl, smiling, doing my best not to come across as threatening.

"What are you doing in here?" the little girl asked. "You don't belong in these here woods."

I couldn't argue with her there. "I'm just...looking for something. Some*one* actually."

As the girl regarded me with suspicion and very little fear, I realized that she must belong to one of the clans of people on the mountain side. Large groups of them were scattered all over, having made the mountain and the surrounding woods their home. Not many knew of the mountain people's existence since members of the clan rarely ventured into populated areas except once in a while to pick up supplies that were unavailable on the mountainside. I gave the woods a quick scan, expecting to see members of the little girl's tribe around somewhere, but I saw no one.

"Ain't no one in these woods that want's to be found," the girl said. "You should turn back."

"And why would I do that?" I asked her.

"Cause if you don't," another voice said from behind me, a male voice that made me spin around, my hand automatically reaching for the pistol under my trench coat. Three men had appeared out of nowhere it seemed. Large, burly men in their twenties with beards and animal skins attached to their clothing. Mountain men, all armed. Two with knives. The biggest of the men--a bear of a man with long dark hair and a bushy beard--came walking forward holding a bow in his hand, an arrow drawn back and aimed right at me.

"Guys," I said, holding my hands up as if I didn't want any trouble, which I didn't. "I'm just out walking in the woods. I don't mean anyone any harm."

"You're trespassing on our land, friend," the man with the bow said. "I've killed for less."

I didn't doubt it. The man looked savage, yet fully in control. Not a man you would want to pick a fight with. He looked like he could easily break me in half given a chance. A chance I didn't want to give him. "Like I said," I told him, thinking now that I was going to have to use magic to defend myself. "I'm not here looking for trouble. I'm here to see the witch. You know where she is?"

The two men behind the guy with the bow both looked at each other when they heard the word witch. I thought I would throw it out there to see what reaction I got. It was evident from their slightly fearful reactions that they knew exactly who I was talking about.

The man with the arrow pointed at me took a few steps closer. "You ain't seeing no witch today, friend," he growled. "Now I ain't gonna tell ye again. Turn around and move on out of here. Otherwise, I'll put this arrow in your chest." As if to emphasize his point, he drew back harder on the bow string.

Clearly, the men were not messing around. If I didn't do what they asked, they were going to kill me. And if I did do what they asked and turned around again, Baal would likely kill Leona. Which meant I didn't have a choice. "She told you to stop any strangers that come in here, didn't she?" I asked, mostly to stall for time while I inwardly recited the words to a spell that would hopefully get me out of the sticky situation I was in. Although as I explained before, magic use in the presence of Sleepwalkers was not a good idea and often caused adverse effects. I didn't think the mountain men would be any strangers to magic, however. Their clan no doubt had a Shaman amongst them, maybe even a few witches or warlocks that dealt mostly in nature magic. Either way, I was confident my magic wouldn't go awry when I used it in front of them.

Used it *on* them.

Which I was already doing, starting with the bow man since he posed the greater threat. As I cast the magic, I saw the look of consternation on the bow man's face, which soon turned to concern and then confusion as he realized he could no longer move his body. "What are you doing to me?" he asked, his voice a mixture of anger and fear.

"Nothing that's going hurt you," I said, stepping to the side, so I was no longer facing his arrow, which he still held in place. It wasn't like he had a choice. His whole body was locked in place now. He couldn't loose the arrow even if he wanted to.

The two men behind him looked confused as they wondered what was happening to their fearless leader and why he hadn't yet put an arrow in me. The two of them tried to walk forward (presumably, so they could stab me with their hunting knives), but gradually slowed to a stop as the magic worked its way into them, freezing the two of them in place like statues. "Witchery!" one of them cried out before his mouth seized up, and he couldn't talk anymore.

"You'll be stuck that way for a few hours," I told them. "Long enough for me to get far away from here."

You might be wondering why I didn't just teleport out of there. Well, for one, teleportation uses up a lot of my magic reserves, and I would need as much juice as possible when it came time to face the witch. I didn't want to be doing that if the tank was half empty, so to speak. There was also the fact that you needed to know where you were going before teleporting anywhere, otherwise who knew where you would end up? As I wasn't familiar with the geography of the woods, I didn't want to risk going off course too much. Besides, I always relished the chance to practice my spells. Spells and magic are like anything else. You either use them or lose them, and I rarely turned down an opportunity for live practice.

"What did you do to them?" the little girl asked from behind me, still standing in the same spot, although now she had a rather large knife in her small hand, which made her look more cute than dangerous. Still, fair plays to her for standing her ground and not running off in fear.

"Don't worry," I said. "They just won't be able to move for a while."

"At all?"

I shook my head. "Not a muscle."

A smile crossed the little girl's face as if she was now thinking about all the devious things she could do to the men and they couldn't do a thing to stop her. "You'd best be moving along, Mister, before any more of my family sees you."

Before I left, I asked the girl about the witch. "You know where she is in here?"

The little girl looked like she knew but didn't want to tell. It seemed like the mountain people were all scared of the witch. Probably with good reason. "She'll turn me into a toad if I tell you anything."

I suppressed a smile as I wondered if the witch had actually said that at some point or if the little girl was just surmising about what might happen to her. Either way, I was sure the witch had said something to keep her neighbors in line. "That's okay," I said after a moment. "You don't have to tell me anything. Have fun with these three, won't you? And remember, they can't move a muscle." I smiled over deviously at the three men and winked. No doubt if they could move their eyeballs, they would have thrown me daggers.

As I was walking away, the little girl called out to me, and I stopped and turned around. "You know," she said, pointing her knife in an easterly direction. "There's some real good rabbit hunting ground over that way, down in the valley."

A smile crossed my face. Clever little girl. "Thanks," I said and altered my course to walk in the direction the girl had pointed in.

# WITCH'S VALLEY

*A*fter the little mountain girl had indirectly told me where the witch was to be found, I headed off in that direction. A few times I had stop and look around, not because I was lost, but because it felt like I was being watched or followed. When I looked around, however, I couldn't see anyone.

Maybe it was the little girl, I thought, although that was unlikely, given her wariness of the witch. Someone else then. Perhaps another of the little girl's clan. I didn't know. Nor did I have the time to flush out whoever was out there.

So I carried on regardless, and it wasn't long before the compass needle began to point in the same direction, which meant I was on the right path. Not that there were too many pathways in those woods, which seemed to get denser the further in I traveled. Then, after nearly two hours of walking, the compass needle began to spin. Slowly at first, then faster the further on I walked. It wasn't long before the compass needle was almost a blur it was spinning so fast, and I found myself on the edge of a kind of valley in the mountain that was maybe the length of a football field, but rounder in shape. Geologically speaking, the dip or valley didn't seem to fit with the landscape. It was like something had come along and taken a massive chunk out of the mountain terrain, and then the forest had grown over the hole. Ordinarily, I wouldn't have thought much of it. But since the needle was spinning like mad and I was looking for a highly skilled witch, the incongruous hole in the landscape was evidence enough for me that the witch had something to do with it.

She was down there in that valley somewhere, I knew. Hiding out under a Cloaking Spell. The trees down below were just a mirage to conceal what was really underneath.

I put the compass into one of my coat pockets and left my backpack beside a nearby tree, intending to pick it up again after I had the witch under control. I imagined things would get hairy from there on out and I didn't need the extra weight.

No doubt the whole valley was boobytrapped. Certainly with magical traps. Perhaps even with physical traps also. Either way, due care was called for.

By that point, the forest had darkened considerably as evening time drew in. Soon enough, it would be difficult to see much through the trees.

*Better get going*, I thought.

As I started to work my way down into the valley, I soon became aware of an odd presence that seemed to be above me somewhere. Picking a path through the trees and undergrowth, it felt like I was being watched again, although not that vague feeling I had earlier. This was more definite and more deeply felt.

I was being stalked.

Hunted.

Stopping, I turned my attention upwards for a few moments, thinking there was something in the trees somewhere. Then a huge black shape passed silently overhead, and I said, "What the fuck?" to myself.

Something very big appeared to be stalking me from the sky. I wasn't sure what it was. My first thought was obviously a bird of some sort since whatever it was flying. But since I was in the witch's territory now, I began to wonder if perhaps she had a guard in the form of some supernatural creature. In that case, there were a few possibilities. A weredragon maybe. Or a low-level demon. Or even some bestial nightmare she had created herself.

Whatever the creature was flying above me, it was not going to let me get much farther into the witch's territory before it inevitably attacked me.

The creature swooped overhead again, lower this time. A dark shadow against the twilight sky, wings making a whoomfing sound as they displaced the air. The thing was huge. Maybe six or eight feet in length was my estimation, though it was difficult to tell it was moving so fast.

Then an ear-piercing screeching sound split the silence and echoed through the forest into my ears, causing me to halt once again and involuntarily shrink away from the sound.

But it was a sound I thought I recognized. A sound I often heard where I grew up in Ireland.

The sound an owl makes when it's on the hunt.

More specifically, a barn owl.

"No," I said, shaking my head. "It can't be a bloody--"

Before I could even say giant owl, a giant owl burst through the tops of the trees and screeched towards me, it's talon's snapping through branches on the way down as they prepared to grip me. I managed to instinctively drop to the ground just as the barn owl swooped over me, its talons missing me by mere inches. It screeched again loudly as it flew back through the trees and out into the open sky again.

"Jesus," I said, hauling myself up and beginning to run now through the woods, although where I was going, I had no idea. My original plan had been to keep walking until I sensed the spell that was keeping the witch hidden, then I would try to break the spell to reach the witch. Not that I expected any part of that plan to be easy since I knew the witch was aware of my presence and would do everything to fight me off--or kill me. Obviously, the giant barn owl was phase one of her security measures.

As I ran, still aware of the owl circling overhead, I pulled out my pistol, thinking I could shoot the owl the next time it swooped in on me. Rather unhelpfully, I also noticed the trees had thinned where I now was, leaving more room for the owl to not only see me but also to fly down at me without any obstruction to its massive body. But I had to keep moving anyway. There was no going back.

A minute later, I entered into a large clearing that brought into view the now dark and starry sky above. Looking up, I searched for the owl but saw no sign of it anywhere.

*Maybe it's gone*, I thought.

I went to walk across the clearing and was stopped suddenly as if I had walked into an invisible brick wall.

*I knew it. A wall of magic.*

Which meant the witch was behind it somewhere, perhaps watching me even now from the other side. Preparing to kill me most likely.

Putting away my pistol, I held both hands out in a peaceful gesture. "I know you can see me," I called out. "I just want to talk to you, that's all."

Yeah right. As if she was going to believe that.

Yet what was I supposed to say? That I was sent by Baal to kidnap her and march her to certain death? I doubted that would have gone down too well. I had to at least *try* and get her to lower her defenses before I started with the strong arm tactics.

"You want to let me in?" I said to the space in front of me.

I waited a moment, and nothing happened. Maybe she thought she was safe as long as she didn't lower the magic walls surrounding her. If that were the case, then I would have to try and lower the walls myself.

Standing back a couple of feet from the invisible wall, I closed my eyes and entered into the Chaosphere in my mind. First I had to see clearly the kind of magic I was dealing with, then I would have to systematically unravel it all until I had made a hole in it, an entrance to the witch's hidden kingdom.

Which all would have been great had I gotten that far. For ten seconds after closing my eyes, a great force thumped into my back and slammed me into the ground, knocking me half unconscious. Then I felt something hard wrap around my body, which a second later lifted me off the ground, carrying my limp body up into the cold night air until all I could see was darkness and the outline of trees below me.

The deafening screech that sounded next told me I was gripped within the talons of the giant barn owl, which gripped so tight I could hardly breathe.

*I'm going to get eaten by a giant barn owl*, I remember thinking as I had the sensation of being swung around in the air.

Probably just as well I blacked out soon afterward.

## EDEN OBSCURED

*W*hen I next awoke, I opened my eyes and had them immediately blinded by bright sunlight. "Jesus," I said turning my head away from the UV rays as they seared my retinas. I shielded my eyes with one hand the next time I opened them, holding my hand there until I was able to keep my eyes open without feeling like someone was shining a light directly on them.

It was green underneath me, and I realized I was lying in grass that felt unusually soft and lush to the touch. Despite the lushness of the grass, I assumed I was still in the forest somewhere. I was also grateful I didn't still have the giant barn owl's talons wrapped around me.

*But wait*, I thought. *It was almost full dark before I lost consciousness after being snatched up by the owl. Now it was daylight. Surely I hadn't been out that long?*

I went to sit up and a pain registered in my back and around my ribs that made me freeze, afraid to move again in case I made the pain worse. The owl's talons had crushed me. God know's what damage the thing had done. Thank God for my trench coat, which seemed to have prevented the owl's talons from piercing my body. Otherwise, the pain and damage would have been a lot worse.

Gritting my teeth, I made another effort to move again, this time managing to sit up and start to look around at where I was.

I was in the witch's little kingdom I had by then realized. And what a kingdom it was. A virtual paradise of lush, exotic vegetation in the form of brightly colored plants and flowers, trees with beautiful reddish-gold leaves and large patches of carefully tended beds of rich soil filled with all manner of herbs, some I recognized, some I didn't. Flowing streams and babbling brooks interspersed all of the greenery, feeding the soil and providing a habitat for the many fish that flashed silver under the surface of the water. Hummingbirds of all types mined for nectar in the hundreds of flowers that seemed to grow everywhere. Insects and butterflies of a type I had never seen before buzzed and fluttered about in the warm air. As I breathed in, my nostrils tingled pleasantly at the array of scents coming from the flowers and plants.

*This is Eden*, I thought in wonder. More beautiful even than the Hanging Gardens in the center of Babylon.

Not the type of place I expected an evil witch to be hanging out in. At the very least, I expected a massive, scraggy castle that was cold and dank inside and which was surrounded by perpetual night and all manner of foul creatures.

Speaking of creatures, where was the owl? Hopefully, outside of the paradise, I was currently situated in. There was no place for a six feet tall barn owl in Eden. Creatures like that should stay in the dark woods where they undoubtedly belonged.

I managed to stand up, grunting and wincing at the pain in my back and ribs. I didn't think anything was broken. Not severely anyway. Maybe a few cracked ribs. Enough to slow me down, though, at least until I had access to my healing ointments, which I reminded myself, where in the backpack I left behind in the woods.

When I sat up, I looked to my right, down the long garden to the quaintest cottage I'd ever seen. With its whitewashed walls, perfectly thatched roof and the immense amount of flowers and shrubs planted around it, I was reminded of those pictures you see in some people's houses. Pictures that depict little fantasy cottages that you just know are too quaint to be true.

Except this one was. Again, I was surprised that I wasn't looking at the walls of a foreboding castle or a dark tower that reached far into the sky.

*What kind of evil witch lives in a place like this?* I wondered. I'd met a lot of truly evil people over the course of my lifetime, and none of them hung out anywhere like the light-filled Garden of Eden I was standing in.

"I suppose you are wondering where you are?" said a voice and I snapped my head around to see that a woman with short blonde hair and a white summer dress had emerged from behind a clump of bushes that seemed to bear a strange fruit that I had never seen before. The woman also had a barn owl resting on her shoulder. A normal sized one. And from the way the owl was looking at me, I knew it had to be the same one that snatched me from the woods.

I just stared at the woman for a long moment as I took her in. Age-wise, she looked to be in her early thirties or thereabouts, although with wizard's it could be hard to tell their real age (as you know already). She was pretty, I'd give her that. More than pretty actually. That much was obvious after just a few seconds of looking at her. Margot Celeste was beautiful, and naturally so. Her frame was slender, her curves perfectly shaped. The woman exuded charm and effortless sex appeal.

But then, most of the witches I had ever met came across the same way. Witches were usually powerful, independent and deeply in touch with themselves and their sexuality. All of that could make them quite alluring and often easy to fall for. If you were able to trust them, that is. My experience with witches had taught me never to trust them. For one, most of them had a deep-seated hatred of men. And for another, they always had an agenda, either their own or that of their coven's if they belonged to one. Or both.

Up until that point, I had no reason to believe that Margot Celeste would be any different. Still, she did not seem at all evil to me right then. And I knew evil better than most.

"You're familiar, I take it?" I said, nodding at the owl on her shoulder before getting to my feet. "For an owl, it makes a good guard dog."

As if understanding what I said, the owl did that thing they all do and swung its head around in a circle as if taunting me before letting out a triumphant sounding screech.

*Screw you Mr Barn Owl*, I thought. *If my Garra Wolf were here, he would make short work of you.*(Linked Comment)

Margot Celeste smiled then. "Oh really? Do you own a Garra Wolf? How very exotic of you."

*What the fuck?! Did she just read my mind?*

"Yes, I did. Your magic, including your wards and defenses, will not work in this place."

"You neutralized my magic?" I was too surprised to be that angry about it. Besides that, I was so enthralled by the witch at that point that I didn't think I would need my magic anyway. Of course, that was just my cock that had me thinking such foolish things. But when the little head demands the attention of the big head, you don't have a choice but to listen, right? *Right?*

"Did you think I would trust that you wouldn't try to use your not inconsiderable magic against me?" she said, then turned her head to the owl and whispered something to it. A second later, the owl launched itself off the witch's shoulder and flew right towards me, pulling up at the last second, so it just missed my head.

"Your familiar has an attitude problem," I said, glad the damn bird had finally flown off to eat a mouse or whatever it was barn owls normally did.

"Barney has served me well over the years."

"Barney?" I couldn't help smiling. "Where you seven when you named it that?"

I could see her trying not to smile. "It's just a name. Speaking of which, what is yours? I could root around inside your head and find out, but I'd prefer to allow you the courtesy of telling me yourself. Despite the fact that you showed me no such courtesy by turning up at my doorstep uninvited."

She had a point, I supposed. "The name's Creed. August Creed."

"August Creed," she said as if my name was familiar to her. "I know you. You have quite a reputation around the city."

"A reputation for what?"

"For doing the things others don't want to do."

I thought about that for a second. "As close a job description as any, I suppose. I'm surprised our paths haven't crossed by now."

She gave me an easy smile as she ran her slender fingers over the leaves of the bush that bore the unfamiliar fruits. I watched as she plucked one of the dark purple fruits from the bush and held it up, the fruit about the size of a tennis ball in her hand. "This fruit is my own creation," she said with a hint of pride. "Most of what you see in here is my own creation."

She tossed the fruit towards me, and I caught it easily with one hand but winced as I strained my cracked ribs. The smooth-skinned fruit felt somewhere between an apple and a plum. "Are you trying to poison me?"

"Poison you?" She laughed as if the idea was ridiculous. "If I wanted you dead you would be dead already."

"And why aren't I?" It was a question I wanted to know the answer to. "You read my mind. You probably know why I'm here. Maybe you even know who sent me."

She came closer then, stopping right in front of me as if I was no danger whatsoever to her. Which I wasn't, not without my magic anyway. "Don't you want to taste the fruit, August?" she asked, her clear gray eyes focused right on me.

I caught her scent as well then, which came across as exotic and as alluring as the scents that permeated the garden around us. Soon it became just her and me as if someone had turned down the dimmer switch on the rest of the world.

Then she seemed to glide forward, and I felt her take my hand, the one that still held the dark fruit, and she guided the fruit towards her mouth and took a slow bite out of it. Juice immediately sprang from the fruit and ran down her chin. Her eyes never left me as she began to push my own hand towards my mouth and I bit into the fruit. I had never tasted anything like it. Sweet. Succulent. Juicy. Everything a fruit should be.

As sticky juices ran down my own chin, I became intensely aware of my desire for the witch. In my mind, I wanted nothing else in the universe but her. I wanted to taste her. To taste every part of her, knowing full well that she would taste even better than the fruit I'd just had.

Before I knew it, her face was right in front of mine, and her mysterious eyes were looking into me. She might have been reading my mind again, but I didn't care. I was so captivated by her presence it felt like I could have stood there for the rest of time and just stared into those eyes. Into that face.

And then she spoke, breaking the spell somewhat. "Come," she said in a soft voice that still carried the hint of desire in it. "Follow me to the cottage. I will fix those ribs of yours." She smiled, light dancing in her eyes as I continued to look into them like I didn't have a choice. "Then we can talk."

That last sentence felt as if it contained a hidden promise. A promise of what, though, I wasn't sure.

But I knew I would soon find out.

# BEWITCHED

*T*he inside of the cottage was even more quaint than the outside if that was possible. The rooms were cozy yet spacious, with dark wooden beams everywhere and slightly yellowed walls of traditional lime plaster. Scents of herbs and what smelled like game cooking filled the place, a scent that tickled my taste buds as I walked into the kitchen behind Margot Celeste.

By that stage, my reasons for being there had all but slipped to the back of my mind somewhere. I knew they were there, but they were just like vaguely distracting thoughts that were unimportant when compared to the thoughts inspired by Margot Celeste's natural beauty and almost breathtaking spirit. Every time she looked at me with those mysterious gray eyes of hers, I found myself pulled in by her stare and intensely interested in the experiences that had given her eyes such mystery and depth.

Margot Celeste had clearly been through a lot in her life. She had experienced great pain and suffering, of that I had no doubt. Speaking as one who had endured such things myself over the years, I could always spot a fellow lost soul. One who still questions their place in the universe, despite everything they have seen and been through that demonstrated they probably didn't have a place at all, and that the universe didn't give two shits about them. In fact, the universe had bluntly demonstrated through means of pain and suffering that nothing really meant anything, and that shit just happened. Yet people like myself and Margot Celeste still chose to cling to the notion that there was some meaning behind their existence, *something* that would eventually bring true peace. Apart from death, that is.

"I can hear your thoughts," Margot said as she gestured for me to sit down at a table that looked like it had been carved from the trunk of an ancient tree, and which I noticed had many Glyphs inscribed into it. "You think we are the same."

I gave a small laugh as I sat down in a chair with a back made of woven reeds. "Not exactly the same. I'm not wanted by an Underworld demon for a start."

She smiled as she brought two glasses and what looked like a bottle of whiskey to the table, setting them down as she took a seat. Then she proceeded to half fill the two glasses. "And now we get to your real reason for being here. Baal sent you. Tell me." She pushed one of the glasses towards me and then lifted her own. "What did you do to end up in his service?"

"I summoned him." Lifting the glass, I downed the contents in one without even considering that it might be poisoned.

Margot shook her head like she wasn't that surprised. "Of course you did."

"I had my reasons."

She snorted slightly as she refilled my glass. "Of course you did."

A frown suddenly crept over my face as I realized something. "Why haven't you killed me yet?" I said it casually as if it was some inane question like, "Where did you get that dress?"

Her eyes focused on me a moment. Then she looked away. "I haven't killed anything in a long time."

It was my turn to stare as things were not adding up in my mind. It almost felt like I was on drugs, and that I was subtly mind controlled. "Did you drug me? Or spell me?"

She formed a tight smile before answering. "In a way. I've warded this place against feelings of anger or aggression. You may want to try and take me away, but you won't be able to. I wouldn't advise it anyway. At least not without your magic, which you don't have access to in here. Is that what you planned on doing? Forcibly taking me to Baal so he could take me to the Underworld with him?"

I thought for a moment, then shrugged like none of it mattered. "Truthfully, I didn't have a plan. I figured something would present itself when I found you. I wasn't expecting any of this. I wasn't expecting...you."

"You thought I would be some vicious old hag? Or cold hearted bitch?"

"I can see you are neither of those things. Which is disconcerting to me because now I'm even more confused as to why Baal wants you so badly."

"I think the better question is, why do *you* want me so badly?"

I almost blushed, which isn't like me. But she was so overpoweringly captivating that I couldn't help it. "It's a case of my soul or yours. Simple math."

"Not that simple. Aren't you forgetting your girlfriend?" She focused on me a second as she read my mind again. "Leona. Leona Lawson."

It shamed me to say that I had completely forgotten about Leona since entering into the witch's kingdom. I will hold up my hands, however, and say that Margot Celeste didn't leave me much choice. Whether she meant to or not, she had me completely bewitched. And without magic to counter her enchantments, there wasn't much I could do about it.

I bit my bottom lip and looked at the floor for a moment. "Leona is the main reason I'm here."

She seemed to look into me again, and then her mouth dropped open slightly, and she looked away, picking up her whiskey glass and holding it there. "Your love for her is powerful," she said, before emptying her glass.

For the first time, I saw some level of bitterness in her that was deep-seated and which obviously had a powerful hold on her, despite her obvious attempts to mask it with all those layers of peace and serenity that she had created around herself. I felt sorry for her then because she had obviously been wronged in the past by someone. Maybe not Baal, but someone else. Something had happened to her that she had never been able to get over. Which was something I knew a little about of course, what with the slaughter of my family all those years ago. "Leona is probably more than I deserve," I said eventually, hinting to Margot that I had some sense of her pain. "I'm lucky to have her in my life."

"But she's not around, is she?" It was a slightly loaded question, maybe designed to piss me off or get at me on some level, I don't know. Her eyes narrowed, and I saw something in her that was dark and formidable, devious and cold-hearted. "She doesn't love you as much as you love her, does she?"

I shook my head. "Why would you say that? Not that it's any of your concern."

She stared hard at me for a second and then smiled, the darkness now gone from her face, the mask of serenity having been slipped back on. "Forget it," she said.

Which of course, I couldn't. There was no doubt she had hit a nerve in me, stirred up my insecurities. Or maybe that was the point. It was hard to tell.

An uncomfortable silence descended in the room. When I looked out the window, I saw it was dark outside. "You did that?" I said, nodding at the window.

She looked almost embarrassed. "I've seen enough sun for one day."

I sighed as I sat back in my chair. "So," I said. "I'm here. You're here. What are we going to do? Obviously, I can't take you to Baal, which means you now have to help me figure out a way to take him off the board before he chops the head of my queen."

She shook her head at my sloppy chess analogy. "Against my better judgment, I find myself liking you, Creed."

"I have that effect on people."

"That's bullshit, of course."

I couldn't help smiling. "And you're right, of course. I'm just good at being a pain in the ass until I get what I want."

"And what is it you want now?"

Our eyes met, and we held each other's stares for a long moment, during which all sorts of delicious desires were stirred up in me. If the situation didn't happen to be so life and death (for Leona especially, you know, the woman I love), I would have found it near impossible to resist her. On her part, she was just being her naturally attractive self. I also suspected she hadn't seen anyone in a long time, at least no one she wanted to fuck. Witch or not, she was still human. As was I and my semi-erect cock. "I think maybe you know the answer to that question," I said. "And I think you also know that I--"

She raised a hand, and my words were cut short, though not through my own volition. "Stand up," she ordered, and I found myself doing exactly as she commanded, totally against my will.

"What are you--"

She raised her hand again as she stood up and then came towards me, her eyes on me as she started brushing her unpainted lips over mine. Her breath, the feel, and smell of her skin was overwhelming as I closed my eyes for a second, still unable to speak.

*Is she really doing this?* I thought. *She can't do this to me. It's unfair and its--*

I could barely think anymore as my desire and a tingling warmth settled inside me, blocking everything else out.

"Turn around," she said in a husky commanding tone. "Walk to the bedroom."

Again, I had no way to resist her, either through words or actions. She had complete control over me. Worse still, I found myself *liking* the fact that she had total control over me. I couldn't deny the perverse sort of pleasure I was getting from the situation as I turned around and began walking out of the kitchen and down the hallway to where I assumed the bedroom was.

"Turn left." Her voice was close to my ear, still with the slightly urgent sounding husky tones.

As I turned left, I tried very hard to resist going into that bedroom. Despite my overwhelming desires, a part of me was still shouting out the wrongness of what was about to happen, of what *was* happening.

But my resistance was pointless because the situation was happening whether I wanted it to or not. And if I'm honest, I wanted it to.

I go on intuition a lot. Sometimes I know things have to play out in a certain way, even if it doesn't make much sense to me at the time, or if the situation seems wrong, but feels right. This was one of those times. My mind was screaming it was all wrong, but a more powerful force continued to guide me into it because it was somehow also the right thing to do. If I wanted the witch's help in taking down Baal (and saving Leona), she had to get what she wanted first.

And what she wanted right then was me.

As I walked into the bedroom, I heard her close the door behind her. The bed was large with an intricately carved headboard and white silk sheets. The light was on in the room, dimmed to a low level. Margot stood leaning against the door for a moment as she stared at me with a kind of playful hunger in her eyes, which now seemed much darker in the low light. "Take off your clothes," she said.

I proceeded to do as she asked as I was still under her influence. As I took my trench coat off and threw it on the floor, I wondered if she were using magic on me because she was worried I wouldn't play with her. I still wasn't sure myself what I would do if she suddenly released me from her spell. Would I gather my clothes up and walk out of the bedroom? Or would I stay?

A moment later, I was standing completely naked in front of her. Walking slowly forwards, she seemed to take in every square inch of me. "Like what you see?" I asked, surprised I could speak.

She came close to me and started running her hands over my chest, tracing her fingers around the edges of my tattoos, feeling the scars she came across. The carnal delight was evident in her smile. "Your body tells of many stories."

I barely nodded as I couldn't help staring at her face. At the beauty of it, and the mystery that lay beneath. I wanted her so bad it hurt.

Then she started to plant gentle kisses on me, moving across my chest, looking up at me as she moved lower down my abdomen, her fingernails raking lightly across my lower back, then grabbing my buttocks as she dropped lower, planting her kisses around the tops of my thighs, her soft blonde hair tickling my skin as she did so.

A shuttering breath left me as her lips made contact with my throbbing cock. There was no turning back now, even if I'd wanted to. Which I didn't by that point. Absolutely fucking not.

Margot spent long moments running her deliciously soft lips all over my cock, occasionally licking me with her tongue which would invariably cause me to gasp with overwhelming pleasure.

When she finally stood up again, she smiled before kissing me, not fully committing, but teasingly. "Take off my dress," she whispered as she turned around.

With slightly shaking hands, I unzipped the dress she was wearing and then watched it slide down over her pale skin and onto the floor, delighted to see that she was wearing nothing underneath. She took a few steps forward then, and my eyes took in the exquisite curve of her lower back and her perfectly shaped ass. Then she turned around slowly, completely comfortable with her nakedness. "You like what you see, Creed?"

"You know I do."

She smiled and came forward again, her hands pushing against my chest as she moved me back onto the bed and then stood over me as she started swaying slightly from side to side, rubbing her hands over perfectly formed breasts, which looked bigger and fuller than they did when she wore the dress. Surprisingly for a witch, she had no tattoos, unless she had removed them at some stage. There were scars, though, the biggest of which was across her flat stomach. It looked like a sharp blade had cut into her once.

I was about to ask about the scar when she came forward and leaned over me with her hands on the bed. Again, she started to kiss her way down my body, but more hungrily than before until she finally grabbed my cock and engulfed it in her mouth. "*Oh, Jesus!*" I gasped, closing my eyes and tilting my head back against the pillow.

Then I felt her kiss me on the mouth, which I instantly responded to for a few seconds before I realized what was happening was impossible as I could still feel her between my legs. When the kissing stopped, I opened my eyes to see her standing over me smiling. But she was also still going down on me with increasing passion. "What the...how are—"

The Margot nearest to me put a finger to my lips to stop me talking. "Don't think," she whispered as the light danced in her eyes. "Just feel."

Who was I to argue?

# 15

# THE MAKING OF A WITCH

$\mathcal{T}$he sex seemed to last an eternity. It was incredible. At one point, there was six Margot's around me, all devouring my body at once like a pack of hungry wolves. I had never felt anything like it. By the end, when I was moving on top of her, there was just one of her, and she screamed and dug her fingernails into my back as she came for the umpteenth time. After that, we fell asleep in each other's arms.

When I next awoke, I found her gone, but she soon returned, still naked, bearing a tray containing bowls of fresh fruit and, I was glad to see, coffee. The serene smile never left her face as she placed the tray on my lap and slid into bed again beside me. "This looks great," I said. "Thank you."

Margot turned on her side and leaned her head against her hand as she picked at the fruit with her other hand. She said nothing for a while as she just seemed to watch me sip at the coffee in between eating pieces of fruit. I was as relaxed as I'd been in a long while like the outside world didn't matter anymore.

"Thank you," Margot said after a while, her eyes sparkling.

"What for?" I asked. "There were six of you at one point, only one of me. I think I got the better end of the deal there. Neat trick, by the way."

She laughed softly. "I'm thanking you because it's been a long time since I lay with anyone."

I realized then that she was lonely. That she had always been lonely, even before hiding herself away inside the little kingdom she had built for herself. A silence soon settled between us for a while, and I inevitably began to think about the outside world again, and all the problems that came along with it.

And Leona, who was probably in New York wondering why she couldn't get a hold of me.

*If she was trying to call me at all.*

A bit unfair of me to think perhaps. She was just busy doing her job after all.

"You're conflicted," Margot said.

I nodded. "You blame me?"

She sat up then. "You don't have to be."

Shaking my head, I couldn't help laughing at my situation, and at the way, things had turned out. "Jesus," I said. "Things were not supposed to work out like this. This isn't..."

"How you envisioned things going? Come on, Creed. Surely you aren't that naive. Nothing ever goes to plan, does it? Things work out the way they are supposed to, not the way you want them to."

"So tell me." I pushed the tray down to the bottom of the bed but kept the coffee in my hand. "Do you think your situation has worked out the way it was supposed to? Are you happy hiding out here in these woods, inside this little kingdom you've constructed with your magic?"

Something dark flashed in Margot Celeste's eyes as she stared at me. "I'm just surviving," she said eventually as she looked away. "Like you, Creed. Like everyone. What else is there?"

"Maybe, but you don't have to be alone while you do it. Believe me, I know."

"Baal has left me no choice."

"There's always a choice, Margot."

Her chest heaved as she snorted. "How right you are. There is always a choice, isn't there?"

I could detect the bitterness in her voice as she pulled the sheets up over herself, covering her nakedness. Which I was partly glad for because I found it to be very distracting indeed. "all right," I said, reaching over to a little bedside table and setting my empty coffee cup there before turning back to her. "I think it's time you told me how you ended up here. Then maybe we can figure a way out of it."

She seemed to consider for a moment, then sighed. "Okay. I'll tell you how I got here. But I'm telling you now there's no way I'm going anywhere. And for that matter, neither are you, Creed. Not if you're smart."

"We'll see about that," I said. "Just start talking."

* * *

MARGOT ENDED UP TALKING FOR A GOOD FEW HOURS, POURING OUT MOST OF her life story, which as I suspected, was pretty harrowing stuff at times. I'll do my best to give you the short version here.

Margot Celeste was born in Blackham City and was orphaned at a young age when both her parents were killed in a freak car accident. No one knew what happened at the time. Her parent's car seemed to go off the road for no reason, hitting a tree and killing both her parents stone dead. Margot was five years old when this happened. She had no family on her father's side, and her aunt on her mother's side refused to take Margot in for reasons that Margot didn't go into, except to say that her Aunt was a total bitch and she hated her. She also intimated that said Aunt got what was coming to her years later, though again Margot didn't go into detail on this. I guessed, though that Margot used her later powers as a witch to take revenge on the woman.

From there, Margot's story was pretty typical. She was taken into care and ended up being dragged through the system, going from foster home to foster home until she was old enough to be on her own. Again, details of her upbringing in these foster homes were sparse, but from what I gathered, Margot didn't have a good time of it.

Her real story began when she was waitressing in a bar in the city one night. She was eighteen years old and trying to establish some sort of life for herself after coming out of the foster system. Her only interest at the time was literature apparently. She loved books and read everything she could get her hands on, which is how she survived her time in numerous foster homes. Now that she was free, she applied for a local college, intending to study English Literature and make good on her dream of writing her own book one day. The waitressing job was intended to help her pay for that.

The night her life changed forever, Margot met a man named Derek Myers while she was working in the bar. "He seemed like a decent guy," Margot told me. "Good looking, about a year older than me. He played football at Blackham University, had a scholarship there. He seemed smart too. He knew his classics, and he sat at the bar most of the night talking to me about his favorite books. I had little experience of men back then, and I found myself smitten by his charms." She stopped and shook her head. "I don't know why I didn't see it..."

"See what?" I asked.

Margot just shook her head again as she went on to explain what happened.

Derek invited her back to his parent's house, who were apparently out of town for the next few days. He told Margot she could come back with him and they could talk all night about books while drinking Derek's parent's alcohol. It sounded good to Margot, who was just glad someone was treating her like a normal person for once.

"What do you mean by that?" I asked her.

"I was withdrawn growing up. I dyed my hair black and dressed like a Goth all the time. I had no friends because no one wanted to hang around with a foster kid. So all the other kids teated me like I was some weirdo outcast, which I was, I suppose. Even when I left high school, I still felt the same way. And then I meet Derek, and he treats me like a normal girl. He even tells me he finds me attractive, which no one had ever told me before." She closed her eyes as if the memories were still painful. When she opened them again, there was a hardness to her stare as she continued.

She went with Derek to his parent's house in Bankhurst. Derek drove them in his brand new convertible. On the way there, Margot thought her life was finally changing. That she was becoming a normal member of society at long last. Which is all she ever wanted. To fit in. To not be treated like a freak and a doormat.

Derek was from a rich family. When they reached his parent's house, Margot couldn't believe that she was about to enter such a grand house. It made every house she had ever been in before then look like a dog kennel. Once inside, Derek showed her around for a bit, glamouring her with the wealth on display. They sat in the huge living room for a while, drinking expensive whiskey and vodka from crystal glasses. Margot felt totally out of place in such lavish surroundings, but Derek made her feel comfortable as he showed her various first edition copies of classic books that she fell immediately in love with.

Then at some point, after Margot had drunk three full glasses of vodka and was feeling more than a little tipsy, Derek kissed her. It was the first time she had ever been kissed by anyone outside of her own fantasies. The drink helped with her nerves, but she still felt herself shuttering when her lips touched his for the first time. She became so breathless that she had to pull away after just a few seconds, then she started apologizing and saying she didn't know what was wrong with her and that she had no business being there with him in that huge house. But Derek had calmed her down by telling her how beautiful she was, how refreshingly different she was compared to all the other girls he knew.

And Margot lapped it all up. Every word. How could she not? Derek was devilishly handsome, like a character from one of her Jane Austen books, and just as charming. More than that, he actually liked her for who she was. As the kissing became more passionate, Margot caught herself thinking that things were finally changing for her. That she was no longer to be the outcast that no one even wanted to talk to never mind be with.

That was probably why she didn't protest when Derek put his hand on one of her breasts and began to squeeze, or when he dropped his other hand down between her legs and did something utterly frightening but wonderful to her with his fingers. When he suggested they go to his room so they could be more comfortable, she barely gave it a second thought and allowed him to lead her by the hand towards what took her a moment to realize was the basement.

"I get more privacy down there than upstairs," he said easily as he opened the door, turned the light on and ushered her down the steps while he pulled the door closed behind them and then locked it. She thought it a little odd at the time that he would lock the door since there was no one else in the house, but she was so caught up with the thought of finally losing her virginity (and to a hunk like Derek!) that she thought nothing of it.

The basement was massive and filled with all kinds of stuff that was boxed up or stacked in piles. When Margot spotted the large bed at the back of the basement, her stomach fluttered with anticipation.

And fear.

"I turned around," she told me. "And Derek was standing near the stairs, but he was different. His smile was different, and his eyes had changed from warm to cold, and he was just standing there staring at me...like a wolf eyeing up its prey."

Confused by Derek's sudden shift in attitude, Margot asked him what was wrong, thinking that she had done something to upset him. "And then I thought to myself, he doesn't want me anymore, that he was just being nice before, and now he was going to kick me out some back entrance and tell me he never wanted to see me again. I actually looked around for another exit, ready to go, and as I did..."

She saw them all standing behind her. Four of Derek's friends. His teammates, including the star quarterback, whom she knew from the news when he was featured for something or other to do with football.

"Everyone of them had the same look on their faces," she said, sounding like she had to drag the words out of herself. "And I knew right away what was happening. Everything clicked, and I knew Derek had been setting me up all along."

She turned around and pleaded with him not to hurt her, but the more she protested, the more she begged, the more Derek's look of predatory pleasure increased as he walked slowly towards her.

Margot was repeatedly raped, beaten and tortured by Derek and his friends for hours, although to Margot it felt like she was in that basement for days as she fell in and out of consciousness. Derek's friends all had their way with her, multiple times, forcing her to do unspeakable things, all the while laughing at her pain.

Then Derek took over. He took his time with her as he raped her, and then tortured her with a live electrical wire, leaving burn marks all over her body. The pain was so intense she blacked out numerous times. Derek used smelling salts to bring her round each time, and then he would go to work with some new tool, like a knife or a pair of pliers. Even his four friends were disgusted by what he was doing, saying they were going to leave, but whatever look Derek gave them forced them all to stay. Margot was half dead by the time he had finished with her.

While she was unconscious for the last time, Derek and his friends took Margot to the edge of town, dragged her lifeless body up an alley and tossed her into a dumpster. It was unclear whether they all thought she was dead. Even if she wasn't, they probably didn't care much. No matter if she was alive or dead, Derek was arrogant enough that nothing could come back on him, and even if it did, it would be nothing the expensive family lawyer couldn't sort out.

"Some homeless guy found me the next day while searching for scraps in the dumpster I was in," Margot said. "I was technically dead by the time I was taken to a hospital. They managed to bring me round, though. Sometimes I wish they hadn't..."

I said nothing as I looked at her with nothing but empathy and concern. It was a horrific experience she had went through which undoubtedly traumatized her forever more. But what do you say? There's nothing you can say. So I let her sit in silence for a while until she felt able to continue.

When she had recovered from her injuries enough to give a statement, she told the cops what had happened, giving them Derek's name and the name of the quarterback, the only other name she could remember. "The two detectives glanced at each other when I mentioned the names," she said. "And I knew right then that Derek and his buddies would get away with it. I just knew. And sure enough..."

They did.

The case didn't even get to court. Margot found herself railroaded by an army of lawyers into signing a statement that said the five boys she initially accused had nothing to do with what happened her and that actually, she didn't know who had assaulted her.

"And that was that. Case dismissed. Now off you go you poor, dirty girl and don't bother the nice rich people again."

Not long after, Margot tried to kill herself by taking a load of prescription pills she bought from some dealer on the street. She swallowed the pills right there and then, washing them down with a full bottle of vodka.

Then she curled up next a dumpster and waited to die.

"As far as I was concerned, death was the only thing left for me," she said, somewhat more in control of her emotions by that stage in her recounting of events past.

"But you obviously didn't die," I pointed out.

"I almost did. Again. But *outside* the dumpster this time." She threw me a glance as if to make sure I was getting the cruel irony of the situation.

A witch found her lying there. Apparently, the witch had been passing by when she sensed someone was in danger and walked up the alley to find the young Margot lying there, unconscious with an empty bottle of vodka beside her, on the brink of death. The witch used her magic right there and then to bring Margot back to full consciousness and also neutralize the drugs in her system.

"I was mad at first," Margot said. "I really did want to die. But the witch, she somehow sensed my pain and pointed out to me that my desire for revenge beamed stronger than my desire to die, and I knew straight away she was right. The thought of revenge had crossed my mind of course, but I paid it no heed because I knew there was no way I could get back at Derek and those other boys. They were all from powerful families, and there was no way I could get near them. So instead of revenge, I chose death."

But the witch explained to Margot that she could enable her to exact her revenge on the people who hurt her. All Margot had to do was go with the witch to her Sanctum, and the witch would show her how. Margot knew the witch was telling the truth. She could sense the woman's power, plus the witch had brought her back from death's door using nothing but magic. Suddenly, Margot was overcome with the notion of getting her revenge on Derek and the others. But unlike before, when revenge was just a silly pipe-dream, the possibility was now very real. And she didn't care what she had to do to exact that revenge. She would sell her soul if she had to.

And as it turned out, that's exactly what Margot had to do.

"Witch's get their power by selling their soul to a demon," she said, which I already knew.

"My mother was a witch," I informed her. "She managed to break her contract, with my father's help. She got free of it."

Margot almost laughed as she shook her head at me. "There is no getting free of it. Believe me, I know. Whatever you were told, it wasn't true. When you trade your soul, there is no getting it back unless you destroy the demon you traded it to. Even when you die, the demon will still own your soul, and you still have to obey it at all times."

I felt my face drop as she said that. Could it be true that my mother was still in service to some demon the whole time I knew her? "But she appeared to me recently," I said. "Her soul is in some other dimension. Not the Underworld."

"She may have found a way to hide. Or she may be still doing the demon's bidding from wherever she is now."

*Jesus*, I thought shaking my head. *The skeletons just keep coming from my families closet.*

It made sense what Margot was saying, especially when I thought about and realized there were numerous times when my mother was gone for long stretches, sometimes days at a time. My father told us our mother was off visiting friends or family, or that she was away sourcing spell ingredients somewhere. We we're kids, so we never questioned it. Could it be that my mother was actually away all those times doing the bidding of some demon? And if so, what the hell did she do?

I decided then it would be best if I thought about all that another time. There were more pressing matters at hand. I prompted Margot to finish her story so we could come up with a plan that would save everyone from Baal. A tall order, I know. But I was nothing if not optimistic.

"I gave my soul to Baal," Margot said with heavy regret. "I wish now I had died by the side of that dumpster. If I thought killing myself now would help, I would. But that would just make it easier for Baal to get to me."

Clearly, Margot thought she somehow deserved to die anyway, though I wasn't quite sure why at that point, not until she told me the rest of her story.

"Baal gave me the power I sought to get my revenge," she said. "Power that I didn't think was possible."

"Magic."

"Dark magic. Exactly the kind of magic I needed right then."

Margot got her revenge soon after. She picked off Derek's four friends first, one by one, and used her newfound powers to inflict horrific pain and do unspeakable things to each of them. She left each one in a dumpster, exactly as they had done to her. Only every one of them was dead by the time they were discarded in the dumpster. Of course, after she killed the first boy, the police came looking for her, tracking her down to the roach infested apartment she still lived in. But the cops could prove nothing, and given the state of the boy's injuries, they concluded there was no way a girl of Margot's size and strength could have done such things. The cops still thought she was involved somehow, though, and they kept a tail on her. Or tried to. With her new powers, Margot easily evaded the cops and was able to kill the rest of the boys without being caught, no matter how much security they had around them. "If anyone got in my way, I either scrambled their brains so they wouldn't remember a thing or...I killed them."

She looked at me then, as if expecting judgment from me, but I said nothing. Not because I condoned the killing of innocents, but because there was nothing to be done about it now. "What about Derek?" I asked.

A slight sneer appeared on her face. "He carried on with his life while his friends were being killed. He acted like he wasn't afraid. Which he wasn't, not until the end. I stopped the car he was being driven home in one night after he had left some club. He had two bodyguards with him. They tried to shoot me, so I killed them. Snapped their necks in an instant. Even then, Derek was calling me all the vicious cunts of the day, saying he was going to rape me until I was dead, and then he was going to fuck my dead body afterward."

"Nice guy."

"The best."

Margot used her powers to force Derek into the trunk of the car. Then she drove the car to an abandoned warehouse near the docks. "I tortured him for days," she said. "I can still hear his screams even now. He was begging for death by the end, but I wouldn't give it to him."

"So what did you do?"

Her face hardened as the memories flooded her mind. "First I dismembered him. Then I made him deaf, dumb and blind. And before I did that, I made sure the last thing he saw was my face. He's probably still lying somewhere, trapped in his own darkness, only my magic keeping him alive."

"Jesus Christ," I said, genuinely appalled. "Remind me never to piss you off."

"He deserved what he got."

As horrified as I was, I couldn't argue with her on that either. Predators like

Derek and his buddies had no business walking the Earth. "So you got your revenge. Then what?"

She smiled humorlessly. "Then I went to work for Baal. Reaping souls."

I shook my head. "Bloodthirsty much?"

"It wasn't like I had a choice," she said, flashing me a look. "Baal wanted souls. I had to get them for him, or else it was unspeakable torment in the Underworld." She paused for a moment. "But you're right. A bloodlust, if you want to call it that, was awakened in me after killing those boys. I'd be lying if I said I didn't enjoy the power I had over them, and the satisfaction of knowing once I killed them that they would never be able to hurt anyone again. It felt like I was reborn. Which I guess I was."

"So how many souls did you reap?"

"Too many to count," she said. "And Baal loved me for it."

"Loved?" It looked like my instincts were right. This was personal for Baal.

Margot let out a long sigh. "A demon can't feel love. Not exactly. At first, Baal was just pleased with my work, and for good reason. Once I was given a name, I didn't stop until I had that person's soul. Many of those names were hard to get to. Some of them were also supernatural. But I still got to them, no matter how much blood I had to spill in the process. Nothing or no one stood in my way. As earners go, I was the best Baal had. I was top of the leaderboard. And he rewarded me with more and more power. You could say he developed a sort of affection towards me. After a while, he took on a mentoring role, teaching me things and telling me things that he really shouldn't have been. Underworld secrets. The weaknesses of certain demons. The locations of hidden portals around the world."

"To what end, though?" I asked. "It wasn't like he was going to die someday and you would assume his place, so why?"

"I think I awakened something in him. A flicker of light perhaps. Something he wasn't expecting, but which he gave into anyway. I didn't care how he looked at me, as long as he kept feeding me power and knowledge, which was all that mattered to me."

"I'll not even ask why. I know why. It's because once you start down that road, it's never enough."

"Exactly."

"So what changed? Why did you end up betraying Baal if he was so generous towards you?"

"It wasn't just one thing necessarily." She stopped and then shook her head. "Well, actually it *was* just one thing. Mostly anyway. I'd had enough of killing, but also Baal..."

"Baal what?" I asked, hoping she wasn't going to say what I thought she was going to say.

"He raped me."

Oh, Jesus. She did say it, and I wasn't sure how to respond, so I ended up saying nothing.

"He had every right to, of course," she said. "He owned me after all. Normal rules didn't apply in that situation. But still, he had never touched me before, and then he just decides he wants me one day. So he took me, and I pretended to enjoy it."

"I can't even imagine..." Actually, I could having seen Baal's true form, and I was sickened.

"Best you don't," Margot said. "Anyway, that was it for me. No amount of power was worth having to endure that all the time. So in secret, I tried to work out ways to destroy Baal before he decided he wanted my flesh again. But I came up empty."

"So you went into hiding instead."

She nodded. "Yes. It was my only option."

"How long have you been here?"

"Ten years," she said.

"Just you?"

"Just me. Until you came along."

I sat back and folded my arms as I let out a long breath. "Well, I'll tell you, I have no intentions of staying here for the next ten years."

Margot looked at me with what seemed like a disappointment in her eyes. "Why not? You'd have everything you need here."

It was a tempting offer to be sure, but my place wasn't in that magic bubble with her. My place was with Leona and Blaze and Ray and Sanaka and everyone else I knew on the outside. Besides, it wasn't my style to hide away from things. I'd tried that before, and it never solved anything. "Sorry, Margot," I said. "But we're going to have burst this magic bubble of yours at some point. Sooner rather than later. Which means we have to figure out how to put Baal down for good."

Margot folded her arms in annoyance. "I just told you, it can't be done. You think I'd still be here if there were a way?"

Yes, actually, but I never told her that. Margot was happy hiding from the world, Baal or no Baal. But I didn't care about that. She could hide if she wanted to, but only after she had done her part to help me.

I got out of bed and started to pull my clothes on. "If there's one thing I've learned after being in some impossible situations over the years," I said. "It's that there is always a way. We just have to find it."

# 16

## UNDER THE GUN

*T*he sun was shining brightly inside Margot's magic bubble kingdom when I went outside and stood in the garden for a while soaking up the warm rays, frankly astounded that Margot was able to replicate the effects of a real sun. Not to mention create the oasis of beauty that surrounded me. It made me wonder how powerful she really was. Baal had obviously bestowed upon her a great deal of magic. But then she was the demon's favorite pet. Until she turned on him, that is.

The witch's story was pretty tragic if you ask me. At one time she was just a normal girl trying to shake off the poverty and abuse that had been thrust upon her by being a number in the foster system. If she hadn't have met Derek the psychopath, Margot's life might have turned out to be very different. But then, as both she and I had pointed out, your plans don't matter when the universe always seemed to have other ideas about where you were going to end up. It was hard not to see the hand of fate in action when you looked back at your past circumstances.

My own tragic past was a case in point. As awful as it was growing up under the despotic influence of my father and then losing my entire family to a demon, in a twisted sort of way, those things had to happen for me to get to where I was.

Still, I shook my head at my attempts to philosophize things when there I was under the gun, having dragged Leona under with me as well.

It was difficult not to think about Leona as I walked slowly through the garden, my hands plunged into the pockets of my trench coat. Whatever the circumstances of the night before, there was no denying that I had cheated on the woman I was supposed to love. For that, guilt was gnawing unremittingly at my insides, more so because I knew Leona's loyalty towards me was unwavering. There was no way she would have slept with anyone else as long as she was with me. She just wasn't the type.

The question I ended up asking myself was, do I tell her or do I just pretend nothing happened and keep it as a dirty little secret? I knew if I told her she would walk. Leona wouldn't allow herself to react in any other way. She had too much pride.

*Just don't tell her*, I thought to myself. *Why wreck a good thing over one night of passion that I never intended to happen in the first place? And it wasn't like Margot gave me much choice, was it?*

No matter what way I thought about things, it did nothing to alleviate my heavy guilt. But guilt or not, I wasn't going to spend any more time dwelling on the matter. There were other much more pressing matters at hand that needed immediate attention.

I turned and headed back to the cottage. Margot's barn owl was perched on the porch roof, and it screeched once at me as I neared the front door. I gave the bird the finger as I went through the door and the owl rolled its head as if to say, "I *know* you just didn't flip me off, motherfucker!"

"Your barn owl familiar hates me," I said to Margot as I entered the cottage to find her at the kitchen table drinking tea. She was dressed all in black, looking much different to the flower girl in the white dress I first saw the day before. Now her hair was gelled back, and she wore dark eyeliner that made her look dangerous and undeniably sexy.

Margot smiled as I sat down after pouring myself a coffee from the tin pot simmering on the stove. "Barney is just not used to company," she said. "He's also fiercely protective."

"I guessed that when he pounced on me yesterday. Thanks for healing my ribs, by the way. I don't even remember you doing it."

"You were too far away to notice."

I shook my head at the sultry and mischievous look in her eyes. "About that."

"Forget it, Creed. You don't have to say anything. I know. You love your girlfriend. You don't have to explain."

A somewhat awkward silence fell as we exchanged looks for a moment.

*And this is why I don't sleep around*, I thought to myself. *The complications are not worth it.*

Margot snorted. "You make me laugh, Creed."

I stared at her a moment, wondering what she was on about. Then I realized. "You just read my thoughts again, didn't you?"

She held a hand up. "Sorry. It was just very loud."

"I'll try to keep it down then."

Her wide smile was warm and beatific. "I'm glad you turned up here, Creed," she said. "I haven't done much smiling for a while."

"Don't thank me yet," I said. "My arrival may yet signal both our dooms."

Margot's smile faded somewhat. "You really know how to kill the mood, don't you?"

"Sorry. The part of me with a gun to my head refuses to sit around any longer."

"And your girlfriend's head."

I glanced at her, thinking she was being snide, but she wasn't. She was merely clarifying the situation, not that she needed to. I was well aware already. "all right," I said, sitting straight in my chair and leaning on the table, so I was facing her. "You know Baal better than anyone. He must have a weakness somewhere. Something we can exploit that will help end him."

A sharp sort of laugh left her mouth. "I don't think you realize the kind of being Baal is. He is no ordinary demon. He's the spawn of primordial beings. A demon like Baal can't be destroyed."

"Everything can be destroyed by something."

She shook her head, adamant that she was right. "Believe me, Creed. I've thought of everything possible over the years. Spells, artifacts, pure magic. That stuff would hurt him, but it wouldn't kill him. You forget how intimately I know Baal. I've seen and felt what he's made off, and there is no killing him."

I sighed and thought for a moment. "All right, so we can't kill the bastard. What if we trap him instead?"

Margot considered for a moment. "It's a possibility," she conceded eventually. "I've thought of it before, but it was never something I would try on my own."

"But the two of us," I said, moving my finger between us. "You think we could pull it off together if we combined our powers?"

Again she thought. "I don't know. Maybe."

I nodded. "Let's assume it's a possibility, that there's at least a chance it would work. How would we do it?"

"Assuming we could hold him long enough, we would have to banish him to another dimension. A dimension he could never escape from."

"Exactly, and I think I might know one. It's called Dimension X and there's nothing in it but darkness. We would have to seal him in somehow, but I'm sure we can figure that out."

Margot shook her head. "You forget one thing. Baal is immensely strong and powerful. Physically restraining him would be impossible. And even with magic, it would still be damn near impossible."

Frowning, I said, "You say he's like the Hulk, physically speaking. But I fought him in the basement of my Sanctum. I got the better of him while he was in his true demon form."

Margot smiled slightly at what she saw as my naivety. "If you got the better of him that's because he allowed you to. Did you think you could beat a demon like Baal in a fist fight?"

Thinking back, I saw she was right. Baal had wanted me to be overcome by the black magic coursing through my system at the time. Driving him back the way I did only served to strengthen the dark magic that was in me. Baal obviously knew that. No doubt if I had gone and chopped the demon's head off with the Sword of Rishanti, I would have sealed my fate, and the black magic would have taken hold permanently. Then Baal probably would have grown a new fucking head or stuck the old one back on. With black magic fully rooted in me, Baal and I would have become brothers in evil. There was no telling what he would have had me do. Devious bastard. "I didn't think too much about it at the time," I told Margot. "I had other things on my mind."

"Take it from someone who knows what Baal is capable off better than anyone." Her blackened eyes focused in on me. "This plan to somehow restrain and then banish him has a slim chance of working. At best."

"I'll take slim. I work with those odds all the time. Slim I'm comfortable with."

She couldn't help smiling. "You are not right in the head. Anyone ever tell you that?"

I smiled back and then stood up. "I hear it all the time. So are we going to do this or what?"

Margot stared up at me as if she was unsure, but I knew she had already made up her mind. "You're going to do it with or without me, aren't you?"

"Yes."

A sigh left her. Then she stood up. "all right, Creed," she said. "I suppose I'm partly responsible for this situation you find yourself in, so I guess I have to help fix it."

"Don't forget your own situation. Baal would get to you eventually, even without me. You know that full well. There's only so long you can hide out."

It was the truth. Her face said so. "You better be as good as you think you are, Creed."

I stared at her a moment, then smiled. "We'll soon see, won't we?"

# 17

# WHERE THE OWL GETS IT

"*I*'m going to miss this place," Margot said while she stood in the garden looking around at the Eden she had created as if it would all disintegrate as soon as she left the place. Which it would, eventually. Without her magic to sustain it, Eden would wither and die.

"You can always start afresh somewhere else," I said, attuned to her pain, but also just wanting to leave the place. I could understand the overwhelming sense of security she felt within the walls of her kingdom. Who knows, given a bit more time, I may have come to feel the same way. But the fact was, there was business to be taken care off. I had to try and save Leona from Baal's inevitable wrath when he realized I was now disobeying his command and standing against him.

And that's if he hadn't realized already. That was another reason I wanted out of the woods. I needed to call Leona to make sure she was all right.

Margot nodded. "Maybe you're right. If I live long enough."

"You will," I said, more confidently than I felt. The truth was, I wasn't sure if Margot and I could take Baal by ourselves. If I wanted to be smart about things, I would enlist the help of Ray and Sanaka, but I didn't want to drag those two into that mess if it meant putting their lives and souls at risk. It was my mess, and Margot's, and we had to clean it up. "Let's go."

Margot raised both her arms then, turning her head slightly skyward as she began uttering words that I couldn't hear. Then she dropped both arms sharply, and the invisible dome over Eden became visible as arcs of light blue magical energy crackled through it for a few seconds and then disappeared. "We can go now," Margot said. "The forcefield is down. It won't be long before Baal picks up on my presence again."

For the first time, I saw fear in her eyes at the prospect of what we were about to do, and at the fact that she was now completely exposed after being under for so long. Stepping close to her, I placed my hands on her shoulders and looked her in the eyes. "Hey," I said. "I'm going to be with you on this, no matter what happens. You're not alone."

She smiled and then nodded. "Why are you doing this, Creed? Why are you helping me?"

It struck me as an odd question. "You know why. Leona's at risk. So am I now."

Her gray eyes searched mine. "You never had any intention of bringing me to Baal, did you? Even before you knew who I was."

She had me there, I supposed. "My instincts about you turned out to be right. I don't sacrifice innocent people to save my own skin."

"But I'm not innocent. I've killed."

"Maybe you'll pay for those deaths one day. You still have innocence in your soul, despite everything. You did the best you could. I get that."

Margot's smile widened further as her eyes became wet and glassy. Then she cupped my face with both hands and kissed me on the lips with a passion that I didn't expect. Closing my eyes, I reveled in her soft touch, in her intoxicating scent, knowing it would be last time I ever did. When she stopped kissing me, she held onto my face. "Thank you," she whispered.

I wasn't sure what for, so I just nodded. "We should go."

Margot stood back as a steely resolve hardened her face.

* * *

As plans went, ours was a fairly simple one. In my experience, when you're going up against the supernatural, its best to keep things simple. With demons and other powerful supernatural creatures, there were enough uncontrollable variables in play without adding a load more in the form of some complicated plan. The fewer variables you brought to the table, the less you had to contend with and the greater control you would have over the situation.

So as far as going up against Baal was concerned, the plan was to get to the Sanctum in the city first, and then to find a spell that would send Baal to Dimension X, hopefully trapping him there forever. That was assuming Baal wasn't waiting for us outside the woods somewhere, or that he wouldn't sense the presence of Margot or me before we could get a chance to set things up.

Before we left Eden, Margot cast a spell that would prevent Baal from sensing either of us. But she wasn't sure how much time the spell would give us. It could be several hours, or it could be several minutes. Such magic worked better when you stayed in one place, as Margot did for years. But when you start moving around the place, the magic becomes less effective at concealing your presence. It was a chance we had to take, however, as was the whole damn plan. Everything we were doing amounted to a massive gamble, Leona's inadvertent involvement putting the sweats on me even more.

When we moved out into the woods, we couldn't help becoming hyper-vigilant as if we expected Baal to appear in front of us at any moment. The woods were still warded, however, so there wasn't much chance of that happening. Regardless, we moved quietly, hardly talking as we made our way through the trees. Above us, Margot's familiar flew overhead, normal sized for the time being. It would fly on ahead for a bit and then circle back, presumably reporting to Margot that it had seen no threats as yet.

375

After a while, I took out my phone and checked the signal, tutting when I got none, even though I knew I wouldn't get a reception until I had left the cover of the woods. It was still playing on my mind that Leona would have been trying to call me. Especially since I realized not long ago that two whole days had gone by while I was in Eden with Margot. My main worry now was that Baal had gotten pissed off at my prolonged absence and had taken his frustration out on Leona somehow.

*Please do not let that be the case*, I thought. I didn't think I would have been able to live with myself after if Leona had come to harm, especially since it would have been my fault if she did.

A loud screech sounded up ahead as the barn owl flew low towards Margot and landed on her extended forearm. I stopped and waited as Margot looked into the owl's eyes for a moment, and then sent it off again with some command I didn't quite hear. "What is it?" I asked.

"There's someone up ahead," Margot said as she moved in behind one of the trees.

I quickly moved in beside her. "Who?"

"Not sure. It could just be one of the mountain dwellers. I'll know in a--"

A hugely loud cracking sound rang out then, cutting Margot off, and I knew immediately it was a gunshot. Shotgun by the sounds of it, and from the look on Margot's face, I knew her owl familiar had been shot down. Margot squeezed her eyes shut for a second and banged the back of her head of the tree.

"Who the fuck is that?" I said, looking out from around the tree and scanning the woods up ahead. Whoever it was they were well hidden because I saw no sign of them. "Some fucking dumb hunter, maybe?"

Margot shook her head. "If it is, they just made a huge fucking mistake shooting my familiar."

Rage flashed across her face, the sudden change in her demeanor stunning me into silence for a moment. *There it is*, I thought as I stared at her. *The face of the Blood Witch. Fearless. Frightening. Cold.*

She pushed off the tree and got ready to go out and find whoever had shot down her owl familiar.

"Wait," I said when I realized what she was planning on doing. "I think--"

But she was away before I could finish, striding through the trees like a panther on the prowl.

And then she stopped dead as if someone had just stabbed her in the back. Her hand went to her neck as she turned around to look at me.

Then Margot collapsed in a heap on the ground.

# IF YOU GO INTO THE WOODS TODAY

*I* stood for one shocked moment as I gazed at Margot lying amongst the undergrowth on the forest floor, her body prone and unmoving. Had she been shot? I wasn't sure, as I had heard no shot unless the person hunting us in the woods had used a silencer, which didn't make any sense after using a shotgun to bring down the barn owl.

Then as I looked harder at Margot, I realized there was something sticking out of her neck. Something that was partially bright red in color.

"A tranq dart," I said aloud.

Well, at least she wasn't shot with a bullet. Frankly, I was a little surprised that the tranquilizer dart even made it anywhere near Margot in the first place. Her powers should have stopped it. Obviously, she was out of practice after ten years of using her magic only to create, and not to attack or defend.

My worry levels went down a bit as I was thankful Margot hadn't been shot by a real bullet. I could use my magic to bring her out of her unconscious state, but I wasn't about to do so when the shooter was still out there. If I went down as well, the game would be over.

And I had no doubt at that stage that whoever was out there in the woods they were there at the behest of Baal. I was starting to think it was a hunter of some kind. It made sense. Baal had obviously hired someone as extra insurance since the demon couldn't enter the woods himself. Then it hit me that the hunter had been following me all along, right since I first entered the woods, and before that on the road.

*Baal, you sneaky bastard*, I thought.

I leaned my head out from around the tree and scanned the woods ahead, still seeing no one. "Whoever you are," I shouted. "You might as well turn back. You have no idea who you're dealing with here."

My announcement was met with a gunshot. A bullet--not a tranq dart--

slammed into the trunk of the tree I was using as cover, exploding bits of bark out near my face. "Son of a bitch!" I cursed, ducking back behind the tree again.

The shooter wasn't messing around. That shot was meant to kill.

I pulled out my pistol and held it by my side. Then I leaned around the trunk of the tree and fired off a single shot in the direction I thought the shooter was. Not that I expected to hit anything, but I wanted to at least warn the hunter that they weren't the only one with a gun.

Seconds after firing, my shot was met with another loud bang, and then another, the two bullets slamming into the tree near my head, causing me to flinch away involuntarily.

*Fuck this*, I thought. I couldn't just stay pinned behind the tree while I waited for the hunter to advance on me. I had to take proactive action of some kind.

Closing my eyes for a second, I cast my enhanced awareness out into the woods in search of the shooter. And while I couldn't exactly see where the person was, I soon got a very good sense of where they where, which was roughly one hundred yards away at my two o'clock. "all right asshole," I said. "Let's see how you react to this."

Switching the pistol into my other hand, I quickly conjured up a fireball in my right hand. Then I stepped out from behind the tree and flung the hot as hell fireball to where I thought the shooter was hiding. The ball of fire streaked through the air, narrowly missing the trees it passed between before exploding into a large clump of bushes, engulfing everything within a three-foot radius around it. A loud scream indicated I had found my target, and a second later I saw a large figure come running out from behind the bushes as he did his best to put out the flames that were now attached to the dark duster coat the guy was wearing. As the hunter moved towards a large tree, he fired two shots at me with the pistol in his hand, and I ducked behind cover again.

Now that I had seen the shooter, I recognized him immediately. He was hard to mistake. A brute of a man, six and a half feet tall and half as wide, always wore a thick beard and his trademark duster and wide brimmed hat. "Damian fucking Gunther," I said as I leaned back against the tree. Blackham's most notorious witch hunter and current head of a family who had spent the last two centuries hunting down every witch they could find. Not only were the Gunther's ruthless and relentless in pursuit of their quarry, but they were also renowned for torturing their captives once caught. Damian Gunther especially was feared amongst the witch fraternity for his cold-bloodedness and almost puritan belief that every witch was a dark stain on God's earth, and therefore deserved no mercy. Obviously, Baal had hired Damian Gunther to capture Margot once I had located her, the demon likely knowing I wouldn't just hand Margot over.

"I know who you are, Gunther," I shouted. "You might as well leave these woods right now or--"

A volley of automatic gunfire blasted into the tree I was using for cover, forcing me to duck down as bits of tree exploded out all around me, a few of the bullets missing the tree and whizzing past me before impacting the ground like mini asteroids, throwing up dirt and debris.

Clearly, Damian Gunther didn't give a shit about my veiled threats. He wasn't going anywhere.

I conjured up another fireball and launched it after the shooting had stopped, ducking back behind the tree again straight after. No scream from Gunther this time, who had obviously managed to avoid the flames.

A silence then descended in the woods. Even the birds had stopped chirping. It was a silence I didn't like. Casting out my awareness, I did a search for the witch hunter. Too late, I realized the bastard wasn't far from me, obviously having run around to my left flank. But I still couldn't see him as I held out my pistol while scanning the undergrowth.

Then I sensed movement out of the corner of my eye. I snapped my head around to see the hulking figure of Damian Gunther appear from behind a tree, a short barreled shotgun aimed right at me. "Drop the pistol, wizard," he barked in a deep, gravelly voice.

I froze as I stared at the massive man standing not ten feet away from me. How the hell did he manage to get around me so fast? "Take it easy," I said as calmly as I could, my pistol still aimed at the witch hunter.

Gunther pumped the slide on his shotgun as he carried on walking towards me, stopping only when he was six feet away. "I said drop that fucking pistol."

*Screw you, Gunther*, I thought as I tapped into my magic, intending to use the same Paralyzing Spell I had used on the mountain men when I first entered the woods.

Gunther smiled as he glared at me. "I see what your doing. Your filthy magic won't work on me. I and my descendants have had plenty of time to find ways to block magic from the likes of you. Now, I'm not going to tell you again. Drop that pistol before I put a hole in your chest."

Son of a bitch. He was right. My magic had no effect on him. I should have known. As someone who hunted witches for a living (and I got the feeling anyone who used magic was a witch to him), it was to be expected that he had found a way to protect himself against most of it. Exactly how, I wasn't quite sure, though I suspected it was mostly a Gunther family trait. Immunity to magic. That's what made them so formidable as witch hunters.

Not having much choice, I lowered my pistol and dropped it to the ground by my feet. "What are you going to do, kill me?" I said. "You even know who you're working for?"

Damian Gunther came closer until he was two feet away, the barrel of his shotgun still aimed at my chest. Poking out of the inside of his worn duster I saw what looked like a machine pistol, which would explain the automatic fire earlier. "It doesn't matter to me," he said, his massively imposing form seeming to block out the sun behind him, his eyes like chips of gray marble set into his lined, bearded face. It was the first time I had met the man in person, having been aware of him and his family's fearsome reputation for years. Seeing him up close, I had to say the man was as frightening as everyone said he was.

"You're working for a demon, a demon who wants to take innocent lives."

Gunther snorted derisively. "Innocent? I don't think so. You know how long I've wanted to get my hands on that bitch lying over there? You know how many people she's killed over the years, how many souls she's reaped?"

"Yeah, and all for the demon you're now taking orders from. There's irony for you."

The barrel of the shotgun moved up level with my face. "I take orders from no one," Gunther growled. "I'm here because it's my job to put down abominations of nature like you and the Blood Witch."

An abomination of nature. That was a new one on me. "There's more to this than you know. You're making a mistake."

Gunther shook his head. "No mistake. The Blood Witch will die at the hands of the demon. As for you, wizard..."

The shotgun barrel came so close to my face I could smell the oil on the metal. There aren't too many things more intimidating in life than having a loaded shotgun pointed at your face. "So that's it, you're just going to murder me here in cold blood?"

Gunther's eyes squinted at me. "That's exactly right, wizard."

"Well then," I said, thinking I could hear his finger squeeze harder on the shotgun trigger. "I guess I'd better--"

I teleported around behind him then, just as he pulled the trigger on the shotgun. With a small bladed knife I had dug out of my trench coat, I stabbed him hard in one of his tree trunk sized legs. Gunther cried out in shock and pain, but the man mountain didn't go down, swinging the shotgun around just as I teleported and appeared behind him once more. Balling my fist, I punched him as hard as I could in the small of his back, wincing as I nearly broke my knuckles on his spine. The blow was enough to send Gunther to his knees. He fell forward as the shotgun slipped from his hand.

As Gunther lay dazed, I rushed forward, knowing if I gave him any time to recover he would be up and on me in a rage. There were a ton of spells I could have used to secure the witch hunter there and then, but as magic in spell form didn't affect him, I had to use raw magical energy instead. The reddish orange energy swirled around my right fist just as Gunther was getting up, growling that he was going to kill me. But before he could get up, I swung my fist at his skull as hard as I could. The impact cracked my knuckles straight away as it was like punching a bowling ball, but I didn't care. The blow rattled the witch hunter's brain so much that he immediately lost consciousness and fell over again to the forest floor.

"Goddamn," I said, wincing at the pain in my right hand. "That fucking hurt."

Margot was still out of it as she lay on the ground not too far away, and I ran over to her, eager to get her awake again before Gunther woke up, which I was sure wouldn't take as long as I thought it would.

After pulling out the dart that was still stuck in Margot's neck, I placed both hands on her chest as I directed my magic into her and uttered the words to a spell that would neutralize the effects of the sedative in her system. I was thankful when she opened her eyes a moment later.

"What happened?" she asked, confused as she sat up and unconsciously rubbed at her neck.

"This?" I said, holding up the dart for her to see. Then I pointed at the still out of it Gunther. "And him."

Margot frowned at the tranquilizer dart. "All of my power and that tiny thing takes me out."

"I know, right? But if you don't see it coming, you can't stop it."

"Clearly not."

I helped Margot to her feet. "We need to go."

She was looking over at Gunther. "Is that Damian Gunther, the witch hunter?"

"Yes. You know him? He says he knows you."

"We've had our run-ins. He was obsessed with taking me down for years."

"Still is," I said, the adrenaline pumping through my system making me jittery. "We should go before he wakes up. Can you teleport?"

She nodded. "Yes, but I need to find my familiar first."

We spent the next few minutes scanning the woodland floor for the body of the shot barn owl. Margot eventually found it, seemingly dead, its once pristine white feathers now stained with bright red blood. The owl's beak hung slightly open, its eyes half-closed. Margot picked up the dead owl and cradled it gently in her arms like it was her dead baby.

"As the owl is your familiar, I'm assuming it isn't completely gone," I said.

"He will come back when he's ready," Margot said, gently stroking the owl's breast with the back of her fingers. When she finally stood up, she cradled the lifeless owl with one arm while she held out her other hand to me.

As I took hold of her hand, our eyes met for just a second, and I got a tingling sensation in my belly that I chose to ignore. A second later we were gone.

# THE PROMISE

$\mathcal{M}$argot teleported us both most of the way across the woods. Then we found the trail that would take us to the road where I had the Cadillac parked.

"Thank you for saving me back there," Margot said. "Gunther would have handed me straight over to Baal if the bastard didn't kill me himself first that is."

"He didn't have much love for you, I'll tell you that," I said as I kept a close eye out in case Gunther had compatriots hiding out somewhere waiting on us.

"I can't say I blame him." Margot shook her head. "I did some terrible things to earn that nickname."

I said nothing as I glanced over at her. It was hard to believe the woman I had spent the last two days with could have been so brutally violent a decade ago. Whatever kind of person she was back then, though, I was pretty sure she wasn't that person anymore. Or at the very least, she kept that part of herself buried deep, in which case she was free to pull it out at any time. Which I hoped she would never have to do, and not just for her sake.

"So has your familiar died before?" I asked changing the subject and nodding my head at the barn owl she held with both hands against her breast.

She sighed. "Many times, unfortunately. Always for me in some way."

"Sounds like a loyal pet."

Margot shot me a look. "Barney is no pet."

"Yes, I know, obviously. I just meant...he's loyal. Blaze, my Garra Wolf, is fiercely loyal too. He died protecting me when I was trying to bring down my father."

"You brought him back?"

I nodded. "I had a special kind of magic in me then. It allowed me to resurrect Blaze. Thank God. It would have been unbearable to lose him."

"Barney has been my only friend in the world," Margot said. "I couldn't be without him."

"You have me now." When I saw the look on her face, I felt I had to explain. "I just mean we're friends."

"Of course."

An awkward silence fell as we continued along the trail, finally nearing the edge of the woods.

"You know," Margot said eventually. "If we get through this--"

"Which we will."

She stopped walking. "If we get through this, I hope we can remain friends, you and I. We won't see each other much, but when we do meet again, I'd like us to be friends. You're one of the good guys, Creed, and those have been few and far between in my life."

I almost blushed as I stared over at her, wondering how Leona would feel if she ever met Margot. Would Leona be able to tell that Margot and I had slept together by some female intuition thing? I hoped not. "I'd like to think we can stay friends," I said. "Besides, I think your owl is coming round to me. He hasn't attacked me since. That's a start, right?" I smiled over at her.

Margot smiled back. "I supposed you could call that progress."

We both laughed before exchanging a last lingering glance, then we made our way down the trail towards the road, and the car soon came into view. I was glad to see the Cadillac again and glad to be getting out of the woods finally. As comfortable as I was surrounded by nature, I was a city boy at heart, and I needed Blackham's familiar ground and surroundings once more. I needed the Sanctum, the place where I had the most chance of figuring everything out with the half-baked plan Margot and I had hatched. "This is us," I said, pointing to the Cadillac. Then I stopped when I noticed a black pickup truck parked just down from the Cadillac. The same truck that overtook me on the way up here. "That's Gunther's truck."

"Looks like he was alone," Margot said.

"Yeah." I wasn't convinced Gunther was alone. Baal had to be close by somewhere. Maybe the demon was waiting for us, knowing we would eventually head for the car.

Then I heard a loud scream that curdled my blood.

"What the hell..." Margot said.

A horrific realization was settling into me as I shook my head. "No..." I said, suddenly sprinting down the rest of the trail towards the road. Margot shouted for me to wait, but I hardly heard her as I carried on running, my heart pounding in my chest, a sick feeling in my stomach. When I finally burst through the trees and out onto the road, I stopped dead when I saw what was in front of me.

Baal stood on the ledge across the road that jutted out from the side of the mountain. He was still in his human host, and he smiled carnivorously when he saw me. But I was hardly looking at him as all of my attention was taken up by what was hanging in the air just out from the ledge.

Or rather *who*.

For it was Leona.

I could only stand and stare for long horrified moments as I tried to work out what I was seeing. Leona seemed to be held in midair by some invisible force that was powered by Baal. Her limbs were spreadeagled as if something was pulling on them. She was also completely naked and covered in blood. Even more horrifically were the large bat creatures that flew around her suspended form. There was maybe a dozen of the bat-things, and as they flew around her, they would bite and scratch her and Leona would scream every time they did so.

"What the...put her down!" I shouted in a rage at Baal as I stormed across the road towards him. But before I got near him (what the hell was I going to do anyway?) Baal thrust out a hand and used the same invisible force to lift me off my feet by the neck and then swing me through the air at a shocking speed, bringing me to a halt right beside Leona past the edge of the cliff.

"Glad you could join us, Creed," Baal said.

I tried to speak, but the grip around my neck was too tight. I could barely even breathe.

"What's that?" Baal mocked. "You were busy fucking the witch in those woods? Ah, I see. Well, at least you are here now, eh?"

Despite the terror of being dangled in midair with the ground hundreds of feet below, I couldn't help turning my head to look at Leona beside me. Her eyes were on me as well, and the sense of hurt and betrayal I saw in them cut me to the bone. "What the fuck have you done, Creed?" she said, barely able to talk but still managing to sound angry.

I was about to say something when one of those fucking bat-things flew in and bit me on the cheek. "Fuck!" I cried in pain, then again as I felt the sharp sting of another bite on my ear. "Motherfucker!"

"You like my pets, Creed?" Baal asked, clearly delighting in his torturing of us. "They came up from the Underworld to lend a hand."

The bat-things continued to whizz around us, biting and scratching at will, although more so on Leona. Baal knew that hearing her pain would hurt worse than feeling my own. "Stop it!" I was able to shout eventually, the grip having loosened slightly around my neck.

Baal merely laughed. "You humans. You never know how to take your punishment, do you?"

"Let Leona go," I said. "She has nothing—"

"To do with it?" Baal finished. "On the contrary, Creed, she has everything to do with it. Didn't I say what would happen if you tried to go against me?"

I said nothing. The bastard had me there.

My eyes went to the woods, and I saw Margot standing just back from the edge, still safe inside the boundary of the ward, still cradling her lifeless owl, looking now like someone who wanted to do the right thing and come forward but couldn't.

Baal saw me looking and turned around, then stared at Margot for a long time it seemed.

"I'll get you out of this," I told Leona.

"Oh yeah?" Leona said as blood dripped down her face. "And how are you going to do that?"

There was venom in her voice. Understandably, I'd say. She was suspended hundreds of feet from the ground and surrounded by blood-sucking bats after all. Plus she knew I had slept with someone else. You could say I wasn't exactly her favorite person in the world right then.

She also had a valid point. The power being used on me (and on her) was too strong for me to overturn with my own magic. And when I say strong, I mean it. I was starting to see that Margot was right about Baal drawing me in back when I first summoned him. In no way did his power feel as strong back then as it did while I was dangling in midair like that. It was just one more thing to put another dent in my already battered morale.

It sunk in then that Baal was about to very possibly kill Leona and me if he didn't get what he wanted, which was Margot. And even then, the likelihood was high that he would still kill us all. "I'm sorry," I said to Leona. "I was just trying to do right by everyone."

"Well, it seems like you really fucking succeeded, didn't you?" she snapped back. "Not that it makes much difference now."

Goddamn it. I couldn't let Leona die. I wouldn't.

My eyes lit on Margot, who was standing safely in the woods, her eyes going from Baal to me. I was afraid she was going to teleport then, never to be seen again. Then there would be no hope for Leona or me. When Margot's eyes caught mine again, I concentrated hard to establish a psychic link with her. As she had already been in my mind, establishing that link turned out to be fairly easy. I just latched onto the trail she had left behind.

"Margot," I projected to her. "I know you're afraid, but you don't have a choice here."

A second later, her voice echoed in my mind. "I do have a choice. I can disappear again."

"No, please don't do that, Margot. If you do, you'll be killing Leona. You'll be killing me. Haven't you got enough deaths on your conscience?"

Leona squealed beside me as she got bit by another bat.

"That's not fair," Margot projected back.

"Maybe not, but it's still true. Be honest, Margot. You've always known you'd have to face the music at some point."

"Yes."

"I know you're afraid, Margot, but you have to hand yourself over to Baal."

"He will probably still kill you."

"He will if you don't."

She went silent as she stared at Leona. She wasn't that far away that I couldn't see the sympathy on her face. The guilt. The shame. "My torture will never end."

"Yes, it will," I said. "I promise you, Margot. I'll find a way to free you from him. I won't stop until I do."

Leona let out another scream of pain, this time louder and longer. When I looked, I saw that one of the bat creatures had landed on her chest and was grotesquely suckling on one of her breasts, blood oozing out of the creatures disgusting mouth.

A scream of frustration left my own mouth.

Baal turned around for a moment to see what was happening. "How cute," he said. "One of my little friends is getting attached I see." Smiling malevolently at me, he turned around again to stare at Margot. "Make her come to me, Creed. Or I will make you watch while I rip your girlfriend to pieces right beside you. She is still your girlfriend, isn't she? Or did you burn that particular bridge? Either way, I will still kill her."

"Margot!" I projected, my face pleading as I looked at her. "Please! I meant what I said. I'll bring you back."

"Is that a promise?"

"Yes!"

She half smiled as she looked over at me. "all right, Creed. You're right. I couldn't live with myself knowing I had a chance at saving you. And the woman you love, of course." Her smile became more forlorn. "You know, Creed, even if you do manage to save me somehow, you should know that there won't be much left to save." She bent down then and carefully laid her owl familiar on the ground. "Take care of my owl for me."

Then she walked out of the woods. Out of the safety of the ward.

The second she did, Baal thrust out a hand and used his power to drag her at speed across the road before halting her right in front of him. The demon stood for a long time just staring into Margot's face. Margot herself tried not to look afraid, but the truth was she was terrified, and there was nothing but abject fear in her expression.

Baal then thrust a hand out behind him, and the next thing Leona was pulled towards him as if she was attached to a rope Baal had just tugged on. She landed in a heap right at the demon's feet.

Baal looked up at me. "You crossed me, Creed," he said. "Despite repeated warnings not to. But I expected nothing less from you. It's who you are." He paused for a second as if considering what to do to me while I stayed suspended in midair, expecting to plunge hundreds of feet down any second. "I'm returning with Margot to my abode in the Underworld now. This whole experience has been very educational. I won't leave it as long next time about coming back here. It's been fun."

He turned towards Margot then, grabbed her by the hair as she squealed and held her down by his side like he was controlling an unruly dog.

My eyes met Margot's again for a second. "Promise me, Creed," she pleaded in my mind, tears and black streaks of eyeliner running down her face.

I never got the chance to answer her, for Baal turned again as if he had just remembered something like he was doing some twisted impression of Columbo. "Just one more thing, Mr. Creed. I'm also taking Leona here to the Underworld as well. I feel it's only fitting, considering your betrayal."

"NO!" I shouted. "*Please don't...please...take me instead.*"

Baal shook his head slightly as he made a face. "A tempting offer, but I'll have to decline."

"*Baal, I'm begging you, please don't take her...*"

"And there you go again using my true name. You humans. You simply don't know how to listen." He bent down and pulled Leona up by the hair, now holding both women by his sides.

Every muscle in my body tensed with helpless frustration and strained against the power holding me. A long scream left my mouth, made up of rage and frustration, of the pain of knowing that Leona's fate was entirely my fault.

"I'll be seeing you, Creed," Baal said, just before he disappeared along with Leona and Margot.

And that's also the precise moment when I started falling through the air towards the ground hundreds of feet below.

20

# FREE FALLING

*a*t the onset of the sudden and unexpected drop, my insides seemed to shoot up as if they were about to explode from my mouth. Within seconds I was tumbling through the freezing air, a deafening wind in my ears. My lungs felt frozen, and I could barely breathe, yet I still managed to scream as I fell. Images flashed across my blurred vision, of the ground below getting terrifyingly closer all the time, of the mountainside and the almost blindingly clear sky. It took me a second or two to comprehend that I was falling fast to my death, and it was all I could do not to let my body go limp as I prepared for and accepted the inevitable.

But then some survival instinct kicked in, and with the ground getting frighteningly closer all the time, I grasped within myself for some form of magic that would save me. *Blindly*. My capacity to think had been utterly suppressed by my panic response. It was absolutely a do or die situation if ever there was one. Therefore there was no time to think. I had one slim chance to do something to save myself. One action was all I would get.

Shutting my eyes, I did the only thing open to me and trusted my instincts.

Magic would save me.

Or at least it fucking better had, given everything I had given to it.

I kept my eyes shut as the sensation of falling through the air continued.

Waiting, praying...screaming.

Then something happened.

I stopped falling. Or at least that's how it felt, but I still had the sensation of moving through the air, and I also felt a familiar clamping around my body as if something had grabbed hold of me. Thinking my magic had done something to save me, I forced my eyes open to see thick, scaly bands of dark gray wrapped around my waist and legs. And as the sensation of falling changed to one of flying upwards, I realized it was talons wrapped around me. Looking up, I saw the massive form of an owl as it flew back up to the mountain ledge with me in its grip.

*Barney, you beautiful bastard!*

When the huge barn owl reached the ledge, it opened its talons and released me about two feet above the ground. I landed with a thump and a loud yelp before rolling across the gravel a few times and coming to a stop. Then I lay there with my eyes closed, pressing myself into joyous terra firma while I took in massive gulps of air. "*Oh, Jesus...*" I said, my body still flooded with adrenaline. My head was giddy with it, and I couldn't help bursting into relieved laughter.

I was alive. I could hardly believe it after feeling certain I was going to die just moments before.

A familiar screeching sound made me open my eyes and roll up onto my knees. The sound was made by Barney, who was back to normal size and perched on top of the Cadillac, his head moving gently from side to side while his black eyes stared at me.

Standing up, I brushed myself off and checked to make sure nothing was broken, and that I still had my pistol and everything else on me, which I had. Then I walked across the road to the car and stopped to look at Margot's familiar. "I see you've made a miraculous recovery," I said. "As good as new."

The owl stared back at me, its large eyes unblinking.

"Lucky for me you're made of sterner stuff, little owl. Thank you for saving my ass. Your timing was impeccable, to say the least."

Tentatively, I put my hand out slowly towards the owl, half expecting it to snap its beak at me. But it didn't. Instead, it let me stroke its pillowy soft breast. "There we go," I said soothingly. "I think you and I got off on the wrong foot. As we now want the same thing—which is to get back the women we love—I think we should stick together from now on. I'm going to need to know what's in that head of yours most likely, and you'll need me to get Margot back for you."

I shook my head as I thought of Leona, hardly able to believe that she was gone. And not just gone, but dragged to the Underworld by a brute of a demon. Even I'd never been to the Underworld. I knew Leona was tough, but how was she going to survive down there? And that's if she wasn't already dead and it wasn't just her eternal soul left. In that case, I would never get her back. She could only remain in this world as a ghost, and neither she nor I would want that. She wouldn't anyway.

The owl must have sensed my emotional state, for it hopped off the car and landed on my shoulder before nuzzling the side of my head with its beak. "I guess we're friends now then," I said looking at the owl and smiling sadly.

I put Barney in the front passenger seat of the car before climbing into the Cadillac myself. Then I just sat there for a while, trying to gather myself after my near death experience and the trauma of seeing Leona tortured and then taken away by that beast Baal.

And then, of course, there was Margot. It wasn't exactly easy watching her disappear either. Despite everything, she did the right thing in the end. She came forward even though she knew would be in for unspeakable punishment at the hands of Baal.

My blood curdled as I imagined what Baal would do to Leona and Margot down there in the Underworld, in whatever domain was his.

*Whatever it takes*, I thought as I stared over at the spot where Leona and Margot had disappeared from. I would do whatever it took to get them both back. Which of course assumed there was much of them to bring back, but I couldn't think in such terms, however great the possibility.

As I started the engine of the Cadillac, intending to drive back to Blackham City for some serious regrouping, I looked over at the barn owl. "Buckle up, Barney," I said. "It's going to be a bumpy ride."

Barney nestled down into the leather of the seat, and half closed his eyes. Turning my attention to the road, I spun the car around and throttled it back towards to the city.

# SYMPTOMS OF THE UNIVERSE

*N*umerous times on the drive back I would be overcome by intense bouts of anxiety fueled emotion that would cause me to grip the steering wheel and shake it hard with my teeth clenched, or else I would start cursing, and palm strike the steering wheel instead. Mostly I was pissed at myself for letting Leona get taken. I should have been able to do something to help her, but for all my magic it still wasn't as powerful as Baal's. Motherfucker made a little boy of me, and I hated it. Hated the control he had over me, even before he suspended me over that ledge.

Since I had left Ireland over thirty years ago, I had gotten used to answering to no one. I had shown enough subservience to last me two lifetimes while growing up in the same house as my father. After I had left, I vowed never again to put myself into situations where other people had a hold over me. Easier said than done of course (the day I got to Blackham I was put over a barrel by Angela Crow, for instance). In my line of work, leverage was often applied to me, but not usually for very long as I was always quick to correct the situation somehow.

But then my father came back on the scene, and ever since I had been under the thumb, first his and then Baal's.

And I was still under Baal's thumb.

That had to change.

Anger and rage started to rule my intentions. I couldn't allow that fucking demon bastard to wreck my life, to take away from me the only person in the world I truly loved (Uncle Ray and Sanaka aside, though I would never tell Sanaka so, even though his response might have been somewhat hilarious).

Although to be honest, I think I managed to push Leona away all by myself when I slept with Margot. Even if I somehow managed to rescue Leona from the Underworld, I doubted very much she would want anything to do with me after that. And I wouldn't be able to blame her one bit if she didn't. But I still had to try and save her, for even if she didn't want to be with me anymore, that didn't change the fact that I loved her and that I would do anything for her.

Even die if I had to, which was becoming a worrying possibility on the near horizon.

Then there was Margot. I had promised her I would save her from the clutches of Baal. So that was two women I was obligated towards saving (as if one wasn't enough).

But first I had to find a way into the Underworld.

*  *  *

I WALKED INTO THE SANCTUM WITH BARNEY PERCHED ON MY LEFT SHOULDER. As I entered the living room, I saw Blaze lying in the corner. When he saw the owl, he sat up and stared inquisitively. The barn owl stared right back at Blaze as if it had every right to be there.

"Blaze buddy," I said, holding my right arm out so Barney could jump onto it. "This is Barney. He's a barn owl as you can tell. He's also like you in that he's a bit special. Bad shit has gone down today, and we all need to work together to fix it." Blaze made a noise in his throat as if to ask what happened. "Leona is gone, buddy. Taken by your friend and mine, Baal. But I'm going to get her back."

I hoped.

I allowed Barney to hop off my arm onto the fireplace and the owl perched on the end of it, looking back and forth from Blaze to me. "Probably not the sort of environment you're used to," I said to the owl. "But with any luck, it will only be temporary. Then you can go back to your woods again, or wherever Margot takes you."

The owl screeched in a sad sort of way.

"Missing her, huh?" I nodded as if I understood. "I know the feeling." I shook my head as pangs of guilt twisted my stomach into knots. Blaze padded over and pressed his big head against my leg, and I sighed as I reached my hand down and ruffled his dark fur. "Thanks, buddy."

For the next while, I found myself pacing frantically around the living room as Blaze and Barney looked on. I was trying to work out what I needed to do next, but it was difficult trying to string thoughts together when all I could see in my mind was Leona's terrified face as she realized what was about to happen to her. And Margot as well, the witch's face pained by knowledge of what she knew she would have to endure. I wasn't sure what would be worse. Knowing or not knowing the kind of pain and unimaginable torture that lay ahead. The only thing I was sure of was that both ways sucked.

It was also difficult to remain objective about the situation. Every thought I had was born out of extreme emotion, and while I knew the motivational power of emotions, I also knew from experience that thinking emotionally could often land you in trouble.

Case in point, whatever I ended up doing, I was planning to do it alone. I intended to venture into the dark Underworld (where I had never been before, remember) alone. That was folly in itself, never mind trying to take on Baal in his home domain all by myself. It was dumb of me to think that I could do any of that on my own, but right then, I didn't care. I just knew the situation was on me, and that therefore I had to be the one to do something about it.

There was also no way I was going to drag Ray or Sanaka into things, putting them at risk as well, however adept they were at handling themselves. Like I said, my guilt dictated that everything was on me and me alone.

*So I might as well get fucking on with it*, I thought to myself.

"What do I need to do?" I asked myself out loud as I continued pacing around the room. "Think, Creed. I need to get into the Underworld first, but how do I that?" I thought for a moment, glancing at Blaze, who was giving me a look he often gave me. A look that said he thought I was mad for thinking of doing what I was about to do. It was also a look I ignored. Madness was what I needed right then (or so I thought). It was the driving force that would make sure I did the ridiculously dangerous things I needed to do to get into the Underworld.

"I need to make a door," I said. "A portal. Do I even have a damn spell for that? I must have..." I stopped and thought about the time it would take to go down into the Library of Dark magic and comb through a ton of books to locate the spell I required. Like I said, I never had much need for such a spell in the past. I mean come on, who in their right fucking mind wants to travel willingly to the Underworld? No one.

But as I was now of unsound mind and didn't have a choice in the matter anyway, I was going to travel willingly into a place that by all accounts (and I had read a fair few, not to mention heard the stories from Sanaka, who resided there for a time) contained every kind of hell imaginable. Including the fire and brimstone land of endless pain and torture that so many Christian Sleepwalker's feared so deeply.

The thing about this universe of ours is that its inhabitants play an active roll in shaping it. If enough beings (and not just humans) believed fervently in something enough, then it would eventually be brought into existence. Which is why such mythical places as Valhalla, Heaven, Hell all existed somewhere in the universe. Gods like Odin, Mars, Yahweh and Zeus resided in real palaces and great halls, in places filled with the souls of believers and those whose lives (soldiers, for instance) made them destined for a particular kind of afterlife.

And although my knowledge of the universe extended quite a ways compared to most, I still only knew an infinitesimal fraction of what there was to know. My mind already struggled to contain what it *did* know. It was a constant battle to keep yourself from being driven mad by having too much knowledge of things that most people didn't even know existed. It often became a heavy burden, but at the same time, it was one I was willing to bear. Such was my unquenchable thirst for knowledge and search for meaning in things.

Being a Sleepwalker might make for a less complicated life, but it also made for a soulless one. Not in every case. Plenty of Sleepwalkers lived meaningful and fulfilling lives. But at the same time, no Sleepwalker ever got to experience the thrill and sense of terrific revelation when the secrets of the universe revealed themselves after much hard work and persistence. Nor could they ever know the delightful but dangerous touch of magic, to sense the infinite possibilities that magic always brought with it. Those were the kinds of things that kept wizard's like myself going. It was about reaching those higher levels of meaning and experiencing the equal parts wonder, joy, and terror at the sheer vastness of the universe itself.

Out of those three, it was mostly terror I felt at the prospect of going to the Underworld. But I couldn't let that stop me.

I wouldn't.

As it would take too long to locate a spell that would open a portal to the Underworld, I came up with another idea instead. Looking over at the barn owl perched half sleeping on the fireplace mantle, I said, "I need to look inside that head of yours. I hope you don't mind."

Barney opened his eyes wide and stared at me. As far as I could tell (I was no owl whisperer), Margot's familiar was giving me consent to enter into his mind. There was no risk to Barney unless I chose to wreak havoc while I was in there, which I wasn't planning on doing.

The owl raised himself up as if it was ready to accept my psychic connection. I stepped forward and gently placed my hands on either side of the owl's head, his skull feeling small and fragile under all that plumage.

Not that this is common knowledge or anything, but owls have photographic memories. It's where they got the reputation for being wise. It's because they remember everything they see in exquisite detail. Of course, you would have had to have walked around inside an owl's head to know this, which most people couldn't do. When I was growing up in Ireland, I used to go out and hunt different animals, all so I could psychically link up with them, often without them even knowing it. Every time, I was left amazed at the rich inner life that all animals seemed to have, from ants right up to rats, foxes, rabbits and deer. Even earthworms had a soul of sorts that was deeply connected to the earth itself, and which guided the worm's every move. It was an amazing experience and one which made the pain of magic practice totally worth it (for a short time at least).

Barney had been with Margot since she became a witch, and I was certain that Margot had been to the Underworld more than once when she reaped souls for Baal. Both of which meant that somewhere inside the owl's head there was a spell for opening a portal.

All I had to do was find it.

## 22

# BARNEY'S MEMORIES

*B*eing inside the mind of another being, either human or animal, was a bit like finding yourself in a giant maze that instead of walls, had banks of images--memories--built up everywhere. Knowing how to navigate your way through such a maze took a lot of practice, especially since you had to navigate in a very instinctive manner.

The images that surrounded me inside the barn owl's mind appeared to be very random in nature. To one side of me, I had images of Margot pottering around in her self-created Garden of Eden with a vaguely sad look on her face. To the other side of me, there were moving pictures of Margot brutally killing people.

It was hard not to fix my attention on those murder scenes. In one scene, Margot is seen using her magic and two long bladed knives to take out a load of men in dark suits that are attacking her. The way she dispatches each of the men is incredible, her every movement self-assured and deadly, the look on her face one of cold-blooded indifference. I watched as Margot killed the last of the men before making her way down a corridor to where another man in a suit stood terrified inside a massive board room. Words are exchanged that I can't make out before Margot uses her magic to pin the man to the wall. She then throws a knife at him that pierces his heart. Slowly walking up to the dead man still pinned to the wall, she moves her hand in front of his chest and again uses her magic to extract the man's soul into a small wooden box. Then she leaves the whole bloody mess behind her.

I saw dozens of such scenes inside the mind of Margot's familiar, who appeared to be present throughout every mission of Margot's. The witch's ruthless efficiency in killing and reaping was frankly staggering. I knew she was capable, but I had no idea just how much until I saw for myself. It was hard not to think of her in a different light, given how many people she had killed, and the often brutal manner in which she killed them. It was like she was killing Derek and his friends all over again, such was the ferocity of her attacks and the look of cold retribution in her gray eyes.

At some point, many of the image banks surrounding me went completely blank, converting to a kind of black static. It was Barney's way of moving me along, and also some attempt to cover up the horrors perpetrated by his mistress. I had seen enough anyway, so I happily moved on, intuiting my way deeper into the passageways of the owl's mind.

After passing by numerous images of Barney hunting in woods and fields, of small and large animals (plus a few humans, including myself) falling prey to his razor sharp talons, I came across more of the owl's memories of Margot, some of which Baal appeared in. Sometimes the demon was in human form, but most often Baal held his true form as he conversed with Margot. I saw him accept the souls she reaped for him, saw him teach Margot how to wield her magic. I even saw the demon having sex with Margot, which I had to look away from after a moment.

I moved on until I finally came across some images of Margot reading from spell books, and then of her doing different spells and rituals, but not the one I was looking for. It took another painstaking search of the owl's mind before I finally stumbled across what I was looking for. I stopped and paid close attention to Margot as she went about opening a portal to the Underworld.

The spell she seemed to be using was nothing too special. A simple Reveal Spell tailored towards finding an Underworld entrance. I paid closer attention to her surroundings, however, because the exact place in which the spell was done was important. Otherwise, the spell would not work. Luckily, Margot's location at the time wasn't too hard to work out. She was in Liberty Hill Cemetery, which was clearly recognizable by the huge Celtic cross that loomed in the background behind her. The cross marked the grave of a well-known Druid that used to reside in Blackham City. The Druid was murdered in mysterious circumstances, his killer yet to be found. I knew the case well because I had been working on it myself for the last decade and a half. It drives me crazy to this day. Some day I would solve it, but only after I got myself out of the mess I was in. If I ever did, that is.

There was one other important detail about the ritual Margot was using to open the portal. She was using a substance known as Red Mercury. It was a substance found only in the Underworld and it was charged with dark magic, which made it useful for a number of things, including making hugely destructive bombs, poisoning water supplies and enhancing the effectiveness of certain weapons ten fold. Clearly, it was also used to create doors to the Underworld.

Having seen enough, I severed my psychic link to Barney's mind and opened my eyes again to see the owl staring unblinkingly at me. "Thanks, Barney," I said. "Much appreciated."

The owl dipped its head slightly and then turned to away to stare out the living room window.

Barney wasn't much of a talker.

"Red Mercury." I stood and thought for a minute, wondering who in the city would have such a rare substance. I never had any use for it myself, so there was none in the Sanctum, unfortunately. There were a few individuals in town that would maybe have Red Mercury, but the most likely person to have it was a man called Peter Franklyn. An old friend who as luck would have it owed me a favor I had yet to cash in.

So with no time to waste, I teleported immediately to Amsterdam Street.

# A DAPPER LITTLE MAN

*A*msterdam Street was in Astoria, which was in the western part of Freetown. The street was once a haven for young artists and bohemian types, as well as those who liked to spend their days doing drugs. It was also the place the Crimson Crow's daughter Jennifer used to hang out in before I helped her escape her mother's clutches by arranging her travel to Babylon (Jennifer still resided there, as far as I knew). Since then, Amsterdam Street and the surrounding area had become completely gentrified. The old pre-war houses had been demolished, and brand new apartment buildings and storefronts had been erected in their place. Whereas once you would have seen a street full of scruffy outcasts, now you were more likely to see a street full of suits and upper middle-class housewives out shopping in the many designer stores that existed there now.

One store that hadn't been closed or demolished in the name of progress was Peter Franklyn's little occult shop. Those behind the refurbishment of the street had, of course, tried to get Peter to shut up shop and move along, but Peter--obstinate little man that he was--refused to go anywhere, and the builders ended up building around him. Now Peter's dark little store was sandwiched between a designer dress shop and a high-end jewelry store. They would never squeeze Peter out as long as he lived.

I teleported straight from the Sanctum and into Peter Franklyn's shop, appearing right in front of the counter where Peter sat in his usual spot, atop a stool with a cup and saucer in his hand. The dapper little gray-haired man cried out when I appeared in front of him, jumping in fright so much he dropped his tea cup, which smashed on the floor. "Dear Lord!" he exclaimed when he realized it was me standing in front of him. "Creed! Damn you!"

I couldn't help my smile of amusement. "Did I scare you, Peter? I'm sorry."

Peter shook his head at me after looking down at his broken tea cup like he had just lost a priceless heirloom. "How many times must you do that, Creed?"

"As long as I keep finding it funny. Which will be forever."

"I'm not speaking to you until you fix my cup. I've had the same one for years. Tea doesn't taste right in anything else."

Pointing the palm of my hand at the pieces of broken china on the red carpeted floor, I did a quick spell and then watched as the broken pieces of china all came together and mended themselves. "There," I said as I picked up the cup and placed it on the wood counter. "Good as new."

Peter lifted the cup and examined it, finally nodding as he seemed satisfied. "Seriously Creed, you are going to give this old man a heart attack one of these days."

"Sorry. I just don't have much time to waste."

"Is something wrong? Are you in trouble?"

I snorted. "When am I ever not in trouble?"

"Good point. How serious is it?"

"Very fucking serious, excuse my language."

Peter didn't like people cursing around him. He considered it uncouth. In fact, Peter Franklyn's whole attitude and appearance seemed to be straight out of a different time like the late nineteenth century or thereabouts. Not that he was that old (he was in his late seventies), but he was somewhat old fashioned, and I always liked that about him. "Well, it must be if you are using that vulgar word around me. I take it you need my help?"

I nodded. "Red Mercury."

Peter seemed surprised for a second. "Why would you need that?"

"To open a portal to the Underworld. As you do."

"Surely you are not thinking of going there?"

"I don't have a choice. Leona is in there. I have to get her back."

His surprise turned to shock, and he slipped off his stool and stood to stare at me in his dark three-piece suit complete with pocket watch. "What is she doing there?"

"Well she didn't go for a fucking vacation, I can tell you that much." My temper took me by surprise. "Apologies. I'm a little tense, as you can probably tell."

"Let me close the shop." Peter walked to the front door, switched the sign and turned the lock. When he had finished, he ushered me past the counter and into a room at the back. The room was large, and every wall had shelves on it filled with stuff that made the place feel closed in.

"No clients today?" I asked him as I browsed the many items on the shelves.

"I have a few readings later," Peter said. "Maybe you want me to read you?"

I shook my head. "I'd rather not know what's in my future, thanks."

The psychic's eyes were on me as I walked around the room. "What happened to Leona, Creed?"

I stopped browsing and sighed as I looked at him. "I did."

Peter said nothing for a moment as he stared at me like a concerned teacher staring at a student he didn't know what to do with. "Will you able to get her back?"

I didn't answer straight away. "Maybe. I hope so. And it's not just her. There's someone else as well. I have to get them both back."

"Who?"

"No one you would know."

"Are going to that place alone?"

"Yes."

Peter shook his head. "You couldn't possibly, Creed. You'll never make it back."

He had a point of course, but I wasn't about to listen to it. "Let me worry about that. Just get me the Red Mercury."

Peter hesitated, but then went to one of the shelves and selected a small glass bottle filled with a luminous red liquid. He didn't hand it to me straight away. "Are you sure you know what you're doing?"

"We'll soon see," I said, holding out my hand.

He passed the bottle to me after a further moment of hesitation. "Why do I feel like I'm facilitating your demise?"

I said nothing as I took the bottle from him. The liquid inside made the glass feel warm to the touch. I slipped it into the pocket of my trench coat.

"Before you go," Peter said. He went to the shelves and looked for a second before taking a spool of silver thread, unraveling a short length, breaking it off and handing it to me. "Take this. Wrap it around your little finger before you enter the portal. As you move through the Outer Reaches the thread will extend behind you so that you will be able to get back to the portal if you get in any trouble."

I took the piece of shiny thread and held it in my hand. "Thanks."

Stepping forward, Peter took hold of my arm for a second. "Thank me when you get back with Leona and your other friend."

Saying nothing more, I teleported back to the Sanctum.

## 24

# PORTAL OF DOOM

*I* didn't need much else to open the Underworld portal. The spell I memorized as I saw it in the barn owl's mind. The Red Mercury had been procured now as well. The only other thing I needed was a plan for when I made it into the Underworld. The problem with that last component, however, was that I had very little idea of what to expect if I managed to make into the place, never having been there before. But I had been to plenty of places around the world where I had never been before then, and one thing I learned to do when I went somewhere for the first time was to try and blend in straight away by staying in the background. Often that meant finding a quiet place to sit and watch, and to see what went, to see how the people in the new place behaved, and also the types of people in the area. More specifically, the dangerous ones. The criminals. The unscrupulous magical adepts. Con men looking for an easy mark. I would give myself time to assimilate. Then I would move around as inconspicuously as possible.

The only problem with that strategy was that it might not work in a place like the Underworld, where unless you were a monster or a damned soul, you would stand out.

"Fuck it," I said after swallowing a large glass of whiskey. "I have no idea what the hell I'm doing. I'm fucked."

Blaze stood up in the living room and made a barking sound as if he disagreed.

"Thanks for the vote of confidence, buddy. But this time...this time I really don't know."

After another moment of intense anxiety, I slammed my empty glass down on the mantle and refused to give in to my fears and insecurities.

*This isn't about me*, I thought.

I tried to remember that.

"All right guys," I said to Blaze and Barney. "You two are coming with me. I need you to guard the portal after I go through. If it gets closed, I'll be kinda screwed. So just to be clear, Blaze, if anyone or anything tries to close that portal while I'm gone, burn those fuckers away." I looked at the barn owl. "Barney, you just grow big and...eat them I suppose."

Blaze walked to the side of me and Barney hopped onto my shoulder, after which I disintegrated us all and sent us through the ether to Liberty Hill Cemetery.

* * *

LIBERTY HILL CEMETERY WAS A MASSIVE PLACE THAT WAS FILLED WITH GRAVES as far as the eye could see. In the center of the cemetery was a grassy hill, on top of which sat the tomb of John Winchester, a sheriff who apparently freed Blackham from the tyranny of criminals back in the bad old days when the city itself was just being built. Winchester cleaned up the festering streets of the fledgling Blackham City and brought liberty for all, except the criminals, whom Winchester brutally murdered, hanging their bodies in the streets for all to see.

That was the story anyhow. Someone more in the know might have said that Winchester was the first vampire to move into Blackham and that he merely rid himself of anyone who might oppose his covert rise to power. Winchester faked his own death. His adoring public believed he was callously murdered by a criminal in an act of revenge. The body was so mutilated no one could tell if it was Winchester or not anyway, but a few whispers in the right ears made sure the body was officially decreed as his. Meanwhile, Winchester changed his appearance and steadily took over the city under the guise of a wealthy industrialist named Marcus Briggs. He stayed in power until the Crimson Crow came along and killed him. It was still Angela Crow who ran the show now, made easier by the fact that she was also the world's only day-walking vampire. Thanks to yours truly.

And that's your history lesson over for today. Now onto business.

The cemetery was steeped in so much bloody history it was little wonder to me that it had become the perfect place to open a portal to the Underworld.

With Barney on my shoulder and Blaze by my side, I trekked through the cemetery as the sky above turned black, and a host of stars started to shine through. If I wasn't so tensely focused on what I had to do, I might have said it was a beautiful night, despite the chill in the air. As it was, I hardly noticed as I focused on locating the Celtic cross I had seen in Barney's memory of Margot.

The cemetery was so big it took me over twenty minutes to finally locate the Druid's grave. From there, I used my memory to pinpoint the spot at which Margot had previously opened the portal, which turned out to be about twenty feet from the Celtic cross, in a spot where there was no grave, and no grass grew. It was a patch of dirt in between two tombstones.

As I crouched down and placed my hand on the slightly damp earth, I immediately felt the energy in the ground. Dark energy. It didn't surprise me that there were was no grave site there. There probably was in the past, until the bodies buried there crawled out of their graves again most likely, fueled by the dark energy that seemed to converge there. No doubt the grave diggers had learned to avoid that particular spot, and indeed probably talked about how they got the creeps every time they stood anywhere near there, or about how strange things would happen.

There are spots on the earth all over the world that most people instinctively avoided walking on or even going near. Black Spots you might call them. Places where dark energies had come to converge over eons. The real problems came when people unknowingly built things on top of these Black Spots, like houses. Once that happened, bad things would soon start happening (*Poltergeist* anyone?).

Barney took off from my shoulder and flew into the night sky like a silent ghost, probably off to scout the rest of the cemetery to make sure we were alone. Blaze began to patrol the immediate area, walking around in a circle, his ears pricked, his yellow eyes alert.

I wasted no time as I took out the bottle of Red Mercury that Peter Franklyn had given me, holding it up so the moonlight shone through the bottle, further illuminating the substance inside. Then I took the cork out of the bottle and carefully began to pour the Red Mercury in a circle on the ground. It took almost the full bottle to make a small, unbroken circle. The Red Mercury lay on top of the earth like normal mercury on a hard surface. As it glistened in the moonlight, it gave off a sharp scent that reminded me of sulfur.

After standing back from the circle, I had another quick look around just as Barney flew down and landed on a nearby tombstone, his black eyes on me as if to confirm that there was no one else around. Satisfied that we were alone, I stood over the circle of Red Mercury and held my hands out in front of me, palms down over the circle below.

As I began to say the words to the spell that would open the portal, I felt the electric presence of dark energy in the air around me, felt it reach up from the ground below and encircle me as if excited by what I was doing.

Halfway through the spell, a bright red light began to beam up from out of the circle on the ground.

The portal was beginning to open, and I paused in reciting the spell for a moment, and then swallowed nervously before continuing.

Arcs of red energy soon began to swirl within the circle of light. Then the ground itself within the circle suddenly gave way, falling into blackness.

A strong wind had picked up and was swirling around me like a banshee, screaming past my ears. So much so that I had to raise my voice while I recited the last few words of the spell.

On the last word of the spell, the red light within the circle intensified to such a degree that I had to shut my eyes against it. The light soon died down, however, and then a high-pitched whine could be heard as the portal seemed to widen by a few feet.

I stood back and stared tensely at the now fully opened portal. All I had to do next was jump into it, and I would be taken immediately to the Underworld, or at least the Outer Reaches, which I was looking forward to even less than the Underworld itself. When I went through the portal, I would still have to navigate my way through the darkness of the Outer Reaches and all the horrors that it contained to find a way into the Underworld itself.

Reaching into my coat pocket, I found the piece of silver string that Peter Franklyn had given me and tied it around the little finger on my left hand. If things went wrong, at least I would be able to navigate my way back to the portal. I hoped anyway.

"All right, Blaze," I said, looking over at the Garra Wolf who was standing just to the side of the portal. "Stay frosty."

Blaze made a small barking sound and raised his head at me. Barney screeched as well from his position on a nearby tombstone.

Then I walked forward into the portal and let it suck me into the darkness on the other side.

# THE OUTER REACHES

*I*t felt like I'd stepped into someone's nightmarish dreamscape when I came out the other side of the portal. Before me was nothing but darkness as far as I could see, and the ground beneath my feet felt hard and unforgiving. After a moment of standing there and being almost afraid to move, my eyes began to adjust to the darkness around me. My jaw dropped in part wonder, part terror as the landscape around me slowly faded into view.

Everything I could see was in shades of black or gray. There was no light to speak off. The sky was near black and filled with a thick blanket of swirling, dark gray clouds. Somewhere behind the clouds, there may have been a sun of some sort, for a trickle of muted gray light seemed to push through the clouds, coating the landscape in a grim twilight and providing a breeding ground for dense shadows.

The Outer Reaches reminded me somewhat of one of Earth's more barren and desolate regions. Across the cracked black earth, I could see mammoth mountains in the distance with lightning arcing around the peaks, the clouds wrapped around the great mountains seeming darker than everywhere else.

It was a black desert as far as the eye could see. Nothing seemed to grow anywhere. It was a desolate world with a barely beating heart, beating just enough to sustain the grim surroundings that seemed to close in around me, despite the vastness of it all.

An icy wind blew everywhere, and I wrapped my coat tighter around myself, which didn't do much to stop the chill from seeping into my bones.

*Where the hell am I supposed to go?* I wondered as the enormity of what I had to do began to sink in. How was I meant to navigate such a vast, barren wasteland? It could have been the size of Earth, or bigger. How far would I have to go to make it to the Underworld?

I turned around and faced the still open portal. *This is madness*, I thought to myself. *What the hell am I doing? I can't do this.*

Then I remembered why I was there. To save Leona. And Margot.

I turned around again. Save them? I'd be lucky even to find them, never mind save them.

*Magic, Creed! You're a fucking wizard! Use your magic!*

It felt like I was crumbling apart inside. The pressure was mounting in me, and the next thing I knew, I was on the verge of taking a panic attack. And I probably would have if a deafening screeching sound nearby didn't force me to focus on my surroundings.

My head snapped to the left where the sound had come from, and I almost jumped back in fear when I saw in the distance something that was like a huge eel slithering through the sky and pushing its way through the clouds. What was even more astounding was the luminescent colors on the eel creature's massively long body. Hues of red, orange, green and blue flashed and pulsed along the surface of the creature's body, reminding me of something you would see in the very depths of the ocean on Earth. The creature was too far away to see me (I hoped), and it soon disappeared into the distance until all I could see was occasional pulses of luminescent light in the clouds.

*Great*, I thought. *The place is full of gigantic creatures that would probably like nothing better than to swallow me whole, soul and all.*

As my eyes took in more flashes of light in different places around the sky, and also on the ground, I did my best to push down my mounting fear so I could focus on thinking of a spell that would help me find an entrance to the Underworld. It was a struggle maintaining focus when the terrifying sounds of the Outer Reaches' inhabitants became more numerous, coming together in a symphony of horror.

Across the whole barren wasteland around me, creatures of all sizes began to light up, illuminating their terrifying shapes. Most of them were too far away to make out properly, but it was clear they were all heading towards me, having been alerted to my presence somehow. I was sure the glowing portal behind me wasn't helping any. I might as well have had a target on my chest or a neon sign above my head saying EAT HERE.

Then, out of nowhere, a humungous creature appeared in the sky before me. It was so utterly terrifying and like nothing I had ever seen before--not even in my worst nightmares--that I can barely describe it. I just remember being transfixed by two glowing white orbs on either side of the creatures face, if you could even say it had a face. The only thing I can be sure of is the bundles of thick tentacles that hung from its head almost down to the ground. Luminescent lights pulsed and flickered down the length of each tentacle. In one way, it was very beautiful to look at. Awe inspiring even. Which could have been the point, for a while I remained transfixed by the all the lights, the creature was reaching out a tentacle to grab me, something I hardly realized until the tip of the tentacle hovered in front of my face like it was supposed to hypnotize me even further. I was vaguely aware of other creatures drawing closer, a mass of flashing lights surrounding me, making me feel like some heavenly dimension was opening up around me.

I didn't even move as the tip of the tentacle opened up like a stunning bio-luminescent flower, showering me with light and feelings of contentedness. Even when a huge mouth opened up within the pretty tentacle--a mouth filled with row upon row of pointed teeth--I still didn't move.

The lights became more intense.

The mouth got closer.

Still, I didn't move.

Not until something tugged on my left hand, pulling me backward and away from the hypnotizing lights.

A sound like a demonic pig drowned out everything else, and I merely watched as the sharp-toothed mouth got closer and closer...

Until I was pulled backward again, with more force this time. A moment of blackness ensued, during which all the bright lights suddenly disappeared, and I found myself staggering into something.

I screamed in fear as something grabbed hold of me, started to shake me.

"August! It's me! It's your Uncle Ray!"

My vision returned as the blackness disappeared and Ray's face came into view before me. "Ray?" I said, dazed and confused.

"Yes. Snap out of it, August!"

I shook my head as if to clear it and soon realized, with utter relief it has to be said, that I was no longer in the Outer Reaches, but back on Earth.

I looked behind me to see that the portal had now gone. I turned back to my uncle. "Ray, how did you..."

Ray let go of me and took a step back, satisfied that I appeared to be okay. "I was for leaving the city tonight. Lucky for you I wanted to say goodbye before I left. I tracked you here. What the bloody hell are you playing at? Going to that place alone. Are you bloody mad, son?"

I looked to see Blaze standing over behind Ray. The barn owl was perched above Blaze on one of the headstones. Suddenly I felt very stupid standing there with all eyes on me. "I didn't have a choice, Ray," I said. "Baal has Leona with him in the Underworld."

Ray sighed and shook his head. "So you thought you would just ride on in there like Clint bloody Eastwood and get her back did you?"

"Something like that. Not that I got very far. The things in the Outer Reaches..." I stopped and shuddered at the realization that I was a second away from being consumed by one of those things before Ray managed to pull me up. "Your timing couldn't have been better."

"I beg to differ," Ray said. "I should have found you before you even tried setting foot in that Godforsaken place. Do you even know how to get into the Underworld from the Outer Reaches?"

I shrugged and shook my head slightly. "Not really," I said quietly.

Ray shook his head again as he stood staring at me. "I know you love the girl, August, but that was bloody stupid. If you'd have asked--"

"I didn't want to drag you or Sanaka into this. This whole thing is my fault. It's my fault that Leona is trapped in that place right now." I looked down to see the piece of silver string still tied around my finger. I reminded myself to thank Peter Franklyn next time I saw him. He may have just saved my life.

Ray stepped forward and put a hand on my shoulder. "all right, son," he said, his tone softened somewhat. "I get why you didn't say anything. But you should know, I'm always here if you need me. You wouldn't be dragging me into anything.

You're the only family I have, and that means it's my duty to help you, no matter the cost."

"Great, so we're a family of idiots then." I laughed slightly, and Ray smiled back at me as he shook his head.

"Let's get out of this bloody bone yard. Then we can figure out how to get your girl back."

It was the best idea I'd heard all day.

# TEA FOR THREE

*R*ay and I, along with Blaze and Barney, teleported to Sanaka's Sanctum, as much so Ray could get his hands on Sanaka's sake as to get us somewhere safe and sound.

"What is going on?" Sanaka said as we stood in the large front hallway. Sanaka was dressed all in black, his hands clasped behind his back as he waited for an explanation.

Ray stepped over beside Sanaka, leaving me standing with Blaze by my side and Barney perched on my shoulder. "Driven by desperation," Ray said, gesturing at me. "My nephew did something extremely foolish and nearly lost his soul forever."

"Again?" Sanaka said deadpan.

I couldn't help making a face at him. "Ha ha, Sanaka," I said. "I think what Ray meant to say was, go and get the sake, please. If you don't mind, that is."

Sanaka held up his hand, and a clear glass bottle materialized into it. Ray went to grab it straight away, but I used my magic to snatch the bottle out of my mentor's hand and into my own before Ray could get his fingers near it. "What happened to respecting your elders?" Ray asked.

"I nearly got eaten by the bastard cross of Cthulhu and a fucking angler fish," I said as I uncorked the bottle. "I need this." I stuck the bottle in my mouth and took a large swallow of the fiery liquid inside. It burned its way down my throat and into my still anxious belly, going some way to dousing the flames of fear that still danced in there. Putting the cork back in the bottle, I tossed the bottle over to Ray, who reflexively caught it with magic first before wrapping his hand around it.

"Who is your new pet?" Sanaka asked as he stared at the barn owl on my shoulder.

"This is Barney," I said.

Ray laughed. "Barney," he mocked. "Give me a break."

"I didn't fucking name him, Ray," I said. "Margot Celeste did. The owl is her familiar."

"Ah yes, the witch," Ray said. "And where is she? I'm assuming since you went to find her that your current predicament is down to her."

"Baal took her as well," I said. "And I don't blame her for what happened. Everything is Baal's doing. He took Leona because he thought I had betrayed him."

"And did you?" Ray asked.

I sighed and shook my head. "I wanted to help Margot."

"You slept with her, didn't you?" Ray said casually before tasting the sake.

I looked away for a moment. Ray and Sanaka exchanged glances. "He would have taken Leona anyway," I said, not very convincingly, not even to myself. Baal could just as easily have kept his word if I'd just done what he asked instead of allowing myself to get bewitched by someone I hardly knew.

*What a fucking amateur I am*, I thought.

Sanaka looked at me then with a rarely seen sympathy in his dark eyes as if he had just read my thoughts. "Come," he said. "You can make us tea. The ritual will calm you."

The last thing I wanted to do was make fucking tea, not when every moment that passed meant more pain and suffering for Leona in the Underworld. But I was wise enough to know that I wouldn't be able to pressure Sanaka or Ray into doing anything until they were ready. It had been firmly established by then that I needed their help to rescue Leona. There was nothing I could do except wait for that help.

"Fine," I said eventually. "But Blaze and Barney aren't big tea drinkers. They need water. And Blaze is probably hungry so get him a steak. And a mouse for Barney. You got any mice in the fridge?"

Sanaka looked at me as if he didn't know if I was serious or not. Eventually, he just nodded. "I'll see what I can find."

Blaze had already walked over to Sanaka's side in anticipation of the steak he was about to chow down on. I told Barney to go with Sanaka as well, and the barn owl flew over and landed on my mentor's shoulder. Sanaka flinched slightly as the bird of prey landed on his gleaming black turtle neck. I wasn't sure, but I didn't think he was a big fan of birds. Something about being attacked by a flock of ravens one time.

"All right then." I grabbed the sake from Ray on the way past and headed for the tea room. Before I got there, though, my phone rang in my pocket, and I pulled it out to see who was calling. It was Brentwood, and I suddenly realized that he would probably be phoning about Leona. "Shit." I clicked accept. "Brentwood."

"Creed, finally," Brentwood said, sounding more agitated than usual. "Don't you ever answer your damn phone? I've called you a dozen times in the last twenty-four hours."

"I've been busy."

"Doing what?"

"I don't think that has anything to do with you. What's up?" A pained look came over my face as I asked the question for I knew what was coming.

"Have you seen Lawson?"

"Leona?"

"How many other Lawson's do you know? Yes, of course, Leona. She's disappeared. I tracked her phone to Morgan County, but there's no sign of her. Is she with you?"

"Eh, no. She's not with me."

Brentwood sighed sharply. "Well have you seen her?"

"Not since she left for New York." I took no pleasure in lying, but I wasn't about to tell Brentwood the truth. He hated me enough as it was.

"Shit!" Brentwood lapsed into angry silence. "I'm beginning to worry something has happened to her. The case she was working on in New York was a difficult one."

"Difficult?" I said, still pretending like I didn't know a thing about Leona's whereabouts.

"The killer is a fucking wizard. You know what it's like hunting you people. You're all dangerous and unpredictable."

"You people?"

"You know what I mean. I'm concerned that whatever psycho she was chasing may have taken her somewhere. Leona's the toughest damn soldier I have, but even she's no match for magic on her own. Can't you track her somehow? She's your girlfriend, after all, Creed."

"Yeah," I snapped. "Thanks for reminding me. I'll call you if I hear anything. Bye, Brentwood."

I angrily stabbed the disconnect button with my thumb, and then in a fit of rage, I threw the phone as hard as I could at the wall down the end of the corridor. "Fuck!" The phone smashed into pieces against the wall, bits of useless plastic scattering across the polished wood floor.

When I turned around, I saw Ray at the far end of the hallway, standing there staring at me. I stopped and held his gaze for a moment. Then I walked off into the tea room.

\* \* \*

SANAKA AND RAY ARRIVED INTO THE TEA ROOM FIVE MINUTES AFTER I HAD started the tea making ritual. Both men, shoeless as I was now, knelt down at the low table and proceeded to sit in silence for the entire time it took me to finish the ritual. That was Sanaka's way of restoring calm. He disliked emotional turmoil, explaining to me many times over the years that it clouded judgment, as well as the flow of magic. I couldn't disagree with him on either front, but Sanaka had been around for a long time. He and Ray had had plenty of time to get a hold on their emotions. I didn't think I would ever get a hold on mine. By their very nature, they took me by surprise every time.

By the time I had finished arranging everything on the table and had knelt down between Ray and Sanaka, I felt a lot calmer than before. Most of my emotions had been brought under control, though that horrible sense of guilt still gnawed at my belly, giving me a sickening feeling that I did my best to ignore.

Besides, I told myself. The best way to alleviate guilt is to make up for it somehow. In my case, the only way to do that was to save Leona from eternal torment at the hands of an evil demon. And to do that, I first needed a plan to do so, which meant hearing what Ray and Sanaka had to say first.

The three of us sat in continued silence for several more minutes, sipping tea, each of us slightly lost in our own thoughts. It was Sanaka who finally broke the silence when he laid his gaze on me. "I will take you to the Underworld so you can try to save Leona," he said in a quiet, measured voice.

I looked back at him for a moment, more grateful than I could say to hear him tell me that.

"I will accompany you as well," Ray said. "There's no way I'm letting you two go there without me. You'll need my help."

Sanaka looked at Ray. "You forget I spent a long time in the Underworld myself."

"I know," Ray said. "But if you're going to take on Baal, you'll need my help. My magic. And to tell you the truth, I'm not even sure if we three will be enough to take down a demon like Baal."

Sighing, I shook my head. "Listen, this is too dangerous for--"

"Stop," Ray said, cutting me off. "Don't even say it, August. I don't care how dangerous it is. I'm not letting you go there alone."

Sanaka nodded in agreement. "He is right. We are...family."

I have to say, a lump formed in my throat when I heard Sanaka say that. It was the first time he had ever referred to me--or to anyone--as family. I respectfully bowed my head at Sanaka, and he did the same.

"All right," Ray said, breaking up the moment. "First things first. We need a way into the Underworld, which, fortunately, I can create for us. Right here in this Sanctum."

"What about the Outer Reaches?" I said. "I fail to see how we could cross it without getting swallowed whole."

"You're right," Ray said. "We would never make it, which is why we aren't even going to try. We can take a more direct route into the Underworld, bypassing the Outer Reaches."

I let out a small breath. "You have no idea how glad I am to hear you say that. I thought I would have to go back to that place again." Then it occurred to me. "I wonder how Margot managed it."

"Obviously her former master granted her safe passage," Ray said.

"Probably via another portal in the Outer Reaches," said Sanaka.

I nodded. "We still have to find Baal once we enter the Underworld. Any ideas on how we're going to do that?"

"The Underworld is very nearly infinite in scope," Sanaka said. "It is expanding all the time, along with the rest of the universe."

"Yes," Ray said. "And within the Underworld, itself are countless other worlds, regions, domains. To find Baal and your girlfriends--"

"Girlfriend," I said. "Margot is not my girlfriend. Just pointing that out."

"Fine, your friends then," Ray said. "To find your friends, we have to find out where Baal's domain is."

"The owl," Sanaka said. "It is the witch's familiar, correct?"

"Correct," I said. "And I know what you're thinking. I've already done it, to find out how to open the portal. You think there might be a clue to Baal's location in the owl's memories?"

"It is worth a try," Sanaka said.

"And if there's nothing?" I asked.

"Then we think of something else," Ray said before smiling at me reassuringly. "Don't worry, boy. We'll find her."

I nodded back, not quite as confident about things as Ray seemed to be. And could you blame me? The task ahead was a mammoth one, and terribly dangerous for all concerned. But if I had to have anyone on my side, it would have been Ray and Sanaka. So I allowed myself to feel some measure of confidence, knowing they would both do everything they could to help me.

No matter what the cost to themselves.

## 27

# NO REST FOR THE WICKED

While Ray and Sanaka worked on extracting information from Barney the barn owl's memory, I teleported to my own Sanctum because there were a few things I needed to get. Now that I was thinking a bit more clearly about the situation, I thought it pertinent that I at least go into the Underworld with some kind of protection on me. There would doubtless be hordes of monsters in the Underworld, and I wouldn't have enough magic to deal with them all. I needed an equalizer. A real weapon of power. Something I could hold in my hands to wield against whatever came at me.

I entered into the Operations Room from the living room. In the far corner was a huge armoire, carved from a fallen ancient oak tree that used to stand in a Druidic field of power in Ireland centuries ago. The armoire had been used by many over the centuries when I bought it at an underground auction nearly three decades ago. I since used it to store whatever weapons I had collected over the years, of which there were many.

Needless to say, the armoire was Leona's favorite thing in the whole of the Sanctum. When I first showed her it--and the tools of destruction inside--she had sat for hours handling each of the weapons, in awe of their very existence it seemed. Her handling was done under strict supervision from me though as most of the weapons had magical properties and could prove to be hazardous in the wrong hands.

I couldn't help but smile at the memory as I crossed the room to the armoire. Then my smile disappeared as I thought, *Jesus, I'm reminiscing like Leona is already dead.*

"She's not dead," I said as I stood in front of the armoire as if saying it out loud kept her in reality.

But she could have been dead all the same.

*Stop it*, I told myself. *She's alive until we know otherwise.*

413

Clenching my jaw as I fought to control my emotions once more, I pulled open both doors of the armoire to reveal the tools of death inside.

Much like the gun locker that Leona coveted so much in her apartment, the weapons in the armoire all had their place as they were attached to the walls and inside doors of the cabinet. I stood there staring for several moments at the array of deadly weapons, wondering which one would be most useful to me. There were four different swords in there, including the demon killing Sword of Rishanti which I had threatened Baal with before. Of course, I didn't know until Margot told me that the sword would have been all but useless against a demon like Baal because he was no ordinary demon, was he? Baal was the spawn of creatures far more powerful than even him. Ordinary means of destruction would therefore not work on him as they worked on some other beings. When it came to Baal, we would have to think of some other way to handle him before he most definitely handled us.

But before we got to Baal, there would no doubt be many of his Underworld minions to protect against as well, which was the main reason I needed a weapon.

Besides the swords, there were other types of bladed weapons. There was also a mace, a battle axe, and a crossbow. Not to forget the nunchakus that used to belong to Bruce Lee, and which were excellent at dispatching the walking dead should you ever find yourself surrounded by them, which I did once (a long story, and one with a messy ending).

I was still deliberating over which weapon or weapons to choose when I heard a faint knocking sound. Frowning, I listened for a second and then went to lift a spiked gauntlet from the floor of the armoire. But before I got my hand on the gauntlet, I heard the rapping sound again, louder this time. Sighing, I realized it was the front door being knocked.

*Fuck it,* I thought. Whoever it was could come back another day when things were a little less life or death. It was probably just Brentwood anyway, come to give me a hard time over Leona. I had no doubt the Division boss suspected that I had something to do with Leona's disappearance. It was instinct with Brentwood to think the worst of me most of the time, despite the help I had given him over the years.

I heard the door knocking again. "Goddamn it!"

Angry and annoyed now, I stomped out of the Operations Room and through the living room to the front door, intending to tell whoever it was standing outside to fucking do one before I turned them into a cockroach.

When I flung open the front door, I was greeted by the sight of an obviously distraught Hispanic woman standing there. She looked about forty, and her eyes were red and puffy as if she had been crying for the last several hours. "Yes?" I asked the woman, trying not to come across as being *too* annoyed in case I upset her further. I couldn't deal with the heavy emotions of others right then.

"August Creed?" the woman asked, her dark skinned face a mask of desperation.

"Yes."

"I need your help." The woman's eyes were wide and pleading. Despite the cold, all she wore was a thin T-shirt and jeans, as if she had run out of her house in a hurry.

I started to shake my head. "Listen, lady, you're calling at a really difficult time and--"

"A monster stole my baby," the woman blurted out before balling her eyes out right there on the doorstep.

Inwardly, I sighed and thought, *I don't need this. Not now. And what the hell does she mean a monster stole her baby?*

I almost told her I know the feeling, but I got the impression she may have taken that the wrong way and attacked me or something. The last person you want to poke with a stick is a mother who's lost her cub. Or baby. You know what I mean.

"I'm not sure how I'm supposed to help you," I said to the woman, still hoping she would turn around and leave.

But she didn't. "Someone told me about you, said you'd be able to help, that you help people like me." The woman stepped forward, her dark eyes a window to her inner pain and desperation. "Can you help me get my baby back? He's all I have. Please, help me..."

As I looked into the woman's face, I couldn't help but feel her pain, the agony she felt over not knowing if her son was alive or dead.

*But Leona...*

The woman's wet eyes were still on me. I felt myself caving. "Look..."

"Bridget. My name is Bridget."

"Look, Bridget, I'm not going to lie to you. You've come to me at the worst possible time. But..." I paused for a second, still on the edge until I saw the hope rising in Bridget's eyes. "I can give you a small amount of time. I can't guarantee you anything either."

Bridget nodded as she did her best to smile, knowing that was the best she was going to get. Doubtless, anyone else had agreed to try and help her anyhow. "Okay. Thank you."

I stood aside and ushered her inside the Sanctum. She held her arms folded tightly across her chest as she walked through the door and into the hallway.

In the living room, I offered her a drink, which she accepted as she sat down in one of the armchairs, trying to keep from staring too much at the strangeness all around her.

"Tell me what happened to your son," I said, wasting no time as I sat in the chair opposite Bridget with a whiskey in my hand. "You said a monster stole him."

Bridget nodded as she sat on the edge of the chair, her glass clasped in both hands resting on her knees, which were pressed tightly together. She was a ball of tension and emotional turmoil. It was uncomfortable, more so because I was probably as bad as her. My legs felt like iron weights they were so tense, and my guts felt ripped out of me. But that's the way it had to be until I got Leona back. Even if I could've relaxed, I wouldn't have.

"I was at home, as usual, earlier this evening," she began. "It was just after dark and I hadn't long put Carlos to bed. He was suffering from a tummy ache all day, so he didn't go to sleep until late. Then I heard a noise upstairs, like someone walking across the floorboards..." Her restraint gave way for a second as her face cracked and fresh tears sprang from her eyes, but she quickly wiped them away and continued. "I was scared by the noise, but I had to check on Carlos. So I went up the stairs and..."

"There was someone there?"

"Yes, a woman. She was all beat up looking and dirty like she lived on the streets. She was in Carlos' room, hovering over him with her...her hands outstretched about to...grab him."

"When you said it was a monster who took your son, were you speaking figuratively or..."

"No," she said firmly. "A monster took my son. Her eyes burned bright red like a demon's and she had...she had fangs. I saw them. And she was so fast. One minute she was there, the next she had gone out the window with...my son in her arms." Her head began to shake as more tears fell.

Assuming Bridget was telling the truth—and I had no reason to believe she wasn't—then it sounded to me like a vampire had broken into her house and stolen her baby son. Which was bad news for Bridget and her son. The vampire had probably drained the baby already. "Bridget, I'm sorry to say this, but—"

"Don't!" she said firmly. "Don't you dare tell me that my son is dead. Just don't."

I shifted uncomfortably in my seat as I stared at her. "Bridget..."

"He is all I have!" she wailed. "My husband never came back from Iraq. He's gone. I have no one except my son, and I want him back!"

*Christ*, I thought. I didn't know how much more pain I could take, either my own or someone else's. I felt for the woman, I did. But the chances of her son being alive were slim. Very slim indeed. However, I also knew Bridget would never accept my word on that. Understandably. Was I not in the same position, having had the person I love most in the world snatched from under me, not knowing if they were alive or dead? Wasn't I grasping onto a slither of hope as well? Didn't I need to know the truth, no matter what the truth was?

"All right, Bridget," I said, standing up. "I'll tell you what. I'll try to track the...monster that took your baby."

Bridget got to her feet as well. "You will?"

"I'll try with the limited amount of time I have. I'm under the gun myself. I really can't afford to be...you know."

Bridget nodded like she understood. "I'm grateful, Mr Creed. You've no idea—"

I held a hand up to stop her. "Why don't you just take me to your home now. The quicker we get there, the more chance there is of picking up a trail." I went to lead her out of the room when I stopped. "Actually, scratch that. I don't have the time. Just tell me where you live, and I'll go alone. It'll be quicker, believe me. You can stay here until I get back."

Bridget looked like she didn't know what to say or do. "Only if you think..."

"I do think. What's your address?" She gave me an address that was three blocks away. "all right, make yourself at home. Drink the whiskey and the tea in the kitchen. Just don't touch anything else. Some of the things in here...just sit tight."

Bridget nodded her consent, and I walked away into the hallway. The second I rounded the corner, I teleported to Bridget's street, a sick feeling coming over me as I realized I was about to track down a possibly dead baby.

Where did it all go wrong, will you tell me, please?

# ON THE HUNT

*A*s soon as I landed in the street where Bridget lived, I realized that if I were going to track a vampire, then I would need a nose that was well suited to doing just that. Not my nose, but Blaze's. So I teleported again to Sanaka's Sanctum and eventually found Blaze, along with Barney, in Sanaka's pristine kitchen area. Blaze lay on the floor, an empty plate not far from him. Barney was perched on top of the fridge half asleep after whatever morsel Sanaka had given him.

"I need your help with something, buddy," I said walking over to Blaze, who immediately bounced to his feet.

Barney's eyes opened wide, and he raised his head as if wanting to know what was going on. I stared at the bird of prey for a moment, then decided I would take him with us. As I didn't have much time, an extra set of eyes might prove useful. I held out my arm, and the barn owl hopped down onto it.

"What are you doing?" Sanaka had appeared in the doorway. "Things are almost set. We should be going soon."

"There's something I have to do first," I told him. "It won't take long."

Sanaka looked confused. "What could be more important than rescuing Leona?"

Nothing. But I still had to do the thing. "I'll explain later."

I teleported back to the street where I had come from, appearing about half way up the street under a tree that shed most of its leaves. I instinctively checked my surroundings but didn't see anyone around. Then I remembered it was nearly four in the morning. Most folks were either fast asleep or wrapped up watching porn at that time. Satisfied no one seen us, I started walking up the street. Barney was now on my shoulder, Blaze in invisible mode by my side, his tail wagging slightly in anticipation of the hunt to come.

The street where Bridget lived was mostly low-rent housing. Every house looked the same except for the cars in the driveways. Bridget lived three doors from the end of the row. I walked through the gate and up the path to the front door, using magic to open the lock. I would have to take it easy with the magic use. All the teleporting had put a drain on my reserves, and I didn't want to enter the Underworld on a near empty tank.

All the lights were still on inside the house when I walked in, the smell of stale cigarettes strong in my nostrils. The interior of the house was well kept. Homely you might say. I noticed pictures on the wall of Bridget standing with a man in uniform (her dead husband I assumed), but I didn't pay them much attention. My only concern was picking up the scent of the vampire who took Bridget's baby son.

I motioned for Blaze to head upstairs and I followed up behind him as he took me straight to the child's bedroom at the end of the landing. Blaze's nose moved frantically over the floor when he entered the bedroom, then he stopped sniffing, looked up at me and made a small barking sound. Confirmation that he had picked up a scent.

"That's the one, buddy," I said.

Blaze dropped his head again and followed the scent to the window. I walked to the window and opened it. A drainpipe led down to the back yard. Beyond that, there was an alley and then more blocks of houses. I didn't think the vampire would have gone too far, not with a probably crying baby in its clutches. It would have attracted too much attention. The creature would have wanted to have holed up somewhere as soon as possible so it could enjoy its meal.

*Christ.*

I shook my head at the thought of the child being no more than a feedbag to the vampire who took him.

One thing I was fairly certain of was that the child-snatching vampire was feral. Feral vampires were all over the city. Most of them were victims of other vampires that simply didn't die in the attack, giving the vampiric virus time to take hold. When a person turned into a vampire, they had to be trained (usually by the vamp who turned them) to control their feral instincts so they could fit in with the rest of society without attracting too much attention. If a person turned and didn't get that training, then as a vampire they would become overwhelmed and ultimately controlled by their baser instincts. Most such vampires didn't last very long. The Crimson Crow had clean up crews who hunted and then dispatched most of them. But sometimes, a few feral vamps could slip through the cracks and avoid detection. Those that did often became powerful predators, learning to hide in the shadows and stalk their prey. Breaking into houses and stealing babies wasn't their usual MO, but from Bridget's description, there was no doubt the child snatcher was a vamp.

Fortunately, the creature wouldn't be too hard to track. Feral vampires tended to develop a very musky smell about them, just like normal animals. That made them slightly easier to track, especially for a tracker like Blaze, who had never failed me in the past.

"All right," I said to Blaze as I turned away from the window. "Let's get down there and get after this thing."

Once we hit the backyard, Blaze was off, moving quickly across the yard with his nose close to the ground, still in invisible mode in case we came across any Sleepwalkers. He didn't even wait for me to open the gate. Instead, he took the route the vamp obviously took and jumped over the chainlink fence into the alley. Needless to say, I didn't follow him. Valuing my groin too much, I walked through the gate instead.

As Blaze pretty much ran north up the alley, I turned my head to Barney and said, "You too. We might need eyes in the sky."

The barn owl screeched as if thrilled by the prospect of hunting and then took off, the faint wind from its wings blowing over my face where beads of sweat had already begun to form. "Fuck this shit," I said as I started jogging after Blaze. Don't ever let anyone tell you that a Mage's life is all books and magic. It isn't, at least not in my case.

I chased after Blaze as he took me through a maze of back alley's that spanned about three square blocks while Barney flew silently overhead. By the time I caught up to Blaze again, he had led me into an abandoned train yard at the edge of the neighborhood and was stood stock still as he stared at part of an old cargo train. I stopped running and walked across the rough ground as I saw Barney land on top of the container, right on the edge. The container door was half open and dark inside.

*The vamp must be inside*, I thought.

As I got closer to the cargo train, I reached inside my trench coat and took out the Killing Knife. Thanks to the Druids who made it millennia ago, the blade would make short work of the vamp.

Blaze had dropped his weight as he continued to stare at the cargo container as if he was getting ready to pounce on the vampire inside should it dare to show itself. I crept quietly across the dirt and stopped just a few feet from the container, my heart pounding from all the running and the added adrenaline that came from stalking a vampire that could quite easily tear me to pieces with claws and fangs that were powered by unnatural strength and speed.

What I needed was a simple plan, and fortunately, I had one that had worked well plenty of times in the past when I had to deal with feisty vampires.

I held up my left hand and conjured a ball of light into it no bigger than a tennis ball. But there was so much UV in the light that the vampire inside the container would think it was in direct sunlight, distracting it long enough for me to kill it with the knife. Simple, like I said, but by no means easy. As Mike Tyson said once, everybody has a plan until they get hit.

I hoped I wouldn't get hit, however, as I stood in front of the gap in the door of the container. No doubt the vamp's heightened senses had already picked up on our presence. It was probably in there waiting to attack whoever came in first, which was going to be me.

Putting one foot on the rusty ladder that led up into the container, I took a breath and then jumped up, keeping my left hand with the light out in front of me to blind the vampire. With the interior of the container now filled with light, I steeled myself for a coming attack, but none came. And as Blaze jumped inside beside me, I searched for signs of the vamp but saw none. Then I spotted a pile of rotting wooden crates at the back of the container, and I realized the vamp must have been hiding behind them. It had to be if the musky stench was anything to go by.

*Strange*, I thought. *Why isn't attacking?*

Carefully, I made my way across the floor to where the boxes were and then thrust my hand quickly over the top of them, the blazing UV light eliciting a scream from the other side.

*Bingo.*

Quickly, I moved around the outside of the boxes, the magic light held out in front of me, the knife in my other hand held at the ready.

The vamp had backed into the corner as it cowered from the UV light, which I shone directly onto it. Smoke rose from the vamp's exposed skin as the light seared it away, causing the vamp to screech in pain.

I held the light over the creature while I looked to see what I was dealing with. From what I could make out, the vamp was once a woman, somewhere between twenty and thirty years old. The clothes the vamp wore were ragged and filthy, her feet bare. By the looks of her, she had been feral for quite a while, living like a nocturnal animal, grabbing food from wherever she could.

The vamp had her arms wrapped around something that was in turn wrapped in a dark blanket.

Bridget's baby son, who didn't appear to be moving or making any sound.

I swallowed down the sick feeling that rose in my throat. *all right*, I thought, gripping the knife tighter. *Let's get this over with.*

Stepping forward, I got ready to stick the knife into the vamp. But I only got one step before something stopped me dead.

A baby's cry.

"*Jesus...*" I breathed.

The child was alive. It must have been sleeping.

My mind boggled slightly as I realized the vamp was protecting the baby in her arms as much as she was trying to protect herself. But why? The vamp had had plenty of time to drain the baby. Why hadn't it done so?

*Now what?* I wondered.

If I made a move on the vamp, she would probably kill the baby before I could save him.

Moving the main beam of the light away from the vamp slightly, I took a few steps back and also ushered Blaze to move around the other side of the boxes so the vamp could no longer see him.

"I know you can understand me," I said to the vamp like I was trying to talk down a jumper from a roof. "I just want the baby back. I'm not going to hurt you."

The vamp turned her head towards me now that most of the light was directed away from her. Her eyes looked severely bloodshot, and her fangs were bared at me, stark white against the dark grime on her face. I wasn't all that sure if she could understand what I was saying. The longer a vamp stayed feral, the more of what once made them human disappeared, including the ability to communicate and understand language. Although by the way she was protectively hugging the baby, she appeared to understand enough.

The baby started to cry then, and the vamp started rocking with it, making strange hissing noises as if she was trying to quiet the child back to sleep.

*Well, if this isn't one of the most fucked up things I've ever seen,* I thought to myself.

And then it hit me what was going on. The vamp had obviously been a mother to a child before she was attacked. Maybe her baby died in the same attack, I don't know. Whatever happened, the woman had somehow maintained some deep level motherly instinct that drove her into wanting to mother a child again. It was the only explanation. Under normal circumstances, baby Carlos would have been drained soon after he was taken. Thankfully for Bridget (and for me, who had no wish to deliver a dead baby to its mother), the child was still very much alive.

As I stood there debating what to do while the vamp clung to the baby in her arms, I reminded myself that I didn't have time to fuck about. Every second I spent standing in that dark cargo container was a second more of pain and torture for Leona. Or at least, that's how I saw it. It's what I chose to believe, the other option (that Leona was already dead) too horrible to even think about.

So I made a decision right there to bring the situation to a swift end in a way that was risky and probably inexcusable. But my back was against the wall, and I didn't have a choice.

Hardly able to believe I was doing it, I suddenly raised the knife in my hand back towards myself and then flung the blade forward. In between releasing the knife from my hand and the blade finding its target, there was a long, interminable split second where everything seemed to slow down, and my heart sat in my mouth, and I thought to myself, *I've hit the baby. Oh, Jesus, I've hit the fucking baby...*

*Bridget, I found your baby, but unfortunately, I stabbed it to death...here you go...oh Jesus...*

Thank the god's things didn't turn out that way.

The blade went into the vamp's skull, pinning her head to the wood of the container wall for just a second until her body began to slowly turn to dust from the top down, her head and face falling apart like a dry sandcastle in a desert wind, the knife staying stuck in the wood behind her.

I rushed forward then as the vamp's shoulders began to disintegrate and managed to grab hold of the baby before it tumbled to the floor with the remains of the vamp. "I gotcha," I said, holding the crying baby tight to me.

A sigh of relief left me as I raised my head to the ceiling and stood there in the now dark container for a moment, grateful that at least something had gone my way for once. Then I felt for the Killing Knife stuck in the wall, pulled it out and dropped into the pocket of my coat for the time being.

Once I got outside again, I told Blaze and Barney to make their way back to Sanaka's. "I got a baby to deliver," I said, then teleported to the Sanctum.

\* \* \*

BRIDGET BROKE DOWN AS I HANDED OVER THE BABY TO HER IN THE SANCTUM. She simply couldn't believe her son was still alive. Neither could I for that matter. If Bridget only knew the dangerous stunt I pulled to get the child back, she might not have been so warm towards me. As it was, she hugged my neck so tight I thought she would break it. "Thank you," she said in just about the sincerest voice I've ever heard, bringing a lump to my throat. "And I hope you succeed in whatever it is you have to do."

I almost cried myself when she said that.

29

# GATEWAY

*B*efore I left the Sanctum to head back to Sanaka's, I went into the Operations Room and grabbed my weapon of choice from the armoire, a Rune Axe that was shaped somewhat like a hatchet with a curved handle carved from mountain ash and a blade that was made from bone, but with metal plates set into either side to strengthen it. Also carved into the blade and handle were runes that gave the axe added power against supernatural foes. I acquired the axe some years ago from an Elven warrior in Babylon (the axe was payment for helping to sort out a sticky situation involving a bunch of angry Dwarves). Since then, I had used the axe to dispatch a fair number of supernatural foes. It was heavy enough to inflict major damage on soft tissue (even to break bone), but also light enough to swing with relative ease. I'd never used the axe against demons before, but I figured demons would bleed like every other creature when I hit them.

I slid the Rune Axe through a specially placed loop in my belt, so the weapon hung securely at my side, concealed by my trench coat until I needed it.

After that, I stood for a moment, trying to think if I would need anything else before going to the Underworld, but aside from a miracle, I couldn't think of anything.

* * *

A short while later, I met with Ray and Sanaka in the living room of Sanaka's Sanctum, which was as sparsely furnished as the rest of the place, the dominating feature being the huge fish tank that was set into the back wall of the room, taking up nearly the whole wall and throwing a glowing light into the room. The aquarium contained hundreds of fish, not all of them from Earth.

"Good of you to join us again," Ray said as she stood next to Sanaka over by the fish tank. Since I'd been gone, Ray seemed to have acquired a staff of some sort from Sanaka. Standing with it, dressed as he was in his ancient duster and shabby boots, he looked like an old traveler about to embark on one last journey.

Sanaka still wore the same black clothes from earlier, except that he had now added a long black leather coat to the ensemble. His sword was also in his hand, the blood red scabbard seeming to glow in the light of the aquarium.

Both of them stared at me like they were waiting for an explanation. "Someone came to me for help," I said simply as I walked into the room. "I couldn't say no."

Both Ray and Sanaka looked at each other, then Ray said, "I didn't think you had time to be a saint."

I sighed and shook my head. "A baby's life was at stake. What do you want me to do? Are we ready to go?" I ignored Ray's face as I focused on Sanaka instead.

Tanaka nodded. "Thanks to the owl, we now have Baal's exact location in the Underworld. We have also opened a gate that will take us directly there."

"All right," I said looking at them both, my adrenaline rising again. "Let's go get Leona back."

*　*　*

SANAKA AND RAY HAD OPENED A GATEWAY TO THE UNDERWORLD INSIDE ONE OF the rooms on the east wing of the Sanctum. The room was in darkness as I followed in behind them. The only light came from the glowing red gateway in the center of the room that made us look like we were all bathed in blood. Also in the room were Blaze and Barney, the barn owl perched on top of Blaze's back. The look the two of them gave me made it clear that they were coming with us. Blaze obviously wanted to help me get Leona back (whom he loved as well). As for Barney, he just wanted his mistress back. I nodded over at them, and Blaze walked over and stood beside me facing the gateway.

The gateway itself had the appearance of liquid blood and stood about six feet high by four feet wide. I stood staring into the slightly mesmerizing ripples for a moment, knowing that once I went through there, I would soon find out if Leona was alive or dead...or worse.

"Let's go through the plan," Ray said. "First, we get face time with Baal."

A laugh escaped my lips. "I didn't know they had iPhones in the Underworld," I said.

"What?" Ray said. "They don't. What does that have to with anything?"

I shook my head. "Nothing. A stupid joke. Continue."

Ray looked at me a moment like I was losing my shit, then dismissed me with a shake of his head. "Anyway. The plan. We get Baal to fight us, then while he's occupied, I'll put a Holding Spell on him, hopefully without him noticing."

"What if he does notice?" I asked.

"Then I hope my magic is strong enough to counter his attempts to release himself."

I nodded, wanting to ask what would happen if Baal was able to resist Ray's magic, but refraining from doing so because the mission already felt like a suicide mission as it was. "Okay. So once you get the Holding Spell on the demon, I do the spell to open a vortex to Dimension X."

"Yes," Sanaka said. "Then we all force Baal into the vortex."

"Hopefully banishing him forever," I added. "Then we get Leona and Margot, and we all go home."

We stood in silence for several moments as if letting the plan hang in the air for inspection. As plans went, it sounded so simple, but we knew it would prove to be anything but. Even with our combined efforts, it was entirely possible that it wouldn't be enough to defeat Baal in his own domain.

It was entirely possible that he would beat us instead, in fact.

"Are we ready then?" Ray asked.

Sanaka nodded affirmatively, but I still sensed his nerves behind his usual composed exterior. Which didn't exactly fill me with confidence, I have to say.

Ray looked neither nervous nor entirely comfortable. He knew what he was getting into. He knew he might not come back from the Underworld. He also knew he was doing it for me, which I think helped quell his undoubted fear somewhat.

As for me, I just wished I had some of that potion that Jack Burton and his crew drank in *Big Trouble In Little China Town*, the stuff that made them all forget their fear and primed them for battle. As I had no such potion (Note to self: invent one if I ever made it back from the Underworld), I just took a deep breath and tried to appear ready for action. "Let's do it," I said.

"I'll go first," Sanaka said, stepping up to the gateway. He paused for a second before walking forward, and then the gateway seemed to swallow him up.

"After you," Ray said, gesturing at me with his staff. "Age before beauty and all that."

I gave him a look. "You're older than me, for fuck's sake."

"I know, but I'm also beautiful. Now get going."

Shaking my head, I walked up to the gateway, paused while I silently prayed Leona was still alive, and then stepped forward, closing my eyes as the gateway pulled me into itself and delivered me into the Underworld and Baal's domain.

# THE LAND OF BAAL

*U*nlike the cold that hung around the Outer Reaches, the Underworld was warm, but not in a good way. In a suffocating, sticky way. The air was so hot it seemed to burn my throat and lungs, like the air itself was laced with sulfur. It was difficult not to cough as I reflexively covered my mouth and nose with my hand.

Sanaka looked around at me as he stood seemingly unaffected by the corrosive atmosphere. Then I remembered that wasn't Sanaka's first trip to the Underworld. He was a former resident of the place, having gone to the dark side at one point in his long past. For as long as I'd known him, Sanaka could be cold and even cruel at times, but it was difficult to imagine him being in any way evil in the way that my father was. From what I understood, Sanaka got lost in black magic at one time. His soul was consumed by it, and he ended up in the Underworld. What his role in the place was, I still didn't know. Nor did I know exactly how long he had spent there before a Dimension Lord stepped in to save him, or why a Dimension Lord should decide to pull him out. I tried pressing Sanaka on the matter a few times over the years, but he was always reluctant to talk about it. And I was beginning to see why.

The dark and smoky landscape that was rolled out before me like some nightmarish painting was possibly the most unwelcoming sight I had ever seen. Less barren than the black desert landscape of the Outer Reaches, and so much more alive and filled with a palpable dark energy that swirled around me like a storm of evil spirits, the wind their screeches, the uncomfortable warmth their touch. The sky was dark with a reddish tinge to it as if the clouds themselves were filled with the blood of the countless souls who must have surely resided there.

And in the distance, the jagged outline of some colossal citadel, looking like it had pushed itself up from the ground itself or had simply emerged all at once at the behest of the ruler of that land.

Which was Baal.

I was so engrossed by what lay before me I hardly noticed when Ray came and stood by my side, having come through the gateway with Blaze and Barney. "That's where we need to go," Ray said as he pointed his staff in the direction of the citadel. "That's where we'll find Baal, and hopefully your girlfriend, Leona."

"She's in there," I said firmly, more because I wanted to bolster the little hope I had of finding her than because I had some feeling that she was in there. I had no such feeling. The only thing I felt was dread. And of course, fear. I was in the Underworld, after all, not Disney Land.

"We should go," Sanaka said. "It is not safe to be so exposed out here."

I couldn't help laughing. "It's not going to be any safer inside that fucking citadel."

No one said anything for a moment as we stood staring at the massively imposing citadel that looked to lie about three miles away. In between us and Baal's lair, there appeared to be nothing but jagged slabs of rock, and what looked like small black lakes in the distance. If I strained my eyes enough, I thought I could see shapes bobbing up and down in these black lakes. I dreaded to think what the shapes were.

Sanaka soon set out across the cracked, arid earth, and the rest of us followed. Ray walked just ahead of me, but behind Sanaka, who led the way. Blaze walked along beside me, his dark fur now split with veins of orange fire as he seemed to be preparing for the inevitable battle ahead. It was good to have Blaze there with me. His presence was always reassuring in dangerous times.

I was also grateful for Barney's presence. The barn owl now stood over six feet tall and was walking along like some feathered dinosaur, its huge talons breaking up the dried earth as it walked. There was no doubt the bird of prey cut an imposing figure, and would likely prove useful in any upcoming battles. Clearly Margot's familiar was fiercely loyal and didn't mind facing possible death or worse if it meant saving his mistress.

"It must be hard for him being back here," Ray said nodding towards Sanaka, who was still walking up ahead.

"It's hard for us all," I said.

"I know that, but you didn't once reside here, did you? You know what it took for Sanaka to come back here? He did it for you, August. He loves you as much as I do. Plus, neither of us could abide your stupidity."

"My stupidity?" I said. "Give me a fucking break, will you? None of this has exactly been easy for me, you know."

"I know it hasn't, but you must learn to separate your emotions --"

"Yeah, yeah. Just leave it, Ray. Now's not the time."

Ray went silent, but more because Sanaka had stopped walking. Ray and I caught up with him. Sanaka pointed the scabbard of his sword out in front of him, but he didn't need to say anything because we all saw what was happening for ourselves. The black lakes I caught sight of earlier were actually lakes of blood, and people were bobbing around inside them. Damned souls, and not all of them human. Some were clearly beings from other worlds, but damned nonetheless, their souls the property of Baal. Every one of them made a kind of low mewling noise as they struggled to stay afloat in the blood pits. And as I looked out into the distance, I saw that the ground was covered in such pits, dozens of them every-where, all filled with perpetually drowning souls.

"Jesus," I said. "Are they being punished?"

"Yes," Sanaka said gravely, staring into the nearest pit several feet away as if he somehow knew what the people inside were going through. "They have displeased Baal in some way. It is a common punishment throughout the Underworld, not just here."

"As long as they stay there," Ray said. "They shouldn't be any trouble for us. We keep going."

We all started walking again, doing our best to avoid the blood pits and ignore the wailing sounds coming from within them. It was difficult all the same, not to catch the eye of the souls struggling around in all that blood. Their eyes pleaded for help, their abject misery and despair written all over their pained faces, faces which were awash with crimson. Hands outstretched as if for help, fingers clasping at the empty air for a moment before the person would sink below the surface of the blood, only to pop back up again a moment later to repeat their whole pathetic plight all over again. It was disturbing but nowhere near as disturbing as what happened next.

All at once, the captives in the blood pits--human and alien souls--began to claw their way out and onto the dry ground. It was like some power had been previously preventing them from leaving the pits. A power that had now released its hold on them. The blood pit dwellers were now free to leave, and every single one didn't appear to be wasting that particular opportunity. And who could blame them for wanting to get out and stretch their legs after so long?

You would think the dripping souls would have been happy to have gotten free from their vicious cycle of drowning in blood constantly.

But no.

The newly emerged souls were not what I would call happy. They looked mad as hell in fact. Like they wanted nothing more than to take all their built up pain and frustration out on someone who hadn't suffered as much as they had. Either that or they were all being controlled by Baal somehow. It was his domain, after all, and I had no doubt he was aware of our presence the second we came through the gateway. Maybe releasing the blood dwellers was his way of ensuring we never made it to the citadel.

Whatever the case, the blood dripping souls closing in all around us didn't seem to care why they were suddenly free. Like a herd of walking dead, they were aggressively focused on me and the others, looking like they wanted to rip us apart.

Instinctively, Ray, Sanaka and I went back to back as the hordes of bodies continued to close in at a disturbingly unhurried pace. Blaze was growling loudly by my side, intense heat and flames now rising from his tensed body. Barney was hovering just overhead like the silent but deadly predator he was.

"Do not fall into the blood pits," Sanaka warned as he drew his sword. "You will never get out again."

"That's comforting," I said, taking out the Rune Axe and gripping it tightly in my right hand. "Considering the fucking things are everywhere."

"We just need to cut our way through them to get to the citadel," Ray said, his staff now held in a defensive position. "Be wary of using magic down here. The

427

dark energy here is so potent and pervasive it may instantly corrupt whatever magic you conjure."

I shook my head. "You might have mentioned that before."

"I'm mentioning it now."

"Stay close together," Sanaka barked.

"And show no mercy," Ray said. "They are already dead. It won't matter."

My eyes run across the bloody faces of the horde closing in on us. Most were human (barely), but many were also alien, clearly from some other world, some other dimension. A few were positively monstrous, in both size and appearance. Baal's reach really did span the known universe.

As the adrenaline coursing through my veins went from feeling like warm piss to hot lava, I became aware of movement behind me and then a battle cry from Sanaka as he sprang into action. The bloody souls had reached him first.

Just beside me, Ray readied himself as an intensely angry looking soul came towards him. "Time to see what you're made of, boy," he shouted before running forward and bringing the end of his staff down on the damned soul's head at a forty-five-degree angle. The movement was quick and precise, and it took me by surprise. It was probably the first time I had ever seen Ray fight without using magic.

But I didn't have much time to stay surprised at my uncle's prowess with a long staff. I had my own angry souls to deal with. Blaze was doing a good job of keeping most of them back, barking and snarling at them. Barney was also swooping down over the horde, screeching loudly as he used his steely talons to knock them over.

The horde wasn't deterred for long, though. Whatever their motivations for attacking us, they probably didn't have much choice in the matter. And they wouldn't stop coming unless we stopped them, that much was clear.

So the first damned soul that came near me—a human man it seemed like, though it was hard to tell in the moment—I swung the Rune Axe at their head, shocked when the axe cut right through as easily as slicing a melon in half. I had forgotten how sharp and powerful the Rune Axe was. I was also thankful that I had chosen the right weapon to take with me.

After that first swing, it was like I never stopped. The damned souls kept coming, and I kept swinging and chopping with the axe, doing my best to keep the Underworld inhabitants at bay. A few times, hands grabbed me. Hands that tried to rip my flesh, pull off my limbs or gouge out my eyes. At one point, Blaze jumped on a damned soul that had me pinned to the ground after I had tripped on a rock. The Garra Wolf's huge flaming jaws practically engulfed my attacker's whole head before biting down, severing the head from the neck. After that, Blaze moved onto the next attacker, a look of terrifying fierceness in his glowing yellow eyes.

The second time I got in trouble, I was surrounded by damned souls. Too many to handle at once. Barney swooped to my rescue, gripping bodies in his massive talons and ripping them apart in an instant.

Sanaka still led the charge up ahead. Occasionally, throughout all the bloody carnage, I would catch a glimpse of my mentor as he cut down bodies like he was slicing through bamboo. He moved at a speed that was breathtaking to watch, his every cut with the sword completely assured and deliberate. It was the first time I had ever seen him seriously use his coveted sword. I didn't think my respect or admiration for the man could have gotten any deeper, and yet it did, right there in that dark hellhole as we were surrounded by foes that wanted only to dismember and eviscerate us and then drag the pieces back into the blood pits with them.

Ray also continued to swing his staff like it wasn't his first rodeo. Which I knew it wasn't obviously, but again, I had never seen my uncle fight the way he did right then. Between Ray and Sanaka, they both gave me the courage to keep swinging, to keep cutting my way through the herd of bodies that never seemed to thin no matter how many we cut down. Souls were still crawling out of the blood pits like there was an infinite number of them beneath the surface of the blood.

"They won't stop fucking coming!" I remember screaming at one point in frustration and near panic.

It seemed like for every damned soul we put down, half a dozen more were ready to take their place. The odds--and the noise--were becoming overwhelming. It was also becoming increasingly difficult to avoid falling into the blood pits, which were everywhere.

Just as despair threatened to overcome me, something happened. Something like a shock wave passed through me, and a circle of blue energy appeared that widened out to pass right through the hordes of bodies surrounding us as well.

I spun around to see Ray standing with his staff planted into the hard ground, and I realized that he had used his magic in a last ditch attempt to keep back the advancing horde.

Everything seemed to stop for a moment, and a stillness fell over us. Then, all at once, every single blood pit dweller fell to the ground like dominos. Everyone waited with bated breath to see if the damned souls would get back up again, but they didn't. They stayed down.

Which would have been something if more bodies were not still pulling themselves out of the blood pits.

We all seemed to have the same idea at the same time, but Ray vocalized it. "RUN!"

The three of us bolted across the hard, rocky ground. Blaze was beside me and Barney screeched as he flew overhead. Soon, I realized the blood pits had ended, but we kept running until the once again growing horde of damned souls was far behind us, and only their continued moaning sounds were audible in the distance.

"All right," I said eventually, hardly able to breathe. "Stop...fucking stop..."

Ray was seriously out of puff as well. Sanaka less so. They both stopped when I did. "The citadel is just there anyway," Sanaka said, his face and hands streaked with blood, as was Ray's and my own.

"What?" I said, focusing forward, surprised to see the citadel a few hundred yards ahead. I was surprised because I could have sworn the citadel was a lot further away the last time I checked. It was like the ominous stone construction had come to meet us half way.

"We should proceed with caution," Ray said, taking huge breaths of the hot air around us in an attempt to keep from hyperventilating, or so it seemed. That could have just been me nearly hyperventilating. It certainly felt like I was.

"I thought we *were* proceeding with caution," I said, or rather gasped.

"Shut up, boy," Ray gasped back. "You know what I mean."

I couldn't help but laugh. For some reason, I found his response funny. So did Ray himself a second later, and joined me in smiling. "What do you always tell me, Ray?" I said. "If you can't laugh in the face of danger--"

"You have no business being there in the first place," he finished.

Sanaka shook his head at us and was about to say something when a hugely loud and terrifyingly familiar voice seemed to cut through everything, instantly wiping the smile of my face. "Gentlemen," the voice boomed. "Welcome to my domain. May it be the last place you ever see."

A cold laughter followed, and my blood chilled.

# FACE OFF

*B*aal was standing up on a turret that jutted out just above the main gate of the citadel. The citadel itself was made from huge stone blocks, and its walls seemed to expand out for miles, encompassing whatever hellish city lay within them. The huge door to the citadel looked to be made from a kind of dark wood that was supported by thick metal straps. Not the kind of door you could knock down in a hurry, even with magic.

As I stood staring up at Baal, who was in his full demon form, his four arms outstretched as if to welcome us, I couldn't help wondering where Leona was. "Where is she, Baal?" I shouted up at the demon in sudden anger.

Baal's glowing orange eyes glared down at me. "Who do you mean?" he asked. "The lovely Leona or the spiteful Margot? Perhaps you mean them both." He laughed then like he was enjoying the whole situation. "Would you like to see your girlfriends, Creed?"

Before I could even answer, Baal raised one of his four hands and clicked his fingers. A second later, two demon figures stepped out of the shadows behind Baal and came forward. My breath caught in my throat when I realized Leona and Margot were being held by the guards. "Leona!" I shouted as I ran forward a few steps.

Leona didn't respond, however. Neither of the women did. Both were naked and covered from head to foot in blood, almost like they had been dipped into one of the blood pits behind me. But I knew the blood was their own, which turned my stomach. "What have you done to them?"

"Nothing compared to what I *will* do," Baal said. "Nothing compared to what I plan on doing to *you*, Creed."

I couldn't just stand there while Leona and Margot were being paraded in front of me like meat puppets. Without giving it much thought, I fired a blast of magic at the massive door of the citadel. It was a move born out of frustration and anger, and not one which I expected to work. Indeed, the blast of magic never even hit the door. Instead, it was somehow redirected back towards Ray, who used his staff to block it at the last second. The force of the magic still knocked him back on his ass, though.

Baal laughed. "This is my world, wizard," he bellowed. "I control what happens here. Not you!"

"Prove it then," Ray said as he walked forward, his attention on Baal. "You want our souls, why don't you come down here and get them yourself?"

"Yes," Sanaka said, also speaking up as he went and stood by Ray. "If you are truly the master of this domain, then you will come down and defend it yourself."

Baal stood with his massive chest pushed out, his four arms held tensely by his side as he looked at each of us in turn. "I had planned to raise one of my monstrously beautiful creations out of the very ground you stand on so I could watch it kill all of you." He paused while he stared at us, then laughed arrogantly. "Filthy humans. You never know your place, do you? Or your limitations. Not until it is too late." He looked at Margot then, who like Leona, could barely stand and was just about able to raise her head enough to take in what was going on around her. "So be it. If it's a lesson in pain and humility you want, a lesson you all shall have."

The demon leaped down off the turret then, landing with a heavy thump on the hard ground below. His burning orange eyes blazed at us, the stripes along his body now cracked open and spurting flames. Baal looked even bigger than he did when I first summoned him, which seemed like a lifetime ago by now. The power and utter conviction of him were terrifying, and I realized then just how much he must have been holding back when I fought him at the summoning. I doubted it would be that easy this time around.

Instinctively, I fell in beside Ray and Sanaka. Blaze stayed by my side, Barney by the side of him. Three wizards, a Garra Wolf and a barn owl. Christ, it was the like the start of some bad joke.

Only it was no joke, not when our souls were at stake.

The first part of the plan had worked. We had gotten Baal to face off against us. Now all we had to do was keep him occupied long enough so Ray could cast a Holding Spell without Baal noticing.

But as Ray had said, magic didn't always work as expected in the Underworld. My attempt to blast the citadel doors was proof of that.

Baal looked like he couldn't wait to get his claws bloody. "I think I will enjoy this," he said, looking at each of us in turn as if marking us for death. "Three legends in their own insignificant lifetimes, about to be wiped from existence like they were never even here. Yes, I will enjoy this."

The demon leaped into the air then like he had rockets on his feet, reaching a height of twenty feet before coming back down again right towards me, his fist drawn back and ready to strike.

*Of course, he would have to come at me first*, I thought in a panic as I jumped back just in time as Baal landed, his massive fist pounding into the dry ground. Even though I managed to avoid him, the sheer explosive energy from his driving fist hitting the ground was enough to blast me back off my feet, and I landed hard on my back, the wind knocked out of me.

I sat up quickly, having no wish to stay lying down so Baal could stomp me with his taloned feet, which he seemed to be planning on doing as he came towards me. "You will pay the price for your insolence, Creed!" he shouted, jumping into the air once more.

But as he came screaming back down again, Barney suddenly swooped in and pushed Baal off course with his feet, sending the demon careening to one side before landing and rolling across the dirt. Baal jumped immediately to his feet and looked up at the barn owl, who was hovering not far above. I then watched as Baal formed a dark energy ball in one of his hands before firing it at Barney. The barn owl veered to one side, but the energy ball clipped his wing and sent him into a tail spin that ended with him crashing into the ground.

Blaze growled aggressively at Baal when he saw what the demon had done to Barney. With a customary lack of fear, Blaze went charging at Baal, the Garra Wolf's body now a burning mass of flame.

"Blaze no!" I shouted, knowing full well that Baal would kill the Garra Wolf as soon as he got his hands on it. Blaze was tough and a fucking fighting *machine*, but there was no way he would win against a demon like Baal.

As Blaze continued his charge at the waiting Baal, I scrambled to my feet and without thinking, threw the Rune Axe that was still in my hand. It was a move I had never tried before, not even in practice, so I was shocked when I saw the bone blade of the axe penetrate into Baal's fiery chest.

The demon screamed when the axe hit, more out of anger than out of any real pain. As Baal gripped the axe to pull it out, Blaze launched himself at the demon. The Garra Wolf's flaming jaws were wide open as they aimed for Baal's throat. Baal had two of his hands wrapped around the Rune Axe that was still buried deep in his chest, but he still had two other hands which he used to catch Blaze in mid air as the Garra Wolf's jaws neared the demon's throat. Blaze was so big and heavy that Baal was forced back, and he lost balance and landed on the ground with Blaze on top of him.

While the demon struggled to keep Blaze from tearing his throat out, my eyes quickly found Ray who was standing some ways behind where Baal lay. Ray's hands were facing Baal as my uncle worked on securing the Holding Spell. It wouldn't be an easy spell to cast considering the power the spell had to hold, so the casting of it would take longer than normal. But if anyone could do it, it was Ray.

Sanaka was now running at the downed demon, having seen an opportunity to inflict some real damage now that Blaze was keeping Baal occupied. Sanaka ran low to the ground with his sword pointing out behind him as he got ready to bring it up and stab it down into Baal's skull.

But before Sanaka could reach the demon, Baal managed to throw Blaze off, and then get immediately to his feet just as Sanaka came screaming at him with the sword. Sanaka swung the sword at Baal's neck and Baal ducked at the same time as pulling the Rune Axe out of his chest with barely a grunt of pain. I was slightly aghast to see the massive wound close itself up in Baal's chest as if it never happened.

Baal laughed at Sanaka as they now circled each other, the demon swinging the Rune Axe around with one hand. "Let's see how good you are with that sword, Sanaka," Baal said.

For someone about to go blade to blade with a demon, Sanaka looked pretty composed and indeed made the first move, charging in with a downward blow which Baal easily sidestepped. Sanaka could have attacked again, but didn't. Instead, he started circling the demon, speaking to it in some ancient tongue. It was then that I realized what Sanaka was doing. He was keeping Baal distracted so Ray could finish the Holding Spell.

And so I could open up the vortex to Dimension X. Which I had almost forgotten about in the heat of the moment.

As I turned around to face away from the citadel, I saw Blaze out of the corner of my eye as he rolled up to his feet, and then I saw Barney swoop over the top of him. At least those two were all right. I'd already lost Blaze once. The thought of losing him again was too much to bear.

Wasting no more time, I raised my hands up and closed my eyes as I entered the Chaosphere within my mind, drawing to me the strands of magic I would need to create the vortex. The only thing I was worried about was the possibility of the magic not working properly. In theory, the magic I was about to use should open the vortex, but magical theory didn't seem to apply in the Underworld. The Underworld had its own rules, of which I was not familiar.

I tried hard to cast the doubt from my mind though, knowing it wouldn't help the magic any. The magic needed my absolute conviction if it was to work as intended.

When I had conjured the required amount of magic in the Chaosphere, I opened my eyes again and immediately looked towards Baal, who was still fighting Sanaka. Although something seemed off about the demon. He was moving slower as if his body were weighted down by some powerful gravitational force. Consequently, he wasn't quick enough to avoid Sanaka's next attack and Sanaka's sword lopped off one of the demon's arms.

Baal roared in pain and frustration as he realized something wasn't right.

And something wasn't, for Ray was lurking in the shadows near the citadel, hiding from Baal as he cast the Holding Spell on the demon.

At some point, Baal must have realized what was going on. The demon soon located Ray and tried to run towards him, but as Ray had almost completed the Holding Spell, Baal could barely move.

"Open the vortex!" Sanaka shouted at me, just before he went running at Baal with his sword held up high at an angle as if he intended to cut the demon's head off.

But Sanaka only got to within a few feet of Baal before some winged creature flew down from the Citadel and grabbed hold of Sanaka before he even knew what was happening. Once the creature had Sanaka secured (which took all of a second), the thing flew up and away into the dark, menacing sky, screaming as it went as if in victory.

"No!" I said as I could only look on helplessly while Sanaka disappeared into the distance.

Then more screaming sounds split the air as the sky above began to fill with screeching dark shapes.

"I will break free of this spell soon enough," Baal shouted. "Until then, your hands will be full."

Instinctively, I ran towards Ray who was standing near the citadel gates. On the way, I couldn't resist looking up to the turret to see if Leona and Margot were still there, which they were, still being held by the two demons. Leona's head was still hanging as if she was barely conscious, but Margot's face was up and seemingly alert now. Our eyes met only for a split second, but it was long enough for me to see something there. A look that somehow promised everything was going to be all right, which I dismissed instantly as a figment of my imagination, for how could she know something like that?

"August!" Ray shouted before I even got near him. "Open the vortex now!"

A demon swooped down above my head, and I ducked just in time to miss its grasping hands. "What about these fucking demons?"

"We'll take care of them," Ray said, with Blaze on one side of him and Barney hovering just above him. "Just open that damn vortex so we can put an end to this!"

Nodding, I stood with my back to the citadel gates, my hands held out before me as I started casting the magic and speaking the words that would open the vortex.

It proved difficult to concentrate, however, what with Baal staring over at me and screaming demons flying overhead. Ray, Blaze and Barney did a good enough job of keeping the demons away from me, but I still had Baal shouting over at me from his fixed position several feet away. "Your bitch thought she had known pain before she came here," he said. "I showed her the true meaning of the word, as I will show you as well, Creed. The depths of your suffering will know no bounds. Your soul will scream for all eternity, and those screams will fall on deaf ears...except your own."

As Baal gave out a rumbling laugh, I did my best to ignore his comments so I could focus on opening the vortex. I was glad a few moments later when the air seemed to split in two in front of me and then pull apart like something was ripping a hole from the other side. As soon as the vortex appeared, I felt the energy of it pull me forwards as if it wanted to swallow me up.

"What is this?" Baal roared, suddenly realizing what I was doing. "A vortex?" As I stood well back from the portal, its swirling dark energy began to pull loose rocks and dirt into itself. When I looked at Baal again, his eyes were full of rage as he struggled to free himself from the Holding Spell that still secured him. "That's your plan? You will never get me into that portal, Creed, you hear me? Never!" Another roar of frustration erupted from him, sounding like a trapped animal now, the hint of panic in the demon's voice unmistakable.

The vortex had fully formed by the time I rushed back over to where Ray was standing, just as he was swinging his staff at a screeching demon hovering overhead. Then I saw Blaze do an almighty leap into the air and latch his jaws around the leg of the demon, who screeched louder in response as Blaze pulled the demon down to the ground and all but disemboweled the thing in a matter of seconds, flames and sparks flying from Blaze's frantically moving head as his jaws viciously tore at the demon's flesh. And while this was happening, demon body parts also began to rain from the sky as high above Barney ripped and tore the demons with his razor sharp talons and beak. I had to jump aside quickly to avoid getting splatted by half a demon body that hit the hard ground with a thump right beside me.

Above us on the turret, the two demon guards still held the women in place, still obeying their master's orders it seemed. I was thankful for the demons' obedience, for otherwise they probably would have taken Leona and Margot deep into the citadel, making it difficult for me to retrieve them.

*Which they yet might do*, I thought.

"All right," I said to Ray. "Let's banish this demon motherfucker for good so we can all get home."

Ray nodded in agreement, but I also swore I saw something in his eyes right then, like there was something he wasn't telling me. I wanted to question him on it, but there was no time.

For Baal was beginning to move again.

# 3 2

# VORTEX

The demon couldn't move much as yet, but he was getting there. The fact that he could move at all was enough for me to want to get the bastard into the vortex as quickly as possible.

The vortex itself was a fearsome looking dark hole, making it look like some giant worm had burrowed its way out of some other dimension. It had its own gravitational pull that I found myself having to actively resist. If we didn't want to get pulled into the portal along with Baal, we would have to be damn careful, that much was for sure. It was bad enough we had to go to the Underworld--to Baal's domain--in the first place. But spending an eternity with the demon in some other desolate and completely isolated dimension just wasn't something I could allow myself to think about, so I banished my worries from my mind and focused only on the task ahead.

Ray was already pointing his staff at Baal, my uncle using his magic to keep a firm hold on the demon. Putting both hands out in front of me, I directed every ounce of my magic towards Baal, setting my magical hooks into him.

In response, Baal roared at us with furious anger. "You will never get me into that vortex! You will never beat me!" Much of the demon's movement had returned, and he struggled furiously against the magic being used to restrain him. I felt the demon's every push and pull, as I'm sure Ray could as well. The demon's own strength and power seemed to ripple back down the invisible magical waves leading back to us, at times weakening the grip we had over him.

*Jesus*, I thought. *We aren't going to be able to do this. He's too fucking powerful.*

Despite my sudden attack of doubt (and fear), I kept up the restraining magic, as did Ray. After some tussling, we were finally able to start shifting Baal towards the screaming vortex. I say shift, I only mean a few feet. We still had about ten feet to go before the vortex's own pull took over and sucked Baal in. But right now, ten feet felt like it might as well have been a hundred feet, such was the demon's determination to resist us.

"We need Sanaka!" I shouted to Ray, whose face by that point resembled that of someone who was trying to push an eighteen-wheeler down the street by himself.

"He's not here!" Ray shouted back. "It's up to us now!"

After Ray had finished stating the obvious, and after wondering fleetingly if I was ever going to see Sanaka again, I doubled up on my efforts at forcing Baal towards the vortex. The demon roared as he resisted against my renewed efforts, but he nonetheless found himself being dragged along by another couple of feet. Then the demon laughed suddenly. "You will exhaust yourselves before I will," he goaded. "It is just a matter of time."

The son of a bitch was right, as much as it pained me to realize it. There was no way I could keep up my current level of effort without expending myself sooner rather than later. Ray could have probably lasted longer, but he wasn't strong enough by himself to control Baal.

Panic started to set in. Thoughts of Baal breaking free any moment and attacking us began to slip into my mind, finding their way through the gaps in my concentration, which were increasing as the seconds ticked by.

Sanaka was supposed to have been there helping us. With his power in the mix, we would have been able to control Baal eventually.

But Sanaka was gone, and there was nothing anyone could do about it.

Then to make things worse, Baal started to move forward. He wasn't just resisting anymore. He was going on the offensive, slowly making his way towards us, and moving further away from the vortex.

Ray and I pushed back at the demon with everything we had, but it was like trying to push the biggest bull in the field using only one hand.

*We're fucked*, I couldn't help thinking. *Baal's going to beat us, and we're all going to pay dearly. Everything would have been for nothing.*

*Everything.*

Baal laughed as if he read my mind. "What's wrong, Creed?" he growled, still inching his way towards us, gaining more ground with every step. "Are you starting to realize how this is going to end? Are you having visions of the pain that awaits you? Believe me, your visions could not hope to match the reality of what you will feel at my hands." He laughed again, his eyes wide and boring right into me, and I felt myself shrink in response.

Then, to break my focus even more, Margot suddenly appeared beside me, holding up a barely conscious Leona. "What the fuck?" I said in surprise. "How did—"

"I have some strength left," she said, laying Leona down on the ground. "Thanks to you."

"Your bitch has come to help you, Creed," Baal shouted, uncomfortably near us now, no more than eight feet away. "How fitting."

I ignored Baal as I couldn't help but stare down at Leona.

"August!" Ray shouted. "Focus!"

I turned my attention back to Baal, who seemed certain he was going to get the better of us.

Then Margot stood beside me and pushed her hands out, a look of grit and determination on her bloody face as she joined in the fight. As soon as she did, Baal stopped moving.

"No!" the demon roared. "You will pay for this bitch!"

"So will you, Baal," she said back as she pushed harder.

Bolstered now by Margot's added power, I felt my own power increase and my focus renew as I pushed hard against Baal. Between the three of us, we were finally able to start forcing the demon towards the swirling vortex, despite Baal resisting with all his might. In just a few moments, we were able to shift the demon to within several feet of the swirling portal. Another couple of feet or so and the vortex would soon start sucking Baal in. Baal himself seemed to realize this and increased his efforts to stand his ground.

"You need to go, Creed!" Margot suddenly said. "Take Leona and go. Now!"

"What?" I said back. "Are you crazy? I'm not leaving you here with that demon."

"You don't have a choice. Once Baal enters that portal, this whole dimension you are standing in will be obliterated. You have to go now."

What? Why hadn't I been made aware of this fact? No one said to me Baal's domain would get sucked into nothingness once he was banished.

"She's right," Ray said, looking exhausted by his prolonged efforts. "But I'm staying to finish him. You two go."

Margot grunted as she kept up her magic against Baal, then said, "No! I started all this. I have to finish it."

She was right of course, but that didn't make it any easier to accept. I may not have known Margot for long, but I couldn't deny the connection I had with her, which was less romantic and more deep friendship and mutual understanding. I didn't want her to die. "I'm sorry, Margot," I said. "I'm sorry I couldn't save you."

Our eyes met then, and I saw the purity in hers. "You did save me." Her eyes welled up with tears, which she didn't let spill over. "Now go before he overcomes us all. I have only so much strength left."

I released my hold on Baal and went straight for Leona, who still lay out of it on the ground, looking like a dreadfully abused little girl in my eyes. I bent down and picked her up, forgetting how heavy she actually was and grunted with the effort of draping her dead weight over my shoulder. A second later, I was joined by Blaze and Barney, both of whom I was glad to see still alive. "Ray!" I said. "Let's go!"

"That's it, Creed," Baal shouted over as he continued to struggle against the magic pushing him and the energy of the vortex pulling him. "Run like the little bitch you are! It doesn't matter where you go, I will find you, Creed, even if takes me all of eternity. I will find you and make you suffer!"

I let Baal's threats go over my head. His words lacked the same power that they once did. He was beaten, and he knew it.

Ray let his arms drop as he released his magical hold on Baal, looking like he was about to collapse at any moment. "Thank you," he gasped to Margot. "Truly."

Margot nodded, her naked form straining with the effort of keeping her magic on Baal. "I can't hold him much longer. Go now. Please." She looked at me then, sadness now in her eyes. "Look after Barney for me."

I wanted to say that Barney didn't need anyone looking after him, but I nodded anyway. "There's time, Margot. You can teleport after--"

"I won't be able to," she said cutting me off. "Please just go, Creed. Save Leona."

Leona. The whole reason I was there in the first place. "Goodbye, Margot."

Margot nodded as she tried desperately not to cry, as did I when I turned away from her to go to Ray, who was now down on one knee, using his staff as support to keep from falling over. "I'm too old for this shit," he wheezed.

"Teleport back to the gateway, Ray," I told him. "Go through. I'll meet you there."

Ray barely nodded. "Don't take long."

"I'll be right behind you."

A second later, Ray vanished.

I turned and took one last look at Margot, our eyes meeting only briefly because she had to concentrate so much on holding Baal to keep him from flying back into the vortex too soon. I wasn't sure how much time I would have once Margot released her hold on Baal, but I was pretty sure it wouldn't be much.

When I looked at Baal, he roared, "This isn't over, Creed! Wherever I end up, I'll get out, and when I do--"

"Fuck you, Baal."

Baal glared back at me as Barney (normal sized now) flew down on my free shoulder. Blaze pressed himself against my leg, getting ready for the teleport.

The last thing I heard before I teleported was maniacal laughter from Baal, and then a scream as he must have gotten sucked into the vortex.

I heard nothing more from Margot.

# SOMEWHAT FUCKED

When I landed after teleporting, I didn't seem to be anywhere near the gateway, which I couldn't see in the dark surrounding landscape. Everywhere I looked there was black, stony ground and huge boulders.

But no gateway.

"Fuck!" I said, still straining to keep Leona's dead weight balanced on my shoulder. My face was covered in sweat as I frantically looked around. It didn't take long for me to realize that my magic had gone awry, either down to me somehow (entirely possible given my adrenalized state), or down to the weird physics of the Underworld dimension I was in.

Barney was hovering above me, and I sent the bird of prey off on a scouting mission to find the gateway.

Just as the barn owl flew off, there was something like an explosion in the distance. A huge ball of reddish-black energy mushroomed and expanded out across the entire broiling sky, creating lightning forks everywhere.

And then the noise came. A deep rumbling noise like the sound of thousands of heavy feet closing in from all sides. As the noise got louder, I realized with horror that the world I was in was falling apart at a rapid rate from the outside in. Every fucked up atom in the place was falling away into a pit of black nothingness. A place I would end up in myself soon enough if I couldn't find the gateway.

Using the mushroom cloud of energy as a point of reference, I judged I had teleported in the opposite direction some fucking how. I had no other choice but to take another chance and teleport again with what little magic I had left in reserve. Moving on foot wasn't an option. The collapsing world would soon catch up with us and swallow us whole.

"Barney!" I shouted, looking around for the owl. Barney appeared a few long moments later, landing on my shoulder again, screeching once to let me know he hadn't seen the gateway anywhere.

Shaking my head, I called Blaze over. Then I closed my eyes and hoped for the best as I teleported us all again.

When I opened my eyes again, I did so almost fearfully like I was afraid to see where I had landed us this time. And after looking around, despair set in once more as I realized it was another fuck up. This time I actually caught sight of the gateway (I think anyway, as it was difficult to tell with all the lightning bolts blasting down from the tumultuous sky), but it looked to be too far away. Maybe two or three miles away with an expanse of stony desert ground in between.

"No, no, no!" I said, about half my remaining energy (which wasn't much by that point) draining out of me like air from a punctured tire, all but deflating me in every sense. If I'd had time, I could have gotten myself and Leona across that desert on foot. But I didn't have that kind of time. In the distance, I could all but see the world I was in collapsing away like crumbling cliffs into a bottomless black sea. At that rate of destruction, I'd be swallowed up before I got near the gateway. I couldn't teleport either. My magic was drained along with most of my remaining energy. I did try, figuring it was worth a shot, but nothing happened.

I fell to my knees then and let Leona slide off me to the ground. Then I took off my trench coat and placed it over the top of her naked form.

I turned to Blaze next, who was standing beside me, Barney sitting on his back. I put my hands on Blaze's head and quickly gave him a tight hug. "You have to go, buddy. You and Barney can make it to the gateway if you go now."

Blaze made a whinging noise and all but shook his massive head as if to say he wasn't going anywhere.

"Goddamn it, Blaze!" I said pushing him away as tears stung at my eyes. "Get the hell out of here! Go! I'm commanding you to go!"

I had never commanded Blaze to do anything before, but I was commanding him now. And he knew it.

Blaze slowly backed away from me, making faint mewling noises in his throat. Barney flew up off Blaze's back and hovered in the air for a moment, his black eyes staring as he screeched almost plaintively at me.

The noise surrounding us was becoming like the the loudest thunder you've ever heard, and the frenzy of destruction was rolling inwards at a rapid rate. "Get the fuck out of here! Run!"

Blaze turned then and bounded off in the direction of the gateway, with Barney flying after him.

The tears that stung my eyes were now rolling down my face as I watched Blaze fade into the distance until it was too dark for me to see him anymore. "Bye buddy," I whispered hoarsely.

Then I turned to Leona, sitting on the ground and pulling her up into my lap, so her head was cradled in the crook of my arm. As I brushed her long fringe out of her face with my fingers, she opened her eyes and looked up at me. "Hey," was all I could think to say, my voice choking up in my throat.

Leona sort of smiled at me, too weak to even move her head. She reminded me of someone who had had a nightmare and was now glad that someone was there to comfort them. Only the nightmare she was in wasn't over. It had just got worse in fact, and I didn't know how to tell her. "You...came for me," she said in a whisper. I nodded, the tears streaming now, hardly able to speak. "I knew you would..."

I put my face down towards hers and kissed her on the forehead, then leaned my cheek against her. "I'm so sorry," I said.

Leona never responded as she closed her eyes again.

When I next lifted my head to look around, my eyes widened in horror as I saw something that resembled a huge tsunami rushing towards us from all sides, swallowing up everything in its wake, leaving nothing but blackness behind. I could barely think straight, but I figured we had about two minutes before the rolling wave of destruction hit us and wiped us out of existence along with everything else in that bastard world we were in.

Two minutes to spend with the woman I loved. The last two minutes either of us would ever spend again.

A kind of peace settled over me then as I accepted the inevitable. A strange sort of calm spread out within me, and I continued to cradle Leona and rock back and forth with her in my arms.

"What's happening?" she barely whispered.

"Nothing my love," I said. "Nothing you need to worry about. Just relax. I've...I've got you."

Leona smiled weakly again. "I love you...Creed."

I all but broke when she said it. The first time she ever tells me she loves me and we were both about to die.

*Fuck you, irony. Fuck you.*

The noise, the tremendous destructive energy closing in on us had now become so overwhelming it was difficult to do anything but stay huddled up against it, bracing ourselves for the imminent impact.

But then I heard Leona's words again, this time in my mind. "*I love you...*"

And I thought, *No, I'm not going to let us go out like this, no fucking way.*

Squeezing my eyes closed, I dug into myself deeper than I've ever dug before until I found what I was looking for. A small kernel of magic buried so deep I had never even used it before. I felt it in myself like some glittering jewel that had been waiting all this time for me to discover it, and now that I had, I was going to use it.

I tapped that small kernel of magic, and I teleported once more, this time with the certainty that I would get us to the gateway.

And by fuck, I did.

I almost burst into tears when I opened my eyes and saw the rippling red gateway just a few feet away.

But the wave of destruction that was swallowing up Baal's domain was also just as close. My joy soon turned to full on panic as I scrambled to get Leona up to her feet.

*We're not going to make it...oh fuck...*

I got us both to our feet, managed to get one step and then tripped on a rock that caused me to fall forward and land just a foot shy of the gateway with Leona lying beside me face down.

I shot out an arm and grabbed hold of Leona as I tried desperately to drag her forward towards the gateway.

Everything was blackness and overwhelming noise.

Then the gateway seemed to disappear altogether, and I knew that was it.

It was over.

Only it wasn't, for the gateway hadn't disappeared.

There was someone standing in front of it.

I looked up.

It was Sanaka.

Sanaka reached down and pulled Leona up off the ground, all but throwing her into the gateway.

As I felt the pull of the destructive force closing in around me, I managed to get to my feet and all but pitch forward into the gateway, helped by Sanaka's guiding hand.

# BACK TO EARTH

*I* burst through the gateway back into Sanaka's Sanctum and landed on the wood floor on my hands and knees, staying in that position for a long moment while I gripped the floor and stared down in disbelief. My mind was having trouble getting to grips with the extreme juxtaposition of being a split second away from total obliteration in an alien world only moments ago to now being alive and safe in my own world again. My head was spinning as it and my body reorientated themselves.

With Sanaka now standing beside me having come through the gateway himself, I finally lifted my head to see Leona laid out on the floor a few feet away with Ray kneeling over her, my trench coat laying beside her. Behind Ray, Blaze lay sprawled out on the floor, his yellow eyes staring at me as he barked his delight at seeing me again. Barney was perched on a table over in the corner, his head down, eyes half closed as if in mourning over Margot.

Ray looked at me with a mixture of relief and concern on his face. "What the hell kept you?" he snapped.

I shook my head as if I didn't want to talk about it, which I didn't. In fact, I would have been happy never mentioning the Underworld ever again. "I got held up."

Ray shook his head before his eyes went to Sanaka. "You made it, old friend."

"Lucky for these two," Sanaka said as he walked over to where Leona lay. Sanaka looked a bit worse for wear himself. His once pristine clothes were now torn and dirty, his face and arms streaked with blood. Despite it all, he still had his sword with him. Whatever else had happened, he hadn't lost it.

"What happened?" Ray asked Sanaka. "You were carried away by that demon."

"I escaped," Sanaka said as he crouched over Leona as if to examine her.

Ray nodded as if no further explanation were needed.

Leona wasn't moving. Her eyes were closed. Her face looked slack. In the brighter light, the extent of her injuries became more obvious. Numerous small cuts and deeper gashes covered her whole body, along with patches of dark bruising. She looked like she had been tortured bad.

*Jesus Christ...*

"Is she..." I said, my voice no more than a hoarse whisper.

"She's alive," Ray said. "But she has a lot of healing to do. It could take days."

"I will examine her fully," Sanaka said. "Then I will heal her."

I crawled forward on my hands and knees and drew myself up beside Leona, lifting my trench coat and draping it over the top of her naked body. Sanaka might help her body, but healing her mind would be a different story. Leona was going to have to do that all by herself.

"I'm sorry, son," Ray said, putting a hand on my shoulder.

"Don't be," I said, shaking my head. "We got her back. That's all that matters."

"And the other one?" Sanaka asked.

I shook my head again. "Margot made a choice. She sacrificed herself to save us."

Sanaka bowed his head slightly as if he was impressed by Margot's honorable actions.

"Speaking of which," I said, looking at Ray. "You knew that place would be destroyed once Baal went through that vortex, didn't you?"

Ray looked at me but said nothing. Sanaka said nothing either, as he would have known the truth as well.

"Let's get the girl to the healing room," Sanaka said eventually, breaking the silence that had developed. He stood over Leona with his hands held out in front of him palms down. Then he used his magic to raise Leona off the floor about four feet. It would be less stressful on her than having to carry her.

"Guys," I said as both Ray and Sanaka looked at me. "Thank you, both. I couldn't have gotten Leona back without you. I'm forever in your debt."

"You're already in both our debts for life," Ray said. "You couldn't possibly be in any more."

I couldn't help but laugh. "Sure, okay."

"I tell you what," Ray said. "Why don't you going and grab us a bottle of sake and we'll call it even, eh?" Ray smiled the way a father would smile at his son. Sanaka also nodded his agreement.

"All right guys," I said, the hope in me already rising from the ashes again. "Sake it is then."

* * *

WHILE LEONA LAY IN THE HEALING ROOM, NOW ON A DRIP FEED OF MEDICINE concocted by Sanaka (who was one of the best healers I knew), Ray, Sanaka and I sat in the living room drinking sake. All three of us were exhausted. Me more so, I had to say. Ray and Sanaka might have been a lot older than I was, but they were made of sterner stuff. In fact, now that the whole Underworld ordeal was over, the two of them now seemed relaxed and relatively unfazed by everything that had happened. It was going to take me a bit longer to get to that stage, however. So much had happened, and with Margot gone and Leona still unconscious, I found it difficult to settle myself in any way. The only upside was that I was so mentally and physically drained that I would soon need sleep, which would at least bring me blessed oblivion for a while.

"You did well in there," Ray said to me as he refilled all our glasses. "You should be proud."

"Proud?" I couldn't help but snort. "Give me a break, Ray, will you? I almost got myself and Leona fucking killed. If it wasn't for Sanaka..." I trailed off as I shook my head.

"Don't be so hard on yourself," Sanaka said. "We all could have died in that place, not just you."

"We worked as a team," Ray said. "And a damn good one at that, I have to say." He raised his glass and waited on Sanaka to do the same.

"To Margot," I said as I raised my glass. "Who saved us all."

"To Margot," Ray said, knocking back his sake.

"Margot," Sanaka said bowing his head slightly.

Ray put his glass on a small wooden coffee table then and stood up, groaning as if his bones ached. "Right," he said. "It is time for me to go. I should have been away days ago."

"You're leaving?" I said, surprised at how disappointed I felt at him saying he was leaving.

"Places to be, people to see," Ray said. "You know how it is."

Sanaka finished his drink and stood up, extending his hand towards Ray. "It has been an honor as always, old friend."

Ray grabbed Sanaka's hand and pulled him forwards, embracing him in a hug. Sanaka stood awkwardly for a second and then patted Ray on the back. "You too," Ray said. "You too."

Sanaka excused himself from the room at that point, saying he was going to check on Leona, leaving Ray and me alone.

"I can't believe you're going again," I said, standing up. "I was just getting used to having you around."

Ray smiled and pulled me into a hug. "I count my time spent with you as my most precious," he said. "And always will."

We pulled apart. "Let's see if you still think that next time you're banging Angela Crow."

Ray laughed. "Angela is indeed a special breed."

"Yes, a special breed of monster. I'll never know what you see in her."

"I could tell you, but..."

"Don't bother."

We both laughed. "Seriously, though," I said. "Don't leave it so long next time."

"And you," Ray said. "When's the last time you went home? I can't even think it was so long ago. You should take Leona and come visit me in Ireland."

I nodded like it was a great idea, despite being repelled by the thought. "This is my home now, but I'll think about going over to Ireland at some point."

Ray stood for a moment as if he wanted to get one last look at me before he left. "Take care, son," he said.

"I will," I said swallowing.

Then he was gone.

* * *

I found an empty bed after that (the same bed I used to sleep in when I lived at Sanaka's Sanctum) and crawled into it, immediately falling into a deep sleep that was occasionally punctuated by nightmares involving Baal and the Underworld. At least once, I awoke with a scream, soaked in sweat, thinking I was still trapped in Baal's domain as it all fell away around me.

When I eventually awoke properly, I got out of the bed (still in my clothes, minus the boots of course) and went straight to the healing room to find Sanaka there tidying up, disposing of blood stained cloths and various empty jars and bottles. I froze in the doorway as I saw no sign of Leona. "Where is she?" I asked frantically.

Sanaka paused with his cleaning up for a moment to look at me. "She left," he said.

A frown creased my face. "Left? What do you mean? Ray said it would take days and--"

"It has been days." Sanaka paused for a second. "Three days."

"Three fucking days?" I shook my head, unable to believe I had slept for so long. "all right, I need to go and see her."

"Creed?"

"What?"

"She instructed me to tell you not to come and see her."

"What? What the fuck? What do you mean? Why would..." I trailed off as the reason why suddenly made itself felt in me like a hammer to the gut. "That's all she said?"

Sanaka nodded. "Only that she would come and see you when she was ready."

I stood for a moment battling the sadness that wanted to send me straight back to bed again. "Thank you for healing her."

"Of course," Sanaka said. "You are free to stay here if you wish."

I shook my head. "Thanks, but I'm just going to go."

Sanaka nodded and went back to his cleaning like I had already gone.

# 35

# AFTERMATH

For the next two days, I holed up in the Sanctum and screened all of my calls (at least the calls that came through on the landline because I had smashed my other phone to bits), having no wish to talk to anyone. The bulk of the calls were from Brentwood, which was no surprise. The Division chief even called at the Sanctum on two occasions, demanding that I open the door so I could get to work on his cult case. Needless to say, I ignored Brentwood's demands. I would get to him when I was good and ready, and I was far from being ready to jump right into another case straight away.

The fact was, I was mourning Margot Celeste, and also the death of my relationship with Leona. Not that I knew for certain that Leona wanted nothing more to do with me, but if I were her, I wouldn't want anything to do with me, not after my betrayal. The only kernel of hope I had left in me was sparked by the fact that Leona had said she loved me back in the Underworld. Of course, she had been half dead at the time, but that didn't matter. She still said it. Which only made me feel worse about the fact that I had slept with Margot behind Leona's back.

So I sat around the Sanctum drinking whiskey and smoking some of Ray's special herb blend that he had conveniently left behind him. It wasn't long before I had sunk into a deep depression. I had spent the last while holding everything in, trying to stay strong so I could do what I had to do. Now that all that was done, I had no reason to keep up my defenses. Consequently, all those emotions I'd been keeping in check flooded out of their hiding places in my mind so they could turn my world black.

A few times in my drunk and stoned state, I tried to call Leona. The furthest I usually got was dialing the number and then hanging up before it could ring. She had said to Sanaka that she would contact me when she was ready, so she wouldn't have been happy with me calling her before that. So I resisted contacting her, as hard as that was.

Then late one evening, the phone rang while I lay drunkenly slouched in the living room making a bottle of whiskey float around by itself. At first, I wasn't even going to answer the ringing phone, thinking it would probably be Brentwood again anyway. But the ringing persisted, and I eventually got up and answered the phone. "Yeah?" I said in the world's weariest voice.

"Creed?"

"Leona." It felt good to hear her voice. Just the sound of it seemed to cut through my depression. "It's good to hear your voice."

She was silent for a moment, clearly unsure of what to say. "Are you drunk?"

"Drunk?" I shook my head. "Not really. A little."

"I was going to come over. We need to talk."

"Okay." I was trying to gauge from the sound of her voice what sort of mood she was in. What sort of mood she was in with *me*. But as always with Leona, it was too difficult to tell. She played her cards close to her chest.

An awkward silence developed, broken by Leona. "Creed? Is that okay?"

"Eh, sure. Yeah. Of course."

"I won't be long."

"Meet me on the roof," I said, deciding I needed fresh air to try and sober up a bit. "I'll leave the front door open for you."

When she hung up, I stood there for a bit with the phone still in my hand, no longer happy that Leona was coming over, but dreading now what she was going to say. Was she coming over to tell me in person that it was over between us? That I had betrayed her, and that she couldn't forgive that?

"Shit," I said replacing the receiver on the phone.

* * *

UP ON THE ROOF, IT WAS A MILD NIGHT APART FROM THE OCCASIONAL BURST OF cold wind. I stood with my trench coat on, arms folded tight across my chest as I stared out over the city, my head somewhat clearer thanks to the fresh air in my lungs.

"Something troubling you, August?"

I looked over my shoulder to see the ghost of Arthur Hendrix coming up behind me. "Hey, Arthur." The old black man looked as he always did in his tailored three-piece suit, which was in stark contrast to his shock of pure white hair. "Why would you say that?"

Arthur saddled up beside me, almost translucent in the moonlight. "Because you only seem to come up here when things are troubling you. What's up? Maybe I can help, as long as it doesn't involve a woman."

"It does."

"Ah, well then, I can't help you, I'm afraid. You're looking at a man who was married and divorced five times in his lifetime."

"Five times? That's a lot."

"You're telling me. I finally realized after the fifth time that men and women are not compatible, except for sex of course. A man should only be married to his business and his money."

"Maybe not the money."

"Of course the fucking money! What's a man with no money? I'll tell you. Nothing."

I shook my head at Arthur's capitalist philosophy. "Shouldn't you be off somewhere haunting your son-in-law or something?"

"I was about to do exactly that before I saw you up here."

"Well, don't let me stop you."

Arthur nodded. "all right, I'll leave you alone. I've got that bastard son-in-law running scared now anyway. You know he hired a ghost hunter? A goddamn ghost hunter! All I can say is, wait until they get a load of this fucking guy!" Arthur went to nudge me with his elbow, and his arm went straight through me.

"Have fun," I said as I watched Leona's black SUV pull up on the street below.

"Hey," Arthur said before he went on his merry way. "What's meant to be will be, and there ain't nothing you can do about that. I learned that one a long time ago."

"Thanks for the advice," I said rolling my eyes at how unhelpful that was. "Bye Arthur."

* * *

LEONA MADE IT UP TO THE ROOF A FEW MOMENTS LATER. I FELT AWKWARD AS I watched her cross the roof towards me. She was dressed in a dark pantsuit, and for someone who had nearly died in the Underworld only days before, I thought she looked pretty good. More than good actually. Up a little closer, though, I saw the haunted look in her eyes, and I immediately felt bad. That look was all my fault, created by trauma that I brought about through my selfish actions. "Hey," I said doing my best to smile at her. "You...look good."

Leona barely smiled as she stood beside me and stared out over the city for one long, tense moment while I waited for her to speak. It was difficult not to just launch into a full diatribe about what an asshole I was, but I knew she wouldn't want to listen to that, so I said nothing instead.

"I'll keep this brief, Creed," she said eventually, and I knew by her tone that I wasn't going to like what was coming next. "I think we should stop seeing each other."

I let her words hang there in the air as they all but confirmed my feelings on the matter, and which were nonetheless devastating. "Can I at least explain..."

"You think I'm doing this because you slept with that witch?"

Somehow her saying it aloud made it seem ten times worse. "Aren't you?"

A sigh escaped her, and she moved a strand of her hair from her face. "She told me she seduced you, that she used her magic on you."

"She did? Yes, she did."

"Whatever. It happened, and it can't be changed. The woman is gone now anyway."

The coldness of here tone stunned me slightly, especially since I still felt the loss of Margot so rawly inside. "A bit harsh, Leona. She saved our lives."

Leona closed her eyes for a second. "I know she did."

A tense silence grew up between us as she continued staring out over the city while I stared down to the street below. Eventually, I couldn't take the silence anymore, and I had to speak. "Look, Leona, I know things have been hard lately—"

"Hard?" She laughed coldly and shook her head. "You have no idea what I went through in that place, no...*fucking*...idea." Tears stung at her eyes as she turned away from me slightly.

"I know, and I'm sorry."

She shook her head again as if sorry didn't cut it. "I've just had enough, Creed. I've had enough of all the supernatural bullshit. I just can't take it anymore. Being kidnapped and tortured by that fucking demon was just the last straw for me."

I wasn't sure what to say to her. It wasn't really what I was expecting to hear from her, to be honest. "What are you saying?"

She turned fully to look at me, her blue eyes vivid in the moonlight. "You're like a magnet for the supernatural, Creed, for trouble. It follows you everywhere. It's a part of you. I'm saying, I can't be a part of that anymore. I can't be a part of...*this* anymore."

"Us you mean."

"Yes."

Once again I stood in silence, unsure of how to proceed. She seemed so adamant I didn't think there was anything I could say to change her mind.

"I'm leaving the Division and joining the FBI," she said. "I already got an interview for tomorrow." She paused for a second. "In Washington."

"*Washington?*" I said, my head spinning now. "You're going to leave, just like that?"

Her face softened slightly when she saw the crushing disappointment in my own face. "I need to get away. Surely you of all people can understand that?"

I did. At one time in my life, I needed to get away as well, and I let nothing stop me from doing that. "I get it," I said quietly.

"Look," she said taking a step towards me, but not touching me. "Give me some time to get settled, then we'll see."

"See what?"

She shook her head, her patience worn thin. "I have to go now. My flight leaves in a couple of hours."

Christ, it was all happening so fast. I didn't want her to go, but I knew there was no point in trying to persuade her otherwise. I knew when she had her mind made up. "Leona?" I called after as she walked away.

She stopped halfway across the roof and turned to look at me. "Yeah?"

"In the Underworld, you told me you loved me."

She seemed surprised to hear this, and a little uncomfortable. "I don't remember saying that."

"Is it true, though? Do you love me?"

She stared at me for a long moment, then said, "I've always loved you, Creed," as if she was just admitting this to herself for the first time, or at least acknowledging it out loud.

Then she turned and walked away.

# SCI-CANE

$\mathcal{I}$ stayed up on the roof after Leona left, watching her drive off in the street below, half hoping she would look up before she got into the car, but she didn't. The screech of her tires had an awful note of finality to my ears, making me think that I was never going to see her again. And the way I felt, I could have easily have believed that were true.

As hard as it was to comprehend, Leona had cracked under pressure. She said it herself, dealing with the supernatural on a daily basis had gotten too much for her. Obviously being kidnapped and tortured by a demon was the final straw for her. And even if I hadn't of slept with Margot, I doubted Leona would have behaved any different. She still would have wanted out.

Did I blame her for wanting out? Of course not. Every other day, I thought about walking again and leaving it all behind me. But I had been there and done that and knew it wasn't the right course of action. I was one of those who was doomed to stay in the game until death. Leona had a choice, and clearly, she chose to exercise that choice by moving away from the craziness that the supernatural brought.

The craziness that *I* brought.

In one sense, I was weirdly proud of Leona for walking, maybe even a bit envious that she had the choice. On a professional level, I didn't hold it against her.

But she walked away from me as well, and that I found harder to take. Christ, she even admitted she loved me. Had always loved me.

Yet not enough to stick around.

\* \* \*

OR MAYBE SHE LOVED ME ENOUGH *NOT* TO STICK AROUND. I DON'T KNOW. THE only thing I knew for certain was the huge hole she had left behind in me. A hole that felt like it was going to swallow me up completely at some point.

The only thing to do was fill the hole with more whiskey. That was my big reaction to the devastating turn of events. To get drunk. It's the Irish way.

As I turned to go back inside the Sanctum again, an earsplitting noise made me jump a fucking mile and violently flinch as if a massive bomb had gone off nearby. I turned around just in time to see a massive flash of bluish-white energy streak across the dark sky as if the energy had been discharged from some huge machine down on the ground somewhere. "What the fuck?" I said, wondering what the hell it was all about.

Then all the lights in the city started to go out as if switches were being flipped everywhere. Within a few minutes, the city was in total blackout.

I stood staring out into the darkness for a few moments, half expecting the lights to come back on again, but they didn't. If it weren't for the huge energy flash across the sky, I would have thought the cause of the blackout to be something mundane like a failed power grid or some other technical hitch.

But the look of the energy I saw suggested the problem was more supernatural in origin. I shook my head. *Maybe Leona had the right fucking idea after all*, I thought.

Then just when I thought nothing else was going to happen, a blue laser shot up from somewhere in the north of the city and pieced the starless night sky. The laser, which looked several feet in diameter, then seemed to cause a violent reaction in the sky itself, which split open and poured out yellowish light from a huge hole.

Only it wasn't just a hole. It was a portal. Somebody somewhere had opened up a portal to another dimension, and as I watched with a fascination I couldn't help, dark shapes began to move down the length of the blue laser light like they were being transported down to the ground. The shapes were traveling too fast for me to see what they were, but I knew it had to be nothing good.

Nothing good at all.

And then as suddenly as it appeared, the blue laser light vanished, and the hole in the sky closed itself up.

A few moments later, all the lights in the city went back on.

I stood shaking my head. "What the fuck did I just see?"

I hurried back inside the Sanctum and lifted the phone, dialing the number of the one person I thought might know what was going on.

"Brentwood. It's Creed."

"Creed," Brentwood barked. "Nice of you to call."

"Spare me the animosity, Brentwood. What the hell did I just see?"

"You're talking about the blackout?"

"Yes, and the fucking light show that went along with it."

"Do you know what that was about?"

"It looked to me like a dimension was opened up in the sky. Why, don't you know what happened?"

"Not really. The only thing we might be sure of is that it had something to do with Sci-Cane. They've been stepping up their activity lately. I need you on this, Creed."

"Any idea of what or who they might have brought down from that other dimension?" I asked, not expecting him to know much at all.

"That's what they did? They brought things back here?" He went silent for a moment as the reality of that sank in. "Christ, it could have been anything."

I closed my eyes for a second and let out a long breath. The choice I had was to stay at the Sanctum and mope around while I drank myself into oblivion, or I could meet up with Brentwood and find out what the hell was going on with this Sci-Cane crew and why they seemed so intent on causing havoc. The former choice seemed much more appealing to me, but my big mouth didn't agree.

"Tell me where you are," I said. "I'll come meet you."

# BLOOD CULT (WIZARD'S CREED BOOK 3)

1

# WELCOME TO DIVISION HQ

*D*riving the Cadillac up to the Department of Homeland Security building, I was stopped at the front gates by a guard in military fatigues armed with an automatic rifle. I slowed the car and wound down the window as the guard came up the side of me and leaned his head down so he could look at me with a very serious face. "August Creed here to see Brentwood," I said.

The guard, a young guy in his late twenties who looked like he barely shaved yet, nodded. "Yes, sir. General Brentwood is expecting you."

General Brentwood. In all the time I had known the man, I don't think I had ever called him General. Calling him that would have just increased the sense of authority he thought he had over me. Brentwood might have operated like he was still in the military, but that didn't mean I had to. The man was operating in a different world now, after all. *My* world, as fucked up as it was.

"Thanks," I said to the guard and waited while he went back to his post and opened the large steel gate to allow me access to the government facility. Which, by the way, was located in the Highlands in the very heart of the grinding machine of state. Normally when I visited Division HQ (which thankfully wasn't that often), I would get stopped at the gate and grilled by whoever was on guard duty as they forced me to show ID and then made phone calls to verify who I was. When they did so, the guard would often come back frosty as if whoever they had called on the phone had told them I was just some annoying piece of shit, but to let me in anyway. This time, there was no such frostiness from the guard on duty. I was temporarily no longer just an annoying piece of shit but a needed, and therefore important, annoying piece of shit. Honestly, I was offended by the change in attitude. So I was great when needed, but a cunt the rest of the time? Story of my fucking life.

When the gates opened, I drove through them, nodding at the guard who just stared back at me like I was an alien being from another dimension. To be fair, I didn't blame the guard for staring because even I had to admit that I looked like shit. The stresses of the last couple of weeks had taken their toll on me. I was at the point now where I felt like something was going to snap inside of me, leaving me broken beyond repair. It had happened to Leona, hadn't it? She lost her shit. Joining the fucking FBI. What was that about? It was a knee-jerk reaction to the trauma she had been through, and a desperate attempt to rid herself of the world of the supernatural. As if that was even possible. After everything she had seen? No way. Once seen, that shit can't be unseen. Even in the FBI, Leona would still be surrounded by the supernatural. It would haunt her every working day. Before long, she would have no choice but to deal with it. So the whole move would be pointless. She might as well have stayed where she was.

Of course, I was only saying that because her leaving Division also entailed leaving me as well. As much as that other stuff was true, the real reason I didn't want her going to the FBI was that it would shatter our partnership. A new normality would set in, of which I wouldn't be a part. Pretty soon, I'd just be some weirdo ex-boyfriend to Leona, and that would be that.

As I drove into the underground carpark of the Homeland building, I welcomed the darkness of the place. The glaring winter sun outside was getting too much, and it didn't suit my mood anyway. The gloom of the carpark felt more comfortable.

After parking the Cadillac, I walked to the elevator to find another armed guard waiting on me. It was protocol for visitors to be escorted into Division HQ, which remember, wasn't supposed to exist. The Division facility was situated underneath the main Homeland building and was a huge fortified bunker consisting of several different floors. What exactly went on at HQ was mostly still a mystery to me. I knew they had a main operations room that I had never seen, and a prison facility on the bottom floor, plus another floor filled with server rooms and tech that was beyond even the NSA. Beyond that, there was still a lot that I didn't know, despite grilling Leona on it over the years, who never told me anything except what I needed to know. I just knew that Division was considered of utmost importance to the government as the threat of the supernatural was so dangerous and so prevalent. Which kind of made me laugh because magic and the supernatural had threaded its way through the government as it had everywhere else in society. Brentwood thought he was the first defense against the supernatural, where really, he was just a glorified monster catcher, there to keep the supernatural psychos from disrupting the flow of commerce.

"This way, sir," the guard said, his tone deferential like I was some VIP to be treated with the utmost respect. Which I got to admit, was a pleasant change from being treated like a mildly dangerous outsider who shouldn't even be spoken to in case they disrupt the sacred military order.

As the doors closed on the elevator and the guard used his ID to get us moving down, an uncomfortable silence ensued as we both faced front and waited awkwardly as people do in elevators. Almost as if to fill the void of silence, my mind turned to Leona and the fact that she had left me. But I blocked those thoughts as soon as they came for I didn't want to think about them. It hurt too much, so I turned to my escort instead. Like most of the people in that place, the guard was young. I put him somewhere in his early thirties. He had dark hair and a square jaw that looked chiseled from granite. I was sure the ladies loved that jaw of his. "So," I said. "Seen any good movies lately?"

The guard barely looked at me. "No sir, not really."

*Well, that's the end of that line of inquiry.*

"Me neither. I feel like I'm fucking *in* one though." I snorted to emphasize the ridiculousness of my life. "Shit just keeps on happening, you know what I mean? Sure you do. You probably served in the Middle East, right? Of course you did. And now you're serving in a different type of war, a supernatural war. You ever think you'd be fighting against monsters when you signed up?"

The guard blinked once but didn't respond.

*Probably not,* I thought.

The lift stopped, and the doors pinged open. "This way, sir," the guard said, looking like he couldn't wait to get rid of me so he could go back and tell his buddies about the fucking weirdo in the elevator.

I followed my escort down a series of corridors, some of which I was familiar with from previous visits, others completely new to me. I passed people in suits and military uniforms, everyone I passed throwing me queer looks and sideward glances as if they thought I had no business being down there in their sprawling underground HQ. The floor I was on seemed to be where most of the important people (read high and mighty) hung out. Most were past middle-aged and seemed like seasoned professionals (read hard-nosed bastards). Their guarded stares said it all. Although to tell you the truth, I was a little miffed at the frosty reception considering I saved all their fucking asses from complete destruction not too long ago. I guess prejudice runs deep. Brentwood's people still couldn't help seeing me as being the enemy. I was the wizard, the dangerous and unpredictable magic-man who often caused as much damage as he prevented. I dealt in the supernatural. That put me squarely on the opposing side, even though in reality, I was closer to the middle.

Eventually, the guard took me down a sloping corridor that led towards a large set of double doors. Before I even got there, I knew the guard had taken me to the very hub of the Division--the central operations room that I knew existed thanks to Leona, but which I had never been in. The guard opened one of the doors and stood to the side to let me pass into the room.

When I entered I stood for a moment to take in the technical wonder that was laid out before me. The room was exactly as you would imagine a clandestine central operations room to be. A huge screen on the far wall was showing shaky cam footage from soldiers on the ground somewhere in the city, probably in the area where the massive blast of energy went off not too long ago. Smaller screens surrounded the bigger one, all showing pictures of various places around the city. And just back from the screens was a bank of computers where several people sat tapping frantically on keyboards and talking into head mics. In the center of the room was a huge oblong table, around which sat several men and women in suits, and a few others in military uniform. Brentwood sat at the head of the table, looking as comfortable as ever in his role as Division boss. He stood up when he saw me standing by the doors and motioned me over to the table. "Creed," he said as I walked over. "Glad you could make it. Welcome to the Central Op room. You've never been in here before, have you?"

I shook my head as I hovered by the table and tried not to catch the eye of everyone else there, who were all staring at me. "No, I haven't," I said. "It's quite the setup. So this is where you do all your spying from is it?"

A few people at the table shifted in their seats when I said that. "We monitor, Creed. We don't spy."

"If you say so."

Brentwood sighed. "You could have left the attitude at home for once."

I raised my eyebrows like a school kid getting a lecture from a teacher. "What can I say, Brentwood? It's a part of me."

"Is this the person you've been telling us about?" a man at the table said, a suit indistinguishable in my eyes from all the rest. "The man who is going to stop these mad scientists?"

The whole table stared at me as if they didn't believe I could help in any way, and that I was probably more of a hindrance than anything. I merely stared back at them all, refusing to be intimidated while I waited on Brentwood to say something in my defense. "Creed wouldn't be here if I thought he couldn't help," Brentwood said to his compatriots.

*You got that right*, I thought.

"He brought down the monster who almost destroyed everything recently," Brentwood continued. "Creed is the best at what he does."

"And what *do* you do, Mr Creed?" a woman in her fifties with severely scraped back blond hair said.

I smiled over at the woman. "Usually the shit you guys can't or won't do."

The blond woman's face hardened slightly as she seemed miffed by my response. Probably because she knew I was telling the truth. These government types, they liked to think that they were all powerful and that nothing could stand in their way. Until something did. Then they were forced to face their own limitations. They could, like the woman glaring at me from the table, become quite resentful when they had to eat cake.

"Eh, Creed," Brentwood cut in. "Why don't we go over here so I can bring you up to speed?" His hand was firmly on my shoulder as he steered me away from the table.

I gave everyone a final smile. "Nice meeting you all."

Brentwood sighed as he walked me over towards the huge screen. "Do you even know who half of those people are sitting at that table?"

"Nope," I replied. "Neither do I care."

"Jesus, Creed. You're in my house now. A little respect wouldn't go amiss."

We came to a stop just at the edge of the big screen, not far from the nearest keyboard tapper, a youngish looking woman who kept throwing me fleeting looks like she was afraid to take her eye off me in case I cast a spell on her or something. I was beginning to feel like the big bad wizard, the dark conjurer who no one seemed to trust. Fuck them. I couldn't wait to get out of that concrete bunker. It was suffocating and sterile. I'd always hated the place. The only thing I wanted was for Brentwood to throw me a lead so I could go to work up top. In the meantime, Brentwood had a point. I was needlessly rude, but that's how I felt like being. I couldn't help it. Still, I apologized, if only to hurry things up. "Sorry. Rough couple of days."

Brentwood stared at me. "So it would seem. What the hell is going on with

Lawson, Creed? Why does she want to leave Division? She wouldn't tell me anything except that she's signing up for the fucking Feds."

"Has she handed in her resignation yet?" I asked.

"Not yet. Later today she said." Brentwood shook his head. "I'm about to lose my best agent, Creed. I'm not happy about it."

I knew how he felt. "I tried to change her mind. At this point, she isn't hearing it. She wants out."

"She should never have hooked up with you, Creed."

Anger rose in me. "Fuck you, Brentwood."

The whole room looked as I raised my voice and Brentwood raised his hand slightly as if to say everything was fine. Which it wasn't. The motherfucker was implying I'd corrupted Leona, led her astray. If he wasn't half right, I might have punched him out. "It's nothing personal, Creed. I just mean relationships make the job harder."

"Says the married man."

"Divorced actually."

I frowned in surprise. "When did that happen?"

"A while ago." It was clear he didn't want to talk about it.

I nodded. "Can't you force her to stay?"

"Lawson? No, how can I?"

"You could if you wanted to. We both know that."

Brentwood shook his head. "We'll discuss this another time. I brought you here to talk about SciCane."

I was happy to drop the subject as well. "Any leads yet?"

"Yes, actually," Brentwood said. "Over here."

He led me over to where the computer guys were, all still in their seats tapping away furiously "What are they all doing?" I asked.

"Trying to hack SciCane," the young woman who'd been throwing me looks said, pausing what she was doing to hold my gaze this time. She was pretty in an unconventional way. Her hair was short and dark with a reddish tint to it, and she had large green eyes that seemed to take in everything. A fierce intelligence was at play behind those eyes, and I could almost see calculations going on inside her head as she continued to stare at me, almost like she was trying to figure me out as if I was some binary driven machine. I couldn't help wondering if she suffered from autism of some kind due to her peculiar detachment. Her smile was tight, almost forced. "I'm Bethany."

"Bethany is our lead analyst," Brentwood said.

"I'm Creed," I told her.

"I know," she said, then turned to stare at the screen in front of her again.

I glanced at Brentwood as if to ask what Bethany's deal was, and he raised his eyebrows slightly as if to say that's just who she is. "Tell Creed about the forum," he said to Bethany.

"Forum?" I said, leaning down to look at the screen, and as I did, Bethany pulled away from me somewhat sharply.

"I don't like to be crowded," she said looking down.

I pulled back. "Sorry."

Bethany just nodded and resumed tapping the keyboard at a speed that made her fingers blur. Keeping my distance now, I did my best to look at what was on the screen, which seemed to be displaying a message board, though I couldn't read the text on it. "This is the website where SciCane posts all their information," Bethany explained. "They post everything from complete spell instructions to the ingredients of some very dangerous substances."

"Dangerous?"

"Explosive in some cases, mind altering in others."

"Drugs and bombs. Typical."

"They have instructions there on how to open portals to other dimensions, for Christ's sake," Brentwood said. "I wouldn't trust half the people in this city to open their own front doors never mind a door to another dimension."

I couldn't help but snort at Brentwood's blatant lack of trust. Not that I could blame him for it. With such dangerous information available to anyone who could find the forum on the dark web, trouble had to be just around the corner, and possibly on a grand scale if enough people started experimenting.

"The admins of the site go out of their way to encourage users to act on the information they provide," Bethany said. "There are numerous long posts here that outline the group's anarchist philosophy. They seem to think they are waking people up so they can start a revolution."

"Setting them up more like," I said, and for some reason, Bethany smiled at that. "If this keeps up, SciCane will get what they want soon enough. Society will just collapse."

Brentwood shook his head as if I had just underlined the potential for disaster. "This is why we need to stop this group and take the whole thing down."

"Can't you shut down the website?" I asked.

Bethany sighed sharply. "No."

"We've been trying," Brentwood said.

"I can't break their encryption," said Bethany, clearly annoyed that something was beyond her obviously considerable skill set. "In fact, I've never seen anything like it. And I mean never. It's like they have their own technology that no one else has."

"They probably do," I said. "They have the Dark Codex after all. They can create anything they want."

"Tell him what you want," Brentwood said to Bethany.

Bethany nodded and glanced around at me. "Although the group operates in secret apart from their public disclosure of information, I did come across a few posts by the main admins, stating that they are willing to allow anyone into the group as long as the person could prove their worth."

"Prove their worth?" I shook my head. "How?"

"You have to be able to demonstrate your abilities. If the group leaders think you have valuable skills that would benefit the group, you get taken in."

"Okay. How does this happen? I assume you can't just contact them."

"No," Bethany said. "You have to post a video on the site here. If your video impresses, the admins will contact you directly."

"Has anyone posted a video?" I asked, curious to know.

"Dozens of people have. I've watched them all."

"And?"

"And most of them are nut jobs. Amateur magicians, hedge witches with very little skill, pseudo-scientists performing weird experiments. Only two people stood out to me."

"Who?" I asked, expecting her to bring the videos up, which she did. In the first video, there was a guy in a baseball cap who was sitting in a darkened room in front of a glowing computer screen while he inputted lines of code onto the screen.

"This is like no code I've seen before," Bethany said.

"That's because our friend here is a technomancer," I said. "He's mixing normal code with magic. It's an art."

"I wouldn't call what happens next art," Bethany said.

I continued watching the screen as the video then cut to Main Street in Camden Town. The technomancer filmed with his phone as money suddenly started spewing from every ATM in the street. Needless to say, people went crazy and started fighting each other to get to the hundreds of bills blowing around the street and through the air. Pretty soon, it was a total riot. The cops came. People were beaten down with sticks, handcuffed and arrested. A moment later, the video finished. "Nice skills," I said.

"Yeah," Brentwood said. "For creating chaos in a busy street. People were hurt. One person was killed after being trampled on."

"What's the next video?" I asked Bethany.

"It's a long one with lots of deranged commentary from the man and woman involved, so I'll spare you the agony of having to listen to it. This crazy couple walks into a corporate seminar full of suited execs--not far from here actually--and turn every last suit into a cow."

"A cow?" I couldn't help smiling.

"Fifty-six cows to be exact."

I shook my head. "Well that's--"

"Fucked up?" Brentwood said.

"I was going to say cool, but fucked up will do."

Brentwood gave me a look. "I'm glad you think fifty-six people being turned into cows is a cool thing, Creed. Those people will live the rest of their lives in a fucking field. They had family, loved ones."

"Yeah, I know," I said raising my hands to calm him. "I was just saying..."

"Saying what?" Brentwood demanded, glaring at me.

I shook my head. "Nothing. Forget it."

"Jesus, Creed. You're as fucking bad as they are."

"Laughing is not the same as doing."

Brentwood shook his head and threw me a sharp look as if I'd uttered a line of philosophical garbage. "Whatever, Creed. The point here is that the video auditions are your way into the group. Post a video that's sure to impress and get a meeting with these fucks so we can find out who they are, and then take them down before they do any more damage."

"You want me to make one of those videos?" I asked, slightly appalled by the idea of such blatant showboating on camera. "Doing what?"

"You're the wizard, Creed. I'm sure you'll think of something."

"A wizard," Bethany said staring at me. "I never thought I'd meet a real wizard. I played D&D for years, and I was always a witch or a wizard."

Brentwood shook his head at Bethany. "Ignore Bethany's starry eyes. She hasn't been here all that long."

"It was nice meeting you, Bethany," I said smiling at her, genuinely liking her. She was down to earth and didn't have a stick up her ass like everyone else in Division.

"Yeah," Bethany said before turning back to her screen.

Brentwood walked me back to the doors as the war pigs at the table threw me looks which I ignored. "Do what you have to do to get into that group," Brentwood said. "I don't care what you do as long as you get a meeting."

"I can do anything?" I asked.

Brentwood sighed. "I can't believe I'm saying this, but I trust your judgment, Creed. I trust you'll keep the damage to a minimum whatever you do."

"I'll try my best."

# 2

# TAKING THE STRAIN

*I*n some ways, it felt like business as usual when I left Division HQ. I had a case to work on, and I could go back to doing what I do. The only thing missing from that normality was Leona. She would be in Washington DC by now, preparing to join the FBI. I had no doubt she would make a good agent, but I also knew it wasn't what she was meant to do. Like it or not, the supernatural existed, and there could be no running away from it once you became involved. Leona would realize that in time. Maybe she would come back to Blackham then. Back to me.

I sighed and shook my head as I drove out of the grounds of Homeland Security, nodding to the guard who had let me in earlier, who nodded back with a look that said he still didn't know what to make of me.

*Fuck it*, I thought. *I have a case now. A big one. Let's just focus on that and let fate sort out the rest.*

"What will be will be, Creed," I told myself out loud as I turned on the radio to a classic rock station in time to hear Judas Priest's "Heading Out To The Highway" which I started singing along to just as the sun broke through the clouds again and filled the gloomy interior of the Cadillac with soothing light.

"*I'm heading out to the highway,*" I sang like someone happy with not a care in the world. "*I've got nothing to lose at all, gonna do it my way, take a chance before I fall...a chance before I fallllllllll....*"

I wouldn't say I had a great singing voice. The old pipes were far from angelic sounding. More crow-like if I'm honest, but I didn't care. Just singing was enough to lift my mood and bolster my resolve to get on with things. I turned the volume up on the song as I headed towards nearby Main Street, ignoring the looks I was getting from expensive suited pedestrians as I sang at the top of my voice with the window down.

"*Making a curve or taking the strain...On the decline, or out on the wain...Oh everybody breaks down sooner or later....We'll put it to rights, we'll square up and mend...Back on your feet to take the next bend...You weather every storm that's coming atcha!"*

When I stopped at a red light, I started banging my hands furiously on the steering wheel as the music continued to play, the sound of screaming guitars and my strangled vocals as I sang the last chorus attracting much attention from passersby and the cars parked beside me, including the disapproving eyes of a woman in the next lane as she stared across from inside her BMW. As the song finished, I banged out the last few beats on the steering wheel and turned to look at the woman who sat next to me. *"Fuck yeah!"* I shouted as I gave her the finger.

The woman in the BMW visibly flinched at my actions and quickly turned away, causing me to burst into laughter. I don't normally go around offending random strangers, but it felt good to do so right then, even if it also felt like I was slightly losing my shit. But hey, nothing new there, right?

I drove into Main Street and then pulled up outside a shop that sold phones. As I had destroyed my last smart phone, all I had on me was a burner phone I had lying around, which as far as phones went, didn't really cut the mustard. That's the thing about upgrading to a smartphone. Once you do, you can't go back to anything else. A bit like magic really. Every upgrade in power and ability became the new norm, and the thought of downgrading in any way felt like anathema.

In the shop, I paid a ridiculous amount of money for the latest iPhone and walked out of there feeling like a tech junky who'd just got his fix. It shames me to say that I actually felt better about myself knowing I had the latest iPhone in my pocket.

I didn't go straight back to the car afterward. Instead, I walked up the street until I found a cafe where I could sit outside in the still bright sunshine while I drank a large cappuccino. Given that I was in the Highlands, I got a lot of looks from people because of my appearance. This was Yuppie Town (do people still use the word yuppie?), and when you looked like a scruffy git in a dark green trench coat that had seen better days, you tended to attract a lot of attention from the clean cut brigade whose territory I was on.

I ignored the looks, however, and I sat in relative contentment drinking my coffee while watching the world go by around me. My eyebrows raised at a bus that drove by, mainly because there was a huge poster image on the side with the face of none other than Angela Crow, smiling like butter wouldn't melt. In giant letters beside her undoubtedly captivating face was the words: ANGELA CROW FOR MAYOR...BECAUSE YOU DESERVE BETTER.

Laughter erupted from me. "Jesus Christ," I said shaking my head. I had to give it to the Crimson Crow. She had balls. Huge fucking balls. If only her prospective voters knew about the sharp fangs concealed behind that charming smile of hers. I couldn't believe she was actually running for mayor of this town. She already ran the place behind the scenes. What was the was the point in her going public as well?

*Who cares?* I thought as the bus disappeared around a corner. My interest in politicians in general and Angela Crow, in particular, ran about as deep as my interest in collecting dried mounds of shit and glazing them for display in my home. They were all just self-serving bloodsuckers as far as I was concerned. Besides, it was my fault the Crow was able to run for Mayor at all. I gave her the power to daywalk after all.

I had a more pressing matter at hand anyway. What was I going to do to impress the SciCane leadership so I could get a meeting with them? Whatever I did, it had to be more than a parlor trick, but not as far as irrevocably turning people into cows, or causing a riot in the middle of town. I had no wish to hurt anyone just to gain entry into the group, even though Brentwood had implied it would be okay by him if I did cause a few casualties. Brentwood might have been fine with collateral damage, but I wasn't.

At the same time, it could be hard to predict how these things went, especially when magic was a big part of the equation. I decided further research into the group was called for, which meant going back to the Sanctum and reading through the SciCane website. And if I was going to infiltrate the group, I had to see what sort of psychology drove it if I was going to make myself a good fit for it.

Leaving the cafe, I walked back to the Cadillac. The second I got inside, my new phone rang in my pocket. Frowning as I pulled the phone out, I wondered how the hell anyone would have my number since I just bought the damn phone, but then I remembered that I kept my old number to save any hassle. I didn't recognize the number flashing up on the gleaming new screen. "Hello?" I said upon answering.

"Hello, Creed." It was a gruff male voice, and it took me a moment to recognize it.

"Big Joe. I don't remember giving you my number."

"You're not the only one who knows how to find people," Big Joe said.

"Well, you got me. What is it?"

"What is it? My cousin, remember? The one who was hexed? You said you would help him."

I shook my head, having forgotten about that. "Now's not really a good time--"

"Don't," Big Joe said. "Don't you fucking try and get out of this. We had a deal, Creed. I give you the flash drive in return for you helping my cousin."

"I have a more important matter to take care of," I said, knowing full well the werewolf wasn't going to take no for an answer.

"No, you don't, Creed. My cousin's house collapsed on top of him yesterday. This thing is getting worse."

"So lock him up in a rubber room or something."

"And then what? Just fucking leave him there until you can get to him? Fuck you, Creed. You do as you promised or I'll bring a world of hurt down on your head. You have no idea of the pain I could cause you."

"Your pack tried that the last time we met," I said. "It didn't go so well if I remember right."

A low growling noise issued from the phone. "You do this," Big Joe growled. "Or you're a dead a man, Creed. It's your choice."

Sighing, I shook my head. The last thing I wanted to do was try and unhex a werewolf who fully deserved to be hexed in the first place. Big Joe's cousin was a woman beater after all. So what if the hex killed him? It would be no great loss to the world. But, I didn't need the hassle of being hunted by a pack of werewolves either. My full focus had to be on getting into SciCane and taking it down. "Christ, all right," I said gripping the steering wheel tight with my free hand. "But you should know, undoing a hex like the one your cousin is under is difficult and not without its risks. He mightn't be the same man afterward."

"What do you mean he mightn't be the same man?"

"I mean a hex is like a disease, and when you cut it out you sometimes have to cut out other parts too."

"Parts? What fucking parts? Are you bullshitting me, Creed?"

"No, I'm not fucking bullshitting you," I snapped. "Your cousin is riddled with dark magic. You didn't really think he was going to escape from it unscarred, did you?"

Big Joe sighed impatiently. "Fine, Creed. You just do what you have to do. I don't think Ace is going to make it through another day if you don't."

"Bring Ace to my Sanctum. I'll work on him there."

"Where's that?"

I smiled as I started the engine. "You said you were good at finding people, so find me." Hanging up the phone, I chucked it on the passenger seat and drove off.

3

## ANARCHY IN THE USA

*W*hen I got back to the Sanctum, I found Blaze in the living room. The Garra Wolf was sitting on the wood floor staring at a single white feather that was on top of the red rug. Blaze's yellow eyes had a hint of sadness in them, I noticed. Frowning, I crouched down and picked up the feather. "So Barney has left us, huh, buddy?" I said staring at the feather. I had left one of the bedroom windows open upstairs just in case Barney the barn owl--Margot Celeste's familiar--wanted out for a flight. Going by the vibes I was getting off Blaze, and the conspicuous presence of the single white feather, I knew straight away that Barney had gone. Probably back to the woods where he had lived with Margot. A brown-stone building in the middle of the city was no place for a barn owl.

I should have known the owl wouldn't be staying after getting back from the Underworld. Barney was undoubtedly more cut up about Margot's death than I was. They were soul mates, after all. I closed my eyes for a second as the memories of the Underworld flooded back into my mind: Baal and his unholy domain; Margot sacrificing herself to save us all; Leona and I almost dying when the world collapsed in on itself. I hadn't had a restful sleep since, plagued as my dreams were by nightmarish scenes that were always accompanied by crippling anxiety, ice cold fear, and unbearable guilt. Sometimes I thought it was a bad thing that magic prolonged the life of its practitioners. What scars would I have fifty years from now? A hundred years from now? What state would my mind be in? Would I eventually break under the strain of having to deal with too much pain and death and suffering?

I opened my eyes when I felt Blaze standing in front of me, his big head level with mine. Ruffling his fur with one hand, I put my head next to his and squeezed for a moment, then I smoothed my hand over his head. "Looks like it's just us again, buddy," I said.

Blaze made a noise in the back of his throat to signal his agreement.

Despite getting off to a shaky start, I had grown to like Barney. The only upside to his absence was the fact that the owl had left the feather behind, knowing I could use it to contact him whenever I needed to. I just had to use some magic on the feather, and I would get an instant psychic connection with Barney, kind of like a feathered phone. It was good to know Barney would miss us as well.

"You hungry, Blaze?" I asked him as I carefully placed the feather inside my trench coat. Something told me I would need to call upon Barney and his unique skills at some point in the future. "Let me get you some steak."

Blaze seemed to perk up at the mention of steak, and he followed behind me into the kitchen, practically gluing himself to my leg as I fetched the steak from the fridge and placed it on a plate for him. "Enjoy big fella," I said, ruffling the fur on his head quickly before heading back into the living room and through the secret door that led into the Room of Operations.

Once inside the Op Room, I sat down at the big rectangular table and opened up the MacBook, logging into the dark web via the Tor browser and typing in the address of the SciCane website which I had memorized at Division HQ earlier. There was a bottle of whiskey on the table as well, and I managed to locate a cleanish glass from under a stack of papers, which I then filled with the whiskey. After taking two large gulps of the stuff, I turned my full attention to the SciCane website.

There was nothing at all flashy about the site. In fact, it looked like a relic from the early nineties. Just a very basic forum format with an article base and a separate section entitled Freedom Files. I decided to click on the article base first, knowing I would find something there about the SciCane philosophy and their manifesto if they had one. And indeed, when I clicked on the link, a whole list of articles popped up on the screen, articles with titles such as the following:

THE SLEEPING TIGER MUST BE AWAKENED
*The People Demand Self-Autonomy*
*Anarchy In The USA*
*magic Is For The Many, Not The Few*
*You Are Not Alone*
*The Universe Awaits You*
*magic Is Science And Science Will Save You*
*The Blood Of The Privileged Will Paint The Streets Red*

I STOPPED READING AFTER THAT LAST TITLE AS I WONDERED WHO EXACTLY THE group classed as privileged. Were they referring to those in power—to those who governed society—or to those who had access to magic? wizards such as myself? Clicking on the article link, I decided to find out as I read the opening paragraphs.

THE RULING ELITE OF THIS WORLD CAN BE BROKEN DOWN INTO TWO SEPARATE *classes: The Non-magical Elite who control things publicly (politicians, corporations) and the magical Elite who control everything behind the scenes, ruling from the shadows (supernatural beings, magical practitioners). Both classes are despicable in their puppeteering ways, controlling, using, and abusing the "Great Unwashed" as they see fit to suit their own nefarious ends. They hide knowledge and truths that rightfully belong to the common man, using it to store up power for themselves, all the while keeping the people below in forced ignorance, corrupting the minds of the people with unattainable desires and unceasing distraction, all to keep the truth from said people. And what is the truth? That there is more to the world than they know. That there is magic in the world and it is theirs--the peoples--by right. The universe is far greater and more breathtakingly magical than people know. It is one of the prime directives of SciCane to open the eyes of the people and awaken them to their true nature, and to the true nature of the world. Once awakened, The Sleeping Tiger will be asleep no more, and the Ruling Elite will be so overwhelmed and so hopelessly outnumbered that they will have no choice but to stand down or have their rarified blood all over the new Streets of Freedom.*

Puffing my cheeks out, I shook my head at what I just read. The online handle of the writer was Crowely666, and I shook my head at that as well. Either the writer was a deluded fanatic, or they were being ironic when they invoked the name of a man who had less to do with real magic and more to do with wanton decadence and the indulging of base desires, all the while reveling in the infamy the ignorant public created around him. Needless to say, I'm not a big Crowley fan. No self-respecting magicslinger is. Whether the writer was being ironic or not, it didn't matter. Neither case made the writer or SciCane any less dangerous.

Going through the other articles, I saw that most of them were written by Crowley666. Every article contained the same anarchist viewpoints, calling for full disclosure of information, and complete self-governance. In the forum section of the site, the call to revolution was espoused a lot by the site members, of which there appeared to be thousands. It was frightening how many members the site had. I had initially thought the group was a localized collective followed by a few dozen fanatics, but reading through the posts, it appeared SciCane had followers from all over the world. And every single follower shared the same philosophy as Crowely666, who I assumed was the leader of SciCane, or at the very least, one of the higher ups. I still had no idea of the group's structure or how they organized themselves. Was the group built on a standard hierarchal system? If so, that would go completely against everything the group seemed to stand for. If they really believed in self-governance, then no one would be in charge, and every member would have the same equal status.

But I very much doubted that was the case. Perhaps on the surface, the people involved saw themselves as being equal. I had no doubt, however, that just a few at the top ran the whole thing, despite the political philosophy espoused on the website. Cults like SciCane (and I didn't doubt that it was just a cult after everything) always had a leader, no matter the philosophy of the cult itself. And if that was the case with SciCane, then didn't that alone prove the infallibility of the whole self-governance thing, when certain individuals still needed to be on top and in a position of power over others?

I shook my head and sat back in my seat as I drank more whiskey. These fucking cults were always rife with hypocrisy, and they almost always were an exercise in ego by whoever led them. Obviously, SciCane was no different. Crowely666, whoever they were, was clearly in charge of everything. If and when I ever met this person, I fully expected to meet a narcissistic megalomaniac who enjoyed using other people to get what they wanted. Though despite the rock star behavior, these people were always dangerous in their own way and had no problem asking their followers to do anything, however horrible or insane.

"Yep," I said to myself with a half smile. "This one's going to be fun all right."

Of course, I still needed to earn the good grace of Crowley666, and to do that I had to record some stupid video audition, something which caused me to shake my head again. I didn't like being put through hoops and made to feel like I was applying for some damn reality TV show with a ridiculously pompous name like The SciCane Protocol, or even worse, a sitcom with a name like Anarchists Next Door or some shit. On the other hand, I understood the need for secrecy and security. What SciCane was proposing—what they were doing—was probably the most dangerous thing any organization could do, which was to try and start a revolution and turn the people against their oppressors. The state, and its well-worn jack boots didn't much like those who did things like that. Which is why the state had their top people on it...or rather person. Me. A burnt out wizard with no love for either side, a man who killed his own father (in saving the world or not, I still did it). A man who cheated on the one person he loved more than any other, the person who willingly put up with his shit the most, the person who had now left him behind like unwanted garbage.

The whiskey glass was refilled as self-loathing and anger ate at my insides like a slow munching worm in my guts. A feeling I was becoming all too accustomed to these days. *Fear And Self Loathing In Blackham City*, starring August Creed. Come and see the show, why don't you? I hear it's a fucking blast.

A loud knock on the front door jarred me from my reverie. "Well," I said, putting my glass down on the table. "I wonder who that could be."

Of course, I knew full well who it was before I even opened the door.

Big Joe was standing there with whom I assumed was his cousin, who was looking a little worse for wear. Blood was streaming down his face actually as if his skull had just been split open. "Creed, you fucking son of a bitch," Big Joe said as he forced his way with his injured cousin into the Sanctum. "In the time it took us to find this fucking place, Ace here has had no less than three disasters befall him."

"Impressive," I said, thinking to myself that Ace fucked with the wrong witch. And you know me. I love a bit of witch.

"Fuck you," Ace spat at me, his words about as charming as he looked. He didn't seem like no womanizer to me. The dude looked like a fucking caveman, to be honest. He was all hair and sinew. What the hell did all these women see in the guy? I couldn't help but wonder to myself as I took in the long beard matted with blood and the thick dark hair stuck to his swarthy face with blood also. Perhaps it was just those werewolf pheromones. It was the only reasonable explanation. I mean, I'm no looker folks (well, just a bit), but this guy? He looked like he belonged in a cave in some forested mountain region somewhere as he survived on freshly killed deer and rabbits, mating with whatever wolf came his way, or any other female creature unfortunate enough to cross his path. "A fucking bowling ball just fell out of the sky and split my skull open."

"A bowling ball," I said, trying to sound like I cared, but probably still sounding as amused as I truly felt. "Looks like it was a strike then."

Ace growled and suddenly went for me like a rabid dog, his eyes now yellow, his fangs bared. But just as he did, Blaze came crashing down the hallway and got between us. Blaze's heckles were up, his massive teeth on display as he snarled at Ace. The werewolf stopped in shock as he stared at the Garra Wolf before him, then seemed to back off almost reverently as if Blaze was some highly thought of Wolf God.

"You have a Garra Wolf?" Big Joe said in amazement, his eyes filled with the same reverence as his cousin's.

"Yes," I said. "And he'll rip you two apart if I tell him too."

Ace raised his hands slowly in front of him. "I apologize," he said, not to me, but to Blaze.

In response, Blaze snapped his jaws at the werewolf. Safe to say, Blaze liked bullies about as much as I did, and given Blaze's upbringing under a sadistic slave trader, that was totally understandable. "Are you two mutts going to behave now?" I asked, weary of them already, and resenting them both for interrupting me while I was working on a case.

"Sure," Big Joe said, clearly disliking the fact that a Garra Wolf was defending me, a creature he would no doubt have seen as his own kind. "Let's just get this thing done so we can all pretend we never even knew each other."

"Big Joe, that's about the smartest thing you've ever said to me," I said. "Follow me."

# 4

---

## CREED AND THE BIG BAD WOLF

*I* took them both down to the basement because that's where most of my spell ingredients were kept. I still wasn't sure what it would take to reverse Ace's hex so I would rather have things at easy reach if I needed them. Blaze followed into the basement as he kept a wary eye on the two werewolves. At any sign of trouble, Blaze would attack without hesitation. I'm not saying Blaze would have found it easy to take down two werewolves at once, especially one Big Joe's size. No doubt the pack leader was an impressive sight when he fully shifted into his wolf form. But Blaze was also a fire elemental, which meant he could burn both werewolves to a crisp if he so desired. I hoped that didn't happen, however, because I didn't want the smell of charred werewolf permeating the Sanctum for God knows how long. Although to be honest, the smell would likely have been no worse than some the offensive odors that had been unleashed in the Sanctum over the years.

"This your little geek den, Creed?" Big Joe asked, thinking he was funny no doubt. "This where you make all your little potions and concoct your fancy spells?"

"Something like that," I said as I cleared the table in the center of the room, removing everything that was on it and placing it all on the floor. "Get up onto the table." I looked at Ace as I said it, noticing how unsure he seemed about the whole situation. He trusted me even less than Big Joe did, which was saying something. But there was no denying the hairy bastard was in a bind, and he, therefore, had no choice but to do as I said. He climbed onto the table and sat on the edge like a really big and really hairy kid about to see the school nurse. Or wizard in this case.

"What are you gonna do to me?" Ace asked.

"Really?" I said. "After everything that's happened to you since being hexed and you're worrying what I'm going to do to you." I chuckled and shook my head. "That's funny."

"Screw you," Ace said. "Just do what you have to do and get rid of this fucking curse so I can get back to my life.

"And what life is that?" I felt like saying. "Drinking and beating up women who couldn't bare to look at you once they realized the mistake they had made?" I said nothing, however, as I went to a shelf on the wall and plucked a small bottle of bright blue liquid from amongst a collection of others.

"What's that?" Big Joe asked as I held the bottle out for Ace to take.

"A precautionary measure, that's all," I explained. "A potion to repress his inner wolf. Things might get a little strained as I try to reverse the hex. I don't want Ace here wolfing out and attacking me."

"Fuck that," Ace said dismissing the potion I held out. "I ain't drinking that shit."

I looked at Big Joe. "Can you please explain to your cousin that if he wants my help, then he's going to have to do as I say. Otherwise, just forget it."

Big Joe nodded and then looked at Ace. "Do as he says."

It was not a request, but a command and Ace knew it. Shaking his head, he held his hand out for the potion bottle. "This shit better be temporary."

"It is," I said. "You'll be free to shift in a few hours again."

Ace grabbed the potion from me, uncorked the bottle and quickly downed the blue liquid inside, grimacing at the acrid taste. He would have grimaced a lot more if I had told him exactly what was in the potion.

"All right, Creed," Big Joe said after glancing at Blaze, who stood just behind the werewolf leader, his head low as if ready to pounce at any second. "Work whatever magic you're going to work so we can get the hell out of this rank-smelling geek den."

I shook my head at him. "If I knew you were coming I would have hung some Magic Trees." I turned away and went back to the shelf, trying to decide the best approach to reversing Ace's hex. Reversing a hex wasn't an exact science. Like everything supernatural related, there were too many variables to fully control an eventual outcome. The best you could do was keep trying things until something worked.

"How will I know if what you're going to do has worked or not?" Ace asked as if reading my thoughts.

"Nothing will fall on you when you step outside," I replied as I sorted through various jars and bottles.

"Funny," Ace growled.

I gave him a sarcastic smile as I came back to the table carrying four different glass bottles containing potions of various colors. "A hex is like a tumor," I said. "Once I get a look inside you, I should be able to find where it is. That's also how I'll know if its gone or not after we've finished."

"A tumor," Ace said disgustedly. "That fucking bitch. I swear, I'm going to hunt her down the second we're done here."

I stopped for a second as I tried to contain the anger that suddenly rose in me. "Maybe you shouldn't get so rough with these women, and they wouldn't do shit like this to you."

"Mind your own fucking business, wizard," Ace snarled, his ice blue eyes staring hard at me. From a few feet away, Blaze growled. Ace glanced at the Garra

Wolf and then back at me. "I'm just saying, what I do or don't do isn't your concern. You owe Big Joe. You don't have a choice here."

That's where he was wrong. I did have a choice. I could choose to prevent Ace from hurting any more women. I could choose to make it my fucking moral duty to do so. "Down the hatch," I said, handing him another bottle, this one filled with a murky red liquid that had the texture of sour milk, and a smell that was just as bad.

Ace recoiled when he smelled the potion. So did Big Joe, their heightened sense of smell under assault. "Jesus Christ," Ace said. "What the fuck is in this stuff?"

"You really want to know?" I asked him.

He stared at me a moment then shook his head. "Fuck it, I don't want to know." He stared at the small bottle in his huge hand for a moment, his face that of someone who was about to drink their own cum. "Shit."

I took some pleasure in watching Ace drink the potion. As expected, he gagged and almost brought the murky red liquid back up again. "Hold it in," I said.

Ace continued to gag. "Easy...for you...to say."

Yes, it was, and I didn't give a shit.

"What's that going to do to him?" Big Joe asked.

"Allow me to see where in his body the hex is," I said. "It will highlight the dark magic in him."

Strictly speaking, it was the opposite way about. The potion would make it possible for me to see Ace in a different light spectrum. Sort of like an x-ray, but much more detailed. Ignoring Ace's groans of complaint, I closed my eyes for a moment and silently repeated the words to a spell that would change my vision to a different light spectrum, helped by the potion that would have spread throughout the werewolf's body by now. When I opened my eyes again and looked at Ace, it was like the werewolf had transformed into a being of pure light. His essential form was now an interconnected network of illuminated nerves and glowing sinew. It was like he had shed his outer shell to reveal the real being underneath. In most cases, this was a beautiful site to behold. The inner form would glow with iridescent colors—hues of yellow, orange, red and blue as if each strand of nerve and sinew contained strings of LED lights inside. If you are familiar with the work of the visionary artist (and wizard, though not many know that), Alex Grey, then you will have some idea of what I am talking about. Generally speaking, the purer a person was, the more beautiful and iridescent they would seem when their outer shell had been stripped away.

But in the case of Ace the woman beating werewolf, his inner form didn't come across as quite so beautiful. The innate darkness in him all but muted the colors of his inner form, turning vibrant reds to muddy browns and warm yellows to shades of muted green and even gray. Where I should have been staring at something akin to a vibrant oil or acrylic painting, I was instead looking at an image that could have been done in charcoal with just the smallest hints of color underneath. It occurred to me then that Ace as a person was much worse than I thought. I doubted anyone but Ace knew just how dark and twisted he really was. There were tones in him that could only have been the result of heinous and unspeakable acts on his part.

"You see it or what?" Ace asked me, referring to the dark magic inside him.

"I see it," I said. "Very clearly."

I did, in fact, see the source of the hex within him. Rather fittingly, it was located in his groin. A dark mass about the size of an orange that seemed to pulsate and send out dark signals around Ace's body, pushing out tendrils of darkness into the air so they could attract the disastrous luck that had been afflicting him.

"Can you get it out?" Big Joe asked, sounding concerned for his cousin. I wondered then if Big Joe knew just how deep the darkness went in Ace. I also wondered how much darkness I would find in Big Joe if I revealed his inner form. Probably not as much as Ace, but still enough no doubt.

"Yes," I said. "This is going to hurt."

*Oh, it's going to hurt all right. For the rest of your fucking life, Ace.*

"Just do it," Ace said. "Get it out of me."

"Lie flat on the table," I ordered. Ace lay back on the table, and I positioned my hands over his groin, above the source of the hex. I looked up at Big Joe. "Hold him down, please."

Big Joe came over and placed his massive hands on Ace's shoulders. "Hang in there, cousin," he said. "You're about to be free of this thing finally. Ain't that right, Creed?"

"That's right," I said, beginning to set my magical hooks into the dark mass embedded in Ace's groin. Once I felt I had a good enough grip, I started to pull upwards, and when I did, Ace cried out like I was ripping out one of his kidneys. "Hold him!"

I pulled harder, the pulsing black mass stubbornly holding on as I tried to get it free from Ace's body. With every pull, Ace would scream like the pulling was also putting unbearable tension on his nerves as well. Not that I cared about the pain he was in. Maybe, if Ace had have been someone else, I would have taken my time and eased the hex out of him. But as it was Ace, I felt no obligation to save him from any pain. So I tugged harder as I ignored the screams, dragging the hex to the surface of Ace's body, and then finally ripping it free from him altogether.

"*Jesus fuck!*" Ace roared as the hex became detached from his nerve endings and got pulled through his sinew and skin until it ended up in my hands. A ball of darkness that was malleable like putty and as cold as a frozen orange in my hands.

"God, is that it?" Big Joe asked, seeming repulsed by the pulsating hex in my hand.

"Most of it," I said. "There's still some left in there. It went deep."

"Oh Christ, there's more?" Ace groaned. "How much more?"

"Enough," I said as I folded my hands around the hex, covering it completely before uttering a few words under my breath. When I opened my hands, the hex had turned to dark smoke which then dissipated into the air before vanishing completely.

"Disgusting," Big Joe said. "All magic is disgusting."

"But disgustingly helpful in this case, eh?" I said shaking my head.

Big Joe said nothing as he continued to press down on Ace's shoulders. "Just get the rest out of him."

"With pleasure," I said.

I positioned my hands back over Ace's groin, the source of his latent sexuality now completely visible since I had removed the hex that was covering it. The source of most people's sexuality was centered around the groin area. It tended to dictate the kind of sexual thoughts a person had, as well as controlling their sexual behavior. And again with most people, this wellspring of sexual energy was normally bright and iridescent. Healthy, you might say.

Ace's sexual energy, however, was not what you would call healthy. It was the same dark, muddy color as the rest of his inner being, though much darker at the center. About as dark as the hex I just removed from him, in fact. "Buckle up," I said. "I'm about to go in."

Just like I did with the hex, I set my magical hooks into the core of Ace's sexual energy and pulled. It came away with little effort. Certainly much easier than the hex. Ace howled as that dark mass of energy pulled free and into my hands. Instinctively, he would know he had irrevocably lost something, but he wouldn't know what. Not for a while, or not until I chose to tell him.

I closed my hands over the main source of Ace's dark, hurtful behavior and made it disappear in a puff of smoke just like the hex.

The wolf was now neutered.

Blaze made a noise and looked away like he knew what I had just done.

"Are we done now?" Big Joe asked.

I nodded as I stood back from the table. "We're done," I replied.

Ace sat up. "I'm finally free," he said. "I can't fucking believe it."

Big Joe smiled and patted Ace on the back. Then he looked at me. "I guess I should thank you, Creed," he said.

"Don't put yourself out," I said. "We're even now, that's all."

Big Joe nodded. "Fair enough."

Ace stood and frowned for a moment, then shook his head. "I feel weird," he said. "Like something is missing."

"There may be some side effects," I said casually as I began to put bottles back on the shelf.

"What fucking side effects?" Ace said, the aggression back in his voice now. "You didn't say anything about side effects."

"I said it wouldn't be easy to remove the hex, and that there might be complications," I retorted, then waited a moment to hit him with the good news. "Your sexual function may be affected."

Ace frowned, as did Big Joe. "What the fuck do you mean my sexual function may be affected?" Ace said. "Are you saying...that I won't be able to *fuck* anymore?"

He looked devastated. Big Joe also looked devastated for the guy. "It was your boner or your life."

They both glared at me, Big Joe's eyes yellow, his fangs showing. "Did you fuck us, Creed?" he snarled. "If you fucked us..."

Blaze growled, and I summoned a silver shard into the air before me and pointed it at Big Joe. "You remember this, don't you? Pure silver, just to remind you."

"I can't fuck anymore," Ace muttered to himself, feeling at his groin like he expected to feel some physical defect.

"You're lucky you even stayed alive this long," I said. "Count your blessings there, Ace."

Ace stood staring at me a moment like he was thinking of boning me by the throat, but then Big Joe put a hand on Ace's shoulder. "Come on, Ace," he said.

"Let's get out of here." His still yellow eyes lit on me then. He knew I had done something to his cousin. He just couldn't prove it. "I'll be seeing you, Creed."

A moment later, and I had escorted them both out of the Sanctum without saying another word. Then I slammed the front door and shook my head at Blaze, who was standing in the hallway staring at me. "You think I went too far?"

Blaze barked once, and I smiled at him. "I don't think so either," I said.

5

# GREAT BALLS OF FIRE

he next day, I went to Gadsden Park with a kid from my local neighborhood called Benjamin, though he preferred to be called Benji. Benji was fifteen and knew exactly what I did for a living. He knew I was a magicslinger and wanted desperately to be one himself. From the moment I met Benji two years ago after he came to the door of the Sanctum and breathlessly asked if he could be my apprentice, I knew I was never going to get rid of him. For better or worse, the kid wanted to be a magicslinger himself, and there was no talking him out of it, even after I explained what it would take to become one, and the endless pain it would cause him in the long run. So while I had no interest in taking on anyone as an apprentice full-time, I could see that Benji wasn't going to take no for an answer, so I offered to give him occasional lessons in the arcane arts, which usually took place at the Sanctum once a week or so. But because things had been so hectic of late, I hadn't taught Benji in over a month. Needless to say, the kid was excited when I called him and asked for his help, jumping at the chance to further his studies in magic.

"Today's lesson has nothing to do with magic," I told Benji when we got to the park after I drove us there in the Cadillac.

Benji, a skinny, slightly awkward kid with a mop of curly blond hair, looked disappointed as we walked towards Blackham City Zoo which was located at the west end of the park. "So what are we doing here?" Benji asked. "And why are you carrying a loudspeaker in your hand? And a placard of that woman? Who is she?"

I smiled, more at the thought of what I was about to do than at his question. "All will be revealed. Here." I took out my new iPhone and handed it to him. "I need you to video what's about to go down. Your job is to be cameraman today. Don't miss a thing, no matter what happens to me."

Benji frowned as he looked a little worried now. "What are you planning on doing?"

"Drawing as much attention to myself as possible hopefully."

"Why?"

"It's part of a longer game. I'll tell you all about it when it's over."

"Another case?" Benji asked, his voice tinged with excitement. He loved to hear about my past cases. For him, talking to me about magic and hearing me tell stories was akin to the excitement some kids his age get from reading a new comic book or watching a new blockbuster movie. Benji wasn't like other kids though. He was obsessed with books, which is how he stumbled across magic in the first place. He was also committed to studying and worked hard to master the small things that I had taught him so far. There was no doubt in my mind that the boy would end up like me. Not totally like me, obviously (God forbid). But he would surely bloom into a full-fledged wizard over time. He was also fascinated by detective work, which is why I'm saying he would end up like me, spending his days chasing leads and wielding magic for the greater good (that's what I tell myself anyway).

"It's a case, yeah," I said. "A pretty big one. You'll enjoy hearing about it if I make it through it alive."

"It's dangerous, huh?"

"Aren't they all? Anything to do with magic is dangerous. Have I taught you nothing?"

"You said magic is dangerous in the wrong hands."

"It's dangerous all the time. Never kid yourself that you control the magic. It controls you. Makes you its slave. It's not a very equal relationship."

Benji nodded. "Is any relationship truly equal?"

I shook my head at him. "You're too wise for your own good sometimes."

Due to his obsession, he knew something of what I said already. But Benji could never walk away from magic. He wanted it too badly. I understood that about him. Still, I made it my duty to inform him of the dangers, so he wasn't going in blind.

A nice mid-morning flow of people was coming and going through the main gates of the zoo, with quite a number of others hanging around outside, sitting on benches eating snacks or walking their dogs around the large field opposite the zoo. *This should do nicely*, I thought as I looked around at the crowds of people. There seemed to be enough bodies around to cause a decent ruckus. No sign of any park cops, but they would turn up soon enough, once I got started. "all right, kid," I said to Benji as I stopped by a park bench just opposite the gates of the zoo. "Head over there and start filming as soon as I start."

"Start what?" Benji asked, slightly exasperated now at the fact that I still hadn't told him what was going on.

"Let's call this a lesson in manipulation and deceit." I stood up on the park bench, pleased to see that I was already getting queer looks from passersby. "Sometimes, kid, you have to make people believe that you're something you're not."

"Why? Isn't that one of the marks of a sociopath?"

I stared down at him. "Just go over there and start filming. And remember, keep the camera on, no matter what happens. You'll have to find your own way home as well. I don't think I'll be around to drive you."

Before Benji could ask any more questions, I raised the loudspeaker to my mouth, the placard I was carrying now resting on the bench beside me, facing out so everyone could see the photograph of the falsely smiling, platinum-haired Angela Crow. It was one of her election placards. The words VOTE CROW was written across the bottom. "Ladies and gentlemen," I said in my most theatrical sounding voice, happy with how well and how far my voice seemed to be carrying. Even the people inside the zoo would be able to hear me. "Good people of Black- ham, I am here today to talk to you about a great deceit—a great *evil*—that is being visited upon you. There is a conspiracy in this town, ladies and gentlemen. An underground network that has existed since this great city was built."

"Fuck off," some man shouted as he was passing by. "No one cares."

"Another fucking nutjob with a loudspeaker," someone else shouted. "Piss off!"

I'll admit, the assault on my ego almost made me get down off the bench right then and go home. But I was doing this for a reason, a very good reason, and so I took the hits and carried on. "Evil runs this town from the shadows," I proclaimed. "The people you think are in charge are not in charge at all. Other's pull the strings in this town, and this woman here." I pointed down at the placard with Angela Crow's face on it. "This is the woman who really runs this town, folks, and I'm here to tell you right now that she is not as she seems. This woman is not who you think she is."

"Who is she then?" a woman's voice shouted out from the small crowd that had now gathered around me. It seems that no matter how mad you were, you could always guarantee a crowd if you stood high enough and shouted loud enough. Maybe someone should let Lady GaGa know that.

"Who is she?" I bellowed back, impressed by my own over the top theatrics. Normally, I would rather cut my own toes off one by one as put myself in front of a crowd like this, but I had to say, I was rather enjoying it, and found the whole experience quite liberating. "I'll tell you who she is." I reached down and grabbed the placard, holding it up so everyone could see Angela Crow's pale but strikingly beautiful face. "This woman here is a bloodsucker, ladies and gentlemen. That's what she is."

"She's a politician," someone shouted. "They're all bloodsuckers."

"I know that," I replied. "But folks, I'm telling you this woman is *really* a blood- sucker. This woman—" I vigorously shook the placard as I paused for effect. "This woman is a *vampire*." I paused again as I let that sink into the crowd, most of whom shook their heads, some making tutting sounds, others walking away. "I'm deadly serious, folks. Vampires exist in this town. More than that, vampires *run* this town."

"He's right," an old guy said at the edge of the crowd, a bum by the looks of it, my little performance probably being the highlight of his day. "I've seen them."

"See," I said to the crowd. "That man knows. He knows."

The crowd didn't seem convinced. The bum wasn't exactly the most credible of sources. Several feet back from the crowd, Benji stood as he filmed everything on my iPhone, a slight look of confusion on his face as he probably wondered what the hell I was up to. But bless him, he played along, loyal little apprentice (sort of) that he was.

"You're crazy," someone shouted.

"No!" I shouted back, holding up the placard again. "This woman right here— this bloodsucking vampire—is crazy. You want to know the other name this woman—this vampire—goes by? The Crimson Crow. And you know why? Because she plucks out the eyes of her victims before she drains them dry, that's why. That's the kind of woman--the kind of vampire--you people are about to elect as Mayor of this great city. Do you really want a vampire in charge? Hell, who am I kidding? She's already in charge. She's ruled this city for over a century. And now she wants more. She wants to rule you from the light now, not just the shadows."

Many of the crowd began to disperse at that point, especially parents who had small kids with them, the parents throwing me angry looks for disturbing the little ones. If anyone were going to phone the cops on me, it would be one of them, the angry, protective parents. But it also seemed that many other people had become interested enough in what I had to say to fill up the gaps left by the ones who had moved on. They all may have thought I was crazy, but at least I was crazy in an interesting way. Even a crowd of goths came over when they heard me mention vampires. Then some smartass shouted out, "If Crow is a vampire, how can she be in the sunlight? Everyone knows vampires can't live in the sunlight."

"You've obviously never seen *True Blood*," a Southern-accented woman yelled out. "Vampires burn up in the sun."

"Not this one!" I responded. "The Crimson Crow is the only one of her kind that can walk in the sunlight without burning up into ashes."

"That's convenient!"

"For her, yes!" I said. "Now she can do things like run for Mayor of this town. Do you really want a vampire to be Mayor of this cherished town? Do you?"

"I think it would be kinda cool," some kid said.

"I don't care what she is," some other guy shouted. "I wouldn't kick her out of bed."

The crowd laughed at that one.

"Go on," I shouted, injecting some righteous anger into my voice now. "Laugh, all of you. We'll see how much you laugh when the Crimson Crow turns this city into a giant blood bank and drains you all dry."

"Screw you."

"That doesn't make sense. What would be the point?"

"You're deluded, buddy! Piss off and shout your brand of crazy somewhere else."

The crowd was getting annoyed now, which is what I wanted. Now for the closing act.

"And that's not all," I shouted louder over the boos and putdowns, at the same time, noticing the park cops driving towards the zoo, which meant I didn't have much time left. "There is magic in this town. Real magic. Magic so powerful you wouldn't believe it."

"And I suppose you're a fucking magician," a young man said.

"That's right," I said pointing at him. "I am!"

More of the crowd began to move away as they'd had enough of my crazy talk, despite the fact that every single word that I had said was true. It seemed people don't really know the truth even if it slaps them in the face.

*Time for the big finale.*

"I can prove it," I said, causing some people to turn back.

"Go on then, David Blaine."

I dropped the loudspeaker onto the bench I was standing on and conjured up a small fireball in my hand, something I was loath to do, but which had to be done.

Just about everybody gasped as I held out my hand, the fireball--about the size of a tennis ball--spinning slightly as it spat out small flames. "Is this magic enough for you?" I said.

Then I launched the fireball at a nearby litter bin, intending to finish with dramatic effect before the park cops came and arrested me. But there were so many Sleepwalkers in attendance that their collective ignorance threw the magic off completely. Instead of hitting the litter bin as planned, the fireball did an abrupt about turn and rocketed into the crowd, slamming into a man's back and exploding into flames on impact. People screamed as most of them ran away in a panic. The few who remained were frantically trying to douse the flames that covered the fallen man's back.

"Oh shit," I said, jumping down off the bench to go and put out the burning man before he got charred to a crisp. But as I jumped down, a voice stopped me.

"Stay where you are!" It was a park cop, his gun drawn and trained one me. I recognized him immediately from the last time I was in the park with Leona when we were there to sort out the kid vampire who was snacking on a golden retriever.

"That man is on fire," I said. "He needs my help."

"It's under control," the middle-aged and overweight park cop said. "Wait a minute. I know you. You were with that ballbuster from Homeland a while ago."

I nodded. "That's me. You going to arrest me?"

"You just set a guy on fire. Of course I'm going to fucking arrest you. Get down on the ground."

"No."

"What?" The cop looked confused.

"I'm not going anywhere until these people acknowledge the darkness that rules this city, that keeps them down," I shouted.

"What the fuck are you talking about?" the cop said. "Are you on drugs?"

"You're the fucking darkness!" someone shouted, and I looked over to see the man who had been hit by the fireball clambering to his feet, his jacket off and lying charred on the ground. Despite the man's anger towards me, I was relieved to see that he was okay. Mostly anyway.

"How right you are," I shouted back. "We are all the darkness! All of us! We're all doomed, doomed I tell you!"

"All right asshole," the cop shouted. "Get down now, or I swear I'll fucking shoot you. Do it!"

I think I'd done enough. I did as the cop said and got down on my knees. Over by the zoo gates, Benji was still filming, and I smiled over at him as the fat cop pushed me down to the ground and cuffed my hands behind my back. In response, Benji just shook his head like he was wondering what he got himself into in hooking up with me.

I couldn't blame the kid.

# 6

# DAYWALKER

$\mathcal{A}$fter getting myself arrested by the park cops, I was bundled into the back of their car (which smelled like fried onions and farts) and driven to the nearest precinct, which happened to be in Mint Ridge just around the corner from the Odeon Theater. The fat arresting officer escorted me inside the precinct building and left me at the reception desk, gleefully informing me before he left that I was probably looking at an attempted murder charge for setting a man on fire. I panicked slightly when I heard him say that, thinking that I was about to get swallowed up by the system and thrown in jail for the next twenty years or so. Then I shook my head at such a ridiculous notion. For a start, Brentwood would never let that happen. He'd have me out of that stinking police station in no time. I only did what he asked me to do after all. And even if I did end up in jail, how long do you think a jail cell could hold me, a practicing wizard with more tricks up his sleeve than Donald Trump?

At the sergeant's desk, the only thing I gave the cop was my name. Then I told him to call Brentwood at Homeland.

"You're not on our system," the desk sergeant said, a slightly built man in his fifties who looked like he couldn't wait to retire so he could spend the rest of his days fishing. "You're not on any system."

"No," I said. "Just call Brentwood. He'll sort this out."

The cop looked at me with tired blue eyes, clearly thinking I was some crazy person. It appeared he didn't believe me. A moment later, I was escorted to a holding cell by another uniformed cop and left there for nearly an hour before two serious-looking men in dark suits came into the station and asked for me. From the holding cell, I could see across to the front desk as the cop and the two suits stared over at me, and I gave them a little wave as if all this was just a big misunderstanding. Initially, I thought the two men were from Division, there to spring me from my jail cell. As it turned out, the two suits were indeed there to spring me, but they were not from Division. They were from a much worse organization.

The Crimson Crow's.

* * *

AFTER BEING BUNDLED INTO THE BACK OF A BLACK SUV, I WAS DRIVEN TO THE Highlands where the Crimson Crow lived in a heavily guarded and fortified building situated a few blocks away from Green Street and the stock market. I can't say I was too put out by the situation as I already knew Angela Crow would inevitably get wind of my little stunt in the park. And now that she was running for public office, I also knew she would be extra sensitive when it came to maintaining a squeaky clean reputation. As I was taken out of the SUV by the two suits and escorted into the huge stone building that was dubbed Crow Enterprises, I had visions of Angela Crow pacing around in her penthouse suite, fuming that I had seen fit to try and sully her reputation. And not only that but to publicly proclaim her a vampire and announce the existence of magic and a powerful shadow government...she was going to be so pissed.

The two suits stood either side of me in the elevator as we traveled up to the penthouse. It was a journey I'd taken only once before, a long time ago. At that time, I thought I was traveling up to meet my death at the hands of the Crow. As it turned out, we struck a deal, and I got to live. I doubt this time she was going to kill me over the stunt at the park. But it was the Crimson Crow. Who knew what she would do? She tended to place a lot of value on her precious reputation, and anyone who damaged that carefully maintained reputation had a habit of disappearing, never to be seen again. So I'd be lying if I said I wasn't nervous as I stood in that elevator sandwiched between two human members of Angela Crow's security team.

I swallowed as the elevator doors pinged open, and then made my way with the security detail down a long corridor that was lined with plush red carpet. At the end of the hallway was a thick wooden door. The entrance to the penthouse. One of the guards knocked on the door and waited. A few seconds later, the door appeared to open by itself as though there was no one on the other side. A little trick I knew the Crimson Crow liked to play to unnerve people before they entered the suite. I had to admit, it did work. As the guards told me to move inside, I felt like a defenseless animal entering the cave of a dangerous predator.

And make no mistake. The Crimson Crow was about as dangerous a predator as I've ever met. She was fucking apex all the way. Not only did she have the physical capacity, but she also had the necessary psychological makeup that allowed her to care for no one but herself. She may have been beautiful, but she was also cold, calculating and brutal in her ways. I'll never know what Uncle Ray saw in her. Come to think of it, I'll never what she saw in him either. There must have been strange magic at work there, I tell you.

"Angela?" I said as I walked into the suite, jumping slightly as the heavy wooden door suddenly slammed behind me. The lights in the suite were dimmed down low, so there was more darkness in the huge room than light. Shadows were cast everywhere like swathes of black velvet. It also didn't help that the windows in the suite were bricked up. Which surprised me, because I thought Angela Crow would have uncovered them when she became a Daywalker. Obviously, she still preferred the dark, probably drawn to it like a nocturnal animal.

I called her name out again, trying to sound like I wasn't afraid. "I can assure you that this whole thing is just a big mis--"

A hand with claws that dug painfully into my neck suddenly gripped me from out of nowhere, and before I knew it, I was being driven back through the air, only stopping when my back slammed into the wall. All the breath was forced out of me, and I went limp as my eyes gradually focused on the two burning red orbs in front of me, and the two impressively long and sharp as fuck fangs that seemed to stick out massively in the gloom. "Not another word," said a voice in pure menace.

The hand around my neck squeezed harder until I could no longer breath. Instinctively, I grabbed the hand as I tried to pull it away from my neck, but the grip was like a vice, the arm like steel. As wooziness began to set in, I tried to call upon my magic, but it was too late for that. I had no time to conjure anything useful. Besides that, my neck would be snapped once the vampire felt what I was doing. The only thing I could do was hold on and hope she didn't kill me.

And just as I was about to black out, the grip around my throat was released, and I fell to the floor like a crash test dummy, my lungs working overtime to replenish my oxygen-starved body again. I sat rubbing at my throat as Angela Crow stood over me like the world's scariest supermodel, dressed as she was in her favorite color of white in the form of a tight-fitting skirt and a jacket that didn't leave much to the imagination. Her platinum blond hair was scraped back and tied up on top of her head, and her lips were painted that deep crimson color she always favored. Her previously burning red eyes had now reverted to their normal cold blue. "Give me one good reason why I shouldn't rip you apart?" she said coldly.

I coughed and swallowed several times before I was able to speak. "Because," I finally replied. "You'd just be killing yourself, remember?"

Angela Crow snarled at me, her fangs still down. "It might be worth it just to get rid of you, Creed. I should have killed you years ago when I had the chance."

I shook my head as I stood up, very glad that I had had foresight years ago to install a magical bomb in the vampire's chest at the same time as I gave her the power to walk in the daylight. Or at least, that's what she thought. She had no way to prove it wasn't true. I'm not saying if it is or it isn't true. It doesn't matter anyway. She thinks it's true. That's all that matters. "Come on, Angela. Don't you think you might be overreacting here just a bit?"

She bared her fangs as she leaned in towards me. "You shouted from the roof tops that I was a fucking vampire!"

"Hardly from the rooftops. It was in the park. Not that many people heard. And anyway, no one believed a word I said. Have you any whiskey here? My throat is a little sore."

The vampire stared hard at me for a moment, then shook her head as she turned away, crossing the shagpile carpet (what is it with vampires and fucking shagpile?) and moving through the shadows towards a large drinks cabinet. "You better have a good reason for that stunt you pulled," she said as she poured two large whiskeys. "In case you haven't noticed, I'm running for mayor."

"I noticed," I said as I walked to the leather corner suite and sat down. "What's that about?"

Angela Crow brought the whiskeys over and handed one to me, which I gratefully received. She didn't bother to sit down, choosing instead to remain standing
as if she always had to maintain dominance. "This city needs me."

I tried to keep a straight face as I stared at her. "Really? How?"

Her lips pursed as she stared at me, and despite her animosity, I couldn't help
but marvel at the pale marble smoothness of her skin, and her exquisitely featured
face. Like all predators, the Crimson Crow was a thing of rare beauty. "Don't test
me, Creed. Just tell me what you were playing at in the park."

"I'm going undercover," I told her. "That little performance in the park was my
way in. Hopefully anyway. We'll see."

"Undercover? Where?"

There was no reason not to tell her. She was hardly one of them anyway. "A
subversive group called the Scientists of the Arcane. Or SciCane for short. Bunch
of nut jobs, but they have power."

Angela Crow tilted her head back as she peered down at me, her jawline
perfect. "I've heard of them. They are on my shitlist, in fact."

"You have a shitlist? That doesn't surprise me. Where am I on it?"

"Not at the bottom anyway."

I smiled. "Good to know."

She shook her head. "I've known about this group for a while. They were relatively harmless until recently. What's changed?"

"They got their hands on a book called the Dark Codex. I'm sure you know it."

"Of course. How in the hell did a bunch of silly subversives get their hands on
such a book?"

"I've no idea. But going by that recent energy blast, it's clear that they did. I've
also been told that they have created their own dimension, and have found a way
for people to enter the Astral Plane without leaving their body first."

"Impossible."

"You would have thought so, wouldn't you? But that's the power of the Dark
Codex. It unlocks secrets of the universe that shouldn't be unlocked."

Angela Crow shook her head and finally took a seat beside me. "This news
worries me."

"It should," I said. "These guys have the potential to do serious damage. They
could destroy everything. And I mean everything. The world. Maybe even the
universe itself. There's a reason that book was kept hidden for so long. It's just too
damn dangerous."

"Clearly," she said. "But you are going to stop the people and recover the book,
aren't you, Creed?"

I stared at her a moment. "You wouldn't be entertaining thoughts about
owning that book, would you, Angela?"

Her face remained impassive. "What do you take me for?"

*Best not to answer that*, I thought. At least not honestly. "Just as long as you
know, as soon as I locate the book, I'm destroying it. Which as an obsessive bibliophile like yourself, will hurt me more than words can say, but it has to be done.
Some knowledge should stay buried."

"At least for now," she said, a hint of a smile on her face.

"Spoken like a true immortal."

Her smile remained, as did mine. While there was certainly no love between

Angela Crow and myself, we did understand each other fairly well, something she seemed to appreciate, despite the fact that she would have happily killed me if she thought she would get away with it. "How's the whiskey?"

"Good, thanks. It's helping with my throat." I rubbed my throat as if to draw attention to it.

"You're a smartass, Creed. Always have been."

"It gets me through. What gets you through?"

"Blood. Money. Power. The usual."

I nodded. "You ever hear from Jennifer?" It was a dumb question, but it just slipped out. Jennifer is Angela Crow's daughter. I helped Jennifer escape her mother's clutches over twenty years ago. Jennifer now resides off-world in Babylon.

Angela Crow's eyes flashed red for a second. "Why would you ask me that?"

I held up a hand. "I'm sorry, it just slipped out in the conversation."

She stared hard at me for a long moment, as if deciding how she should proceed. Her next question surprised me though. "Have *you* heard from her?"

"Yes, actually," I said nodding. "She came through on a trans-dimensional link a few months ago."

"And what did she say? Did she mention me?" She was trying to appear uncaring, but I could see she felt more than that. She may have treated Jennifer like a piece of property once, but it would seem her daughter's long absence had somehow made itself felt in Angela Crow, perhaps in the form of a yearning for her only kin.

"She asked how you were. I told her I didn't see you that much. Not at all, in fact."

Angela Crow nodded, then a small sigh escaped her lips just before she drank some of her whiskey. Clearly, she missed her daughter. It was also true that Jennifer missed her mother, despite everything that had happened between them. As I knew full well, family ties were hard to break. Perhaps even impossible to break. "I haven't spoken to her in over twenty years. Not since she left me."

For once, I felt some sympathy for the Crow, even though I really shouldn't have. She only had herself to blame for her only daughter leaving her. The way she treated Jennifer was unforgivable, much like the way my father had treated me and my family was unforgivable. But who knows? If my father had of been still around and wasn't quite so evil and twisted as he was in the end, I may have been able to salvage a relationship with the man. Which would have been better than killing him as I did. "If it matters to you, I can tell you that Jennifer might be open to talking to you at some point. That's just my opinion, I have to stress. She hasn't actually said so."

Angela Crow's face seemed to soften after I said that. "You know, Creed," she said. "I'm not the monster you think I am." *Could have fooled me.* "I have good reasons for doing what I do." *Serial killers have good reasons for doing what they do as well.* "My kind are not human. Jennifer always refused to accept that fact."

"She just wanted to be someone different," I said, still somewhat cautiously in case I invited her rage again. "That's all."

"Did you want to be someone different, Creed?"

"I became someone different."

She smiled. "Of course you did."

A silence fell for a few moments as we both sat drinking our whiskey, her in deep thought, me hoping I could leave soon.

"I'd like to help you in taking down this SciCane group," she said, breaking the silence.

I was surprised to hear her say it. "What's in it for you?"

She rolled her eyes at me. "Can't I help protect my own city? I'm going to be mayor soon after all."

"Fair enough. Just as long as we're in agreement that I destroy the Dark Codex when I find it."

"Of course."

"Good," I said, though I still wasn't sure if she was working an angle, maybe to try and get her hands on the book. I knew better than to underestimate the Crimson Crow's lust for power. The Dark Codex would certainly be a big prize for her.

She stood up then. "I'll get all the information I can and pass it along."

"Thanks." I was still slightly weirded out by the fact that she was helping me, though I had no doubt as to her sincerity. I just couldn't help thinking that she was working an angle that would become clear at some point down the line. Despite my trepidation, however, I gladly accepted her help. With the almost infinite resources she had at her disposal, I was hoping she would prove to be a valuable asset in the case.

Angela Crow crossed the room at that point and turned up the lights. For the first time, I noticed there was a naked girl hanging from the ceiling with the rope around her wrists. The girl looked dead, though I couldn't be sure. "Now," Angela Crow said. "If you'll excuse me. It's lunch time."

I took a last look at the poor girl about to be drained dry by the Crimson Crow. "I'll leave you to it then," I said and left the room.

# 7

# KILLING TIME

"So was everything you said true?"

Benji called at the Sanctum after I phoned him and told him to come around with my iPhone, which contained the video footage he shot of me at the park. We were down in the basement, and I was replenishing the potions that I had used on Ace, who was probably finding his libido a bit flat these days. He'd be half the wolf he used to be by now, which didn't bother me in the slightest. "All true," I said to Benji as I mixed up ingredients in a small clay bowl.

"That woman is really a vampire?" Benji looked a little disturbed by this.

"There's a lot I haven't told you." Lifting the bowl, I poured the contents into a small glass bottle. "This city, and this world are not what you think." I was trying to ease Benji into the world of the supernatural. He was just a kid, and I didn't want to overload his brain with too much information in case it drove him insane, which was a real possibility.

"I already know the supernatural exists." He wrinkled his nose at the strong smell coming from the bottle I was pouring into. "I know there are monsters out there already."

"Yes, but we still have to get along with them," I said, corking the bottle and placing it on a shelf. "Most of the time anyway."

"So if that mayor woman is a vampire, why didn't she kill you for doing what you did?"

I couldn't help but smile. "Believe me, she wanted to."

"Why didn't she then?"

"I have my leverage. Plus, things aren't always so black and white, kid. The supernatural world is as gray as it gets. There are shades of gray you've never even seen before. That's what makes it all so complicated."

Benji thought for a second. "So how do you tell right from wrong then if everything is gray?"

I smiled at him, never failing to be impressed by his wise mind. "Good question, and one I wish I had the answer to." I shook my head at the notion of trying to see things in such cut and dried terms. "I guess you just have to go with your gut."

"Is that what you do?"

"Always. Doesn't always mean I'm right though."

"You still mess up a lot?"

My laughter was tinged with bitterness as my mind tried to flash memories of my fuckups over the years, but which I shut down immediately. "Oh yes, I fuck things up quite a bit. It's the human condition. I've come to accept that. Mostly anyway. It still hurts like fuck."

"What does?"

"The pain and consequences of making the wrong choice." I couldn't help thinking of Leona at that moment. "It never gets any easier."

Benji frowned to himself as he seemed to mull over my words. But it didn't matter how much he thought about it, he would never know the pain I spoke of until it stabbed him in the belly one day. He was still young and largely innocent, and not for the first time, I questioned whether I should be helping him steer towards a life of pain and sometimes impossible choices. Life as a Sleepwalker was challenging enough. Life as an awakened adept was damn near impossible sometimes. But who was I to stand in the way of anyone if that's the life they wanted? Benji had already made his choice. It was my duty now to make sure he didn't live to regret the choice he made, to fortify him against the worst that would inevitably be thrown at him. "So can you teach me something today?" he asked as if affirming his commitment to the path he was now on.

Despite my reservations, I was pleased by his enthusiasm and desire to learn. He reminded me of myself long ago. "Sure thing, kid," I said.

* * *

AFTER GLADLY GIVING BENJI THE MAGIC LESSON I'D PROMISED HIM AND sending him away with a bundle of books to read as homework, I went straight to the Op Room and plugged my iPhone into my Mac so I could watch the video footage of myself at the park. As soon as I saw myself on camera, I flinched at my appearance and at the shock of seeing myself on the video in the first place. For as long as I can remember, I've hated having my photo taken, or being filmed in any way. In my family home in Ireland, there exists a number of old home movies that my father shot over the years, and in most of them, I can be found hiding behind a book or walking out of the room, only to have my father insist that I reveal myself to the camera, which I would do, awkwardly, probably coming across like some kid who was being made to entertain a sexual predator. Not that my father was that way inclined, not that I knew anyway. Which was probably just as well, because his everyday abuse was bad enough. I didn't know what I would have done if he had sexually assaulted me and my brother and sister on top of everything else. *Christ, I'm messed up enough as it is*, I thought, forcing myself to turn my mind away from such dark, depressing thoughts.

The image of myself on screen was depressing enough. Jesus, I looked like a

494

fucking madman standing up on that park bench as I waved around the placard with Angela Crow's face on it, shouting that the woman was a vampire and that she would bleed everyone dry. It was no wonder the crowd assembled around me didn't believe a word I said. I wouldn't have believed it either.

I cringed again when I watched through squinted eyes myself launching the fireball that ultimately impacted the poor guy in the crowd. Then I burst out laughing when the park cops showed up, and the fat cop arrested me. "What a fucking pantomime," I said shaking my head. "If nothing else Crowley666 will laugh their ass off. Christ...the things I fucking do."

Logging into the dark web, I brought up the SciCane website and then uploaded the video to the site, leaving a comment underneath that said I would like to join the fight against tyranny and to make magic available to all. I also added that as a wizard and accomplished alchemist, I would be a valuable asset to the group.

Now all I had to do was wait.

* * *

Fuck waiting. It felt like all I did these days was wait around. Bad thoughts came when I sat around with nothing to do, which was usually followed by too much whiskey, which I was trying to cut back on for the sake of the case. So to stay on the move, I drove over to Division HQ and was granted access immediately this time. And since Brentwood had given me a security card, I didn't need any escorts once I went inside.

I took my time as I made my way down to the Central Operations Room as I wanted to get a better idea of the inner workings of the place. This was the first time I had unrestricted (mostly anyway) access to the place, so I was making the most of it. Division HQ was made up of three floors, the bottom floor being mostly a maximum security holding wing for whatever supernatural miscreants were brought in, of which I was one at one time. I still remembered how grim and clinical it was down there, with each prisoner being held in separate cells with reinforced glass windows. You couldn't help but feel like Hannibal Lecter as you stood in the small cell, with guards, doctors and lab techs walking by as if you weren't there at all. The interrogation rooms were also on that floor, which I was also familiar with.

The next floor up was a series of large rooms where Division agents trained in weapons and tactics. Leona used to say it was her favorite place in Division, and where she spent most of her time while she was there, either training or instructing others. The final floor was the one I was on now. It was mostly office space, and also were the Central Op Room was, which I was currently heading for. I noticed on this visit that the dirty looks were fewer in number, most people having accepted that the scruffy wizard guy was part of the team, at least for now.

When I walked into the Op Room, I found it to be almost empty. No sign of Brentwood or the gaggle of top brass that sat at the huge table on my last visit. Only a few tech people sat around the massive screen at the front of the room. And Bethany, who glanced over her shoulder at me and then quickly turned away again as if I was of no interest to her whatsoever. I didn't take her cold manner personally. Bethany was atypical as far as personality and behavior went. My kind of person, in other words.

"Where's the boss?" I asked Bethany as I came up behind her to find her watching the video I had uploaded to the SciCane website.

"This is my fifth viewing," she said in her blunt sort of way. "It's really hilarious."

I smiled, unsure of how to feel about that. "Thanks, I guess."

"Have you always been nuts?"

"What?" I snorted.

She glanced over her shoulder at me. "I like nuts."

Snorting again, I shook my head. "Okay..."

"Would you like to get a cup of coffee with me? We can go to the cafeteria. The coffee sucks, but there's nowhere else."

"This place has a cafeteria? Why didn't I know that?"

"What, you think we just order pizza?"

I shook my head at her bluntness. "Of course not."

She stood up and faced me without much direct eye contact. "So are you coming?"

I nodded. "Sure. We can discuss the comedic merits of my little video."

Her wide mouth shifted into a smile of sorts. "There aren't any."

"You said it was hilarious."

"Unintentionally only."

"Okay," I said nodding. "And that's bad obviously."

"Only for you, as you have to suffer the humiliation while everyone else laughs."

"Jesus." I shook my head. "I'll bet Brentwood loves you."

She frowned. "Why?"

"You're blunter than he is."

She shook her head as if she didn't understand. "I'm just being honest."

"I know." I smiled. "Come on. Let's get a coffee, and you can tell me all about how you ended up in this place."

Bethany nodded awkwardly and then led the way to the cafeteria, which turned out to be on the same floor, not too far from the Central Op Room. The cafeteria was empty except for one woman working the counter and a few Division personnel seated around the place who looked up briefly as Bethany and I walked in. Bethany ordered herself a chocolate muffin and a cappuccino. I got myself a sandwich because I hadn't eaten in a while and a pot of black coffee. I also paid for everything. "Thanks," Bethany said as we sat down at a formica table.

"No problem," I said before biting into my sandwich, which actually didn't taste too bad. It would do to fill the hole.

We sat in slightly awkward silence for a while as I devoured my sandwich and Bethany picked at her muffin, then she said, "Agent Lawson is your girlfriend, right?"

I stopped chewing for a second before putting the rest of the sandwich back on the plate, having lost my appetite. "She isn't Agent Lawson anymore," I said as I wiped my hands. "Well, she is, but not here."

"The FBI. I know."

"Did you know her?"

Bethany nodded as she continued to pull bits off her chocolate muffin. "Of course."

I waited, then asked, "Were you friends?" I didn't recall Leona ever mentioning anyone named Bethany, but then Leona was never in the habit of discussing work unless it involved me, or she needed help on a case. Division politics rarely if ever came up.

"Not really."

"You didn't like her?"

Bethany made a pained sort of face. "It's not like that. I just..." She trailed off as she stared intensely at her plate, then she glanced briefly at me and gave a tense smile. "I'm not good with people."

I smiled. "You're in good company then. Neither am I." Which wasn't exactly true. I was good at negotiating with people, but emotionally speaking, I got a little lost most of the time.

"No," she said shaking her head. "I mean I have this personality that..." She trailed off again as she shifted in her seat.

"Hey." My tone was casual. "No need to explain. I get it. Why don't you tell me instead how a smart girl like you ended up in a place like this."

She smiled, slightly more comfortable now, her huge green eyes like shimmering pools in her pale face. "I hacked the Division mainframe. It was go to jail or go to work here."

"Not much of a choice. You used to be a hacker?"

"I'm still a hacker."

"Why'd you hack Division?"

She stared down at her plate again. "My brother and I were walking home one night when we got attacked by a werewolf. My brother died."

"I'm sorry."

She shrugged, looked like she was going to cry for a moment, but held it together. "I didn't know it was a werewolf at the time. I just knew it wasn't an ordinary creature. So I did what I do best, I started digging until I found proof that werewolves existed. When I hacked this place, I got my proof and a whole lot more."

"But Brentwood nabbed you."

She nodded. "That was six months ago."

"You seem to be doing okay here. Brentwood seems to like you."

"I get the job done. That's all he cares about."

"Tell me about it."

"I read your record," she said as she sat back in her chair, seeming slightly more at ease now.

"My record?" I didn't know why I was so surprised that Division had a file on me, but I was.

"You've done a lot of shit."

I laughed. "You could say that."

"You seem cool, though."

I smiled. "Thanks. I'd say you're the coolest cat in this fucking place."

She looked embarrassed as she looked away. "It's not hard, is it?"

"Don't sell yourself short."

She dared to make eye contact with me, holding it for a long second, her wide eyes revealing much depth and intelligence, and of course pain. There is always pain.

Bethany seemed almost glad when her phone pinged. She took it out of her pocket and smiled as she looked at the screen. "We just got a hit from SciCane," she said, then smiled. "It seems your audition was successful."

# INVITATION TO MADNESS

*B*ack at the Sanctum after leaving Division HQ, I was about to prepare for my upcoming meeting with SciCane when I got a call I wasn't expecting. When I saw the caller ID, I stopped dead in the living room and stared at the phone for a long moment, unsure whether to even answer or not. Eventually, I did as I sat down. "Hey," I said into the phone, my voice reserved.

"Hey," Leona Lawson said back, her voice as restrained as mine was. Despite it only being a phone call, I could still feel the tension between us.

A brief silence ensued, though it felt longer. I hardly knew what to say to her. She had made her position very clear the last time we spoke, leaving me with the lasting impression that there wasn't much more to say on the matter. It's not that I didn't want to discuss things with her--I did--but I knew there'd be no point. "What's up?" I tried not to sound angry or bitter, even though I felt it.

"Nothing." She paused for a second. "I just needed to talk to someone."

"What about your new friends in DC?"

"Forget it. I shouldn't have called."

"Wait." I sat forward in my seat. "I didn't mean--"

"Yes, you did, Creed."

"You're right. I'm sorry. I just...don't like how things have ended up between us."

"And whose fault is that?"

*Who's the bitter one now?*

I said nothing.

Leona sighed. "I'm sorry," she said. "This isn't all your fault."

"Yes, it is," I said. "If I hadn't of...you know..." It pulled at my guts even to mention what I now thought of as the "dirty deed", which only made me hate myself even more because I didn't really believe the night I spent with Margot was dirty at all, at least not in the worst sense.

"You think this is all about you sleeping with that witch?"

"Well, yeah. I do. Mostly."

"I can live with what you did, Creed. I know you were pressured into it."

*Pressured? Be honest now, Creed. Were you pressured into sleeping with Margot? Could you have stopped her?*

*I'll take the fifth on that one.*

"It still shouldn't have happened," I said. "And I'm sorry."

"As I said, that's not why I'm in Washington. I just had to get away from Blackham and all the madness there."

"You've been through a lot, Leona. I can't even begin to imagine how you felt or what you went through in the Underworld."

"No, you can't."

Shit. That meant it was bad. Really bad. But what the hell did I expect anyway? That she sat down there having tea and biscuits and playing backgammon with Margot and Baal while she waited on me rescuing her?

"You should've stayed, Leona," I told her. "I could've helped you get through this. Division probably have people as well--"

"A bunch of shrinks? No thanks."

Can't say I blamed her there. "I still could have helped you deal."

"How?" she asked bluntly.

I was on the spot now. "Well, I..."

"You don't even know, do you? That's because you don't deal with anything, Creed. You just move onto the next case."

"It's not like you're any better. You just apply military grit to everything. You moved to Washington and a different job. How's that any different?"

"I'm not saying it is. But at least here, I don't have to deal with the supernatural bullshit as well."

"You could've just took a break for a while. You didn't have to run."

"I'm not running."

We both knew that wasn't true. "Whatever you're doing, it doesn't matter. I just know that I love you, Leona. And I know that you love me. I want us to be together. We were made for each other. Who else would put up with our shit?"

She laughed softly. "No one."

"Exactly." A wave of hope washed over me and it felt like a weight had been lifted off my chest.

Then she said, "That still doesn't change anything. I can't go back there, Creed, to that city, to the madness. I'm sorry."

I sank back into the chair, most of my hope now dashed. "Are you saying you never want to come back here?"

She didn't answer for a long time, and when she did, I wished she didn't. "Yes."

I thought about telling her I would move to Washington, but Blackham had been my home for the last thirty odd years. It was the only place in the world where I felt truly comfortable. My life is here. To make myself feel better and prevent an emotional freefall, I told myself that she would change her mind eventually, once things had settled down a bit and she had got her head on straight again. Whether or not she would, remained to be seen. "You just need some time, that's all," I said eventually, hating how weak and pathetic I felt.

Leona sighed. "You're wrong, Creed. My mind is made up."

I listened hard, trying to detect the faintest hint of doubt in her voice. I wasn't all that convinced. Leona could be stubborn about things, but she had been known to change her mind down the line.

*She did about me, didn't she?*

I thought about telling her that, but she would only say it wasn't the same thing, so I said nothing about it. "all right," I said. "Let's just leave it at that for the time being anyway. We can still talk though, right? About other stuff."

"Of course."

"Good. I'll call you then. You going to be all right?"

"Don't worry about me, Creed. I know you're working a case for Brentwood."

"I am."

"Then go do what you do best."

* * *

As I sat in the Op Room, I was happy to have retained some of the lightness of being that returned to me while I spoke with Leona. The phone call had made me realize how much I was missing her. Pushing aside my feelings like I always do only served to weigh me down, a feeling I always found myself getting used to all too quickly. Before you know it, dragging your feet through mud becomes your normal state of being, and life is hard enough without that.

So feeling like I could give most if not all of my attention to the SciCane case now, I opened the MacBook and logged into the SciCane site. I had already done this back at Division with Bethany, but I left no reply to the posted invitation then, preferring to do so at the Sanctum before committing to anything. The invitation came with a few conditions attached, some of which were expected, others were not.

The video I posted had managed to attract dozens of comments and reactions. Comments like, "*Yeah! Stick it to that bloodsucking bitch!!!*" and, "*Glad someone is standing up to that power mad vamp!!*" There were many other comments, most along the same lines, congratulating me for standing up against the "*tyranny of our oppressors*". One guy from Poland said he wished the man in the park had burned to death so his charred body could make a bigger statement. Someone else from Ireland of all places said I should have fireballed the entire crowd. That would have shown the bastards apparently. I shook my head as I read over the comments, most written by no more than keyboard wizards and wannabe anarchists who would probably shit their pants if they came into contact with a supernatural creature of any kind, never mind a vampire, never mind the fucking Crimson Crow herself.

In my forum inbox, Crowley666 had left me a message:

*Hello there Creed000. Thank you for posting that very entertaining video. We are impressed by your, albeit rather unfortunate, use of magic, as well as your commitment to your beliefs. You are the first person we have ever seen publicly speak out against the tyrant Crow. For that alone, you deserve entry into our family, but only if you can meet the following conditions:*

501

*1. You must meet us at a time and place of our choosing, which you will only be notified of a very short time in advance via this private message board.*

*2. You will come to the meeting alone. If we suspect anyone else is with you, things will end badly for both you and the people you are with. Please do us all a favor and bear this in mind before our meeting.*

*3. At our initial meeting, you must be prepared to be as open and as honest with us as possible. You must also be prepared for a very probing line of questioning. If for any reason we feel you are dishonest in your answers to our questions, or that you are lying about your motivations for being there, our response will be less than forgiving. If you are as smart as you no doubt think you are, you will know exactly what we mean by this.*

*4. You must also know that if you are accepted into the group that there will be no turning back for you. Once in, you cannot leave. The reasons for this are obvious, we would imagine, so no explanation is necessary. If you are not prepared to commit fully, don't show up at all.*

*If you are willing to adhere to these conditions, Creed000 then you need do nothing else but wait on our contacting you on here again. If not, reply to this message immediately, and we won't contact you again.*

*Good day to you, Creed000. We await your decision.*

*Crowley666*

I sat back in my chair and thought about what I'd just read. I still wasn't sure if whoever wrote the message had a flair for the dramatic, or whether they were deadly serious with their conditions. I guess I'd know soon enough when I met up with them.

Speaking of "them" it appeared that Crowley666 was not an individual, but a collective. Either that or someone just liked to use the royal we when they spoke, perhaps to make themselves sound more serious, as people online had a habit of doing. Whatever the case, nothing I'd read so far gave me any less cause for concern. The bottom line was that SciCane were up to serious shit, and had some serious firepower in their hands in the form of the Dark Codex, which at the end of the day, had the potential to be many times more powerful than the most destructive of bombs out there. That alone made SciCane a serious fucking threat, even if they did turn out to be a bunch of disorganized, deluded fools who reveled in the melodrama of being in a secret organization.

I'd had dealings with many cults over the years. Blackham was still full of them. Most of them were small and deceptively unthreatening, passing themselves off as outcasts or loonies who believed crazy shit and lived a crazy lifestyle. But the one thing they all had in common was their potential for causing great harm in the long run. Such harm wasn't always the physical kind like murder--though there was much potential for that as well. More often the harm came to the many lives ruined by the cult and their brainwashing ways. Hundreds, thousands of lives claimed through mental cruelty and abuse. Thousands of families torn apart in the process, their sons and daughters lost to the madness spread by the cult leaders.

SciCane was potentially worse than all of the Blackham cults put together. SciCane was taking power and putting it into the hands of those who couldn't handle it. It was bad enough they were preaching magic to Sleepwalkers, awakening those who probably shouldn't be awakened. It was worse that SciCane themselves were reaping information and knowledge from a source that was much too dangerous for anyone to handle. Period.

Did I say all cults have one thing in common? I meant they have two things in common, the last of which is this:

They all need taking down.

And the sooner, the better.

*A* few hours later, I got another private message from Crowley666:

HELLO, CREEDOOO. AS YOU NEVER RESPONDED TO OUR LAST MESSAGE, WE ARE NOW *assuming that you want to go ahead with our meeting. In that case, please proceed immediately to the park where you made your audition tape. Sit on the same bench you stood on. Someone will make contact once you do. Please make your way there now. We look forward to meeting you Creedooo.*

CROWLEY666

THE PARK? I THOUGHT AFTER READING THE MESSAGE. WERE THEY INTENDING to give me the run around first before making contact like out of some thriller movie? Was I to be shuffled around half the city before meeting anyone? I hoped not. I could understand their paranoia and need for secrecy, but a simple address would have done. What did they think I was going to do? Bring half the city's law enforcement with me?

"All right," I said as I stood up. "I'll play your little game, Crowley666."

I stood for a moment in the Op Room as I drained the last of the whiskey bottle and thought about what I should take with me to the meeting. No point in taking weapons, as whatever I had on me would likely be confiscated at the meeting. So my trusty six-shooter was out. I left the Killing Knife on the table as well, just in case I never saw it again if it became confiscated by SciCane. No point in bringing anything to the meeting but myself and my magic. That

BLOOD CULT (WIZARD'S CREED BOOK 3)

would have to suffice as far as protection went, but hopefully, I wouldn't need any.

Night had fallen as I stepped out of the Sanctum and headed for the Cadillac parked on the street. There was also a chill in the air, and I pulled the collar of my trench coat up, so it covered my neck.

When I hit the street, I suddenly saw a dark figure emerge from behind a black van. It was too dark to see the person's face, but I saw clearly enough that they were pointing something at me. Too late, I realized it was a gun. Before I could think about employing any defensive magic, I felt the impact of something hitting me in the chest, and I looked down to see a dart sticking in me.

Then the world went funny, and I fell into a black hole of oblivion.

\* \* \*

I AWOKE TO FIND MYSELF SITTING IN A CHAIR INSIDE A DARKENED ROOM. THE only light source was an annoyingly bright spotlight on the ceiling somewhere in front of me, the near-blinding beam of light shining right on me.

*What the fuck is this?* I thought, half panicked by the fact that I had no idea where I was, or how I ended up there.

Then I remembered getting ambushed outside the Sanctum. Instinctively, I put a hand on my chest where the tranq dart had hit me. So much for being given the runaround. Obviously, when Crowley666 told me to go to the park, it was only to get me to leave the Sanctum. Abduction had been their plan all along it seemed.

I put a hand out to kill the glare of the spotlight shining on me. "Hello?" I called out. "Anyone there?"

Seemingly not, for no one answered my call. Surprised that I wasn't strapped to the chair, I got up and walked around the room, which is when I realized that there was no need to strap me into the chair because the room had no doors or windows from which I could escape. The matt black walls were all smooth with no sign of anything that resembled a doorway.

*Fuck's sake*, I thought. *Was there any need for this?* I was beginning to feel like a prisoner at a CIA black site. "Hello?" I called out again as I walked around the room. "I didn't come here to be held like a damn prisoner. Frankly, given the anti-oppressive philosophy we share, I'm surprised at your level of...paranoia here."

I kept looking around as if searching for a face while I waited for a response that never came. Shaking my head, I sighed sharply in annoyance. I didn't appreciate being held prisoner by anyone, nor blatantly ignored. Fuck them, if that's the way they wanted to play it. I'd get out of this room myself, using my magic.

Only when I went to tap into my magic source, I realized that I couldn't. Something was blocking my access, and I didn't know what it was. It could have been magic, but it felt more like some sort of technology that was in effect.

I shook my head again, anger replacing my annoyance. "Seriously? Are you guy's sure you aren't government because it's sure beginning to fucking feel like it."

"Hello, Mr Creed."

The male voice was loud, and it startled me slightly when it sounded in the room, seeming to come from everywhere at once like the voice of some omnipotent deity. I stood for a second before answering back. "What is this?" I asked the voice. "The abduction thingy I can understand. You didn't want me to know your location yet. Although to be honest, a blindfold would have done just fine. But holding me prisoner? A notch too far, I think."

"Apologies if you feel uncomfortable," the voice said. "A security measure, that's all. We don't know if we can trust you yet. I'm sure you can understand...August Creed."

I smiled slightly at the mention of my name. It was no great surprise that they had done their homework on me. Not that I was worried. There wasn't much to be found on me outside of the Blackham City Online Grimoire. Officially, I was a ghost and had no legitimate records of any kind. Which just left my reputation around the city. Depending on how connected SciCane was, they could have gotten a pretty good representation of me by asking around. "So you know who I am?"

"Of course. Your reputation precedes you."

"Then you know I'm the real deal."

"Yes. The question we want to know, however, is why you are here when your dealings with the supernatural elite are well known?"

"Yes," I said, more relaxed now that I knew this was just an initial interview. All I had to do was tell them what they wanted to hear and I would be released from the room soon enough. I hoped so anyway. "I've dealt with the supernatural elite, as you call them. I've also dealt with the government, with Division. That's why I'm here. I'm sick of their oppression and controlling ways, and the fact that they all think they have the right to do whatever they want, no matter who they hurt in the process." I didn't have to try very hard to get the right amount of conviction in my voice. My outrage at the powers that be was never far below the surface at the best of times. But my philosophy had always been that's it's better to work with the people at the top instead of trying to overthrow them. It was better to play smart and subvert from within when the opportunity arose.

The voice went silent for a moment before booming into the room again. "Why should we believe you? How do we know you aren't here on the elite's behalf? Division perhaps?"

I snorted as if the very idea appalled me, which it did anyway. To be clear, I wasn't there on anyone's behalf but my own. "Undercover? Seriously? Do I look like ooCreed to you?" I laughed at my own joke. The voice didn't respond. "Seriously though. I'm here because I saw an opportunity when I came across your organization."

"To do what?"

"To finally make a difference and change the power balance. The people of the world have been enslaved for too long, and I'm not just talking about the supernatural oppressors. I'm talking about all of them--the corporations, the churches, the governments. The whole damn system of oppression. We need to wipe it all out and start again, only this time, the people are in charge of themselves, with no one looking down on them or squashing them into the ground with a jackboot when they don't play by the rules. I'm blessed with abilities and knowledge, and as I said, I'm sick of using those to help the elite with their problems. I want to use the power I have to help the people."

"But you help people already, do you not?"

I nodded. "Sure, but I mean on a grander scale. A global scale. I want to help the people help themselves. That's what your organization is all about, is it not?

Putting power back in the hands of the people so they can govern themselves from now on?"

"That is correct. That is what we are working towards."

I held out my hands. "Great. Then there's nothing more to talk about except what we are going to do to achieve that goal."

A long silence ensued, during which I wondered if my performance had been up to scratch, and whether my interrogator believed me or not. Then just as I was starting to think that I had somehow failed their little test, the whole room suddenly changed like someone had hit a switch to reveal the real room concealed behind the black walls. In the space of a few seconds, the room was transformed into a lounge containing leather furniture and a small, fully stocked bar. It felt like I was now standing inside a room in some exclusive club. Slightly confused and fairly impressed, I stared around me as I tried to work out how that little trick had been done. It seemed like magic. Maybe a Concealment Spell that had been over the room to begin with. But it felt like there was more to it, like some kind of technology had been involved in the transformation, though I couldn't be sure.

There was now a doorway in one of the walls, and after a moment, the door was opened and in walked a very beautiful but stern looking woman who was dressed in black trousers and tight-fitting turtleneck. Her bobbed auburn hair framed a face that I imagined was highly photogenic thanks to the woman's large clear blue eyes, perfectly sculpted nose and cheekbones, and wide, thick-lipped mouth. In some ways, she reminded me of Leona--her straight-backed seriousness mostly--though that could have just been me projecting my emotions onto her. She paused by the door for a brief moment while she stared intensely at me as if gauging my threat level, which is exactly the kind of thing that Leona would have done. I wondered if the woman was ex-military as well. She seemed in good shape, her body tall and slender, her muscles no doubt toned and hard under her dark, sexless clothing.

I stared back at the woman, saying nothing as I took her in, and she did the same. Then without saying a word, the woman walked to the shining, dark wood bar. As she slipped behind it, I saw the semi-automatic pushed into the back of her trousers. It seemed she was taking no chances. "Drink?" she asked as she held up a bottle of whiskey.

I nodded. "Yeah, sure."

The woman poured two tumblers of whiskey and slid one down the bar to me. Then she downed her own drink in one and placed the empty glass on the bar before coming around the other side and sitting on one of the bar stools.

"Where are we?" I asked after tasting the whiskey.

The woman smiled, her lips painted in bright red lipstick. "You mightn't believe me if I told you."

I raised my eyebrows. "Try me."

She smiled again. "Why don't I introduce myself first?" she said. "Then we'll get to where we are, and why you are here."

"I thought I already explained why I was here, but anyway. Go ahead. What's your name?"

"My name is Jordan Grayson."

*Grayson*, I thought. *Where do I know that name from?* I couldn't remember, but I was sure it would come to me. "Well, you know my name already."

"August Creed."

"You say that like my reputation precedes me."

"It does. To be frank, I was shocked when you posted that video."

"Why?"

"You seem like the kind of man who is perfectly happy with the way things are in the world."

"Not really."

"Then why have you never tried to change anything? Your considerable skills are well-known."

"What was I going to change on my own?" I said as I now sat two stools away from her. "I've been waiting for an opportunity like this for a long time."

She nodded and then stared at me a moment as if she could see right through me. A slight wave of panic arose in me as I began to fear my act wasn't coming off as well as I had hoped. "I'm still not convinced. You don't strike me as the sort of man who would join an organization like SciCane. You seem too...independent."

"That's because I am," I said without missing a beat. "And I want to remain so, which is why I'm here. The ones in power are making it more and more difficult for people such as myself to operate independently. They are constantly trying to drag me into their control mechanisms where they can keep an eye on me. I don't like that, obviously."

Jordan Grayson gave me a small smile. "Obviously."

I relaxed a little now. She seemed to be warming to me, or at the very least, giving me the benefit of the doubt. Which was a start, I guess. Though I got the impression Jordan Grayson didn't fully trust anyone, not even herself. "So tell me," I said. "Who is Crowley666? You or the man whose voice was speaking to me from out of nowhere it seemed?"

"Crowley666 is a convenient handle for our online activities," she said. "Nothing more."

"An in-joke."

The slight smile again. "Something like that."

"So who's in charge of the operation here? Are you head of this organization?" I knew she wasn't before she even answered. Not that I thought her incapable of leading SciCane—she probably did for the most part—but because I knew there had to be some other megalomaniac behind everything. Probably the man whose voice I heard earlier.

She grabbed the whiskey bottle from the bar before speaking again. "Firstly, Mr Creed—"

I stopped her right there. "Just Creed will do. No need for formalities now that we're friends."

She gave me a look as she refilled my glass, indicating that my slightly sarcastic tone wasn't lost on her. "First of all, Creed," she said. "There is no organization. SciCane is merely a collective, a gathering of individuals who share a desire for a common goal."

"Okay. So how many are in the collective?"

"Enough. More than you would think."

I wasn't sure I liked the sound of that. Given the extreme nature of SciCane's philosophy and political views, everyone involved had the potential to cause a great deal of trouble and damage. "So the collective is growing." I nodded as if I approved. "That's good."

"Yes," Jordan said, her deep blue eyes never leaving me. "We intend to make an impact, and we need the numbers to do that."

*Not necessarily*, I thought. They had the Dark Codex. Really, they didn't need anyone. One page of the book could do more damage that any amount of blind followers and fanatics. Though I wasn't about to say that to Jordan. The second I mentioned the book, she would know something was up. "Of course. So who's in charge of everything? You?"

"I'm in charge of all our operations," she said. "Planning and logistics. Tactics and strategies."

I nodded as if impressed, which I was. You know me. Always a sucker for a strong woman who knows what she's doing. Not that I had an eye on Jordan Grayson or anything, even though she was highly attractive if a little closed off. I couldn't help wondering what sort of pain she was masking under the black clothes and her almost corporate manner. "And who do you report to then?"

She looked towards the ceiling for a second as if someone was watching us through a camera from somewhere else. "All in good time," she said. "Before we can trust you with anything, you will have to prove your loyalty to us."

I frowned. "Prove my loyalty? I thought I already did that."

Jordan shook her head. "You will have to go farther than that."

"How much farther?" I was beginning to get worried. Was she going to ask me to kill someone, or do something that was going to injure a lot of people? I hoped not, though the thought had crossed my mind before the meeting that I would most likely end up having to do things that went against my nature if I was to be convincing enough in my role as an undercover operative. I knew the only way I was going to get anywhere near the Dark Codex was if I first got close to whoever had the book in their possession. Which meant gaining that person or persons confidence and getting them to trust me. And given the nature of the "collective" I was now a part of, gaining confidence would necessarily involve highly deviant and dangerous actions.

"You'll find out soon enough," Jordan said, her eyes giving nothing away as she stood up, making me wish I still had my magic so I could read her mind, though something told me her mind would be a goddamn steel trap. "In the meantime, you should come with me. I will show you to your quarters."

"My quarters?" I stood frowning at her.

"Did you think you would be heading right back home after this meeting?" She shook her head as if my commitment was in doubt again. "As I said, you're all in, Creed, or else..."

"Or else what?"

The corners of her wide mouth turned up into a humorless smile for a moment. Then she turned and walked to the door, opened it and waited patiently for me to walk through it.

Inwardly, I sighed as I walked towards the door with one dominant thought in my mind:

*What the hell have I gotten myself into here?*

# MESSIAH

*S*till slightly miffed at the fact that I was now being forced to stay in whatever place I was in (what did I think, that I could come and go as I pleased? I was undercover now, which meant staying undercover), I walked beside Jordan Grayson as she led me through a maze of hallways that made me think I was in some massive manor house or stately institution. Not the sort of place I was expecting SciCane to be based in. I was expecting somewhere a bit grottier, a bit more industrial perhaps like an old warehouse. Certainly not the stately charm of this place. In almost every hallway, the dark wood walls were adorned with old paintings and often lined with bookshelves filled with aged looking books. For a group that supposedly shunned the decadent luxury of the ruling elite, SciCane was sure hanging out in style. "You mind telling me where the hell we are?" I asked Jordan as we turned down yet another hallway. Jesus, how big was this place?

"This is our headquarters," Jordan said.

"Yeah, I figured that. I mean where are we on the map? Are we still in Blackham?"

"Not exactly." Jordan stopped halfway down a wide hallway and opened one of the doors, beckoning me to go inside. "This will be your quarters from now on."

The room had the same dark wood floors as the rest of the place, and a large four poster bed of all things. I snorted. "Really?" I said smirking at Jordan.

"What? Would you prefer something a bit more basic? We have a basement."

I shook my head. "This will be fine. I have to admit, though, this isn't what I was expecting."

She stared at me patiently. "And what were you expecting?"

"Some place a bit more gritty."

"Just because we are outsiders doesn't mean we have to live like dogs."

*Outsiders?* I thought. Was that how they all viewed themselves? I guess it was an accurate enough description, and one I was comfortable enough applying to myself. "I guess not." I walked further into the room while Jordan stayed by the door as if going any further would somehow give me the wrong impression. "So what now?"

"There's a meeting in an hour," she said.

"A meeting?"

"Yes. You will get to hear our leader speak then."

I nodded, not bothering to ask who the so-called leader was since I knew she wouldn't tell me. She still hadn't told me where the fuck I was yet. "I'll just hang here until then, will I?"

"I'll send someone to collect you in an hour."

When she went to leave, I stopped her by saying, "What about my magic? You're still blocking it somehow. When will you unblock it?"

Jordan smiled a smile that had no warmth behind it at all. "One step at a time. I'll see you at the meeting in an hour." She walked out and closed the door. A second later I heard a key being turned in the lock.

*What the fuck? Is she locking me in?*

I stood shaking my head as I couldn't escape the feeling that I was being held in some high-end prison. Taking out my phone, I went to check my location but wasn't surprised to find that the phone had no signal whatsoever. Convenient.

I sat down on the edge of the four-poster bed, having nothing else to do but wait.

* * *

SOMETIME LATER, THE DOOR TO MY NEW QUARTERS WAS UNLOCKED AND OPENED to reveal a man standing there. The man was small in stature and baldheaded with a scrunched up face. I did a double take as I got up off the bed to walk to the door. "Wait," I said. "I know you. You're..."

The little man was nodding his head as if to say, "I know, I know..."

"Sam, isn't it?"

"That's me," Sam said, rather excitedly.

This was the same Sam who tried to use bitchcraft on me in the park in Little Tokyo not too long ago. He'd been running around in his dead daughter's plastic wizard cape like some nutcase. Now he was dressed a bit more respectably in dark trousers and a brown suede jacket. "What the hell are you doing here?" I asked him. "I seem to remember giving you a pass to a very respected school of magic. What happened?"

Sam looked down the corridor for a second then stepped inside the room a bit. "I went to the school as you said, but I didn't fit in there. Everyone looked down on me."

"Looked down on you?"

He nodded. "Yes, both literally and figuratively."

"I see."

"I tried, I really did, but that place just wasn't for me."

"And this place is?"

"Yes," he said, his eyes widening. "SciCane accepted me for who I am. They treat me like I have value, and that I'm worth something to the world."

Inwardly, I sighed. Poor Sam. He was so desperate to belong somewhere that he couldn't even see when he was being used. Or perhaps he did see, but his self-worth was so low that any form of attention would do. I felt like telling Sam to leave immediately and save himself from any future pain, but I was supposed to be undercover, and therefore an avid supporter of all things SciCane. Besides, it was possible we were under surveillance at all times, so I had to be careful about what I said. "Well, you made the right choice, Sam."

Sam beamed back at me. "You really think so?"

I walked past him into the corridor. "I do. We're going to do great things here. We're going to change the world, Sam."

"Yes, we are." Sam closed the door to my quarters. "Follow me. You will now have the honor of meeting our great leader. A man of pure vision he is."

I smiled. "I'm sure. I can't wait. What's the meeting about?"

Sam looked around as if to see if anyone was listening. The hallway was empty, so no one was. That we could see anyway. "We're going on a mission," he said in a low, excited voice.

"What kind of mission?"

"No one knows yet. But I think we're about to find out."

"Awesome."

"It sure is. This way."

I followed beside Sam as he directed us down a series of hallways. "How long have you been a part of this, Sam?"

"Well, that's the thing," Sam said. "In Earth time, not that long. But in here, time is different. I've been in here for a while now."

I stopped. "Wait, Earth time? Where the fuck are we, Sam?"

Sam stopped as well. "No one told you?"

"Told me what?"

He smiled as if he was about to reveal something awesome. "We're in a different dimension. A pocket dimension actually, created by our amazing leader."

*A pocket dimension*, I thought, letting it sink in. Then I remembered Brentwood saying something about SciCane having their own dimension. Clever bastards. No one could touch them here. No doubt the Dark Codex helped with that. "Okay, cool," I said nodding as if I wasn't fazed. Looking at Sam, I could see he was brainwashed and in total awe of whoever was in charge. The fearless, charismatic leader that I was apparently about to lay eyes on for the first time.

"It's more than cool," Sam said, now walking again. "We're going to change the world, Creed." He smiled up at me. "I'm glad you're here. Fate has brought us together again."

I nodded as I wondered if everyone around here was as zealous as Sam, which I had no doubt they were.

A few minutes later, we came to a set of ornate double doors that Sam could barely push open by himself. When the doors opened, they did so into a great hall that was filled with people. Maybe a hundred or so people all standing around in small groups. Almost all of them looked at me as I entered the hall with Sam, and I did my best not to seem affected by their stares. The crowd was a mix of men and women, both young and old, but mostly youngish looking. Staring back at them, I thought everyone in the room looked completely normal. No one was dressed funny. None had robes or cultish garments on them. They could have been there just to hear their favorite author do a reading. Except they obviously weren't. They were there to fuck shit up in the name of SciCane, in the name of change.

I followed Sam through the crowd as I nodded my head at those who made eye contact with me, trying as I did so to get a read on them. For the most part, the others in the room seemed normal in an outcast sort of way. A few I got danger vibes from. Those could have been soldiers. Or gangsters. What united them all, though, was their interest in and knowledge of the arcane arts. Otherwise, they wouldn't have been standing there at all.

Sam stopped by the front of a large stage. "He'll be on soon," he said excitedly. "I can't wait to hear what the next mission is."

"The next?" I said. "How many missions have you done, Sam?"

"Quite a few. Small stuff mostly. Disrupting some things, subverting other things. Apparently, though, the missions are being stepped up. Some of the things we've been doing lately though...it's crazy."

"Like what?"

Sam looked at me like an outsider for the first time. "I probably shouldn't say. You haven't been fully vetted yet."

I shook my head at him. "I see."

"But you will be," he hastily added. "With your skills, you'll be a real asset."

"So I've been told."

At that point, Jordan Grayson walked onto the stage, and everyone went silent. It was like someone had flipped a mute switch in the room. Clearly, Jordan commanded a lot of respect and authority from the group members. She spotted me as she came to the center of the stage, briefly held eye contact before shifting her gaze to the rest of the crowd, staring out at them with the calm assurance of someone who knew everyone there would follow her every order to the letter. Glancing briefly around, I could see the fervent adoration and respect in the eyes of the crowd. "Change-bringers," she announced in a voice that wasn't too loud, but which still carried to the back of the room. "It is time to kickstart the revolution and bring the prison of Earth crashing to its knees."

The crowd cheered at that, then settled down when Jordan made a movement with her hand. "Now let me welcome the man who will lead the charge in this revolution of ours." Her head turned to the side of the stage. "My father, Dr Gordon Grayson."

From stage left, a tall man in his sixties wearing a robed outfit came walking out, and the people in the hall started cheering and clapping, including Sam beside me, who judging by the awe and reverence in his face, looked at Grayson as some sort of messiah figure. Everyone in the room did, in fact, except me of course. I merely clapped and put on a polite smile as I was aware of Jordan staring at me from the side of the stage as if gauging my reaction to the man who was not only her leader but also her father, which come to think about it, was no great surprise. Her devoutness to the cause and seriousness of manner started to make sense now. She was Daddy's little girl, and she tried hard to please him.

Gordon Grayson stood for probably longer than he should have so he could absorb the adoration being thrown at him by his followers. If you're familiar with cult behavior, you will know scenes like this are commonplace. Cult leaders enjoy giving sermons to their followers, not just to refresh the faith of said followers each time, but also to bask in the messianic glory that came from the blind adoration of people who couldn't steer their own ship and needed a captain like Grayson to do it for them. I couldn't help but wonder if these people could see the irony in what they were doing. SciCane was all about self-governance and autonomy, yet the people involved were completely subservient to the hierarchy put in place by Grayson and his daughter. As I sneaked the occasional glance at Jordan, I also wondered if she was really as committed to the cause as she seemed, or had she just been brainwashed by her father like everyone else here? Time would tell, I guess.

Eventually, Grayson--dripping with the false modesty of a true false prophet--made motions with his arms as he quieted the crowd. Soon, the hall was completely silent, and you could have heard a pin drop as everyone waited with fervent anticipation on their leader to speak.

"Comrades," Grayson said in a voice that came across as strong and self-assured. *Nice touch addressing the sheeple as his comrades*, I thought. Make them all think he's right there with them while deflecting from the fact that he is really ruling over them like any other despot. "The time has come to put our plans for change into action. It is time to awaken the sleeping tiger so we can finally hear it roar!"

The crowd cheered at that. By sleeping tiger, I assumed Grayson was referring to the clueless masses, the Sleepwalkers. *Not a good idea*, I immediately thought. Tigers had a tendency to bite when you rudely woke them from slumber.

There was no doubt Grayson played the messiah role well. He came across as self-deprecating, yet strong and in control at the same time. Staring at him, I could see he had similar features to his daughter, including the same color blue in his eyes. He still had all his hair, which was gray and cut short in a rough sort of way as if he did it himself. And considering his age, he still cut an imposing figure. Even with the shapeless robes he wore, I could tell he was in good shape underneath.

"Comrades," Grayson said, addressing his followers again. "Let us not waste any more time. There are people on Earth who need wakening up, and you--" He pointed out to the crowd. "You will wake them. You all know what you have to do. Now go and do it! Go and create change in the universe, brothers and sisters! Be the angels the people of Earth need!"

More cheering and clapping, and then a moment later, the crowd seemed to disperse as everyone went to leave the room. Sam also left, while I hung around the stage wondering what the hell I was supposed to do now.

"Mr Creed." Grayson addressed me from the stage. "Why don't you follow me to my quarters so we can talk." He was smiling, but he still seemed ominous to me.

I nodded and then climbed on the stage to follow Grayson, who was already walking away. And as I followed behind him, it suddenly hit me where I knew Grayson from.

He was the killer of seven people.

# 11

# GORDON GRAYSON

$\mathcal{I}$ followed Gordon Grayson down a few hallways and into a large study where Grayson seated himself behind a big oak desk, at the same time gesturing me to sit in the seat opposite. "I'm just realizing," I said as I sat down, trying to maintain the air of a man who had nothing to hide. "There are no windows in this place."

Grayson smiled. "No. We are situated in a small pocket of time and space. There wouldn't be much to see."

"I guess not." I sat back in the leather seat and crossed my legs as if settling in for a long, meaningful conversation, hoping I was putting out just enough reverence without seeming too eager about it, and without coming across as some starstruck groupie. If I wanted him to trust me eventually, I would have to act like someone who could be trusted, someone who was not too weak to think or stand up for themselves. I had to be a man he could respect.

Grayson stared at me for a long moment, just as his daughter did, and probably for the same reason. To get the measure of me. "I must say, I'm pleased to have a man of your caliber here with us," he said eventually, sounding genuine enough. Under other circumstances, I might have been flattered that such an accomplished scientist thought of me in those terms. And yes, Grayson was a scientist, at least until he managed to kill seven people who were voluntary subjects in one of his experiments. I remember the story being in the news at the time because it happened not too long after I came to Blackham. Grayson went on the run rather than face the consequences of his actions, and hadn't been heard from since. Until now, that is.

"A man of my caliber?" I gave a self-deprecating laugh. "Nothing compared to you, I'm sure. Your work on the nature of consciousness was quite brilliant. I would have said a few more years, and you would have cracked the consciousness code, so to speak."

515

"So you know me then?" Grayson said nodding, not sounding too surprised. "Then you must also know what I did back then."

"Of course. I'm sure you didn't mean it. Did you?"

"What do you think, Mr Creed?"

I didn't hesitate. "I believe you didn't kill those people on purpose. What did happen? It was never made clear in any of the reports."

Grayson sighed slightly as if he was hesitant to talk about it, but he did so anyway, probably just to get it out of the way before we could get to the real order of business, which I had to assume involved deciding if I was trustworthy or not. "It was just another experiment," he said. "We'd done dozens of them by that point. It simply involved putting the subjects into a deep trance so we could more easily study their brain activity. More specifically, the special behavior that goes on at that level. At that level of consciousness, our brains run on--"

"Magic."

He nodded. "You would, of course, know that, being a wizard. I didn't at the time."

"So what happened?"

Grayson stared down towards the floor for a moment as if remembering back to thirty years ago. "We didn't know this at the time, but when a person's mind is in that deep trance for a prolonged period, doorways can be opened in their minds. Doorways that lead to other worlds. One of the subjects opened the door to one such world, and something bad came through the door. An evil spirit of some kind that went from one subject to the next, draining their life-force as it went. We didn't notice until it was too late, and even then, we didn't know what to do. The only reason we knew what was happening was because the spirit revealed itself after draining the last person. It was like a dark shadow with burning eyes, and it seemed to leer at us, knowing there was nothing we could do. And then it just disappeared as if it were never there in the first place."

"Leaving seven dead bodies behind it," I said.

Grayson looked angry for a moment, his blue eyes seeming to go darker as his brow creased. "Those people should never have died," he stated. "If the powers that be hadn't of kept us in ignorance--shielding the true nature of the world from us, keeping us ignorant of the supernatural horrors that exist--we may have been able to stop that evil spirit before it killed those seven people." His stare was intense as he focused on me as if he considered me as one of those who kept the truth hidden, which I did of course, for which I make no apologies for. "That incident opened my eyes. At that moment, I decided to never again live in ignorance and that I would show the world the truth that had been kept hidden from them. I've spent the last three decades searching for and uncovering that truth."

*Searching for the Dark Codex more like*, I thought. Too soon to mention that yet, though. "You ran."

Grayson nodded. "I was looking at life imprisonment for something I didn't do. Wouldn't you?"

"I suppose."

"Sometimes running is the only option."

I couldn't disagree with him. "I know."

"I've no doubt you do, Mr Creed."

"Please, just Creed will do."

He nodded. "Why are you here, Creed? Tell me the truth."

His bluntness almost caught me off guard, and I shifted in my seat slightly. "Like everyone else here, I want to see change, of course."

"Come on," he said, his eyes narrowing like he knew there was more to it. "Half these people here are crackpots. You must have seen it. Most are only here because I need bodies. They are working towards the greater good, even if they don't quite see it. But you, Creed, are no crackpot."

I smiled. "I can give you a list of people who would likely disagree with that. A long list."

"I'm not saying you aren't a little crazy." Grayson snorted. "Hell, men like you and me, we're all a little crazy, right? We have to be. It's how we get things done when no one else can, am I right?"

"Sure."

"But you know more than all these people put together. Maybe you even know more than me."

Puffing my cheeks out, I said, "Jesus, stop. I just fucking do what I do, same as you. Same as anyone. It's like I told your daughter, I'm here to help."

"I have no doubt about that." He pointed his finger at me then. "But to help who, that's what I'm unsure about."

"You think I'm here to disrupt things?" I laughed as if the idea was absurd.

"Yes, I can't help but think that. You just don't strike me as the type of man to get involved in a revolution such as this. I'd even go so far as to say that you are a part of the system we are trying to bring down here."

Shit. I had obviously overestimated my ability to hide my true nature. That and my far-reaching reputation, which never had revolutionary attached to it at any point. "I've always bucked the system in my own way," I said, again feeding him mostly truth since I figured it was the best way to tell a lie, to conceal it under truth. "I just never thought it could be changed until I came across SciCane. Sure, the whole cult thing you got going here is not to my tastes at all, but you seem serious about changing things, and you make me believe that things *can* be changed. Hell, you can't make them any worse, can you?" I laughed as I leaned forward, eliciting a deep chuckle from Grayson as well.

The man in charge sat back and thought for a long moment while I stared right back at him as I held my conviction that I belonged there with him. "I must admit," he said eventually. "I do like you, Creed. You don't give a fuck, and I need people like that. People who don't give a fuck. But—" He seemed to pause for dramatic effect. "I can't shake the feeling that you're here to do damage to us. Maybe for that shit-heel organization, Division. You have ties with them."

I made a show of snorting loudly. "Division? Give me a fucking break. I hate those guys. They've been busting my balls for years. Sure, I helped them out with a few things, but only so they'd leave me the fuck alone. They would have locked me up otherwise."

"Maybe that's why you're here, so they don't lock you up."

I sighed as if there was nothing more I could say. "You'll just have to take my word on that, then won't you?"

Grayson nodded sagely, his broad chin jutting out. "I suppose I will. But the truth is, it doesn't matter. The revolution has begun, and there is nothing you or anyone else can do to stop it."

He seemed so damn sure. I wonder why? Dark Codex much? "I hope that's true."

Smiling, Grayson said, "Oh, it is. You want me to trust you, Creed?"

"Of course."

"Then here's what you are going to do for me."

# 12

# MISSION OBJECTIVES

nside one of the rooms of the sprawling mansion, there was a gateway that led back to Earth, similar to the liquidescent (and if that's not a word, it is now) gateways in Sanaka's Sanctum, such as the one I went through recently to get to the Underworld. As I stepped through the bright blue portal after Jordan Grayson, I shook my head at the potent magic her father had obviously tapped into via the Dark Codex.

When I came through the gateway, Jordan was waiting for me inside a sewer tunnel. "The sewers?" I said wrinkling my nose at the smell, which reminded me of rotten socks.

Jordan, serious as ever, said, "It's important we stay hidden. We couldn't just create a gateway in the open for someone to find."

I nodded. "Fair enough."

Jordan was dressed in a tight-fitting red dress that showed just how lean and lithe she was underneath. She looked stunning, in fact, though obviously uncomfortable. I got the impression she didn't dress up much, and only when it was required of her. Like now, for the mission. She didn't seem to have a problem with what we were about to do, however.

For the record though, I had a major problem with the mission objectives. For reasons that will soon become clear.

In the meantime, I had my magic back, so that was something at least. I smiled as I conjured a small sphere of blue energy in the palm of one hand.

Jordan didn't seem too impressed as if she had seen it all before. "You do magic?" I asked her, though I knew she didn't. I would have felt it otherwise. Her father, however, was a different story. Grayson had a ton of magic coursing through him, which I immediately felt when I first saw him. It felt unnatural though like he had gotten it all at once instead of building it up over years of practice.

519

"I dislike magic," Jordan said as we trekked on through the sewer tunnels, Jordan knowing exactly where to go as if she had come this way many times before.

"Why?" I asked as the energy ball disappeared in my hand. "When you are actively trying to put magic in the hands of the people?"

Jordan nodded as if the irony wasn't lost on her. "It's the only way to change things, to level the playing field so the people can protect themselves against their oppressors, supernatural or otherwise."

She wasn't wrong, hypothetically speaking. The Sleepwalkers wouldn't stand a chance against the combined might of the state and corporations, not to mention certain factions of the occult underground, unless they had the power to protect themselves and fight back. My biggest worry about that was what was going to happen afterward, if and when the Sleepwalkers defeated their enemies. What then? Was everyone just going to live their lives in peace? Were they fuck. Chaos would ensue. Widespread and unbridled use of magic would see to that. Instead of freeing the people, the Grayson's would plunge the entire world into another dark age.

But I couldn't exactly argue against their philosophy and tactics when I was supposed to be a part of the team, now could I? The only thing I could do was hope that I managed to stop their crazy plan before it came to fruition. Though I have to be honest, what I was about to do with Jordan wasn't exactly going to help matters on that front. Not only was my loyalty being tested, but I was also being used to kickstart the "grand plan". I could've informed Brentwood, but there wasn't much point. Mission priority was to obtain the Dark Codex. And the only way to get it was to get close to the Graysons. Having them all arrested at this stage wouldn't help much as neither would likely give up the book's location anyway.

It wasn't long before we exited out of the sewer tunnels and into a disused subway station that eventually led us out to a backstreet in the north end of Freetown near the river. I continued to follow Jordan out of the backstreet just as dusk began to settle in the city. I wasn't sure how long I had been in the pocket dimension, but it felt good to be walking around Blackham again. "We haven't really discussed the plan yet," I said to Jordan as she took us into a small parking lot where a beat up old van was parked.

"There isn't much to discuss," Jordan said as she went around the driver's side of the van and opened the door. Once inside, she opened the passenger door for me, and I hopped in, shivering slightly at the cold inside. The van had obviously been sitting for a while.

"There isn't much to discuss?" I was slightly incredulous at her seeming lack of worry over what we were about to do. "We're about to try and snatch a werewolf and a vampire. I don't know about you, but I have little experience in kidnapping, especially bloody beasts with teeth and claws that will almost certainly fight back."

Jordan turned her head to look at me. "They won't fight much, not if we do things right."

"Which is how? Hypnotize them into coming with us?"

She smiled. "Something like that. Once we chose our victims, we can con them out to the van, at which point we restrain them and toss them in the back."

I snorted and shook my head. "Have you ever tried to restrain a werewolf?"

"Yes."

The immediacy of her answer surprised me a little. "Really?"

"I've been down many dark roads, Creed," she said. "Along the way I've had to deal with all kinds of creatures, as you have as well, I'd imagine."

"Of course, but I usually talk or bargain with said creatures."

"And if they don't listen?"

"Then I use magic. Or my gun. Or my knife. Depends on the situation."

"We need these creatures alive."

"Yeah, I know." I tried not to let my consternation at that show. Gordon Grayson wanted the supernaturals for a little show that he had planned, in which I was being forced to play a leading role. Not something I was happy about, especially since said show would be broadcast on every social media channel around the world. My current good standing in the occult underground would take a serious hit. I wasn't even sure if my reputation as an independent would ever recover.

"You seem hesitant about this," Jordan said as she eyed me suspiciously. "That makes me question your loyalty." Her hand moved down to the pocket in the door, where no doubt she had a gun stashed.

"Hey," I said raising my hands. "I'm just naturally cautious. I can't help it."

She shook her head. "Nothing is changed by being cautious. Boldness changes things."

"I agree. That's why I'm here after all."

I was glad to see her hand return to her lap. Christ, was she really going to shoot me there? Her blue eyes focused on me. "The life you once lived is over," she said. "There is no going back to it, no matter what happens. Even if you could go back, it wouldn't last long. Things are going to radically change in this world, and that's all there is to it. It's inevitable."

"You seem so sure. Is that just faith talking or do you have something that is going to guarantee our success?"

Her eyes narrowed. "What do you mean?"

"I mean your father must be getting his power from somewhere. You don't just wake up one morning and know how to create a whole new dimension in the universe."

As soon as I saw the gun, I knew I had pushed things too far, alerting her suspicions. "What do you know?" she demanded, pointing the gun at me.

I raised my hands again as if I didn't know what she was talking about. Although even if I didn't know, I would now, because her reaction said it all. She was thinking about the Dark Codex. "I'm not sure what you are talking about. I just mean I don't know anyone who can successfully create their own dimension out of nothing, and I know a lot of very learned people, including myself. So you tell me. What do you know?"

Jordan stared for a long time, then put the gun closer to my face, the barrel seeming huge so close up. "Tell me the truth, Creed. Are you with us or not?"

I didn't hesitate. "I'm with you. Of course I am. Now can you lower the damn gun, you're making me nervous."

She lowered the gun, but only slightly. "I realize that you might want answers to certain things, but you must also realize that you must earn our trust first before we open ourselves up to you. Successfully completing tonight's mission will be a start to that process."

I nodded. "Sure thing. I understand."

"Good." She retracted the gun and put it back in the pocket of the door. "Now tell me where we can find a good werewolf hang out."

## 13

### STING PART ONE

*I* ended up taking us to a bar I knew in downtown Freetown called Dark Riders. It wasn't exclusively a werewolf hangout as it had more of a mixed crowd most nights, but I was fairly certain we would find at least one werewolf inside who we could target. Inside, bikers lined the bar and hogged the pool table. Most of them seemed human, but I spotted a few lycans amongst them. Also in one corner was a crowd of young people. Students, I think. There for the excitement of drinking in a dive bar with a shady reputation. Jordan and I got some suspicious looks as we walked inside and took a table in one of the far corners, although most of those looks turned to desire as they eyed up Jordan in her tight fitting dress. "Do you know these people?" Jordan asked me as we sat down.

"Not exactly," I said, staring back at the werewolves gathered around the two pool tables. "They probably know me though."

"You seem to have a big reputation around this town." Jordan sat straight as she stared intensely around the bar. She didn't seem too comfortable like she wasn't used to frequenting bars such as this one.

I nodded. "You could say that." Although after tonight, said reputation was going to take a major battering because of what Gordon Grayson wanted me to do.

"At least the beasts are here." The way she said it, it was clear she had no love for werewolves, but then who did? I was pretty sure her disdain extended to all supernatural creatures, though.

"Yes," I said as I eyed up the large men by the pool table, who had gone back to their game now, their stares going from constant to only occasional now. Maybe they knew if I was around then something must be up somewhere. If so, they had good instincts. "Let's have a drink before we do any abducting."

Jordan looked at me like I was breaking some rule. "You're going to drink now?"

523

"Sure. We have to look natural if you want this to work." When a busty barmaid came over to take our order, I asked for two whiskeys.

"Make that one," Jordan said to the waitress.

"Eh, they're both for me," I said. "What are you drinking?"

"Ice water," she said.

I looked at her. "Ice water? You don't want anything stronger, honey?"

"Honey?" she said staring at me.

I smiled at the waitress. "We just argued. You know how it is. That's what happens after being together for so long, right honey?"

Jordan was frowning at me like she thought I was going mad. She also looked somewhat embarrassed as she nodded once and said nothing.

I looked back to the waitress. "Two whiskeys and ice water it is then."

"Back in a moment," the waitress said, shaking her head slightly as she walked away.

"What was that?" Jordan asked.

"Cover," I said. "Trying not to arouse suspicion. Haven't you ever done this before?"

"I've done plenty." Her head turned away as she looked around the bar.

*Jesus, she is a strange one*, I thought. Brusquer than even Leona and that was saying something. She reminded me of someone who had lived at a monastery her whole life, someone who didn't quite fit into normal society. I wondered what her deal was as I settled back into my seat, happy to chill for a while before we had to make a move on one of the shifters. "So tell me about yourself," I said. "You haven't always been second in command in SciCane, so what did you used to do?"

She frowned at me as if she didn't understand the question, but really she was just loathed to talk about herself or reveal herself in any way. Jordan was clearly a woman who was used to playing her cards close to her chest for whatever reason. "There isn't much to tell."

I sighed. "Look, if you're going to sit there staring over at those guys like you're about to arrest them all, they're going to get suspicious. Trust me. I know what I'm talking about." The waitress arrived with our drinks, and I handed Jordan hers. "Sit back and enjoy your...ice water."

Jordan shook her head but nonetheless sat back in her seat, looking only slightly less uncomfortable now. Then she surprised me by saying, "Give me one of your whiskeys."

I couldn't help smiling. "That's the spirit." I held up my glass after I handed her the other one. "To SciCane and changing the world."

Jordan raised her glass slightly. "To SciCane." Then she downed her drink in one.

"So you do like to drink," I said before downing my own whiskey and signaling to the waitress again.

"Sometimes." It was almost an admission of guilt the way she said it, and I wondered why she seemed so pent up all the time. Was it the strain of helping her father run things? Or was something deeper keeping her locked up tight? Her extreme guardedness seemed to be more than just professional. It was a way of life and one that I couldn't help but recognize.

"You've done a lot of traveling, haven't you?"

The question seemed to take her by surprise, and I knew why. It was because her traveling was connected to the Dark Codex. Shrugging, I said casually, "I can just tell you've been around. I used to go around a lot, a long time ago."

Jordan stared and then raised her perfectly smooth chin as she nodded. "I've been to places."

"What kind of places?"

She seemed hesitant to reveal anything as she said nothing. Then the waitress arrived with two more drinks and placed them on the table. When the waitress walked away, I looked at Jordan, still expecting an answer to my last question. She shook her head. "Places you wouldn't believe," she said finally, before looking away.

"Try me," I said as I lifted my whiskey glass.

Jordan shifted in her seat slightly as she stared intensely towards the bar. "I've been to many dark places in the world."

"For what reason?"

"Why do you care?"

"I'm just making conversation," I said shrugging. "Unless you want us to sit here like a couple of mutes and draw attention to ourselves. We have to appear natural for this plan of yours to work."

Her stare remained as stony as ever for another moment, then she sighed, grabbed her whiskey from the table and sat back in her seat as she retracted her thorns somewhat. "Fine. I was searching for something, along with my father."

*Well, all right.*

"Searching for what?"

"Something that would help us change the world."

"And I take it you found it, given the things you've done recently?"

She nodded. "Yes."

"How long were you searching for?"

Jordan sipped her whiskey and looked away. "My whole life."

Jesus. She looked to be in her mid-thirties now. A long time to be on the road. It made my six years look like the blink of an eye. "Was it worth it?"

She frowned. "Was what worth it?"

"The thing you were searching for. Was it worth devoting your whole life to?"

Staring as if she didn't know what to say, she quickly blurted out, "Of course." Then she looked away, and I practically saw her guard come up again.

*That's the end of that conversation,* I thought as I finished off my whiskey. No point sitting much longer. "all right, let's do this," I said, slamming my glass down onto the table loudly enough for the werewolves by the pool tables to notice and throw hard stares my way.

Jordan seemed slightly shocked by my sudden turn in attitude and my rising aggression as if she had forgotten about the plan for a moment. Then her face changed to one of extreme distress and tears immediately flowed from her eyes. I have to say, I was impressed by her acting skills. So much so, I had to repress a smile. "Please," Jordan wailed suddenly in a loud, very convincing voice. "Just go! Leave me alone!"

Out of the corner of my eye, I noticed the half dozen or so werewolves all raise their heads to take notice of what was going on. "You cold bitch!" I shouted back as I shot to my feet, almost knocking over the table. "I'll just go and find someone else who *is* willing to put out occasionally. Frigid cunt!"

Jordan flinched at those last two words as if genuinely stung.

"Hey asshole!" one of the werewolves shouted. "Leave her the fuck alone!"

"Hey, don't worry," I said back, still all attitude. "I'm leaving this dump right now."

The werewolves seemed to take great offense at me calling their hang out a dump, and all at once began to head towards me like a pack of, well, wolves. At that point, I decided a quick exit was in order before I had to defend myself against a load of angry werewolves.

*It's all up to you now, Jordan*, I thought as I made a speedy exit from the bar and walked quickly to where the van was parked down a side street.

All I had to do now was wait.

While I hung around the outside of the van, I took out my phone and checked it for messages. It was the first chance I'd had since leaving the SciCane Dimension (when did my life become like a Sci-Fi Channel movie?). I wasn't surprised to see two messages from Brentwood asking how things were going. There was also another message from Leona. A picture message, showing an image of an FBI ID badge with her name on it. I shook my head and sighed. She went ahead and did it. She joined the fucking FBI. I had to admit, it stung a little--a lot actually--looking at that badge with her name on. And why the hell did she send me the picture? Was she trying to make some kind of statement? Shaking my head again, I dismissed the message, having no time or inclination to engage in the ongoing drama. For a woman who often kept her emotions on the back burner, and who wore her no bullshit attitude like a badge of honor, Leona was fairly getting into the melodrama that seemed to have sprung up in place of our previous relationship. I didn't appreciate it, and I didn't know why she was acting so different, despite her explaining her reasons.

But fuck it. I had a job to do as well.

"It's me," I said into the phone after calling Brentwood's number.

"Creed," Brentwood said. "Hold on a second." The sound of a door closing. "Go ahead. Give me an update. Any sign of the Dark Codex yet?"

"A little early in the game for that, but I'm getting there." I looked down the street. No sign of Jordan yet.

"I take it you're inside?" Brentwood asked.

"Yeah," I replied. "I'm on a mission now so I can't really talk too long."

"A mission?" Brentwood sounded concerned. "What kind of mission?"

I puffed my cheeks out when I thought about it. "You'll find out soon enough."

"I don't like the sound of that, Creed."

"You'd like it even less from my end, but hey, anything to get the book."

"Will there be expected casualties from this mission they have you on?"

*Just my reputation.*

"Maybe," I said, hearing voices approach. "Probably. I gotta go now, Brentwood. Did you know Leona got her badge?"

"Did she?" He sounded surprised, though I don't know why.

"She did. Bye Brentwood."

I slipped the phone in my pocket and ducked around the side of the van just as Jordan came walking up the street with a man the same height as her, but twice as broad. One of the werewolves from the bar. I smiled when I realized her planned seduction had worked. I didn't think she had it in her, which made me wonder about what other hidden depths Jordan Grayson had.

*Careful, Creed. You know where that kind of thinking leads. Next thing you know you'll be noticing how sweet she seems when she smiles, how taut her muscles are...how long her legs are...*

Shaking my head at the thoughts running through my mind, I focused on pouring out a sizable amount of white powder from a small vial into the palm of my hand. No, I wasn't about to get coked up. The powder was for incapacitating the werewolf. It should put him to sleep for a good long while so he wouldn't give us any trouble until we got back to the Grayson Dimension. The last thing I wanted was for an angry werewolf to go nuts in the back of the van. We still had a vampire to abduct as well, which would cause even more friction if they were both awake and conscious enough to hate and fight with each other.

Jordan was still playing the role of dissed girlfriend. Easy meat for the werewolf. Or so he thought. I heard Jordan giggle as she came up on the van. A strange sound coming out of her mouth as she didn't strike me as a giggler. More of a scowler like myself. "What do you say, big boy?" she said to the werewolf. "You want to fuck my brains out in the back of that van?"

Standing on the other side of the black van, I shook my head at her crassness, though I was none the less turned on by her sexual bluntness. *Maybe she'll say that to me later*, I thought, then shook my head again.

*Stop it...*

"If it's fucking you want," the deeply voiced werewolf said. "It's fucking you're going to get."

*Cheeseball.*

Jordan gave a dirty laugh in response. "Good to hear."

As she opened the back doors of the van and stood back, glancing at me as she did so, I quickly came around to confront the werewolf. The guy was young looking, maybe early twenties, with thick stubble and dirty blonde hair. The look on his face said he wasn't surprised to see me, which was somewhat disconcerting as I considered what that meant. Surely I was the last person he should have expected to see, given that I had stormed out of the bar earlier? In fact, the young werewolf smiled when he saw me, almost like he was expecting me to appear at some point. "So Ace was right," he said, his eyes turning yellow now as he growled at me.

"Ace?" I said, knowing now that something was wrong. "What about--"

Before I could finish, the werewolf lunged forward and grabbed me by the lapels, his superior strength and power forcing me back into the wall as he held me there close. My arms were trapped, so I couldn't even lift my hand to blow the powder in his face.

Then I heard a clicking sound. Jordan was standing behind the guy with her gun pointed at his head. "Let him go," she said, her voice reverted to stone cold seriousness now.

The werewolf holding me didn't seem concerned by the gun, and a second later, I knew why as I saw three other men appear behind the van. "Drop it, sister," one of the men said, obviously pointing his own gun.

Then I heard a familiar voice approach. "Well, well," the gravelly voice said. "If it isn't August Creed. Just the man I wanted to see."

"Ace," I said in a defeated voice. "What are you doing here?"

Ace motioned for his mate to let me go as he moved in front of me instead. "I think the question is, what are you doing here? What the fuck are you and you're girlfriend here playing at?"

"She's not my girlfriend," I said.

Ace stuck his thick, hairy forearm across my throat and snarled. "I don't give a fuck whether she is or not. You two are up to something, and I want to know what it is. I heard all about your little performance in the bar, and knew straight away something wasn't right."

"What are you doing here, Ace?" I said, noticing Jordan had handed her gun over to one of the other men. I also noticed she didn't look too afraid, which considering the circumstances, must have meant she was good at holding her shit together under pressure, which I was glad to see. "Isn't Red Hill your territory?"

Ace grinned and revealed his fangs. "This whole city is my territory. I go where I want."

*Of course, because you're an arrogant fucker with no respect for anyone.*

"Let me go," I said. "I can explain what's happening here."

"Oh, I'm sure you can," Ace said. "But to be honest, Creed, I don't really care what you and Olive Oil had planned. I only care about making you pay."

"Pay? What for? I saved your damn life, remember?"

Ace snorted. "Yeah, you saved me all right." He applied more force to his chokehold and leaned his head in closer to my face so I could smell his whiskey breath. "But you also took something from me, Creed."

"I didn't take anything," I said, my voice straining against his hold. "That was the hex."

"Bullshit!" He spun me around then and slammed me into the side of the van with such force that my hand flew open, and I lost the powder I'd been holding. "You did that on purpose. Don't fucking lie to me."

"Ace, I--" I shook my head in annoyance, having had enough of being pushed around by Ace and his crew. A blast of magic left me and knocked Ace right back into the wall with enough force to dislodge a lump of plaster.

Once I did that, Jordan launched into action against the other three men. I was too busy keeping an eye on Ace to see much of what Jordan was doing, but going by the blur of movement and the cries of pain, it seemed like she was kicking those guy's asses. Even Ace seemed astonished as he looked for a second at his mates taking a battering. Then he gave a loud growl and sprang to his feet, his facial features now changed as the wolf in him came out. As he sprang at me, I moved quickly to the side, at the same time conjuring up a thin shard of pure silver that I sent flying towards Ace's leg. The shard pierced his thigh all the way through, and the werewolf howled like a bitch, falling to one side for a moment.

"Back off, Ace!" I shouted, another silver shard already floating in the air in front of me. "Or the next one goes in your black heart."

Ace roared, partly out of aggression, partly out of frustration because he knew I wasn't joking. Then gripping the shard of silver in his leg, he ripped it out and roared again, this time in pain. "You're dead, Creed!"

"No, you'll be dead if you don't back off," I warned him, moving the shard of silver closer to him.

There was still much scuffling going on at the other side of the van as Jordan continued her fight against the other three werewolves. Then all the activity stopped in the space of a few seconds as if they had all given up. Jordan appeared beside me a second later with blood on her face. Her breathing was heavier than normal, but otherwise, she seemed okay. "Your friends are all down," she said to Ace.

"Bitch!" Ace spat back.

"Charming," Jordan said like she was facing some snot-nosed kid who'd given her the finger. "I hope you keep that charm when you're on camera later."

Ace looked confused for a second, and I took the opportunity to reach into my pocket and grab another handful of the knock out dust. "What are you talking about?" he asked.

"Don't worry," I said as I took a step towards Ace and blew the dust from my hand into his face. "We'll make sure to film your good side. If you have one, that is." I couldn't help but chuckle and look at Jordan, who actually smiled.

Ace was coughing and spluttering because of the powder I'd blown in his face, and before he could even ask what is was, his eyes rolled back into their sockets and he keeled over onto the ground. Jordan and I stood looking down at him for a second as if we'd just bagged our prize. "You took out those three on your own," I said to her. "Impressive."

Jordan shrugged as she wiped the blood from her nose. "They weren't that hard," she said.

"It was three werewolves."

She shook her head as if she didn't know what more to say. "Let's get sleeping beauty into the van. We still have a vampire to get."

# 14

# STING PART TWO

*W*e still had a vampire to get. As if it was going to be that easy. As if getting a damn werewolf turned out to be that easy. "Have you had much experience with vampires?" I asked Jordan as we cut across the city toward our next destination.

She looked at me and frowned for a second as if she thought I was being sarcastic. I wasn't. Okay, maybe just a little. I like to think I'm the only experienced one sometimes. The truth was, I didn't really know what kind of world Jordan existed in, or what world she came from. I had no doubt she had been through the mill like the rest of us, but in what way I had yet to find out. So it was a legitimate question. "I'm no stranger to vampires," she replied, directing her gaze back to the road, the headlights of oncoming cars and the neon signs of Gomorrah illuminating her face, which in combination with the blood streaked across her one cheek, made her look scary like a stone cold crazy psycho bitch from a horror movie.

I nodded at her answer. "And what does that mean exactly? You've been around them? You know how they operate? How scary powerful they can be?"

She mashed her lips together as she threw me a glance. "Are you questioning my ability to handle the next part of this mission after I just put down three very large werewolves all by myself? Werewolves that wouldn't have been there if it weren't for your past indiscretions. What did you do to that guy anyway?"

A smile creased my lips. "It's a long story," I said. "Let's just say I hindered his ability to go balls deep."

"Why?"

"Because he deserved it. He hurt too many people. Too many women. So I castrated him." When Jordan raised her eyebrows in shock, I added, "Figuratively speaking. Mostly. I removed his desire ever to have sex again."

"With magic, I'm guessing."

"Correct."

"He seemed like a real asshole anyway."

I smiled at her, and she gave me a smile back. At least I was getting somewhere with her. She was starting to trust me, if not completely like me. Hopefully, once my loyalty had been established thanks to the mission, her father would trust me too. Then I could make inroads towards getting the Dark Codex.

Outside the van, the night was full and black but illuminated on all sides by the neon landscape of Gomorrah. Gomorrah was the nickname given to the city's sex district, which consisted of three square miles of real estate dedicated solely to accommodating Blackham's abundance of sex workers and even greater number of consumers. Needless to say, Gomorrah was a favorite haunt of supernatural predators, especially vampires. When someone was killed or went missing in Gomorrah, not too many fucks were given, quite often because the victims were nobodies with no family and no one who would miss them. Low rent hookers were most at risk in this regard because they represented easy pickings for hungry vampires and other predators who fancied a quick meal. I directed Jordan to the east of Gomorrah and the fringe where most of the low-rent streetwalkers could be found selling their ravaged wares, usually just to fund their drink or drug habit.

Jordan parked the van around the corner from one of the back streets. "What's your plan?" she asked. "I intended to lure a vamp out of one of the clubs like I did with the werewolf in the back there."

"Too much trouble," I said as I shook my head. "This way will be easier. All you have to do is pose as a prostitute and lure one to you. I'll be waiting to take them out."

She didn't seem amused by the plan. "You mean you want to use me as bait?"

I shrugged. "Isn't that what you did with the werewolf? What difference does it make?"

"None, I suppose." She looked down the street to see two hookers standing at the street corner. Both had on ridiculously short skirts and tight fitting tops that left their scrawny midriffs exposed. "I'm not exactly dressed for the part."

"I know, which is why this will work. Any vamp that lays eyes on you will think their luck is in, believe me."

Jordan seemed to flush slightly as she quickly looked away, and I couldn't help but smile at her bashfulness. Obviously, she wasn't used to compliments. Like someone else I know. "I can't believe I'm about to pose as a prostitute." She shook her head. "I suppose it isn't the worst thing I've ever done."

"What is then?"

She turned to look at me. "What's the worst thing *you've* ever done?"

"I killed my own father. Does that count?"

Jordan couldn't keep the shock off her face. She also seemed somewhat disturbed by the notion of someone killing their own father. Who knows, maybe she had considered the same thing herself? With a typically domineering father like Gordon Grayson, I couldn't blame her if she did. "Why?" she asked.

"He was about to destroy the whole world," I said, a disturbing image of Mr Black popping into my head as I spoke. "I didn't have a choice."

"Wait, this was recent, right? That's what that portal in the sky was about, with the giant fucking tentacle poking through?"

I nodded. "Yep."

"That was your father doing that?" She shook her head. "We kept a close eye on that situation, though we didn't know it was your father doing it."

"No one did. It was a version of my father really. I called him Mr Black."

"And how do you feel about...killing him?"

I snorted. "Ask me again when I've figured that out for myself." Jordan went quiet as she stared at me, clearly disturbed on some level. "What about *your* father?"

She shifted in her seat. "What about him?"

"Do you have a good relationship with him?" I knew what her answer would be before she even said it. My meeting with her father told me all I needed to know about the man. I was too familiar with his type--a borderline sociopathic megalomaniac with delusions of grandeur to put it bluntly--not to recognize it. I also recognized the behavioral signs of someone with a tyrant for a parent. Seemingly obedient and loyal on the outside, but underneath torn and conflicted, and full of self-loathing.

"I love my father," Jordan said like a good, loyal daughter.

"You can love someone who is still a complete bastard."

Her face hardened as instinctive anger flashed in her eyes, which I was offended by. Her anger was not at me, but at the fact that she knew I had a point, which stirred up the self-loathing she had at continuing to remain under her father's thumb. I could have been reaching, but I didn't think so. Given everything, it wasn't hard to work out. "Mind your own business," she snapped.

"Hey," I said. "It's fine. I understand completely."

"You talk too much." She took her gun out and popped the clip, checking it before slamming it back in again.

"Okay, a conversation for another day then."

"I don't think so." Jordan popped the gun into her bag and opened the van door.

"I'll be close by," I said. "Don't worry."

"I won't. Go wherever you want."

She left the van then, slamming the door behind her. I let out a sigh as I watched her walk away and then turn up a narrow side street. I had pushed one button too many there. The more time I spent with Jordan, the more I felt sorry for her. She seemed to have given over her whole life to serving her father, and was no doubt feeling the pinch of that giant commitment. Already, I wanted to help her, my lack of resistance to a damsel in distress kicking in once again. Jordan was a good person. That much I could tell. She also didn't seem to hold the same conviction for the cause as her father did. She was just following his orders like a loyal daughter. I decided right then that I would do my best to save Jordan when SciCane inevitably fell. The whole thing was Gordon Grayson's doing, and I had no doubt Jordan had suffered enough for his ambitions. Hopefully, things would work out that way, but I knew better than anyone that things often didn't. Look at what happened to Margot Celeste. I thought I would be able to save her as well. And of course Leona, who I saved but who isn't the same person anymore.

I shook my head, wishing I had my whiskey flask with me (it was still in a bag in Red Ridge Forest somewhere), but as I didn't, I merely took a deep breath to center myself and jumped out of the van. Then I walked to the side street Jordan had turned up earlier. As I peeked around the corner, I saw her standing about halfway up, not far from another lone woman that had on something closer to a belt than a skirt. The hookers around there were so low-rent they didn't even have a pimp, which was good news for us because it meant we wouldn't have to deal with some angry slimeball shouting that we had muscled in on his territory.

Jordan spotted me looking around the corner, gave me a hard stare and then turned her back to me. Still tetchy, it seemed. I couldn't blame her. It was a natural reaction to someone drawing attention to the fact that you were a part of an abusive relationship. As much as the relationship itself hurt, it hurt more when other people talked about it.

Across the street, there was a liquor store, the bottles in the window not only giving me a thirst, but also an idea, which was perhaps a mere justification to sate my craving for the hard stuff. But who cares? So I went across the road and bought a fifth of Jack Daniels, and then went and sat fifty yards from where Jordan stood leaning against the wall like a lost high-class escort. I raised the bottle at her as I sat down on the pavement with my back against the wall, and she shook her head at me as if to ask what the hell was I doing. "Ignore me," I said, just loud enough for her to hear. "I'm just a bum."

She made a face as if to agree with me on that one, then turned her back to me once again. Up the street, the other hooker headed off somewhere with a John.

Over the course of the next two hours, Jordan was approached by no less than four different men who wanted to pay her for sex. Two of the men walked off when Jordan politely told them to go fuck themselves. The other two men fled when Jordan pulled her gun on them. All four men completely ignored me, so I guess I was doing a good job of pretending to be a bum. Some might say I didn't have to pretend too hard. Those people, although they might have a point, can go fuck themselves.

The fifth man to come along seemed slightly different to the other four. This man was taller than Jordan at over six feet, and athletically built. He also wore a dark suit as if he was a resident of The Highlands who had wandered too far across town. Except this guy didn't wander anywhere by accident. He was there by design, seeming to almost glide through the darkness with the practiced prowess of an experienced predator. As he glided by me, he approached Jordan almost silently like a Jaguar approaching its prey. Jordan had spotted him of course and obviously knew immediately that the man was a vampire. Even in the darkness with only a single street lamp for light, I saw the momentary look of fear on Jordan's face. She was smart enough to know that vampires were highly dangerous. It wasn't for nothing that they were apex predators and top of the food chain in Blackham and most of the rest of the world.

"Well, this is a surprise," the vampire said as he walked up to Jordan. "Are you sure you aren't lost? Such a lovely specimen does not belong in a back street such as this." The vampire held out his hand. "Come, why don't you? My limo is parked just around the corner. I can take us somewhere more fitting for a woman of your...class."

As I slowly got to my feet so the vampire wouldn't notice, I saw Jordan hold out her hand to him. "Let's go then."

Was she playing along, or had she been glamoured by the vampire? It was hard to tell. It didn't really matter. As long as she kept the vamp's attention so I could blast him with magic first, and then finish him by throwing a handful of Oblivion

Powder in his face. There were spells I could have tried that would render the vampire unconscious or incapacitated, but the thing about vampires is that many of them were smart enough to keep themselves warded against magic spells. A long time ago, the vamps realized that being just powerful wasn't enough to thwart a magical attack from an accomplished wizard or witch. So the vamps developed means to protect themselves against such devious attacks, and such knowledge was handed down to every new vampire, including the one standing by Jordan, no doubt. If I tried any spells and they failed, the vamp would be alerted to my intentions, and I would have a fight on my hands. A fight I didn't fancy my chances in with no gun and no knife to even the odds.

A magic blast however, was a straight physical attack, and one which the vampire couldn't block if he didn't see it coming.

The attack would have worked if I hadn't have underestimated the vamp. The bastard had obviously sensed me as a threat from the beginning. As soon as I unleashed a large blast of vermillion magic, the vamp sidestepped in a flash and Jordan took the full force of the blast, which lifted her off her feet and sent her flying back into a nearby dumpster with a loud thud. Then she hit the ground and lay there unmoving. "Shit!" I said, preparing another blast as the vampire turned to face me.

"I'm not sure what this is," he said in a calm voice. "But whatever it is, did you think it would really work?"

My answer was to send another blast his way, but he was so fast he managed to reach me before the blast even got halfway towards his previous position. In a flash, his hand was around my throat, lifting me clean off my feet, his steel grip crushing my windpipe and the arteries in the side of my neck.

"Stupid human," the vampire said, his eyes now burning red in their sockets, his fangs fully out as he sneered at me. "You can be my starter tonight before I have the woman for my main course. Then maybe I'll take your ID, find your family, and have them for desert."

*Good luck with that*, I thought, or think I thought anyway. My head was so fuzzy I couldn't tell. Then as unconsciousness raced towards me, my left hand twitched slightly, and I remembered I had something in it. I couldn't think what it was, but some instinct was telling me to throw it at the vampire.

So I did. I took what was in my hand and threw it in the vampire's face. Through slits for eyes, I saw the vamp recoil as a cloud seemed to form around his face. Then mercifully, his grip around my neck loosened for a moment as he coughed and spluttered. Finally, he let me go, and I fell to the ground. Two seconds later, the vamp fell to the ground beside me as I was choking and trying to deal with the massive rush of blood and oxygen going to my head as consciousness fell back into the driver's seat again. "Oh, fuck..." I said as I rubbed at my neck. "Motherfucker."

The vamp was out cold on the ground. I guess he wasn't expecting me to throw a handful of Oblivion Powder in his face.

*Live and learn, asshole. Live and learn.*

I startled as I remembered Jordan. When I looked up the street, I saw she was still on the ground in the same position as when I last saw her. "Shit," I said as I got to my feet and rushed over to her. "Jordan...can you hear me, Jordan...wake up." Jordan stirred as I gently tapped her on the face. Then her eyes flew open suddenly, and she recoiled away from me. I held up my hands. "Relax. It's just me."

"What happened?" she asked, looking confused and still a bit afraid.

"You were knocked out...by my magic."

She frowned. "Why?"

I shrugged. "The vamp avoided my attack. You took it instead."

"The vamp?" She jumped to her feet then and looked down the alley. "Where..." Then she spotted the figure on the ground. "Is that him over there?"

"It is. He's taking a nap right now."

Jordan looked at me then, something like admiration in her eyes. "You took him down by yourself?"

"It's like I said. This isn't my first rodeo. You think your father will be pleased?"

Her eyes grew slightly defensive as she obviously remembered our conversation from the van. "I'm sure he will be," she said with a slight bite to her voice.

"Good," I said back. "Because the last thing I want to do is displease him."

Jordan stared for a moment, then shook her head. "Let's go," she said. "We still have a show to put on."

# 15

# POKING THE SLEEPING TIGER

*T*he Grayson Dimension. I don't think that was the official name for the little off-world enclave created by Gordon Grayson, but the name seemed fitting as at times I felt like I was trapped in a soap opera. One of those eighties shows like Dallas or Dynasty with power-mad characters at the center. Gordon Grayson could have been the J.R. Ewing of his own show except for the fact that he wasn't interested in oil or money or playing the system for all it was worth. He was more interested in destroying said system and letting the people build their own replacement. So he said anyway. I still wasn't sure if his motives were not more nefarious and narcissistic than he was letting on. Either way, as the star of his own show, he was doing a good job of running things. Every member of SciCane that I came across seemed to be totally subservient to the guy. His followers worshiped him like he was some sort of visionary. And maybe he was. There was no denying the man was a force to be reckoned with. He had managed to find the Dark Codex, after all, a book that no one had laid eyes in seemingly forever. People were not even sure of its existence, but yet somehow, a lowly scientist (albeit a brilliant one in his time) had found the damn thing. With significant help from his number one follower, of course. His daughter.

Back in the Grayson Dimension with our two captives in tow (and after I teleported all of us right to the dimension gate), I was starting to see what an efficient team Grayson and his daughter made. Gordon would float around inspiring everyone with his presence while Jordan gave orders and organized the "crackpots" so things could get done.

And what was being done was a show within a show. Everyone was back in the main hall of the mansion, having returned from their respective missions. Those missions, as it turned out, were the same as the mission Jordan and I had returned from. Only the monsters were different. And all of the monsters, nearly a dozen of them, were lined up on stage. Their limbs were bound by magical energy--thick bands of purplish light that encircled the ankles and wrists of each supernatural being. The bonds were powerful and somehow stopped the captives from moving anywhere. Each one was forced to stand beside the other like prisoners awaiting execution. What was really freaking me out was the fact that none of the captives had a mouth anymore. Where their mouths should have been there was now only bare skin as if their mouths had never existed. I knew Grayson's acquired magic was responsible for the change in anatomy. Looking at him in his pristine white robes as he stood to the side of the stage looking intensely at the supernaturals, I noticed small arcs of purple and violet energy crackle off him like static electricity. Only it wasn't anything as benign as electricity. It was pure magical energy. Unbelievably, Grayson had so much magic in him he was struggling to contain it all as it leaked out of him. *Hopefully, not like a damn about to burst*, I thought to myself as I stood to one side of the hall while watching everything get set up for the show. It was entirely possible for a person to take on too much magic, to the point where that magic made them explode like supernovas. It was a well-documented condition. I had a feeling though that Grayson had found a way to contain the energy within himself, again thanks to the knowledge in the Dark Codex. It did beg the question, however, of how much magic Grayson intended to take on board, and why he would need so much magic in the first place.

I didn't have time to dwell on such questions though, as Jordan beckoned me over towards the stage. I moved through the groups of people standing around staring at the supernaturals on stage and practically bouncing with excitement and anticipation at what was to come. Jordan stood by one of three digital film cameras that were mounted on tripods by the front of the stage. "We're almost ready," she said. "You know what you have to do?"

I nodded. Just destroy my reputation, that's all. "I got this."

"Good." She seemed nervous, more tense than usual.

"You all right?"

"I'm fine. It's just we've waited a long time for this moment when we would finally awaken the world to the horrors that surround it."

The zealousness was there, but I wasn't feeling the conviction. Deep down, I didn't think Jordan agreed with any of what was going on or anything her father was doing. So deep, in fact, that she wasn't even aware of it. I was though, and I was glad to know it. It meant I had a chance of turning her, maybe even enlisting her help to get the book. We'd see. "Relax," I told her, touching her arm and smiling. "Everything will go fine. You should be proud for getting this far."

Her smile didn't come immediately, and when it did come, it faltered slightly. "Pride has nothing to do with it. It's necessity and doing what's right."

We both looked at each other for a moment, the look in her eyes not exactly matching her words. Which she knew, but didn't really try to conceal. Then she looked away when the people in the hall suddenly started clapping just as Gordon Grayson walked to the center of the stage, stopping directly in front of one of the cameras. Cameras I assumed were now rolling.

*Showtime*, I thought, wishing I didn't have to take part, but knowing I didn't have a choice.

Grayson stood tall and proud with just the right amount of modesty, so he didn't come across as too arrogant. Tiny sparks of magical energy still emanated from him, and on occasion, I saw veins of dark purplish light show up on his face and arms as if the magic within him was constantly fluctuating and traveling around his body. Behind him, the restrained and mute supernaturals struggled futilely against their magical bonds, but no matter how much power and strength any of them possessed, they would never break free. The vampire's eyes were seething. Ace the werewolf's face was full of disconcertedness. A female shapeshifter looked scared and confused. Another man who was a Wendigo also looked scared. The wererat and the two demons seemed to be staying calm as if they knew it was futile to be any other way. And finally, the Blood Beast, a giant of a man who could transform into something resembling a Sasquatch, stared hard at the crowd in the hall as if he wanted to rip all their heads off. Grayson had chosen each supernatural because of the radical transformations they could enact. Which of course, would make for great TV.

As the crowd in the hall fell silent, Grayson addressed the camera. "Good people of the world," he began in a voice that conveyed his confidence and the promise of revelation. "I speak to you today as a concerned citizen, and as someone who has had enough of the lies and coverups perpetrated by those in charge. I am speaking to you now because I feel it is my duty to show you the truth about the world you all live in, and the threats around every corner that you are not even aware of. Today, I will make you aware of those threats, of the monsters in our midst, so that you may rise against them and take back the world which is rightfully yours. Once you see the truth, you can never go back. But don't worry, because I will also enable every one of you with the power to stand up against your oppressors and your hidden enemies. But first things first. Let me first reveal to you the monsters--the *real monsters*--that live in your midst, and who have been hunting people like you since forever with complete impunity."

Brentwood would be having a fit by now, I thought. It was Brentwood's job to keep the supernatural under wraps. His worst nightmare was someone broadcasting the existence of monsters across the world's media. And what was worse was the fact that there was nothing Division and all of its resources could do to stop the broadcast. Grayson had the power of the Dark Codex behind him, and he had manipulated the technology--crude technology in comparison to what he probably discovered in the Dark Codex--so no one else could. The man was in complete control of everything.

Grayson spent another few minutes talking about SciCane and what the organization represented, calling upon the people he addressed to join him in the fight, which he felt sure they would once they saw what he was about to show them.

Or rather what *I* was about to show them.

When Grayson had finished his speech, he beckoned me with a smile up to the stage. *Here we go*, I thought, nervous as hell as I stood in front of the camera like I had planned to do with Grayson. "Hello," I said. "My name is August Creed. Some of you might know me already. I've spent the last three decades dealing with the supernatural and living in the occult underground. I'm now a member of SciCane, and I am about to show you the monsters that you've always suspected lived under your bed and hid in your closet, but which you never really knew existed for real." I stood to the side of the camera then as I waved my arm at the supernatural captives behind me. "Behold. These people look like ordinary men and women, but I assure you, they are far from it, as I will now show you."

My stomach churning, I had an overwhelming urge to dash off the stage and run from the Grayson Dimension never to return. In a moment of clarity, it hit me then how much had changed recently, and it tore at my guts that I could never put things back to the way they were, and that now things were about to change again just as drastically, and perhaps even disastrously.

"As you can see," I said while I walked in front of the captives. "The mouths of these monsters have been...sealed, to keep them quiet. This was done with magic, ladies and gentlemen." Ladies and gentlemen? Where the fuck did I think I was, *Letterman?* "That's right, I said magic. You'll be hearing more about that shortly. In the meantime, I will now use my own magic to force these creatures to transform themselves into their true monstrous forms."

That last part was a lie. I still didn't have access to my magic within the Grayson Dimension because Gordon Grayson was still blocking it somehow. Obviously, the man didn't yet fully trust me, which was slightly annoying, given what I had done for him so far. So I now had to make a show of doing magic when really it was Grayson, standing by the side of the stage, who would be forcing the captives to transform via his own magic. I stood before the struggling captives and made a few exaggerated gestures with my hands as I spoke some words in an ancient language that was actually two lines from a poem written by an old mystic from Babylon. Once I'd finished, the struggles of the captives increased as Grayson's magic forced them all into their transformations from human to supernatural creature. In a matter of moments, there was now a fully transformed werewolf, a raging vampire, a seething wererat, a massive Blood Beast, two grotesquely misshapen demons, a roaring Wendigo and a shapeshifter who continually shifted from one form to another uncontrollably, moving through the forms of every person she had ever taken on. Despite the changes, the bonds still held the creatures in place, expanding to allow for the bigger growth in limbs in some cases. Each of their mouths was now also uncovered, and every one of them screamed and roared with rage and frustration as they continued to struggle futilely against their bonds.

I addressed the camera once more. "Behold!" I said theatrically. "The monsters in your midst!"

At that point, with sweat forming on my brow and soaking my armpits, I exited the stage and went and stood beside Jordan again, who only glanced at me briefly as she kept her eyes on the stage as if she were afraid that the creatures might get loose. "Nice performance," she said.

"Really?" I countered. "I thought I was a little stiff."

Jordan shook her head as if she was unable to tell if I was serious or not, which I was and I wasn't. But no matter about the quality of my performance on stage, there was no denying that my reputation was now shot. If I ever managed to resolve the situation I was in, I wasn't sure if I would ever work again as a wizard. Who would want to work with me after what I just did? Every supernatural I knew would want me dead for exposing them.

*Fuck it*, I thought. I'd find a way to sort things. The important thing now was that I had hopefully earned the trust of Gordon Grayson. With any luck, it wouldn't be long before I was able to locate the Dark Codex. And who knows, maybe there would be something in the book to help fix a tattered reputation.

Grayson was back on center stage, smiling smugly at the raging supernatural creatures behind him. Then he turned to face the camera again. "Behold the truth!" he proclaimed, his arms outstretched. "These are the monsters that live in this world, that control this world, which feed off you and your children! And I submit to you now, people of the world, that these foul creatures must be stopped. They must all be wiped out, and that includes—especially includes—the ones at the root of our power structures. Those that rule from the shadows, and who work every single day to keep you—the good people of the world—in ignorance. It is time to awaken, people! It is time for you to rise up against your supernatural oppressors, and to take back the power that is rightfully yours! It is time for each man and woman of this Earth to rule themselves instead of being ruled by those who don't belong in this world! By those who belong in the depths of Hell!"

*Nice,* I thought. *He's playing the religious card.* People will see those creatures on stage, and that's the first thing they would think. That all of the creatures were from Hell. The fear of God would be put in their souls, and Grayson knew that. He was smart to play on it. It would make his audience more susceptive to what he had to say.

"You might now be asking yourselves," Grayson went on. "How are you going to protect yourselves against such powerful, terrifying creatures? Well, fear not, for I will soon give you all the power you will need to crush these creatures and destroy the supernatural underground once and for all. For the most important revelation I have to reveal to you is that magic—real magic—exists in this world, and always has." Grayson held out his hand's palm up then and conjured a sphere of bright purple light in each hand. "This is the magical energy that I will give each of you access to. This is what you are going to use to change your destiny, and most importantly, the world." He paused for a moment, for dramatic effect no doubt. "Be ready, people, for soon I will bestow the gift of magic on you all. Then we will take back the world. Together!"

"And cut!" someone by the cameras said.

Grayson smiled to himself as magical energy sparked off him. "Excellent," he said, now addressing the people in the hall as they started cheering and clapping. "The Sleeping Tiger has been awakened at last!"

Jordan was clapping and smiling along with everyone else as she gazed up at her father, though I couldn't speak to her conviction. I still wasn't entirely sure if she fully believed in what they were all doing. If she didn't believe, she certainly played the part well of someone who did.

"Now," Grayson said. "Time to dispose of the filth on this stage."

He turned to face the still raging captives, spreading his arms out wide as he reared his head back. Then he held his hands out and arcs of purple energy shot from his hands and into the chests of each of the bound creatures. The roars of rage soon turned to screams of pain and fear, and within seconds, every one of the creatures seemed to spontaneously combust all at the same time, the flames so intense they were reduced to piles of blackened ash in a matter of seconds.

"Jesus Christ," I breathed, astounded at the power Grayson had at his fingertips. I didn't know of any wizard who could do what he just did. Not even Sanaka, and he was one of the most powerful wizard's I knew. What the hell was in that book that could give Grayson access to such power? Whatever it was, it had no place in the hands of someone like Grayson, nor anybody for that matter.

As soon as I found it, I was burning the fucking thing to ash.

# PARTY TIME IN THE GRAYSON
# DIMENSION

*N*eedless to say, after the SciCane broadcast, the world went slightly crazy. The government, of course, tried to suppress the video footage of the supernaturals being outed, but that was impossible since Grayson's media reach was wide. By the time the government and the occult underground knew what was going on, the video had already gone viral around the world. Some people thought the whole thing was a hoax, but most who saw the footage of the transforming monsters and Grayson's use of magic couldn't deny that it was all real. In trying to suppress the footage, the government only made things worse. People knew then that there must be something to it if the government was trying to cover it up. Just in case, Gordon kept the broadcast going on a loop on his own social media channel that absolutely no one could switch off but him. Such was the power of his reach now, and all thanks to the book, of course. The book I needed to get my hands on soon before Grayson turned the world upside down if indeed he hadn't already done so.

There was no doubt in my mind that the occult underground would be gunning for me after my appearance on the video. Most would see me as a traitor. Some wouldn't know what to believe. Others, like Angela Crow, would know what I was up to, but the public outing would still grate on them. The Crow was probably seething right now, thinking I had taken things a step too far. She was probably paranoid her kind would be hunted now.

That was the whole point of the video as far as Gordon Grayson was concerned anyway. He wanted the supernatural element to be running scared. While vampires and other supernatural creatures may have been powerful and numerous, they were still outnumbered many times over by the Sleepwalkers. No matter how powerful the supernatural element was, they couldn't defend against that many people gunning for them.

And going by the media reports, it seemed the hunt had already begun. Across the world, Sleepwalkers were banding together like groups of vigilantes to flush out the monsters in their neighborhoods and kill them. They gave interviews on local news stations where they voiced their outrage that such creatures were in existence all this time and no one had saw fit to warn them. "Our kids are not safe!" they would scream. "We won't stop until every last stinking creature is dead!"

You couldn't blame the people for being so outraged. Their actions were motivated by fear, which Grayson knew was one of the most powerful motivators. If you wanted to stir up a revolution, then stirring up fear first was a good way to start one.

And while the world was going mad, the members of SciCane were partying on down in Grayson Manor. As you do, of course, when you've just turned the world upside down. Nearly a hundred people occupied the great hall, all of them guzzling from bottles of wine and strong liquor that Grayson had obviously provided to them. To keep his followers happy, of course.

I grabbed a bottle of whiskey and hung out with Sam and his dorky friends for a while. They looked at me like I was some kind of awesome revolutionary like fucking Che Guevara. Their naivety was painful to watch as they discussed in drunken slurs how different, and how much better, the world was going to be when they had finished enacting their leader's plans. Looking around, I saw a hall full of rejects. People who didn't belong in normal society for one reason or another, hence why they ended up joining Grayson's cult, having no idea (or simply not caring) that their great leader viewed them as nothing more than minions to do his bidding and carry out his dirty work. But for the time being at least, everyone I spoke with in the hall felt like they belonged for the first time in their lives. Not only that, they felt like they were making a real difference. They were changing the world. Which they were, of course, but maybe not in the way they thought. They thought that once the playing field had been leveled and magic and the supernatural became commonplace, and the traditional power structures had been torn down, that the world would be some harmonious, magical place where everybody would get along and be free to do their own thing without interference from above. They thought the human race would evolve into this wondrously magical species who would go on to spread knowledge and goodwill throughout the universe. I don't know whether this was wish fulfillment on their parts, or whether Grayson had filled their heads with utopian fantasies, but either way, it was complete nonsense.

The only thing certain about Grayson's plan was that it would plunge the world into complete chaos, especially when phase two was put into place. It was bad enough that the Sleepwalkers had been awakened, but Grayson was planning on empowering them with magic. What kind of magic or how much, I still didn't know. I just knew any amount of magic in the hands of the uninitiated would end in disaster. A fucking blind man could see that. Grayson himself surely saw it, which made me wonder if he didn't have some hidden agenda, though I couldn't speak as to the nature of such an agenda. Maybe he wanted to rule the universe. He seemed the type to want to do so, and in my experience, all power mad motherfuckers like him wanted to either rule or destroy the world. They couldn't help it, because when you have that much power (like Mr Black had), it became a question of one or the other. Rule or destroy. The question was, which one was Grayson going to pick?

When I was finally able to tear myself away from Sam and his best buddies, I took my by now half empty bottle of whiskey and started to head to my quarters. As I was doing so, I spotted Jordan from across the hall. She seemed to have the same idea as she slinked away through one of the exits with a bottle of something in her hand. Right then, I thought it a good idea to follow her and join her in her room if that's where she was going. If nothing else, it was a better idea than going back to my own quarters and drinking alone.

"Jordan," I called when I spotted her going down a long hallway. "Wait up."

Jordan stopped and turned around as I jogged down the hallway towards her. "What do you want?" she asked, clearly not in the party mood.

"Nothing much. I just thought you could use some company." I held up the bottle in my hand and nodded at the one in hers. "Better than drinking alone, right?"

"Says who?" She started walking again, and I followed her.

"Says someone who drinks alone all the time." I caught up with her and fell in beside her as we turned a corner into another wood-paneled hallway.

"Maybe I like drinking alone."

"No one likes drinking alone."

She shook her head and then stopped by a door in the hallway. "Fine," she said. "One drink, and that's it."

I smiled and nodded, her inference that there was to be no funny business not passing me by. "Okay." She opened the door, and I walked into her quarters with her, closing the door behind me. The room was a lot bigger than mine, and the bed in the center was also a four poster, though again bigger than mine. It didn't look like it had been slept in recently though. The sheets were still immaculate.

"You weren't enjoying the party?" she asked as she grabbed two glasses from a cabinet in the corner of the room, coming back to hand me one.

"Not really," I replied as I accepted the glass and sat down on the chaise lounge while she sat on the other end. "It was like Jack Nicholson had dropped them all of in the bus for the school disco." Jordan burst out laughing, which surprised me. "You've seen *One Flew Over The Cuckoos Nest?*"

"Of course," she replied, still smiling. "Hasn't everyone?"

"I guess so. I just thought you'd have been too busy over the years to watch movies, what with the whole quest thing with your father to find...what was it again?"

Her smile faded, though not completely. She'd drunk too much already to keep up her usual guarded seriousness. Which I was hoping was the case when I decided to follow her.

*And that's not the only thing you were hoping, eh? Wink, wink, nudge, nudge...*

I paid the thought no heed. Just my sex-starved brain and it's wishful thinking. I blamed all the recent adrenaline.

"I didn't say what it was," Jordan said.

"Come on." I relaxed back into the chaise lounge and took a drink. "I thought we were on the same side now. The least you can do is fill me in. If nothing else I'd like to hear about your adventures up till now."

She snorted. "Adventures? I wouldn't call them that."

"What then? What would you call them?"

Jordan stared for a moment as if deciding if she could really trust me. In the end, I think a combination of the alcohol she'd consumed and a desire to connect with another person other than her father pushed her into opening up. And if the only other people she had to talk to were the one's in the great hall, I didn't blame her. "all right, Creed," she said, settling back into her seat in a resigned sort of way as if she thought it would somehow do her good to talk to someone. And of course, I was happy to listen, not only because I hoped she would discuss the Dark Codex and its whereabouts, but also because I was genuinely interested in Jordan Grayson. And attracted. Don't forget attracted. "What do you want to know?"

"I want to know what brought you here," I said. "I want to know how you ended up in the Grayson Dimension."

"Fine, but afterward, *I* want to know how *you* ended up here."

I nodded. "Deal."

"Needless to say," she began. "I'm here because of my father..."

# JORDAN'S STORY

Thirty-seven years ago, Jordan Grayson was brought into the world by Gordon and Marie Grayson. Gordon was a research scientist of little note at the time, and Marie was a respected defense attorney. As an only child, Jordan led a happy life for the first seven years of her existence. She excelled at her private school, always staying in the top few percent of her class, showing a particular talent for art. Her drawing skills were apparently well beyond her years, and she spent many hours each day sketching and painting. To balance things out, her mother enrolled her in a gymnastics class, and also a martial arts school, both of which Jordan took to immediately, showing great promise in martial arts in particular.

Then Jordan came home from school one day to find her father crying in the living room. Immediately, Jordan knew something terrible had happened. She had never seen her father cry before, not even when both his parents died within months of each other the year before. Jordan dropped her school bag to the floor as her own tears began to flow, and she asked her father what was wrong. Although somewhere inside, Jordan already knew what was wrong. Something had happened to her mother, she knew.

And something did happen. Her mother was attacked at her office by a man she put away a few years before, a psychopath named Tommy Farnes who went down for assault. When he got released, the first thing he did was seek revenge on the lawyer who put him away, Marie Grayson. Farnes beat Marie Grayson over the head repeatedly with a stapler that he grabbed from her desk. He didn't stop hitting her with it until another lawyer walked in and restrained him. But by then it was too late. Marie Grayson went into a coma and never came back out of it. She died a month later when the machines keeping her alive were switched off.

Needless to say, things changed for Jordan after that. She lost all interest in her studies and dropped to the bottom of her class. She stopped drawing and painting as well. The only thing she kept up was her martial arts training, and only because she had this idea in her head that she would one day get revenge on the man who killed her dear mother.

Gordon Grayson threw himself deep into his work after his wife died, switching the focus of his work to the nature of consciousness. He thought if he could isolate a person's consciousness, then perhaps he would be able to download it some way and save it somewhere until another body was found to put it in. It was pipe dream stuff no doubt, but Gordon was motivated by grief, and the desire to save his little girl should anything happen to her in the future. He wanted to create a backup of her consciousness should it ever be needed, as well as his own.

The result of all her father's constant working was that Jordan rarely saw him. She was looked after part time by a hired nanny. The rest of the time she looked after herself, which she soon became good at. The desire for revenge never left her either. She spent her days hating the man who ended her mother's life, often fantasizing about killing him in horrible ways. After many months, it was all she could think about, until one day she decided that something had to be done.

"I was about eight years old," Jordan told me as she lay on the chaise lounge and continued to drink vodka while I guzzled my bottle of whiskey. "And all I could think about was killing that son of a bitch that took my mother from me." She shook her head. "I blamed him for everything, for taking everything away that was good in my life."

"That's some heavy shit for an eight-year-old to be carrying around," I said. "Didn't your father notice what was going on with you?"

"I kept it well hidden. He thought I was getting on with things. Not that he gave it too much thought anyway. All he cared about was his work. Sometimes I thought he resented me for being alive, that he thought it should have been me who died and not my mother."

"I'm sure that wasn't true."

"You don't know my father. He can be spiteful, resentful. Mean even."

"I know the type."

"Your father was the same?"

"You could say that, but we'll talk about him later. Continue."

Almost three years after her mother's passing, two things happened that would change Jordan's life forever.

The first thing was that she saw Tommy Farnes one day on her way back from her martial arts class in downtown Los Angeles where she used to live. She stopped dead when she saw him, knowing there was no way it wasn't him because every detail of his face was burned into her brain by then. But he was supposed to be in jail. Why was he out walking around without a care in the world with some woman hanging off his arm?

"It turned out, Farnes had been given an early release for helping the Feds with some case," Jordan said. "The bastard had made a deal. I didn't know that at the time though. I just thought it was incredibly unfair and unjust that he should be out walking the streets. It felt like a snub from God, even though I've never believed in God, but that's how it felt. And I got so fucking angry, seeing that man smiling with his girlfriend as he walked into a cinema..." She trailed off and shook her head as if the feelings she described were still fresh in her. Which I knew they were. Such feelings never went away. They just got pushed to the back of your mind over time where they sat festering until you thought about them again.

"So what did you do?" I asked her.

"Something came over me. It was like a coldness, and all my other emotions shut down except for this burning desire to kill Farnes. I knew right then that I had to do it, if not for me then for my mother."

"And did you?"

"I followed Farnes and his girlfriend into the cinema. A few other people were there, but I hardly noticed them as I took a seat right behind Farnes. I sat there for a while, shaking like a leaf, terrified that he would turn around and notice me, even though he wouldn't have known who I was. But I had it in my head that he would know when he looked in my eyes, that he would somehow recognize my mother in me. But he didn't turn around because he was too busy groping his girlfriend." Jordan stopped and took a shuttering breath as if she was going to cry. "I'm sorry. I've never spoken about this to anyone before."

"That's okay," I said, refilling her glass for her. "Take your time. I know how hard this stuff is to talk about."

Jordan nodded, sipped from her glass, and then continued. "After a while, the fear I felt going in there just seemed to leave me, and I felt calm because I knew what I had to do next. I'd never been more certain of anything in my life, in fact. I reached down into my training bag where I had a sai that I trained with. You know what a sai is?"

I nodded. "An Okinawan piercing weapon. I have a set at home."

"Well, I took the sai out of the bag, and I held it for a minute while I waited for Farnes to stop kissing his girlfriend. Eventually, he did. Then..." She trailed off as her eyes focused downwards as if she was reliving the whole event. "I thrust the sai into the back of Farnes' head, in the hollow of his skull. He didn't know what hit him as I kept the sai in his skull for a minute. As his girlfriend started screaming, I leaned over and looked into Farnes' eyes just before he died. 'For my mother,' I told him, then I pulled the sai out of his skull at the same time as the smell of shit and piss filled the air around me. I felt nothing at the time, apart from the satisfaction of knowing he was dead, the man who took my mother from me."

It was hard to believe that an eight-year-old girl could do such a cold-blooded act of murder, but I knew from her eyes she was telling the truth. "What happened after?"

What happened was she got home to find her father in a state, babbling that everything had gone wrong and that they were all dead. They being the seven people who were killed by the evil spirit he inadvertently allowed into this world. Of course, he didn't explain any of that to Jordan at the time. He just told her they had to go. Jordan, having just killed a man, wasn't particularly stable herself, mentally speaking. In her mind, running made perfect sense because that way, if anyone came looking for her for killing Farnes, she wouldn't be around and therefore wouldn't go to jail.

"But little did I know that the rest of my life would be one long jail sentence," she said, sounding drunk and more than a little bitter.

"That bad, huh?" I asked.

She smiled exaggeratedly and nodded her head. "Fucking...bad."

I stared at her a moment before speaking. "I don't get it, Jordan. Why have you stuck around for your father's crusade all these years when you clearly don't believe in it."

"I believe."

"I don't think you do."

"All right, Creed," she said, waving her glass antagonistically at me. "Tell me why you think I don't believe."

"I think you know the answer to that already. You followed your father because you had to, because you were only a kid at the time, and because you thought the police were going to be after you for killing the man who put your mother in a coma. You probably feared going to jail for the rest of your life, so you gladly ran along with your father. And over the years, you've stuck with him out of guilt, because you somehow see this as being your punishment."

Jordan stared at me for a long time after I'd finished, her face going from angry to sad, and then to drunken stoicism as she flopped her head back on the chaise lounge. "You don't know me, Creed. Killing Farnes, that's not even the worst thing I've done. If you knew some of the things..." She trailed off and looked away.

"Things you've done for your father, you mean?"

"Yes, but it makes no difference. *I* did those things, not him. *Me*."

After refilling my glass, I sat in silence for a while as I contemplated Jordan and her story. She had more darkness in her than I initially realized. A lot more. But I had no doubt that her darkness grew out of her loyalty to her father, and her deep-seated guilt over killing a man at age eight. Fuck, she was just a kid. How could something like that not fuck her up? I also couldn't be sure, but I was pretty certain Jordan's father used her guilt over that incident, and her fear of getting caught, to control her, and to force her to do whatever he asked of her. It was hard not to feel sympathy for Jordan. She was just another damaged soul, abused and taken advantage of by someone who should have been looking out for her instead of using her for his own ends. Let's just say I could relate.

"You know," I said eventually as Jordan wiped tears from her eyes. "You can just leave all this. There's nothing to say you have to stick around any longer."

Jordan snorted derisively and shook her head. "It's not that easy, and you know it."

"Maybe not, but what's your alternative? Be a slave till you die?"

"What do you want me to do, Creed? Kill my own father?"

"I did," I said quietly.

"Yeah, and look at you."

I couldn't help but feel shocked. "What's that supposed to mean?"

"No offense, Creed, but you're not the most well-adjusted person I've met."

"Well, considering what I've been through recently, I think I'm doing fine, so..." I looked away, angry for a moment as all of my problems presented themselves in my mind at once.

Then I felt Jordan's hand on my leg. "I'm sorry."

"Forget it. You're probably right anyway. I don't know how I haven't gone insane by this point."

"Too late," she said, and laughed, and I laughed along with her.

"So, this thing you said you spent the last twenty odd years searching for."

Jordan released her hand from my leg. "What about it?"

"I'm not going to lie to you, I know it's the Dark Codex."

Her head snapped around to look at me. "How did..."

"Did I know? I had heard rumors before I got here. And given the power your father wields, he couldn't have gotten it from anywhere else."

Jordan frowned then as if realizing something. "Is that why you're really here?" she asked. "To get your hands on the book?"

"Of course not," I lied. "I have no interest in the book. I'm just making sure we're on the same page, so to speak."

She stared for a moment as if trying to tell if I was lying to her. Then she focused on her vodka bottle as she refilled her glass. "That fucking book has been the bane of my life." Her bottle was empty now, and she tossed it onto the floor where it rolled across the boards, coming to a stop near the bed.

"Why?" I asked though I knew the answer already.

"Why?" She laughed bitterly. "The search for that cursed book turned me...into a monster. I've kidnapped, tortured and killed people just to get one step closer to finding it. You have no idea..."

"I'm shocked you found it all. There has never been proof of its existence even. Until now that is."

"My father believed in its existence," she said, quite drunk now as she slurped from her glass. "Sometimes I wonder if his blind faith alone brought the book into existence."

"Stranger things have happened."

Jordan drained what was left in her glass and then dropped the empty glass to the floor. "Would you like to sleep with me, Creed?" she asked out of the blue, her eyes on me.

Slightly taken aback, I hesitated before answering. "You're drunk, Jordan."

"And? You've never taken advantage of a drunk girl before?"

"Not really," I said, smiling politely.

"Of course you haven't, because you're a perfect fucking gentleman, right?" She laughed somewhat manically and then buried her head in her hands as she almost fell off the chaise lounge.

I set my glass on the floor and gently laid my hands on her shoulders, surprised at how hard she felt under her clothes. "Come on. Let's get you to bed."

She didn't resist as I helped her over to the big four poster bed and lay her down on it. When I went to leave, she quickly grabbed my hand. "Don't go. Please."

Looking down at her, I was hit with a wave of sympathy for her. She had probably never known real love, and she was also clearly desperate to connect with someone, which I was happy to do, tonight at least. "all right." I took my trench coat off and lay it on the back of a chair. Then I lay on the bed next to Jordan, and she rolled into me, placing her arm across my chest as she held me tight. I wrapped my arms around her. "Sleep now."

Jordan mumbled something into my chest that I didn't catch, then fell asleep a moment later while I lay there awake for a good hour thinking mostly about Leona and the Dark Codex, neither of which gave me good dreams.

# 18

## THE UNIVERSE AND OTHER THINGS

*W*hen I awoke the next morning, Jordan was gone, and the first thing I thought was that I had to get the Dark Codex. And soon, before Grayson unleashed magic upon a world that wasn't ready for it, and probably never would be.

I winced as I rolled off the bed, the previous night's whiskey consumption now making it feel like a whole building crew had moved into my skull and were now going at it hammer and tongs. The first thing I did was check the whiskey bottle on the floor, but it was empty. Probably just as well. If I were going to make a serious play for the Dark Codex, it would help if I was sober.

Sitting on the edge of the bed for a moment, I looked around at Jordan's room. For its large size, there was very little in it, especially in the way of personal possessions that weren't just practical in nature like combat boots, a laptop and a number of weapons strewn around. There were no photographs, no quirky or weird items. Nothing to suggest that only Jordan alone lived there. It could have been anybody's room. Of course, it was possible that Jordan kept her most valuable possessions back on Earth, but something told me she didn't have any such possessions. People who spend all their time punishing themselves over past wrongs didn't tend to have that much stuff around them beyond the bare necessities. Possibly a single item that reminded them of what a terrible person they were, but I saw nothing in Jordan's room. Knowing her, it was a picture of her mother, which she no doubt kept on her at all times.

But as drawn as I was towards Jordan, I knew I would have to shift my focus to the book. So I stopped thinking about damaged women and started thinking instead about even more damaged men, specifically Gordon Grayson.

*Where would a bastard like him hide his greatest possession?* I asked myself. *Up his own ass, perhaps? Down the toilet? Maybe under a nest of vipers under the floorboards?*

*Fuck's sake. Be serious.*

Serious. I could do serious.

I would get the Dark Codex even if I had to kill to get it. There. How's that for seriousness?

Then I thought, how commendable, but that means nothing against someone like Grayson. He had all the power, and thanks to him, I had none. There was no way I could strong-arm him. I probably couldn't outwit him either, since thanks to his no doubt greatly expanded intellect, he would doubtless have every base covered.

*Including me.*

It was a thought that made me freeze in realization for a second. *Son of a bitch*, I thought. *How long had he been playing me?*

Then as I stood up, the door opened, and Grayson himself was standing there. "Did you enjoy your night with my daughter?" he asked, seemingly serious.

I stared back at him, slightly lost for words for a second. "We drank."

He smiled then, and magic arced somewhere inside his mouth. "I'm just messing with you. Come with me. I want to show you something."

My suspicion showed as a frown on my face. "Show me what exactly?"

Grayson smiled again as he made a movement with his hand and I found myself gliding against my will across the floor towards him. "It's something I think you might appreciate, Creed."

When he laid a hand on my shoulder, I got the familiar sensation of teleporting, and then I found myself somewhere else completely, with Grayson standing beside me in his shimmering white robes like some god-like figure. "Holy..." I said, my mouth open wide at the scene before me, unable even to form any more words.

"Holy?" Grayson said. "I wouldn't degrade the magnificence of the universe by calling it holy. There simply are no words to describe what you are seeing, or at least, none that do it justice."

For the first time since I'd met him, Grayson was absolutely right about something—words could never do justice to the wonders playing out before my eyes. But in the interests of full disclosure, I'll try to set the scene for you.

We appeared to be standing on some other planet or moon, surrounded by space. Somehow, I was able to breathe normally, which was no doubt Grayson's doing. Before us, there appeared to be a gigantic tear in the fabric of space, and the tear revealed a kaleidoscope of furious energy that intertwined and exploded at speeds beyond normal comprehension, the exploding energy renewing itself many times over before I could even blink. The sheer power on display—the mind-boggling energies at work—terrified me like nothing ever had before. And yet, at the same time, there was something strangely comforting about being in the presence of such unexplainable forces. Things were happening that I couldn't even begin to understand, that was so far beyond my comprehension they rendered me dumbstruck in the truest sense of the word. It was akin to taking someone who had known nothing but peace and love their whole lives, and suddenly transplanting them into the middle of a battlefield, knowing nothing of war or hate or even violence. That person simply wouldn't be able to process what was going on around them. Which is how I felt standing there.

Then Grayson's calm and almost reverent voice found its way into my melted mind. "What you are seeing," he said. "Is the inner workings of the universe itself. This is the power that lies behind everything, which creates everything, and ultimately destroys it, only to renew it again. Even I can't comprehend the full glory of it all. I can only witness it like you are doing now. A small peek behind the curtain is all we get." He paused. "But I aim to change that."

The sensation of teleporting again and the wondrous view is gone, replaced by four walls. Grayson's office. "No," I said, crushed by sadness. I spun around to Grayson, who was seated behind his desk by then. "Take me back."

Grayson smiled and shook his head. "I know," he said. "It's hard to let go of all that wonder and amazement, isn't it? When I first made that tear in space, I spent to what amounted to years, off and on, just standing there staring. Mere minutes here and on Earth of course, but out there...many years."

I took a seat across the desk from Grayson as I struggled to find focus again. The images of all that power and energy at work were burned deep into my brain. "I feel like my mind is melting."

"That will pass. In fact," Grayson stretched out a hand, and a charge of magic went into me, causing me to jolt. "Let me quicken the process."

Immediately, I felt like myself again. I was still in awe of what I had just seen, but I was in control of it. "How?" I asked.

"How," Grayson repeated, then shook his head. "Come on, Creed. Let's not play any more games. We both know why you joined us here. I have the Dark Codex, and you want it. Or rather your Division puppet masters want it."

"I'm nobodies puppet."

Grayson laughed as his eyes filled with purple magic. "You're *my* puppet, Creed. Or haven't you realized that yet?"

I shook my head, unwilling to give him the satisfaction of seeing me look worried, which I was a bit, to be honest. "That book is dangerous, and you know it."

"Dangerous?" Grayson said, scowling now. "Dangerous for whom, Creed? You? The rotten power structures that seek to rule over us? Certainly not the people. The Dark Codex will set the people free. It has already started setting them free."

"You think telling people that monsters and magic exist will empower them? It won't, it will just make them scared, and when people get scared, they lash out."

"Indeed they do," Grayson said. "Indeed they are. Right now, back on Earth, people are lashing out all over the world as they force out the monsters and kill them."

"And how many innocents are going to die in the process?"

"Be real, Creed. You know you can't have a revolution without some sacrifice."

I shook my head in disgust. "You remind me of someone I used to know. He talked a lot about sacrifice as well."

"I assume you speak of your father?" He nodded. "I know your whole story. Your mind is an open book to me."

"Well, that's fucking comforting." *Bastard*, I thought, becoming steadily more angry and desperate against his overwhelming power.

"Your father seemed like a very driven sort of man. I can respect that."

"Next you'll be saying he was just misunderstood."

"All men of power are misunderstood," Grayson said. "Except by those who have power themselves."

"And you seem to have that in spades, don't you? Thanks to the book."

"The book, yes..." Grayson sat back in his seat as if relaxing. "You know, I've always believed that the answers to unknowable questions were out there in some form, even before I had ever heard of the Dark Codex. I knew there had to be some source of knowledge that would explain everything. After all, why not? We always assume that knowledge must be scattered around all over the place and must be painstakingly uncovered before any truths could be revealed. I never bought that. I always believed in the ultimate source." He smiled almost whimsically. "And as it turns out, my instinct was alway right. My destiny has always been intertwined with the book. I just never knew it until those people died and I had to run."

*Fuck it*, I thought. I wasn't going anywhere soon. I might as well settle in and wait for an opportunity to arise if one ever did. "If this is going to turn into a story, maybe you could conjure me up a drink," I said. "I'm sure the book taught you how to pour whiskey." I smiled sarcastically as Grayson waved his hand and a bottle of Johnny Walker Red and a single glass appeared on his almost bare desk. "At least it's the good stuff."

"Knock yourself out."

After I had poured my drink, I sat back in my leather seat and tried to appear relaxed as I focused on Grayson. "So tell me. How'd you ever hear about the Dark Codex? What set you on the path to finding it, considering it's always been just a myth?"

"A myth?" Grayson said. "I assure you, it was never a myth to me..."

# 19

# GRAYSON AND THE DARK CODEX: A LOVE STORY

*F*or as long as he could remember, Gordon Grayson had an interest in science, and in the acquisition of knowledge. From a young age, Grayson questioned the world in which he lived, and was endlessly curious about everything. Later, as he moved into high school and then university, that curiosity manifested into a burning desire to unlock the secrets of the universe. As a scientist already, he knew the current understanding of the universe barely scratched the surface when it came to revealing satisfactory answers. Grayson's burgeoning ego at the time made him believe that he would one day unlock every secret the universe held. It was just a matter of time. He also came to believe in an ultimate source of knowledge. He didn't know what form such knowledge took, but he had a deep feeling that it was out there somewhere just waiting to be discovered by someone committed enough to go after it. At that point, however, going on the hunt for this source of knowledge was no more than a dream. To embark on such a journey, he would need to amass the resources to do so first. So in the meantime, he embraced science, and throughout his academic career, managed to collect several doctorates and diplomas in various branches of science, including in the branch he later came to specialize in, which was neuroscience.

Despite his demonstrated brilliance, however, Grayson was never really welcomed by the scientific community, and this was largely due to his unconventional theories in the fields of physics and neuroscience. His theories about the origins of the universe and the laws that governed it were a bit too out there for most, especially a staunch scientific community that cared more about maintaining the status quo (and their grants) than in considering theories that tore apart and completely contradicted the ones they accepted as near gospel.

"A bunch of conservative fools," Grayson said dismissively as he continued to languish in his red leather chair. His ego was clearly enjoying the chance to tell his story and do himself the justice he obviously thought he deserved. Not having many other options, I drank and let him speak while I listened and hoped an opportunity of some sort would arise, though in what form I didn't know.

"I know the type," I said, commiserating despite myself. "Change isn't their thing."

"Like any power structure, the academic world tries to maintain and perpetuate itself by whatever means necessary, even if that means going against the very reason for their existence in the first place, which is to find answers. They were less interested in answers than they were in their own confirmation biases. Not that any of that matters now, of course." He smiled, pleased with himself that he thought he had somehow finally proved all of his old academic colleagues wrong.

"No, I guess not."

After the seven people had died during Grayson's experiment, everyone was obviously gunning for him, the law especially. Grayson wouldn't allow himself to be thrown in a prison cell over something he saw as being an accident, however tragic. So he took the only option open to him--besides turning himself in--and he went on the lamb, taking his eight-year-old daughter with him.

"Destiny is a funny thing, Creed," Grayson said. "I would never have wished for those seven people to have perished the way they did, but in one respect, their deaths became a catalyst that would push me further down the path of my destiny. You see, Creed, I'd been planning for years to go in search of the ultimate source of knowledge. The Holy Grail if you will. I put money in a secret bank account for years. I mapped out travel plans based on leads I had come across over the years. I even had a private plane sitting waiting to take me wherever I needed to go. Not my plane of course, but one with a pilot who had already agreed to fly me. The only problem was, I could never find the courage just to get up and go. It would have meant leaving my wife and daughter behind, abandoning my career, such as it was. I couldn't do it."

"Why didn't you do it after your wife died?" I asked him.

His eyes darkened and magic arced off him like he didn't appreciate me bringing up his dead wife. "I see Jordan has informed you of some things."

I nodded. "Just the broad strokes."

Grayson looked away for a moment as if considering his daughter. "She was the reason I didn't leave back then. She needed me. I needed her. It seemed like the wrong time."

"Jordan killed that guy Farnes on the same night as you--sorry, the spirit--killed those seven people. Maybe there *was* some destiny at play." I paused, then smiled. "Or maybe it was just a coincidence."

"My daughter did what had to be done," Grayson said, his confident demeanor faltering slightly. "What I myself could not do at the time."

"You thought about killing Farnes yourself?"

"Worse. I ignored him as I chose to throw myself into my work instead."

I nodded. Said nothing.

To Grayson, his daughter murdering a man was her awakening as his guardian angel. That's how he put it, what he called Jordan. His guardian angel. He knew he would need someone to help him and keep him safe in his quest, and Jordan would fit the role perfectly. She was young of course, but while Grayson kept them both sheltered for a few years in the wilds of Canada with the money he had saved, he also trained her to be his bodyguard. Every day, Grayson would train his daughter in all manner of disciplines, including armed and unarmed combat, surveillance, how to tail people, how to set people up for abduction and murder, how to con people into doing anything. Grayson didn't do this personally. He only oversaw things. To help him, he paid an ex-CIA operator to train Jordan instead. By the time she was twelve years old, Jordan was a deadly weapon. Her unarmed skills were lethal and based largely around simple, fundamental strikes that combined with her deadly speed and agility. Which meant she could take on opponents much bigger than herself. She could also shoot with any gun you put in her hand, could handle a knife like a seasoned butcher, and had senses so keen you just could not sneak up on her, but she could sure sneak up on you. On top of this physical training, Jordan was also educated to a high degree in the use of technology, psychology, and chemistry. She also spoke five different languages fluently.

On hearing all this for the first time, I sat there in Grayson's office dumbfounded, and also sickened by what he had put his daughter through at such a young age, and all for his own ends. I could hardly imagine how brutal her regime must have been to get her to the level that Grayson needed her at. And she was still just a fucking child, for Christ's sake! "What is it with you people?" I said, unable to hold my anger. "You think people are just puppets, and that you can pull their strings as you see fit? She was your daughter, Grayson."

"Yes," he shouted back. "And I ensured she served a higher purpose in life!"

"Your purpose, you mean?"

His eyes flared up with magic then, and I found myself wishing I still had my own magic so I could blast the cunt out of his fucking chair. But I didn't, so instead, I had to sit there while Grayson reached out a hand and seemed to clamp an invisible vice around my heart. I dropped my glass to the floor as I clutched at my chest with both hands as if I was having a heart attack. Then as I was about to fall out of my seat, the pain stopped.

"Don't dare judge me, Creed," Grayson half snarled. "Everything I have ever done has been for the greater good, for the good of humanity. And the same goes for my daughter. She played her part more than you will ever know. Besides, a man like you is in no position to judge anyone."

A man like me? That hurt my feelings. Sure, I'd made some mistakes, a lot of mistakes, but I would have liked to have thought that the good I did over the years outweighed any bad I may have caused. That was the only thing that kept me going sometimes, in fact, and I wasn't about to question that for Grayson or anybody else. I could have told Grayson to go fuck himself and stop being a hypocrite. That he and men like him were experts at justifying their actions and linking them to some imaginary greater good that was no more than a fantasy in their heads. A fantasy they would go to any lengths to see realized. A fantasy that always had a grab for power and control at its heart. I could have hit him with all that, but what would have been the point? Men like him also never listened or let themselves be swayed by mere moral arguments. They listened only to their own twisted desires and what they saw as being right. So instead, I sat back in my seat and calmly refilled my glass with the expensive whiskey, then said, "Point taken. Please don't do that again."

Grayson snorted and shook his head at me. "You know I had you all wrong, Creed. I thought you were a man of principle, despite working each day to facilitate the status quo. But now I see that you are really just a man who is very good at taking a lot of shit and then getting back up again. You must have proved very irritating to your foes over the years."

"You have no idea."

Narrowing his eyes, Grayson stared at me a moment. "Well, I can tell you this much, Creed. You won't be getting back up against me, should I decide to put you down."

I shook my head slowly as if weary and accepting of the control he had over me. "Just finish your story," I said. "I promise to be a good boy and listen." I held up my hand. "Scouts honor."

Grayson shook his head slightly at my sarcasm but nonetheless continued talking while I continued to wait for an opportunity to arise, even though I knew none would. But you had to have hope, right?

"After nearly four years of training," Grayson said. "Jordan was ready to go on the road with me. So off we went to Europe."

In Europe, Grayson started his search for the Holy Grail. I say started, but he had already put things in motion while in Canada, cultivating leads and mapping out likely places to search in Europe where he thought he would most likely find the Dark Codex.

"I didn't even know what I was looking for at that point," Grayson told me. "I had never heard of the Dark Codex until I was several years into the expedition. Up until that point, I was still trying to find proof that the idea of the Holy Grail of knowledge even existed. The second I stumbled across a mention of the Dark Codex in another book, I knew it had to be real. I knew it had to be the thing I was searching for."

I shook my head at his crazy commitment. "So you go to all that trouble initially, turning your daughter into your bodyguard, going on the road for years, before you even knew the book was out there?"

"Yes."

"That's some kind of faith."

"Indeed," Grayson said. "Sometimes I wonder if my very belief brought the Dark Codex into existence."

"I doubt that," I said. "Considering it had already been a thing for centuries."

"Yes, but no one had ever laid eyes on it, had they? So no one could be sure it even existed at all."

"I suppose not."

"Whatever the case, there is very little doubt that the book would have remained hidden forever if I hadn't of found it."

A bit of a stretch, but I could see his point. "So how did you find it?"

Very early on, Grayson's expedition steered him towards the occult underground in Europe. After all, if you want to find a magic book, you go where people might know about that sort of thing. Not that Grayson had been previously aware of any occult underground, or even of the supernatural. Barring his encounter with the evil spirit who killed Grayson's seven guinea pigs, the man had had no previous contact with anything supernatural. But as he and Jordan started their search in Paris, they kept running into things they couldn't readily explain. magical occurrences. Strange people with glowing eyes and sharp teeth. Men who looked like wolves. People who could do impossible things. It didn't take long for Grayson to realize that there was a whole other world hidden within the everyday one. A world of the supernatural. And instead of being scared by this, he embraced it, even became excited by it as he knew the answers he sought lay in that realm of the unnatural. That's when Jordan really had to become her father's bodyguard apparently. As Grayson led them further into the occult underground, they inevitably started rubbing shoulders with dangerous beings. Vampires. Werewolves. Witches and wizards. Luckily for Grayson, his daughter's skills were up to the task, and she kept him safe against all manner of supernatural creatures that for whatever reason, wanted to kill Grayson.

"Driven by my desire to find the book, I pushed hard," said Grayson. "I asked questions and didn't care who that upset."

"Because you had Jordan to protect you."

"Yes, but I developed my own defenses eventually as well. As soon as I discovered magic, I had to learn it, if for no other reason than the scientist in me was curious about it."

"Nothing to do with the power it gave you then," I said, telling myself to slow down on the whiskey lest I become too pissed to function at my best, which admittedly, I was little off from anyway.

Grayson gave me a tight smile. "Don't be a hypocrite, Creed. You've spent your whole life studying magic. You couldn't live without it."

He wasn't wrong. "So you taught yourself."

"Yes. I found I had a knack for it. It came easy."

As his magical power grew, and as his daughter became more of an accomplished killer, the two blazed their way through Europe for a further decade, leaving a trail of bodies behind them. The bodies of those who tried to stand in the way of Grayson's crusade. "It's surprising how many never wanted the book found," he said, seeming genuinely baffled by this. "I think I'm proving it can be a force for good, no?"

Christ, he was serious. Or was he? Maybe he was just enjoying playing the role of revolutionary, and he secretly had other plans. I didn't exactly know. Not that it mattered. He would still have to be stopped. "You can't really believe this will all end well, do you?" I said. "You're going to end the world as we know it, and not in a good way. You'll destroy everything. The people will destroy themselves."

"Some of them will, but others will rise like phoenixes from the ashes, and those people will rebuild the world again."

"Rebuild it how?"

Grayson shook his head. "I don't know. That remains to be seen. It's what makes this all so exciting. I have faith this will work out."

Fuck, is he really that deluded? I was finding it hard to believe that he was. "So what about you, Gordon, where do you fit into all this? What's your role in the new world order going to be?"

"My role?" he said as if he had never considered it, which of course he had. Many times, no doubt. "I see myself as purely a facilitator of change. A guiding light, if you will."

I couldn't keep the smirk from my face as I shook my head. "Forgive me, Gordon, if I remain somewhat skeptical when it comes to your motives and apparent modesty. I simply don't believe you."

Grayson almost smiled. "And why not?"

"Because I've come across your type a thousand times over the years, and to put it bluntly, you are all selfish bastards. You only want more power."

"My, your father did a number on you, didn't he?"

"Tell me I'm wrong then."

"You're wrong."

"I still don't believe you."

"Well," Grayson said. "Only time will tell."

"It sure will. It always does."

Grayson smiled as if he found me amusing. "Would you like to hear how I found the Dark Codex?"

"Sure," I said, genuinely interested, but maintaining my sarcastic tone. "Why not."

Grayson's first real lead on the book came roughly fifteen years into his search. Say what you like about the guy, you couldn't fault his commitment. Most sane people would have given up trying to find something that clearly didn't want to be found, but not Grayson. He refused to give up, no matter what the cost. Even at the cost of damaging his only daughter beyond repair.

While in Rome, Grayson met an old priest who claimed to have been privy to the secrets of the Vatican vaults, where apparently all manner of religious and magical objects were kept, supposedly for safe keeping, but mostly because the items, by their very nature, contradicted the church doctrine, and the Vatican couldn't have that, of course. Grayson met with the old priest, who was in his eighties by then, and the priest told Grayson that he used to maintain the inventory of the vaults, so he knew exactly what was down there at all times. The priest told Grayson that the Dark Codex was once on the inventory, decades ago, but disappeared one day without a trace. Or so it seemed. The priest claimed that the book was actually appropriated by a secret and shadowy group known as the Protectors of Light, of which no one knew anything about except that they were linked in some way to the Knights Templar, and they took it upon themselves to protect certain artifacts that were deemed too dangerous for the world, of which the Dark Codex was one.

"It took me another few years to finally track down the Protectors of Light," Grayson said. "They were hard to find, let me tell you. Most people who knew about them also feared them. Most were prepared to die before they gave up any information."

I refilled my whiskey glass one last time, deciding I'd drunk enough. "And let me guess, you were happy to oblige those people."

"We did what we had to do."

"You mean, Jordan did. I'm assuming she did all the torturing."

Grayson stared at me for a moment, and I wondered if that was guilt I saw in his eyes, or anger at me. Probably both. "Jordan did her job as she was supposed to. Very well, I might add."

*Sickening*, I thought as I shook my head. How mentally scarred Jordan must be after everything her father forced her to do. Then I thought, forced her? Why didn't she just run? That was something I would have to ask her when I next saw her.

Eventually, Grayson found someone who was willing to talk under duress. The victim gave up a lead, a location in the Himalayas. But by that point, the Protectors of Light had already gotten wind of Grayson's intentions to get the Dark Codex, and the group took preemptive action. When Grayson and his daughter arrived in India, they were attacked shortly after that. Jordan managed to defend them, as did Grayson with his magic, but Jordan almost died in the confrontation as they were attacked by figures who resembled ninjas in dark hoods. Grayson went into hiding after that while he nursed his near dead daughter back to health using medicine and magic.

"I almost lost her," he said.

"So why didn't you stop?" I asked.

Grayson looked away in silence for a moment before carrying on with the rest of the story as if I'd asked him nothing. *Bastard*, I thought. *Even if he'd lost Jordan, he still would have carried on.*

After the attack, Grayson took precautionary measures and used magic to prevent the Protectors of Light from tracking them any further. Grayson and his daughter effectively became invisible to their hunters, which allowed them to carry on with their quest. It took them a further two years to track the Protectors of Light down in the same Himalayan mountain range but in China. Grayson, unwilling to take any chances, hired a small army of local Chinese mercenaries and led them into the mountains along with Jordan. Once there, they located the Protectors of Light's secret hideout on one of the highest mountain peaks, and there, an epic battle ensued. The Protectors of Light were essentially warriors, so they weren't easy to take down. Grayson had more men with him, however, and after nearly two days of fighting on highly dangerous ground, all of the mercenaries Grayson had hired were killed by the end, and only one of the Protectors remained standing. Grayson himself went into the huge cave hideout and killed the last Protector himself with lightning magic.

"The cave was like a treasure trove of magical items," Grayson said, his eyes lighting up at the memory. "I'd never seen so much magic in one place."

"Let me guess," I said. "You took it all."

Grayson shook his head. "That's where you are wrong. I only took what I was there for. The book."

"So you finally found it, after nearly twenty years of searching."

"A lifetime of searching."

"Was it everything you hoped it would be?"

A wide smile appeared on Grayson's lined face as he spread his arms out. "We're here, aren't we?"

*Yes*, I thought. *Unfortunately, we are.* "So what now, Gordon?" I asked. "Are you going to kill me?"

"Kill you?" He shook his head. "Why would I kill you, Creed? I don't see the point. There is nothing you or anyone else can do to stop what's happening anyway."

*We'll see about that*, I thought, though I wasn't exactly filled with confidence. "So what then? You keep me prisoner here?"

Grayson considered a moment. "I'll be releasing the magic formula soon. You are free to leave after that. I have no doubt the people on Earth will need your assistance and expertise. The new world order will take a while to settle."

I almost laughed. "Take a while to settle?" Then I did laugh. "You crack me up, Gordon, you really do."

Grayson merely smiled at me like I didn't bother him one bit. And once again, I got the impression he was hiding his true agenda. "I'll see you in the great hall, later, Creed."

I got up to go, then stopped. "What about the book?"

Grayson frowned. "What about it?"

"I'd like to see it."

A smile spread across Grayson's face. "You really know how to push your luck, don't you?"

I shrugged. "I just thought, you've told me so much about it, you've demonstrated its power to me. After all that, I'd really like to see the thing for myself. See what all the fuss is about."

Sitting back in his chair, Grayson considered my request for a long moment, then he said, "all right, but before I do." He stood up. "If you try anything untoward, I will simply vaporize you in an instant, and it will be as if you never existed. You know I have the power to do that."

I didn't doubt him. "Understood."

"Good." Grayson smiled then as if he was looking forward to finally showing someone else the book he gave half his life, and most of his daughter's life, to get. He made a series of complex hand movements in the air, and a few seconds later the Dark Codex materialized into view, and then floated down onto the desk. Grayson stood over it like a proud father. "Isn't it the most beautiful thing you've ever seen?"

For once I had to completely agree with Grayson as I stood there in near awe staring down at the Dark Codex sitting on the table. It was indeed one of the most beautiful things I had ever seen. Regarding dimensions, the book was about the size of a MacBook, but obviously much thicker since there were hundreds of pages between the covers. The book cover itself appeared to be made from a hard, white substance that could have been bone, but much whiter, and much smoother. On the cover itself, intricately detailed patterns were carved, along with symbols that I had never seen before, and the whole book seemed to give off a whitish glow that just made you want to stare into it while you got lost pondering over what mysteries the book contained inside. I was lost for words.

"When I first found the book," Grayson said. "I spent days just sitting there staring at it like you are now. I literally couldn't take my eyes off it. Little did I know that this is a final security measure to prevent people from opening the book even if they managed to find it." Grayson clicked his fingers then, and I snapped out of my daze like some chump on stage with a hypnotist. "I've just released you from the book's hold."

He wasn't lying. I found I could look away from the book now if I wanted to. Not that I really wanted to anyway. The bibliophile in me was busy having multiple orgasms at the sight of that wondrous book. "I've never..."

"I know," Grayson said. "Very few have. You can thank my daughter for allowing us both to see it."

"I don't understand."

"It was she who found a way to break me free from the trance I was in at the time. She didn't stare at the book long enough to become entranced herself, probably because she hated the book before she even laid eyes on it, but that's...something else." Grayson looked down for a moment. "Anyway, smart girl that she is,

Jordan used a magic ritual from one of my spell books to bring one of the Protectors of Light back to life for a brief time, long enough to learn how to break the trance. As it turns out, you had to be wearing a special pendant, which each of the Protectors had around their necks. Not that I need such silly trinkets now, of course." He gave a small laugh as purple magic danced around his eyes like an indicator of his supreme power.

"Can I open it?" Christ, I was like a kid at Christmas, seriously.

Grayson laughed at me being me again. "No, Creed, you most certainly cannot." He waved his hands over the book then and made it disappear once more.

"Spoilsport," I said to him.

Sitting back down in his chair, Grayson made the door open behind me with a wave of his hand. "You've had your fun, Creed. Now get out."

I stared at him a moment longer, seeing the dark seriousness in his eyes now and thinking, *Yes, there it is. The real Gordon Grayson, hiding in there behind a mask of civility.*

As I left the room, one thought dominated my mind:

*How long would it be before the real Gordon Grayson came out to play?*

# 20

# WALKING AWAY

*A*s I walked away from Grayson's office, I couldn't help but feel defeated. There had been almost no point in me infiltrating SciCane in the first place since not a single thing I'd done so far had helped put a stop to Grayson and his plans. Hell, I'd *helped* the man with his broadcast to the world, which no doubt amused Grayson, especially since he'd known all along I was there to try and stop him. Sure, I'd verified that he had the Dark Codex in his possession, but the book might as well have been kept at the other side of the universe. There was no way I could access it, and definitely not without magic. Indeed, without magic, I felt castrated and powerless to do anything. Getting my magic back had to be my main priority for now and to do that, I would have to find a way to leave the Grayson Dimension and then return to it once I had a plan in place. Only trouble was, Gordon and Jordan were the only ones who could open the gate to Earth, and I wasn't sure if Jordan would be willing to let me out of that prison. Only one way to find out, I supposed.

I checked the main hall first because that's where everyone seemed to be as they prepared for the next broadcast. Sam was there, and he came running up when he saw me. "Isn't this exciting?" he beamed. "Everyone in the world will soon be able to use magic."

"Yeah," I said, still looking around for Jordan. "I can hardly contain myself."

A frown replaced Sam's smile. "What's wrong, Creed? You don't seem excited."

I sighed as I looked at Sam. "That's because I'm not, and neither should you be, Sam. All you people need to wake up and get the hell out of here."

"What? Why?"

"I don't have time to explain. Grayson is not who you think he is, Sam. It's not safe here. Once the broadcast is finished, he'll have no use for any of you anymore."

Sam shook his head like it was blasphemy coming out of my mouth. "Creed...I thought you were one of us."

"Fuck's sake, Sam." I grabbed him by the shoulders. "Wake up! Nothing about this is right. Grayson is on his way to ending the fucking world. Can't you see that?"

Sam shrugged out of my grip. It was the first time I'd ever seen him angry. "You've been lying," he said before pointing his chubby finger at me. "You're not one of us." Then he raised his voice as he looked around at the others in the hall. "He is not one of us!"

Every head in the room turned to look at me then with angry suspicion in their eyes. Then they all pointed at me and said in unison, "Not one of us!"

*Fuck me*, I thought. I felt like Donald Sutherland in the final scene of *Invasion Of The Bodysnatchers*, about to be mobbed by a bunch of brainwashed freaks. "Stay back!" I shouted as I went to move back out of the hall. But I was surrounded by the SciCane loyalists, and every one of them still pointed their finger at me as they shouted, "Not one of us! Not one of us! Not one of us!"

Creepy motherfuckers. I'll bet Grayson was watching this from somewhere, highly amused by it all, not caring if his crowd of freaks decided to rip me apart with their bare hands, which they seemed like they wanted to do as they inched closer, closing in around me. No matter what way I went to move, my path was blocked. *How the fuck am I going to get out this?* I wondered. I had no magic, no weapons to defend myself. Nothing. I could probably use my fists, but there were too many of them, and this wasn't some Korean action flick where the main star kicks the ass of dozens of bad guys one after the other until they were all down. Unfortunately, real life didn't work that way. In reality, I would probably get a few punches in before getting jumped and dragged to the ground. Then I'd be stomped to death like a giant cockroach.

Just as my mind was turning over that pleasant thought, a voice somehow managed to cut through the chanting of the crowd. "Enough! That's enough! Stand down! Now!"

There was some commotion nearby as the crowd parted and I saw Jordan push her way through towards me. I'd never been more relieved to see anyone at that moment. "Thank Christ," I muttered.

The crowd had stopped chanting as all eyes went to Jordan. "Get back to work!" Jordan shouted with impressive volume and authority in her voice. If I was a SciCane puppet, there was no way I would defy those orders. And indeed, the freaks did as they were told, lowering their pointing fingers and shuffling off back to whatever they were doing. Sam narrowed his eyes at me and then shook his head at me. "Traitor," he spat before walking away.

*And that's the thanks you get for helping people*, I thought. *Traitor indeed. Seriously.*

"Let's go, Creed," Jordan ordered. "We have a place for traitors like you."

Traitors like me? I frowned at her and shook my head. Her as well? "Really, Jordan?"

Jordan motioned with her head. "Let's go, I said."

I sighed. "Fine."

Jordan led me out of the hall then, through a side door and out to a narrow corridor. "It's time for you to go," she said staring at me with her strangely emotionless blue eyes.

I couldn't help but think about everything that her father had told me. About the bloodstained life Jordan had led for so many years. Was still leading. "Go where? Some dark hole somewhere?"

She shook her head. "Back to Earth."

"You're letting me go?" I was surprised as she no doubt knew by now the real reason I was there. If she didn't figure it out the night before while we were drinking, her father had probably informed her by now. Either way, she didn't seem all that pissed about it. No more pissed than usual anyhow.

"Would you rather stay and be ripped apart by the mob? They'll do it, you know."

"Oh, I know. Why are you helping me?" She began walking then, and I started after her. "Well?"

"Does it matter?"

I fell into step beside her. "You should come with me."

She snorted and shook her head. "No."

"No?" I couldn't understand her reluctance to leave. "Why not? There's nothing left for you to do once your father unleashes magic to the masses. Speaking of which, can't you stop him?"

Jordan turned a corner into a wider hallway. "And why would I do that?"

"Because what your father is doing is wrong, and you know it is."

"I don't care."

I grabbed her by the arm then to stop her, and she quickly pulled out of my grip and gave me a hard stare like she was going to attack me, so I held up my hands. "Hey, I'm just trying to make you see sense here, Jordan. I know what you've been through--"

"No, you don't. Stop pretending like you do."

"All right, I know some of what you've been through. Your father told me a lot as well. The point is, there's nothing here for you, Jordan."

"There is nothing anywhere for me," she said in a flat voice, then she walked off, and I followed after her.

"You only think that now," I told her. "There's still time for you to have a normal life."

Jordan stopped suddenly and slammed me into the wall with shocking strength and speed. "Just fucking stop, Creed. I don't need your help. I don't need anything from you. I just want you gone."

"Why?" I asked defiantly. "Because I make you uncomfortable? Because I have the nerve to point out a different path for you?"

"There is no different path. No redemption road. All roads lead to pain."

"Maybe so, but some paths also lead to other things as well."

"What like? *Love?*" She shook her head derisively.

"Maybe. The point is, possibilities exist. There are no such possibilities here, and you know it."

"Did it ever occur to you that I don't care, or that I might be happy with that?"

I shook my head as she let me go and took a step back. "Well, if you're happy with that then there is something seriously wrong, Jordan."

Jordan stared at me for a long moment like I didn't get it, then she shook her head. "The gate is this way."

She led me there without saying another word, entering the room where the gate was and standing to the side so I could walk towards it. But instead, I turned to her. "You should know," I said. "I'm not going to stop until I have the Dark Codex. It's just too dangerous, and I'll be damned if I leave the equivalent of a nuclear bomb in the hands of..." I trailed off.

Jordan made a face. "It's okay, you can say it, Creed," she said, her voice tinged with bitterness and self-loathing.

Sighing, I took a step towards her. "You're not at fault, Jordan. Your father is."

"I made my own decisions."

I shook my head. "No, you didn't."

A scowl creased her forehead, and she looked away for a moment. "Just go, Creed."

"We can make this right, Jordan," I persisted. "You can help me get the book and then--"

She pulled out her gun and pointed it at my head. "I said go. Now."

I held her gaze for a moment, then nodded. "all right. I'll go." I walked towards the shimmering gate and stood in front of it, paused for a second and then turned to look at Jordan again. "You're wrong about all roads leading to pain. Not all of them do."

Gun still in hand, Jordan's face softened for a second, and her blue eyes glistened as if she was going to cry, but I didn't wait for her to do so. Instead, I told her she knew where to find me, and then I stepped through the gate to see what kind of world Gordon Grayson had created with his outing of the monsters.

# 21

# WTF!

*I* have to admit, I was dreading teleporting out of the sewers after I came through the gate. I had visions of angry mobs stalking the streets in search of supernatural beings so they could kill them and hang the bodies from lamp posts as a warning to others. I was expecting the city to have gone crazy with fear and bloodlust, but when I landed in an alley and walked out into the main street, things appeared to be normal. No hanging bodies, no crowds of monster hunters, no blood washing the streets. But that didn't mean things hadn't changed. Underneath the apparent normality, I could sense the uneasiness that seemed to permeate the air. The fear even. There was no doubt that Grayson's broadcast, helped by me, had had an effect. As I stood in the early evening cold, I noticed there were few if any supernaturals walking or hanging around. The vampires would usually be out by now, getting ready to hunt their dinner. I saw none amongst the crowds of Sleepwalkers. I didn't see any werewolves hanging around the bars either, nor any other supernatural. A few demons in stolen meat suits. That's all.

As I walked down the street, I noticed people were cagier than usual. Many of them were staring at me and did double takes. Then I realized they recognized me from the broadcast. Shit. I was so caught up with everything I'd forgot my face had been plastered on every screen throughout the world. And just to verify this, I stopped by an electronics store that had several TV's in the window, all showing the same video footage of the SciCane broadcast, which was interrupted only by reporters and commentators as they discussed aspects of the broadcast. One news headline read: ARE THE MONSTERS REAL? Another banner headline read: MAN KILLS REAL LIFE VAMPIRE! AMAZING FOOTAGE! Above the headline, a video of a man shooting and then staking a young vampire was playing over and over. A message flashed on the screen: IS IT LEGAL TO KILL A MONSTER? DO YOU CARE? CALL US! LET US KNOW!

And then on the biggest screen, I cringed when I saw a still picture of me from the broadcast as I stood on the stage with the restrained supernaturals behind me. The headline underneath said: DO YOU KNOW THIS MAN? CALL NOW!

Something told me it would be best if I got off the streets.

"Hey, mister!" There was some teenage kid behind me when I turned around. "That's you, isn't it? It's really you. Oh my God!"

"Piss off, kid," I said as I started to walk away.

Then someone else said. "It's him, the monster hunter from the video!"

Before I knew it, there was a crowd of people closing in on me, all talking at once as they asked if the video was real, and what's the best way to kill a vampire and what's your name and are we all going to get eaten by monsters and is the world going to end and--

I ran into the nearest alley. Once there, I teleported to the only place I ever felt truly safe.

The Sanctum.

* * *

THERE WAS NO SIGN OF BLAZE WHEN I MADE IT TO THE SANCTUM, SO I ASSUMED he was out somewhere in invisible mode, probably stalking small animals in the park, a favorite pastime of Blaze's. In the living room, I poured myself a whiskey and sat down on the chair nearest the fireplace. Then I let out a long breath and sank back into the seat for a few moments while I closed my eyes, grateful for the safety of the Sanctum, at least for a little while. I still had much to do.

Taking my phone out of my trench coat pocket, I expected the device to be chock full of messages and missed calls that I wouldn't have received in the Grayson Dimension, and would only have come through when I left. And indeed, I had dozens of messages and missed calls from people. I hardly needed to look at the messages to know what most of them said. The text from Forsyth, my vampire friend, summed things up nicely: WTF??!!

The rest of the text messages were a mixture of threats and disbelief that I could do such a thing as expose the supernatural underground to an unsuspecting world. *Goddamn it*, I thought. Maybe I should have tried some other way to get Grayson and the Dark Codex. By going undercover, I had made things worse it seemed. But thinking about it, I didn't know what else I was supposed to do. Grayson was practically untouchable with all his magic power and increased knowledge. Plus, he existed in another dimension, which made him hard to get to.

*Fuck it. At least I confirmed Grayson has the book, and I know where he keeps it. Sort of.*

As far as I could tell, Grayson kept the book inside a pocket dimension that only he had access to. As far as security went, it was the safest place in the universe.

Unless I could figure out a way to crack the safe, so to speak.

It was an idea I had already given some thought to, and I had already decided to go and see Sanaka about it, the one man I knew who could possibly help me.

But first, I decided to call Forsyth and explain what was going on before he sent out a lynch mob to hunt me down. After that I would call into Division to give Brentwood an update, who going by the string of missed calls and texts I'd received from him, was also probably considering sending a mob to find me by that point.

Forsyth's phone rang twice before he picked up. "Hey, Forsyth," I said rather sheepishly. "How's it going?"

"Don't you fucking hey Forsyth me," the vampire said in an angry tone, which was saying something because Forsyth rarely got angry about anything. "You have some nerve calling me after what you did."

"Forsyth, calm down. I can explain. It's not what you think."

"Not what I think?" He laughed coldly. "You fucking exposed us to the world! Seems pretty fucking clear to me, Creed."

I shook my head, wondering if everyone I met from now on was going to be equally as caustic. I couldn't blame them if they were. "That was going to happen with or without my participation. There was no stopping it. Come on, Forsyth. You know I would never do something as mad as that unless I had to."

"Had to?"

"I went undercover in SciCane to try and stop them."

Forsyth laughed. "And what a great fucking job you did at stopping them. You ended up helping them. Fucking SciCane. I mean, who are these loonies anyway?"

"It's really just one guy. Gordon Grayson. And he has the Dark Codex."

"What?" Forsyth went silent for a moment. "That's impossible. The Dark Codex is just a stupid myth. Everyone knows that."

"It exists. I've seen it."

"Great. So that's where this Grayson motherfucker is getting all his power, is it?"

"That's why I have to get the book before he does any more damage. Although in saying that..." I trailed off as I remembered something.

"What?"

"At some point today, Grayson will broadcast to the world again, and when he does..."

"Well don't keep me in suspense, Creed. What's this crazy motherfucker going to do next?"

"He's come up with a magic ritual that will give anyone who completes the ritual magical powers, and he intends to make said ritual available to everyone."

"Oh fuck." Forsyth went silent as he probably considered the implications of such a move.

"My thoughts exactly."

"Well, can't you stop this asshole? I have resources, whatever you need."

I shook my head. "It's not that simple. Grayson is untouchable. He exists in his own dimension that only he controls access to. He also keeps the book in a separate dimension. Plus, the power he's gathered already, the knowledge he has...he's too formidable to take on."

"So what the hell are you going to do?" Forsyth asked. "Just let him use the damn book to wreck everything?"

"I have a plan." I didn't. Far from it. But I had to calm Forsyth down some way.

"A plan? What plan? You said he was untouchable."

"Let me worry about that," I told him. "You focus on keeping your people in line."

"In line? You cheeky bastard. My kind is being hunted by rednecks with bows and wooden-tipped arrows. Gangs of stake happy bastards are roaming the streets in search of vampires. In search of anything supernatural. And now you tell me that said bastards will soon have magical powers to back up their genocidal crusade. Fuck you, Creed! My kind will tear those bastards apart if they don't cease."

"Calm down, Forsyth. Just fucking lay low for a while, that's all I'm asking. I'll sort this mess out soon enough." I shook my head as I said the words, knowing full well I wasn't anywhere close to stopping Grayson. Certainly, there was no way to stop the next broadcast. In that respect, the world was fucked. Magic would tear it apart.

"You'd better, Creed, or there's going to be all-out war before long. Vampires and the rest of the supernaturals will not hide for long. Sooner or later, they are going to fight back, and then the world will be painted red."

"No pressure then."

"No pressure."

After I had hung up the phone, I sat for a few moments as I considered calling Leona to see how things were in Washington, but then I remembered that she had sent me a picture of her FBI badge like some sort of statement I didn't fully get, and I found myself pissed at her again, so I didn't bother calling. Besides, I had more pressing matters to deal with.

Like updating Brentwood for one.

## 22

# REGROUP

*A*fter I had told him about everything that happened in the Grayson Dimension, conveniently leaving out the part about me cozying me up to Jordan Grayson in her bed, Brentwood was left in a foul mood. It wasn't like he had been in a good mood in the first place mind (it wasn't like he was in a good mood ever, but no matter). The secret he had been trying to keep maintained for years had now been revealed to the world, and that was going to make Brentwood's job a lot harder if he had to deal with newly clued up Sleepwalkers on top of everything else. I had no doubt he was also taking shit from his superiors over the whole SciCane debacle. It was Brentwood's job, after all, to keep magical sociopaths like Gordon Grayson contained, and if not contained, then dead. As with all these situations, someone had to be to blame. Heads would inevitably have to roll, and Brentwood's neck was on the chopping block at that moment, the guillotine poised to come down on him. Come to think of it, that's how I thought of the world as I knew it as well. Fucked.

"Fuck, Creed," Brentwood barked as he paced around behind his head of tech, Bethany, who was sat in her usual chair within the Central Ops room. "This is a goddamn unmitigated disaster. Why the hell did I ever listen to you?"

I shook my head twice. "Eh, excuse me? Everything I've done so far has been to your plan. It was your fucking idea to put me undercover in the first place. For all the good it turned out to be since fucking Grayson had me pegged from the get go." Now I was angry as well as I stood with my arms tensed by my side.

Brentwood stared at me with bulging white eyes as if he was about to attack me. But then he sighed sharply and turned away for a moment while he seemed to gather himself. "You're right, Creed. I'm sorry. I just don't know what to do about all this."

I must admit, it was disturbing to see Brentwood so unsure of himself. He had always been the most cocksure motherfucker I'd ever met (besides myself, of course), never wavering even for a second. But now he was wavering, something I would have taken pleasure in under different circumstances. But since things were so tense and dire, it didn't seem appropriate to be reveling in the man's zero hour. The world's zero hour. "Fuck it, forget it," I said. "Let's just figure out a way to stop Grayson and get the Dark Codex. That's all that matters."

"Agreed," Brentwood said.

"Speaking of messianic assholes," Bethany piped up from in front of her screen. "Here's everyone's favorite about to broadcast again."

Brentwood and I turned our attention to the massive screen a few feet in front of us, to the huge figure of Gordon Grayson, standing on stage in the hall of his mansion, dressed as always in his pristine white robes, the purple magic practically fizzing off him. At the rate his magic was increasing, I wondered how long his physical body would be able to contain it before it just exploded with all that power inside. I had heard of cases before where adepts took on so much magic power that they ended up transforming into pure energy, their physical bodies completely obliterated. What happened to them after that was anyone's guess because they were usually never heard from again.

Grayson's deep voice boomed out of the speakers around the screen as the broadcast started. "People of the world," he began, the hubris dripping off him turning my stomach. "The time has finally come for you to empower yourselves so you can claim back the freedom from tyranny and deception that is rightfully yours."

Brentwood shook his head as he scowled at the screen. For some reason I expected him to say the words, "Hippy scum," but he didn't. Instead, he said to Bethany, "Are you sure there's no way to pull the plug on this asshole?"

"I'm sure," Bethany replied. "Whatever magic the guy is using has the worlds comms locked up tighter than my Aunt May's pussy."

An involuntary snort left my mouth. "Seriously?"

Bethany shrugged. "She's seventy-eight and never married."

I shook my head at her and looked back to the screen to hear Grayson talk. He was currently gabbling on in that self-righteous tone of his, talking about the new world order and what it would mean for everyone and blah blah. It was all just words. By that point, I was convinced Grayson didn't give a shit about anything that he was talking about. The man had his own agenda, and something told me it would reveal itself very soon, but not before he sent the world into a state of growing chaos. After another few minutes of pointless pontification, Grayson finally got to the point of the broadcast. "And now," he said. "It is time for you to embrace destiny and change your life forever. If you go now to the following website--" He gave the name of a site that was just an alphanumeric sequence. "--You will find there a complete set of instructions that will tell you how you can access magic. More power than you can dream of, in fact. What you do with this power is up to you, but it is my great hope that you use the power to change the world around you, and to change it for good rather than bad."

"Bethany?" I said.

"Already on it," Bethany said as she brought up the website Grayson was referring to.

I looked over her shoulder at the computer screen in front of her to the lines of text on the otherwise blank screen. Each short paragraph was numbered sequentially one through six. It didn't take me long to read over the instructions. Grayson wasn't kidding when he said he would make it easy for people to access magic. He had outlined a short ritual that consisted mostly of an incantation, and then a few simple hand movements.

"That's it?" Bethany said. "But anyone could do that."

"I think that's the point," Brentwood said, a note of defeat in his otherwise stoic voice.

"Yeah," I said distractedly as I mulled over the instructions. They made no sense. They were meaningless, in fact. And then I realized that the instructions themselves didn't matter. When you did the ritual, you were not mysteriously tapping into some magical force, you were actually tapping into Grayson's own magic, or whatever magic he was channeling. Going through the ritual was basically a way to give Grayson the thumbs up so he could fill you full of magical power. "Jesus Christ..."

"What?" Brentwood asked.

I shook my head. "It's just the sheer scope of what Grayson is doing. Imbuing so many people with magic. Fulfilling all those inevitably millions of requests. Only..."

"Only what?" Bethany asked with her full attention on me.

"Only a god could wield such power," I finished.

"Fuck," Brentwood said. "You're saying Grayson has the power of a god now?"

I nodded. "That's what I'm saying, and I have a feeling he's only going to get more powerful."

"Great," Brentwood said shaking his head. "Now we know exactly why the Dark Codex has been kept a secret for so long."

"Why would anyone even create a book like that?" Bethany asked. "Who would even have the knowledge to do it?"

It was a question I hadn't really considered, and at that point, I didn't care. "It doesn't matter who made it," I said. "All that matters is we get it out of Grayson's hands."

"And then what?" Brentwood asked. "You said it yourself. Grayson has become a demigod. How are we supposed to stop someone like that?"

"We don't," I replied, then paused as the thought came to me. "The Dark Codex does."

Brentwood stared at me a moment as Bethany reduced the volume on Grayson's talking. It didn't matter what the mad man had to say anymore. All that mattered was what he had put into motion. "Are you saying we can use the book to stop Grayson?"

I turned to look at Brentwood. "I'm saying it's likely the only play we'll have, assuming I can get the book in the first place."

"Then what's to stop you making yourself into a god like Grayson?" Bethany asked.

I thought she was joking, but she wasn't. "You'll just have to trust me on that one."

Both Bethany and Brentwood looked like they didn't love with the idea of trusting such power in the hands of someone like me. But fuck them. They didn't have a choice.

"All right, Creed," Brentwood said. "I'm going to admit that I'm all out of options here, so what's your next move? Tell me you have a plan to stop this maniac."

*Everyone wants a plan*, I thought. But you know what they say about plans, don't you? They never survive contact with the enemy. Not that I had much of a plan anyway. "There's someone I need to see," I said. "I'm hoping he can help us."

"Who?" Brentwood asked.

"The biggest pain in the ass I know, besides myself, of course. Tetsuo Sanaka."

# 23

CITY GONE MAD

*A*fter leaving Division HQ on foot, I decided I should take the scenic route to Sanaka's Sanctum. For one thing, the damage was done as far as the broadcast was concerned. Grayson had fully enacted his plan, his public plan anyhow, so I didn't feel much of a sense of urgency to get to him. For another thing, I wanted to see for myself the effect his latest broadcast was going to have on the city. At first, as I walked through The Highlands in the dark of night, everything seemed normal. Things were quiet as they normally were at that time of night in that area of the city, especially with all the vampires now keeping a low profile. Then as I was walking past a small parking lot, I spotted a few expensive looking cars parked there with about half a dozen people standing around them. College kids it looked like, every one of them in the process of conjuring energy balls in their hands and throwing them across the parking lot like flaming baseballs where they either fizzled out in the air or landed on the ground in an explosion of sparks. The college kids roared with delight at this and high-fived each other. "This is fucking awesome!" one of them shouted. "I feel like the fucking Hulk!"

And then it happened. Just a few seconds after the kid said it he suddenly transformed into a giant green-skinned man that must have stood at least twelve feet high. "Oh, Christ," I said as I watched the Hulk pick up one of the cars and fling it across the parking lot like it was nothing. The car exploded when it landed, and the other kids stepped back from the Hulk in fear and wonder. Then they all cheered, and the Hulk roared.

I could hardly believe what I was seeing. There was never any doubt in my mind that Grayson's instructions would work, but knowing and seeing are two different things. It was inconceivable to me that a bunch of kids now possessed the magic power of a high-level wizard, and that they could seemingly do things without the need for spells or rituals. It seemed all they had to do was think about what they wanted and it would happen. This fact was demonstrated further when the rest of the college kids affected their own transformations. In the space of a minute, each of them had turned themselves into their favorite comic book character. I was now looking at the movie versions of Spiderman, Iron Man, Storm and two Wolverines, and none of them wasted any time in trying out their new powers. The two Wolverines proceeded to use their claws to tear up the remaining car, the sound of metal tearing metal screeching across the parking lot. Spiderman slung a web onto the nearest building and swung off into the night, while Storm, well, she caused a storm by inviting a small tornado into the parking lot that lifted up the remains of the car destroyed by the two Wolverines and flung it into the side of a nearby building. Iron Man was long gone, shooting off into the night sky like a ballistic missile.

"This isn't good," I said as the newly transformed superheroes fled off into the night, no doubt to fuck up as much shit as they could. "Not good at all." If the kids in the parking lot were anything to go by, the world would soon be fucked. Grayson had effectively given people the means to bend reality into whatever shape they pleased just by thinking about. Knowing magic as well as I did, my mind boggled as to how exactly Grayson had achieved such a feat given that magic always came with rules and regulations. Thanks to the Dark Codex, Grayson had given people a way to bypass all of said rules so they could just get to the good stuff.

Still in shock over what I just saw, I started walking again, and as I did a stretched limo pulled up alongside me. *Who the fuck is this?* I wondered. *Some dick who'd done Grayson's ritual and who had decided to become Patrick Bateman?*

The passenger window of the limo buzzed down, and I saw it wasn't Patrick Bateman inside, but someone equally sociopathic. The Crimson Crow.

"Creed," Angela Crow said, her pale face half in shadow inside the limo. The door opened. "Get in."

I sighed but got inside the limo. As the limo began to drive off again, I turned to look at Angela Crow. "I just saw a bunch of college kids turn themselves in superheroes from the X-Men. We're all fucked."

"No thanks to you," the vampire said. "I know you said you were going undercover, Creed, but I didn't think you'd get quite so involved."

I shook my head. "Give me a break. I did my best in there. Besides, I'm not sure you realize how much power Grayson has at his fingertips."

Her blue eyes seemed to light up for a second, and then become incensed by the idea of a power greater than her own. "So he really does have the book."

"Yes," I said as I poured myself a whiskey from a crystal decanter. The other decanter was filled with blood. Of a fine vintage, no doubt. "I've seen it."

Again, she was unable to keep the glow from her eyes. "What's it like?"

"Beautiful. I literally couldn't take my eyes off it. Grayson had to break the spell it had over me."

Angela Crow shook her head in what seemed like wonder. "Can you get it?" she asked.

I explained Grayson's security measures to her. "I have to find a way to get through them," I said. "Anyway, I was half hoping you had some useful information for me or didn't your bottomless resources turn anything up?"

The vampire made a face, her eyes reddening slightly. "That's where you are wrong, Creed. I did turn something up."

I froze with my glass half way to my mouth. "You did?"

She nodded slowly. "There's a way to destroy the book."

I registered surprise for the second time. "How?"

Angela Crow smiled, and then licked her lips. "Please, Creed. You know I'm not just going to hand you that information. Not without something in return."

I shook my head. "Surprise. What do you want?"

"It may surprise you to learn, Creed, that I know my limits. I'm well aware that the Dark Codex is too much power for one person. Grayson is proof of that."

"Agreed."

"But I still want to see the book for myself," she said, a tinge of excitement in her voice. "I want one look at it before it is destroyed."

I smiled as I shook my head. "Leave it to you, Angela. The world is hanging by a thread, and your kind is being hunted like animals, but you still have to conduct business."

Her smile was almost playful. "If it weren't for business and general skullduggery, I would have died from boredom centuries ago."

"You do remember that I hold the detonator to the bomb in your chest," I said. "I could force you to tell me what you know."

The Crimson Crow snarled as she showed her fangs, and for a second I thought she was going to lunge at me, but she soon relaxed. Thankfully. "Let's stop playing games, Creed. We both know you've been bluffing all this time."

"Are you willing to take that chance?"

The tension in her face returned. "You need me, Creed. This city needs me. I'm the only one keeping order here. Not you and certainly not fucking Division. Me. Without me, this city would fall into chaos, and you know it."

"Have you looked out the window lately? Kids are transforming into movie characters. I dread to think what else will follow."

"I'm sure you will find a way to contain it," she said. "You always seem to."

"Is that a compliment? Or a sarcastic referral to the whole Jennifer situation?"

"Let's call it both."

I shook my head. "You know, back when I was growing up in Ireland, if you'd have said to me that I would one day be in America, sitting in the back of a stretched limo across from a fifteen-year-old vampire, while outside college kids turned themselves into their favorite comic book characters, and a mad man with the universe's most powerful book holds the world to ransom, you know what I would have said?"

The Crimson Crow rolled her eyes at me. "What would you have said, Creed?"

"I would have said you were insane. But insanity has become the norm for me now, so..."

"What are you saying, Creed?" she asked shaking her head in annoyance.

A bit of a laugh left my mouth. "I'm not really sure. Maybe that I would only agree to a deal like yours in a mad, mad world, and that this is indeed a mad, mad world we find ourselves in."

"In your own meandering, infuriating way, are you agreeing to my terms?"

I nodded. "I guess I am."

Her smile was immediate. "I'm very glad to hear that."

"Don't get your hopes up," I said as I put my glass back where I found it. "I still have to get the damn book first, either before or after I find a way to take down Grayson. And that's if the world hasn't ended by then."

"I have faith in you, Creed. The full extent of my resources is also at your disposal."

"I'll bear that in mind. Now tell me how to destroy the book."

She laughed. "Not so fast, Creed. After I see the book. Not before."

I knew she would say that. It was worth a try I suppose. If she had spilled, there was no doubt I would have destroyed the book rather than give it to her. "Very well then. If I make it through this shitstorm, I'll be in touch."

She knocked the window for the driver to stop. "Don't bother," I said. "Bye, Angela."

A second later, I was standing on the sidewalk near Little Tokyo, having totally underestimated how long it would take people to power themselves up with Grayson's instructions it seemed. It was like people had been waiting since the first broadcast to get their magic on. Everywhere I looked, I saw people who had managed to transform themselves running around as ninjas, samurai warriors in full battle dress, their favorite movie and even cartoon characters. I counted at least three Deadpools scampering around fighting with other superheroes, a full-size real-life version of Bugs Bunny who was getting it on in the street with Wile E. Coyote, numerous X-Men characters and at least one Stag Demon from Hannibal, which disturbed me greatly as it trotted down the middle of the street. And that's not to mention the numerous other people who were conjuring fireballs and energy spheres, making money appear out of thin air, lifting cars above their heads with one hand and bringing magical unicorns into existence so they could ride around on them like it was something they had dreamed of doing their whole life. It was all very bizarre, to say the least. Grayson had effectively given people the power to make their every dream and whim into a reality, and given how messed up in the head most people tended to be, this made for some really weird and disturbing shit. The city wouldn't last another day at that rate before it came tumbling down under the weight of its inhabitants unrestrained whimsy. Already there were explosions going off all over the city. People could be heard screaming as superheroes laid waste to entire buildings, blew up cars and had epic battles with each other.

"Jesus fucking Christ," I said as I stared around in dismay. "I'm trapped in a teenage fantasy world."

Just then, one of the many Deadpools running around came somersaulting towards me, a baton in each hand as he landed a few feet from me. "Let's dance, motherfucker," he said, holding some sort of ridiculous fighting stance.

I took one look at the red-suited comic book character and fired him a sarcastic look. "Let's not," I said, about to teleport the hell away from that madness when I suddenly got swept up by something that was flying hard and fast. Within seconds, I was carried up into the night sky, memories of my last nearly fatal free fall still disturbingly fresh in my mind. Only this time, it wasn't a giant owl that had me, but a person. Another fucking superhero it seemed. What the fuck was wrong with people? They had the power to do anything, but instead, they go right for the fucking comic book characters. A sign of the times, I tell you.

"Don't worry," my Savior said in a very gruff voice, who I now realized was Batman. "I've got you."

"I can see that," I said loudly over the sound of the wind as I was carried over the rooftops below, although exactly where the guy was going was anybody's guess. He seemed to be flying towards the river for some reason. "You can put me down anytime."

"The city isn't safe. I'm taking you to my lair."

"You're taking me to the Bat Cave?"

Batman had me wrapped in his arms underneath him. His black mask looked down for a second. "How do you know about that? My lair is a secret."

I didn't answer straight away. "Lucky guess. Seriously though, you can put me down on the ground. I can take care of myself."

"Not when the Joker is out there causing chaos."

*Oh fuck, is he for real?* I thought. *Fuck it. I'll just teleport, which I should have done minutes ago.* But before I did, I decided to fuck with the guy a little. "Which one are you?"

"What?" Batman growled.

"Which Batman are you? Please don't say Val Kilmer. Or George Clooney. Definitely not one of those two. Are you Michael Keaton? He was the best Batman in my opinion."

"I..."

"Christian Bale then. Of course you are."

"I don't know those names."

"Oh, I see. You're in character. I get it. Then riddle me this, Batman. What do you have now that you soon won't?"

"I don't know what--"

"Me," I said, and then teleported out of the arms of Batman and into the grounds of Sanaka's Sanctum, shaking my head as I walked up to the front door. "The shit just got very fucking weird."

# TEA FOR TWO

"*E*xcuse my language," I said to Sanaka as he met me in the spacious front hall of his Sanctum. "But it's like the fucking Marvel slash DC Universe out there. Not that that would mean much to you--"

"I'm a fan of the Punisher," Sanaka said, completely flooring me as he stood in black robes, the crimson red sheath of his sword in his hand.

I shook my head. "How the hell...I've never...you don't...I mean, the Punisher, seriously? I thought maybe Doctor Strange would be more your kind of superhero."

Sanaka smiled. "The Punisher reminds me of the person I once was long ago, in a different time. I am reminded not to go back there."

"Right," I said nodding. "You know you are still a mysterious son of a bitch, Sanaka, even after all these years."

"Come," he said turning around. "We shall have tea."

*Tea*, I thought as I watched Sanaka disappear down a corridor, his steps silent on the hardwood floor. Always tea in a crisis. And guess who gets to make it?

Sanaka was already seated as I entered the tea room. I didn't bother to moan or ask if he would do the tea ritual for a change because I knew there was no point. Sanaka would remain kneeling at the small table until the ceremony was complete. So despite my resistance, I took off my trench coat and folded it, placing it on the floor next to the table containing everything I needed to make the tea. My resistance persisted for the first five minutes as I prepared the water for heating, but as always it melted away once I brought my full focus to the ritual and the many small, precise movements I had to perform as part of it. This was the reason Sanaka always brought me to the tea room in a crisis. He knew it would calm me before I had to explain things to him. Though I was sure he was already up to speed on most of what was happening. Sanaka had very little contact with the outside world or at least the normal parts of it. Even more so than I, he moved in a twilight world that was mostly hidden behind a veil of normality, but which underneath was anything but. Still, Sanaka always seemed to know what was going on in the city and elsewhere. The important stuff anyway. Like when mad scientists get their hands on a dangerous book and then try to bring about a new world order with it.

"So," I said after kneeling and serving the tea. "I assume you know what's going on out there, and that you've seen both broadcasts."

Sanaka nodded. "I saw."

"And that you know Grayson has the Dark Codex. Did you know that book even existed?"

"I did."

"Of course you did. I guess I don't need to tell you the shit we're in then. With Grayson I mean. What's happening outside is bad enough, but I don't think we've seen the worst yet. Grayson is a power mad fucker. He isn't going to stop."

"I agree," Sanaka said after carefully sipping his tea. "But if you are here expecting me to tell you how to stop him, you are wasting your time. Nothing can stand up to the limitless power of the Dark Codex."

"Yeah, I sort of figured that already." I paused before saying the next part. "Nothing except the Dark Codex itself."

A faint smile appeared on Sanaka's bearded face. "Indeed."

"Why are you smiling?"

"Because only you could think of using the book against itself, or at least against this man Grayson."

I shook my head. "It's not like there's any other choice, is there? I doubt a nuclear bomb could stop Grayson at this point. He'd probably just absorb its power to make himself stronger."

"Theoretically, that would be possible."

"Theoretically? There is no theoretical anything for Grayson. Everything is possible for him now. Things you and I probably don't even know about, and that's saying something."

Sanaka sat in silent contemplation for a moment, then asked, "So how do you propose to get your hands on the book?"

I sighed as the enormity of the problem came crashing down on me. "Well, Grayson keeps the book in a hidden dimension within another dimension—the Grayson Dimension—that he controls access to, and where only his magic seems to work. So it's going to be like trying to crack a couple of uncrackable safes, with no tools to speak off...and only one of the safes can be located." I threw my hands up. "Fucking impossible, in other words."

Sanaka narrowed his eyes at me and he did that face he always does when he thinks I've disappointed him in some way, a face I knew all too well by that point. "I thought I taught you better than that."

"Yeah, yeah, I know. Nothing is impossible. There's always a solution. But in this case..." I trailed off as I shook my head. "It's like I told Brentwood. We're dealing with a self-made god here who can do whatever he wants with no one to stop him."

"No one is unstoppable, not even the most powerful of beings," Sanaka said. "I would have thought your encounter with your father and Rloth would have taught you that."

I nodded and made some sort of face that signified I more or less agreed with him. "Okay, fine. Maybe I'm being a little histrionic, but I can't help it. My head is fucked, Sanaka. I'm actually starting to think that Leona had the right idea when she decided to run away and start again."

"You are talking nonsense. Stop it, please."

Sanaka stared at me as I was about to protest, then I just looked away and sighed. "all right," I said eventually. "Fuck it. I'm sure between us we can come up with a plan to get the book. Right?"

"Curse one more time in my company and I will throw this scalding tea in your face. Right?"

"Sure." I dropped my gaze for a second like a scolded schoolboy. "The stress is getting to me."

Fucking hell, what's the big deal? It's just a fucking word. All these years and I still don't know why he has such a problem with so-called course language. Now I have to watch my every fucking word, and every other word is going to want to be be fuck just because I can't say it. Fuck.

Sanaka finished his tea and then got to his feet. "Come," he said. "There's someone I think you should meet."

A frown crossed my face as I stood up. "Who?"

"The person who wrote the Dark Codex."

# ATHELSTAN

"*What* the fuck? Are you serious?"

It was a stupid question. Sanaka was always serious, even when he was joking. Even when he promised to reprimand me for cursing in his presence, which he did by slapping me around the face with invisible energy from his hand. It was like being slapped with a wet towel and it stung like hell. Lesson learned. "Why are you so surprised?"

I shook my head in astonishment. "Well, because you are just now mentioning this, and because the writer of the book actually exists and you actually f—you actually bloody know him. Or her. Or it. Who is it?"

Sanaka came around the table and placed a hand on my shoulder after he had picked up his sword. "You are about to find out," he said.

He teleported us to the midst of a tropical jungle, the heat and humidity making its suffocating presence felt immediately. "Where the hell are we?"

"An island." Sanaka looked around for a moment until he located a pathway through the jungle. I say pathway, it was more of a barely noticeable trail. Sanaka used the scabbard of his sword to push aside the thick jungle foliage. "This way."

"The author of the Dark Codex lives here?" I said as I grudgingly traipsed after him, doing my best to avoid the snap back of branches he was pushing aside. "How could anyone live here? It's like a fucking bug infested hothouse. Ow! Something just bit me on the arm. Motherfucker!"

"Keep up," Sanaka called as he forged on through the jungle.

I shook my head, thinking the author of the Dark Codex had to be an insane nut job to be living in a place like this. Hell, he wrote the fucking book. He had to be insane to even do that in the first place. "This is going to be a waste of time, I know it," I said to myself as I pushed my way through the jungle foliage. "Can't we just teleport to wherever we have to go?"

"Too many wards."

"I don't see any wards."

"You wouldn't."

"What does that mean?"

No reply.

Eventually, after what seemed like hours of clawing our way through unrelentingly thick jungle, we finally emerged into a large clearing. Sanaka stood, sweat dripping down his face as he stared towards the small mud hut in the center of the clearing.

"Thank fuck for that," I said, emerging from the trees like I'd repeatedly been raped by vines, with cuts and bites all over me, buckets of sweat stinging the hell out of every last one of them. I stared at the hut in near disbelief. "This person lives in there?"

Sanaka nodded. "Yes."

I puffed out my cheeks as I wiped the sweat from my face. "Well, I just know they are going to be batshit crazy then. They'd have to be to live in this circle of hell."

"I completely agree," said a voice from right behind me, and I jumped away in fright to see a naked man with a long beard standing within the trees. As he walked out to the clearing, I was relieved to see the man had on some sort of loin cloth. Things were awkward enough without having to avoid staring at the dude's junk as well.

"Athelstan," Sanaka said bowing. "I apologize for this intrusion."

"That's all right," Athelstan said, who seemed remarkably cheery, and dare I say it well adjusted, considering he lived alone in the eighth circle of hell.

Athelstan brought his gaze to me. Underneath the long scraggly beard, I saw a young guy in his late twenties at most. His hair was dark and curly, and his eyes were large and green and somehow trustworthy. There was definitely something about him, but I failed to see how he could be the author of a book that is rumored to be over a thousand years old. Unless there was magic at work, and let's face it, there was *always* magic at work somewhere. "And you are?" he asked.

"August Creed," I said, extending my sweaty hand, which Athelstan took and casually shook before letting go as if the whole encounter was awkward for him as well. I was guessing he didn't do much socializing in this place.

"You are a wizard, like Tetsuo here." It was a statement, not a question.

"Yes," I said. "He was—is—my mentor."

Athelstan smiled, and his eyes reflected the hint of craziness that I was expecting from him. Not that much, but then it was just a glimpse. Something told me there was more to Athelstan than the easy going Robinson Crusoe act he was putting out. "No better teacher than Tetsuo. I had the pleasure of being his student also, many years ago."

I wanted to shake my head but didn't. It still stuck in my craw that Sanaka had known the origins of the Dark Codex all along and hadn't bothered to let me know. Everything that happened could have been prevented.

Athelstan narrowed his eyes at me. "I know what you're thinking," he said. "And events could not have been prevented."

*Of course he can read my fucking thoughts.*

"Why not?" I asked, still slightly incensed, made worse by the sticky heat boiling my every molecule.

"Come into my hut," Athelstan said. "And I will tell you why not. But actually, before you do. There is a pool at the far edge of the clearing. You should go cool yourself off there first. Maybe lose the clothing as well. You'll be more comfortable."

"You got a spare loin cloth, Tarzan?"

Athelstan smiled. At least he had a sense of humor. "Maybe just keep your trousers on."

I nodded. "Good idea."

He was right about the pool. It did cool me off. The crystal clear water was glorious in fact, and when I got out, I pulled my trousers and boots back on, gathered up my shirt and waistcoat and headed to the hut in the center of the clearing. The inside of the hut would have been spacious if it weren't for the fact that Athelstan and Sanaka--and now me--were filling up the space, along with towers of white paper that were stacked around the dark brown walls like wonky skyscrapers. "What the hell?" I said, casting my eyes towards the nearest paper stack. "Are these all manuscripts?" I looked at the top of the pile and saw the words FLIGHT OF THE HAWK, and then underneath, BY MAXWELL PERKINS. "Who the hell is Maxwell Perkins?"

"That would be me," Athelstan said. "Just one of my many--many, many--pen names."

Athelstan sat crosslegged on a pile of animal pelts. Sanaka sat kneeling just across from him, sword by his side. I sat down in the middle to form a triangle as Athelstan offered me a crudely carved wooden bowl filled with a milky liquid. "What is it?" I asked.

"Probably not the right question to ask," Athelstan said. "Just drink."

"Will it send me on a trip? I don't need any trips right now. I'm on enough of one."

Athelstan laughed. "That's a good one. No, nothing trippy. It will calm you though. I sense you need calming."

I tried the drink. It tasted bitter, like juice from a plant, and it burned my throat on the way down. I made a face as I swallowed. "Good shit," I choked out.

Athelstan seemed pleased. "Glad you like it."

I placed the bowl on the ground beside me, unsure if I should drink anymore. Whatever was in the concoction, it was making me feel slightly drunk already. Not that I was complaining as he was right, it was calming. "So this is what you do?" I asked. "Sit in here and write books with that ancient typewriter over there?"

"Yes," Athelstan said. "Writing is the only thing that keeps me going, even after a thousand years."

"A thousand years? Really?"

"He is immortal," Sanaka said.

"You're clearly not a vampire," I pointed out. "So I'm guessing magic?"

"More like bad luck," said Athelstan. "I never asked to be this way. Immortality is not all it is made out to be. You know how many times I've died and come back? Guess."

"I wouldn't...I don't know. A lot?"

A crazy laugh came from Athelstan as he almost doubled over, then he stopped laughing abruptly and focused his wild gaze on me. "Two hundred and sixty-five times."

I made a whistling noise. "That's a lot of dying."

"I've experienced every kind of death imaginable," Athelstan said. "Most of them painful. All of them frightening in their own way. And I just keep on coming back."

"Why?" I asked. "Is it something to do with the Dark Codex?"

Athelstan's dark eyes grew even darker at the mere mention of the book. He directed his gaze at Sanaka. "So that's why you are here," he said. "And here I thought I was just getting a simple visit from an old friend."

Sanaka bowed his head slightly. "Forgive us, but we need your help, Athelstan. The Dark Codex has fallen into the wrong hands."

"Again?" Athelstan exclaimed, leaning back as if he was about to fall over. "I knew something was wrong. I knew it."

"Wait," I said. "Did you just say again?"

"This isn't the first time the book has fallen into the wrong hands," Sanaka said.

I shook my head in disbelief. "When?"

"Most recently, Hitler had the book in his possession, but thankfully not for long. Long enough to bring about a world war though. Fucking weasel that Hitler was. A few others have gotten their mitts on the book as well. The stories I could tell you..."

"I'm sure," I said, not really interested in hearing about his exploits or historical anecdotes. "How did you get the book back at those times?"

"How did I?" Athelstan said, then laughed. "Oh no, I didn't get the book back. I'm just a writer, always have been. I may have written the book, but I don't look after it. Never have."

"So who usually gets it back?"

"It depends. There's always some do-gooder person or group willing to sacrifice themselves if need be. The protectors have varied over the years. I don't pay much attention."

It was starting to dawn on me that Sanaka may have made a mistake coming here. Clearly, Athelstan didn't know very much, at least not the information I was after. A small sigh escaped me, and I looked at Sanaka for help.

"The book has been found again," Sanaka said to Athelstan. "The world is at risk once more."

"I see," said Athelstan. "Lucky I'm holed up in this place then, eh?" He laughed like the whole thing was a big joke, which pissed me off slightly.

"As long as you're all right," I said, about to stand, but Athelstan put a hand on my leg to stop me.

"Stay seated," he said, a sudden note of authority in his voice. "I might be able to help you."

"You better not be bullshitting," I said. "I don't have time for bullshit. Neither does the rest of the world."

"Are things that bad out there?" he asked. "It's been a few years since I've been off this island. I tend to go a little...crazy out there in the world after a while."

"Yeah, well," I said. "The world will do that to you."

Athelstan nodded. "Yes, which is why I spend most of my time in isolation these days. It's easier."

"I'm sure it is."

"You are judging me," he said. "Fair enough. You don't know me. But believe this--I gave enough of myself to this world over the centuries, including my blood. Lots of my blood."

"I'm sorry," I said. "I'm not here to judge you. I just want some answers, that's all."

"I can give you answers," Athelstan said. "But I don't know if they'll be the ones you seek."

"We'll see," I said. "Why don't we start with how you came to write the Dark Codex."

Athelstan tugged at his long beard for a moment as if agonizing over something. "Fine, I will relive that ancient pain again, just for you, August Creed."

I nodded and sipped at the concoction in my bowl as Athelstan spoke. "I was a simple scribe in Medieval England," he said. "A monk actually. I used to spend my days copying scripture. A slow and painful process, but still an enjoyable and satisfying one for someone like me, someone who loves language and books as much as I do. Then one night as I was praying in my quarters before bed, I was suddenly struck with the Holy Spirit. A great light filled my whole body, and I fell on the floor in near rapture as I thought the Lord had come to me."

"I take it wasn't the Holy Spirit?" I said.

Athelstan shook his head. "It was not. That much became clear when the voice started speaking. It was this deep, booming voice speaking in what seemed to come from all directions as it spoke in Anglo-Saxon. I knew immediately the voice didn't belong to our Lord, so then I became confused, and then frightened. It occurred to me that I might be being possessed by a demon. Demon possession was common back then."

"It still is," I said, suddenly remembering with a wave of sickening anxiety that I still bore the mark of a demon myself. "Bastards never change."

"I tend to avoid all contact wth the supernatural," Athelstan said, zoning out for a second. "It's just easier that way. I tend to arouse their curiosity, which is always unwanted." He shook his head. "Anyway, I knew the power that had invaded me was unlike any power I had ever known at that point. I feared for my soul, but the voice explained that it didn't want my soul, only my skills as a scribe. It said it would not leave me until I had written down everything that it was going to dictate to me. Out of fear, I had to agree to the entity's terms, but I did ask what would happen if I refused. The entity said it would find someone more willing to do its bidding and it would leave me alone."

"So why didn't you refuse?" I asked.

Athelstan sighed. "Because despite the fear and the crushing weight of its presence, I still felt like I had been chosen to complete some important task. A holy task, even if the entity in me had nothing to do with God, which it didn't. Back then, I longed to feel important, to feel valued as something more than just a pen monkey who spent his days in dark rooms toiling away by candlelight." He shrugged. "I had self-esteem issues. So I said yes to the entity and agreed to do the work it was asking of me."

Athelstan left the monastery he had spent his whole life in up to that point and found a room at a local inn to stay in. "I never left that room for over three years," he told me. "The landlord would bring me food, and I would pay him each week with money that magically appeared on my writing table whenever I needed it. All

I did was work on the book being dictated to me. Night and day, that's all I did until the book was completed."

"Did you know what you were writing?" I asked him.

"Yes and no," he said. "It was weird. I understood what was being said by the entity, but I never really thought about it as I was too busy making sure it was being properly transcribed. I was in a kind of trance most of the time, and I could also never remember what I had written the previous day. It was like the words just faded from my memory the moment they were written down."

"So you finished the book. Then what?"

Athelstan took a deep breath then let it out slowly. "I was given instructions on how the book should be bound, and I also sketched out the design of the cover, based on what the entity told me. I had a local craftsman bound the book and make the cover, which took months of work as the design was so complex. The material used to make the cover was also not of this world. A huge block of this glistening pearl white substance appeared in my room one day, and I carried it all the way to the craftsman so he could shape it. I also paid the man a considerable sum to keep the work he was doing secret. Although an hour after he had finished the work, he fell over stone dead. I had no doubt the entity inside me had killed the man, and I obviously began to fear that I would die too, once the entity had finished with me."

"So this entity," I said, trying to understand. "Did it tell you anything about itself, where it was from, why it was getting you to write the book?"

"Nothing," Athelstan said. "And I didn't ask. The identity of the entity remains a mystery to me to this day."

I shook my head. "Very strange."

"Strange? Yes. Even stranger that it left me alive—immortal in fact—because it said I would be needed again at some point in the future. It never said what for. I was told to give the book to a particular group of people back then, who would keep it under their protection. And although the book has changed hands many times over the years, that was the last I saw of it."

"So you've just been floating around ever since," I said. "Writing more books?"

"Mostly, yes."

I looked at Sanaka, who was still calmly kneeling and listening. "What's your take on this?"

"What do you mean?" Sanaka asked.

"I mean why do you think the entity made Athelstan here immortal? What do you think its plan is?"

Sanaka shrugged. "I have no idea."

I shook my head. "Seriously? None?"

Sanaka just looked at me and said nothing.

"Well, do you at least know how to destroy the book that you wrote?" I asked Athelstan.

"Destroy?" Athelstan shook his head. "It cannot be destroyed. I thought you knew that."

I gritted my teeth and closed my eyes for a second. "That fucking bitch."

"What?" Athelstan said.

"Nothing," I said shaking my head, thinking I should have known better than to trust Angela Crow.

Sanaka snorted slightly as if he knew about my conversation with the Crow. I was going to say something, but I let it go.

"I'm not really sure why you are here," Athelstan said, looking like he'd had about enough of our little unannounced visit. It was clear he wasn't really a people person. Otherwise, he wouldn't be living alone on some far-flung tropical island in the middle of a jungle, would he? "Everything I've told you, Sanaka here knows already." He looked at Sanaka. "You know everything already."

Sanaka shook his head slightly. "Not everything."

Frowning, Athelstan said, "What do you mean?"

"We do not know your exact power over the Dark Codex, nor your connection to it," Sanaka said. "You have made no contact with the book since you wrote it, but I believe you have power over it. I believe you can locate the book, and possibly destroy it completely."

Athelstan snorted. "Pure conjecture."

"Are you denying you have an innate connection to the book?"

A weary sigh escaped Athelstan, and he began to tug nervously at his beard. "I have a sense of the book, yes, I'm not denying that."

"A sense?" I said. "What does that mean?"

Athelstan released his beard as he looked at me with thinning patience. "I can feel the book at all times, no matter where I am. The closer I am to the book, the more intense the feeling until I can hardly stand to be anywhere near it because it feels like a wretched fire is burning out my insides." He shook his head as he seemed to relive the feeling. "I realized a long time ago that I am not meant to have any contact with that book. The pain is self-explanatory."

I thought for a second as I stared intensely at the former monk. "That only goes to support the theory I posited a moment ago," I said. "I still think if you and the book come together, the book will be destroyed somehow."

"And so will I," Athelstan said quietly. "Do you think I haven't thought about exactly everything you have said. I've had a thousand years to think about it."

"That's a lot more than most people get," I said.

"So you are asking me to die now?" he said.

I shook my head. "You don't know if you'll die. You don't know anything at this point. But I'll tell you what I do know. If we don't try and put a stop to the book's new owner, and then the book itself, there won't be a world left for you to live in, Athelstan. At least not one you'd want to live in, and there is no island far-flung enough for you to hide out in. There'll be no one left to read all those books you wrote. So even if there is a chance that you'll die, so what? You've had a fucking thousand years. Are a few more years of reclusive living worth the fate of the whole goddamn world?"

Athelstan stared at me a moment, and then slowly turned his head towards Sanaka. "You didn't tell me your apprentice was a crusader. He reminds me of a character I used to write in an adventure series. His name was--"

"Don't care," I said, raising a hand to interrupt. "Seriously, have you not been listening to me?"

"Yes, I've been fucking listening," Athelstan snapped. "You sit there and ask me to go with you to my likely death and expect me to be happy about it--"

"No one said you had to like the idea," I said. "And you're not the only one putting your life on the line, either. Fucking Christ, you've already died and come back hundreds of times. Who is to say you won't do so again?"

"The book," he said. "I've always known it would be the cause of my final death if I ever had one. Why do you think I've spent the last one thousand years avoiding the cursed thing? And besides, the book has always been retrieved in the past, albeit too late, but still retrieved and protected once more. Why is this time any different?"

"It *is* different," I said. "This time the book has made a god that will wreck everything. Maybe the whole damn universe, I don't know. The potential is certainly there. I'm also not willing to wait until the damage has all been done, either. Things move faster now than they did in the past."

Athelstan nodded almost nostalgically "Yes, I'm afraid they do."

"Then you know you don't have a choice," I said as gently as possible. "Maybe this was your destiny all along? To destroy the very thing you had a hand in creating."

"Leave the poetic irony to the experts, Mr Creed," he said making a face at me just before he stood up suddenly and began tugging at his beard again. "all right, fine. I'll go on this crusade, or suicide mission or whatever it is with you, but on one condition."

"Really?" I said, glancing at Sanaka. "What?"

"You must grant me another half a day so I can add what might very well be the last chapter to my memoirs," Athelstan stated.

I puffed my cheeks at the balls on the guy. The fucking world was about to collapse in on itself, and he wanted to finish writing his fucking memoirs. "all right, fine," I said, looking a Sanaka, who just nodded like he didn't mind at all. "Just make it quick."

Athelstan looked down at Sanaka. "He's very pushy your apprentice."

"I'm not his apprentice," I said, shaking my head in annoyance.

"Whatever," Athelstan said. "I'm blaming all of this on you in my memoirs, Tetsuo, I hope you know. You knew things would turn out this way before you came here."

Sanaka sat and made no acknowledgment of Athelstan's accusations, even though I knew the former monk was completely correct.

As Athelstan threw Sanaka and me out of the hut so he could get to typing, I stood outside in the baking heat and considered giving in to my frustrations so I could throw a temper tantrum. But then I saw Sanaka walking towards the pool, calmly disrobing and sliding inside like he didn't have a care in the world. "Fuck it," I said, heading over there myself. "What's good for the goose..."

26

# AT THE GATE

*W*hen Athelstan finally emerged from his hut several hours later, he had a distant look on his face like he had just woken up from a dream. "Finally," I said marching over to him. "Can we go now then?" By that point, I had had enough of the sticky heat and the biting insects. I wanted back to civilization if it even still existed and the world hadn't completely crumbled under the weight of excessive magic use by then.

"I suppose so," Athelstan said, then stared intensely at me. "You must promise me something."

"What?" I asked as Sanaka came to join us, hardly a bead of sweat on his brow.

"If I don't make it back," Athelstan said. "You must promise to come back here and retrieve my memoirs from the hut."

"Sure," I said. "Providing I live to do so myself."

Athelstan nodded. "That will have to do then."

Sanaka took hold of our arms. "Ready?" he asked, his sword now on his back.

"Ready," Athelstan said with not much enthusiasm.

"Wait," I said, looking at the former monk. "You're leaving like that?"

Frowning, Athelstan said, "Like what?"

"You're wearing a loin cloth. You look like a naked tramp. Style issues aside, you'll need a bit more protection than that around you."

Athelstan sighed. "Fine," he said, then walked back into the hut. A moment later, it was like a different person emerged. "What about now? Do I still offend your sense of style, Apprentice?"

"I told you, I'm not an apprentice," I said shaking my head. "And yeah, you look...more ready now." Athelstan no longer looked like Robinson Crusoe's junky brother. His dark hair was now short and combed, his beard trimmed to leave a thin mustache and a short, pointed bit on his chin. He also wore a light colored three-piece suit that looked like it was made several decades ago, but which looked

591

good on him nonetheless. I didn't ask how he managed such a dramatic transformation in such a short time inside a mud hut devoid of anything but manuscripts and a typewriter. I knew magic had to have something to do with it.

"Back to the world again," Athelstan said as Sanaka took hold of his arm. "It always scares me going back."

*You should be scared.*

"Trust me," I said with a smile. "You're gonna love it."

* * *

"OH MY GOOD GOD," ATHELSTAN SAID AS SOON AS WE LANDED BACK IN Blackham. Per my request, Sanaka had teleported us smack into the middle of Main Street in Freetown. I thought Athelstan needed to see for himself the extent of the Dark Codex's reach this time, or rather Gordon Grayson's reach, as it was him directing everything.

"Told you," I said with a grim smile that I couldn't keep from my face. Even Sanaka looked shocked at the chaos happening all around, and that was saying something because I don't think I've ever seen Sanaka looked shocked at anything. You name it, it was walking or running around the streets like it had been there forever: unicorns in all colors (including a rainbow one), naked porn stars, celebrities, transformers, cartoon characters, bloody Surfs and every character our modern culture has thrown up, not forgetting the massive troll like creatures straight out of Warcraft, and monsters that could only have come from video games or movies, huge fucking things indiscriminately killing people and fucking whatever took their fancy. Either someone had transformed into one of those things, or they had somehow used their newfound magic to conjure one up. Whatever, the effect was the same. Total fucking chaos added to by the epic battles going on between monsters and superheroes, wizards and demons, giant Furbies and real life Pokemon characters.

"What the actual fuck?" Athelstan said as he gaped in awe, looking half afraid that something or someone was going to attack him at any moment, which was highly likely because the whole city seemed to have turned into a giant free for all. A huge battle arena straight out of some big budget fantasy movie. I could only imagine what was happening in the rest of the world. Something very similar no doubt. "What is happening?"

As I was about to answer, Bugs Bunny (un huh) sprinted by us, almost knocking Athelstan over and then shouting over his shoulder, "Sorry Doc!" I turned just as Elmer Fudd came running up (uh huh un huh) with a shotgun in his hand. "It's wabbit season, and I'm hunting wabbits," Elmer said gleefully, then ran off after Bugs Bunny.

I stood shaking my head. "Seriously. What the fuck is wrong with people?"

Athelstan looked deeply disturbed as he stood with wide eyes. "I've been here for two minutes, and already I feel like I'm insane. Again. Get me out of here. Let me go, Sanaka, please. I want to go back to my island."

"Sorry," I said, grabbing his arm, and then Sanaka's. "But you're staying until we're done."

"Until I'm dead or insane, you mean?" Athelstan moaned.

"Like the rest of us," I said just before I teleported the three of us down into the sewers where the gate to the Grayson Dimension was.

*Was* being the operative word, for the fucking gate was gone. "No," I said. "Grayson, you motherfucker."

"I'm assuming Grayson closed the gate," Sanaka said as we stared into an empty sewer tunnel. Or at least it was empty until the fucking Teenage Mutant Ninja Turtles came running up it, shouting, "Cowabunga dudes!" as they somersaulted by.

Athelstan looked like he was about to cry. "Who...what..."

"Don't ask," I said, then turned to Sanaka. "Any ideas?"

Sanaka shook his head. "Not as yet."

"Fuck," I said, gritting my teeth. Suddenly, I wished Leona were there with me. I don't know why she popped into my mind at that moment. Maybe because she always kept me calm, or because anything seemed possible when she was around. Either way, I realized with almost knee-bending emotion that I missed the hell out of her. *Was she okay?* I wondered. What if she was in trouble in DC? What if she needed my help? What if I never saw her again? It was all I could do not to turn tail, grab the nearest superhero and force them to fly me to DC so I could be with the woman who would have my heart always and forever.

But then something distracted me. A voice in the shadows of the tunnel behind us. "You looking for the gate?" Jordan Grayson stepped forward into the light, dressed in black and as striking as ever. "It's gone, but I know how to get it back."

I nearly ran to her just to hug her for saying that, but I knew she wouldn't appreciate it. "Jordan? What are you doing here? Why aren't you with your father?"

She snorted and shook her head as she stood several feet back from us. "I don't have a father anymore." A dark look crossed her face. "I don't think I ever did."

A wave of sympathy went through me, and I went to her this time to put a friendly hand on her shoulder, which she didn't immediately shrug off. "I'm sorry, Jordan. I know exactly what you're going through."

"Yeah," she said. "You never did dish the dirt on that, did you?"

I smiled. "Hey, not my fault you passed out."

Something of a sad smile appeared on Jordan's weary face. "Thanks, Creed."

"What for?"

"You made me realize what a cunt my father is, or rather, what a cunt he's been to me over the years." She shook her head. "I can't believe it's taken me this long to accept that he never loved me, and he only used me."

"I'm sure some part of him does love you," I said, aware that Sanaka and Athelstan were standing behind waiting.

"I don't care anymore, Creed. I'm through whatever."

"Through?"

"With everything."

I frowned, slightly disturbed by her tone. "You're going to make it through this with the rest of us, Jordan. Trust me on that."

*More promises you can't hope to keep, eh, Creed?*

"And then what? I have nothing, Creed. I have no one." Tears began to form in her eyes, but she wiped them away.

I placed both hands on her shoulders. "You'll figure it out. I'll be there to help you."

She looked doubtful. "Will you?"

"We're friends. Right?" I doubted she even knew what friends were.

"Sure," she said after a moment. "I guess."

"Well then, I always look after my friends. You'll learn that about me. I'm a caring guy."

She laughed, and her near perfect face lit up for a moment. "You make me laugh, Creed."

"I think you said that already, back in your quarters," I said.

"Well, you do, and no one has ever made me laugh since my mother died."

"That's a long time."

"Yes, it is."

"Eh," Athelstan shouted over. "It's not that I'm at all anxious to meet my possible demise or anything, but this waiting around is killing me. So if you two could hurry the fuck up, that would be great. Just saying."

"Who the hell is that guy?" Jordan asked.

"Would you believe the guy who wrote the Dark Codex?"

Jordan looked shocked for a second. "Get the fuck out of here. That guy?"

"That guy. You should have seen him earlier. He lives on an island all alone like Robinson fucking Crusoe. Long beard and loin cloth and everything. Lives in a mud hut writing novels. You believe that? He's also immortal, in case you're wondering."

Jordan nodded. "I was actually. Can he help stop my father?"

"Possibly," I said turning around finally to walk back to Sanaka and Athelstan. "We'll see."

"See what?" Athelstan said. "And who is this?" He pointed at Jordan.

"This is Jordan Grayson," I said.

"Belfoir," Jordan said. "I'm going by my mother's name from now on."

"Good call," I said, then looked at Athelstan. "Jordan can open the gate for us."

"Your father," Sanaka broke in. "What protection does he have?"

"Are you kidding?" Jordan said back, looking at Sanaka and probably wondering who he was. "He has the power of the universe at his fingertips, and if that somehow isn't enough, he has about a hundred armed followers who are willing to kill and die to protect their messiah. They are all his disciples, even though he doesn't give a shit about any of them...about any*one*."

"I don't think we should be focusing too much on Gordon, not until we get the book," I said.

"And then what?" Jordan asked.

"Then I try to find something in the book to help us take down your father," I said.

Jordan shook her head. "Are you mad? You're going to read that book?"

"I don't see any other choice," I said. "Your father can't be stopped by conventional means. He's too damn powerful. The only place to access equal or greater power is in the book." I registered her look of concern. "Don't worry. I'm not your father, Jordan. I'm not going to make myself into a demigod. Once I'm done, Athelstan here will hopefully be able to destroy the book for good."

"And most likely myself along with it," Athelstan said, looking like he hadn't quite accepted his possible imminent demise just yet.

"Well," Jordan said. "That all sounds great, as long as my father doesn't kill you all first. And what about magic? You know you can't use it in there."

"We're hoping Sanaka here will find a work around, otherwise..."

Jordan shook her head. "You all are lucky I showed up. I can lower the wards my father put in place. I know all of his security systems, providing he hasn't changed anything."

I could have kissed her. "Maybe you could buy us some time as well," I said. "Give Athelstan a chance to locate the book."

"If I can," Athelstan said. "I've never tried before. Although, my connection to the book feels stronger here, so maybe we are close."

"Just get the coordinates," Sanaka said. "I will retrieve the book myself."

"Maybe I should," I said. "The book puts you in a trance if you look at it. It's the Medusa of books." I chuckled slightly, then shook my head as everyone just looked at me. "Anyway, Gordon has already made me immune to the trance state, so it shouldn't be a problem."

"We will see," Sanaka said.

"All right then," I said. "Jordan, open the gate please, then lower the wards. Let's get this done."

Jordan closed her eyes as she seemed to concentrate. A moment later, the shimmering gate to the Grayson Dimension appeared behind us. Jordan and I stepped up first. She didn't look too thrilled about going through. "My father will know why I'm here," she said. "I already told him I was walking away."

"Tell him you changed your mind," I told her. "That you've nowhere else to go."

"The sad thing is, that's the truth," she said, then looked at me. "He'll know you've come the second you step through that portal. You know that, right? He sees everything now."

I nodded. "I figured as much. I'm counting on his ego telling him we aren't worth bothering with."

"Maybe," Jordan said.

"Are we going through now?" Athelstan asked anxiously. "Or should I call Dr Phil so you two can continue to work out your daddy issues?" When everyone gave Athelstan a funny look, he smiled awkwardly and shook his head. "Apologies. I'm a little tense."

"Don't sweat it," I said. "We all are." I looked at Sanaka who appeared as calm and composed as ever. "Most of us anyway."

There was nothing more to say by that point.

Taking a deep breath, I stepped through the gate into the Grayson Dimension and my possible doom.

# GRAYSON MANOR REVISITED

hings had changed since the last time I was in the Grayson Dimension. A lot. As it happened, we didn't even get the chance to carry out our plan to split up and locate the Dark Codex. When we came through the gate, we came through straight into a gigantic chamber that looked like the great hall of a huge palace. The floors were made of white marble, and the walls appeared to be solid marble as well, with great gold pillars lining each side. Gathered in the hall were Grayson's disciples, the ones who tried to kill me the last time I saw them. About a hundred pairs of angry and suspicious eyes turned to look at us as we stayed by the gate. "So much for the plan," I muttered to myself as I spotted Grayson at the front of the huge chamber. He wore his usual white robes as he sat in a great iron throne. Or at least I think it was iron. It reflected the light in a strange way, as did the smaller throne beside his, on which a woman with long dark hair and white robes also sat. I didn't recognize the woman at all, although Jordan seemed to.

Jordan stopped dead on the marble floor and gaped at the woman like she had seen a ghost. "No," she said. "It can't be..." There were tears in her eyes as her face twisted with various emotions.

"Jordan?" I said. "Are you all right? Who is that?"

Her mouth opened, but she couldn't speak.

"Creed," Gordon Grayson said loudly from his throne. "I had a feeling I hadn't seen the last of you. And I see you've brought guests."

A few of Grayson's disciples--now wearing black robes and hoods like a bunch of Satanists--came to escort us to the front of the hall. Each of the escorts had a long knife in their hands. I pulled away when one of them tried to grab me. "Go fuck yourself," I snarled, and then I looked at Grayson. "Tell your brainwashed drones to keep their hands off."

"We have our own minds," one of the drones said, a man whose face I could hardly see under the hood. "We serve of our own free will."

"Even worse then," I said back.

"Jordan," Grayson said as he stood up, a strange sort of smile on his face like he was about to show off a new toy he had acquired. "Look who I brought back from the afterlife."

It clicked then who the woman next to Grayson was. It was Jordan's mother, still the same age as when she died. "Jesus..." I said.

"Mother?" Jordan said, her voice breaking as she pushed her way through the hooded disciples to get to the front of the hall.

"What now?" Athelstan said falling in beside me.

"Can you sense the book?" I asked quietly.

"Yes," he said. "It's near. Very near. It feels like my blood is boiling. Most unpleasant actually."

"Good," I said. "Try to get an accurate location. Then I'll retrieve it."

"How? Him up there won't allow it."

"I don't expect him to."

"Then how?"

"I'll think of something."

Athelstan didn't look convinced. "You'll think of something? I don't--"

"Let's just go," I said cutting him off. I looked at Sanaka, who had both hands on the scabbard of his sword, obviously expecting trouble from Grayson's disciples. So was I, but not yet. I knew Grayson would want to boast for a while first, and I was happy to let him if it gave Athelstan time to pinpoint the pocket dimension in which the Dark Codex was being kept.

When we reached the front of the huge hall, Jordan was standing staring at her mother as her mother stood up slowly with tears in her eyes, obviously unable to believe that she was now staring at her daughter. No longer the little girl she would have remembered, they were both now around the same age. Gordon Grayson stood by his throne and looked on with a prideful smile on his face. "This is what you've always wanted," he said to his daughter. "And I am finally able to give it to you."

Jordan approached her mother slowly, almost cautiously like she was walking into a trap. "Jordan?" her mother said, then put her arms around Jordan. After a moment, Jordan hugged her back, and they stayed hugging for a long time as if they were afraid if they let each other go they would never see each other again.

I glanced away to see that Grayson was staring at me. "I take it you are here for the book," he said. "Of course you are."

"You have no need for it anymore," I said. "You've got all the power of the universe in you now. Why don't you just hand it over?"

Grayson shook his head. "The book belongs to me and me alone. I'm surprised you thought I would just hand it over, Creed."

I didn't, but I thought I would try. "I thought you would see reason, Gordon."

"Reason?" He laughed. "Trust me, Creed, I am far beyond petty human constructs such as reason."

"You're a god now, is that it?"

"If a god is one with ultimate power, then yes, I am a god. In fact, I was just about to let everyone know that." He sat back down again and smiled at his wife and daughter, who now stood staring at him like he was some kind of monster.

I sensed Grayson's mood begin to darken as he didn't take too well to the anger and resentment coming from his wife and daughter. In an effort to prevent a possible outburst, I got his attention again. "By everyone, you mean the whole world," I said.

Grayson turned his attention to me again, his face still darkened, purple magic arcing all around him. "You are correct. I thought what people needed was independence. Freedom from those who oppressed them. I thought the people needed power, the power to make things better themselves. But I see now that I was wrong. What have they done with the power I gave them?"

"Became superheroes and conjured rainbow unicorns," I said, echoing his disgust.

"Indeed," Grayson said. "They are squandering the power I gave them on nonsense. People don't need freedom, Creed. I realize that now. The people need to be ruled. By me."

"You want to know what I think?" I said, hoping Athelstan would get a bead on the book soon. "I think this was your plan all along, Gordon. You knew this would happen, and that you would have to step in."

Grayson said nothing for a moment as he half smiled at me. "As far as the people of the world are concerned now, I am their God. In fact, I'm out there now, all over the world, telling everyone about the new regime change."

"But you're here."

"I am everywhere all at once, Creed. I am a god, remember?"

As if to prove it, a replica of Grayson appeared right in front of me, while his original self continued to smile over at me from his throne. "Nice trick," I said, taking a step back from him.

"Observe," he said as he waved his hand in the air. Above the heads of the gathered disciples, a number of shimmering windows appeared that showed various locations around the world, and in every one, there was Grayson standing by various landmarks, including the Eiffel Tower, the British Parliament buildings, the Roman Colosseum and of course, the White House. In every location, Grayson had made himself huge so that he was almost as tall as the buildings he was standing beside. "I am your God now," the various versions of himself proclaimed in a booming voice. "You will all serve me now. Your world will be dismantled, and a new world order will be constructed by me, which you will all follow. Nothing can stop me. Your weapons are useless. Try to use them, and you will incur my wrath. Serve me faithfully, however, and you will be rewarded in ways you cannot yet imagine."

Grayson waved his hand again, and the images in the air disappeared.

"So we're all supposed to just follow you from now on?" I asked.

Grayson nodded. "And you will."

I was going to say, "Or what?" but I already knew the answer. Without the Dark Codex, there would be no standing up to him.

"Stop this, Gordon," Marie Grayson said as she stood beside Jordan.

"Mom, don't," Jordan said, knowing full well her mother was wasting her breath.

The Grayson in front of me disappeared suddenly, and the Grayson on the throne turned to look at his wife. "Stop?" he said as if he couldn't fathom what she was asking. "Why?"

"It's wrong, Gordon," Marie said. "You know it is."

Grayson snorted. "Wrong," he muttered to himself as he shook his head. "There is no such thing as right or wrong, my love," he said. "There is only me and the laws I hand down. Either you obey, or you don't."

"This is why you brought me back?" Marie asked. "To watch you become a tyrant?"

"I brought you back so we could rule the world together," Grayson said, his madness seeming to come to the fore now. "The three of us. Together. Can't you see that?"

Marie shook her head. "I'd rather be dead again."

Grayson's face darkened as he stared at his wife. The arcs of energy surrounding him became more agitated as he stood up and seemed to grow in stature until he was towering above everyone. "So be it."

"Athelstan," I hissed. "The fucking location. Now."

"I have it," Athelstan whispered back as he stood close to me. "I have the exact space-time coordinates."

"Give me them," I said just as Grayson reached out a hand and grabbed the top of his wife's head, causing Marie Grayson to suddenly start shaking as purple energy flashed from within her body.

"No!" Jordan cried. She pulled out her gun and fired upon her father, but the bullets disintegrated even before they got near him. Then the gun itself disintegrated also, and Grayson put his other hand on top of Jordan's head, causing her to immediately shake and vibrate like her mother as similar energy flashed from within her.

"What is he doing?" Athelstan asked after he had given me the coordinates of the Dark Codex's hiding place.

"Killing them," I said, then looked at Sanaka, who had his eye on the now encroaching disciples behind us. "Help them!"

Sanaka turned to look at Grayson and outstretched his hand as a pure red sphere of energy formed in it, which he then blasted at Grayson. The high-speed energy ball hit Grayson in the head, causing purple and red sparks to explode as if out of his skull. Grayson cried out and was forced to release his wife and daughter, who both fell to the floor.

At that point, I seized the opportunity given to me by Sanaka to close my eyes for a second so I could enter the Chaosphere and form the required magic for a retrieval spell powerful enough to retrieve something from a different dimension. It only took me a few seconds to conjure the magic. The hard part would be getting the magic to reach across time and space to the exact coordinates given to me by Athelstan. It was something I had never done before, so I wasn't even sure it would work. But as always with magic, I never let my doubts interfere in the process. When I cast the spell, I did so with the absolute conviction that it would work.

As I continued to work the spell in as discrete a manner as possible, Grayson was staring angrily at Sanaka. "You are powerful, wizard," he said, his voice now more of a growl as it seemed to have dropped an octave, although it could have been the magic interfering with my perceptions, which sometimes happened. He glanced down at Jordan, knowing full well she had lowered the wards that previously blocked the use of magic in the place apart from his own. I had to give it to Jordan. For someone who professed to hating magic, she had certainly picked up a few tricks along the way. "Surprisingly so, but nowhere near powerful enough to defeat me."

"I don't have to be," Sanaka said calmly.

"What?" Grayson asked, seeming confused for a moment.

"He says he doesn't have to be," I shouted, just as the Dark Codex in all its shining beauty came falling out of the air and into my waiting arms. The book was heavier than I thought, and I almost dropped it as I clinched it to my chest.

"Very good, Creed," Grayson said. "Enjoy your little moment of victory. It won't last long, I assure you."

*We'll see about that,* I thought as I prepared to teleport out of the Grayson Dimension, taking the Dark Codex with me. But a second later, our surroundings changed, the walls and ceiling falling away to reveal a different location, one that I instantly recognized as being Liberty Square in Bankhurst, characterized by the giant obelisk in the center and surrounded by grand stone buildings. Needless to say, the place was already in chaos as people ran around in fear and bewilderment at their unexpected change in circumstances. They no longer had access to the magic that had previously allowed them to become like gods in their own right, and they were also clearly terrified of the giant Grayson God who towered almost as high as the obelisk.

Surrounded by Grayson's hooded disciples, my first instinct was to teleport out of there, but I quickly found that I couldn't. A smugly smiling Grayson standing amongst his disciples told me why I couldn't. "I should have disposed of you long before this, Creed," Grayson said as he reached out his hand and used his magic to rip the Dark Codex from my grip and into his own waiting hands. "You simply don't have the power to go up against me. No one has."

"So you keep saying," I shouted angrily, and then sent a blast of magic his way, which he just absorbed into himself.

"Prepare to die, Creed," the giant version of Grayson boomed. "Kill him! Kill them all!"

The order was to his disciples who now completely surrounded Sanaka, Athelstan and myself. I could see no sign of Jordan or her mother, so I assumed they were still back in the Grayson Dimension. Probably for the best.

To say I felt vulnerable as the hooded disciples closed in would be an understatement. Every one of them was armed with a bladed weapon, and I had nothing but my magic if it even still worked in this Grayson world. Neither did I have my trusty trench coat on me, having left it back at Sanaka's Sanctum, so that meant I would have no protection at all from the knives about to stab me to death.

I tried to teleport, but nothing happened. "Shit!" I looked at Sanaka and Athelstan. "Can you use your magic?"

They both shook their heads as the disciples moved in closer. "No," Athelstan said as he looked frantically around. "But then I'm immortal, so what do I care, right?" Despite his joking bravado, he still looked afraid.

Sanaka had his sword out and ready. I would have said he could save us, but I knew he couldn't, despite his unmatched skills with the sword. There were just too many disciples surrounding us, and now I could see that they all had magic in their eyes as well. "Fuck this!" I shouted as the odds of survival lessened with every passing second. "Fuck you, Grayson!"

Then the disciples closed in, and the stabbing began.

## 2 8

# FACE OFF

*I* awoke to the taste of blood in my mouth, pain all over my body and to the sound of someone calling my name. "Creed?" the familiar voice said, a voice I hadn't expected to hear again. "Wake up, Creed, damn it."

My eyes gradually came into focus, and there she was kneeling over me. A beautiful sight. So beautiful, I thought I was hallucinating. "Is it really you?"

"It's me," Leona said. "Who'd you think it was, the Virgin Mary?"

I tried to laugh but my stomach hurt too much, and I cried out in pain instead. "*Oh, Jesus...*"

"Stay still," Leona said as she ripped open my shirt. "You've been stabbed. Multiple times."

"Sanaka?" I mumbled. "Athelstan..."

"Sanaka is nearby. I don't know any Athelstan."

Then I remembered Grayson's hooded disciples descending on us, violently stabbing and slashing at us with their long knives. I remember trying to defend myself, but being completely outnumbered, despite Sanaka trying to keep the crowd at bay with his sword. Then I remembered falling to the ground and seeing the pool of blood oozing out around me. My own blood. "Grayson?" I said.

"Not far away," Leona said as she held up a bottle of something. "He's changing the city. Turning it into a giant prison." Leona began to pour whatever was in the bottle over my wounds, causing me to scream as the liquid burned its way in. "Sorry, Creed. This is the same stuff you used on me on that island. You remember? Hey, Creed, stay with me!"

"I'm...here..." I said as consciousness threatened to leave me again.

"You'd better be," Leona said as she continued to pour the healing potion on the rest of my wounds. "I didn't come all the way back here just to watch you die on me, you hear?"

Even through the pain, I smiled. "You're...back?"

Her face hovered over mine for a moment. "Let's face it. You need me. I leave for two minutes and now look at you."

I tried to laugh, but couldn't. "I...really missed you..."

"Tell me how much later, once you take down that fucker Grayson."

"But I can't..."

"No," said another familiar voice. "But we can."

"Ray?" I said, hardly able to contain the emotions that had by then built up in me as my uncle's grinning face hovered over mine.

"Did you think you'd have to do this alone?" he said, then gave a dismissive laugh. "Come on, son. This is too big for even you. You haven't been the only one working on taking that bastard Grayson down. In fact, I've brought a few friends along to help us."

I managed to lift my head an inch to see a large crowd of people standing behind Ray. "Who are they?" I asked.

"wizard's, my boy," Ray said. "The best in the universe." He put his hands on me then and used his magic to finish the healing process that Leona had started. Within a few moments, most of the pain I'd been feeling was gone, and I sat up.

"You don't understand, Ray," I said. "Grayson has so much power behind him."

"Maybe," he said, helping me to my feet. "But there's enough of us here to keep him occupied while you get that damn book off him."

I looked past to crowd of wizards and witches standing behind him, a veritable sea of magic obsessed weirdos. There must have been nearly a hundred of them. I looked back at Ray. "I guess it's the only shot we have."

"Then we'd better make it count," Ray said.

I turned to Leona then, who was standing two feet away, dressed in the leather outfit she always favored while working for Division, including her twin custom Berettas which were strapped to each leg. God, she looked amazing, and even more bad ass than ever. I went to her and threw my arms around her, hugging her tight to me as she did the same. "We don't have time for this," she whispered, her soft skin and warm breath on my neck.

"We're having a long talk later," I said as we pulled apart. "A *long* talk."

"Sure," she said smiling. "I'm sure you've plenty to say. As always."

I smiled back and shook my head. "You know it. Sweetheart."

She shook her head. "I'll let you get away with that this one time."

"all right," Ray said, barging forward in his battered trench coat, his long gray hair tied back in a ponytail. "We need to do this now before there isn't a world left to save."

I looked out into the distance to see the giant version of Grayson about a mile away as he walked along, rearranging whole city blocks as he went, occasionally sending the odd burst of magical energy down below, presumably to help round up the herd into the prison he was building. "all right," I said, just as Sanaka joined us. "Let's do this."

"I cannot find Athelstan," Sanaka said.

"Shit," I said. "We need him to destroy the book."

"I'll find him," Leona said. "He can't have gone far."

After giving Leona a description of Athelstan, Ray, Sanaka and I led the army of magicslingers down the street towards Grayson. It wasn't long before Grayson noticed us marching towards him. Within seconds, he had teleported his towering form high in front of us. "What is this?" he asked, seeming amused by the gathering in front of him. Then he spotted me. "You really are a cockroach, Creed, aren't you? You just won't die, will you?"

"You'll die before I do, Grayson," I shouted back as I stood with my ripped and bloody shirt blowing around me.

"Bold words for a man about to take his last breath," Grayson said. "All of you are about to take your last breaths."

"Now!" Ray roared suddenly, and all at once, the gathering of magicslingers, including me, focused all of their magic on Grayson, aiming to hold him for as long as possible. It was unheard of for so many wizards to be gathered in one place, and even more so for them all to combine their power and focus it on a single target. The magical energy hitting Grayson must have been immense and too great for him to block. And indeed it seemed to be so as the giant Grayson became rooted to the spot, unable to move as he strained against the power holding him, and within a few moments, he was brought to his knees.

*Jesus*, I thought. *It's actually working.*

"Now, August!" Ray said. "Get the book!"

He didn't have to tell me twice. By that point, I was mightily pissed off with Grayson and his fucking godwalking antics. The only thing I wanted to do was go home with the woman I loved, and that bastard Grayson was getting in the road of that.

I didn't need Athelstan to tell me where the book was this time because it was obvious where it was. It was embedded in Grayson's chest, glowing like a beating white heart. I shifted all of my energy and concentration onto the book and began to pull it from Grayson's chest. But as soon as he felt me go for it, a surge of anger must have gone through him, enough for him to get back to his feet and to begin sending out blasts of purple energy into the crowd of magicslingers behind me. I saw one of the wizard's get hit with the purple energy, which instantly incinerated them. Short-lived cries of pain could be heard all around as Grayson continued to pick off those who stood against him. Before long, there wouldn't be enough of us to hold him, and then that would be that. He'd kill us all.

So I redoubled my efforts. But it still wasn't enough. Grayson kept picking off the magicslingers while smiling balefully at me as if he knew it was just a matter of time before he was able to break free and annihilate us all.

And it would have been just a matter of time.

If the monsters hadn't shown showed up, that is.

# THE POWER AND THE GLORY

*J*ust as all hope of defeating Grayson started to leave me, and as the number of wizards standing against him got less and less, something incredible happened.

Every supernatural in the city seemed to come from nowhere all at once. Vampires, werewolves, even bloody demons and some very rare weredragons came charging out of the streets and clambering over roofs as they went tearing towards Grayson. Hundreds of bodies launched themselves at the wannabe demigod, swarming over his giant form like insects, biting and tearing and ripping and shredding him. Grayson was so taken by surprise he stopped firing out his energy blasts and crashed down to his knees once more under the weight of the supernaturals surrounding him. It was an amazing sight, and for a few moments, I could only look on in awe.

"I hope you are not going to waste this opportunity by standing there scratching your bollocks," a familiar voice said, and I turned to see The Crimson Crow standing beside me, looking as glamorous as ever despite it being a borderline apocalypse.

"You," I said. "I have a bone to pick with you."

"Pick your bones in your own time," Ray shouted at me then. "Just get that bloody book, so we can finish this bastard."

I turned back towards Grayson then and focused everything I had on getting the Dark Codex out of him. Thanks to the swarm of supernaturals keeping him busy, Grayson's defenses were tied up enough that I was able to snatch the book from his chest, and a few seconds later, the Dark Codex came whizzing into my hands. Immediately, I clutched it to my chest and pulled my torn and bloody shirt over it. "No one look at it," I said. "Especially you, Angela."

The Crow made a face at me and then turned away. "Get on with it then."

I ran across the road and huddled inside a shop doorway with the Dark Codex. My breathing was erratic, and my heart was pounding as I opened the book.

Only to find that every page was blank.

"What the fuck?" I said, thinking that Grayson had made a dummy copy and still had the real book somewhere else.

"The book will answer your most burning questions."

I looked up to see Athelstan standing there with Leona. "You're alive," I said.

"After coming back from the dead twice, yes, I'm alive," Athelstan said as he gazed upon the book like it was a very old former love.

"Whatever you're going to do, do it now," Leona said as she stood with her back to me. "Grayson is pissed off, and he seems to be gaining ground again."

Athelstan came closer and stood over me. "The book will sense the answers you are looking for," he said. "The full text is never revealed to anyone. You learn only what you need to learn."

"Okay," I nodded. "Got it."

I turned to the first page of the book and stared at it. Then after a minute, text began to appear on the page, and as the exquisitely written words became visible, my jaw almost hit the floor as I read what it said. It was not the answer I was expecting. Instead, it was the answer to a completely different question that had been haunting me for decades: Where in the universe are the souls of my mother, brother, and sister?

"I can't believe it," I whispered.

"Did you get what you need?" Athelstan asked urgently.

"Yes," I said, half dazed. "I mean, no, not yet."

"Anytime, Creed," Leona said just as huge balls of purple energy began to explode around the place. "Grayson is back on his feet."

*Shit. All right, Creed, concentrate for fuck's sake.*

A moment later, more text appeared on the pages of the book, and as I read over it, I realized with relief and excitement that it was the answer I needed. I shook my head. "This is...beautiful," I said as I read. "So simple, so eloquent. Why have I never thought of this?"

"Forget being a fucking bookworm," Leona said, genuine concern in her voice now. "And just fucking stop this fucker, will you?"

I jumped to my feet, leaving the book on the ground. "Guard the book," I said to Athelstan and then pushed past Leona as I stepped out into the street.

Grayson was back on his feet and looking furious. He was still being attacked by several brave werewolves and vampires, but the attacks were having little effect on Grayson now. Then, in a burst of pure anger, he sent out a massive blast of magical energy that knocked back everyone and everything within a twenty-foot radius. Bodies flew back and slammed against buildings as cars overturned and trees fell. Leona, Athelstan and I were outside the blast radius, so we remained standing while Sanaka, Ray and the wizards that were left all fell back onto the road like fallen dominos.

Filled with confidence now that I had the means to defeat Grayson, I stepped boldly into the middle of the road and shouted, "Grayson!"

Grayson turned around at the sound of his name being called and glared at me with his glowing eyes. "You!" he boomed. "You really are pissing me off!" He lifted one huge arm and aimed his hand at me, ready to blast me with unspeakably powerful magic that probably would have obliterated me in an instant had I given him a chance to use it. "Die!"

I thrust my own hand out in front of me then, aimed at the giant Grayson. "Not today...*Gordon*."

It was then that I used the spell outlined in the Dark Codex. The spell was a truly sublime piece of work that effectively tapped the very power of the universe itself. For it to work, I had to manipulate my own magic just so, and once I did, a vast reservoir of magic became opened up, and along with it, a massive feeling of god-like power the likes of which I had never felt before. It even eclipsed the power I felt when I defeated Mr Black, and that's saying something.

Wasting no time, I directed the new power at Grayson with the intention of draining his own away from him. The second I did, every atom of my body seemed to transform into pure energy as I began to suck Grayson's enormous power out of him as easily as directing a high-powered magnet at a mountain of iron filings.

Grayson looked shocked and stunned as he froze on the spot the instant he felt my power being directed at him, and he looked down with anger and helplessness as a stream of purple energy jetted from him and straight into my hand, where it seemed to collect in that bottomless reservoir that had formed within me. "What?!" Grayson exclaimed. "NO!"

He put up a resistance then, using everything he had to try to pull back the power I was sucking out of him. For a moment, he actually managed to reverse the stream, grinning at me as he did so. But I doubled my efforts and quickly managed to get the energy flowing back into me again. I'd had quite enough of Grayson's bullshit by that stage. That and the fact that I knew I was going to be with Leona again gave me ample motivation and strength to drain every drop of power that Grayson had. By the time I had siphoned out the last drop of energy from him, Grayson was back to his normal size and on his knees as he stared at his hands as if expecting to see some remnant of magic arcing off them, but none did.

Grayson, as a demigod and as a man, was finished.

Or at least I thought he was finished. The Crimson Crow had other ideas. In a blur of impossibly fast movement, the Crow rushed at Grayson, and within seconds, she had ripped Grayson's head of his body with her bare hands. Then she stood as she held up the severed head like it was some great prize. Blood dripped from the torn neck into the Crow's mouth, running over her chin like red syrup. Then her supernatural brethren cheered like they had won some great battle. Everyone else was slightly repulsed by the whole act, except for Ray, who if I didn't know any better, seemed quite turned on by the Crow's brutal act.

I shook my head and turned away. Now I was left with a monumental amount of magical energy in me, and I gotta tell you, it felt awesome. It felt like I had the power of all creation in me, and that I could do anything I wanted to do, even find my family.

Because I knew exactly where they were now.

The question was though, did they want to be found? Was it right for me to find them, even though they had moved on from this world a long time ago?

Those were questions I would deal with later.

As I looked around me, I noticed that everyone was keeping their distance from me, watching me warily as if I was a suicide bomber with my finger on the kill switch. When I looked down at myself, I saw why. Much like Grayson was, I was now being consumed in a way by the huge amount of power within me. I was in effect, transforming into pure energy.

"August, son," Ray shouted over. "You need to dump what's inside you before..."

"Before what?" I asked.

"Let's not go there," Ray answered. "The book will tell you what to do."

I turned to look towards the shop doorway where Athelstan was still guarding the book, though he still seemed to be keeping a wary distance from it. I reached out a hand, and the book came flying towards me, stopping in midair right in front of my face, the pages opening as if knowing exactly what I needed. And indeed, within moments, text appeared on the page as I was given full instructions on how to dump the power I had collected. It was a simple enough procedure, no more than an incantation that would release the energy back into the ether and out into the universe again where it belonged.

But I hesitated.

So much power.

*Why get rid of it?* I asked myself. *Think of the good I could do with it. The changes I could make.*

"August," Ray warned. "I know what you're thinking. It's too much power. Let it go, boy."

Ray was right. It was too much power for one person. It ripped my guts out to do so, but I recited the incantation, and the instant I had finished, all that power went rushing out of me, jetting up into the night sky like a giant proton beam before dispersing into space.

And then it was done. The only power left in me was my own. The book closed and gently drifted to the ground.

Then everyone around me clapped and cheered. People came forward and patted me on the back like I'd just scored a winning goal, which I guess I had in a way. It was all very embarrassing, to be honest, and I noticed Leona smirking over at me, knowing full well how I felt about so much attention on me.

Eventually, I called Athelstan over. He came trudging over like a man on Death Row. "You ready, buddy?" I asked him, keenly aware that I was asking him to die.

Athelstan stared down at the book. "We don't even know if this will work," he said somewhat hopefully.

"Eh, yeah, it will. I already checked."

The former monk nodded for a moment, then breathed out sharply. "Okay then. My time is finally up. Make sure my memoirs get to my publisher, will you?"

"You have my word on that, Athelstan. You will not be forgotten, I promise you that."

After looking over at Sanaka and nodding his goodbyes, Athelstan said, "Hand me the book."

With everyone watching, I picked up the book and somewhat reluctantly handed it to him. "Thank you," I told him.

Athelstan smiled and nodded. "Thank *you*, Creed."

I was about to ask him what for when he suddenly closed his eyes as white energy beamed from the book and into Athelstan himself, separating his atoms and taking them into itself until there was nothing left. Very soon, both Athelstan and the book had dissipated into nothing.

I let out a long breath. It was finally over.

Leona was standing nearby, and I went straight to her, putting both hands on her cheeks as I kissed her passionately on the mouth. "Let's go home," I said.

"I sold my apartment," she said.

"That's okay. You can stay with me."

"You expect me to live in that ratty Sanctum with you and Blaze?"

"Yes."

She smiled again. "all right then."

My smile was wider as it felt like all my dreams had come true at once. "You just made this wizard very happy."

As we went to head away, one of Grayson's hooded disciples came running out of an alley. I assumed they had all been killed or dispersed somewhere. Leona pulled out one of her guns and pointed it at the fleeing disciple. "Stop, or I'll blow the back of your head off," she shouted.

The hooded figure stopped dead and turned around, a look of shame on his familiar face. "Don't kill me, please."

"Lower your gun," I told Leona.

"But these fuckers tried to kill you earlier," she protested.

"I know, but they were all brainwashed by Grayson, and I know this one."

Sam pulled his hood down and stared shamefully at me with tears in his eyes. "I'm sorry, Creed," he said. "I thought...he seemed...I didn't mean..."

"It's okay, Sam," I told him. "I get it. Just go. And take those robes off before someone does shoot you."

Sam nodded as he took his robes off, leaving himself naked but for a pair of pale blue boxers. "I really am sorry," he said again, then turned to go.

"Sam?" I said.

He stopped and turned around. "Yes?"

"Do me a favor, will you?"

"Anything."

"Stay the hell away from magic."

# 30

## A NEW DAWN

*I* spent the next two days holed up with Leona in the Sanctum, screening all calls and refusing to open the door to anyone. Most of those two days were spent in bed making love and watching news reports on the MacBook. Needless to say, the world was not the same place that it was pre-Grayson. The existence of the supernatural was now a commonly held fact in the world. People accepted now that vampires and such lived among them, and also that magic was real. There were no more Sleepwalkers it seemed, and now the world had to find its feet again as norms became reshuffled and ordinary people found a way to live with their supernatural cousins.

Taking the helm in this matter was Angela Crow. It came as no surprise to anyone who knew her that she not only outed herself as a vampire to the world (to those who didn't know already), but she also made herself the leader of a brand new organization called The Council Of The Gifted (yes, really), whose main goal was to look after the interests of the very large and expansive supernatural community. To back up her status as the accepted leader of the supernatural world, the Crow paraded Gordon Grayson on the world stage, telling people it was her and her supernatural brethren that had brought Grayson down and thus saved the world. "That fucking bitch," was what I had to say to that, but at the same time, I didn't care. I was no glory hunter and was in fact glad that the Crow had taken credit for bringing Grayson down. Despite her blatant play for power, what she was doing was necessary in these new times. Order had to be maintained somehow.

"It looks like Grayson did affect a new world order after all," I said as I lay in bed with Leona while we pigged out on pizza. Even Blaze, who sat on the floor at the foot of the bed, had a slice.

"Seems like it," Leona said. "It's crazy to think that everyone knows the truth now. How will that pan out, do you think?"

"Time will tell, I guess. Where does that leave Division?"

Leona shrugged. "I don't work for them anymore, so I don't know."

"I thought you'd be going back?"

She shook her head. "I have other plans."

"Oh, do tell."

"Well," she said. "There's this crazy wizard guy who wants me to go partners with him."

I nearly dropped my pizza. "No. Seriously?"

"As I said, the guy has issues, and he's not even that good looking."

"Fuck off," I said, still smiling from ear to ear. "I hear he's handsome as hell and handy with magic."

"Well, he's handy with magic."

She laughed, and I elbowed her gently in the ribs. "But seriously, you're going to partner with me?"

"Look," she said. "When I was in DC, and Grayson showed up to take over, everyone there was running around terrified and not knowing what to do. The FBI was fucking clueless, and the Division branch there wasn't much better. I just remember thinking about you then, about how you were probably back here working like crazy on finding a way to stop Grayson instead of running scared like the bureaucratic weasels I was surrounded by. That's when I knew that I was destined for this kind of work and that I was destined to do it with you, Creed. So I got on a plane."

"Destined, huh?"

"I guess we're stuck with each other."

I leaned in and kissed her. "I guess we are. So are we going to have a business name? Are we getting cards done? What about offices. I was thinking--"

"Creed?"

"Yes?"

"Shut up and fuck me again."

* * *

AFTER SPENDING TWO FULL DAYS ALONE WITH LEONA (MOSTLY IN BED, I HAVE to say), I was feeling good. All of my previous emotional turmoil seemed to have dissipated, and I was left with a calm, peaceful feeling inside which was punctuated by the excitement I felt at properly partnering up with Leona. There was a little fear as well. I mean, what if things didn't work out? What if working together wrecked our relationship? But those were just commonplace worries, and certainly preferable to the gargantuan pressure I'd been under for what seemed like a life-time now, ever since Mr Black had first made an appearance. Things just hadn't stopped since then. I was glad now that my life seemed to be heading in a normal (normal for me anyway) direction once more.

When Leona was sleeping in bed, I went downstairs and made myself some coffee. It was early evening, and I felt pleasantly refreshed and calm. Calm enough to make some phone calls, the first of which was to Brentwood, whom I'd had numerous missed calls from as usual. When he answered, the first thing he did was thank me for helping to take Grayson down, telling me the world owed me another debt. His goodwill was short-lived, however, after I told him Leona wouldn't be coming back to work for him. He was pissed off because he had assumed that she would return to Division now that she was back in Blackham. He became even more incensed when I told him Leona and I would be working together from now on. I'd poached his best agent as far as he was concerned, despite the fact that Leona had left Division anyway. So Brentwood was quickly back to hating me again. "I'll see you around," I said before I hung up on him.

Next, I called Ray, but he didn't answer his phone, so I sent him a text saying I would meet up with him in the morning, assuming he was still in Blackham, which I had no doubt he was. He would either be lying drunk in Sanaka's Sanctum or drunk in Angela Crow's bed. Whatever the case, I told him to call me.

Then finally, I called Jordan Grayson on the number she had given me a while ago. I didn't think she would answer, but she did. "Jordan," I said. "It's Creed."

"Creed," she said, sounding much different than I remembered. Her usual tone of dark seriousness seemed to have been replaced by a more lighter tone. The tone of someone who had found peace, and perhaps even happiness. "I've been meaning to call you. Are you all right?"

"Never better actually. I should thank you for helping us with your father."

"Please, I should be thanking you."

"Are you with your mother?"

"Yes," she said, still sounding like she could hardly believe it. "She's here. We're going to Mexico soon. To start over, away from everything."

I nodded and smiled. "I'm really glad to hear that, Jordan. I'm happy for you. Don't be a stranger."

"You too. You still owe me a story."

"Yeah, I forgot about that."

"Maybe you and your girlfriend could come down to Mexico in a few weeks, once we get set up."

"I'd like that," I said.

"All right. I have to go, Creed. And Creed?"

"Yeah?"

"I'm glad I met you."

"Me too," I said smiling, and then she hung up.

I sat for a while in the living room after that as I drank my coffee, realizing that Leona would want a proper coffee machine in the Sanctum now that she was moving in. I could still hardly believe it, and once again the excitement in my belly was tinged with fear.

But that was nothing compared to the almighty invisible force that slammed into my chest a second later. It was like a freight train had come through the living room window and run me over. My coffee cup shattered on the floor, and for long seconds, I couldn't breathe at all as it felt like something was crawling around inside me. Then all at once, my body relaxed again, and I was able to breathe. "What the fuck?" I said holding my chest like I'd just had a mini heart attack.

An awful feeling hit me then, as I realized what just might have happened, but I was praying I was wrong.

Unfortunately, though, I wasn't.

A very deep voice began to issue a sinister laugh from within me. Then the voice said, "August Creed. My name is Dagon. I'm the demon who tore apart your family. Nice to meet you. Again..."

The demon began to laugh once more.

And it was all I could do not to cry.

# BLOOD DEMON (WIZARD'S CREED BOOK 4)

*To my dad and sister, for pulling through like champions.*

"We are doomed to all kinds of nonsense: the pain nonsense, the nightmare nonsense, the sweat and slave nonsense, and many other shapes and sizes of insufferable nonsense. It is brought to us on a plate, and we must eat it up or face the death nonsense."

— THOMAS LIGOTTI

# NOTE TO READER

Dear Reader,

As you know from the last book, our hero Creed has been possessed by a demon. From my perspective as the writer, this situation presented some technical challenges when it came to formatting dialogue between Creed and the demon. To simplify matters, I chose to use normal formatting, even though the conversations are telepathic and not spoken aloud. So, unless otherwise stated, you can assume that all of the dialogue between Creed and the demon takes place telepathically.

# PROLOGUE

*T*his is your first real foray onto the filthy streets of Earth since donning your new flesh suit. *It's been too long*, you tell yourself, as you stroll down the street, taking in every detail of your surroundings: the lit buildings, the loud traffic noise, and even louder voices of the people that pass you by as if you were just another human. A few of those people even nod as if they know you, and you smile at them and nod back courteously as if you know them as well, ignoring the strange looks you get in return. It seems the meatpuppet you are occupying is well known in these parts. *Good*, you think. That should allow for more fun down the line. That's why you're here, isn't it? To have fun? Hell, you're on fucking vacation! Your domain in the Underworld can go fuck itself for the time being. Everybody needs a break, right?

You spot a strip club called Filthy Nasties, and decide to go inside and have some fun. You move through the crowd, occasionally nodding at people who nod at you, not all of them human. When you find a seat near the main stage, you sit down. A naked girl asks you what you're drinking, and you tell her Long Island Ice Tea. Last time you visited Earth, you got a taste for Long Island Ice Teas. How long ago was that? You smile when you realize you are beginning to think like a human again. Where you're from, there is no concept of time; just an endless *now*. It can get tedious, which is why you are here.

When the naked waitress arrives back with your drink, you smile and thank her, taking in the curves of her body as you do so. *Ah yes*, you think, *the pleasures of the flesh*. Your main reason for being here. You can hardly take your eyes off the girl, her ass jiggling enticingly as she moves away in high heels. The feel and taste of human flesh is exquisite, especially when one is occupying another human body, as you are now. But the smell you are not so keen on. Humans stink, as far as you are concerned. That's all there is to it. It can take some getting used to. The first few times you broke through to Earth millennia ago, you couldn't stop your human

621

body from convulsively being sick over and over. You thought you were going to die, that something was badly wrong. Thankfully, you got used to the smell after a while. You can tolerate it now without wanting to vomit.

Another girl is dancing on stage, wrapping herself around a steel pole for the pleasure of all the men watching, her long dark hair almost touching the stage floor as she arches her back in a near impossible way, gripping the pole with only her muscled thighs. *My*, you think as you taste the Long Island Ice Tea, *humans are a crude lot, but they sure know how to entertain each other*.

As you watch the dancing girl, you begin to feel the cock of your meatsuit stir and come to life. A slight shiver runs through you, and you close your eyes for a second to enjoy it. *There it is*, you think. That singular feeling of sexual pleasure that only humans seem to experience so deeply. You've possessed the bodies of many a different creature in your time, but none seem to do sex in the way that humans do. Humans are *built* for sex. They are equipped to feel every nerve impulse. Which also makes them good at feeling *pain*, which to you is the same as pleasure...at least when *you* are giving it.

You sit drinking for a while, as you marvel at the skills of the dancers. Your cock is semi-erect as you anticipate the pleasure soon to come, tasting and feeling all that warm, pliable flesh once more. But first, a little exercise of power is in order, just to make sure everything works as it should. Not every human host is built to withstand the pressures of channeling your power through their weak bodies. Some collapse immediately under the strain, which can be a real inconvenience. In the case of your current unwilling host, you don't think you will have that problem, as his body is already used to channeling large amounts of powerful energy. It is perhaps one of the strongest bodies you have ever been in, and you are glad you decided to let this one live years ago. Still, a quick test is called for, if only to blow out the cobwebs, to use one of the many strange human expressions you find so despicable, yet amusing.

The girl with the dark hair and big natural tits is still working the stage, while the men sitting near you shout things like, "Yeah baby!" and "Shake that ass!"

*Let's up the intensity of this show a little*, you think.

You begin to focus your concentration on the dark haired dancer with the dragon tattoo on her leg. You wait until the girl finishes collecting money from the men around the stage, allowing them to tuck bills into the elastic of her G-string. When she walks back to the pole, you begin to direct your power at her. You see the confusion and slight consternation on her face, as she realizes she can no longer move herself away from the pole. It's as if someone has glued her hands to the metal. Professional that she is, however, the girl keeps moving the rest of her body to the rhythm of the music. But she is also looking to the back of the stage for some sort of help, and soon another naked girl walks onto the stage and dances her way over to the girl by the pole. The two girls exchange words, and then they both look confused as the dark haired dancer continues to try and unstick her hands from the pole, but to no avail.

Smiling, you decide to up the ante, and you begin to manipulate the girl's entire body this time. The dancer lets out a frightened squeal that only seems to excite the crowd more, as you start to wrap that delectable body of hers around the pole. The girl's hands stay in place as the rest of her moves in the opposite direction. You see the pain and distress in her face as her body is pulled around the metal pole. Then you hear the crack of bone as the girl's wrists snap, followed by her forearms, the broken shards bursting through the girl's skin, spraying blood all over the stage, and over the blonde girl who was trying to help her.

Soon the mangled girl is screaming in agony as her body continues to twist and fold around the metal pole. The sound of more bones breaking causes the people around you to draw back in horror from the stage, yet unable to keep their eyes off the grotesque performance that is happening. The music has now stopped, and the stage is full of people who try in vain to unwrap the screaming dancer from the pole. But there is no moving her, and the people on the stage soon realize this, as they step back from the girl in helpless horror.

More of the dancer's bones break as you continue to force her body around the pole, stretching and tearing her skin. The lit stage is now awash with the dancer's blood. She only stops screaming when her spine breaks. Even then, you continue to manipulate her broken body, until it ends up looking like some disgusting creature has wrapped itself around the pole.

But you are not finished yet. The crowd needs a finale, and you shall give it to them. You focus on the blonde dancer who is still on stage and screaming in horror at her friend. When your power hits her, the blonde dancer is upended and slammed onto her back. Before anyone knows what's happening, she is sliding at speed towards the flesh covered metal pole. Her legs are wide open when she hits, and the sound of her pubic bone shattering makes people scream. Some of the men standing behind you begin to vomit.

But they ain't seen nothing yet.

You slide the screaming blonde dancer back across the stage, causing those around to jump out of the way. When the girl is a good ten feet away, you rocket her towards the pole, with her legs wide open once again. The girl's face is a picture as she speeds towards the pole. She knows exactly what's coming, the pain she is in for, and that makes things all the more pleasurable for you.

The metal pole splits the girl open to her belly when she hits it, throwing back a great wave of blood onto the stage that covers some of the people still standing there. The sound of increased screaming only makes you smile wider.

But you are not done. One final movement is called for in this symphony of blood.

You slide the now dead girl across the stage again. Then you slam her into the pole once more. This time the pole cleaves right through the girl's body, splitting her in two in the most brutal manner possible. The two halves go flying out either side of the stage, and you are hit with a spray of hot blood that is shocking at first, but then immensely satisfying.

Standing up, you begin to clap. "Bravo!" you shout as everyone stares at you aghast. "Bravo!"

A rough hand grabs your shoulder and spins you around. A large man dressed in black now has you by the throat. Security, you presume. You grab the man's wrist and twist sharply. The man screams as a shard of broken bone bursts from his skin. As the bouncer falls to his knees and screams in agony, you grab him by the head and pull. His head rips from his body easily. Like pulling a grape from a vine. You stare at the head for a second, as if you are fascinated by it. Then you throw it onto the stage, which already looks like a bloodbath.

Smiling as you look around, no one else approaches you. Not even the handful of supernatural creatures in the room. They recoil when you look at them, and you are aware that your human eyes are now glowing red. "Thank you all for a wonderful evening," you say, just before draining the last of your Long Island Ice Tea, which now has blood mixed into it. "I bid you all a good night!"

As you go to leave the strip club, someone shouts out, "You won't get away with this, Creed!"

A smile crosses your lips. "I think you'll find that I will."

# RIDING WITH THE DEVIL

*I*n terms of terrifying things that have happened to me over the years, getting possessed by a goddamn demon has to rank up there with one of the most terrifying. It's not just your body the bastards possess, even though that's bad enough. It's also your mind and soul. The fuckers invade every tiny part of you. No corner of your mind is too dark or remote not to be violated and merrily explored by the demon possessing you. Within moments of the invasion, the demon will know your every dirty little secret, your every repressed memory, and anything you have tried to hide away over the years, even from yourself. At the same time, the demon's dark essence seeps deeper into your soul, making you feel so dirty and unclean that you just want to squirm your way out of your own body to escape.

Physically speaking, things aren't much better. Once inside, the demon has full control, as it settles firmly into the driver's seat. You still have the sensation of moving around, but you are a prisoner in your own body. It's like being paralyzed inside a moving machine, where you have no choice but to go where it goes.

In the end, possession is the ultimate form of rape. A human will never feel so violated as when they are possessed by a demon.

That's what I had to put up with for over a week after being possessed. I remained a paralyzed prisoner in my own body, unable to communicate in any way. I couldn't speak, and I could barely muster a thought. I remained trapped while the demon strode around town doing whatever the hell he wanted, without fear of reprisals and to whomever the hell he wanted.

Let me tell you, he did a lot of things to a lot of people.

Over the course of those long days, I became a spectator in the life of an immensely powerful serial killer. Or so it seemed. The demon tortured, brutalized and killed so many people, I lost count. It had to have been dozens, and that wasn't even including the scores of people he caused to have unfortunate "accidents". If he saw someone walking across the road, he would direct a car in the person's path. If he saw someone on a ladder, he would cause the ladder to fall. For the fun of it, he would also invade the minds of random people and force them to do crazy things, like begin to assault and rape the person nearest to them, or to murder some other random person in a variety of creative ways. All for the sheer fun of it. I may not have been able to access the demon's thoughts, but it was still clear the bastard was enjoying himself as much as a master butcher in a kill house.

After witnessing dozens of horrifying incidents, the fear that this was now my existence began to permeate every fibre of my being. The demon no doubt allowed this fear to spread in me, just because it amused him. How long was I going to be a prisoner in my own body? Would the demon just kill me after it had finished using me? Such questions burned within me, but I had no means of communication to ask them.

I don't think I would have gotten very many answers anyway. That was the other infuriating thing about it all. The demon was completely ignoring me. After those first words when he initially invaded my body, he went on to act as if I wasn't there at all. It was like he didn't want the distraction of having to acknowledge me. The fucker was on vacation, and he had slapped a big DO NOT DISTURB sign on my face.

The only times the demon even remotely acknowledged my existence was when someone recognized me. That is to say, when someone recognized the face being worn by the demon. To everyone out there who saw, it was August Creed walking around, not some demon. So when the demon did bad shit, like force a woman to throw her baby into oncoming traffic, people saw me at the scene, and not the demon. Luckily, he was mostly subtle about his public displays of power. Most people didn't realize it was him manipulating matters. They only knew when the demon wanted them to know, like in the strip bar when the bastard wrapped that poor dancer around a pole, and then used the same pole to split another dancer in half. People thought *I* did that shit!

But there wasn't a damn thing I could do about it. The demon could fuck Donald Trump to death on national TV for all to see, and there wouldn't be anything I could do to stop him (admittedly, in that particular case, I don't think I would stop him).

I was fucked basically.

The cops couldn't stop the demon either. Despite the trail of blood left behind, the cops—or even Division for that matter—never got near him. He proved expert in avoiding the authorities, who were no doubt going all out to try and catch the depraved serial killer who was painting the town red.

Then one day in an expensive hotel room in the Highlands, the demon said out of the blue, "I think it's time we had a little chat."

Just like that, I had control of my body again. The move was so unexpected, and I had forgotten what my body felt like by then, that I immediately collapsed onto the expensive carpet like a puppet whose strings had just been cut. I lay there gasping and making strange sounds with my mouth, as I struggled to get used to being me again. The whole experience was as overwhelming as the initial possession, and it took me a good few minutes before I could even stand up, and a further few minutes before I could work my brain properly again.

What really threw me, though, was the fact that some other me was standing staring...at me. At first, I thought I was hallucinating, as my mind struggled to right itself. But the other me was smiling, his eyes were glowing red. He also wore the same dark clothes as me, right down to the dark green trench coat. It was me all right, but a much more evil version of me.

"That's right," other me said. "You are looking at yourself. Or rather, at a representation of *me*, the demon who possessed you. Who *still* possesses you."

A rush of pure anger hit me, and instinctively I went to use my magic on the other me, but as I did, a great pain went through my whole body, and I tensed as if being electrocuted, before falling to my knees.

Evil Creed came walking toward me. "Make no mistake, I still very much own your body. What you see here, this form in front of you that reflects your own, it is just a mirage for your benefit. Only you can see it, for the most part. I just thought it might be a helpful way for us to communicate. So you can put a face to the voice, in a way."

I shook my head as the pain dispersed, and I got back to my feet. "As handsome a devil as I am, you couldn't have chosen a different avatar?" I said. "Like maybe Jenna Jameson?"

Evil Creed shook his head. "I don't know who that is."

"She's a porn star."

"Ah, I see." He smiled, or rather sneered at me. I never realized I could look so damn evil. "No, Creed, as you like to be called. This particular form seems more fitting to me, and a lot more fun. You should see your face. Oh wait...you can." He chuckled to himself like it was all one big game to him, which it probably was.

"Fuck you."

"Now, now. No need for hostilities. You should be thanking me for releasing you at this time. Or would you rather I take you over completely again?" His eyes flashed red. "I can do so in an instant, believe me."

I shook my head. "What do you want from me?" I asked wearily, unable to believe that I was once again trapped in a situation that wasn't of my own making. After everything I had been through recently, I thought I was due at least some respite from the madness. But apparently not. Apparently the multiverse thought I was due a bit more, because you know, the multiverse is an uncaring cunt. Ligotti is right about that much, I can tell you from experience.

The demon sat down in a chair by the large window that looked out over the financial district. He had a drink in his hand that I didn't see him pour. "You're just a vessel, a meatsuit to be abused, until it is worn out," he said.

I went to the minibar and found a small bottle of whiskey, which I cracked open and drank all at once, hoping the alcohol would calm my nerves. "That's it? That's all I am to you? Some cheap suit off the sale rack? Nothing more?"

The demon looked confused for a second. Then he smiled and nodded. "Ah yes, I see. You are referring to the fact that I marked you years ago."

"Yes, and the fact that you slaughtered my fucking family." I gritted my teeth against the fact that the demon responsible was now in the same room as me again —was now *in* me, for fucks sake. "Why did you do it?"

His red eyes glowered at me. It was difficult to even look at him, given that I was also looking at myself. "Because that's the kind of being I am. A demon, as you humans like to call us. And also because your wretched father planned to trap and destroy me after he had drained me of all my power."

I frowned, unable to remember my father ever mentioning that he had planned on trapping the demon. I was under the impression that a deal had been made between them. "That's news to me."

"Of course it is."

"But that still doesn't explain why you had to kill the others. They were innocents, only there because my father forced us to be there." I shook my head. "You didn't have to kill them..."

The demon laughed in a slightly deeper voice than mine. "Careful, Creed. You are beginning to sound naive, which I know you are not. Surely you know how things work with us by now? We don't fuck around. Human lives mean nothing to us."

*Don't I know it*, I thought.

"So you left me alive just so you could come back and possess me?"

"Yes. I like to mark certain humans for future use. For when I come here on vacation."

"Vacation? You've got to be fucking kidding me." I grabbed another mini bottle of whiskey and cracked it open.

"Not at all. Even demons need a break sometimes."

He was smiling, so I couldn't tell if he was serious or just fucking with me. Not that it mattered. All that mattered to me was getting rid of the bastard so I could go back to my life. Speaking of which, Leona was probably out of her mind with worry, no doubt wondering where the hell I was, not to mention angry as fuck, knowing her. She probably also had people scouring the city looking for me. Given the sometimes very public acts of carnage perpetrated by the demon in my body, I was shocked Leona wasn't able to locate me. I guessed the demon was good at not being found.

"The answer is yes," he said. "I, or rather you, was approached on several occasions by people claiming they knew you. I simply killed them. You probably don't remember. I can read your every thought, by the way, just so you know." A wicked smile crept over his face.

My stomach churned as panic struck me. "Leona. Did you..." I couldn't even say the words.

"Kill her?" The demon shook his head casually. "No, though I would have had I come across her."

I let out a sigh of relief, though I still felt sick at the thought of the demon killing Leona. Of *me* killing her. I sat down on the edge of the bed and stared at Evil Creed. "Are you done with me and your little vacation now?" I asked hopefully. "I mean, you've had your fill, right?"

The demon snorted. "I'm nowhere near done," he said. "In fact, I'm just getting started."

*Jesus Christ...*

"So you plan on using my body to kill more people, is that it?"

"If it tickles my fancy." He smiled. "My fancy is always tickled."

I probably would've laughed at that had I not felt so sick. Instead, I shook my head at him. "And when you're done?"

"Then I kill you and move on."

The casualness of the statement made it obvious he wasn't lying. "So I'm fucked."

"Maybe not completely fucked."

"What the hell does that mean?"

Evil Creed stood up and walked towards me, leaving his empty glass on a table. "It means two things. Firstly, despite what you think, I don't just possess you humans so I can kill other humans, as much as I enjoy doing that. No, I'm also interested in some of you, the kind of human's you are, the lives you lead here, however petty and inconsequential they are most of the time. As I said, it's a break from the norm. That's why I marked you all those years ago when you were still a boy." His eyes narrowed, and he looked at me kinda weirdly, as if perhaps I amused or intrigued him on some level. "I must say, you do interest me, Creed. You've grown up to be quite powerful for a human. You destroyed your demonized father, for instance. You also managed to banish that old goat Baal to Dimension X. You even managed to save this world from a madman bent on destroying it. You get shit done, Creed. I can respect that."

"So you're a Creed fanboy now, is that what you're saying? You just want to hang and be friends?"

Evil Creed's eyes flashed a deeper red than before. "I don't like your tone. I'm trying to give you a chance here, which you clearly don't appreciate."

I held my hands up and nodded. "All right, I apologize, before you go treating me like a meatpuppet again to prove your point. What's the second thing you meant?"

Evil Creed kept staring with glowing red eyes for another moment, as if he was contemplating ripping me apart just to be done with me. Then he shook his head, and his eyes went back to normal again, which is to say, less red. "The second thing is that I know you are planning on finding the rest of your family. You know where they are, yes?"

For a second, I wondered how the hell he knew that. Then I remembered he could read my mind. "Yes, I do."

"Good, because I would like to know how they escaped from my domain in the Underworld. No soul escapes from my domain. *Ever.*"

"And yet my family did."

"Yes, somehow. I should like to speak with your mother again, to find out how she managed it. How they *all* managed it."

"Then what? You take them back to the Underworld with you?" I shook my head. "I won't allow that to happen. You might as well kill me now."

"Answers will be enough."

"You expect me to believe that?"

"What choice do you have? You either take me along, or I take your soul to the Underworld after I've used up your body, which won't take as long as you think."

I sat and thought for a moment. He was right. I didn't have a choice. "Okay," I said. "But there has to be ground rules."

"Rules?" He looked disgusted. "I don't do rules. I do what I want."

"If you want answers, there has to be rules. It's the only way this is going to work."

Sighing, he shook his head melodramatically. "Fine, let's hear them then. What are your silly rules?"

"For a start, you can't control me all the time," I said. "You can ride along, but I'm in control."

"So when do I get to have fun, hmm?" He shook his head. "No can do."

My fingers gripped the edge of the bed and squeezed. "Then we compromise."

"Compromise? A hateful word if ever there was one. How?"

"You only get to use my body some of the time."

"Oh really? When?"

"I don't know."

"Twelve hours each."

"Twelve hours? That's..."

"Fair is what it is, and I'm not known for being fair, so take it or leave it."

I stared back at the demon and saw he wasn't going to compromise any further. Like it or not, I would have to give myself over to him for a full twelve hours each day. I wondered if Dr. Jekyll was this perturbed at giving half of his life over to Mr. Hyde. At least Jekyll didn't remember anything Hyde had done. I wished I could say the same about—"What do I even call you?"

The demon smiled. "You can call me Max."

"Max?" I said back, thinking things couldn't get any more surreal.

"Yes, Max will do. Your human tongue won't allow me to say my real name. So Max it is. I like Max."

"All right then, *Max*. I guess we have a deal."

"Good," Max said. "I'm glad to hear it. This should prove to be fun, don't you think?"

"Oh, definitely, yeah. A whole load of fun indeed."

"That's very sarcastic of you to say so."

I stood up. "There's one other thing."

Max's eyes narrowed. "What?"

"As you've been riding around in me for over a week, I need my body back so I can sort out the undoubted devastation you've left in your wake."

Max snorted. "Good luck with that."

"I need forty-eight hours."

"Two whole days?" He stood for a moment as he considered my offer. "Fine, but just remember, Creed. I'll always be inside you watching your every move. Any attempt to screw me, such as attempting to exorcise me, will be met with severe punishment. Do you understand?"

I nodded. "Yes."

"Good," he said, just before his Evil Creed avatar disappeared. "Your time starts now."

## 2

## UNFRIENDLY WELCOMES

*O*nce Max had disappeared, I immediately teleported out of the hotel room in the Highlands to my Sanctum in Freetown. I reappeared in the living room, half expecting to see Leona sitting in there fraught with worry, or more likely, seething with anger at my unexplained and very sudden disappearance. But Leona wasn't in the living room. Neither was she to be found anywhere else in the Sanctum.

Blaze was there, though. He walked in from the kitchen and paused a few feet from me, which wasn't like him, because he normally came to me so I could greet him with a hug. But he kept his distance this time, and I knew why. "Relax, Blaze," I said. "It's me."

Blaze's yellow eyes seemed to narrow as his mouth curled into a snarl, and he started growling at me. Obviously, he could sense the demon in me. Blaze hated demons, especially after Baal and Demon Black. His snarl got nastier as his heckles raised, and thin lines of fire began to break out all over his body.

*Shit, is he going to go for me here?*

"Blaze, seriously," I said holding my hands up to try and calm him. "It's really me. I know you can sense the demon that's inside me, but you have nothing to worry about. I have it under control."

*Yeah right.*

Blaze continued to growl and snarl as he bared his large teeth at me. He wasn't backing down, despite what I said.

Then he did something I thought he would never do. He attacked me. He came running at me like I had seen him run at countless monsters before. But I was no monster, or at least that's what I told myself. The recent string of dead bodies left behind in my wake told a different story.

A sadness washed over me as Blaze, my faithful companion for the last fifteen years, bounded across the wood floor in attack mode, heading straight for me. But before he could reach me and start tearing at me his teeth, and burning me with his elemental fire, I teleported out of there.

I landed outside on the steps leading up to the Sanctum, and stood there for a moment shaking my head in dismay, unable to believe that my best friend was about to attack, and possibly kill me.

"Don't take it personally," I heard a voice say then. A voice in my head that sounded just like mine only deeper and snarkier. Max the demon's voice. "The mutt was going for me, not you."

"Christ," I said. "Am I going to have to put up with your fucking running commentary in there on top of everything else?"

"You know you are talking out loud? You don't have to, unless you want to seem insane. Just think your reply, and I will hear you."

"Fuck you. Did you catch that thought?"

"Loud and clear." He hit me with a burst of pain in my head then, that made me slap both hands to my skull in case it exploded. "Did *you* catch that one?"

Gritting my teeth against the residual pain, I snarled out loud, "That was uncalled for."

"So was being rude to me."

"Rude? Are you fucking kidding me? You're a demon. You're not supposed to take offense."

"I know, I'm just fucking with you." His laugh chilled my blood. "This is all good fun, isn't it, Creed? I'm glad I chose you to possess this time."

I shook my head. "Yeah, I'm real fucking glad as well. Wanna be BFF's?"

Max went silent for a second. "What is BFF's?"

"Christ. Forget it."

"Ah, I see. You were being sarcastic."

"What the fuck do you think?"

"What is a BFF anyway? A Big Fucking Fish? A Bereaved Female Ferret? A Battered Femoral—"

"Oh fuck, enough!" I shouted. "God! It's a fucking Best Friend Forever, all right? Now just shut the fuck up and let me fucking think. Please!"

Max started tittering to himself. "Best Friends Forever," he said. "That's amusing, Creed...and strangely sickening."

"Someone fucking shoot me now," I implored as I turned around slowly to face the street.

Then froze.

In front of me on the street was a group of heavily armed men. Some in dark suits, others in tactical gear. "Get down on the fucking ground!" one of the men in a dark suit said as he advanced towards the steps aiming a handgun at me.

Instinctively, I raised my hands in the air. "I think you're making a mistake..."

"Get down on the ground and put your hands behind your head!" the dark suited agent bellowed again, this time adding, "If you don't comply, we will be forced to shoot you. Do it now!"

Holy fuck. Can this hellish week get any worse?

"I'm willing to bet that it will," Max said cheerfully, as if he was standing right beside me. Frankly, I was surprised his Evil Creed avatar hadn't made another appearance, just to fuck with my head further.

"I'm sure you are," I muttered back silently at the same time as deciding it was time to teleport to somewhere that didn't have men pointing guns at me. Only, when I went to use my magic, it didn't work. Nothing happened. "What the fuck?"

"Last chance, Creed!" the gunman shouted.

He said my name. He has to be from Division.

"Division?" Max said. "What's that?"

"Shut up. You caused this. You're the reason they're even here and about to fucking shoot me."

"I could wipe them all out in seconds..."

"No! Don't do that. You'll just make things worse."

"I know," Max said gleefully.

"Please, listen to me--"

Max started laughing. "You're so easy, Creed. All your kind is. I'm not going to miss the chance to see you squirm under questioning as you try to explain the blood trail you left behind."

"That you fucking left behind!"

"Same difference."

"No, it's fucking not the same!"

"I'M ABOUT TO FUCKING SHOOT YOU, CREED!" the Division agent balled.

"All right!" I shouted. "I'm complying!"

I dropped down to my knees as the lead agent came running up and slammed me face first into the ground. In seconds, I was surrounded by a forest of legs in heavy combat boots, some of which ended up kicking me in painful places.

"They're a rough lot, aren't they?" Max said as if he was watching the whole scene play out on TV.

Ignoring the demon inside me, I said to whoever would listen, "What's this about? Did Brentwood send you?"

I was cuffed and hauled to my feet before I got an answer from the heavily built blonde haired agent who arrested me. "Yeah, motherfucker, he did."

"Why?"

The agent shook his head in disgust, as did several other agents. "Because you're a sick motherfucker, that's why."

He punched me hard in the stomach then, and I would have went down if it were not for the agents either side of me holding me up.

"They don't like you very much, do they?" Max said. "I wonder why?"

"I'm glad you're finding this funny."

"Oh, I am, Creed. Believe me I am."

I was hauled down the steps and dumped into the back of a meat wagon with two armed guards either side of me. The blonde haired agent stood by the doors. "Oh, and I suppose you're wondering why you can't use your magic on us? That's because we switched it off." He clicked his fingers. "Just like that. Enjoy the ride, Creed."

*No way...*

Once again, I tried to use my magic, but nothing happened.

*What the hell have they done?*

As the heavy metal doors slammed shut, so to did my mind.

3

# THE DEVIL MADE ME DO IT

*J*was taken to Division HQ, where I was brought to an interrogation room and handcuffed to a table. Then I was left alone there.

"What the fuck?" I said to no one. I had at least expected Brentwood to have given me the benefit of the doubt, considering all that I had done for him recently. I was being treated like a dangerous mass murderer. To make matters worse, Max's avatar—still in the form of Evil Creed—appeared in the corner of the interrogation room, and stood there with his arms folded, that fucking annoying, sneering look on his face.

*Christ, I hope I don't actually look at people like that...at least not all the time.*

"How does it feel to be treated like a criminal, Creed?" Max asked with blatant delight in his voice.

I was about to answer out loud when I realized there was a camera in the room. It probably wouldn't help my case if I was seen talking to someone who wasn't really there. Division probably thinks I've snapped and gone insane, having buckled under the pressure of the last few months. Although that did pose the issue of how I was going to explain myself without sounding like I'm off my rocker. "This isn't the first time I've been treated like a criminal," I said telepathically. "Certainly not the first time by Division. What the hell are you doing here anyway? You said you would fuck off for forty-eight hours, and yet, here you are."

"I just enjoy seeing you suffer, Creed. There's something uniquely satisfying about human suffering in general." He smiled. "It hits the spot."

"Fuck off."

Just then the door opened, and in walked someone I wasn't expecting to see. At least not yet, and certainly not in Division HQ. "Leona," I said in a voice somewhere between shock and relief. "Thank God. What are you—"

I never got to finish the sentence, because Leona's right hook to my jaw stopped me talking any further.

Max started to laugh. "Oh, yes," he said with delight. "This is getting interesting now."

"That's for running out on me," Leona said as she paced the room for a moment, before coming to sit in the chair across from me. She was dressed in her tactical leather outfit and long leather trench coat, which meant she looked sexy as hell and I couldn't help noticing, despite the fact that she looked ready to punch me again if she didn't get a satisfactory answer to her next question, which was, "What the hell happened, Creed?"

"What happened is, my usual bad luck kicked me in the balls again," I said, resisting the urge to glance over at Max who stood leering in the corner.

Leona made a face and shook her head. "What are you talking about?"

"Yes, Creed," Max said, staring at leona as if she could hear and see him. "What *are* you talking about?"

I took a deep breath, deciding just to come out with it. "You know how I told you I was marked by the demon who killed my family?"

Leona nodded. "Yes."

"Well, that demon came to collect a week ago."

"Came to collect? You mean--"

"It possessed me."

Leona drew back away from me as if in defense, a move that made me reach out to her, only to have the chains around my wrists tighten and snap my arms back. "Are you seriously telling me you've been possessed by a fucking demon?"

I nodded as I stared angrily at the chains holding me. "Yes."

She stared into my eyes, soon realizing I was telling the truth. "That's fucked up, Creed."

"You're telling me."

"She believes you," Max said.

"Stay out of it," I told him.

"It would also explain a lot," Leona added.

"You mean...the bodies?"

"Everyone thinks you killed those people," she said.

"Does Brentwood think that?"

"He doesn't know what to think yet."

"Is that why he sent you in here, to get the truth?"

Anger flashed across Leona's face. "He didn't send me anywhere. I asked him to let me talk to you first, as a favor to me."

"What are you even doing here anyway? Are you back working for Division?"

"What?" She shook her head. "God, you're such an asshole at times. I work with *you* now, remember?"

"Of course I remember," I said. "I'm sorry. It's just this whole fucking mess. Can you get me out of these chains?"

The door opened then. Brentwood walked in wearing his usual serious scowl. "You're lucky you aren't in a containment cell right now," he said, then looked at Leona. "Give us the room."

Leona knew better than to argue with her former boss. She nodded, giving me a quick look before she left the room. Brentwood sat across from me. His stare was long and hard.

"General Brentwood," Max said, as if a new player had just entered his game.

"He's much more intimidating in person than he is in your thoughts, Creed. You don't give the man enough credit."

"I'm guessing you heard everything I said to Leona," I said to Brentwood, while ignoring Max.

He nodded his bald head. "The devil made you do it? That's seriously your defense?"

"Why would I lie about something like that?" I was genuinely annoyed that he didn't believe me.

"You tell me, Creed. You never were the most stable of individuals, and with the kind of insane life you lead, who's to say you didn't suddenly crack under the strain? I've seen it happen enough times. Some guy's, they just snap one day and do crazy fucking shit, like go on a killing spree around town. Maybe they also don't want to believe the bad shit they've done, so they concoct some cock and bull story to cover up their madness."

The consternation on my face grew as he spoke, until I finally shook my head in dismissal of his beliefs. "Look at me, Brentwood. Do I look fucking insane to you?"

"You always look a bit insane to me, Creed. It's hard to tell."

Max laughed at that.

I sighed sharply. "Fuck off," I told him, having to stop myself from shouting it out loud.

"So you've really been possessed by a demon?" Brentwood said. "That's what you're telling me?"

"That's what I'm saying."

"Can you prove it?"

"Yes, Creed," Max said, now standing behind me somewhere. "Can you?"

When I said nothing, Brentwood took out his phone. "Because I can prove to you that you killed over a dozen people, Creed."

"What?" I said, dreading what he was going to show me.

"Oh," Max said. "This should be interesting." He went around behind Brentwood so he could stare at the phone. I tried not to look at him while keeping my eyes on the table.

"There," Brentwood said sliding the phone toward me. "Recognize anyone in that video?"

I sighed as I picked up the phone, dreading what I was going to see. It was security cam footage of me inside an elevator somewhere, with an older woman standing beside me. I watched myself on the video reach out and press the stop button on the elevator, before proceeding to viciously attack the woman, biting and clawing at her face like some wild animal. "Jesus Christ," I said, wanting to look away, but watching until the end, which seemed to take a long time. Before the video ended, I could be seen standing over the bloodstained body of the woman, as I smiled at the camera inside the elevator.

I looked at Brentwood, and shook my head emphatically. "That's not me."

Brentwood took the phone. "Well, it sure fucking looks like you, Creed."

I shook my head. "Come on, Brentwood. Do you really think I would do something like that? Do you think I would blatantly look at the camera like that if someone wasn't making me do it?"

Brentwood merely stared at me as he slid the phone across the table again. "Take a look at those. Crime scene photos of the people you killed."

Even though I didn't want to, I picked up the phone and went through the slideshow of horror that depicted one mutilated body after another. Some of the bodies were so cut up, they reminded me of the work of Jack the Ripper. "Nice work," Max said chuckling to himself as he stood looking over my shoulder.

"I didn't do any of this," I said. "I'm not a murderer."

"Try telling that to my superiors," Brentwood said. "They want your head on a stick, Creed."

"They wanted my head on a stick even before this."

Brentwood sat back in his chair and sighed. "I'll be honest with you, Creed. I don't think you killed those people. You're crazy, but not crazy enough to slaughter innocent people. I don't think anyway."

"I didn't do it."

"Well, whether you did or you whether you didn't, I don't have much choice but to hold you here."

"What?"

"Even if you are telling the truth about being possessed by a demon, there's no way I can let you go free so your demon can murder more people."

"So I'm your prisoner now?"

"It looks that way."

"Fuck's sake," I said clenching my fists. "You can't keep me locked up in this place."

"Can't I? Everyone thinks you're a murderer, Creed. A sick bastard. What do you want me to do? Someone has to pay for all those deaths."

"Oh dear," Max said as he leaned in close behind me. "Did I get you into trouble, Creed? I'm sorry."

Max's cold laughter caused me to strain against the chains holding me as I tried to get to the bastard. "Fuck you!" I screamed aloud.

"Creed!" Brentwood said. "What the fuck are you doing? Sit down!"

Feeling like an angry idiot, I sat down again and tried to quell my emotions as I clenched and unclenched my fists. "This can't be fucking happening," I muttered to myself.

"What was that?" Brentwood asked. "Can you see the demon who possessed you?"

"Unfortunately," I said.

Brentwood drew back almost in fear for a second. "It's here in this room right now?"

"Over here," Max said as he started waving at Brentwood, as if Brentwood could see him.

"Unfortunately," I said again.

Brentwood shifted in his seat, as he seemed to be considering leaving the room. Evidently, he didn't feel safe in the company of a demon. The moment Brentwood stood to leave, I felt Max take over my body, and then snap the chains holding my wrists as if they were made of paper. I was then dragged along helplessly as he used my body to attack Brentwood. I felt my hands wrap around Brentwood's throat, as my fingers began to squeeze his windpipe. Brentwood was strong, but Max was much stronger, and easily held Brentwood down on the floor. "What the fuck?" I screamed at Max helplessly from within. "Stop it!"

I was relieved when my fingers released themselves from around Brentwood's throat. Max relinquished control again, appearing in the room once more as Evil Creed, laughing while I stood in shock, and Brentwood scrambled to his feet. Then a second later, the door burst open and four armed guards came storming in pointing automatic weapons at me, screaming for me to get down on the ground. "I'm sorry," I said to Brentwood as I sank to my knees, and the four guards rushed me. "That wasn't me..."

My hands were zip tied behind my back, along with my legs. "Take him away," Brentwood said in a hoarse, pissed off voice.

I resisted the guards, turning to Brentwood as I remembered something. "My magic," I said. "How were you able to block it?"

Brentwood snorted once. "Technology, Creed," he said, sounding a little too smug for my liking. "It's catching up with magic. Get used to it."

That wasn't enough for me. "How?"

"We can use satellite technology to target any adept, then we put a block on their magic. As you know, it works...just like magic."

*Bastard.*

"Where did you get the tech, Brentwood? No one in Division is smart enough to come up with something like that."

Brentwood glared at me, but he knew I was telling the truth. "Outside contractors. That's all I'm going to say." He looked at the guards still holding me and nodded at them. "Take him to his cell."

Before the guards took me away, I shouted, "Just remember who you're dealing with, Brentwood. You might be able to hold me now that you can block my magic, but you can't block the power of the fucking demon inside me..."

Brentwood got to his feet quickly. "Is that a threat, Creed?"

I said nothing as the guards took me away.

# 4

## LOCKED UP

They locked me up in one of the cells on the bottom floor of the facility. The cell was a small room made out of reinforced concrete, except for the front wall which was made of thick plexiglass. "I hope you're happy now, asshole," I said to Max as he stood staring at me in the corner of the room. I sat down defeated on a bench that seemingly doubled as a bed, even though there was no bedding anywhere in the room.

"Happy?" Max said screwing his face up. "I don't really do happy the way you humans seem to. There is a certain inherent satisfaction in the situation, however."

"Even though you're locked up in here as well?"

"I'm not worried about that. I can break us out of here after I grow bored with your predicament."

I nodded. "Great. That'll really help matters."

"We could go off-world. I know some interesting dimensions where we could go."

"No thanks."

Despite what I said, breaking out off Division could end up my only option if Brentwood and his superiors insisted on keeping me locked up. By their reckoning, I was too dangerous to be let out, at least not while I was possessed by a demon. It was looking increasingly likely that I wasn't going anywhere soon.

"So is this what you normally do to the people you possess?" I asked Max. "You fucking ruin their lives before killing them?"

"Usually," Max said. "You are just playthings after all."

I shook my head. "You're a total cunt."

"Oh, come now, Creed. All is not lost. And besides, didn't I agree to help you find the souls of your family members?"

639

"The ones you killed, you mean? Yeah, you did, but that was before your serial killing got me thrown in *here*."

Just then, Leona appeared in the corridor outside, standing by the Plexiglass as she looked in at me sadly. "Hey," I said going to the glass. "I'm really sorry about this. I feel like fucking Hannibal Lecter in here. Quid pro quo, Clarice... did the cries of the lambs bother you?"

Leona gave a slight smile and shook her head. "Weirdo. It's not your fault."

"That I'm a weirdo?"

She laughed. "No, Jesus...of course you're a weirdo, but that wasn't what I meant."

"Thanks."

"I meant it's not your fault you're in this place."

"I'm sure Brentwood isn't thinking that."

"His back's against the wall on this one. He says he can't release you."

I sighed and shook my head. "What a nightmare. I bet you wished you'd stayed in Washington."

Smiling, Leona put her hand to the plexiglass, as did I. "You'll figure this out, Creed. You always do."

"The damage is done, and there's a string of bodies to prove it. I don't see how." I shook my head as the seriousness of the situation hit me like a ton of bricks. "All those people dead...because of me."

"Hey," Leona said firmly. "You're not responsible for killing those people. It wasn't you."

"I wouldn't be so sure of that," Max said from the back of the room.

I couldn't help but turn my head as I telepathically said, "What the hell do you mean?"

When I turned back to Leona, she was frowning at me. "What's wrong, Creed?" she asked.

"Nothing," I said.

Leona looked past me into the room as if trying to find something. Or someone. "Can you see it?"

"You mean the demon?"

She nodded. "Yes."

"Well, the motherfucker is standing right behind me," I said. "Or at least a projection of himself. Or rather *myself*." I shook my head as if the whole situation was a confused mess. "I mean, he copies my image."

"So you...see yourself?"

"Yes. A more evil version of myself, as joyful as that sounds."

"That's fucked up."

"Yes, it is rather fucked up, isn't it?" Max said gleefully.

"Is it talking to you right now?" Leona asked, unable to keep from looking past me into the room.

"Unfortunately," I replied. "He's an annoying fucker, I'll give him that."

"He?"

"He calls himself Max. You believe that? A fucking demon that calls himself Max."

"Would you have preferred I call myself Veltron or Belthane or some other ludicrous name instead?" Max asked.

"I couldn't give a fuck what you call yourself, asshole," I shouted aloud, not caring anymore who heard me. "I just want you fucking gone."

"Yes, all in good time," Max said. "Provided I get what I want."

"Well, maybe if you had consulted me first before going on a fucking killing spree, we might have been able to come to an arrangement sooner, and we'd be on our fucking way now," I shouted back, again out loud, after spinning round to face him. "But you didn't. No, you had to be the big bad demon and kill a load of innocent people, just so you could feel big or superior or whatever the fuck it is you get out of picking on defenseless beings. You're nothing more than a child killing fucking cunt!"

Max stood in front of me with his eyes blazing red, his face dark and tense. "I should just rip you apart right now in front of your bitch girlfriend and be done with it," he snarled. "There's plenty more meatsuits out there for me to wear."

"FUCKING DO IT THEN!" I bellowed as I threw my arms out. "PUT ME OUT OF MY FUCKING MISERY!"

Max's stare intensified just as all of my joints seemed to pull painfully away from my body.

*He's going to fucking do it*, I couldn't help thinking in shock. *He's going to end me.*

But then Max smiled, and his stare became less intense, as did the pain in my joints. "You aren't getting out of this that easily. I'm going to stick around to see you suffer for another while yet." Sneering, he backed off into the corner and stood with his arms folded as if to say, *Your move, motherfucker.*

"Creed!" Leona shouted through the glass. "Are you all right in there?"

When I turned around there were two armed guards standing beside Leona, and they all drew back in slight horror when I looked at them. "I'm fine," I said, before taking a deep breath to calm myself. "Just releasing some steam. Nothing to see here."

The two guards stared hard at me as they looked like they were about to burst into my cell to restrain me. Leona, however, said something to make them back off, and they both nodded before heading back up the corridor, disappearing out of sight. "What was that?" Leona asked when the two guards had gone.

"What was what?" I asked.

She shook her head like she was in no mood for any bullshit. "You know what. Did you just dare that demon to kill you? You know how fucking stupid that is?"

I shook my head. "I was just straightening some things out, that's all."

"Indeed," Max said, as if Leona could hear him.

Leona stared at me a moment, and then looked away. It was rare to see her upset, and I felt terrible about it. I walked to the glass as Leona wiped a few tears from her eyes, before straightening herself up and resetting her face into its usual stony expression. "Did you know your eyes were...glowing red, when you were arguing with the demon?"

I sighed and shook my head. That would explain why Leona and the guards drew back when I looked at them earlier. "No, I din't know."

"I'm worried, Creed," she said.

"I know you are," I said, putting my hand back on the glass. "But I'm going to fix this. I promise."

Leona's deep brown eyes stared into mine. It was a look I often thought she had perfected while working as an interrogator, a look that made it seem as if she was looking right into your head, like a mindreader. "That's the thing, Creed," she said quietly. "I'm not sure you *will* fix it this time."

5

# AS THE CROW FLIES

*W*hen Leona had gone to talk to Brentwood again about releasing me, even though we both knew it would be a waste of time, I had nothing else to do but sit on the bench in my cell. Max, or at least his avatar, had disappeared for the time being. I could still feel him inside me though, monitoring my every movement, my every thought and feeling. It was like being under twenty-four surveillance by a cold, faceless entity. There was nowhere to go to be alone, not even with your thoughts. Nothing was private anymore unless Max chose not to pay attention. But as the constant knot of anxiety in my stomach was telling me, Max was paying attention to everything. Mercifully, he was refraining from giving any snarky rebuttals to my thoughts, or to the fact that I was trying very hard to ignore his presence, which naturally proved impossible.

My biggest fear was him taking me over again. I hated the absolute loss of control. It was terrifying knowing Max could do anything he wanted with my body, and there wasn't a damn thing I could do to stop him.

Max owned me.

And he knew it.

\* \* \*

I SPENT THE NEXT SEVERAL HOURS IN THAT CELL JUST SITTING AROUND, OR pacing the floor as I wracked my brains trying to figure a way out of the situation I was in. Of course, I was well aware that Max was listening to my every thought, like some sleazy spy on a morally dubious assignment. He didn't seem to mind that I was blatantly plotting against him, though. He was confident there was no way for me to get rid of him without killing myself in the process. Or rather, without *him* killing me before I got a chance to take any real action. The first line of an exorcism to come from my mouth would result in my death. Any kind of spell or ritual designed to hurt or hinder him would be met with swift punishment in the form of extreme pain or death. Max had made that abundantly clear by now, several times.

In my defense, I was trying to think of a way in which we could both get what we wanted, and he seemed okay with that. The occasional thought of revenge would often hitch a ride on my train of thought, though, sometimes traveling for a good distance before I realized exactly what it was: an invitation to extreme pain or death. Max let these occasional lapses slide without repercussion. In fact, if I was reading him right, he was quite enjoying watching some of the scenarios that would play out in my mind. They seemed to amuse him. Going by the laughter I heard in my head, his favorite revenge scenario was the one where I used my magic to rip his spirit out of me, at which point the Ghostbusters would direct their proton streams at Max's vengeful spirit, being careful not to cross the streams of course, before directing Max into the ghost trap on the floor. The scene finished when Max's contained spirit was dumped into a containment unit. Just one of the more satisfying scenarios I cooked up.

Revenge fantasies aside, it soon became clear to me—if indeed it wasn't clear before—that whatever path toward resolution I chose to take, it would hinge upon first getting out of the cell I was in, and that wasn't about to happen anytime soon. Max once again offered to bust us out, but that would involve killing more people, and there was no way I was going to let that happen. Max had killed his last innocent, at least in my body. He begged to differ, of course. But fuck him. I would kill myself first before I let the bastard go on any more killing sprees.

I had just about given up on any hope of escaping or being released from my prison, when I heard movement in the corridor outside. Thinking it was either Leona or Brentwood, I went to the plexiglass to see.

Imagine my surprise when Angela Crow appeared on the other side of the glass. She was a gleaming vision of white, dressed in an eighties style power skirt, and bright red high heels the same color as her lipstick. Her platinum blonde hair was wrapped in a bun on top of her head, which allowed her large predatory eyes to beam out of their sockets unshaded. When she smiled, the tips of her fangs showed. "Hello, Creed," she said, stepping close to the glass. "What a mess you've got yourself into this time."

"What are *you* doing here?" I asked suspiciously. "Are you worried I'm going to fall victim to foul play? We both know what happens if I do." I tapped my chest and gave her a suggestive look.

She shook her head. "Yes, Creed, I'm well aware of the supposed bomb you have in me."

"Not supposed."

"Whatever. I don't think that's any way to talk to the person who's going to get you out of here anyway."

My eyes widened. "What?"

"You heard her," Max said, his disembodied voice in my head. "This delectable specimen is going to free us."

"How are you going to manage that?" I asked Angela. "Brentwood has made it clear I've to stay locked up."

"I have my ways, Creed. You should know that by now."

I narrowed my eyes at her. "You're not going to have your minions storm this place, are you? If so, forget it. There's enough blood on my hands."

"Really? I thought you considered me to be more subtle than that."

"Subtle?" I barely smiled, unwilling to piss her off with any sarcastic remarks. "How are you going to manage it then?"

"You forget the influence I have, now that I'm head of the Council of the Gifted." She smiled, showing her fangs again. "I could make things very difficult for Division, if I wanted to. Brentwood will simply be made aware of that fact."

"And if he doesn't go for it?"

"He will."

"You seem sure. Though perhaps you haven't heard—I have a demon problem."

"Yes, I know," she said. "That won't matter. Still, you're always getting into sticky situations, aren't you, Creed?"

"This one's a little more than sticky. Dire, I'd say."

"You're referring to the body count you left behind recently?"

"Not me. The demon."

"Whatever," Angela said. "I could care less about a bunch of dead humans. You know me, Creed. I'm not one for sentiment."

"So why are you here?" I asked her. "Am I to believe you are getting me released out of the goodness of your heart?"

Angela smiled. "Whatever else you think of me, Creed, I do show some loyalty toward those who deserve it. As much as you are a pain in the ass, you've done more than most to help this city, and dare I say it, even me."

My jaw nearly hit the floor. For a full ten seconds, I was literally lost for words. Then I said, "Those are words I never thought I would hear coming out of your mouth, Angela. Are you sure you haven't been possessed by an angel?"

Angela shook her head. "Balk if must. You always do."

I smiled somewhat wickedly. "What do you want, Angela? It must be important considering the strings you would have to pull to get me out of here."

"It is," she said. "I want you to go to Babylon, and bring my daughter home to me."

Again, I was almost lost for words. "Why?" was all I could think to ask.

Angela moved her face right to the glass, her piercing blue eyes now staring right at me. "Because she is my daughter, and she should be with me. It's time she came home."

"Who said she wants to come back here?"

"You did, Creed."

"I don't think so."

"Yes, you did. In our last few conversations you mentioned that Jennifer had softened her position somewhat when it came to me."

"That's not the same as saying she would want to come back here," I said. "And why would she if you're just going to treat her like an underling again?"

Angela's mouth tightened as she scowled at me. "It wouldn't be like that. Jennifer would be by my side as an equal. One of the benefits of living so long is that you have plenty of time to learn from your past mistakes."

"Or be doomed to repeat them."

She snarled at me this time, her eyes flashing red for a second. "Why are you so quick to think the worst of me, Creed?"

My expression softened for a second as I looked away. Maybe Angela had changed as much as she was putting across. There was no doubt in my mind that she missed her daughter. What I was worried about was reuniting her with Jennifer, and then the same old patterns of behavior emerging. I pulled Jennifer out of that life before, and I had no wish to do it again if I could help it.

On the other hand, I was looking at imprisonment for the foreseeable future. Keeping me locked up was helping no one. The only way I would get Max out of me was to give him what he wanted, or at least what he said he wanted. You never know with demons. They're such lying, manipulative bastards.

"And humans aren't, I suppose?" Max piped up in my head.

"Butt out of my goddamn thoughts, will you?" I shot back.

"I can't believe you are even debating this creature's offer," he said. "Just fucking reunite her with her bitch daughter, and then we can go on our little adventure together."

"You've got serious fucking issues, you know that?"

"So have you. I guess we're a match made in heaven."

"Fucking *hell,* more like."

"Oh yes, that sounds much better."

"Fuck off," I said out loud without meaning to.

"Did you just tell me to fuck off?" Angela said as anger rushed into her face.

"No," I said holding up my hands. "I didn't mean to say that out loud. I was just talking to the demon...as you do."

Angela shook her head. "I can only imagine the kind of conversations you are having."

"Trust me. You'd stake yourself rather than put up with a demon inside you —*inside your head.* Especially one named Max."

"Max? The demon is called Max?"

"Catchy name for a demon, don't you think? I would have preferred Cunt, or Annoying Prick, but I didn't have a say in the matter."

"I'm offended," Max said.

"Anyway," I said to Angela. "I've considered your offer."

She raised her eyebrows slightly. "And?"

"I'll do it."

She couldn't keep the smile from her face, which sort of threw me. She actually looked happy. "Thank you."

"But on one condition."

"Yes?"

"If Jennifer says she doesn't want to come back here, then that's it. You have to respect her wishes and leave her alone, which means no abducting her."

"It wasn't something I was considering," she said, sounding offended. "But of course I will respect my daughter's wishes whatever she may decide."

I nodded. "All right, now get me the fuck out of here."

"There's one more thing," Angela said.

I gave a small sigh. Here we go. "What is it?"

"If Jennifer comes back, I want you to make her a Daywalker, like me."

"A Daywalker? That's...I'm not even sure I could do it again."

"Don't bullshit me, Creed. We both know you can do it."

She was right. I *could* do it. I was just pondering the implications of doing it *again*. It was a lot of power to hand to one vampire, and normally, I would've refused to do it. But since it was Jennifer, and since I didn't have a choice...

"Fine," I said. "But I'll only do it for Jennifer. No one else."

"Of course."

"All right," I said. "Are you going to get me out of this fucking cell...you know, before I adopt the roach in the corner as my pet?"

Angela shook her head. "I'll go and talk to Brentwood," she said, before walking away. "Don't go anywhere, will you?"

"Oh, ha ha..."

Max chuckled to himself. "I *do* like her."

"Screw you, Max."

6

# MAKING PLANS

$\mathcal{B}$rentwood didn't seem too amused when I walked out of Division HQ alongside Angela Crow, but the order to release me came from above his head, so there was nothing he could do about it. Given that I expected a bit more trust from Brentwood in the beginning, I couldn't help but smirk back at him on my way out the front door just to piss him off even more. After everything I'd done for him, he should have given me the benefit of the doubt, instead of tossing me in a fucking cell.

"Well," Max said. "You did try to strangle him, did't you?"

"No, motherfucker," I replied. "That was you."

Max laughed. "Oh yes...it was, wasn't it?"

"Asshole."

"Speaking of assholes, I'd bet her's is just delightful."

I assumed he was speaking of Angela Crow, whose slender ass was wrapped tight in her white pencil skirt. "You want to cut her up like you cut up those other people? Trust me, she won't fucking let you do that."

"Powerful is she?"

"Very."

"But still powerless compared to me."

"I wouldn't be so sure."

"I'd like to find out."

I shook my head. "Christ, give it up, will you? Not every flesh parcel you see is fair game, you know."

"Actually, it is."

"Well, there's more important things to worry about besides getting to know the Crimson Crow's asshole."

"For you maybe," Max said. "Remember, Creed. I'm just along for the ride; for the experience, and the pleasures along the way. No matter what happens, I have nothing to lose. You, on the other hand, have everything to lose. Your body, for instance...or your soul."

I stopped on the way to Angela's limo. "What the hell is that supposed to mean?" I said aloud.

"I'm just pointing out the stakes. Eventually, this body of yours will begin to break down, as it won't be strong enough to contain my presence anymore. Then you will die, and I will naturally claim your soul."

"How long?" I asked as Angela and her guards stood staring at me with confused looks on their faces.

"Before your body dies?" Max said. "Most of the fleshsuits I inhabit break down within a week. Some of the stronger ones last a bit longer. You're pretty strong, Creed, with all your magic. I'd give you two weeks."

"Two fucking weeks?" I tried to say quietly through gritted teeth.

"Creed?" Angela said, seeming bored by what was happening. "Are you all right?"

"Fine," I muttered before addressing Max again. "We had a deal, Max. We find my family, you get your answers, and then you leave."

"Yes, that's still the deal...if you make it that far."

"So what the fuck are you talking about then?"

"I'm just pointing out that time is of the essence, and that I won't be helping you in any way. I am merely an impartial observer here. I just enjoy seeing you squirm under pressure, Creed. It gratifies me."

Angela was looking agitated now. "Creed, are you coming or not?"

"I'll make my own way," I told her. "I'll be in touch."

"Suit yourself." Along with her guards, she walked away to her limo.

"Hmm," Max said. "I can't *wait* to see her again. Delectable piece of flesh that she is, vampire or not."

"That's all anyone is to you, is it? Just flesh?"

"Yes. You humans and your supernatural subspecies are just playthings to me, and others like me. In the grand scheme of things, this realm and its inhabitants are small and insignificant."

"Well," I said. "For something so small and insignificant, you and others like you sure seem to spend a lot of time with humans." For the first time, Max was silent, and I laughed and shook my head. "What, no comeback?"

"We just enjoy playing with our toys, that's all."

"Yeah? You know who else enjoys playing with toys?"

"Slutty housewives?"

"Kids, that's who."

"If I were human, I might take offense to that, but seeing as how I'm not..."

I sighed. "Whatever, Max."

I looked around the parking lot for a moment feeling slightly lost, as if I was marooned on an island with a psychopath, with no chance of help coming from anywhere. My first instinct was to go to the sanctuary of the Sanctum, but then I remembered that Blaze attacked me the last time I went there, so going back didn't seem like a good idea. I didn't blame Blaze for what he did. As special as he was, Blaze was still an animal. He was still a wolf. When he attacked me, he was just following his instincts, probably out of fear, which may have blinded him to the fact that it was me he was attacking, and not the demon inside of me.

"Actually, you're wrong about that," Max said. "Your little wolf friend, or pet or whatever he is, can see me. When he looks at you, he doesn't see you. He sees me, or at least the energy I put out." Max laughed. "So it looks like there won't be any ruffling of fur or playing of fetch any time soon."

I puffed my cheeks out in exasperation. "You're a total bastard, you know that?"

"Again, that's where you are wrong."

"What?"

"Well, all this talk of flesh has, shall we say, stoked my desire. I'd like to get my hands...*dirty* again, if you know what I mean. Or should that be bloody? Bloody dirty, perhaps..."

Panic hit me like a ten ton hammer as I had visions of having to helplessly watch Max as he butchered more innocents. "No," I said. "No more killing."

"Relax," Max said. "I won't be killing anyone else. Not while I'm in your body at least."

I didn't like the sound of that either. "Wait, what do you mean?"

"Well, I've been thinking. I have no desire to be trapped in a cell with you again, which would likely happen if you were seen around town with your hands dripping with blood. Plus, I'm rather looking forward to our coming adventures. I didn't think I would be, but I am. For some strange reason, I find you interesting, Creed. You're not like most of the humans I possess, who tend to be weak and afraid all of the time...but more on that later. Just know that I will be using some other body when I want to indulge my taste for the flesh."

"You mean you're going to possess some other poor sod just so you can kill people?"

"Yes. I thought you'd be glad."

I shook my head. "Glad that you're going to kill more innocent people?"

"Would you rather it was *you* who killed them?"

I shook my head again, this time in shame. "No."

"Well, then. Stop your whining, and don't look a gift horse in the mouth. You'll be free of me, Creed, for a little while at least. Isn't that what you wanted? No need to answer. I know it is. I can feel it."

At that point, my mind was so mangled, I just wanted him gone. "Go now. Just fucking go."

"Remember, Creed," Max said, turning up the pain dial in my chest just a little, a sinister tone to his voice inside my head. "I can come and go from you as I please, and there is nothing you can do to stop me. You have been marked, which means there is no spell, no magic that can undo that. I own you completely until I decide not to. So while I'm gone, don't waste your time looking for ways to stop me. If you do, I will know, and I will take it personally that you chose not to listen to me. Do you understand?"

I nodded as I winced at the stabbing pain in my chest. "Yes."

"Good." He stopped the pain. "Then I shall see you soon."

A second after he finished speaking, Max's invisible spirit shot out of my chest so forcibly, it felt like my guts were being pulled out along with it. When he had gone, I breathed a huge sigh of relief as I bent over and leaned my hands on my knees, feeling like I was finally able to breath properly after so long. Then, when my lungs were filled, I shot up straight, threw my head back and let out a long, agonized scream.

\* \* \*

Despite what Max said about not scheming behind his back to have him exorcised, or prevented from re-entering my body, I teleported over to Sanaka's Sanctum and let myself in. It took me a few minutes to find Sanaka in one of his training rooms practicing his sword katas. He didn't miss a single beat when I slid back the door and walked into the room, minus my boots of course, which I left outside the Sanctum. I remained by the door respectfully while Sanaka continued to perform the sword kata, his movements graceful and masterful in their execution, but also laden with tremendous power and strength. I admire those who wield such skill with weapons. When it comes to edged weapons, I'm more of a hack and slash guy. Less Miyamoto Musashi, more Jason Voorhees. That was me. My mind is my main weapon, along with my magic, and always has been. Sometimes I even wield both like I know what I'm doing.

"Why would you bring a demon into my Sanctum?" Sanaka asked as he stood in the middle of the room, dressed in white robes and still holding his katana.

"I haven't," I said. "The demon is gone for now. That's why I'm here."

"You want to know if you can stop it from possessing you again."

"Yes."

"You can't."

I sighed at his bluntness. "Seriously? There's nothing to be done to stop this motherfu—I mean, demon, from possessing me again? There must be *something*."

Sanaka remained seemingly unaffected by my plight, his calm composure as infuriating to me as ever in these tense situations. When my back is against the wall, I like people to scream along with me. It makes me feel less alone. Not that Sanaka cared about any of that. "If there is, I do not know about it."

"So I'm screwed then." It was more of a statement than a question.

"I hear it's the same demon which marked you years ago," Sanaka said, walking forward. "The one who killed your family."

I nodded. "Yes."

"I'm sorry. It must be hard."

"Are you sympathizing with me? You never show me any sympathy. Ever." I paused for a second as I realized something. "I must really be screwed."

"The demon will kill you and take your soul when it is finished with you," he said.

"No," I said shaking my head. "We made a deal."

Sanaka raised one eyebrow at me. "You made another deal with a demon? Remind me again how the last deal you made with a demon worked out."

"Point taken." I shook my head. "What the hell was I thinking? I can't trust the son of a bitch. Not that I had much choice. I was screwed anyway."

Sanaka shook his head at me as he left the training room with his sword. I followed behind him as he made his way to the kitchen, where he began to prepare Sushi from a freshly caught sea bass. My nose wrinkled as he began to gut the fish. While still Sanaka's apprentice, I grew to hate the smell of fish, for he fed it to me everyday, telling me it helped the flow of magic around the body. Something about the essential oils, I don't fucking know. Whether it does or not, I still don't know. Sometimes I think Sanaka just enjoyed fucking with me at times. "The best I can do is try to find a solution to your problem," he said eventually. "But I don't think there is one. Some things just can't be changed, even with magic."

"Yeah," I said. "Don't I know it."

* * *

WHEN I LEFT SANAKA'S SANCTUM, I WALKED OUT INTO THE PARK AND CALLED Leona on my phone. "Hey," I said when she answered. "Where are you?"

"The Sanctum," she said. "Where are you? With that Crow woman?"

The vitriol in her voice was unmistakable. Leona had no love for Angela Crow, or any other vampire for that matter, but especially Angela, whom Leona thought I was too close to for my own good. "No. I was with Sanaka trying to find a solution to my demon problem."

"Any luck?"

"No."

"Figures."

"Are you all right, Leona? You sound...pissed off."

"That's because I am, Creed. I know this getting possessed by a demon from your past thing is not your fault, not exactly anyway, but it's still—" She stopped in frustration like she couldn't form the words.

"What?" I said, feeling like shit that I had dragged her into something again.

"I'd just like things to be normal for once, or as normal as they can be with you."

"It sounds like you regret moving back here...or getting back with me."

She sighed. "It's not that, Creed. I don't do regrets, you know that. What's done is done. But once again, there's a very real chance that you might..."

"Die?"

"Yes. Again."

"Look, I'm not going to die. I'll figure a way out of this. I always do."

Leona went silent. I could picture her back at the Sanctum, staring hard at the floor as she tried to keep her emotions under control. "So what's your next move?" she asked eventually.

"To see you," I said. "Is Blaze there with you?"

"No. He left earlier."

Blaze was probably out hunting somewhere, which meant he would be gone for most of the night. "All right. I'll be there in a minute."

After hanging up the phone, I went and sat on one of the park benches, as there was something I had to do before Max showed up again. Max couldn't know that I had been talking to Sanaka about trying to get rid of him. I couldn't afford to piss Max off, so I would have to conceal the memory of my conversation with Sanaka. Closing my eyes, I focused on the memory, and then wrapped it up in a bit of concealment magic. Then I pushed the memory far back into the recesses of my mind. It was like taking an old video tape and stashing it in a box in the basement. As long as Max wasn't looking for it, he shouldn't find it. Once I had pushed the memory to the depths of my mind, I could barely recall it myself. With that done, I teleported to the Sanctum to see Leona.

\* \* \*

LEONA WAS SITTING IN THE LIVING ROOM OF THE SANCTUM, STILL DRESSED IN her field gear. In front of her was my centuries old chess table. On this highly prized, and ridiculously expensive, table was one of her custom Berettas, stripped down to its various components, which Leona was cleaning with an oil cloth. It was something she liked to do when she was stressed, to calm herself and regain her focus. The fact that she was in the middle of doing it now, spoke volumes about the effect my current situation was having on her. Once again, guilt stabbed at my belly like a knife. When Leona came back from Washington, she did so on the understanding that it was to be a fresh start for her and us. That fresh start lasted barely two days before things went belly up. It was beginning to seem that Leona and I were fated to be together only in strife. Normality was a foreign concept for us and our relationship. Unless of course, this *was* normality.

"Hey," I said as I stood feeling like a stranger in my own Sanctum, knowing that if Blaze decided to walk in now, he would most likely attack me again. Or maybe not, since Max wasn't in me at present. But I had no doubt screwed with Blaze's head the last time, and the poor guy probably didn't know what to think now. He might attack just out of pure confusion.

Leona stopped what she was doing long enough for us to look at each other, as if to say, *Well, here we are again in the midst of another shitstorm...*

"Are you okay?" I asked her.

"You're the possessed one," she replied.

"Not right now I'm not." I crossed the room to pour myself a glass of whiskey from the bottle on the mantle. "Max has decided it would be unwise to use my body for any more killing, so he fucked off into someone else's body instead, so he could do his killing without any negative consequences to me. Or him for that matter."

"Jesus. You know how fucked up that sounds?"

"Believe me, I know."

"Can't you keep the demon out, now that he's gone?"

I shook my head as I filled my glass for the second time. "I wish. There's nothing to be done on that score. Me and Max, we're like two fucking peas in a pod until he decides otherwise."

"What about Ray or Sanaka? Surely they must be able to help?"

"Sanaka is a dead end, I think anyway. I can't quite..." I shook my head dismissively. "As for Ray, I'll see him when I get to Ireland."

"Wait, what? You're going to Ireland?"

I nodded. "I have to. It's a condition of my release."

"Why did the Crow get you out?" Leona asked, somewhat suspiciously, I thought.

"So I could go to Babylon and bring her daughter home to her. Ray has direct access to the place, which is why I'm going to Ireland."

Leona shook her head. "You're going away again."

"Yes," I said. "I don't have a choice. It's either that or stay locked up at Division."

"And then what?"

"Well, assuming I manage to persuade Jennifer Crow to come back here, then I have to go to where the rest of my family are, or at least their souls."

"What for?"

I frowned. "What do you mean, what for?"

Leona frowned and moved the table aside as she stood. "Your family is dead, Creed. Wherever they are, they've moved on. What do you hope to achieve by tracking down their souls?"

It was a valid question, despite the defensive anger that rose in me when she asked it. Truth be told, I hadn't really considered what I would do when I tracked down my family. Neither did I know anything about their situation in the multiverse. I just knew I had to find them. After that, I didn't know.

"Closure," I said eventually, in answer to Leona's question.

"I thought you got that when your family appeared to you last time," she said.

"They were ripped out of this world before their time, Leona."

"Lots of people are taken before their time, Creed. It doesn't mean we have to track their souls half way across the universe to do...whatever it is you plan on doing."

"Are you telling me you would pass up the chance to see your brother again?" I asked her, knowing I'd be hitting a nerve.

Her face set in anger for a moment as she stared hard at me. "Fuck you, Creed."

"Hey, I'm just saying. I know there's not much logic in finding my family when they've been dead for so long, but this isn't about logic or common sense—"

"Nothing ever is with you."

I nodded. "Fair point, but it's just something I have to do."

"Is your demon tagging along with you, then?" She sat back down and started purposely cleaning her gun.

"That's the only reason you're even talking to me," I said. "Otherwise I'd still be out there killing people, until I ended up dead myself."

Leona looked up at me briefly. "What do you mean?"

"I made a deal with the demon. Luckily our interests intertwine."

"So the demon will leave you alone once it gets what it wants, is that it?"

"That's the plan, yeah."

"And the plan always works out, right?"

I sighed. "What do you want me to do, Leona? I'm working things out as best I can here."

Leona stopped oiling her gun and sighed as well. "I know. I'm sorry."

I crossed the room so I could give her a hug. "We can get through this," I said.

"We?"

I pulled back to look at her. "Yes, we."

Leona went silent for a moment, before saying unexpectedly, "Brentwood offered me my old job back."

*That motherfucker.*

"What did *you* say?" I asked as calmly as possible.

"I told him no, and that I was partners with you now."

I wanted to kiss her, but it didn't seem appropriate somehow. "You've no idea what that means to me."

"I know what it means. That's why I told Brentwood no. I'm with you, Creed, but on the understanding that we are partners, and partners don't keep shit from each other, or do foolish things behind each others backs. From now on, I want complete transparency from you."

I nodded. "Of course. That goes without saying."

"Good."

"You're a real hardass, Lawson, you know that?" I said, smiling as I moved in to kiss her. But just as I did, a familiar force slammed into my back, and a dark presence filled me.

"Hey, Creed," Max said. "Did you miss me? Let me show you what I've been up to..."

# 7

# TROUBLE IS BACK

$\mathcal{I}$t was like being trapped in a chair while being forced to watch a nightmarish film reel, or some awful snuff movie, as Max gleefully fed me his most recent memories. I had to watch through the eyes of a stranger—the person whose body Max possessed—as the demon used the person's body as a tool for murder. The first image I saw was of a young woman, possibly a prostitute, lying spreadeagled on a filthy looking motel bed. The woman was stripped naked, and her stomach was cut open, her intestines removed and placed on the blood soaked bed beside her. I don't know how, but the woman was still alive. She was screaming, but little sound left her mouth, as her tongue had been cut out, and most of her teeth had been removed, presumably with the bloody pair of pliers that lay on the beside table next to her. A large butchers knife came into view, and I watched as the hand holding the knife began to slice off the meat from the woman's legs, as garbled noises came from her mouth. It was bad enough that I had to watch this horror unfold. What was worse was that I could *feel* everything that Max was feeling as he mutilated his victim. His pleasure was as intense as his hatred for the victim, and it was difficult for me not to get swept away in those feelings, to the point where I smiled and began to relish the next cut with the knife...

Then the memory changed to a different one. This one was of a tramp in an alley, as Max brutally bludgeoned the man with an iron bar, hitting the tramp repeatedly over the head as the old guy lay dead on the ground. Again, I felt the palpable pleasure coursing through Max as he smashed the tramp's skull open with the iron bar, and then keep hitting until the tramp's brains were mush. The tramp also had a little dog with him, which yapped and nipped at Max's ankles. Max looked down at the dog in annoyance, before lifting his leg high and bringing his boot down hard on the dog's head...

After that, the memories came thick and fast, until it felt like *I* was the one doing all the killing: an old man is thrown into the path of an oncoming truck as people stand around screaming; a child is fatally stabbed at the zoo; a woman has her breasts bitten off one agonizing bite at a time; a cop is shot repeatedly in the head with his own gun; a prostitute is raped by a gang of mind controlled dogs, and then eaten afterward...

The horror went on and on, until...it just stopped, and I was back in the living room of the Sanctum again, with Leona.

And Max, of course.

He was laughing inside me like he'd just played some supremely funny practical joke on me. "Did you enjoy the show, Creed?" he asked.

"Fuck you!" I snarled as I fought to get my bearings again.

"Creed!" Leona said as she held my arm. "Are you all right?"

I nodded. "I'm fine."

"I take it your demon is back?" she said.

"You better believe it, baby," Max said, sounding like he was on a high after his latest killing spree.

"Listen," I said to Leona. "I should go now. I don't trust this asshole around you."

"And rightly so," Max said. "Hmm, the things I could do to that sweet—"

"Don't even fucking think about it!" I shouted aloud, startling Leona. "I'll slit my own throat before I let you—"

"What, Creed?" Max said.

"You know what," I said, silently this time. "Leona is out of bounds, you hear me?"

"I think you are forgetting who is in charge here, Creed. Do I need to show you again?"

"No. Just please keep her out of this."

"Humans and their silly feelings for each other. Fine. I'll do my best."

Knowing that was as much of a promise as I was going to get from him, I dropped the matter and went to Leona so I could kiss her goodbye. "I'm not sure how long I'll be gone for," I told her. "Hopefully not too long. I'll call you."

"Don't worry about me," she said, looking at me like I was a complete basket case, which is how I felt. "I have a case to work on anyway."

"A case?"

"Don't look so surprised. A woman came here while you were...away. She wants help with something that has taken up residence in her basement. Something small and demon-like apparently."

"A Yattering," I said straight away. "Not all that dangerous, but the little bastards can cause trouble if they want to. Mostly they just like a place to hideout while they cause mischief. They've driven many people insane."

"I already figured it was a Yattering."

I smiled. "Of course you did. That's why we're partners. Just be careful. How are you going to handle it? I usually—"

"I'm going to kill it."

"Oh, right. Sure. That'll work, I guess."

Max laughed. "I'm liking her more all the time."

"All right," I said ignoring Max. "I'm going to go now." I kissed her one more time, much to the disgust of Max. "I love you."

Leona smiled. "I love you too, Creed."

My heart warmed when she said it. "See? We're getting better at this whole boyfriend-girlfriend thing. Next we'll be going on dates and camping trips and—"

She punched me on the shoulder, slightly embarrassed now. "Get out of here."

I smiled once more before teleporting out of the Sanctum.

* * *

OUTSIDE IN THE STREET, I PHONED RAY AND BRIEFLY EXPLAINED MY SITUATION to him, telling him I needed to go to Ireland so I could use his access portal to Babylon. He sounded busy, whatever he was doing, and merely told me that was fine, and that there would be a private jet waiting for me at the airport. Then he hung up without giving me any lectures, or lamenting me for being in deep shit once again. I frowned at the phone in my hand for a moment after Ray had hung up, wondering if my old uncle was okay. I guess I'd see when I got to Ireland.

Which I wasn't looking forward to, by the way. It had been many years since I last set foot in Ireland, for obvious reasons. Too much bad shit had happened there, and I never saw the point in going there just to relive a load of painful memories.

"You've been reliving them ever since anyway," Max said in my head.

"I'd appreciate it if you wouldn't invade my mind like that," I said as I walked to the Cadillac parked just down the street. The airport was too far away to teleport, so I decided I would drive there. I fancied the drive anyway, thinking it might clear my head a little.

"Em, duh." Max sounded like me doing an impression of a teenager, which I found disturbing. "I've possessed you, you know. I can do whatever I want with you."

"Fine, whatever." Christ, now I was doing the stupid voice.

As I was about to get into the car, I sensed movement not far behind me. When I looked over my shoulder, I saw nothing. Not at first anyway. Not until a shape materialized out of the darkness.

A wolf shape.

Blaze stood there staring at me, his yellow eyes full of mistrust. We stared at each other for what seemed a long time, and then Blaze finally turned away, becoming invisible again as he did.

"Heartbreaking," Max said. "The bond of trust between a man and his dog...*broken*." He laughed like it amused him greatly.

"First of all, Max, he's not a dog, he's a wolf," I said. "And second of all, he won't come near me because you're here."

"He's a smart doggy then."

I gritted my teeth for a second as I griped the door handle on the Cadillac, slamming it behind me as I got inside. As soon as I sat down, Evil Creed appeared in the front passenger seat beside me. "Oh, God...really?" I said. "You're going to sit there for the whole drive?"

Max smiled. "Of course. This feels like a road trip."

"We're going to the airport."

"Still, it's a chance for us to chat. To get to know one another."

I couldn't tell if he was being serious or not. "You have access to my entire mind already, and I have no desire to know you, so..." I shook my head at him and started the car up. "There's nothing left to say."

Just as I was about to drive off, something massive crashed down onto the hood of the car, causing me to cry out in shock.

Max never flinched. "Well, what do we have here?" he said calmly.

What we had, was a fucking huge werewolf on the hood, staring in at us with glowing yellow eyes. I barely had a chance to react before the beast launched itself at the windshield, smashing one sinewy arm through the glass, and grabbing me by the throat with its huge paw.

*"Oh, shit..."*

# 8

# THE BEAST

$\mathcal{F}$ully transformed werewolves are frankly terrifying monsters, with the power and strength to rip a man apart in seconds. Coming face to face with one, as I have many times, is always a frighteningly intense experience. This time was no different.

As I was pulled through the windshield of the car, my head breaking the glass on the way through, I couldn't help but panic that I was about to be torn apart and eaten by the monstrous werewolf who had me by the throat. The werewolf's paw was so big it completely wrapped around my neck. One quick jerk is all it would take to snap my neck like a chicken's.

The werewolf stood up to its full height on the hood of the car, holding me out in front of it like I was nothing but a nuisance to it. It's reddish-yellow eyes burned fiercely within its massive head, and it opened its mouth to reveal possibly the biggest teeth I have ever seen. Those things could bite my head off with one quick snap, which I thought the creature was going to do as its head came towards me. But it roared instead, its hot breath blasting my face, the noise of it causing my heart to stop for a second as terror ran through me unabated.

But I didn't even have time to be scared, because the werewolf then turned and threw me into the air like a rag doll. When I came down, I bounced over the road, grunting in pain until I came to a stop next to a parked car. I could only lie there dazed as massive shadows seemed to close in around me.

The rest of the pack.

*Great.*

As I regained my vision, I made out the shapes of about six more towering werewolves, every one of them roaring down at me. The noise was deafening, and completely overwhelming. Under such an aural assault, the last thing I was thinking about was employing defensive magic. But of course, the werewolves knew that would be the case. Who said werewolves were dumb anyway?

"Well, this was most unexpected," Max said calmly within me. "These things really want to *eat* you, Creed."

I could barely hear his voice over the noise the werewolves were making. Not that I wanted to hear it anyway.

A few seconds later, some of those surrounding me stood aside, and the pack leader who had ripped me out of my car came stomping over and picked me up by the lapels, holding me so our faces were level. As I looked into those rage-filled eyes, it didn't take me long to work out who the werewolf was. "Big Joe," I said. "I know it's you—"

The werewolf pulled me closer and roared in my face, coating me in hot saliva. I guess it was Big Joe after all. He was here about his cousin, Ace, whose death I had facilitated on live TV. Clearly Big Joe wanted payback, and although I could understand why, there was no way I was going to let the werewolf kill me over the head of his sociopathic sexual sadist of a cousin. Ace got what he deserved in my book, and killing me wasn't going to bring him back. Not that Big Joe cared about any of that. He just wanted revenge.

Well, there was no way I was going to just roll over for these hairy fucks. It was time to use my trusty Silver Needles Spell. That should slow the bastards down a bit, long enough for me to get the hell out of there anyway.

Only, when I went to tap into my magic, I couldn't. It was like something was blocking me from doing so. Even when I tried to teleport, nothing happened.

Then one of Big Joe's huge paws slammed into my chest and sent me flying back onto the road again. Half conscious from hitting my head on the hard asphalt, I could only lie there and wait for the werewolf to come get me so it could continue beating the shit out of me.

But then several loud bangs roused me out of my daze, and when I sat up I saw Leona on the sidewalk near the Sanctum. She was firing continuously with her two custom Berettas. She had already downed two of the werewolves, though I wasn't sure if they were dead or not. Maybe, if she was using silver nitrate bullets.

As I watched from the middle of the road, I saw one of the werewolves go bounding up Leona's blindside. "Leona!" I shouted, but she was too busy firing at the other beasts to hear me.

The werewolf got to within feet of Leona before I saw Blaze come to her rescue. He ran down the steps of the Sanctum and leaped in the air, launching himself at the werewolf about to railroad Leona. Blaze's body was a mass of flame by this point, and the second he leapt on the werewolf, the beast's fur immediately ignited and began to stick to its flesh. The werewolf howled in pain, but Blaze didn't stop until he had torn out the beast's throat, and its body was a charred, smoldering mess that filled the night air with foul smelling smoke.

Out of the corner of my eye, I sensed something running toward me. When I looked, I panicked when I saw Big Joe bounding toward me on all fours. There was no doubt the werewolf was about to execute a kill stroke. Perhaps decapitate me with one powerful swipe of his massive paw. Desperately, I searched for my magic again, but it wasn't there.

Then, as if someone had pulled my strings, I found myself jumping to my feet as I stood to meet the incoming werewolf head on. Now I had the by now familiar feeling of being a mere passenger in my own body as Max took over.

When the werewolf came rushing at me, my arm shot out and stopped the huge beast in its tracks, as if the werewolf had run into an invisible wall. For the first time, I felt a new form of power coursing through my body. The dark power of Max, from which he drew a shocking amount of strength. My body did not give an inch as Max held Big Joe up by the throat, holding his head in place to keep his snapping jaws away from my face.

A huge rush of blood lust then took over, and Max went to work.

Using my body, he slammed Big Joe down into the road with so much force the asphalt broke underneath the werewolf's body. To Max, Big Joe was no more than a bothersome animal that needed to be put down. I felt my knee drop onto Big Joe's chest, pinning him to the ground. I felt my hands grab a hold of those snapping jaws and begin to pull them apart. Even though I didn't necessarily want Big Joe dead, there was still something satisfying about prying those huge jaws of his until a loud snap was heard, followed by a howl of pain.

Max didn't stop there. He kept pulling until the jaws began to extend back over Big Joe's head, finally ripping his face off, spraying blood everywhere. "There," Max said in my voice. "No more howling at the moon for this beast."

Before Max could even chuckle to himself, the remaining three werewolves moved in to attack. Completely unconcerned by the fact that three massive beasts with teeth and claws were advancing toward him at speed, Max smiled and counter-rushed the werewolf to his left. My body moved at such head-rushing speed that I could barely comprehend what was going on. I felt Max operate my limbs in ways I never knew possible, and all at the same blinding speed. For a few long seconds, my vision was taken up by the towering bodies of the werewolves that became stained with swathes of dark crimson blood, as Max proceeded to rip each of them apart, effortlessly tearing off their limbs and ripping their heads from their shoulders. For me, trapped inside my own body, the rush of all that power and speed and brutal violence, it was at once terrifying and exhilarating, like being on the world's scariest rollercoaster. You only think you know power until you have experienced what other beings such as demons are capable of. It's a humbling experience, to say the least.

When Max had finished his flurry of violence, he stood in the middle of the road with blood dripping down his face, looking around at the scattered body parts of the werewolves. "Well, that was fun, eh, Creed?" he said joyfully. "Did you enjoy the ride in there?"

If I could, I would have shook my head and said nothing. As it was, I just said nothing.

Max then looked over to Leona, who was standing on the sidewalk, a look of horror on her face. I doubted her look of horror had anything to do with the gore on the road. It likely had more to do with the fact that she just watched me rip apart three werewolves like they were made of Playdoh. Of course, it wasn't actually me that did it. It was Max, but I'm sure it didn't seem like that to Leona.

"What's wrong, Leona?" Max called over with a smile on his face.

"Stop it!" I said. "Leave her alone!"

Leona shook her head. "I don't even know who I'm talking to."

"It's me, it's Creed," Max said in a soothing tone.

"You bastard," I said.

"That wasn't you who ripped those werewolves apart," Leona said.

"Oh, but it was, dear," Max said slipping back into his own snide tone. "You see, me and Max are the same now."

Leona stared hard, her guns still in hand. "You're not Creed," she stated bluntly.

"Good girl," I said within myself, as much to annoy Max as anything.

Max chuckled. "You're right. Creed doesn't have the power to do what I just did. The same as he doesn't have the power to do this."

Max raised his arms, and I felt a massive surge of his power go through my body.

"What the fuck are you doing?" I asked him.

"Wait and see," he replied aloud. He was still staring at Leona as he continued to draw on his power.

"Don't you fucking hurt her, Max. I swear—"

"Silence!" Max commanded, and I found myself in the position of not being able to form thoughts anymore. The only thing I was capable of now was to experience everything as it was happening, and no more. To Max, I was now unable to communicate and interrupt him.

When he turned away from Leona, his attention went to the body parts of the werewolves scattered all over the road. As I watched, all of the detached limbs and severed heads began to come together like iron filings to a magnet. Arms, legs and heads began to knit into torsos, to form a monster that was far more terrifying to look at, and far bigger, than any of the werewolves were by themselves. This new creature stood upright on six legs, which were attached to a bunch of squashed together torsos. Heads and arms from all seven werewolves were attached, seemingly randomly, all over the grotesque torso, with three heads mounted together on the top to form one giant, misshapen head that roared from three different mouths.

"Isn't it handsome?" Max said as he presented the Beast like a proud father.

Leona was already pointing her guns at the Beast. She emptied two full clips into it, and although the Beast roared in what sounded like pain, it didn't seem that fazed by the bullets.

"It will take more than a few bullets to stop this beast," Max said. Then he turned to the creature. "Go!"

The Beast roared once more, and then went bounding down the street away from us, surprisingly fast considering its twisted form.

Leona's guns were now pointing at Max.

At *me*.

Max merely smiled. "Are you really going to shoot me, the love of your life?"

"You're not the love of my life...demon."

"It's like I said, Creed and I, we're one and the same now. You better get used to that, Leona. Oh, and before I disappear, good luck with the Beast. I hear he can get a bit...violent around people. Bye, Leona. See you soon." He blew her kisses. "Love you..."

He chuckled to himself as he teleported away.

# 9

# HOME SWEET HOME

*M*ax teleported us right to the airport, near a baggage cart that was parked on one of the runways. After a few seconds, I realized that I was back in control of my mind and body again. A huge surge of pent up anger went through me, and I turned around and punched the luggage on top of the cart. "Fuck!" I shouted, attracting the attention of a couple of baggage handlers strolling down the runway toward me. Before the two men caught up, I teleported to the runway where I knew the private jet was waiting. But before I headed towards the waiting plane, I stopped on the runway to talk to Max.

"I'm sensing some anger," Max said in his smug voice that made me want to strangle the cunt.

"What the fuck was that?" I demanded, telepathically of course.

"What was what? Oh, you mean the Beast. Yes, a—"

"I mean with Leona, asshole. You don't fucking talk to her, you hear me? You don't even fucking look at her, or I'll—"

"Go on," Max said. "You'll what, Creed? What will you do?"

I shook my head in frustration. "Leona has nothing to do with any of this. Just leave her alone."

Max sighed as if I was being overly dramatic. "I was merely speaking with her. If I wanted to hurt your pretty girlfriend, I would just—"

"Stop. I don't want to hear it. Just keep her out of this, all right? I'll do whatever you want me to do, but Leona is off limits."

"Off limits?" Max laughed as if I was a silly little boy. "Haven't you realized yet? Nothing is off limits to me in this world. *Nothing.*"

"Look, I'm just asking you to leave Leona alone. That's all. It's the fucking least you can do considering you're wearing me like a cheap suit."

Max laughed. "A cheap suit. That's funny. That's actually how it feels sometimes."

Shaking my head, I started towards the waiting jet. "Let's just get on the fucking plane," I said aloud.

"Can I ask why we are getting on a plane?"

"What? You know why."

"Yes, I know, but the fact is I can get us to Ireland much quicker."

I stopped. "You can teleport that far?"

"Of course. Like I said, nothing is off limits here."

"You might've mentioned this before."

"You never asked."

I sighed. "You really are a cunt."

* * *

IN BARELY THE BLINK OF AN EYE, I FOUND MYSELF STANDING OUTSIDE A SMALL cottage in the middle of the day, with nothing but green fields surrounding it. Although I hadn't laid eyes on the tiny cottage for many years, I knew immediately it was Uncle Ray's Sanctum. If the talismans hanging over the door weren't enough to give it away, the sight of Ray himself as he opened the front door was. "August?" Ray said, staring at me quizzically. "You weren't due to arrive for another ten hours at least."

"I know," I said. "Didn't you hear? I got myself a new way to get around. My own personal demon."

Ray nodded. "Right enough. At least they're good for something, right?" He chuckled.

"Cheeky bastard, your uncle," Max said.

"Did he hurt your feelings, Max?" I said as I went inside the Sanctum. "I'm sorry."

"Two cheeky bastards in one family. Who would have thought?"

As small and quaint as Ray's Sanctum was on the outside, on the inside it was like a grand castle fit for any lord or king. It was positively cavernous inside, with stuff everywhere. Every artifact and thing of interest that Ray had ever procured on his extensive travels, ended up inside his Sanctum. Everywhere you looked there were things like old wooden trunks and suits of armor, ancient weapons, and even a sarcophagus, which God knows where he got that from. Ray's place always reminded me of an antique store that no one bought from, so the stuff inside just kept piling up everywhere. It had gotten worse since my last visit. It was like he was building a whole other structure inside, based upon a crazy blueprint that only he understood.

"Does this man ever throw anything out?" Max asked.

Ignoring Max's question, I addressed Ray inside his huge living room, which was also full of stuff, though slightly more organized stuff. "It seems like every time we meet these days it's under dire circumstances. You must be sick of helping me sort out my problems."

Ray smiled as he sat down on a well worn leather armchair, taking his pipe and tobacco pouch from out of his brown waistcoat. "That's what I'm here for," Ray said as if it was nothing. "Will you be visiting the old family home while you're here?"

I shook my head as I sat down in the chair opposite him, next to the roaring open fire. "Not this time."

"Or any time is the impression I get."

I gave a tight smile as I stared into the fire. "I have no wish to go back there."

"Well, at least sell the place then." Ray lit up his pipe, filling the room with a sweet smelling smoke.

"I will, eventually. I've got more pressing matters to take care of first."

"Like getting rid of the demon that's possessed you?" He stared hard at me, as if he was trying to see the demon inside. "What's it like?"

"You mean the demon?" I shook my head. "I don't even know where to start."

"Oh, come now, Creed," Max said. "I was looking forward to your summation of me."

"He's an asshole," I told Ray.

"Bastard," Max said.

"Aren't they all?" Ray said as he offered me the pipe, which I refused. My head was messed up enough without smoking some of Ray's special blend. "How do you plan on getting rid of it?"

"We worked out a deal."

Ray raised his eyebrows. "A deal?"

"Yeah, I know. My deals with demons don't usually go that well."

"Just be careful, son."

"I'm trying to be," I said, directing it more at Max than Ray.

Max laughed within me as if the whole situation was a joke to him.

"So you want to go to Babylon?" Ray said. "On behalf of our mutual friend."

"You think I'm wasting my time?"

Ray shrugged as a cloud of smoke drifted around him. "I barely know Angela's daughter, so I can't say how she'll react. Angela does want the girl home, though."

"You think she genuinely misses Jennifer?"

"I do. Thirty years apart has only filled Angela's heart with yearning. A surprising development, I have to say."

"Maybe she's more human than she lets on."

"Angela has many sides to her that most don't see."

"You're the one that sleeps with her every chance you get. You should know."

Max chuckled. "Really? Well, who'd have thought it?"

"I'm not ashamed to say that no other woman compares," Ray said smiling. "You'd have to have been there to know what I mean."

"I'll just take your word for it," I said, pushing back unwanted images of Angela Crow behaving sexually.

"How's Leona?"

I nodded. "She's okay. Struggling to cope with my latest mess, I guess."

"She's a strong woman. She'll be fine."

"I know she will."

We sat in silence for a few moments while Ray continued to puff on his pipe, his eyes becoming slightly droopy as the herbs had their psychoactive effect on him. "Right, then," he said eventually as he got to his feet. "I can see that time is pressing. Let's get you to Babylon."

* * *

As Ray travels so extensively throughout the multiverse, he has gone to the trouble over the years to create a whole wing in his Sanctum that houses nothing but gateways that lead to other worlds and dimensions. There are hundreds of individual rooms in the wing, each room containing a portal leading to a different place in the multiverse. wizard's, and other people in the know, often come to Ray's Sanctum just so they can access one of his portals. It's easier to do that than to go to the trouble of creating their own. Thanks to all these traveller's, Ray has amassed quite a few favors in return, making him one of the most connected wizard's anywhere. "Passport, please," he said as he opened the door to one of the rooms.

"Funny," I said, not smiling at all.

Ray chuckled anyway. "You should learn to smile more, son. Everything is better with a smile."

"Yeah, Creed," Max said. "Let's see you flash those pearly whites."

*Fuck you.*

I moved past Ray into the small room, which was as basic as it gets. Four stone walls, and a shimmering portal in the middle that resembled an upright pool of glistening, orange-colored water. "This will still take me to your Sanctum in the center of the city, right?" It had been a long while since I'd stepped through the portal.

"Yes," Ray said. "Everything is still the same, although the city itself has gotten somewhat...dystopian."

I frowned. "Dystopian? How?"

"The corporations have taken over, as they are want to do. It's like this realm, only worse."

"Whatever. I'm sure I won't be staying long."

"Be careful anyway. The violence levels have gone up since the corporations started running things."

"You know me," I said. "I'm always careful."

Ray just looked at me. "Of course you are."

I walked up to the portal and looked at my uncle before stepping through. "See you soon, Ray."

# SECRETS AND LIES

$\mathcal{R}$ay's portal took me through to his Babylon Sanctum, located in the very heart of the city. The Sanctum was nestled in the center of a huge tower block, and on the outside it looked like any of the other apartments in the building. Inside of course, was a different story. There were many rooms, most of them containing more of Ray's stuff that he had piled around everywhere. I swear, if Ray ever decides to keep all of his books in one place, such a library will be the biggest in all the realms. It will also probably contain every key piece of knowledge, magical or otherwise, known to man. As it is, Ray prefers to keep his valuables scattered around in different places, because he thinks it will be safer that way. He's probably right. The realms are full of those who spend their time stealing other people's most valuable possessions, and keeping all your shit in one place just made it easier for said people to steal. Hence why the Babylonian Sanctum looked like a storage facility in parts.

I walked through the nondescript living room and out onto the balcony. It was still daylight outside, and I took a few moments to look out over the city, to see if it had changed as much as Ray said it had. On the surface at least, the city looked the same to me, save for a few extra skyscrapers that had been erected since my last visit. The tallest of the skyscrapers was right in the center, and it stood higher even than the fabled Tower of Babel, which had always been the city's centerpiece. Now the skyscraper stood alongside it like a bully trying to intimidate or push out the smaller kid. The arrival and placement of the huge skyscrapers spoke volumes. The Tower of Babel was occupied by the Babylonian royal family, who had historically ruled over the city since it rematerialized in this new dimension. It now seemed that the corporations were trying to muscle out the old rulers, if they hadn't done so already. Not that I cared that much. I didn't live in the place after all, and as soon as I was done, I'd be gone.

"Did I mention Babylon is one of my favorite playgrounds?" Max said, now standing beside me on the balcony as Evil Creed. "Such fun to be had here."

"Fun?" I said. "You mean killing?"

Max smiled. "They are one in the same."

"Of course they are. Fucking psycho demon."

"Says the human with the hypocritical moral code. It's laughable. At least I am true to my nature. Can you say the same, Creed?"

"If being true to my nature means being an evil, murdering bastard, then I'm happy as I am."

Max shook his head. "You humans will never understand the true meaning of life in the multiverse. You think you have it all worked out, but you don't."

"And demons have?"

"There is nothing to work out in the first place," he said. "One simply becomes what they are, and acts like they were born to act. It's not complicated. Only humans make living complicated."

"So we should just live like animals, is that what you're saying?"

"Better than how you live now, with all those repressed feelings of guilt and shame, and whatever else. It makes me sick."

"*You* make *me* sick."

Max smiled at me. "You are always so defiant, Creed. I like that about you. I think you would make an excellent demon."

"No thanks."

"Many of the greatest of our kind started of as human."

"Did *you*? I dread to think what kind of person you would have been."

"I was never human. The mere thought turns my stomach."

"So you were just excreted from the darkness, is that it?"

"In a way, yes. I was born evil, as you humans might say. I prefer to think of myself as pure, rather than evil."

"Pure?" I couldn't help but smile. "You can be a pretentious cunt at times."

Max's eyes flashed red for a second. "And you can be an insolent swine at times."

"Then I guess we're both assholes."

"Your self-loathing is palpable."

"So is your dickishness."

Max frowned as if he didn't know what that meant. "Whatever."

"Yeah, whatever. Are you going to be tagging along inside me for this whole mission, or will you be jumping ship for a while?"

"I haven't decided yet."

Not that I wanted anyone else to die at the hands of Max, but I couldn't help wanting rid of him while I made contact with Jennifer. "Just don't get in my way."

"Saying something like that only *makes* me want to get in your way, you know."

"What if I said please?"

"It wouldn't matter. At all."

"Fuck you, then."

"Fuck you, too."

"Dick."

"Twat."

I almost smiled, but didn't want to give him the satisfaction. "I'm going to do what I came here to do," I said walking away. "You do what you want."

* * *

U<small>NFORTUNATELY, DESPITE MAKING IT PLAIN</small> I <small>DIDN'T WANT HIM AROUND WHILE</small> I went to meet Jennifer, Max tagged along anyway. He made his presence keenly felt as I first teleported across the city, and then walked the few hundred yards to where Jennifer lived. Or at least, where she *did* live last time I saw her, which would have been a few years ago. She may have moved since then for all I knew.

"You could have called this girl before coming here," Max said.

"And tell her what? That I was coming to bring her back to her mother? She would have shut me down straight away, and then when I came here she probably wouldn't want to speak to me. Face to face is better. Anyway, you're in my head all the time, you should know this."

"Contrary to what you might think, I don't spend all my time sifting through the sad remnants of your mind, Creed. That would just be tedious and supremely bloody boring."

"So what do you look at in there?" I asked, genuinely curious about the answer.

"Just the stuff that matters," Max said as I opened the glass door to the apartment building, which was made out of sandstone blocks, and was shaped like a pyramid. "Like your memories of me slaughtering your family."

I stopped dead in the foyer, my boots squeaking on the mosaic floor. "You had to bring that up, didn't you?" I said aloud as my face set in anger. A second later, images of the very incident he was talking about flashed across my mind like blood splashing over a wall.

"You forget I'm here to torment you, Creed. Did you think I was here to be your partner in this little buddy movie you call your life?" He chuckled like that was funny.

"Fine," I said as I did my best to keep my voice level. "Just do me a favor, and leave the tormenting until after I've convinced Jennifer to come back with us— with *me*. Don't forget I'll end up in prison again if I fail here, which means so will you. I'm sure neither of us wants that."

"This doesn't give you power over me, you know. I'm happy to watch you squirm as I torment you in that cell again. But—" He paused, for effect no doubt, to cover up the fact that he knew I was right. "—I don't get out that often, and I would rather not spend all my time breaking your mind in a prison cell, which I would do...eventually."

"How many souls have escaped from your domain in the Underworld?" I asked him.

The question seemed to jar him. "What?"

"How many lucky souls have managed to free themselves from your chains in the Underworld?"

"I see what you're doing."

"Just answer the question."

"Four souls, all of them your family members," he said, unable to keep the anger from his voice.

"Just the four in...how old is your domain? Very fucking old, I'd say. And in all that time, no one has ever escaped, until—"

"Your wretched family came along!"

"I know, right?" I said nodding. "That must really *bug* you, not knowing how they did it. I mean, you said the place was impossible to escape from, right?"

A sudden stabbing pain in my chest caused me to stiffen up. "Stop it," Max growled, his voice no longer human.

"I'm just saying," I said wincing with pain. "You want to make sure...no one escapes again...right?" The pain stopped as suddenly as it began, and I breathed out sharply.

"You've made me angry now, Creed." His voice sounded human again, but it was still deeper than normal. "I feel like killing something to vent my frustrations. Maybe I'll use your body to do it."

"Wait," I said. "I wasn't trying to piss you off. Okay, maybe a little. But I was just trying to make you see that we both have a stake in things going smoothly. I mean, could you really go without finding out how my family escaped from your domain?"

"What's to stop me from going to them now and getting those answers myself?" Max said. "You know which realm they are in, which means I do to."

I shook my head. "Even if you found them, they would never tell you anything."

"I wouldn't be so sure of that. You have no idea how persuasive I can be. Just ask your mother."

"What the hell does that mean? That you tortured her?"

"Tortured? In the beginning, yes. Of course."

I shook my head. "In the beginning? So then what, you tried to wine and dine her?"

"That's actually not too far from the truth. In some small way, I found Brenda to be fascinating. For a human, I mean."

"Wait a minute. Brenda?"

"Much time passed during her incarceration. Many conversations took place. She spoke of you a lot."

It felt like my head was spinning. "You're fucking with my head again."

"Yes and no," Max said. "Yes, I am always fucking with your head, Creed. But also no, on this occasion I am not really. I speak the truth. I probably know your mother better than you do." He laughed, finding this funny.

"Jesus Christ," I said, my stomach tying itself in knots at the thought of him being in any way intimate with my mother. Whatever she did, she must have did it so she could play him. Maybe that's how she eventually escaped.

Thankfully, Max didn't appear to pick up on this thought. "There is much you don't know, Creed. Maybe I'll fill you in sometime. Or maybe I won't."

"Fill me in about what?"

"Secrets and lies. It's what makes the world go around."

"Could you be any more cryptic?"

"You go and retrieve vampire girl," he said. "I'm off to kill some people. There's more meat here besides humans. It would be a shame to waste it."

Before I could even protest, his spirt burst out of my body, and he was gone, just like that. I stood in the foyer for another moment, trying to wrap my head around everything he had said about my mother. Was he telling the truth, or was he just trying to fuck with my head again? In any case, it didn't matter. All that mattered now was persuading Jennifer Crow to come home.

The other stuff could wait.

# 11

# JENNIFER

*I* was slightly nervous when I knocked on the door to Jennifer's penthouse suite, and not because I was turning up unannounced. I knew she would be fine with that, and had always been pleased to see me in the past when I'd dropped in. Rather, I was more nervous about what I had to say to her. While I knew Jennifer's attitude toward her mother had softened over the years, I wasn't sure if she would go so far as to move back to Blackham to be with her again. It could be that was a line Jennifer never intended to cross again, in which case, it was back to prison for me. Unless of course, I went on the run instead. Or stayed here in Babylon perhaps. *No*, I thought. My life's in Blackham, along with the love of my life, Leona. I couldn't just clear off, never to be seen again as I constantly looked over my shoulder. If Angela Crow didn't hunt me down, Leona surely would for leaving her high and dry.

I cleared my throat as I heard footsteps nearing the door inside the penthouse. Then I smiled as the door opened, and Jennifer was standing there. "Surprise," I said lamely.

Jennifer froze for a moment, like she couldn't believe who was at her door. Then she returned my smile, and ran forward to throw her arms around me, gripping me tight. "I can't believe you're here," she said, sounding tearful.

*Neither can I*, I almost said, but thought better of it. "Are you going to invite me in?"

Jennifer let go of me, and stood back and smiled. Needless to say, she hadn't changed at all since I last saw her. Being a vampire, Jennifer didn't age the way humans did. She was forty-six years old, but didn't look a day over twenty-five. Her long dark hair shone under the lights of the hallway, and her slightly wet brown eyes reflected the light like dark pools. She also wore a black business suit that made her look grown up and professional. I say that because I met Jennifer when she was just fifteen and still a kid. She has tended to remain that way in my mind over the years, even though she is far from being a kid these days.

Jennifer stood aside so I could enter the penthouse, the interior of which was spacious and spotlessly clean. The complete opposite of my Sanctum back in Blackham. All the windows in the place were covered by heavy curtains, but the doorway leading to the balcony outside was open, allowing a gentle night breeze to drift in. The only slightly messy part of the penthouse was the far corner near the kitchen, which contained an easel and stacks of canvases leaning against the walls. "Still painting, I see."

"Of course," Jennifer said in a voice that was just the right side of husky. "It's what keeps me sane, you know that."

I nodded. "I do."

A silence ensued for a moment that felt awkward, made worse when Jennifer asked, "What are you doing in Babylon, Creed?"

"I came to see you, of course."

She stared a moment, then smiled. "I know you, Creed. There's more to it. And to be frank, you look like shit. What's going on?"

I sighed and shook my head. "Get me a drink and I'll explain everything."

* * *

THREE DRINKS LATER AND I WAS DONE EXPLAINING TO JENNIFER THE PURPOSE of my visit. Once I told her that her mother wanted her back in Blackham, Jennifer sat in stunned silence for a few moments. Then she got up and walked out onto the balcony. When I'd finished my drink, I put the empty glass on top of an expensive looking table, before joining Jennifer outside. Standing beside her, I was grateful for the cool breeze blowing my skin, and I stood in silence for a moment just enjoying it. It was the closest I felt to being free since...forever it seemed like.

"I knew this day would come eventually," Jennifer said after a while. "I didn't think you would be the one to come and get me, though."

I shook my head, feeling like shit about the whole situation. "Believe me, neither did I. This was the last thing I wanted to do. I know you're happy here, and that you probably don't want to go back to Blackham. Why would you?"

Jennifer nodded. "Why would I indeed?"

"What do you mean?"

"I mean maybe I'm not as happy here as you think."

"Really? I thought you liked it here. I thought you were content."

"I was, but things changed."

"Like what?"

"Take a look out there, Creed," she said. "Babylon is not what it was when I first came here. When I came here it was a free city, full of art and history. It had a really great vibe."

"And now?"

She shook her head. "Now the city has been taken over by the big corps. They moved in from other worlds and just took over. All but crushed the small corps that were here to begin with, and turned the city into a place of pure commerce, splitting it in two, making the gap between rich and poor even wider. Art is barely tolerated anymore, unless its being used as currency. I'm not sure I can live in a city that doesn't tolerate art."

"You look like you're doing okay here," I said.

"I got a job with one of the big corps after they bought over the other corp I was working for." She shrugged. "It was okay for a while. But then things got serious. Corporate espionage is a huge thing here now. It's like an ongoing war. People die all the time, and no one blinks an eye. It's fucking creepy, and wrong."

"Sounds like it."

She turned to look at me, her hair billowing behind her in the breeze. "And now you're here, asking me to go back to Blackham and my mother."

"She's changed," I said, not sure if I really believed that or not myself. "She genuinely misses you."

"It's been thirty years. She should."

"You know what's been happening lately back on Earth? Things have changed."

"Changed how?"

"The supernatural is no longer underground for a start. Sleepwalkers are a thing of the past."

Jennifer looked shocked for a second. "How?"

"It's a long story," I said. "But your mother is now in charge of a group called the Council of the Gifted, if you can believe that. The Council now oversees the supernatural world."

"Of course it does," Jennifer said nodding. "And of course my mother is in charge."

"She wants you there alongside her, to help her run things. As her equal."

"Her equal? She said that?"

"More or less."

"I don't know, Creed. Do you believe her?"

"Believe her about what?"

"Well, that she won't try to control me like she did before."

I shrugged. "I'm sure she will, but it's up to you to stand up to her. You're a grown woman now, Jennifer. She has to respect that, and I'm sure she will...eventually."

"Yeah, eventually."

"Look," I said leaning my elbow on the balcony railing. "My opinion is that the Council needs someone like you to stop it from becoming just another power hungry group. It needs someone who will at least try to do the right thing. This could be good for you as well. Plus, there's the other thing."

"What other thing?"

"Your mother wants me to make you a Daywalker."

Jennifer drew back a little in surprise. "You would do that? You've always said you would never make anyone else a Daywalker. That one is enough."

I nodded. "I know, and I still probably feel that way..." I trailed off for a second before speaking again. "I feel like I need to come clean about why I'm really here." I meant to explain everything to her earlier, but when it came to it, I chickened out, thinking it would upset her too much. Now it didn't seem to matter, given that she didn't seem too averse to going home.

A frown came over her face. "What do you mean?"

"To cut a long story short, I've been possessed by a demon."

"What?" Her eyes widened. "You have a demon in you right now?"

"Well, not right now. He's actually off...doing stuff. He'll be back soon enough, though, you can be certain of that."

"I've never met a demon before. Does it control you? Like completely?"

I nodded. "When it wants to, yes. In fact, that's what I'm trying to tell you. While the demon controlled me, it killed a number of people. As it used my body, I'm being held responsible. It was your mother who got me out of jail."

"In return for bringing me home to her," Jennifer said, then smiled and shook her head. "That sounds just like her, using desperate people to do her bidding."

"What can I say? She plays the game to win. She always will. Although, she did say she would still keep me out of jail, even if I failed to return with you, but..." I made a face. "I don't really believe that she will. So really..."

"You have no choice," Jennifer finished, then shook her head. "That's the sort of behavior that motivated me to leave in the first place. I was sick of her manipulating and hurting people to get her way."

She wasn't making things easy for me, especially as she spoke the truth. "Look, I'm not saying your mother is, or ever will be, Mother Teresa. She is who she is. But the fact is, she maintains order in Blackham. Soon enough, her reach will extend across the world thanks to this new council she's heading up. I really can't think of anyone better suited to the job. Except you."

"What makes you think I'm a leader?" Jennifer asked.

"Because like it or not, you are your mother's daughter, Jennifer. You're a vampire princess, for fuck's sake. You were *born* to lead. Aren't you a leader here in the corporate world?"

"Of sorts. I'm not as ruthless as some. My morals get in the way."

"Yes," I said. "And that's precisely why the New World Order needs you. It needs a moral center, which you can provide."

"*If* I go with you."

"Yes."

Jennifer stared at the city below for quite a long time, as I had all but forced her to consider her options and possibly make a life changing decision. Eventually, she turned her back on the city to lean against the balcony. "I can't believe you're possessed by a demon," she said with a slight look of amusement on her face. "How does that even happen to the great August Creed?"

"It was set in motion a long time ago," I said. "There was nothing I could've done."

"And now?"

"I'm working on it."

She nodded. "Which means working on *me*, right?"

I laughed. "You make it sound so..."

"Manipulative?"

"I was going to say dirty. I didn't come here to manipulate you into anything. If you choose to stay, I'll just find another way to save my ass. I'm usually good at that, if nothing else."

Jennifer smiled. "Like I would ever refuse you help, Creed. I'm coming with you."

I was glad to hear the words come out of her mouth, but all the same, I had to be sure. "I don't want you doing this just because I asked you to. It has to be your decision."

"I owe you a debt that I've never really paid, Creed," she said as she took my hand. "I know you think I don't owe you anything, but I do."

"You really don't—"

In a flash of blinding speed, she put her finger on my lips to stop me from speaking further, and for a second I was reminded of how powerful a vampire Jennifer was. She was powerful enough when I first met her over thirty years ago. Time would only have increased her innate powers, especially as she was a pure blood. *Royal* blood no less. "I've made my decision," she said, an almost playful smile on her crimson lips. "It's time I stopped hiding anyway. It's time I embraced my true destiny."

I gently pulled her hand away. "Which is?"

Her smile widened. "I guess we'll find out, won't we?"

I smiled back. "I guess we will."

Jennifer went to turn away to walk back inside, but the second she did so, blood exploded from her chest as she was knocked back onto the floor.

Before I could even shout her name, a huge force hit me on the back, and I went flying forward, landing on the floor next to Jennifer, who was groaning in pain and shock. At first, I thought Max's spirit had forced its way back into my body. But given the sharpness of the impact, and the fact that Jennifer was lying bleeding on the ground, I quickly came to the conclusion that we had both been shot by a sniper, who was probably perched on one of the buildings across the way. When I realized what had just occurred, I became thankful as fuck that I was wearing my trench coat, which as I mentioned before, is bullet proof thanks to the demon skin the coat is made out of.

Through my own pain and confusion, I saw movement inside the apartment. I counted three people dressed in black tactical gear with masks over their faces. All of them held automatic weapons. "Targets are down!" I heard one of them say.

"What the fuck is this?" I barely had time to say before two of the intruders stood over me, aiming their guns at my head.

"Say goodnight, motherfucker," one of the intruders said.

Then he pulled the trigger.

# 12

# ASTRO CORP

*T*he gun went off, and I braced myself for a bullet to the head which thankfully, didn't come. It did however, strike the ground next to my head, sending sparks and chips of concrete stinging into my face, not to mention the bang of the shot itself, which left my left ear ringing in pain. When the shot rang out, I instinctively closed my eyes. When I opened them again, the shooter was still standing over me, but his guts were spilling out onto the floor right next to me, as if his belly had been slit open by a knife.

Which it had, in a way, because it was Jennifer's razor sharp claws that had slit the man's gut open, and she was now using those same claws, combined with lighting speed and supernatural strength, to decapitate one of the other hitmen. When she swiped at the guy, his head went rolling over the balcony to fall out of sight.

The last remaining intruder had by now raised his gun to fire at Jennifer. As he squeezed off a round of shots, Jennifer moved quicker than any human eye could see, dodging every one of the bullets flying at her. Then, with the same speed, she moved around behind the human, and twisted his head so far around he was almost looking at her when his neck snapped. Jennifer let the body drop to the ground, and at that moment, another sniper bullet slammed her in the chest and sent her staggering back.

All of this played out in a matter of seconds, so I was still lying on the ground at that point, as more sniper bullets zinged above my head. I knew if I didn't do something about the sniper, that I would run the risk of being shot myself, an inconvenience I didn't need.

"Time to give this motherfucker a taste of his own medicine," I said as I crouched on the balcony. "Jennifer? You all right?"

A groan came from Jennifer's mouth that signaled she was in pain. "Fine," she wheezed. "Just two big fucking holes in my chest. Nothing to worry about."

"Glad to hear it."

I stood up to face the buildings across the way. Going by the trajectory of the recent bullets, I figured the shooter was in one of the apartments straight across, though I couldn't see any sign of them, until I saw a muzzle flash coming from the window of one of the top apartments. I already had a magical shield erected in front of me, which stopped the bullet dead in mid-air.

"Let's see how you like this, asshole," I said as I used my magic to send the bullet whizzing back along the exact trajectory it had previously travelled on, and at the same speed. If the sniper was in the same position, the bullet would travel up the barrel of the rifle to give the person a nasty shock.

When the shooting stopped, I became satisfied the shooter had been taken care of. Going to Jennifer, I helped her to her feet. "We should get inside in case there are more snipers out there," I said.

Jennifer nodded as I helped her inside the penthouse, sitting her down on the red leather sofa. "Fucking Astro Corp," she said as she gingerly fingered the holes in her chest.

"Astro Corp?" I said while checking the penthouse for more intruders, and finding none.

"One of the big players. Probably the biggest. As you can tell, they aren't averse to taking people out who are in their way...or those who have crossed them."

I walked back to the sofa. "*Did* you cross them?"

"Yes. It's a long story, so don't ask."

"Looks like I arrived here just in time. Things are dangerous here for you now."

"You could say that."

"We should go now then."

"After I've healed. I need blood first."

"Well," I said. "There are three blood bags out on the balcony. Take your pick."

Jennifer got up and dragged in one of the bodies from the balcony. Then she knelt down beside it and sank her fangs into the neck of the corpse. It didn't take her long to drain the whole thing dry. When she had finished, she took a deep breath and wiped the excess blood from her mouth. "That's better," she said, her fangs still out.

"I forgot how fierce a fighter you are," I said. "You made short work of those guys out there."

"They left me no choice."

"I'm surprised this Astro Corp didn't send a lot more men. Surely they know what you are?"

Jennifer stood up and proceeded to remove her torn and bloody clothes, stripping down to her underwear.

*Yep...she's all woman these days.*

I did the decent thing and turned away.

"I never had you down as the bashful type," she said, a note of amusement in her voice as she headed to the bedroom, presumably to get fresh clothes.

"I'm not. I'm just being a gentleman."

"Not many of those around these days," she shouted out from the bedroom.

"We're a rare breed."

Jennifer reappeared wearing dark jeans and a black leather jacket. "That you are, Creed."

I returned her smile. "You ready to get out of here now?"

"Sure, once I do one last thing."

"What's that?"

"Give someone a message." She walked to the body she had recently drained and unclipped a radio from the dead man's vest.

"You're radioing the people who just tried to kill you?"

She nodded. "Just to let them know their ill-advised assassination attempt didn't work." She clicked a button on the side of the radio. "Come in. Anyone there?"

The only sound that came over the radio was static.

"Maybe they're out," I said, half joking.

Jennifer spoke anyway. "I'm guessing you assholes know who this is. I'm just letting you know that I'm still alive, and all your men are dead. I'll be leaving Babylon soon. Don't try to track me, or you'll be sorry."

She was about to toss the radio when a voice came over the line. "You have something we want," said a male voice that sounded educated and arrogantly well mannered.

Jennifer shook her head at the radio. "I know I do, and you will never get it."

"Don't be so sure," the other voice said. "We have our ways. You know this better than most, Jennifer."

"Yeah, I do," Jennifer said, her voice full of contempt for whoever she was talking to. An Astro Corp executive if I had to guess. "But you should know that I have my ways as well. Don't test me." She tossed the radio on the floor, and looked at me. "Let's go."

"What was that about?" I asked as we headed out the door, Jennifer not looking back even once.

"I have something they want."

"I gathered that. What do you have they want so badly?"

"The most valuable thing to any corporation—information."

"About what?"

"Believe me, Creed," she said. "The less you know the better. The less *anyone* knows the better."

Needless to say, I was immediately intrigued by what she was hiding, but I knew better than to push her on it. Not the right time. Definitely later, though, if there ever was a later.

"Not the right time for what?"

I stopped dead when I heard Max's voice in my head. Then I turned away from Jennifer slightly as I spoke telepathically back to him. "What the fuck, Max? How long have you been—"

"In you? I just got here."

"Why didn't I feel you going in? Jesus, that sounds disgusting. I think I'm going to barf..."

"I thought I would slip in silently," Max said with an exaggerated note of salaciousness in his voice. "You know, like slipping it to the wife when she's sleeping."

"What? That makes no—"

"Creed?" Jennifer said. "What the hell?"

"Sorry," I said to her. "My demon is back."

Jennifer drew her head back slightly as if she was trying to see the demon in me. "So are you going to like, demon out on me now or something?"

"No," I said shaking my head. "It's not like that. I—"

"I can see the resemblance," Max interrupted. "The daughter is delectable as well, but in a different way that I can't quite—"

"Shut up!" I said aloud.

Jennifer flinched and took a step back. "Are you demoning out?"

"No, I told you—"

"I know," Max said. "She has hidden depths. The mother keeps nothing hidden."

"Yes, well observed, Max," I said. "Now will you shut the fuck up for a minute? We need to get out of here."

"I'll teleport us to wherever—"

"No. I got it, Max."

"Fine."

"Can we go now?" Jennifer said.

"Yes," I said.

"Creed," Max said. "Remind me to show you the movie of what I was up to here in Babylon. Let's just say things got a little...*freaky*."

I sighed and shook my head. "Shoot me now," I said aloud, and then teleported us out of there.

# 13

## RAY

*R*ay was in the living room puffing on his pipe with a book in his lap when I arrived back at the Sanctum with Jennifer. "My dear!" Ray said as he put the book he was reading aside, and struggled up out of his chair. "How lovely to see you again."

Jennifer smiled as Ray made his way over and hugged her. "Hello, Ray," Jennifer said. "Long time no see. You haven't changed a bit. Still as handsome as ever."

"Stop," I said. "His ego is big enough."

Ray shook his head at me, before turning his attention back to Jennifer. "My," he said as he seemed to marvel at her in a way that I didn't think was entirely appropriate for a man of his considerable age. "You have grown a good deal since we last met. You look so much like her now."

"By her, I assume you mean my mother?" Jennifer said. "You still sleeping with her, Ray?"

"A gentleman never tells," he said.

"He is," I said, walking away to find the drinks cabinet.

"What's wrong with you?" Ray asked me. "Why are you so grumpy? Is that demon playing you up?"

"I thought I was being a good demon," Max said.

"Keep quiet, Max," I said as I poured myself a large measure of Glenfiddich, which was also Ray's favorite brand of whiskey. Then to Ray, I said, "We ran into some trouble in Babylon. I got shot. Jennifer got shot twice."

"Shot?" Ray said looking at Jennifer. "I didn't think you capable of making such enemies. Who shot you?"

"Corporate shills with no soul," she said. "I got into business with the wrong crowd."

"Unfortunate," Ray said. "But easily done. Do you think you've left your unfortunate business behind now?"

Jennifer puffed her cheeks out as if she was overwhelmed by everything that had happened. There was no doubting that things were moving fast for her. "I'd like to say yes, Ray, but I doubt it."

Ray nodded. "Trouble does have a way of following you wherever you go. Right, August?"

I just shook my head at him. "Sure, Ray."

"My nephew is having his own troubles," Ray said to Jennifer.

"I know, he told me," Jennifer said as she gave me a look of sympathy. "I can't imagine what it must be like to have one of those things inside you."

"Things?" Max blurted within me. "That's rich coming from a bloodsucking vampire!"

"Shut up, Max," I said aloud.

"What?" Jennifer said.

"Ignore him," said Ray. "He's just admonishing his demon. Come and sit down, my dear. August, get the lady a drink. It's terrible that I have to even remind you."

"What's your poison?" I asked her.

"Absinthe would be nice," Jennifer said as she sat down on an ancient looking sofa.

"Interesting choice," Ray said. "Bottom shelf, August. There's a bottle of real absinthe there that I picked up on my travels recently. Not like the piss they sell in most places these days."

I found the bottle Ray was talking about and poured three shots of the bright green Absinthe, just the fumes of which brought tears to my eyes. Then I carried the shot glasses over and gave one each to Jennifer and Ray. Ray raised his glass. "Welcome home, Jennifer," he said with a broad smile. "May things work out for you."

"Let's hope," Jennifer said.

I raised my own glass. "Welcome home, Jennifer. It's good to have you back."

Her dark eyes smiled back at me. "Thank you, Creed. It's actually...good to be back."

As we drank, I hoped she would feel the same way after spending time with her mother in Blackham. Not that that was my biggest concern at that point. I had other things on my mind now, like traveling to the realm where my family was. Or at least their souls.

With the absinthe burning my stomach like liquid fire, Ray sent me to fetch another round. When I returned, he had that look on his bearded face. The one that said he was waiting on me to tell him something. "What?" I said.

"There's something you are not telling me," he said. "I can always tell with you. You're even more standoffish than usual."

A sigh escaped me as I sat down next to Jennifer on the sofa. "I was going to tell you anyway."

"Tell me what?" Ray asked as he began stoking his pipe up again. "Is Leona pregnant?"

I couldn't keep the shock off my face as I nearly choked on my absinthe. "What? No, of course not. Jesus, the thought..."

Jennifer tittered to herself beside me. "You should see your face, Creed."

Shaking my head, I said, "A kid, really? In my line of work? No way."

"You have to think about carrying on the family line sometime," Ray said.

"Why haven't *you* then?" I asked him.

"Who says I haven't?" Ray replied, as he casually lit his pipe.

"What?"

Jennifer laughed this time. "Your face, Creed..."

"You're squirming inside here," Max said. "A strangely pleasant sensation for me..."

"Are you serious?" I asked Ray as I ignored Max.

"No," Ray said smiling. "Maybe. Who knows?"

I shook my head. "I wouldn't put it past you."

"Neither would I," Ray said. "But we're talking about the fruits of *your* loins, August, not mine."

"We're not talking about mine either, for fucks sake," I said. "I think there's too much fucking absinthe going around here."

Again, Jennifer laughed, given credence to my last statement.

"Relax, son," Ray said. "I'm just playing with you. Although it *is* something you should certainly consider in the future."

"Yes," I said. "When I'm done being possessed by a demon, sure I'll give it some thought, Ray."

A chuckle left Ray's mouth. "All right then, son," he said. "Enough talk of procreation. For now."

"For bloody ever," I said.

"What's really going on with you?" he asked.

I hesitated and stared at the floor for a moment. This was something I had been dreading telling Ray about, simply because I knew what he was going to say. "Well," I began. "You remember how I used the Dark Codex to learn how to defeat Grayson?"

Ray nodded warily. "Yes."

"Well, I also used the book to find out where the souls of my family are. Currently, they are in the Realm of the Dead."

"And let me guess, you're going to find them?" Ray shook his head. "Not advisable, August. It's a bad idea to interfere with the souls of the dead. I thought you knew that."

"Why?" Jennifer asked.

"Because, my dear," Ray said. "They are in the Realm of the Dead, which is no place for the living. It is too easy to have one's soul hijacked there. There are many souls who would like nothing better than a second chance at life, even if it is in a different physical body."

"I'm not worried about that," I said. "I'll figure out some protection spells before I go. Plus, my body and soul have already been hijacked. Isn't that right, Max?"

"Indeed they have," Max said. "Aren't you the lucky one?"

"I sure am."

"Yes," Ray said. "Your demon might actually be an asset in this case. It will be like having an attack dog with you."

"So people go to this Realm of the Dead when they die?" Jennifer said. "Then what?"

"Most get taken to the Underworld, or to the Celestial Heavens," Ray explained. "Whichever afterlife they are destined for. Others never leave the Realm of the Dead at all."

"So who decides where a soul gets taken?" Jennifer asked.

"No one is entirely sure," Ray said. "Apparently you just get sent where you need to go. Greater universal forces are at play than mere mortals can understand, even the more knowledgeable amongst us. The multiverse is a vast place, my dear, full of unknown entities who wield unimaginable power. It's like a great machine that operates in the background, keeping things running and sorting out the infinite souls of the beings who inhabit the multiverse at large."

"It's best not to think too hard on it," I said. "If you value your sanity."

"Yes," Ray said nodding. "Plenty have gone mad trying to understand things that are so far beyond their understanding, as to be forever out of reach."

Max sighed inside me. "Stupid humans with your minuscule intellects," he said. "I have no idea where you all get your smugness from. You know nothing, at the end of the day."

"Thanks for pointing that out, Max. Is it hard to breathe all the way up there in your ivory tower?"

"I can breathe just fine, thank you."

I shook my head at Max, then said to Ray, "Look, I just know my family is in the Realm of the Dead somewhere, and that I have to find them. When they appeared to me that time at the factory, I got the sense that something was wrong."

"Good," Max said. "Serves them right for screwing me over."

"Fuck you, Max. You were screwing *them* over, not the other way around."

"That may be true," Ray said. "But I still think you should leave it. It's too risky. You may never return."

"That's a chance I'll have to take," I said. "Trust me, I don't have a choice here."

"What do I always say, son?"

"That there's always a choice."

"That's right. In this case, I don't think you're making the right one."

"Well, that's on me, isn't it?"

"Careful, son. You're beginning to sound like a martyr, and we all know what happens to martyrs. They get crucified."

I couldn't help but laugh. "Sure what's new? At this point, the fucking cross is stuck to my back permanently."

"I could go with you," Jennifer offered.

"Thanks," I said shaking my head. "But no. Like I said, this is on me. I'm not risking anyone else's soul. Besides, you'll have enough on your plate when you get back to Blackham."

"All right," Ray said as he stood up. "If you are going to go on this crazy trip, at least let me give you something that might help. Hold on."

Ray left the room and arrived back a few moments later with something in his hand, which he placed on the table between us. The object was about the size of my hand, and made of metal that appeared intricately engraved with various symbols. In the center was a metal cog, and in the center of that was a dull green gemstone that resembled a skull. An arrow pointed out from underneath the metal cog. "It's a compass," I said. "I already have a similar one. It's for finding people, right?"

"Not people," Ray said. "Souls."

"It's beautiful," Jennifer said.

"The Realm of the Dead is vast," Ray said. "Trying to find a soul in somewhere that size would be like trying to find a needle in a haystack. That's where the compass comes in. All you have to do is focus on the soul you want to locate, and the compass will lead you to them."

I took the compass off the table and held it. It felt surprisingly heavy in my hands. "Thanks, Ray," I said. "I appreciate you giving me this."

"I expect it back," Ray said, his gray eyes focusing on me. "You hear me, son?"

I locked stares with him for a moment, and then nodded. "I hear you."

Ray nodded. "Good."

After a moments silence, I stood up. "We should go now," I said to Jennifer. "Your mother will be waiting."

Jennifer gave a tight smile, but didn't stand. "I'm not sure I can do this now," she said.

"Nonsense, my dear," Ray said. He went over and took hold of her hands, gently pulling her to her feet. "I know for a fact that your mother will welcome you with open arms."

Jennifer nodded in response, but said nothing. She knew she didn't have a choice anyway. If she thought anything like me, she would probably have thought her destiny was just catching up with her. Some things in life you just can't avoid, no matter how far you run, or what you do.

"Teleport us back to Blackham," I said to Max.

"And what if said no?"

"Then you'd be an even bigger dick than I already consider you to be."

Max chuckled. "It's more fun being a dick."

"Whatever. You want your answers, you'll take us back."

I turned to Jennifer. Thanks to her nerves about going home, she now reminded me of the young, vulnerable girl I had saved all those years ago.

"Only to now throw her back in the lions den," Max said smugly.

"You ready?" I said to Jennifer. "My demon hijacker will be teleporting us back."

Jennifer nodded as Ray released her hands. "I'm ready."

Ray patted me on the shoulder. "Good luck, son," he said.

"Thanks, Ray. I'll hopefully see you soon."

As we were about to vanish from the room, Ray said, "And August?"

"Yes?"

"Get rid of that bloody demon."

I couldn't help but smile. "I'm working on it."

14

# THE GROPE

$\mathcal{A}$ s per my instructions, Max teleported us back to Blackham, landing us outside the gray stone fortress that Angela Crow had called home for decades now. It was the middle of the night, and there was no one around but the four guards posted at the entrance to the building. "It's good to be home," I said despite my current circumstances.

"I wish I could say the same," Jennifer said.

I put a hand on her shoulder. "That's just the nerves talking. You'll be fine."

"Will you come in with me?"

"What? I..."

"Please, Creed. I'd feel better if you were there. Just until I see how things go."

"All right," I said. "I'll come in with you. Your mother will probably kick me out again anyway."

"No, she won't," Jennifer said as we walked to the entrance of the building, the four guards already standing to attention as we came toward them. "I won't let her."

I couldn't help but smile. "Is this new no-bullshit attitude a sign of things to come?"

"Well, it won't be like before, I can tell you that much."

"Glad to hear it." It would be interesting to see how Angela responded to sharing power with her daughter. Something told me it wouldn't all be plain sailing.

One of the burly, black suited guards stepped forward from the rest as we approached. I knew his face from my numerous visits over the years, a face that hadn't aged at all since the first time I saw it. He still looked like a lumberjack in a suit, thanks to his thick beard and massive frame. Normally, the guard, whose name is Bradley, would throw me a few hostile words when he saw me. But this time, his focus was completely on Jennifer. It was the first time I had ever seen

686

Bradley's face anything but stoney. He looked like he was going to cry. "Princess Jennifer?" he said in a deep voice. "Is that really you?"

"Hello, Bradley," Jennifer said. "Yes, it's me."

Bradley stepped bent his knee to bow. The other three guards behind him swiftly bent the knee as well. "Welcome home, Princess."

Jennifer seemed uncomfortable as she shifted her gaze away from the guards. She clearly wasn't used to such devoted loyalty after thirty years away. "I'm here to see my mother," she said, after first clearing her throat slightly nervously.

"Yes," Bradley said. "She's expecting you. This way."

I went to walk behind Jennifer, but Bradley stood in my way, projecting his imposing demeanor once more. "Not you, Creed," he growled.

"He's with me," Jennifer said. "Step aside, Bradley."

The vamp held my gaze for a moment as if he was going to refuse Jennifer's order, but then he stood aside.

"Thanks, Bradley," I said cheerfully as I smiled at him.

One of the other guards held the door open for us. When we were in the foyer, Jennifer dismissed Bradley, saying she could take it from here.

"But, Miss—"

"That's an order, Bradley," Jennifer said holding his gaze.

Bradley soon relented, throwing me a dirty look as he went back outside.

"Well," I said. "It didn't take you long to find your authority again."

Jennifer smiled. "Old habits."

We took the elevator up to the penthouse suite and walked down the carpeted hallway to the front door. Or at least, I did. Jennifer stopped a few feet back from the door. "What is it?" I asked turning back.

Jennifer let out a shuttering breath. "I don't know if I can do this." She shook her head as she shifted her weight back and forth.

I went and laid my hands on her shoulders. "I'm here with you," I told her. "You'll be fine. And just to remind you, you're under no obligation here. You can walk away at any time. It's not going to be like before, trust me."

She nodded. "I hope you're right, Creed. If you're not, I'm gone."

Jennifer walked to the carved wooden door and knocked it twice. Her mother would already be alerted to the fact that we had arrived, of course. But it wasn't like Angela was going to be waiting for us by the door like some soccer mom waiting for their kid to come home from summer camp. No, she would be inside, sitting patiently, playing things the only way she knew how, which was cool.

I was about to place a friendly hand on Jennifer's shoulder, but as soon as I raised my arm I lost control of it, and I suddenly felt my hand clamp over one of her sizable breasts instead. Before Jennifer could even register her shock, my other hand grabbed her other breast so that I was now squeezing and kneading both of them at the same time. "Oh shit, I'm—"

My mouth stopped working as I lost control of my entire body.

"Creed!" Jennifer said. "What the hell are you doing?"

"Max!" I shouted telepathically, since I couldn't speak anymore. "What the fuck are *you* doing?"

Max didn't answer me. Instead, he said to Jennifer in my voice, "Your tits are so firm and lovely," as he continued to squeeze them like stress balls. Then to make matters worse, Max pressed his—my!—groin against Jennifer's ass, and started grinding against her. "Oh yeah, that ass is amazing too. Oh yeah..."

The door opened then, and Angela Crow was standing there. Her delight at seeing her daughter again lasted only a second as she took in what was happening.

If I had control of my body, the blood would have drained from my face. Max continued to grind harder against Jennifer's ass, as he kept my hands firmly on her breasts. "I want to fuck your daughter until she squeeeeeals, Angela..."

"Oh fuck," I moaned trapped within myself. "You didn't just say that, you fucking—"

Jennifer twisted and pushed me away, just as Max gave up control of my body. "What is—" Jennifer started to say, but then stopped when she must have realized it wasn't me groping her.

Able to use my arms again, I held them out in front of me. "I'm sorry, that wasn't me, that was the demon..."

Jennifer shook her head. "That was really fucking weird, Creed."

"You're telling me?" I said, a slight laugh escaping me, which I cut short immediately when I remembered Angela was still standing there. "Angela, I'm..." I trailed off when I realized Angela wasn't listening. Her focus was on her daughter, which I guess was a good thing for me.

"Jennifer?" Angela said in just about the tenderest voice I've ever heard her use.

Jennifer turned around to face her. "Mother," she said with much less affection.

Angela continued to look stunned for a moment, before stepping forward and hugging her daughter, gingerly at first, and then tight. Jennifer went slightly stiff as her mother pulled her in, but after a moment she put her arms around her and held on.

At that point, I decided it was time to make my exit. There was no need for me to be there, and besides that, I didn't think Angela wanted me there.

Even so, as I went to walk away, Angela caught my eye and nodded her thanks. I nodded back and started walking down the hallway. "Max, you fucking cunt, what the fuck was that stunt about?"

Max's laughter echoed inside my skull. "Just amusing myself," he said.

"You're lucky Angela didn't eviscerate me on the spot."

"Now *that* would have been funny."

"Yeah," I said. "Fucking hilarious."

15

# SPITTING BLOOD

*B*efore I made arrangements to travel to the Realm of the Dead, I knew I had to see Leona first. I couldn't just bugger off to some place I might never come back from without seeing her. I called her and got her to meet me at a bar downtown that fitted the description of my usual haunts, which is to say the bar—called McGuigans—was dark inside, and full of dodgy looking characters. Leona was already there waiting on me as I walked in. "No funny stuff," I said to Max. "Or I swear I'll banish myself to the Abyss, and you along with me. Even demons don't escape the Abyss."

"You would never," Max said, slightly shocked that I would even suggest such a terrible thing.

"Try me, asshole."

A whiskey awaited me on the table as I sat down, a much needed one, I have to say.

"How was Babylon?" Leona asked. "Did you find who you were looking for?"

"I did," I said as I downed the whiskey in one, and then signaled to a blonde waitress for another.

"That's good. I haven't long finished cleaning up the mess you left behind."

"The mess?" Then it hit me. "Oh yeah, the Beast."

"That fucking thing killed over a dozen people before we could bring it down," Leona said, her blue eyes full of anger.

Max tittered to himself.

"That wasn't me as you know," I said.

She shook her head and turned away as she drank her orange juice.

"Looks like someone is in the bad books," Max said.

"No thanks to you."

The waitress arrived with my drink. When I asked Leona if she wanted another orange juice, she shook her head, and the waitress left.

689

Neither of us spoke for another minute, and I wasn't sure exactly why. Leona looked seriously put out, and I didn't think it was all down to the Beast and the death and destruction it caused. "What's wrong?" I asked her eventually.

When she finally looked at me, her eyes seemed tearful, which wasn't like Leona. She was usually better at keeping her emotions in check. "Am I ever going to see you again, Creed?"

It wasn't a question I was expecting, to tell the truth. "What? Of—"

"Don't say of course, Creed. Just don't."

I frowned at her. "What's wrong, Leona?"

"I think she's sad, Creed," Max said in a ridiculous voice. "Whatever will she do without you?" He laughed then, the bastard.

"I did some research on this Realm of the Dead place you're going to," Leona said. "From what I've read, its a one way trip. Once a soul enters into that realm, they automatically get processed. So your soul could end up in the Underworld as easily as the Celestial Heavens. Or it could get trapped in the Realm of the Dead forever."

Inwardly, I sighed at the fact that, since moving in, Leona now had full access to my libraries. "Technically, that is true," I said, trying not to sound too concerned. "But you're forgetting I'm a wizard. It's my job to find ways around these things."

"And have you?"

"Of course."

Leona's eyes narrowed. "*You* forget I used to be an interrogator. I know when people are lying, and you're lying. You get a twitch around your eyes when you lie."

"Do I?"

"Yes."

I laughed then, trying to lighten the mood. "Look, you need to trust me on this. I'll make it back safely."

Leona sighed and shook her head. "Is it going to be like this for the rest of our lives? Always living on the edge, tempting fate, poking monsters?"

I laughed again. "Poking monsters."

"You know what I mean. Sooner or later, one of us is going to come to a horrible end."

"That never bothered you before, being a soldier and all. Warriors are supposed to accept death as an inevitability."

"I know." She shook her head. "But in the army, I had no emotional ties."

"You didn't have me, you mean?" I said smiling.

"You don't have to be so smug about it, but yeah. Emotional ties complicate things."

"That they do, but the alternative is worse, I think. Going through life with no one. That's no way to live. Don't you agree?"

"I guess."

"You guess?"

"I mean yes, I agree. I'm not as sensitive to these things as you are, Creed."

"You saying I'm a wet blanket?"

She chuckled. "You are."

I shook my head and drew back in mock offense. "It's not a weakness to have a heart, you know."

"I know," she said. "Truth is, I admire the way you handle your feelings. You don't run from them."

"I wouldn't say that."

"You're about to risk your soul just so you can see your family again. How is that running from your feelings?"

"There's more to it than that," I told her, before draining the whiskey left in my glass. "Before, I had a choice. Now, I don't. Not only has my dark passenger put the screws on me, but I also have a feeling my family are in trouble somehow. They need my help. It's the least I can do."

"Their deaths were not your fault," Leona pointed out. "You're under no obligation."

"I know that, but I still feel responsible somehow. Maybe it's just guilt over the fact that I lived and they didn't." I shrugged and shook my head. "Whatever the case, there's no getting out of the situation now, even if I wanted to. Max would only kill me and steal my soul anyway, isn't that right, Max?"

I felt Max take over as he focused on Leona, who drew back away from him when she realized it wasn't me anymore. "You better believe it, baby," he sneered at her.

Leona shook her head in disgust, refusing even to look Max in the eye. "I'm not talking to you, asshole," she said.

Max laughed to himself. "Playing hard to get. I like it." He reached out and tried to stroke her face. Leona's reaction was to grab his wrist and twist hard as she brought her other forearm down on his elbow joint, driving Max's face down onto the table.

"Fuck's sake, Max!" I shouted helplessly from within. "Piss off now!"

Max started laughing. "Oh, the fun we could have," he said to Leona.

"Max, seriously," I said. "She'll break my damn arm."

Max relinquished control then, his presence drawing back as he laughed to himself.

"I'm back, Leona," I said. "You can let go now."

"How do I know it's you?" she asked.

My face was planted flat against the table, making it difficult to speak. "Do I need to bring up the deep sea diving again?"

Leona sniggered, but still kept the lock on for another painful moment before finally letting go. As she did so, the bar owner approached the table. "Everything all right here?" he asked, obviously used to such incidents.

"Fine," I told him as I rubbed my elbow. "Just a misunderstanding."

The bar owner looked at Leona, who nodded at him, which must have been good enough for the bar owner because he walked away.

"That thing better be gone by the time you get back," Leona said, now sitting slightly further away than before. "It fucking creeps me out."

"It creeps *you* out? Try having it inside you."

She shuttered. "No thanks."

"Max and I have an understanding. Once he gets what he wants, he's gone. Right, Max?"

"Oh, of course," Max said within me. "Absolutely."

"I'm not really feeling the trust here, Max."

691

"I don't really care. I'm under no obligation to make you feel safe and secure, Creed. Quite the opposite, in fact."

I sighed. "Are you saying you will renege on our deal?"

"It was never a deal, Creed. It's sweet that you thought that, though."

I noticed Leona staring at me then, a slight look of disdain on her face. "You're talking to it now, aren't you?"

"Just straightening some things out, that's all. It can wait."

Leona drank the rest of her orange juice and set the glass on the table. "I gotta go anyway."

I couldn't hide my disappointment. "You're going? Where?"

"I have two more cases to handle."

"Really? You seem to be getting into the swing of things."

She shrugged. "As long as I stay busy, that's all that matters."

When she stood up, I stood up along with her, moving around the table so I could put my arms around her.

"I'll be back," I told her as I stared into her eyes. "I could never leave you alone."

When we kissed, it felt as if it was the last time we would ever do so. After we'd finished, Leona said, "You better not."

As I went to step away from her, I felt a sudden pain in my belly, as if I'd just been stabbed with a rusty knife. The pain was so intense that I cried out, doubling over as I fell to my knees while clutching my abdomen.

"Creed!" Leona said as she held me up, preventing me from falling onto the floor. "What's wrong?"

"I...don't know," I gasped.

I coughed, and blood sprayed from my mouth onto the floor.

"Jesus!" Leona said.

As the coughing continued, more blood came from my mouth. The pain grew so intense that I thought I was going to die right there.

But a few seconds later, the pain died down to a dull ache, and I finally stopped coughing. "Fuck me," I said wiping my mouth with the back of my hand. "That fucking hurt."

"What did?" Leona asked. "What's wrong, Creed?"

Everyone in the bar was looking over at us, and I held a hand up to them. "It's okay," I said. "Just a coughing fit."

Once I said that, most people went back to what they were doing, no longer interested in the crazy coughing man.

"Are you sick or something, Creed?" Leona asked.

"Not as far as I know."

"Then what? You were coughing up blood, for fuck's sake."

"I think I can answer that," Max piped up within me. "Remember I told you that human bodies struggled to contain my spirit? Well, your body is struggling, Creed."

I shook my head. "It's fucking Max," I told Leona. "He's...slowly killing me."

Leona stood with her hands on her hips and shook her head. "Your situation can't get any worse, can it?"

"It's okay," I said still holding my stomach. "I'll be leaving my body behind when I go to the Realm of the Dead, so Max won't be in it anymore."

"No," Max said. "I'll just be merged with your soul instead." He laughed. "The fun will continue."

Inwardly, I sighed. "I can't wait."

# A LITTLE APPRECIATION

*I* said goodbye to Leona outside the pub as she got into my battered Cadillac. She gave me a final look of plaintive concern before driving off, leaving me to stand on the sidewalk in the cold dark, feeling sorry for myself as Max thought it funny to chide me for being such a soppy bastard when it came to Leona. I can't tell you just how annoying it is to have the voice of another continually chattering and making snide remarks inside your head. It's like a radio you can't turn off. Even when Max wasn't speaking to me directly, he was always making some comment or other about the people I crossed paths with, or the city itself. He even provided running commentaries on the memories he pulled from the depths of my mind, reminding me of those annoying chatterboxes on Youtube who comment on video games as they play them. The bastard never stopped, which I was sure was part of his plan to drive me insane, if my body didn't fall apart under the pressure beforehand that is. I still had the acrid taste of blood in my mouth, and it felt like a mild acid solution was slowly burning its way through the lining of my stomach.

"Shut up, Max," I said wearily as I began to walk down the street. "Just shut up."

Max ignored me as he carried on commenting on a memory I had of my final confrontation with my father. "This is quite the showdown," Max said. "The only thing missing here is the popcorn."

I sighed as I turned the corner and carried on walking down the next street as a light rain began to fall. Pulling the collar of my trench coat tighter around my neck, I shoved my hands into my coat pockets as the rain got heavier. "When it rains it pours," I muttered to myself.

"What?" Max said distractedly. "I didn't hear you there. I'm just at the part where your father throws your dog at you. It's fucking hilarious actually. You take quite the battering, don't you, Creed? But you still keep coming back from it."

"You'd do well to remember that, Max."

"Oh yes? And what do you mean by *that* exactly?"

"You're the one with the supposedly superior intellect. I'm sure you can work it out."

Max laughed. "You humans. So funny."

I shook my head as I turned my attention to my upcoming trip to the Realm of the Dead. As I would have to separate my spirit from my physical body, I would need a safe place in which to leave it while my spirit was in the other realm. There was only one place in the city where I would feel comfortable leaving my body, and that was Sanaka's Sanctum. My mentor would watch over me while I was away, and hopefully be on hand with his skill and expertise if anything happened.

Deciding to walk the couple of miles to Sanaka's Sanctum, I crossed the road and headed towards Little Tokyo. Thanks to the rain that continued to lash down, and the late hour of the night, the streets were almost empty of people. I liked the city when it was quiet like this. It was peaceful, and gave me cause to remind myself how much I loved the place. I couldn't imagine living anywhere else in the world. Especially not Ireland. Just being there brought back a plethora of memories and feelings that I had kept pushed down within myself for years. That, combined with Max's continual rummaging around inside my head, had left me feeling raw and scraped out. I simply wasn't used to being shaken around like a fucking snow globe, as long buried thoughts and feelings swirled around me unabated. Normally, I kept that part of myself locked down tight, and for good reason. The past was the past, and that's where it should stay.

Max sniggered. "Says the man who is about to embark on a journey to find the souls of his long dead family members."

"Fuck you, Max," I said aloud. "If I want your opinion, I'll fucking ask for it. Which I don't."

I stopped dead in the middle of the sidewalk then, which wasn't my doing, but Max's. "You know what?" he said. "I think I'm in the mood for a killing spree. What do you think, Creed? You want to get a little blood on your hands?"

"All right, Max," I said, trapped in my own body once more. "I get it. You're in charge."

Max backed off, giving me back control once more. "Don't interrupt my TV time again."

I started walking. "You interrupted *me*, for fu—just forget it."

Somewhere inside me, Max laughed quietly to himself, causing me to grit my teeth and shake my head as I rounded the next corner. As I did so, a black limousine pulled up on the road alongside me. Even before the darkened window rolled down, I knew who it was. "A word, Creed," the voice of Angela Crow said from inside.

*Great. What the hell is wrong now?*

Sighing, I got inside the limousine, at least glad that I could get a drink while I was in there, which Angela already had waiting for me. She knows me so well. "What's up, Angela?" I asked her as I accepted the whiskey she handed me. "If this is about earlier with Jennifer, I told you—"

"It's not about that, although you are lucky I didn't tear your head off, molesting my daughter like that. It was a disturbing sight."

"I agree, it was. It was also the work of the demon inside me."

695

"Terrific work as well," Max said.

"You need to get rid of that thing."

I refrained from making a duh sound, even though I wanted to. "Yes, I'm working on it. What do you want, Angela? There's somewhere I have to be. More to the point, how did you find me? You always seem to know where I am."

Angela, dressed in a white evening dress, wearing high heel shoes the same shade of red as her lips, smiled. "I think you forget sometimes that I tasted your blood long ago, when we first met. I can find you anytime, Creed."

"That's comforting. Thanks for reminding me."

"I *was* going to contact you directly, psychically, but I thought it better if we speak in person."

I swallowed a mouthful of whiskey and nodded. "Well, I'm glad you didn't. One voice inside my head is enough."

A slight smile appeared on her face. "You will get yourself into these situations, won't you, Creed?"

"I try not to. This one was out of my hands."

She nodded slowly as she continued to smile. There was something different about her. She wasn't normally so avuncular. "The reason I wanted to see you is because I want to thank you properly for bringing Jennifer home to me."

"How is Jennifer?" I asked, curious to know.

Angela hesitated for a second before answering. "She's okay. She's still getting used to being back. Many years have passed."

"And you two? How are you two getting along?"

Again she hesitated, as if she wasn't sure. "Better than I hoped, I suppose. She at least doesn't hate me anymore."

"Well, that's something."

She narrowed one eye at me. "Are you being disingenuous, Creed?"

"Disingenuous?" I shook my head. "No. I'm glad things are working out between you and Jennifer. You know how much I care for her. I want her to be happy, if happiness is at all possible in this world."

"I see you're feeling the pinch," she said. "You've been through the wars lately, Creed."

I snorted. "I'm still in the fucking wars, and about to go into an even bigger one."

"What do you mean?"

I explained to her where I was going and why. "You aren't the only one who misses their family."

"I don't understand what you hope to gain," she said. "Your family is gone, Creed."

I then explained to her the deal I made with Max. "Besides that, I think my family is in trouble. At the very least, I can help them move on to their rightful afterlife."

Angela sat staring at me a moment, then said, "We've had our ups and downs over the years, Creed, but I consider you a friend. You know how many true friends I have?"

I wanted to say none, but I just shook my head.

"Very few."

"Well, thanks Angela. I appreciate that."

"You're a good man, Creed. You deserve some happiness."

"I'll be happy when I help my family move on, and I get rid of you know who."

"Are you talking about me again?" Max said. "I have a name, you know."

*Yeah. Asshole.*

"Is there anything I can do to help you?" Angela said. "Besides keeping you out of jail?"

"Yes, actually," I said. "You can give me a lift to Little Tokyo."

She shook her head. "That's it?"

I fixed my eyes on hers. "Just don't hurt, Jennifer."

She held my stare, and for a moment I thought I had made her angry as her eyes briefly flashed red. Then she turned away and looked straight ahead. "I'll try not to."

# THREE'S A CROWD

t took me a while to find Sanaka when I went inside his Sanctum. At first, I thought he wasn't home, but I soon sensed his strong presence, so I set out to find him. The trouble, as I said before, is that Sanaka's Sanctum is huge inside, containing more rooms than your average municipal building. There are hundreds of them, and probably many more that I don't even know about, so finding Sanaka can be a problem sometimes. Eventually I did find him, though, in the south wing of the Sanctum. Though technically, he wasn't in the Sanctum at all, but in a forest environment that was only accessed via one of the rooms. When you opened the door, you stepped straight into lush forest that had rays of sunlight streaming through the trees, and a babbling brook running through it. Sanaka was sitting crosslegged in the grass, his eyes shut as he seemed to be meditating. I knew better than to disturb him, so I sat with my back against a tree and waited.

"He has quite the abilities, your mentor," Max said. "As humans go, he is one of the most powerful I've come across."

"Is that admiration in your voice, Max?" I asked him as I allowed the sounds of the forest to wash over me.

"Merely an observation. In the grand scheme of things, he is still a pawn in a much larger game. Like you, Creed."

"That's good to know."

I was barely paying attention to Max. My mind was on the upcoming trip to the Realm of the Dead. More specifically, I was wondering how my entry into it was going to work, and whether I would be able to enter the place in my physical body as I did to the Underworld recently. Then it occurred to me to ask Max. No matter how well versed I, or even a master wizard like Sanaka, was in the ways of the multiverse, I could never hope to know as much as a pure supernatural being like Max.

"The answer is yes," Max said, eavesdropping on my thoughts as usual. "You may enter the Realm of the Dead in your physical form, but I wouldn't advise it."

"Why not?" I asked.

"I would see a physical form as a liability. It's a dangerous place. Why take the risk?"

"You're just worried something will happen to me before you get your answers."

"Precisely. Up to you, though. At least if you die, your soul won't have far to travel."

I shook my head. "Hopefully it won't come to that."

When Sanaka finally emerged from his trance-like state, he didn't seem surprised to see me when he opened his eyes. He said nothing as he got gracefully to his feet, and then picked up his sword off the grass.

"Now why would a man like that need to carry a sword in his own Sanctum?" Max asked, his Evil Creed avatar having now appeared next to me, never failing to creep me the fuck out.

"It never leaves his side," I said quietly. "That's just how it is."

"Sort of like how I never leave your side, eh, Creed?"

I nodded and gave a tight smile. "Yeah, sort of like that, Max."

Max laughed, his eyes now on Sanaka as he came towards me.

"You look tired," Sanaka stated bluntly, his eyes dark pools of pure calm.

"Haven't been getting much sleep lately," I said.

Sanaka nodded. "Come. One last tea ceremony before you depart."

Aside from the fact that I didn't even mention why I was there, his choice of words disturbed me a little. One last tea ceremony, as if I would never get the chance to do another.

I fucking hoped otherwise.

* * *

When I served the tea, I sat down across the low table from Sanaka. Max sat to the left side of me, also in a kneeling position. Taking the piss, the cunt.

"Where's mine?" he asked.

I was about to answer in the normal telepathic manner when Sanaka did something I didn't expect. He turned his head slowly, and looked Max right in the eyes. Then he said, "Tea is reserved for the pure of heart, not for demons."

My eyes widened, as did Max's.

"Did he just speak to me?" Max asked. "I think he did."

"You can see him?" I said to Sanaka.

Sanaka looked at me and nodded. "Yes."

I shook my head. "How? I thought only I..."

Sanaka gave the merest of smiles and said nothing.

"I told you this motherfucker was powerful, didn't I?" Max said, his disturbingly wild eyes now on Sanaka. "I knew I shouldn't underestimate you, old man. My instincts were right. I'm surprised you haven't tried to banish me yet."

"And let you kill my student in the process?" Sanaka said.

I was a little miffed by him calling me his student, even though I should've been used to his bluntness after twenty years. "Did you cast a spell?" I asked him.

Sanaka sipped from his tea cup before placing it carefully on the table. Then he nodded. "An All Seeing Spell," he said.

"Of course," I said. "I should've known you would. If nothing else, Max here cuts a dashing figure, right?" I chuckled at my lame attempt at a joke.

Sanaka didn't crack a smile, but Max did. "Very good, Creed," he said laughing. "Lucky for me your mentor here didn't pass on his sense of humor along with his sorcery skills, or I would've lost out on such wit."

"Yeah?" I said. "Well, lucky for me I got possessed by such a snarky mother-fucker, because that's just what I needed. A demon to take the piss out of me all day long."

Max laughed and looked at Sanaka. "We're like characters out one of those buddy movies you humans seem to like so much, aren't we? Like *Lethal Weapon* or *Tango and Cash*."

"Really, Max?" I said shaking my head.

"Sorry," Max said. "My references probably aren't up to date. I haven't been here in a while."

"No shit."

"Maybe we could hit the cinema when we get back, eh, Creed. There's this—"

Sanaka's fist slammed onto the wooden table. I all but jumped, and Max snapped his head around. "Enough!" Sanaka said in a gruff voice.

A tense silence ensued that lasted about ten seconds, before Max cut in. "He looks calm, but he has a lot of rage in him, your mentor, doesn't he?"

I puffed my cheeks out, shaking my head as I sheepishly looked at Sanaka. "This is the kind of crap I have to put up with all day. Just banish him. I don't care if it kills me."

"Do not tempt me," Sanaka said, his normal composure now frayed around the edges slightly. Such was the effect Max had on people, when he wasn't senselessly killing them, that is.

"All right," I said as I got to my feet. "I think it's time for me to go."

Sanaka nodded and stood up. "I have already prepared a room for your body to stay in while you are gone," Sanaka said.

I followed him out of the room and down the hallway to another room that had a magic circle drawn on the floor. "I thought just being in the Sanctum would be secure enough," I said. "You didn't have to go to all this trouble."

"The circle and the spells I've cast will help me recover your soul quickly should you need to get back here in a hurry," Sanaka said. "Also, one can never be too careful."

"Agreed. But how will you know if I'm trouble or not?"

"I will be able to monitor the state of your soul from here. If I feel any signs of extreme distress, I will try to pull you back here as quickly as possible."

"Extreme distress?" I couldn't help snorting at that. "Something tells me that extreme distress will be my normal state once I get to this place. You know how these missions go. Especially with a demon traveling with me."

"I will use my judgement," Sanaka said.

I nodded. "Okay. I trust you."

Sanaka gestured towards the magic circle. "Lie down in the circle."

I did as he asked, and lay back on the wooden floor with my feet inside the circle. All I had to do now was cast a Disembodiment Spell to detach my soul from my body. Then I could leave the Earthly Plane altogether.

"Thanks," I said as Sanaka stood over me. "I know you and Ray think I'm crazy for doing this."

"You do what you must," Sanaka said.

"Wise words," Max said. "Wise words."

*Shut up, Max.*

"And one more thing?" I said to Sanaka. "Could you keep an eye on Leona while I'm gone? She can handle herself, but just the same, I'd feel better if..."

"I will watch over her," Sanaka said.

"Thanks."

Our eyes made contact for a short moment. I couldn't be sure, but I thought I saw a hint of worry in my mentor's eyes.

I didn't know whether to be flattered by that, or bloody scared.

In the end, I chose scared.

18

JOURNEY TO THE REALM OF
THE DEAD

*I*n terms of esoteric lore, what I did when I left my physical body was astral project. My soul, or intermediate body, separated itself from my physical body so I could travel through matter and the Earthly Plane, until I reached the Astral Plane. Generally, when a soul departs the Earthly Plane because the physical body has died, that soul will travel automatically to the River of Souls, located in the Astral Plane. From there, the soul will travel down the river to the Realm of the Dead, where they will await processing. Obviously, I did not want to join the myriad other souls floating down the river, so I had to make my own way to the Realm of the Dead.

I was already familiar with the Astral Plane, having travelled there on a number of occasions for various reasons. I even have a Sanctum in the Astral Plane, a place where I mainly go to practice casting some of the more dangerous spells in my repertoire, so I could do so without the negative consequences that might arise if I did the casting on the Earthly Plane. I have a pretty good handle on my magic abilities these days, so I rarely visit the Astral Sanctum anymore. Besides which, the Astral Plane itself can be a dangerous place. There are plenty of predators roaming around the ether looking for stray souls, or souls who deviated for whatever reason from the entrenched pathways. Souls like my own.

"Don't forget me. I'm still here." Max's disembodied voice still echoed inside my head, though it sounded more distant and discombobulated than it did before, almost like he was speaking to me from underwater. It was weird, to say the least.

"How could I forget?" I as I traveled through the misty ether, well aware of the shadowy shapes that often passed me by, some of which were massive. Most of these shapes were creatures who live in the Astral Plane. They may once have started life as something else, human for example, until they ended up trapped, or just unwilling to go anywhere else. Eventually, the ether changes these souls into creatures who hunt other souls. If one of these things eats your soul, that's you gone forever, and there is no shitting you back out. Given how easy it is to get lost in the Astral Plane, travelers often fall prey to these creatures as they try to find there way in the ether. The winds are strong and constant in the Astral Plane, making you feel like a ship lost at sea sometimes, all the while blowing you toward some astral monstrosity just waiting for its next meal. It also doesn't help that it is so hard to navigate in the Astral Plane, as it is nothing but ether with pockets of land that float around the place like something from a Dali painting.

It was because of these navigational dangers that I cast a Mapping Spell, which manifested a thin silver thread that trailed off in front of me into the distance. All I had to do was keep following the silver thread and it would eventually lead me to the Realm of the Dead. Lucky for me, magic didn't stop working just because you had no physical body anymore. If anything, my magic felt stronger without the confines of the physical body to hinder its flow.

Although of course, there was still Max. That motherfucker would hinder anybodies flow.

"Well, this is pleasant," Max said as I continued to follow the thread. "A nice stroll through the Astral Plane. You do seem to get around a lot for a human, Creed, I'll give you that."

"You seem to get around yourself a lot," I said. "For a demon."

"Yes, well, we all need a break, don't we?"

I snorted at that. "That just doesn't sound right coming from a demon. Tell me, Max, where do you come from? What darkness where you born in?"

"You couldn't fathom the place of my birth. It's a place of pure darkness that no human mind could conceive of."

"Try me."

"Unlike most demons," Max said, "I was never something else. Many demons were human once, or some other benevolent creature before the darkness corrupted their souls, turning them into conduits for evil."

"Is that what you are, Max? A conduit for evil?"

"I am a conduit for the Great Darkness. The Great Darkness knows no right or wrong. It just is. That's what many of you humans fail to understand. There is no stopping evil, because it is a part of the very fabric of the multiverse. It's a form of energy as pure as that of the energy of creation."

"Sounds like you're a slave to it."

Max went silent for a moment, just as a large dark shape passed silently overhead, although that wasn't why he went silent. "I am as much a slave to my nature as you are, Creed," he said eventually. "That's why I can't understand your constant condemnation of me. I'm just being what I was created to be."

"An evil annoying bastard, you mean?"

"You're lucky I don't have feelings, Creed, or I might just take offense to that."

"And no sense of humor either."

"I dispute that one."

"Really? I've yet to come across a demon who does stand-up."

"Ha ha. Your own sense of humor leaves a lot to be desired."

"So I've been told...on numerous occasions."

"Anyway," Max said. "The point is, my motives are pure, even if, as a human, you choose to label them as *evil*. That doesn't change what I am."

"You ever think about trying something else? Like *not* being evil for a change? Maybe just going against your nature a bit, to see what happens?"

"No. Have you?"

I thought about that for a second. "Not really."

"Then why would you expect me to?"

I had no answer to that.

Max gave an exaggerated sigh. "You humans," he said. "Such hypocrites at times, expecting the forces of the multiverse to bend unyieldingly to your will, when you yourselves refuse to budge on anything."

"Most of us do our best," I said. "We are who we are."

"My point exactly! And besides, I think I've been more than accommodating with you, have I not, Creed?"

"If you call using my body to kill all those people accommodating, then yeah, you've been very helpful."

"Sarcasm aside, I think you know I speak the truth. I could make things a lot worse for you, Creed. A *lot* worse. As it is, I'm helping you locate your long lost loved ones. How much more accommodating could I be?"

"Well, you could stop possessing me, and take yourself back to the Underworld. That would help."

"Eh, no. Not going to happen."

"Worth a try."

"You'll see, Creed, that my presence in you will be a good thing. You'll be stronger when I leave...if I don't kill you first."

"Kill me? I thought we were over that."

"I do what my nature demands of me," he said. "But I am also fair. If I think you deserve to live, I will let you live, assuming your body doesn't fall apart under the strain of having me."

"I'm not *in* my body, strictly speaking, remember?"

"Oh, right, you don't know do you?"

"Know what?" I asked, just as another shadowy shape passed underneath me. It was starting to feel like I was being hunted.

"Part of my essence remains in your physical body back on the Earthly Plane," he said. "Which means your physical body will continue to deteriorate, albeit at a slightly slower rate."

I shook my head. "That's just great."

"I suggest keeping our little trip short...if you want a body to go back to."

I screamed in frustration into the ether. I couldn't help it. Being constantly bent over a barrel was taking its toll on my mental state. Although in hindsight, giving away my location to astral predators probably wasn't the smartest move in the book. Within moments of my scream, I saw a large, dark shape coming up towards me out of the depths like a Great White shark. In an effort to avoid the monster coming at me, I sped up my travel, but the thing coming at me kept getting closer. Then it disappeared, and for a moment, I thought it had gone. *Thank Christ for that*, I thought.

Until the astral monster burst out of the ether right in front of me. A high pitched squealing noise came out of its huge maw as it came barreling towards me like a giant squid. It even looked like a squid with its thick tentacles and large flashing eyes. As the creature lunged at me, I managed to bank to the left just in time to avoid the huge mouth that snapped at me.

"It's a feisty one!" Max said with way too much glee in his voice.

"You do realize if I get eaten by that thing, so do you," I shot back as I looked around for the creature, which seemed to have disappeared again.

Max laughed. "A crude creature like that could never hope to consume me. I'd destroy it from the inside out. Besides, the only soul here is yours, Creed. I'm just a spirit."

"Oh, well that's all right then. Maybe you—"

I stopped mid-sentence when I caught sight of the murky black entity coming at me from the left side. This time I was ready for the creature, having already primed my magic in preparation for an offensive attack. As the creature came squealing toward me, I thrust my hand out and blasted the ugly bastard with a sphere of magical energy that put a hole right through it. Something that was half way between a squeal and a howl came from the creatures twisted mouth, and it sank down into the ether like a sinking ship, its black eyes glowering at me as it did so. A second later, the injured creature was set upon by the other predators in the area, as they proceeded to devour it in a frenzied attack that brought more horrible squeals to my ears.

"Nicely done, Creed," Max said. "We sure showed that thing who was boss."

To be honest, I was surprised at the strength of my magic. I'd forgotten how amplified magic could get in the Astral Plane. I hovered in the ether for a moment, waiting to see if the creature would attack again, but there was no sign of it. Hopefully it got the message that I wasn't to be fucked with.

I wish I could've said the same for the dozen or so other astral predators that seemed to be swarming around me now. The noise of the previous creature must've attracted them all. "Shit!" I said, feeling like a lonely herring surrounded by hungry Barracudas.

"I suggest fleeing," Max said, sounding completely unconcerned.

"For once, Max, I have to agree with you."

Trying to take on so many predators at once would have been folly. Even if I did manage to fight them all, my magic reserves would be severely drained. As I would probably need all of my magic in the Realm of the Dead, I decided to do the only sensible thing, which was run. Or rather, barrel off through the ether as fast as I could, still following the silver thread that stretched out before me.

Several squeals and roars sounded behind me as the predators realized I was making a run for it, almost like they enjoyed the excitement of the chase.

My astral form was rocketing through the ether as fast as any bird of prey on the Earthly Plane, but the creatures were keeping up, a few of them managing to come alongside and below me. If one of the grotesquely formed creatures got too close for comfort, I would send a blast of magic at them, which seemed to be enough to keep them at a safe distance.

Until, that is, I felt a pressure around my leg that stopped me in mid-flight. I turned to see a thick, dark tentacle wrapped around my left ankle, and the creature it belonged to hanging in the ether not far behind it. Without thinking, I conjured a Flaming Sword in my hand—a sword of pure magical energy that burned a magenta color—and used it to slice through the tentacle holding my leg. The severed appendage dropped out of sight into the ether, the creature it belonged to now mad as hell as it came rushing at me. I waited until the attacking creature was just a few feet away, before quickly moving out of its path and swinging the Flaming Sword, which cut the creature clean in half.

No sooner had I done this when two more of the astral vermin attacked at the same time. I used the sword to cut the head from one of the creatures. The other I stabbed in the abdomen before slicing it in half.

My defensive actions had made the other stalking creatures wary about approaching now, but they still hung around nearby, their dark shapes passing through the ether like moving shadows. It wouldn't be long before instinct got the better of them and they started attacking again.

Using my small window of opportunity, I began to follow the silver thread once more, this time keeping the sword in my hand in case I was attacked again. When I turned to look, I saw the creatures were still following, but they were keeping their distance. For now at least.

"Impressive skills," Max said. "I think they got the message not to fuck with you."

"No thanks to you," I said. "Feel free to help out sometime. You know...with all that power you keep harping on about. So far, the only power I've seen is the power to sit on the sidelines and not shut up."

Max didn't seem offended at all. "But, Creed," he said. "It is much more fun watching how *you* handle these situations."

"And if I die? What will you do then? How will you get your answers?"

"I'd get them myself, of course."

"From my family?" I snorted. "They'd never tell you anything."

"They told me lots during their stay with me. Talked a lot about you, Creed."

I didn't take the bait. "For all their talking, you still didn't know they planned on making their escape, did you? Which means they kept it from you. Which means they only told you what they wanted you to hear. Which also means, they will tell you nothing about how they escaped if they don't want to. They might even use such information to their advantage somehow. But *me*, they'd tell me everything..."

"Yes, yes. You've made your point, Creed. You can shut up now."

I couldn't help a slight smile of victory appearing on my face. A smile which got wider when I suddenly noticed a huge, swirling vortex of deep red energy up ahead. The silver thread was leading right toward it. I hovered in the ether for a moment as I stared in wonder at the gigantic portal up ahead, and at the flood of souls that went from the river below, and into the vortex. Countless balls of light being drawn into the mass of swirling energy like migratory eels, all heading for the Realm of the Dead for processing.

"Looks like we're here," Max said.

The astral predators were still lurking behind me, so I didn't hang around. Following the silver thread, I headed straight for the portal...and the Realm of the Dead.

19

· · · · · · · · · · · · · · · · · · · · · · · · · · · · · · · · · ·

# THE GRAY LANDS

*W*hen I went through the portal, I fully expected to be greeted by hundreds of congregated souls from the sheer number pouring through. But that wasn't the case. Instead, as I stood on the barren earth in the Realm of the Dead, I watched the torrent of souls come through the portal, and immediately take flight into the gray sky. I assumed the souls were being pulled elsewhere for processing, perhaps to set them up in some mysterious way for their stay here. The processes of the afterlife were all new to me, so I wasn't too sure what was going on. It was eery, though, watching all those spheres of brilliant light take to the skies.

"It's something, isn't it?" Max said as I continued to watch the light show. "All those souls...they are making me hungry."

"Try and restrain yourself," I said. "We're not here so you can load up on souls."

"You needn't worry. The powers that be in the multiverse have seen fit to forbid me from taking any soul from the Realm of the Dead. I may only take *living* souls."

I turned away from the flood of souls pouring through the blazing red portal, and focused my attention on my immediate surroundings. It appeared I was standing in a desert of sorts, that stretched as far as my eyes could see. Not that I could see that far, because the mist surrounding everything made it hard to see more than several feet ahead. As I began to walk across the hard, slightly damp earth, I wondered where all the souls were. If this was the Realm of the Dead, then surely it should have been packed with the souls of people? Not only could I see no one, I could also hear nothing that suggested people might be anywhere near. In fact, I heard nothing at all; there was nothing but the eery silence. "Well," I said half to myself as I made my way through the mist. "This is creepy."

"It's the Realm of the Dead," Max responded. "What did you expect, a theme park?"

I shook my head at his sarcasm. "I expected *something*. Not nothing at all."

The Realm of the Dead is also known as the Gray Lands, if I didn't mention it before. I was starting to understand why. I'd never seen a drearier place in my life.

I stopped then and took the Soul Finder Ray had given me out of my pocket. It appeared that everything was now a solid form since entering the Gray Lands. I no longer had a translucent astral body, but a solid one, as if I was back on Earth. With all my knowledge of things magical and esoteric, it still amazes me how the universe works, and how the entire physics of a world can be completely different to another. I don't think any one person is meant to know or understand everything, though. For all my questing after knowledge, I know my limits (most of the time anyway). Gordon Grayson didn't know his limits when he sought after the Dark Codex, and look what happened to him. So if things in the multiverse want to change from one place to the next, that's fine by me. I don't need to know the ins and outs of everything.

"That's very philosophical of you, Creed," Max said. "I'm sure the powers that be in the multiverse appreciate your understanding."

I sighed and shook my head as I looked at the Soul Finder in my hand. "Are you always listening to my thoughts? Doesn't it get tedious? *Boring?*"

"No, not really," Max said. "My mind does not work the way yours does, Creed, or like any other human. It is true, you beings are tedious bastards most of the time, repeating the same thought patterns over and over until you die, but..."

"But what? You get some sort of twisted enjoyment from people's abject misery and lack of understanding, as we flounder like dying fish on the ocean bed called Earth?"

"That's actually not far wrong, and quite poetically put, Creed. Anyone would think you were learned hearing that. You left out one thing, though."

"Oh yeah? What's that?"

"The fact that I am a balancing force in the multiverse."

"A balancing force? Sounds pretentious."

"I don't care how it sounds to your sensitive ears, it is nonetheless true. Without beings like me—"

"Evil fuckers, you mean?"

"Call us what you will—demons, monsters, Titans...evil fuckers. We are all the same. We are all born of the great multiverse, and brought forth for a reason."

"To provide balance." I shook my head. "Because the world just has so much good in it, that it needs parasites like you to keep it in line. Right. Okay."

"Is that how you think of me, as a parasite?"

"Don't go getting offended now, Max. In spite of your pretentious reasoning for your existence, you *are* a parasite at the end of the day...currently feeding off me."

Max went silent, and for a dreaded moment, I thought he was going to retaliate by causing me horrible pain, or taking over my body again, neither of which I wanted to happen. But I wasn't going to listen to his bullshit and not counter it with the truth. I may have been under attack by a demon, but I still had my dignity and integrity, neither of which I was prepared to give up just because some demon liked hearing the sound of his own voice...or rather my voice.

"Think of me however you like," Max said eventually. "Your words mean nothing to me anyway."

"I don't know, Max," I said with some glee that I didn't even try to hide from him. "It sure sounds like they do mean something. Maybe all this time around humans is beginning to...rub off on you."

"Nonsense."

I couldn't help but smile. "Your affected tone says it all."

Inside, I could practically feel him seething. "I'm warning you, Creed—"

"Okay, stop right there, Max. Can we just quit the bickering for a minute so I can figure out where we have to go from here? That way, everyone gets what they want sooner rather than later. Is that all right with you, or do you want to waste more time with your petty tortures?"

"Fine," Max said like a scolded child, just as a stabbing pain in my stomach that lasted a splitsecond caused me to double over. "Just remember who is in charge here."

"Jesus, was that really necessary? Are you that fucking insecure that you have to hurt me every time you want to make a point?"

"Pain is a great motivator. I've learned that about humans."

I sighed. "Put it in your definitive guide to humanity then. In the meantime, I'll just wait for the Soul Finder to get its bearings, and then we'll be off...somewhere. Into the fucking mist that is everywhere."

Max backed off for the time being, while I stared down at the Soul Finder, which was part mechanical and part magical. I was beginning to wonder if perhaps the realm we were in was interfering with the device in some way, or maybe interfering with the flow of magic in general. To test my theory, I tried to form a sphere of energy in my other hand. The energy appeared as expected, but it looked weak, and not as vibrant with color as it should've been. Which told me that magic worked in the Realm of the Dead, but the magic itself was only half strength at most. This worried me for a moment, but then I decided there wasn't much I could do about it. Hopefully, I wouldn't need to use much magic anyway, if at all.

Time would tell, as it always does.

In the meantime, the arrow on the Soul Finder began to move gently around, before settling down as it pointed in a northerly direction while glowing light blue. "I guess we go this way," I said as I began to walk in the direction the arrow was pointing.

As I walked across the desolate earth, a strange feeling stirred in my belly that had nothing to do with Max being inside me, and everything to do with the fact that I was finally on my way to see my beloved family.

\* \* \*

I WALKED FOR HOURS THROUGH THE GRAY MIST AS THE SOUL FINDER POINTED the way. Despite the device, more than once I wondered if I was heading in the right direction, because in all that time, I came across absolutely nothing in the way of life—no people, no organic lifeforms, unless you included a few dead trees, and certainly no buildings or dwellings of any kind. The place was dead as dead can be. "I know this is the Realm of the Dead," I muttered. "But this is ridiculous. There's fucking nothing here."

"Patience, Creed," Max said annoyingly. "I think you forget how big this realm is. There are vast stretches of desert here that are vast beyond comprehension. It leaves room for expansion, I suppose. Humans keep dying, after all."

"Like your recent victims, Max. Maybe you'll—"

I stopped suddenly as I noticed something rising out of the mist not too far ahead. From this distance, it appeared to be a huge block of shadow, but as I started walking again, drawing closer to the change in scenery, I saw that it was in fact a building up ahead. *Finally*, I thought as I quickened my pace.

The building itself was huge, and constructed from gray stone blocks. It also wasn't the only building. There were more, each one uniform in its dimensions, being rectangular and stretching high into the sky, like the skyscrapers back on Earth. I could also hear sounds for the first time, which cut through the heavy silence I had grown used to. The sounds of people.

Excitement and apprehension grew in me in equal measure as I walked quickly towards the buildings up ahead.

"Looks like we've arrived at the Gray City," Max said, sounding intrigued. "It seems very...gray."

"Is that supposed to be a joke?" I said.

"Not really. Just alluding to the fact that everything is so very...gray here."

"I'm sure your domain in the Underworld is a fucking rainbow delight."

"Not exactly, though it isn't...*gray*. There's lots of red where I come from."

"Sounds awesome."

"Better than this faded memory of a place."

The Soul Finder was still pointing north as I made my way into the Gray City, which didn't appear to have any set boundaries, and seemed like it was in a constant state of expansion as it spread into the desert. I even saw the first signs of people as I stepped onto a road that seemed to grow out of the desert itself. People were coming and going in and out of the buildings nearest to me, some of them rushing off deeper into the city. Anyone who noticed me gave me a strange look, and it didn't take me long to figure out why. So far, every person I had seen looked the same, in that they were gray in appearance, as if all the color in them had faded over time, or as if they had stepped out of an old black and white photograph. I, on the other hand, had retained my normal colors, and while not exactly vibrant, I still stood out against the grayness of everything else.

"So much for keeping a low profile," I said as I caught the stares of more people.

"Not being truly dead has afforded you a bit of color," Max said. "You'll be like a beacon walking around here."

I sighed. "Fuck it. What's the worst that can happen? I mean—"

That's as far as I got before I got jumped and thrown to the ground.

# SHADES OF GRAY

*W*hoever jumped me was now wrestling me onto my back after shoving a few unwelcome knuckle sandwiches into my face. Before I knew it, my assailant was straddling me, their considerable weight on my chest making it hard for me to breathe. When I finally got the chance to look up and see my attacker, I saw the gray figure of a middle-aged man dressed in a blood stained suit. His eyes were intensely focused on me, almost like he was looking right through me.

"What is this?" I asked with hardly enough air to finish the sentence. "What... are you doing?"

"Silence!" the man growled, more than a hint of excitement in his wild eyes for some reason. "I can't believe I've found one...after all this time..."

"What are—" A slap to the face shut me up.

"You're a living soul! I can use you to get back!"

My suited assailant planted one hand on my forehead, as he seemed to recite some sort of spell. Whatever magic he was using, I felt it invade my body, creating a highly unpleasant sensation that was reminiscent of the time when Max first possessed me.

And then it hit me what my assailant was doing.

The fucker was trying to possess me so he could use my body—my body in this realm anyway—as his ticket back to Earth. He was no doubt intent on stealing my actual physical body when he got there.

The whole thing was happening so fast, and my magic was so slow to respond, that he may just have succeeded in his bid to use me as his way out of the Gray Lands.

Except he wasn't counting on one thing.

Max.

"Sorry," Max said to my assailant as the man's gray form began to push its way inside me. "But you are trying to fuck with forces your puny brain could never hope to understand, and indeed you will feel those very forces as they fuck you up in just a moment. But in the meantime...fuck off!"

With a burst of sudden energy that blasted its way out of my body, Max used his power to throw the man off me. It was like my assailant (more like fucking rapist!) had just received a massive electric shock that propelled him several feet into the mist, before he landed with a heavy thump on the ground.

Immediately, I sat up and rubbed at my chest. "Glad to see someone's power is working fine," I said.

"It seems to be," Max said before I felt him take over my body and jump to his feet. "And I know one gray bastard that is about be on the wrong end of it."

Max used my body to stomp to where my assailant now lay moaning on the hard earth. The bloodstains on the man's suit looked fresh, or at least I thought so. It was hard to tell when everything was so damn gray. "Please don't," the man said looking up, probably seeing the hatred and anger Max had written all over his—*my*—face. "I just wanted to go home..."

"You want to go home?" Max chided. "I can certainly help you out with that."

The man frowned. "You can?"

"Of course! Now hold still, won't you?"

"What are you going to do?"

"Just this."

Max brought his boot down on the man's head, stamping his skull into the ground.

"For fuck's sake, Max!" I protested powerlessly. "Stop!"

One of the man's eye sockets was now crushed, and dark blood was oozing from it. Aside from the lack of color, the blood was as real as any back on Earth. If I didn't feel so disgusted, I may have wondered why the man was bleeding at all, or why he was afraid of dying when he was already dead. As it happened, the dude answered at least one of those queries. "Please," he spluttered. "If you...kill me...I'll have to start all over again..."

Even Max was intrigued now. "Start what all over again?" he asked.

The man shook his head like we didn't understand. "This..."

Max frowned for a second, then shook his own head. "Sorry, I don't know what you mean. Come to think of it, I don't care either..."

Max's boot came down on the man's head once more. Then again. And again. And again. Soon he was stamping nothing but bloody mush.

"Stop!" I shouted. "Fucking stop!"

Max stopped after one final stamp. "There," he said. "He won't be jumping any more unwary strangers, will he?" He took a deep breath and smiled. "That sure felt good. I was getting pent up in there. Now I feel better."

"Was there any fucking need for that?" I demanded to know.

"Of course there was. The man was a parasite. He needed stamping out." He laughed then. "Stamping out...you get it, Creed?"

"Fucking hilarious, Max. Now give me back my body so I can do what I came here to do."

"Fine." He gave me back control then. "I'll be here to save you again when you need me to, don't worry."

"I won't," I said as I wiped my boot along the ground to try and remove the clumps of skull and brains stuck there.

"We'll see, won't we?" Max said smugly.

As I started walking again, I realized I didn't have the Soul Finder. "Shit," I said. The device must have fallen once I got jumped. I looked around for the next few minutes, peering through the mist as I scanned the ground for the device, finally finding it safe and sound. But when I went to pick it up, a voice made me stop dead.

"You won't last another hour here," the female voice said in an English accent.

I slowly straightened up and put the Soul Finder in my coat pocket for safe keeping, before turning my attention to the newcomer. "Who are you?" I asked her.

The woman was as gray as everything else. Her dark hair spilled down over the long cloak she was wearing. I saw no obvious signs of injury, so I couldn't say how she died and ended up here. "Someone who can help."

I hadn't been in the place for long, but long enough to know that I should be suspicious of everyone. "Why would you help me? I suppose you're after my body as well?"

She shook her head. "You have a choice. Stay out here on your own so someone else can jump you, or come with me now before more Soul Jackers arrive."

"Soul Jackers?"

"You just met one...before you crushed his skull."

I looked away for a second. "That wasn't me..." I muttered.

"It sure looked like you."

"It's complicated."

Through the mist, distant voices carried, heading our way. "You coming or not?" the woman asked.

"I don't trust her," Max said.

"You don't trust anybody, Max," I said telepathically before addressing the woman again. "What's your name?"

The woman hesitated a second before answering. "Moira."

I walked toward her. So far, the woman seemed genuine. She also had a point about me hanging around in full technicolor for all to see. It was clear that I would have to cover myself up somehow if I was going to survive this place. It also occurred to me that Moira had probably been a Gray Land's resident for a while now, and that she may be able to help me navigate the place. The realm was obviously more perilous than I first thought. "The name's Creed. Lead the way."

Moira nodded, her face pretty even rendered in gray tones. "Follow me."

She proceeded to lead me further into the city through a series of back alleys, before going inside one of the gray stone buildings. To be on the safe side, I took out my gun, Moira raising her eyebrows at me when I did. "Just being cautious," I told her.

She nodded. "That's a good policy in this place."

The inside of the building was like any other you would expect to find on the Earthly Plane, though it appeared abandoned, and eerily quiet. "What is this place?"

"Just a derelict building," Moira said. "A good place to hide out."

"From what?"

She glanced at me over her shoulder as she led me down into the basement. "Lots of things."

I shook my head. The Gray Lands were seeming more perilous by the minute.

"Shoot her if she tries anything," Max said. "Or I'll rip her apart myself."

"I don't think it will come to that, Max," I said.

"This might be trap."

"Maybe, or it might be a much needed safe haven for me to get my bearings."

On the way down to the basement, Moira unhooked an oil lamp from the wall and lit it with a match. Using the dimmed light to find her way, she led me further into the basement, before stopping in a large opening, a place she obviously called home judging by the mattress on the floor and the canned food scattered around.

"You live here?" I asked her.

"It's safer than up there."

"Safer? What kind of realm *is* this place?"

"Probably not what you think," Moira said as she sat down on an old wooden crate and removed her cloak. I was surprised to see two short swords criss-crossed on her back, and a small crossbow clipped to her belt.

"You run into trouble often here?" I asked her as I looked around the room, wondering why she would be living in a disused basement.

"A bit, yeah." She narrowed her eyes at me then. "What are you doing here? Are you another traveler? Travelers don't last long here."

"I'm here on business, actually."

She frowned and shook her head as if that didn't compute. "What business could you possibly have in the Gray Lands?"

"You ask a lot of questions," I said, grabbing a crate and sitting opposite her.

"I just like to know who I'm dealing with."

I nodded. "Fair enough."

"Tell her nothing," Max said. "The bitch will likely betray you."

"She seems okay," I said to him. "At least she's helping me."

"Bringing you to a darkened basement, probably so her compatriots can come along and jack your soul."

"You have serious trust issues," I told him. "I'll be on my guard though, if it makes you happy."

"Just don't blame me when things go tits up."

"Things have already gone tits up. We're here, aren't we?"

"So why would you risk your soul to come here?" Moira pressed.

"My family members are trapped here. I think anyway."

"And you've come to save them?"

"That's the plan."

Moira snorted and shook her head. "You have no idea of the kind of place you just walked into."

"I'm hoping you'll tell me. Is it even possible for souls to get trapped here?"

"Of course. Some don't seem to move on, like me. Others..."

"Others what?"

"Others get held prisoner." She looked away then, as if she knew someone in that very predicament.

I frowned. "Held prisoner? By whom?"

"Someone you don't want to mess with if you value your soul."

"This person sounds dangerous."

"He is."

"He?"

Moira sighed. "You ask a lot of questions yourself."

"It's in my nature," I said smiling.

A slight smile appeared on her face as well for the first time. "Mine too. I was a detective before...I died, and ended up here."

"Were you any good?" I knew she would have been. She looked the dogged and determined type, and as gray as her eyes were, I could see the experience in them.

"I was," she said.

"What happened?"

"How did I die, you mean?"

I nodded.

"Heart attack. You believe that? Thirty-eight years old, and I die of a fucking heart attack. Stress of the job, I guess."

"I'm sorry."

"So am I. I've been stuck in this miserable realm ever since."

"How long?"

"How long have I been here?" She shook her head as if she didn't know exactly. "At this point, it feels like years. There's no time here, so it's hard to keep track."

"Any idea why you're being kept on hold?"

"No idea. Maybe there's no room left in Hell."

"I suspect you'll go in the opposite direction."

She threw me a look. "How would you know? You don't know what I've done."

I shrugged. "Maybe not. We've all done things, though."

"Yeah. Maybe I would've been more careful if I'd known this afterlife shit was real. I mean, you'd think we would've been *informed* of the afterlife's existence on Earth. It would have made things easier."

"I doubt it," I said. "We are who we are. Some things are destined."

"Like you?"

"I don't follow."

"Well, you've landed here, in my lap, so to speak."

"And?"

"Maybe you can help me."

"Help you do what? I can't exactly speed up your processing."

"I don't mean that."

"What then?"

"Here it comes, Creed," Max said. "She's going to ask you to risk your soul to save hers. I can see it written all over her miserable ashen face."

Moira tilted her head forward slightly to stare intently at me. "If I help you with your business here—and you *will* need my help—you give me a lift back to Earth."

"Told you!" Max said. "Fuck her...fuck you bitch!"

"Jesus, calm down, Max. She does have a point. I need her knowledge of this place."

"She'll screw you, Creed," Max said. "She *will* do it!"

"Sounds like you're the one with the problem, Max. Pipe down in there, will you?"

"Fine. Don't come running when she jack's your soul."

"How can I give you a lift back to Earth?" I said to Moira. "I don't think that's possible."

Her gray eyes lit up for a second. "It is with magic."

"Magic? You're an adept?"

She shook her head. "You can get whatever magic you need here...for the right price."

"So if that's the case, why don't people here use magic to escape?"

"Because it can't be done apparently. The only way out of here is in the body of a still living soul."

"Of which I am one."

"Yes. That makes you as valuable as anything here."

"Tell her this seat is already occupied," Max said. "There's no room at the inn... no seats on the bus...no—"

"Yes, all right!" I said. "I get it, Max."

"Are you all right?" Moira asked. "You seem...tense."

I smiled at her. "I'm interested in taking your deal, but there's something you should know first."

"What's that?"

"Me, bitch!" Max shouted, nearly fucking deafening me from within, to the point that I flinched. "That's what!"

I wanted to scream out loud for Max to shut the fuck up, but I managed to keep my cool as I said to Moira, "I'm eh...possessed...by a demon."

Moira frowned as if she didn't know what to make of that. "Okay..."

"Yeah, I know it's weird," I said. "But it's true. If you were to somehow hitch a lift with me, so to speak, you'd be sharing my body, or astral body, or whatever form this is...with a demon...and I don't think he's up for sharing."

"Hell no!" Max stated.

"I see," Moira said as she considered this.

"I would fear for your immortal soul," I said.

"And quite right, too," Max said.

"Shut it, Max," I said. "You're being an asshole. I'm not sure we'll be able to navigate this place safely without Moira here, and if we can't do that, neither of us will get what we want..."

"You don't need this grayed-out floozy," Max retorted. "I will make sure you come to no harm until this is done."

"Really?" I said. "You think I didn't notice the reduction in your power when you used it earlier? You're hobbled here as much as I am. Clearly spells, and not innate magic, rule the roost in this place."

"I have plenty of power left, believe me..."

"No, you don't. I would feel it if you did, and I don't feel it anymore." I looked at Moira, who was now staring at me weirdly, like everyone else when they found out for the first time that I was possessed by a demon. "Face it, Max. We need her."

Max sighed. It was the first time I'd ever heard him do it. "Fine, but I'm fucking her up if she tries anything...anything at all."

"Jeez, Max...anyone would think you were starting to care about me. Maybe you've been in there too long..."

He made a spluttering sound. "Nonsense. I care for nothing and no one."

"Keep telling yourself that."

Moira made a coughing sound to get my attention. "You look like you are in silent conversation with yourself," she said. "It's...kinda creepy, actually."

I smiled at her. "You should try being on *this* side of things. It's *really* creepy over here..."

Moira chuckled, and then smiled back. "So do we have a deal...Creed?"

There was nothing more to consider as far as I was concerned. "Yes," I said nodding. "We have a deal. Now maybe you can tell me where a man can get a drink around here..."

# CLOAK AND DAGGER

"*There's* no fucking whiskey in this place? At all?"

I sat staring at Moira as she smiled back at me. "Sorry to disappoint you," she said. "There's no food or drink of any kind in this hell hole. The souls of the dead have no need for snacks or tasty beverages, I'm afraid, so..."

"There's no whiskey."

Moira snorted and shook her head. "I know, right? Considering how grim this place is, you would have thought there'd be a bar at least."

"Fuck that. I might have to go home again."

Moira laughed out loud this time. "You might have to."

I sighed. "I can wait."

"When I first got here, all I thought about was coffee. It was all I wanted. Ridiculous, right?"

"Not really," I said shaking my head. "These are the things that make life bearable, after all."

"Bearable, yeah..." Moira looked down and shook her head, the image of sadness in her gray state.

"So what do people do here to pass the time?" I asked her. "At least tell me there's some good drugs going around?"

She looked up and smiled. "Not drugs exactly...magic."

"Magic?"

"There are spells that can...take you away somewhere else."

"On a trip you mean?"

"Something like that. The trips are quite real. Vivid. It can get addictive." She looked away for a second, as if in shame. I let it slide.

"So who comes up with these spells?"

"Most of them come from LeBron. He basically runs this city, through his minions."

"Who is he?"

Moira sighed as if she didn't want to talk about it. "Not someone you want to mess with, that's for sure. He has a way of making people...disappear. Don't ask me how. People are kidnapped and never seen again."

"Sounds sinister."

"It is. There's talk that LeBron runs an energy bank inside his mountain lair, which is apparently where he keeps people locked up."

My curiosity peaked upon hearing that. *Maybe that's where my family is?* I thought. "What do you mean by energy bank?"

Moira took her two short swords from the scabbards on her back and placed the swords on the floor, stretching her back as she did so. "Energy is currency around here. It's about the only thing people have to trade, so most trade theirs for spells. This place is junky central."

"Are you talking about soul energy?"

She nodded. "What else? That's all anyone is here, just a soul manifested in partial physical form."

"Surely it would be detrimental to give away the energy of your soul?"

"Of course it is. You'll see when you venture outside. Half the souls here have faded away to nothing because they've traded away so much of their energy."

"Let me guess," I said. "LeBron acts like a pusher, and get's people addicted to the trips."

"I saw it all before as a cop," Moira said. "It's no different here."

"So what does this LeBron get out of it? What does he do with all the energy he takes?"

Moira shook her head. "No one knows. No one has even seen LeBron, as far as I know, not even the people who do his bidding apparently. He lives inside Crystal Mountain, on the outskirts of the city."

"Crystal Mountain? Sounds like something from a fantasy novel."

"I suppose you could say it is. It's a huge mountain that is partially formed out of crystallized energy, which LeBron has fashioned into a fortress of sorts. As far as anyone knows, he never leaves the place."

"Yet he still manages to dominate the Gray Lands."

"Yes," Moira said. "He has plenty of souls working for him. You work for LeBron, you get all the trips you can handle. That's the word on the street anyway."

I nodded. "There's always a tyrant, isn't there? Everywhere you go."

"The nothingness I expected would have been better than this."

"Who's to say you won't move on to somewhere better?"

"I'd be there by now if I was, and anyway, I'm just as likely to end up somewhere worse as better. You hear so many horror stories going around this place about the Underworld and the horrible demons..."

"Why is it always the horrible demons?" Max protested within me. "Humans are more wretched than demons are, and that's a fact."

"You've upset the demon," I said to Moira.

She looked like she didn't know what to say to that for a moment. "What is that like?"

"Great," I said with sarcastic cheer. "We have fun all day long, Max and I."

"Really?" Moira said looking unsure.

I snorted and shook my head. "Of course not, it's a fucking nightmare."

"Once again, Creed, I am offended—"

"Whatever, Max."

"What?" Moira said.

"Oh, did I say that out loud?" I said. "I'm sorry. Sometimes I forget..."

"Why do you call it Max?"

"He named himself that."

"Weird."

"You have no idea..."

The conversation lulled at that point, and we sat in silence for a few minutes while I considered this LeBron character. By the sound of things, all trouble in the Gray Lands linked back to him, which must mean that if my family are in trouble, then LeBron must have something to do with it. Quite possibly, he might be holding my family in his mountain lair. I would soon find out anyway, once the Soul Finder took me to their location.

Speaking of Soul Finders, I showed the device to Moira, and explained to her that we wouldn't have to turn the city upside down looking for my family. The device would take us straight to them.

"That's good," she said as she handled the device for a moment, before handing it back to me. "This is a big place. You may never have found your family if you had go out there blind. I could've used a device like that when I was a cop. All this magic stuff could've been helpful, but instead it was kept from people, except those in the know."

"Not anymore," I said. "Things have changed back on Earth. The supernatural is out in the open now, including magic. It remains to be seen what kind of world we end up with because of it."

"You mean everyone knows about magic and...everything else now? Wow..." She shook her head. "That will make things interesting for my return."

Moira seemed to be pinning all her hopes on getting out of the Gray Lands and back to Earth. I felt like mentioning that these situations often don't work out the way we want them to, but I said nothing because I didn't want to dash whatever hope she had. Although I was curious about one thing. "Say you make it back to Earth. You realize you'll be just a spirit on the Earthly Plane."

She nodded. "I'm aware of that."

"You're happy to live as a ghost?"

"It has to be better than staying here."

I thought for a moment, then said, "There are ways, you know..."

"Ways?"

"Ways to not be a ghost."

"What do you mean?"

I was hesitant about saying anything, but I knew of a way to possibly solve her problem if she made it back to Earth. "There's a way around it, if you don't mind living in the body of someone else, that is."

"Possession, you mean?"

Max laughed. "Taking a leaf out of the old demon playbook, Creed? I must be rubbing off on you."

"Sort of," I said to Moira. "You inhabit the body of a dead person."

Moira nodded. "So I'd be walking around in a corpse? I don't think that would be very...pleasant, do you?"

"No, it wouldn't be like that. Your life force would reanimate whatever body you'd be in. You'd be very much alive."

Tears suddenly filled Moira's gray eyes. "I would get another chance..."

"Yes, but let's not get ahead of ourselves," I said. "There's a lot to do before that can happen."

She wiped her hand across her cheeks. "Well, then," she said standing, grabbing her two swords from off the floor. "Let's not waste anymore time, then, eh?"

I nodded, glad to have someone who knew the local terrain on my side. I just hoped nothing happened to her because of me. My past history didn't exactly fill me with confidence in this regard. Anyway, the deal was her idea. She made her own choices. "Right on," I smiled. "Once we get outside, I can use the Soul Finder to direct us, though I have a feeling I know where it's going to lead us."

"Crystal Mountain?"

"Right on again."

* * *

ONCE WE GOT OUTSIDE, THE SOUL FINDER INDICATED THAT WE SHOULD HEAD in a northerly direction, which happened to be right through the center of the Gray City. Before I left Moira's basement hideout, she tossed me an old gray cloak and told me to put it on. "You need to cover up the fact that you are a living soul," she said. "You'll attract less attention wearing the cloak."

So now I was walking alongside Moira through the winding streets of the city, which were alive with grayed out people, most of whom seemed to shuffle along with the gait of someone who had lost their purpose in life. The need now was for escapism from the grim reality of their situation, rather than the need to prove themselves in some way. One thing I did notice, was the shady characters who seemed to populate every back alley and street corner, reminding me of drug pushers from Earth. Indeed, after several surreptitious glances in their direction, I managed to catch sight of what they were pushing—small glass vials filled with a glowing substance, the color of which seemed to vary depending on which pusher was selling. In return, the ghostly customers would hand over a vial containing a bright white substance.

"Are those people buying the magic you talked about?" I asked Moira.

"Yes," Moira said, her hood covering most of her face. "Most here have learned how to siphon the energy of their own souls, cutting out the need to go to any energy bank. It saves time, and they can buy their trips quicker."

I noticed many of the customers who bought the trips were almost completely transparent, as if they were fading into nothing. "It's like they are trying to destroy themselves one trip at a time," I said. "Some of them barely have any energy left to maintain their form."

"That should tell you how fucking grim this place really is." Moira shook her head at the ghostly figures gathered around the pusher. "It's a slow suicide."

"And the people selling the trips, they work for LeBron?"

"Yes, they are LeBron's slave monkeys, no better than the poor souls they sell to. They're only doing it for the free trips."

721

Many of the buyers didn't even wait until they were alone to take their trip. Most of them shuffled off and bedded in somewhere on the street nearby. Everywhere you looked, there were people lying around, their eyes closed, their jaws hanging slack as whatever magic they took transported them away to some other reality. That's all anyone seemed to do. The trip business seemed to be the only business in town. "What's inside all these buildings?" I asked Moira as we walked down a wide street flanked with grand stone buildings, the Soul Finder still leading us north.

"More escapism," Moira said, a slight note of disgust in her voice. "Anything recreational from back on Earth you can think off: cinemas, strip clubs, casinos, gyms...even fucking shopping malls."

I snorted. "Shopping malls? Really?"

"They're like virtual shopping malls. None of the stuff you buy is real. This whole place, in fact, is just one big virtual reality simulator, a way to pass the time until you continue on your way."

"Or not."

"Or not," Moira said plaintively. "Some things are real here, though. The cloak you're wearing, the weapons I have...other things. LeBron started introducing real world items into the simulation. I think he wants to make this world as real as Earth eventually. Lately, I've even seen cars driving across the desert."

"LeBron seems to have a real grip on this place," I said. "How the hell is he getting away with it, though? I mean, surely the powers that be in the multiverse wouldn't tolerate a mere human corrupting a realm like this?"

"Sounds like a conspiracy afoot," Max said. "I actually quite like it here. It's full of hopelessness, which is my kind of place. Anyone would think we were in the Underworld."

"I'm glad you're enjoying yourself."

I became wracked with sudden pain at that moment, which sent me to my knees, and forced a scream out of my mouth as I clutched my stomach.

"Creed!" Moira said grabbing onto me to stop me from falling. "Are you all right?"

"No..." I said through clenched teeth. "Max...stop it..."

"I'm afraid it's not me this time," Max said. "Or rather, it is me, but it's not intentional. My presence in your physical body back on Earth continues to corrode you from within. You are just feeling the effects here."

"Feels like...acid...burning through me..."

"Yes," Max said. "I hear it's quite painful. It should pass, though."

"Comforting..."

"Creed!" Moira said. "You need to get up. You're attracting attention."

I was able to turn my head to see what she was talking about. Two grayed-out young thugs were watching me intently from the doorway of a building. After a moment, they started walking in my direction. Something glinted in the hand of the biggest pusher, and I realized it was a knife. After spitting a mouthful of blood out onto the ground, I hauled myself back to my feet.

"You there!" the pusher with the knife said in what sounded like a Russian accent. "Don't move!"

Rather than let my would-be assailant get any closer, I decided to take preemptive action, and hit him with a magic blast to buy some time so we could make a run for it. But when I went to conjure the energy in my hand, only the weakest of spheres materialized. "*Shit...*" I said.

"Your power is getting weaker, Creed," Max said.

"Yeah, no thanks to you."

"I'll handle this," Moira said as she reached behind her for her swords.

The two pushers stopped a few feet away, the bigger one now pointing his knife in my direction. "You can't hide under that hood," he said. "I see what you are..."

At that point, several other of LeBron's men came out of the mist in various places. We were now completely surrounded.

*Fuck it*, I thought. *There's no way I'm getting soul jacked or killed by a bunch of grayed-out thugs. My magic may not work, but my pistol certainly does work.*

As the knife wielder advanced toward me, I reached under my cloak and pulled out my pistol, aiming it at the guy's head. "Not another step," I told him.

The thugs were all impressed by the fact that I had a gun, it seemed.

"You shouldn't have done that," Moira said, her swords now out as she kept looking around her. "They'll kill you just for the gun."

"Not if I kill them first..."

I shot the thug in the head, the one holding the knife. Fuck it. He was dead anyway, so what did it matter? I was done pissing about.

The fact that one of their own had just been shot didn't seem to deter the others any, because they all kept moving forward. There was maybe a dozen of them now, most of them holding knives.

"I hope you can fight," Moira said as she readied her swords.

"I may not need to," I said, watching as the chaos bullet I put into the thug started to take effect.

"What?"

"Get ready to run."

I wasn't sure how great an effect the magic in the chaos bullet would have, given that magic itself wasn't as strong in the Gray Lands as it was on Earth. But it didn't have to be that strong. Just enough to create an opening would do, an opening we would need, because the pushers had increased in number, with more emerging from the mist all the time. I even felt one of them attempt a bitchcraft move from afar, using a spell of some kind to try and suck out my soul energy.

"Allow me," Max said as I went to prepare a counter to the spell. Max took control of my body for a moment, and then used his own power to send a blast of dark red energy at the pusher engaged in the bitchcraft, sending the guy flying back into the mist. "That one was on the house."

The magic in the chaos bullet was taking full effect now, as bolts of blue magical energy began to shoot from the body of the pusher. The blue bolts shot out in all directions, hitting several of the surrounding thugs. I couldn't help but smile. Chaos bullets never get old.

At that point, maybe in a panic at all the magic flying around, the rest of the thugs attacked en masse. Moira didn't wait for them to get any closer. With a loud shout, she sprang forth with her swords, swinging them at the thugs with impressive speed and skill, cutting down at least two of LeBron's men in her initial attack.

I still had my pistol in my hand, so I thought, *Might as well...*

The thug closest to me got a bullet in the chest as he tried to attack me. Then the next closest one got a bullet in the throat. The chaos magic in the first bullet exploded the body of the guy I shot in the chest, spraying blood and gore everywhere. The guy who got shot in the throat was lying on the ground clutching his neck as blood erupted from his mouth. Within seconds, he appeared to be completely consumed by blue magic that swirled around him, before lifting him to his feet and spinning him around at great speed, until all you could see was a whirling blue dervish. This mass of magic began to dart around the place in all directions, spinning like a tornado, sending bodies flying as it crashed into them, knocking them down like skittles.

*Awesome*, I thought.

"Creed!" Moira shouted. "Let's get out of here!"

For a second, I thought about trying to teleport us out, but then thought better of it when I remembered my magic levels were low, so I opted to make my escape the old fashioned way. I sprinted off into the mist, following behind Moira as she took us through a series of back alleys, until we reached an abandoned looking street with only a few trippers lying around. Then we stopped to catch our breath.

I couldn't help smiling as endorphins rushed around my body. "Well, that was fun," I said.

Moira shook her head. "I'm glad you think so. That could have gone so much differently..."

"Yeah, but it didn't, did it?" I still had my pistol in my hand, I noticed, so I put it back in its holster.

"That's an interesting gun you have."

"Not the gun, so much as the bullets. Infused with chaos magic, as you no doubt saw."

"Now why didn't I have one of those when I was a cop?"

"Because you didn't know about magic then."

"I do now, that's for sure."

I reached into my pocket and took the Soul Finder out. "It's telling us to go west."

"West?" Moira said.

"Yeah. Is that a problem?"

"Only if you consider LeBron a problem. Crystal Mountain is the only thing that lies west."

I nodded, unsurprised. "Well, then," I said. "Let's go pay LeBron a visit, shall we?"

## 2 2

# CRYSTAL MOUNTAIN

*I* don't know why, but for some reason I thought it wouldn't take us that long to get to Crystal Mountain, especially when we left the city and headed across the wastelands. After a while though, I soon realized that LeBron's lair was quite a distance away.

"I've never been to the mountain," Moira said, a little defensively, I thought, as we made our way across the mist shrouded wasteland. "Why would I go there?"

"I just assumed..."

"I just know it lies west. That's it."

"Well," I said. "It's lucky I have the Soul Finder, otherwise how the hell could you navigate through all this fucking mist?"

"I guess you wouldn't. It's not unheard of for people to get lost out in these wastelands. Don't be surprised if we cross paths with some of them."

The depressing grimness of the Gray Lands, like many of the other off-world places I'd travelled to, made me appreciate just how good I had things on Earth. I couldn't wait to get back there and see Leona, at which point I would take her to the little cabin I owned in the woods, and we would hide away in there for a few days while fucking our brains out and taking long walks through the forest in between. That was the dream anyway.

"Hmm, sounds good," Max said. "Except the walking part. Did I mention I hate walking?"

"You hate everything," I said.

"Not everything..."

"Oh yeah, I forgot about the torturing of humans."

"My favorite pastime."

"So if you hate walking so much, can't you teleport us to where we need to go?"

"Sorry," Max said. "Not enough power here to take both of you."

"Or maybe you're just conserving yours for things to come."

"What things?"

"You think LeBron is just going to allow us entry into his mountain lair? You think he won't try to jack my soul, or lock Moira and I up so he can drain us of our soul energy, or whatever the fuck he does? You'd be trapped along with me."

"Perhaps, but it would just be a temporary state. I'd find a way out. This land is no place for a demon, after all."

Moira gave me a look. "You having one of your silent conversations with your demon again?" she asked.

"Just trying to formulate a plan, for when we get to the mountain. Any ideas?"

Puffing her cheeks out, Moira shook her head. "As I said, I've never actually been to the mountain, so I'll be going in as blind as you are."

"Okay, so as a cop, how would you approach this?"

"I'd have a SWAT team on site ready to storm the place."

I nodded. "Of course you would. But since we don't have a SWAT team on hand, and no back up at all..."

"Don't forget me," Max said.

"I refuse to rely on you for anything. Stay out of this."

"Cranky..."

"Then I guess we play it by ear," Moira said.

I couldn't help laughing. "Funny you should say that."

"Why?"

"Playing it by ear is my usual plan of attack."

"Oh yeah? And how does that usually work out for you?"

It was my turn to puff my cheeks out. "It varies."

Moira nodded as she smiled. "Comforting..."

"If my girlfriend were here, she would probably come up with a decent plan of attack."

"Your girlfriend?" Moira seemed slightly put out by my mentioning this, perhaps because she was trapped in a grim existence with no one to comfort her.

"Yeah," I said. "She's a super soldier...and sexy as fuck."

Moira shook her head. "I'm sure being sexy really helps when you're shooting people."

"Of course it does. It helps me."

Laughing, Moira said, "Seriously..."

"Did you have someone back when...you know..."

"When I was still alive?"

"Yeah."

"No, not really. I was married to my job."

"Is that something you regret?"

She threw me a look. "What do you think?"

I nodded. "I know what's it's like. I'm lucky I have someone who understands."

"Yes, you are."

I put a friendly hand on her shoulder. "Hey, if we make it out of this place, you can start again. Rectify all those past mistakes."

"Or make them all over again."

I couldn't help but smile at the truth of her words. "Hopefully not."

\* \* \*

THE MOUNTAIN WAS A LOT FURTHER AWAY THAN EITHER OF US INITIALLY thought. It felt like we had been walking across the gray featureless landscape for days, and more than once I wondered if the Soul Finder was faulty in some way. Moira, however, assured me that we were going in the right direction. "How do you know?" I asked her. "You said you'd never been out here before."

Moira sighed. "I may have lied about that."

I frowned. "What do you mean? Why would you lie?"

"Because," she said shaking her head. "I may have worked for LeBron at one time."

"Ha!" cried Max suddenly. "I told you, Creed, didn't I? She's a lying, untrust-worthy bitch!"

I stopped to stare at her. "Doing what? Pushing trips?"

She nodded. "Yes, I'm ashamed to say. It was just something I fell into, because...I guess I didn't know what else to do, or..." She trailed off as she looked away.

I said nothing for a moment, and then continued to walk. "No need to explain. I get it. But why lie about it?"

"Because it isn't something I'm proud of, and I thought if you knew, that you would think I was playing you somehow."

"Are you?"

"Of course not."

I nodded. "Then we don't have a problem. Although, there is one thing I'd like to know."

"What's that?"

"Given the distance Crystal Mountain obviously is from the city, how the hell do LeBron's people get back and forth? Are you seriously saying you walked every time?"

"No. LeBron installed a teleportation pod in the city. That's how his people get back and forth."

"You might have mentioned this before," I said. "We could've used it instead of traveling by foot."

Moira shook her head. "It's guarded all the time, and anyone who arrives at Crystal Mountain is greeted by guards. We would've been caught straight away."

"LeBron has guards? How many?"

"Enough."

"Have you ever seen him? LeBron, that is."

"A few times. He locks himself away, so he's rarely seen by anyone, except for those who do his bidding."

"Okay. So you know how to get into his lair?"

"There's only one main entrance. It's not going to be easy."

"It never is," I said. "We'll figure something out."

"Are you pissed at me for lying?"

I shrugged. "No. Your knowledge of the place will work in our favor."

We carried on walking through the thickening mist in silence for another while, before Moira started asking me questions about my family. "Who are they to you?" she asked.

"My mother, brother, and sister," I told her.

"What happened to them?"

"They died." We both laughed despite ourselves. "I mean, of course they did."

"So what do you plan on doing once we get to Crystal Mountain? Are you going to try and break them out, assuming they're in there?"

"That would be a start, yes."

"Then what?"

I didn't answer at first, because I wasn't sure myself. In the back of my mind, I had the notion that I would take all three of them back to Earth with me somehow, so they could start again the way Moira planned to. "I'm not sure. I guess that's up to them."

"You miss your family." It was more of a statement than a question.

I nodded. "Of course I do. Don't you have family who died?"

"I had a son. He was twelve years old when..." She trailed off, the emotion too much for her.

"I'm sorry," I said. "What happened?"

Moira let out a long breath, as if answering was going to be hard. "I was working on a case, trying to catch a serial killer who was terrorizing Manchester at the time. The killer used to contact me a lot. It was like a sick game to him. He thought we had some sort of connection. You know how these sick fucks think."

I did. All too well. "So what happened?"

"Well, in an effort to catch the bastard, I went on live TV and tried to draw him out by undermining him, saying he was just a sad loser who would soon be caught, and that he would rot in prison for the rest of his natural life. It seemed like a good idea at the time, and we were desperate for a break in the case, so we figured we had nothing to lose. Except...I did." She paused for a moment as if to contain her emotions. "It's entirely my fault. I should've had round the clock protection on my house. The nanny was killed, my son was taken. We never recovered his body until we caught his killer. I had to watch as they dug my son up from a boggy field. His little body..." She squeezed her eyes shut, like the memory was still fresh in her mind.

I put a hand on her shoulder. "It's all right," I said. "You don't have to go on."

She nodded and wiped her palm across her face. "Before you ask, I've looked for him here. I can only hope my son has moved on somewhere better."

"I'm sure he has."

After that exchange, neither of us felt like speaking again, until we noticed the mist beginning to clear somewhat. Which I thought was unusual, until I realized that the infamous Crystal Mountain was looming up ahead like a giant fortress. It was odd seeing a single mountain in the otherwise featureless landscape, as if the massive clump of rock had been dropped there from another realm. The huge crystal formations that jutted out from the rock, as if they had at one time rained down it, ensured the mountain earned its name. "Inside Crystal Mountain," I said. "Where evil takes its form..."

"What?" Moira asked, still slightly broody after talking about her dead son.

I shook my head. "Nothing. Just a song I heard once."

"There's a song about Crystal Mountain?"

"Yes, but not this one."

"It's an impressive structure," Max said. "It reminds me of the citadels in the Underworld."

"I'm sure you feel right at home," I said.

"Never mind that," Max said. "How are we getting inside?"

From what I could see, the only entrance was a huge double door set into the front of the mountain. "I guess we go in the front door," I said, more to Moira. "Unless you know another way in?"

Moira shook her head. "That's the only way in or out as far as I know. But we would never get in without being seen."

"Lots of people must come and go here," I said. "Couldn't we pretend to be pushers and just walk in?"

"You'll be seized the minute they clock your face. So will I."

"I have an idea," Max piped up within me.

At that point, I was open to all options. "Go on," I said cautiously.

"We simply knock on the door."

I immediately shook my head. "That's your big plan? Knock on the fucking door? That would never..."

"What would never?" Moira asked. "You have a plan?"

I didn't realize I was speaking aloud. "Max has a plan. Apparently we just knock on the front door like cub scouts selling cookies."

"Jesus," Moira said shaking her head. "This was pointless. I should never have brought you here. It was a bad idea..."

"Hey, don't worry about it," I said. "We'll figure something out."

"My plan is a good one," Max said. "And the only one you have, I might add."

I said nothing as I stared at the door in the distance.

"Eh, Creed?" Moira said.

"I'm thinking..."

"No, Creed, you better look..."

"At what?" I said, annoyed at her for breaking my concentration. But as I took my focus off the door and placed it on my immediate surroundings, I soon saw what she was talking about.

Dark figures in the mist surrounding us. At least a dozen.

*Shit.*

"Maybe you won't have to knock after all," Max said. "Maybe they'll march you straight in."

One of the figures stepped out of the mist behind us to reveal themselves. It was a woman, and she held what looked to be a machete in her hand. "Are you two lost?" she asked in an Australian accent.

"Shit," Moira said as if she recognized the woman.

"No," I replied immediately, seeing an opportunity. "We want to work for LeBron."

The woman laughed as she came closer. She would have been pretty if she wasn't so gray...and didn't have a gaping wound running down her face, as if she had been sliced with a knife only minutes ago. "Oh, really? And why would a living soul want to work for LeBron?"

*Crap.*

"And you, Moira..." The woman laughed. "Yeah, I know it's you. We've been tracking you two since you left the city."

I sighed and shook my head. How the hell did I not realize we were being followed this whole time?

"It's the mist," Max said. "It seems to have a way of cancelling everything out, magic especially."

"We didn't come here looking for trouble, Charlotte," Moira said as she took her hood down.

"Is that right, Moira?" Charlotte said. "I seem to remember you causing a lot of trouble last time you were here, what with killing all those people because you thought you were too good for this place."

"They shouldn't have tried to stop me leaving," Moira said.

"Well, no one will try to stop you this time," Charlotte said. "Because this time you won't get the chance to leave. LeBron will make sure of that." She shifted her gaze to me. "And as for you, Mr. Technicolor, LeBron has plans for you..."

The way she said it, it was like LeBron knew all about me. Given the Gray Lands were his domain, it wouldn't have surprised me if he had clocked my presence the second I came through the portal. Something I should've considered at the time, but didn't.

"All right," I said taking off my cloak and letting it drop to the ground, hearing the gasps of the gray souls surrounding me as they looked on with envy. Even Charlotte's eyes widened as she gazed upon me as a potential ticket back to the living. "We'll come quietly. Just take us in."

"Bad idea, Creed," Moira whispered.

"Let's hope not," I said.

## 23

# BACK TO SQUARE ONE

*T*he huge double doors set into the front of the mountain were opened, and the massive weight of them creaked as two men pushed from the inside. As I walked through the doors with Charlotte prodding me with the tip of her machete, I couldn't help thinking I was going into somewhere that was straight out of *Indiana Jones and the Temple of Doom*. It felt hot inside, as if lava were boiling just below the surface of the rock. We moved into a cavernous opening, from which pathways and tunnels veered off in every direction, giving the impression of walking into a giant termite nest. The rock itself was veined with collected soul energy, and it was this energy that gave the whole place a ghostly pale blue glow. The ghostly light made the people lying around everywhere look even more ghoulish, as they lay slumped on the floor or against walls, their eyes closed as they tripped in a different reality. Those who walked around the place simply stepped over the trippers as if stepping over a pile of rubbish.

"Welcome to Crystal Mountain," Moira said with more than a note of bitter sarcasm. "The place of dreams."

"Or in your case, Moira...welcome back," Charlotte said, now walking beside us. "I'm sure LeBron will be pleased to see you again."

I snapped my head around to look at Moira. "You know LeBron?" I asked. "You told me you'd never met him."

Moira closed her eyes for a second before looking away. "It's complicated...I'm sorry..."

Charlotte sniggered. "What, she didn't tell you she used be one of LeBron's playthings? His favorite by all accounts."

"See!" Max practically screamed inside me. "I told you, Creed, didn't I? You couldn't trust her!"

"Christ, relax Max, will you? Who gives a fuck if she used to...do whatever with LeBron? She helped, didn't she?"

"What the fuck has she done, Creed?" Max said. "Tell me! How has she helped us exactly? We could've easily got here by ourselves, and you know it."

For once, Max wasn't wrong. All Moira had really done was tag along. I could've walked here and got captured all by myself. Still, I couldn't deny her heart seemed to be in the right place, even if her desire to leave the Gray Land's made her overplay her hand a little. She could still be useful inside this place.

"I say we kill her," Max said. "Better yet, *I'll* kill her."

"No one's killing anybody," I said. "At least not her."

"I see what's going on here. I know you inside and out, Creed. You have a soft spot for this bitch. In fact, you have a history of having soft spots for bitches that don't deserve it."

"Hold on a—"

Charlotte pushed me forward, cutting short my rebuttal to Max. "Keep moving, Mr. Technicolor," she said, directing me towards a long tunnel off to the right, that seemed carpeted with trippers.

"This place feels like a giant crack house," I said as I started down the wide tunnel, Moira no longer walking by my side, but behind me.

"That's a very astute observation," Charlotte said. "It is kinda like that. But it's also much more."

"More?" I said stepping through the mass of bodies on the floor, noticing the doors made of iron set into the walls in places, and wondering where the doors led to.

"Much more. Not that you need to worry about that."

"And why's that?"

Charlotte stepped in front of me, blocking my path and bringing me to a stop next to one of the iron doors. "Where you'll most likely end up, you won't be seeing or doing very much, at least not in this world."

I frowned and nodded as if her threats didn't concern me, and then smiled at her. "There's something you should know about me," I said.

Charlotte raised her once blonde eyebrows and cocked her head like she was mightily interested in what I was going to say next. "Oh yeah, Mr. Technicolor? And what's that?"

I leaned toward her slightly. "I have a way of getting out of these things, and bringing the house down along with me. It's a special skill that I have."

Charlotte snorted and shook her head, though I could tell she was shaken slightly by the conviction behind my words. "Well, we'll just have to see about that, won't we?"

"I guess we will."

"In the meantime, though..." She turned and pulled opened the door we were standing beside. "You need to go in there."

I glanced quickly inside the room and saw nothing much in it. "It doesn't look very inviting. What if I refuse?"

"For fuck's sake, Creed," Max said. "We could kill this bitch and all these other docile bastards lying around. What are we waiting for?"

"Not yet, Max. There are too many of them. We're playing the long game here..."

"You and you're fucking long games," Max all but screamed. "Throw caution to the wind for once...take a fucking chance!"

I tried not to look irritated by Max's childish behavior as I continued to stare at Charlotte.

"There are many here who would drain you dry in seconds," Charlotte said. "If I tell them to." She placed a hand on my chest, and I felt an immediate pull inside as a tiny strand of my soul energy was stolen by her. "Hell, I could do it myself right now. In seconds, it would be like you never existed."

"But you wouldn't, would you?" I retorted. "I don't think your boss would be very happy if you siphoned me off by yourself. I'd say he'd be pissed."

Charlotte shook her head dismissively. "You think because you are a living soul that you are special?"

"Well, yes..."

She laughed. "No, you are not. Or at least, you won't be..."

I frowned. "What does that mean?"

"You'll find out soon enough, Mr. Technicolor," she said. "Now get inside before I cut you. Pain is as real here as it is on Earth."

She held up the machete as she glared at me. Giving her a look back, I walked inside the room, with Moira being pushed in behind me. Then the heavy door was shut and locked.

Max laughed. "Congratulations, Creed," he said. "You have now landed us back in jail. Fantastic job."

"Shut the fuck up, Max!" I barked out loud. "It won't be for long."

"I think you said that the last time as well..."

"I got out, didn't I?"

"Yes, and now you're here, aren't you?"

I sighed. "I'm not talking to you anymore."

Moira was standing in the corner of the dimly lit room, her arms folded as she refused to look at me. "All right," I said to her. "Start talking..."

She shook her head in anger. "About what?" she snapped. "About the fact that I used to be one of LeBron's whores because it was a way to get free trips? About the fact that he enjoyed doing despicable things to me, and that I let him? Or about the fact that he gave me magic so I could be with my son inside some fantasy trip where my son always died at the end?"

Moira's gray eyes glared at me as they filled with tears. "You've upset the bitch," Max said. "Just break her neck now and get it over with."

"All right," I said to Moira, backing off slightly. "It just feels like you've been lying to me this whole time. Although now I can see why."

Saying nothing, Moira sat on the dirty floor with her back against the wall.

"At least ask the stupid bitch if she knows where your family is," Max said. "She must know, given how familiar she is with this place."

"Do you know where my family is being held?" I asked her.

She shook her head. "If they are here at all, they are most likely in the Draining Chamber, if they aren't like all the other trippers here."

"The Draining Chamber? What's that?"

"The place where LeBron keeps his captured souls so he can slowly drain them of their soul energy." A sigh left her. "He does it slowly, allowing the energy of the individual to replenish, before draining them again. That way, he has a constant supply."

The thought of my family being drained of their soul energy didn't sit well with me. "You know where this Draining Chamber is?"

"Of course, but we're locked up in here, in case you didn't notice."

"Not for much longer," I said going to the door.

"Even if you get the door open, there will still be people outside to stop you."

"Let them try."

"That's the spirit, Creed," Max said. "Let's get out there and show that grayed-out filth what real violence is."

I said nothing as I held my hand over the lock in the door, my anger helping to focus my weak magic on unlocking it. It took a fair bit longer to move the lock than it would have done had my magic been at full strength, but I got there in the end, and the lock finally turned with a heavy click. "Let's go," I said to Moira with my hand on the door handle.

Moira got to her feet, but she didn't move toward me. "What about LeBron's people? There are too many of them..."

"Wrong," I said, my face setting into a determined scowl. "There's not enough of them."

Pressing down the handle, I opened the door and stepped outside.

24

# MAKING A BREAK FOR IT

*I* may have mentioned before that I am not a fighter. That's not strictly true. Under ordinary circumstances, I have nothing to prove. I'm not one of these guys that constantly has to brow beat people, or beat the shit out of them in order to prove my superiority over them. There are usually better, smarter ways to handle a confrontation, or to make a fool of someone.

But the circumstances I was in now were far from ordinary. I was stuck in a colorless, depressing land, surrounded by the souls of the dead. My family were most likely being drained of their soul energy as we speak, and I had a demon inside me that didn't know how to shut the fuck up. On top of that, I was missing Leona, and I was also tired of fucking predators taking advantage of the ones I loved.

Needless to say, I was pissed as hell. Even at less than half of my magical strength, I was going to show these dead motherfuckers what a wizard scorned really looked like.

I started with the first person who approached me when I walked out of the prison cell. Some burly guard with a long knife strapped to his leg. Before the guard could even reach for his knife, I shot him with a blast of magic that sent him flying back into the wall, knocking him unconscious in the process. I stared down at my hand for a second, slightly shocked by the power of the magic blast.

"Your anger is fueling your magic, Creed," Max said, sounding like he was enjoying every second of me going psycho. "Use it! Lay waste to these cretins!"

Max's words, which normally would have annoyed me with their blatant encouragement to do harm, spurred me on this time. My anger soon turned to fury as more grayed-out motherfuckers came running at me. Encouraged by the strength of the last magic blast, I sent another down the tunnel. The blast caught one guy in the chest, forcing him back so hard he knocked over half a dozen other people like skittles.

Behind me, I sensed someone approaching, and when I turned, I saw a woman charging at me with a knife, a look of feral aggression on her gray face. I still wasn't sure if these people were intending to kill me or just bring me down, but it didn't matter to me either way. As the woman thrust her blade at my belly, I slid quickly to the side and punched her hard in the skull, sending her veering away from me. Then I finished her with a kick to the chest that sent her slamming into the wall, where she dropped the knife and slid to the floor.

When I turned, I saw Moira standing next to me, both her swords out. "You're a crazy motherfucker, you know that?" she said.

"Crazy is what we need right now," I said, my eyes wide as I looked around. "Which way?"

Moira pointed down the tunnel toward the front entry. "That way. We have to get to the top of the mountain. That's where the Draining Chamber is."

"And LeBron?"

"He's up there to."

We didn't get a chance to say much else, as more people came charging at us. I was about to use my magic again when I felt the all too familiar sensation of losing control of my body, as Max took it upon himself to take me over. "I can't let you have all the fun, now can I?" he said.

"Fuck it," I said, knowing there wasn't much I could do to stop him. "Whatever. Knock yourself out."

"With pleasure."

As the group of Grays were almost upon us, Max thrust out his hand and grabbed the man in the lead by the throat, picking him up off the ground and tossing him hard against the wall. The others hesitated, but then kept coming, albeit more cautiously. Max, however, gave not one fuck for their caution, and charged at them like a madman, roaring as he went in a voice so deep I could hardly believe it was coming from my throat. From there, he started grabbing those nearest to him so he could tear off their limbs like a child who had become bored with a raggedy old doll. He punched one man so hard in the face that his fist came out the back of the man's skull. He gouged out the eyes of someone else, tore the balls off another, shoving said balls into the mouth of another, before biting the person's nose off and spitting that at someone else.

It didn't take long for the Gray's to start backing off out of sheer terror, and I didn't blame them. Even if they couldn't really die, and always came back from whatever "death" they experienced here, being torn apart by a raging man-demon probably wasn't high on their list of most pleasurable experiences. So they ran screaming in fear. Even some of the trippers lying around were woken out of their alternative realities by all the commotion and violence taking place around them. Most of the awakened trippers snapped their eyes shut again when they saw what was going on. Those who dared to keep theirs open looked like someone who was, well...having a bad trip.

"Nice job, Max," I said. "Now hand over the keys."

"I don't think so," Max said aloud. "I'm not done yet. I'm just getting started, in fact..."

"Max, come on! Our priority is to get upstairs, not to cause as much bloodshed as possible."

"We can do both."

"Goddamn it..."

"You all right, Creed?" Moira asked me.

"Creed is fine," Max told her. "You have me for the time being..."

Moira drew back as she realized who she was talking to. "Where's Creed?"

"In the back." Max gave her a sneering look. "Don't worry...I won't bite you...yet."

"Leave her alone, Max!" I shouted. "Just fucking move forward."

Max was about to do so when he caught sight of Charlotte standing at the end of the tunnel. In her hand was a staff with a glowing ball of whitish energy on the end. "I suggest you get back in your cell," she shouted. "Or I'm going to have to put you back in. That means you too, Moira."

"Who does this bitch she think she is?" Max said dismissively as he began to walk toward her.

"Wait!" Moira shouted.

Max didn't listen. He kept stomping toward Charlotte.

"Be careful, Max," I said. "I think that's—"

I never got the chance to finish the sentence before Charlotte shot a blast of energy from the staff she was holding. The sphere of energy moved so fast that even Max had no chance of blocking or avoiding it, so he—that is I—took the full impact of the blast in the chest. Not only did the impact lift me clean off my feet, sending me flying, but it also felt like it had burned a hole right through me.

"She's all yours," Max said after he had given me control of my body back.

I couldn't even think of a sarcastic reply, never mind speak one. I was too concerned that I had a massive hole in my chest. When I barely lifted myself up to check, I was relieved to see my chest still intact, despite the tendrils of smoke rising from me.

Charlotte was standing over me, staff in hand. "Didn't I tell you to get back in your cell? You should've listened."

In spite of the pain, my anger didn't relent. "Screw you...Gandalf."

"I'm going to enjoy killing her," Max said. "I'll shove that staff right up her pussy until it comes out of her mouth."

"Up you get, asshole," Charlotte ordered, now standing back as she aimed the glowing tip of her staff at me.

"A gift from your boss?" I asked when I was finally able to stand up.

She smirked. "Something like that. I can use it to kill you if I want."

"So why don't you then?" I said, stepping defiantly toward her.

"Don't fucking tempt me," she warned.

"She's bluffing, Creed. She won't kill us. She's not allowed to."

"We both know your boss wants me alive," I said, trying to be reasonable now. "Why don't you just save everybody some trouble and take me to him now?"

"Forget it, asshole. You don't call the shots around here." She motioned with the staff then. "Get back in your damn cell before I zap you again."

"Zap me? That's cute." I deliberately smiled at her as I took another step forward. "You know, Charlotte, in your haste to assert your dominance over me, you forgot about one thing."

"Oh yeah? And what's that?"

"Me!" Moira said as she came up behind Charlotte, stabbing her in the back with one of her swords.

A look of shock registered on Charlotte's face as she dropped the staff and looked down at the blade sticking out of her chest, her dark gray blood dripping onto the floor. "No..." she said shaking her head.

"Enjoy forgetting any of this ever happened," I told her just as Moira pulled the sword out of Charlotte's back. Charlotte then dropped to the ground, seemingly dead.

"Fuck!" Max screamed inside me. "I wanted to do that!"

"Reign yourself in, Max," I told him. "Who cares who killed her? We have a job to do."

I could almost feel him sulking inside me. "Bunch of bloody spoilsports..."

"Whatever."

Moira was staring down at Charlotte's body. "I've been wanting to do that for a long time."

"What exactly will happen to her soul now?" I asked. "How does it work again?"

"I thought we had a job to do," Max said in a childish voice. "There's no time for you to indulge your inner nerd..."

"You die here in this place, and then you just materialize in the desert like nothing ever happened," Moira said. "You forget you were ever here before. It's like you just arrived."

"So technically, this might not be your first rodeo here?" I said.

Moira shrugged. "That's a possibility, I suppose."

"Some souls could've been in this place a lot longer than they think," I mused.

"You're depressing me. Can we go now? I'm surprised we haven't been surrounded yet."

I frowned as I looked up and down the tunnel. "Good point. Why hasn't everyone here descended upon us by now? The ones that aren't tripping anyway."

"It's LeBron," Moira said. "I know it. He wants us to come to him."

I nodded. "All right then. Let's give the bastard what he wants."

## 25

---

# THE DRAINING CHAMBER

$\mathscr{I}$t was a measure of LeBron's confidence that he allowed Moira and I to make our way up through the labyrinth of passageways that made up his vast mountain lair. There was apparently an elevator that led right to the top of the mountain, but after giving it some thought, I deemed getting inside a reinforced steel box to be too dangerous. It would've been too easy for LeBron to trap us inside and do God knows what to us, and I didn't want to give the bastard that opportunity. So I opted for the scenic route instead. This route would've taken much longer if it hadn't of been for the fact that my magic was still running high from the encounter outside the prison cell. My anger had calmed somewhat, but there was still enough of it left to replenish my magic, at least enough so I could teleport Moira and I almost to the top of the mountain. There were very few people in that part of the lair. Those we did meet along the way generally stood aside to let us pass.

"This seems too damn easy," I said after a while. "I expected more...resistance."

"You don't know LeBron," Moira said, the deep scowl on her face signifying her discomfort as we neared the top. "He won't see you as a threat because he thinks he's all powerful here, and that no one is a threat to him."

"He hasn't met me yet."

"Or me," Max chipped in.

"Let me handle LeBron," I told him. "You'll get what you want soon enough, Max."

"I'd better."

"How far are we from the Draining Chamber?" I asked Moira.

"Not far," she said. "You want to got there now?"

"I do."

Moira sighed. "If LeBron let's us."

"Fuck LeBron," I said. "I need to see where my family is being held."

"You won't like it."

I shook my head. "Yeah, I don't expect to."

Moira wasn't lying when she said the Draining Chamber was near. After walking down another two tunnels, we emerged into a huge cavernous space. Several feet into the vast chamber, I stopped and stared, first in amazement, and then in disgust as I realized what I was looking at.

Bodies suspended in the air. Thousands of them, stretching back as far as my eyes could see.

"This is it," Moira said quietly, almost like she was in some sacred place. "Welcome to the Draining Chamber."

"My God..."

"Magnificent," Max said.

"Not the word I would fucking use."

"Of course you would be offended by this callous, not to say flagrant, mass abuse of humanity, dead souls or not."

"Forgive me for not being a demonic cunt like you."

"Sticks and stones, Creed..."

"Fuck you."

Max continued to talk, but I wasn't listening. My full attention was on what was in front of me, at the uniform rows of suspended bodies. Each body was releasing tendrils of soul energy to be collected somewhere high above. As I began to walk forward and past the first few rows of bodies, I saw that each person was suspended without using any external mechanism to hold them up. Somehow, LeBron was using soul energy, or just plain magic, to keep what amounted to thousands of bodies completely suspended and unconscious. The drain on his energy had to be stupendous, which meant LeBron had access to a metric fuckton of it. "I've never seen anything like this," I said to myself.

"Every one of them is under a spell," Moira said from just behind me. "Everyone you see here is tripping in some other reality."

I shook my head. "It's like the fucking Matrix in here."

"Do you think your family is here?" Moira asked. "How will you find them? There are so many people..."

I took out the Soul Finder. "With this."

"No need for your crude gadgets here," a voice suddenly boomed from behind us. "I can locate your family for you."

I spun around with one hand out, ready to unleash a magic blast at whoever was behind us, knowing full well it had to be LeBron. The man standing by the entrance to the chamber was tall, and not gray like everyone else here. This man wore, of all things, a burgundy colored suit made from a shiny material, that gave him the appearance of some hipster gangster. His greased back dark hair only added to the facade, as did the gold tipped cane he was carrying. I was left with the impression that while everyone else here was wallowing in gray misery, LeBron was living in colorful luxury. He stood there with his wolfish grin and sharp blue eyes, arrogantly putting out that he was the king of these lands.

"No one told me Willy Wonka was going to be here," I said, my hand still out and ready to unleash a blast of magic should the need arise, though something told me LeBron wasn't interested in fighting, at least not yet. His appearance in the

Draining Chamber was merely about introducing himself, and probably putting me in my place.

His grin faltered only slightly at my sarcastic remark. "Then welcome to my chocolate factory," he said with more than a trace of an Eastern European accent, spreading his arms wide while walking forward. He then started to laugh like the whole situation was a joke to him.

"This is no fucking chocolate factory," I said. "You're draining these people. Where is my family?"

LeBron frowned and shook his head as if he didn't know what I meant. "Your family? You think they are here?"

"I know they are."

"What are their names? I know the names of every soul in here."

I didn't answer at first. My anger was beginning to boil up again. All I wanted to do was blast LeBron with magic, and then run over and shake some answers out of him before...

"I see your thoughts," Max said quietly. "Violent...bloody. I approve."

"Brenda, Fergus and Roisin McCreedy," I said to LeBron through gritted teeth.

LeBron thought for a second, then he nodded in recognition. "It seems you are right. Your family is here."

I took a few steps toward him. "Release them right now."

A smirk crossed LeBron's face. "Or what? What will you do? I see you have magic, but your power is no match for mine in this place. There's nothing you can do that could possibly hurt me."

To test the waters, I sent a blast of high velocity magic towards LeBron, who merely stood with his arms out and allowed the magic blast to hit him on the chest, before absorbing the energy into himself.

"That was about the best I've got at the moment," I said to Max.

"Lucky I'm here then," Max said. "He is a living soul, and therefore—"

"Open to possession," I finished. "Go get him, Max!"

Max's spirit shot out of my body, an invisible force that a second later embedded itself into the body of LeBron. LeBron looked shocked as he reeled back clutching his chest as if he'd been blasted with a shotgun. "What...is this?" he stammered.

"Just my pet demon," I said walking towards him. "He wanted to say hello and—"

LeBron suddenly shoved his chest out forcefully, as if to expel the unwelcome presence inside him, which he did with a shout of effort. "I take your stinking demon, and I spit it right back at you!" he said.

"He...he...shouldn't be able to do that," Max said, now inside me again. "It's not possible..."

"He just fucking did," I said.

"Are you quite finished now?" LeBron asked. "Because if you are not, I will simply turn you into a human battery like the rest of the souls you see hanging in here. Like your family..."

I took one step forward as if to go at LeBron again, but I was able to quell my anger this time. He was the one with all the power in this place, so there was no point antagonizing him further if it meant I would end up incapacitated. I would at least wait until I freed my family. "Fine," I said as calmly as I could. "You win.

Just let me speak to my family, then you can do what you want with me, I don't care..."

"With *both* of you," LeBron said as he looked past me. "I can see you skulking back there, Moira. Come forward."

I turned around to see Moira emerge from behind a suspended body, where she had been hiding since LeBron appeared. She came and stood beside me, but not before giving me a look that said she felt betrayed by me. She was obviously expecting a little more from me in terms of handling LeBron. Clearly she had a lot to learn about playing the long game, something I know quite a bit about. "I knew I shouldn't have trusted you," she said to me.

"Moira, my darling," LeBron said. "It's good to see you again. I've missed our little...soirees."

Moira grunted. "Is that what you call them? Rape parties more like..."

"Call them whatever you want. As I've said to you many times before...normal rules don't apply here." He smiled. "Thank God!"

*Another sick motherfucker*, I thought.

"Screw you, LeBron," Moira said. "I'll destroy myself first before I let you get your hands on me again."

LeBron thrust his hand out, using his power to drag Moira toward him, until the same hand was around her throat. "You were saying?" he said, a note of nastiness in his voice that more than hinted at his capacity for sadism. "You forget I own you, as I do every soul here." He threw me a dark look as well. "Including you now, Mr. McCreedy."

"It's Creed, actually," I said. "You can own my soul if you like, as long as you release my family first."

"You're giving me ultimatums now?" He let go of Moira's throat and pushed her down onto her knees, again using magic.

"Look," I said, trying to sound reasonable. "I'm offering you my services in return for releasing my family. I have skills that might be useful to you."

"What are you doing, Creed?" Max said. "Tell me you are not negotiating with this animal."

"Shut up, Max and let me handle this."

"What makes you think I need anyone?" LeBron said.

"This is a big place. Lots of souls to control. You need people you can trust to help you run it."

LeBron laughed. "And I can trust you, can I?"

"If you release my family."

"You are right, I do need trusted souls, otherwise things can get a little...overwhelming." His eyes narrowed as he stared at me. "I could see you being useful, but then so would your living soul..."

"So that's it? You just want to drain me like all the rest in here?"

"Maybe, maybe not. The population of this place is about to...blow up very soon." He chuckled as he found that funny for some reason. "I'll have my hands full then."

"What do you mean, blow up?"

LeBron smiled. "Why don't you come with me now, and we can perhaps discuss your future here? If you even have one, that is."

"What about my family?" I demanded.

LeBron sighed as if I was becoming a major inconvenience to him. "You can see them later, once I release them."

I stared back at him, wondering if he was telling the truth, then realizing it didn't matter whether he was or not. It was his show now, and I had no choice but go along with it.

# 26

# ROOM WITH A VIEW

*L*eBron teleported me to his living quarters at the very top of the mountain lair, leaving Moira behind in the Draining Room. Before we left, LeBron looked at Moira and said, "I'll find you later, my dear. Don't run away again, will you?"

Moira glared at me as if I had betrayed her in the worst way possible, but for the time being, there wasn't much I could do except shrug just before I disappeared.

"Make yourself comfortable, Creed," LeBron said when we got to his living quarters, which were not what I expected. It was like he had just teleported us into a room at the Four Seasons. Unlike the rest of his lair, the walls in his living quarters were smooth and painted a deep red, and the room itself contained furniture that would have cost a pretty penny back on Earth. Unbelievably, he also appeared to have a television mounted on the wall that was showing a news channel from Earth.

"So this is what you do with all that soul energy you collect?" I said looking around the huge room.

"Partly, yes. Why live like a rat when you don't have to?" He was standing by a drinks cabinet, arranging two glasses. "What's your poison? You look like a whiskey man to me."

"That'll do."

LeBron smiled. "I knew it. I'm a gin man myself."

"None of us are perfect."

He hesitated in pouring the drinks to throw me a look. "We don't often get travelers like you coming here, you know. I'm surprised you even made it this far without getting soul-jacked."

"I had help."

"Yes, from Moira. A very capable woman, in more ways than one." He smiled.

"She has a problem with authority, though."

"I thought her problem was with being used as a sex slave..."

LeBron said nothing as he left my drink on the table, and carried his own outside to the balcony. I went and grabbed the glass, chugging the whiskey down in one, surprised at how good it tasted. I poured myself another large measure before joining LeBron out on the balcony. From such a high vantage point, you could see right across the desert to the Gray City and beyond, the stone buildings rising ominously out of the mist in the distance.

"Tell me," LeBron said as he stared out. "What do you see?"

I wasn't in the mood for games, but I knew I would have to play along until I figured out a way escape this place, preferably with my family. "I see a depressing place full of miserable souls who wished they weren't dead."

LeBron nodded. "Of course you do. You want to know what I see?"

"I'm sure you're going to tell me."

"I see a vast potential, a place to make a world unlike any other."

"*Your* world, you mean?"

He nodded. "Indeed."

"And how do you plan on doing that? By draining those who live here of their soul energy?"

"Partly, yes."

"It sounds like you have a grand plan," I said.

"I do."

"Care to share it?"

He turned his head to look at me. "In time, perhaps."

"Okay. Care to share how the hell you're getting away with all this then? Last time I checked, the Realm of the Dead wasn't up for grabs. I mean, it's the Realm of the Dead..."

"You would've thought so, wouldn't you?" he said. "But yet, here we are..."

"Here *you* are, you mean?"

"Yes, here *I* am."

"How did you end up here? Your physical body is obviously alive and well somewhere. Why are you here?"

"You are right, my body is safe in a place where no one can find it."

"On Earth?"

"Yes. I don't mind telling you that. You know why?"

I shook my head. "Because you think I'm never leaving this place?"

"Well, to be frank, that is true. You will never leave this place, but maybe not for the reason you think."

"What does that mean?"

LeBron smiled after sipping from his glass. "Don't worry. You will find out what that means soon enough...along with everyone else."

"Sounds predictably ominous," Max said.

*It always is.*

"I can't wait," I said. "In the meantime, what about my family?"

He turned to me, leaning one elbow on the stone balcony. "Men of magic like you and me are a rare commodity here," he said. "Most of us manage to avoid the afterlife in one way or another."

"Why didn't you?"

He raised his eyebrows for a second. "Let's just say I ran into some trouble on Earth. I had to leave in a hurry, and the portal I rushed through happened to lead here."

I nodded. "I get it. This place is so joyful and spiritually fulfilling that you couldn't bring yourself to leave, right?"

LeBron suppressed a smirk as if he wasn't sure how to handle my sarcasm. "I saw potential here where others didn't. I still see it."

"Potential for what? Even greater misery and degradation?"

He stood up straight suddenly, as if incensed by my criticism. "I've given the people here a means to escape their misery while they await processing. I've also given meaning and purpose to those who have been forced into staying for an extended period."

"By turning everyone into pushers and junkies?"

His blue eyes bored into me. "The man who carries a stinking demon around inside of him is taking the moral high ground with me?" He laughed and shook his head. "Please..."

The truth is, I didn't much care about what LeBron was doing. I was there for one reason only, to try and save my family. Everything else was just an inconvenience, including LeBron. It only remained to be seen just how big an inconvenience he was actually going to be. "Look, whatever," I said. "I have no interest in getting in your way. I just want my family, that's all."

LeBron smiled as if he just realized something. "You do understand that you are never getting out of this place, don't you, Creed? Or has that not dawned on you yet?"

I stared back at him. "You've already said. You're going to try and keep me here?"

"Not try. I will, same as I've kept your family here."

I rushed forward suddenly in a burst of anger, my face only inches from his now. "You'd be making a big mistake trying to keep me here."

"Would I?" LeBron said scowling back. "And how would you stop me, hmm? Only I can harness the soul energy here. I've made sure of that. Whatever magic you might have here is not enough to stop me from doing anything, least of all from making sure you remain here, and under my employ." He moved his face closer to mine then. "You don't get to gatecrash my kingdom, and then leave when you feel like it. I'm in charge here. I'm in charge of *you* now. I suggest you get used to that."

I breathed hard through my nose as I gritted my teeth in angry frustration. The motherfucker was right. At least for now. So I backed off slightly, knowing I would have to bide my time with him. "How the fuck do you have so much power here anyway?" I asked him. "You really expect me to believe the greater powers in the multiverse are okay with you fucking hijacking the Realm of the Dead? I don't buy it."

"Believe what you want," LeBron said. "The so called greater powers that you speak of have yet to interfere. When have you ever known the powers that be to step in on anything? They simply don't care, or they work to a greater plan that none of us can comprehend. Whatever the case, I'm here. So are you. Get used to it."

"You might want to mention the small problem of your weakening body on

Earth," Max said. "Going by the constant pain I can feel in you, I don't think you have much time left before my lingering presence kills you. I'd say a few days at most, if the concept of days even exists in this place, which I don't think—"

"I get it. Just shut up."

"Just trying to be helpful, because you know, either way, I'm still getting out of here at some point, even if you don't..."

I felt like closing my eyes and sighing, but I didn't want to look weak in front of LeBron, which was proving difficult, given the almost constant pain running through every part of my body.

"Would you like to see your family now?" LeBron asked me, somewhat unexpectedly.

As much as I hated him, I couldn't deny that his offer filled me with joy. The manipulative bastard probably knew it would as well. "Yes," I said.

LeBron smiled like a gracious host. "Why don't you go inside and relax? I'll have your family brought up here so you can all spend some quality time together. I'm sure it's been a while."

Max laughed inside me. "Who's the sarcastic one now?"

# FAMILY REUNION

Once LeBron left, I found myself pacing nervously around the room. Under ordinary circumstances, I might have paid more attention to the plush carpet, the pictures on the walls, or the odd trinkets lying around, but my apprehension over seeing my family again made it difficult for me to think of anything else. The last time I saw them didn't really count in my mind, given the circumstances at the time. This time, I didn't have my father to deal with. There was LeBron, of course, but I had a feeling he would stay out of the way, at least for a while. The man was demanding my loyalty, and allowing me to see my family would, in his mind, perhaps make me more willing to give him that loyalty. Which was bullshit, of course, because there was no way I was staying in the Gray Lands to work for LeBron.

"If your body gives up and you die, you won't have a choice," Max said. "You'll end up having to stay here anyway."

"It won't come to that," I said aloud, wincing at the grinding pain in my bones. "I don't plan on being here much longer."

"So what's your exit strategy?"

"I don't know yet. I'll find a way. I always do."

To be honest, escaping the Gray Lands was the last thing on my mind at that point. My eyes kept going to the door as I waited on it to open, and my family to walk through. I was looking forward to seeing them so much, but I was also afraid, because I was unsure of the reaction I would get from them. Apart from that brief meeting months ago, I'd had no interaction with them in so long, that I was worried I would be a stranger to them now. That's not even taking into account everything *they* had been through, and the ways those experiences might have changed *them*.

"Don't forget," Max said. "I get to grill your mother on how she escaped me."

"Grill? I don't think so."

"Speak with her then...you know what I mean. And don't worry, Creed, I'll let you have your little moment with your family before I butt in."

"You'll get your chance to ask your questions, Max. In the meantime, back the fuck off or—"

I cried out in pain as I doubled over, and then dropped to my knees. The liquid lava was flowing through my veins again, and the jackhammer was pounding on my bones...or so it felt like. "Fuck..." I said through gritted teeth.

"It's getting worse, Creed..."

"*Fucking...really...dick...*"

"Just saying..."

The door opened, and LeBron walked in to see me kneeling on the floor, my arms folded over my stomach as if I'd been stabbed. "Having a spot of bother there, are we?" he said, sounding completely unconcerned. "Never fear, though, because mother is here...and brother...and sister..."

Still in agony, I managed to lift my head up enough to see three ghostly forms enter the room. Three gray, translucent souls. The last vestiges of my immediate family.

"Dying vestiges it looks like," Max said.

It was hard to disagree with him. All three of them looked quite literally like shadows of their former selves. Much more faded than the last time I saw them.

"August!" It was my mother, rushing over to help me, but her soul was so weak that she barely had any real physical form, so she was barely able to touch me. Her hand passed right through my arm at one point as she tried to help me up.

*My family are ghosts...*

"I'll leave you all to it, shall I?" LeBron said. "I'll be along in a while to offer each of you a proposition. It's one I hope you will accept, but we'll see."

The door closed as he left, and it was just the four of us in the room. Five if you included Max, who thankfully was keeping to his word, and not appearing as Evil Creed...yet.

As the pain finally began to subside, I was able to look properly into my mother's face, and what I saw there was more pain. *Her* pain. "Mother..." I said, my voice a mix of emotions. "It's really you..."

She smiled, her once soft pink lips now colorless. "Yes, it's me, son. What are you doing here, August?"

"You shouldn't have come to this bloody awful place," my brother Fergus said as I stood up.

"Aye," my sister, Roisin, said. "You never could help yourself, could you?"

I stood smiling at the three of them. "I didn't think I was ever going to see any of you again."

"By rights, you shouldn't," Roisin said, then smiled as she came forward to hug me. "But it's still good to see you, Gus."

Fergal came over next and gave me that cocky smile of his that I always remember. "Come here, little brother, and give your big brother a hug," he said standing with his arms out. "Be careful you don't fall through me. We're all a bit... drained at the moment."

"Aye," Roisin said. "Thanks to that bastard LeBron. You'd think after escaping from the Underworld and that other bastard, Santos, that we'd catch a break. But no, that would be too much to ask, wouldn't it?"

"Santos?" I said. "You mean Ma—" I stopped when I realized they wouldn't know who I was talking about.

"Yes, dummy, they mean me," Max said. "They asked for a name, I gave them one."

"Mean who?" Fergal asked me.

"No one," I said shaking my head, then frowning as I realized something. "You are all dressed in the same robes."

"Bloody awful, aren't they?" Roisin said.

"I'm surprised the bastard things are even staying on us," Fergal said. "Given our lack of physical form and all that."

"How did you even end up in that room?" I asked them.

"Because," my mother said. "We refused to work with his lord and master, LeBron, that's why."

"We've had enough of being ordered around by Underworld tyrants," said Roisin. "We didn't need more of it in the afterlife as well."

"LeBron suspended us in that draining room," Fergal said. "Supposedly to teach us a lesson. I think maybe he forgot about us. It seemed like we were in there a long time. Whatever trip he had me on, it put me in some fucked up alien world."

"Same here," Roisin said. "It seems like I've spent years running from monsters."

"I was back on Earth," my mother said. "In Ireland before...your father..."

"Aye, the less said about that cunt the better," Fergal said. "I'd spit if I could form saliva."

"What happened after we appeared to you?" Roisin said.

"I hope you destroyed the cunt," Fergal said. "Tell me you did, Gus."

"I did," I said. "Thanks to you guys."

"That's my little brother," Fergal said. "I always knew there was a tough guy inside all that softness."

"Leave him alone," Roisin said. "He's proved us all wrong, haven't you, Gus?"

"I always knew you would do great things," my mother said.

I shook my head in embarrassment. "Great things? Not really. If you knew some of the things I've had to do..." I shook my head again.

"I know more than you think, son," my mother said.

"What?" I asked frowning.

"She's been spying on you," Fergal said. "Ever since we got to the Underworld."

"What?" I was confused. "How?"

My mother smiled slyly. "Do you forget I'm a witch?" she said. "We tend to know a few things."

"I didn't even think that was possible," I said.

"It is if you find the right people and things to help you," she said. "I was able to drop in on you, so to speak, several times over the years. How do you think I knew you were in trouble with your father?"

I still couldn't believe it. "I was wondering about that. When else?"

My mother smiled her reassuring smile. "It doesn't matter. All that matters is, you weren't truly alone all those years, even if it felt like it to you."

"But I never noticed anything..."

"Your wolf did. Blaze, is it?"

I nodded. "Yes."

"I couldn't believe it when I heard that you have a pet fucking wolf," Fergal said. "You know how fucking cool that is? I always wanted a wolf."

"Language, Fergal," my mother scolded him.

"Really, mother?" Fergal said. "After everything, you're still admonishing me for cursing?"

"You know how I feel about it," my mother said.

Fergal sighed and turned away as if he was tired of hearing it.

"You see what I have to deal with, Gus?" Roisin said. "It's cats and dogs all the time with these two."

"It's because I'm not her favorite," Fergal said. "You are, Gus. It was always you."

"Stop it, Fergal," my mother said, annoyed now. "There's no need for that. Not now."

I could only stand there and smile. "God, I've missed this," I said as I felt tears roll down my cheeks.

"Och, Gus," Roisin cooed when she seen me crying. "Come here."

When she tried to hug me, I fell through her. "Shit..."

"Oh, for fucks sake!" Roisin said. "I can't even give my little brother a hug!"

"How much fucking soul energy did that bastard LeBron take from us?" Fergal said, looking down at his translucent hands. "There's hardly anything left of us!"

"Calm down," my mother said. "All of you. The soul energy will replenish over time, as long as we don't end up in that draining room again."

"I hope you're right, mother," Roisin said. "I've never felt weaker. I can barely feel my magic anymore."

"Same here," Fergal said as he tried to conjure energy in his hand, forming only faint blue sparks.

"That should return as well," my mother said. "I think the more pressing issue is what we are all going to do now. I think it's clear that we have to go along with LeBron, for now at least, and then—"

"Wait a minute," Fergal said as he held up his hand to interrupt my mother. Then he looked at me. "Gus, what the hell are you doing here? Seriously. How did you even find us for a start?"

"That's a long story involving the Dark Codex," I said.

"The Dark Codex?" Fergal said frowning. "It exists?"

"Not anymore," I said. "But it did exist, and I learned of your whereabouts from it."

Fergal shook his head. "You have quite the adventures, don't you, little brother?"

"Sometimes it works out like that," I said, rather ridiculously grinning like a Cheshire cat. Growing up, Fergal was always the cool one, and I used to look up to him. Now it seemed, he was looking up to me, which made me feel weirdly proud.

"Okay," he said. "So you find out that we are here in this misery hole...and you just decide to come visit?"

I felt like a kid again, getting grilled by my older brother. "There's a bit more to it than that."

"What do you mean?"

I raised my hands like it was obvious. "I came to take you home, of course."

Neither of them said anything for a long moment as they stared at me. My mother was the first to speak. "Oh, August..." she said as she looked at me sadly.

"Why the hell do you all look so sad?" I said. "We can all get out of here, we can all go back to Earth and you can start again, live the lives you deserve..."

"But..." Roisin said. "We're dead, Gus." She let it hang there in the air, as if waiting for the penny to drop.

"Jesus," I said. "I know that, but it doesn't matter. I can still take the three of you back with me."

"And then what?" Fergal asked. "You'll get us new bodies to walk around in?"

"Yes," I said. "You know it can be done."

"We do know," Roisin said.

I shook my head, not understanding their reticence. "So why am I sensing there's a problem here?"

"Look, August," my mother said in that gentle voice she always used to use when she had some heavy truth to impart. "You must understand, we've been dead a long time, or at least we've been gone from Earth a long time. A lot longer than it seems to you, in fact."

"A lot longer," Fergal muttered.

"And?" I said.

"We just want to move on," Roisin said. "To our proper afterlives, if that bastard LeBron would ever let us. Can you understand that, Gus?"

I looked at each of them in turn, and they all had the same confirmation in their eyes. Shaking my head, I said, "So you don't want to come back with me?" It was more of a sad statement.

"Sorry, little brother," Fergal said. "Our lives on Earth are just a distant memory to us now. That time has passed, and I'm afraid there's no going back."

I could only stand in shocked silence for a moment as what they were telling me sunk in. I felt angry at first, and then a deep sadness settled over me as tears began to roll down my cheeks. "I've had this dream," I said staring at the floor. "A fantasy, if you like. It first came into my head when I left Ireland, when I realized that I was completely alone in the world. I had Ray, of course. I still do. But back then, Ray wasn't around much. It was just me. So to get myself through, I would have this movie in my head of all of us being together again, and..." I looked up at them to see faint tears running down their translucent cheeks. "So when I found out you were here, I thought...we could all finally be together again." I shrugged. "But I guess not, eh?"

No one really knew what to say after that. It was clear that they had no desire to return to Earth. It was also clear that it had been arrogant of me to assume in the first place that they would even want to.

But before we could discuss the matter any further, a loud voice broke the silence, and I realized Max had appeared in the guise of Evil Creed. "All right," he said. "Enough of this maudlin bullshit already. It's depressing."

"Oh, Jesus..." I said shaking my head.

"What the fuck?" Fergal said turning around suddenly.

"Who..." Roisin began.

"No..." my mother said.

Max smiled. "I'm glad you recognize me, Brenda," he said. "Even in this guise.

Do you like it, by the way? He cuts a dashing figure, your son, especially when *I* wear him." He laughed then, as if his great moment had finally come.

Both Fergal and Roisin were looking at me now, the real me, while my mother still stared in horror at Max. "Gus, what is this?" Fergal asked, a hint of fear in his voice, though he probably didn't know why at that point.

"I was planning on getting to this...at some point," I said.

"He was taking his sweet fucking time, is what he was doing," Max said.

"Shut up, Max!" I barked. "Let me fucking explain, will you?"

"Oh, go ahead," he said. "This should be fun, although I think your mother has already worked it out, haven't you, Brenda?"

My mother turned her head slowly to look at me. "August?" she said. "This can't be what...*who* I think it is?"

I puffed out my cheeks and held up my hands. Christ, I hardly knew where to start. "Basically...I've been possessed...by a demon..."

"Jesus Christ, Gus," Fergal said. "How'd you let that happen?"

"I couldn't stop it," I said.

"Why not?" Roisin asked.

My mother answered the question for me. "Because it's Santos," she said in horror.

Fergal and Roisin looked at each other, then at me, and then finally at Max.

"Surprise motherfuckers!" Max shouted, his eyes glowing red now.

My brother and sister instinctively backed away from him. "What the fuck?" Fergal said aghast.

"How can this be?" Roisin said in horror.

"Ask your mother," Max said. "She knows. Or ask your little brother. He knows better than anyone." A wicked smile came across his face as he looked at me.

"The fucker marked me after he killed all of you," I said.

"Yes," Max cut in. "He's only alive right now because he said he was coming here to—" He sniggered to himself. "—*rescue* all of you. Of course, you all know why I'm here, don't you? Especially you, Brenda. I imagine it was your doing that you all managed to escape my domain." He shook his head, and then instantly appeared beside my mother, pressing his face toward hers. "I need to know, Brenda, how did you do it? Tell me now!"

My mother took on a frightened look as she stepped back, and then at the same moment, the door opened and LeBron walked in. "I'm back!" he announced, as if we'd all somehow missed him.

In the blink of an eye, Max disappeared. "Goddamnit!" he screamed inside me.

"What's the matter, Max?" I said. "Afraid of LeBron?"

"Fuck you, Creed!"

"He can hurt you, can't he?"

"He can fucking try!"

"You'd best behave then."

"Screw you! Screw all of you!"

I couldn't help but laugh out loud.

"I'm glad you are in good spirits," LeBron said as he came forward. "I think it's time we all talked now..."

# ULTIMATUM

"$\mathcal{A}$ll right, boys and girls, let's get started," LeBron said like he was some school teacher about to teach a class. He stood in the center of the room, still wearing his shiny red suit. He smiled and clasped his hands together as he was about to speak again. "As I said, I have a proposition for you all...the McCreedy family..." He smiled again as if that was funny to him.

"Are you going to ask us to work for you again?" my mother said.

"Yes, as a matter of fact," replied LeBron. "And much like last time, you will not have much of a choice. But let's not get ahead of ourselves just yet. Let me first explain to you what I have planned for this place."

"You mean the Gray Lands?" I said. "The place that doesn't actually belong to you."

"We've already discussed that," he said. "Like or not, I own this place, and that's how it will stay."

*Jesus*, I thought. *The arrogance of thinking he was getting one over on the powers that be.*

"Well, he is, isn't he?" Max said.

*For now.*

"Anyway," LeBron went on. "I have big plans for this place, but I will need more energy, in the form of souls, to bring those plans to fruition."

"So you need to create more draining chambers," Roisin said.

"Yes," LeBron said. "That will be necessary."

"So where do you plan on getting more souls?" I asked. "I would have thought the millions you have here already would suffice."

"If only that were so," he said. "But alas, my plans call for a lot more than that. I need *billions* of souls."

"*Billions?*" I said.

"Yes, and when I can harness enough soul energy, I am going to make this place into a new Earth, only better."

"One which you control, of course," my mother said.

LeBron nodded his head slightly. "Of course, my dear. It will be my playground, after all. But not just mine; it can be all of yours too. Think about it, a place similar in every way to the Earth you knew, only magic won't be hidden like it is on Earth. For magicians like you, that would be a blessing, to say nothing of the blessing of getting a second chance at life. A life that will last an eternity, because well...you are already dead."

"And to live in this paradise, all we have to do is work for you," Fergal said. "Doing what?"

"Whatever I require of you," LeBron said. "Magic will play a big part in my new world, and I will need accomplished magicians to help me run it. I'm humble enough to admit that such a massive undertaking as creating a whole new world might be too much for me to handle alone. I will need trusted acolytes to help me, and in return, said acolytes could have anything they wanted."

My mother sighed and shook her head. "LeBron, we have no interest in staying here to help you build your fantasy world. Please, just allow us to move on. I have no doubt there are plenty of others here that you could ask for help."

LeBron's smile was strained. "You would think so, but there really isn't. Magicians are rare in the Gray Lands, and I will need people of your skillset."

"So that's a no then?" Fergal said, already knowing the answer.

"I don't know how many more times I have to say it," he said beginning to pace the room. "None of you are getting out of here. Ever. Including you." He pointed at me. "So you either agree to help me and live out your afterlife in complete luxury, or I put you all back in the Draining Chamber, and you will still contribute to my new world, only in a much less enjoyable fashion. I will drain every one of you until there is nothing left." He stopped pacing and looked at each of us turn. "So you see, you don't really have a choice, do you? Unless the Draining Chamber holds some special appeal that I'm not aware of, does it?"

No one answered as we stared at him.

"Well, does it?" he shouted.

We all shook our heads then, and my mother sighed. "No," she said, speaking what we were all thinking.

"I can't believe you are going along with this nonsense," Max said. "The man is clearly fucking deranged."

"Yes," I thought back. "He also holds all the cards at present. I don't have a choice until I can find a way out."

Right then, my whole body spasmed in pain as it felt like my ribcage was being crushed, and hot battery acid had replaced my blood. It wasn't long before I hit the floor screaming. "What is this?" LeBron demanded to know as my family gathered around me in concern.

"He has a demon in him!" my mother snapped.

"Oh yes, the demon," LeBron said. "That filthy thing is still here?"

"Yes, and it's killing him!" Rosin said.

"You can get rid of it," my mother said. "Do it! Before it kills him!"

"I can rid him of this parasite," LeBron said. "If you all agree to my terms."

"No!" Max screamed inside me. "He can't! Tell them, Creed! If he sends me back, I'll rip your fucking body to pieces! Tell them!"

"Wait..." I said, barely managing to raise a hand. "You...can't."

"Why not?" my mother asked. "We need to send that bastard back to the Underworld now!"

"He'll kill me," I gasped through the pain. "Part of him...is still in my body...on Earth..."

"Yes, that's right, motherfuckers!" Max shouted. "It's called insurance!"

"Fuck!" Fergal shouted. "That demon bastard!"

"What does it matter if he dies or not?" LeBron asked. "His soul will end up here anyway. In fact, I can guarantee it will."

The pain began to subside, and I sat up. "What the fuck are you talking about?" I asked him.

LeBron's smile became wider than usual. "I haven't told you yet how I plan on acquiring those billions of souls." He paused as if for dramatic effect, his eyes full of glee at what he was about to say. "I'm going to kill everyone on Earth."

He let that hang there for a long moment as we all stared at him. "What?" I said eventually.

"You heard me," he said. "What do you think I've been doing with all the soul energy I've been collecting here? I'll tell you. I've built a fucking bomb! The bomb to end all bombs! A bomb so fucking powerful, it will wipe out every single person on Earth in an instant, and then billions of souls will come flooding into this place, providing me with the energy I need to build a new world."

"You're fucking insane," Fergal stated.

LeBron drew back as if offended. "Insane? I don't think so. A visionary is what I am."

I had no cause to believe that LeBron was lying. I barely knew the man, but I knew his type, and I knew him to be completely capable of such a massive act of... what would you even call what he planned on doing? Terrorism? Theft? Complete and utter fucking madness?

My first thought was of Leona, and then Ray, both of whom would die like everyone else when LeBron triggered his bomb. My own body would be destroyed, and I'd be stuck here too.

"Think about it," LeBron said as he looked at me. "What would you really be losing, Creed? Your loved ones would still be with you here. It would be just like they were alive on Earth. I would see to it." He held his hands out like some politician delivering a speech. "People, there is no downside to what I'm proposing here. I am offering you everything in exchange for your loyalty, that's it. But, if you are foolish enough to turn me down, there is always the Draining Chamber, and your eventual, inevitable wiping out of existence." His wolfish smile widened. "I know which option I would choose..."

"You're crazy if you think you could ever get away with such a thing," my mother said.

"My dear," LeBron said. "I already have."

"What do you mean?" I asked him as I stood up, albeit weakly.

"It means that my bomb is built, and ready to be transported by me to Earth," he said. "In a few hours, there will not be a single living soul left on Earth, and that...that is a fact, boys and girls. Now are you with me or not?"

My mother shook her head. "We could never be complicit in such a heinous, unspeakable act of terrorism," she said.

LeBron snorted and shook his head in disappointment. "You know what?" he said, a hard edge to his voice now. "Maybe you are not the smart people I thought you were. Maybe—"

He got no further, because I pulled out my gun and shot him in the forehead with a chaos bullet. My mother and sister screamed in shock at the sudden loud noise, and Fergal cursed out loud.

LeBron staggered back a few steps, his face registering his complete shock at being shot point blank in the head...as you would. It was my last bullet, or I would have shot him again. But it was also a chaos bullet, so I didn't think I would have to anyway. I had yet to see anybody, supernatural or otherwise, stand up to a chaos bullet.

Though as it turned out, LeBron became the first person to do so. He leaned over as he gripped his head with both hands, crying out in pain. Then the bullet that should've been still embedded in his brain, squeezed its way out of the entry wound and fell to the floor with a small thudding sound. LeBron then stood up straight and breathed out forcefully, as if he'd just did a massive line of coke. "Fuck!" he shouted as the hole in his head began to close over. "That hurt! But also...what a fucking rush!"

Before he could fully recover, I tried a Paralysis Spell on him, backed up first by my mother, then by Fergal and Roisin as we all said the words to the spell together, putting all of our combined magic behind it. If we could paralyze LeBron for even a minute, it would give me enough time to finish the bastard properly with my knife. Being a living soul, if he dies here so to would his body, wherever it was. Of course, his soul would end up here once more, but by the time that happened, it would be too late for him, because I would release all the soul energy he'd been using to gain power. He'd be just another soul then.

Which would've been all well and good, had the Paralysis Spell worked on him. It should have worked, given that four powerful adepts were casting it. But all four of us were extremely weakened, and as it turned out, no match for someone of LeBron's power. With one angry wave of his hand, he sent us all flying across the room, smashing us into the wall.

"Fools!" he cried. "Did you really think your puny magic would be enough to hold me? You are even stupider than I thought."

"No," Max said as I lay dazed on the floor. "Just desperate."

LeBron walked over to us. "And to think I had such high hopes..." He shook his head in disgust. "My men will be along shortly to escort you all to the Draining Chamber. In the meantime, I have travel plans."

"You can't do this!" I shouted.

LeBron thrust his hand out and used his power to lift me off the floor, pinning me against the wall. "Don't dare tell me what I can and cannot do. You are speaking to a soon to be god."

I laughed then. "You know I met a guy like you just recently. He thought he was a god as well."

"Oh yeah?" LeBron said. "What happened to him?"

"I stopped him. He's dead now. Probably in the Underworld somewhere, which is where you're heading. I'll see to it myself."

LeBron laughed and shook his head at me. "You know, I *was* going to finish you all and be done with it...*right now*. But I don't think I will. I think I'll keep you around so you can see the world that I build. I might even find every soul you've ever loved or cared about, and I might make you watch as I make their lives a living hell, worse than anything the Underworld has to offer. Then, and only then, will I consider destroying your souls for good. How does that sound?"

He let me go, and I fell to the floor, my body wracked with pain once more from the demon possession. "I'll come after you, LeBron," I said wincing. "You know I will. Your fucking minions won't be able to keep me here..."

LeBron bobbed his head from side to side. "I beg to differ, but just in case..." He closed his eyes for a moment, his body stiffening slightly. I could see he was working his power, but I wasn't sure what for.

"There," he said after opening his eyes. "I just created a little insurance policy to make sure you stay here, Creed."

"What are you talking about?" I asked him.

"Well, it's like this, Creed," he said. "If you try to leave this realm and come after me, your family will cease to exist. Their survival is completely dependent on you remaining in this realm. I know you desperately want to be the hero and stop me from wiping out billions of people on Earth, but we both know you won't go down that path if it means your mother dearest, and your two siblings, die...for good. We also both know you would never be able to stop me anyway, even if you did somehow manage to come after me, so...you might as well get comfortable. All of you. I'll be back soon enough...with several billion souls in hand."

"You're bluffing," I said.

"Am I? Why don't you test the theory, Creed?" He smiled then, as if he'd thought of something. "I tell you what, Creed. Let's make this interesting, shall we? I will instruct my men to let you leave this realm not long after I do. They won't try to stop you. So now, the only two options you face are: option one, save your family, or option two, *try* to save several billion people on Earth.

"So what do you think, Creed? Am I bluffing? What will you do, I wonder?" He laughed as he started to walk away. "I look forward to finding out..."

"LeBRON!" I roared after him. "YOU FUCKING BASTARD!"

# GOODBYE

*I* was on my feet, pacing the room, fucking beside myself over what to do. There was very little doubt in my mind that LeBron was telling the truth. What sliver of doubt did exist was based only on the spurious notion that he had seemingly cast such a powerful spell so quickly. There would have been a lot of intricacies, and a lot of power required, to cast the spell in such record time. It *could* be done, *if* you had access to nearly unlimited power, which LeBron had in the form of the soul energy he had collected.

"That fucking asshole!" Fergal said, back on his feet now as well, along with Roisin and my mother. "He's really going to mass harvest billions of souls."

"Just so he can build another world here," Roisin said.

"One that he controls," my mother added.

I turned and looked at them at all as if they had a screw lose in their brains. "Who the fuck cares about his motives?" I said shaking my head. "Don't you know what he's done?"

The three of them looked at each other as if they shared some common consensus, then they looked at me. "We know what he's done," my mother said.

"Then why the fuck are you not freaking out?" I asked.

My mother smiled and walked up to me, placing a hand that I barely felt on my cheek. "August, my son," she said. "You know what you have to do."

I looked right into her faded eyes and shook my head, even though, deep down, I knew she was telling the truth. "No..." I said. "I'm not...I can't..."

"You have to, Gus," Fergal said as he came toward me. "That crazy fool is going to wipe out the Earth's entire population. We all know he isn't bluffing about any of it. We know he has the means to do it."

"And he will do it, Gus," Roisin said, coming closer as well, making me feel like they were ganging up on me. "You know he'll kill all those people."

"Including Ray," Fergal said.

"And Leona," my mother added, surprising me.

"How do you know about Leona?" I asked, then shook my head. "Never mind..."

"Just go, little brother," Fergal said. "You're the only one who can save all those people."

"But..." Tears streamed down my cheeks. "You'll all die...you'll cease to exist anymore."

Roisin was crying now too, and I really wasn't sure if they were tears of joy or sadness. "We know," she said.

I looked at Fergal, and the second I did, barely visible tears rolled down his cheeks. "Brother..." I said, suddenly realizing I was going to miss him all over again, only worse this time.

The three of them moved toward me, and we huddled together as a family one last time, our heads slightly bowed as we looked at each other through wet eyes. "August," my mother said, barely managing to hold her reassuring smile. "I am so proud of the man you have become, of the things you have done to help others. You turned out exactly how I thought you would, how I always hoped you would."

"Mother..." I could barely speak.

"I love you, Gus," Roisin said. "My little brother..."

Fergal gripped the back of my neck, and I actually felt his hand squeeze as he pulled my head against his. "I'm proud of you, little brother, you hear me?"

I could only nod.

"You go now, and you get that bastard," he said. "You make sure he suffers for what he's done, all right?"

"Oh...he'll fucking suffer all right," I said through gritted teeth. "I'll make sure of it."

We all stayed hugging for what seemed like too short a time, until it became obvious that I would have to leave them to their fates if I was going to have any chance at all of stopping LeBron. My mother stepped back first, then Roisin, and then Fergal.

Leaving me standing alone.

My mother smiled her beautiful smile at me, and I knew it would be last time I ever saw it, a fact which seemed to rip my guts out going by the pain I felt there. "Go now, son," she said. "Do what I brought you into this world to do. I love you."

"I love you, Gus," Roisin said.

"Love you, little brother," Fergal said.

With the tears still pouring from my eyes, I said, "I love all of you..."

Making myself move, tearing myself away from them, was the hardest thing I have ever had to do. I just kept thinking to myself that it wasn't supposed to be like this, that they were supposed to come home with me...

The only thing that got me moving was the deep anger I felt for LeBron, and the thought of him doing what he was going to do.

I didn't have a choice.

I had to try and stop the bastard.

I *would* stop him. I was damned if I was going to let the deaths of my beloved family members be in vain.

As faded as they now were, I gave each of them one last loving glance, before turning my head and walking toward the door.

I barely got two steps before I heard the voice of Max behind me. "Not so fast," he said. "I'm not leaving until I get what I came here for."

About to turn around, my condemnation for Max was curtailed when the door opened and Moira walked into the room looking beat to hell. She could barely walk as she came tumbling into the room. "Moira!" I said as I ran to her. "Are you all right?"

Moira held out a hand as she straightened up. "I'm fine..."

"You don't look it," I said. "What happened?"

"LeBron left me with some of his men, saying he would be along later to see to me." Dark gray blood ran down her face as she spoke. "I managed to escape. Then I hear that LeBron has left. Is that true?"

"It's true." I looked behind me to see Max listening intently as my mother spoke to him. Then I turned back to Moira. "You still after a lift home?"

"More than ever."

I nodded. "We have to go now then."

"What's going on? Where's LeBron?"

"I'll explain on the way." I turned around again, and shouted to Max. "Let's go!"

Max disappeared, and then spoke within me. "Don't have a heart attack on my account, Creed," he said.

"You get what you need?" I said staring at my family, the pain of doing so killing me, but I didn't care if I was getting to see them. "Like I even care."

"Yes, I did, though it wasn't what I expected—"

"Don't care."

My family all waved to me. After waving back, I looked at them one final time, and then turned and left the room, rage and sorrow about to boil over in me. Which I hoped they did.

But only when I caught up with LeBron.

Then I would teach him the meaning of pain.

# 3 0

# NO TIME

$\mathcal{W}$e made it out of the mountain lair without much trouble. A few of LeBron's more loyal men tried to stop us, but I swiftly dealt with them using only my fists, which I was more than happy to do, except for the fact that I was now on a clock. LeBron was probably on Earth by now, preparing to set the bomb to end all bombs.

"We're never going to make it," I said when we got outside to the desert. "There's not enough time. By the time we cross the desert on foot..." I shook my head in despair.

"I can teleport us to the portal," Max said.

"What?" I said aloud.

"What?" Moira said.

"Max said he can teleport us to the portal, even though he said he couldn't teleport us on the way here," I said.

"So I lied," Max said. "Big deal. I'm a demon. Now do you want a lift or not?"

I sighed and shook my head. "Just fucking do it."

As soon as I grabbed Moira's arm, we vanished and reappeared in front of the portal leading to the Astral Plane. Torrents of souls still poured through it, and I couldn't help but think what a cruel joke the whole cosmic system was.

Moira stood staring in wonder. "I've never seen this. I can barely remember coming through it."

"Fascinating," I said bluntly. "Jump aboard now, come on..."

"What?" she said staring at me. "I don't know how."

"Just think of me as a portal and walk inside. I've already used a spell that will allow me to receive your spirit."

She nodded like she was unsure of the whole thing. Under normal circumstances, I would have gently lead her through the whole process of inserting her spirit self inside of me, but these were not normal circumstances, and I didn't have the time or the patience to fuck about. "Okay," she said. "I just walk...into you, right?"

"Yes, just come forward..."

"What if it doesn't work?"

"For fuck's sake..." I stamped forward and pulled her roughly toward me. She then disappeared as if she had fallen into a black hole.

"Fuck, this is weird," Moira said from inside me. "It's like being you...only not."

"Don't crowd me please," Max said.

"I'm sorry, I don't—"

"I said don't crowd me!"

"How am I—"

"Enough!" I shouted aloud. "The two of you, shut the fuck up!"

"Feeling a bit enraged, Creed, are we?" Max said.

"I'm fucking warning you, Max," I said. "If you don't stop I will make it my fucking mission to hunt you down in the Underworld and destroy your demon ass, even if you fucking kill me, I'll still find a way. You hear me?"

"He can be very convincing when he wants to be," Max said quietly to Moira. "He'd make a great demon..."

I closed my eyes for a second as I took a deep breath. There was no time to be pissed at Max. Max could wait.

Running toward the portal, I jumped off the ground and dived into the swirling red mass of energy, soon finding myself once more in the shadowy Astral Plane. Then, once I'd cast a Direction Spell, I sped off toward the Earthly Plane, praying that I wouldn't be too late when I got there.

\* \* \*

THEY SAY THE JOURNEY ALWAYS SEEMS QUICKER ON THE WAY BACK. THANKFULLY in this case, that turned out to be true. My journey back through the Astral Plane seemed to take half the time it did before, perhaps because I wasn't attacked by any astral predators, or maybe just because Max wasn't talking incessantly this time, or perhaps even because my every action was being fueled by pain and rage. More so because, for a second there before I left the Gray Lands, I actually thought there was a slim chance that LeBron really was bluffing. Not about the bomb. I was certain he wasn't bluffing about that. But about my family ceasing to exist once I went through the portal. The second I went through, though, I realized I was kidding myself if I thought my family was still in existence. A man like LeBron, though mad as a hatter, didn't kid when it came to using his power to hurt others. He was a classic sadist, and was probably loving this little game he had going with me, more so than if he had killed me outright. But that is always their biggest weakness, isn't it? Hubris. The need to prove their dominance over others. The need to be the smartest one in the room at all times.

Only they aren't always the smartest.

Are they?

\* \* \*

I EXITED THE ASTRAL PLANE THROUGH THE PORTAL IN SANAKA'S SANCTUM.

Landing in the room, I was met, not by Sanaka, but by Ray, who was sitting on a chair next to my physical body, which still lay on the floor in the same position.

"It's about bloody time," Ray said standing and stretching as if he had been sitting for ages. "I thought you were never coming back."

"Ray?" I said in surprise. "What are you doing here? Where's Sanaka?"

"I was worried about my only nephew," he said. "I had to come, to make sure you were all right."

"And Sanaka?" I said looking around and seeing no sign of my mentor.

Ray shook his head, as if he didn't quite know how to explain where Sanaka was. "He had to leave...on an emergency."

"Emergency? What kind of emergency?"

Ray came forward and placed his hands on my arms. "Don't worry about him, he's fine. You know Sanaka, always the mysterious type. The important thing is, you're back."

There seemed to be more to the story than Ray was letting on. Sanaka would never have left my side unless he was forced to, which told me whatever had caused him to leave suddenly, it must have been serious. I decided to let it slide for now. There were more important things to worry about. If Sanaka was in some kind of trouble, I was confident he could handle it himself.

I smiled somewhat forlornly at Ray. "You know me, Ray, I'm like a bad penny..."

"Well, your body is waiting, son." He gestured down at my physical form. It was like looking down at a corpse. I hardly recognized myself. It seemed like Max's presence had been taking its toll on my body while I was away. My skin was an ashen gray, and my eyes looked sunken. Pretty much what I would have looked like as a ghoul, had my father's curse taken full effect at the time.

"Is that a fucking boil on my neck?" I said in disgust.

"Yes, that's a common outbreak on the possessed," Max said. "It will clear up once I'm gone."

"You're actually leaving?"

"Yes. Itchy feet. Count yourself lucky you survived me, Creed. You're the first."

"I'm flattered."

Moira chose that moment to make her exit, or should I say, entrance. "Are we...on Earth?" she asked as she looked around the room.

"Who is this?" Ray asked, more bemused than surprised. "Did you pick up a hitchhiker, August?"

"Something like that," I said. "Ray, this is Moira. She needs a body."

"What's wrong with the one she has?"

"Eh, she's a ghost..."

"I'm just kidding. I suppose you want me to..."

"If you could, yeah. I've got a more pressing matter to deal with." I walked forward and lay down on top of my physical body, as it and my astral form became one again.

"Anything I can help you with?" Ray asked as he took my hand and helped me up. My body felt stiff and sore, and shockingly weak. I didn't know how I was supposed to hunt LeBron in this state, never mind stop him.

"Yes, actually," I said, wincing at the pain in my body. "First, I need to find someone right away, and second..." I trailed off as wooziness made me unsteady on my feet.

"Woah," Ray said grabbing my arm. "You can barely stand. You need to rest and recuperate."

I shook my head. "There's no time...I can't."

"Why not? What's going on, son?"

I shut my eyes as I became overwhelmed, not only by the pain and weakness, but by the despair that came from the fact that I was in no state to go after LeBron. I couldn't even fucking hold myself up!

"It's me doing that to him," Max stated as bluntly as ever as he now stood next to me in the form of Evil Creed.

"No shit!" Ray said glaring at Max, showing a rare glimpse of anger. Obviously Sanaka had passed on his All Seeing Spell to Ray before leaving. "I think it's time you left, demon. I trust you got what you wanted already?"

Max nodded. "I did actually, which surprised me because I thought—"

"I don't care what you thought, demon," Ray snarled. "Leave my nephew and go back to the Underworld where you belong."

"No..." I barely managed to say. "I need him..."

"Need him?" Ray said. "What the bloody hell for?"

"LeBron...teleport..."

"You're not making sense, August. Who or what is LeBron?"

"I think he's trying to say that he needs me to teleport him to LeBron, the fool who is trying to blow this world up," Max said. "As neither of you two can teleport far enough if need be. Am I right, Creed?"

I nodded. "He stays..."

Ray shook his head, confused now. "If he stays much longer he'll kill you, son."

"I hate to say it," Max said. "But your uncle is right, Creed. You're on your last legs, my old son."

They were both right. I was dying. There was no doubt about that. Max had to go. At least until I could heal. "Possess Ray instead," I said.

"What?" Ray said still holding me up. "Absolutely not! There is no way in fucking hell I'm letting that filthy, disgusting thing inside—"

"Ray!" I said clutching at his chest. "This is life or death...trust me."

"Then possess someone else," Ray argued.

"THERE'S NO FUCKING TIME, RAY!" I screamed suddenly. "THERE'S NO TIME...THERE'S—"

The world went black.

## 31

# BATTLE READY

*I* woke up half screaming in a panic, to find myself lying on a chaise lounge in Sanaka's living room. Moira, or at least her ghost, was standing over me. "It's okay," she said reassuringly. "You're safe, Creed."

I sat there blinking for a moment as my focus gradually recovered, and I soon realized that I was feeling physically a whole lot better than I did before. "What happened?" I asked Moira.

"You basically collapsed into a coma," Ray answered. I hadn't realized he was in the room. He was sitting over by the fireplace puffing on his pipe. "I worked my magic on you, though. You can thank me later."

"Thanks, Ray," I said as I swung my legs off the seat. "What about..."

"The demon?" Ray said. "Oh, he's right here inside of me, driving me fucking crazy for the last hour. August, son, how did you put up with him for so long?"

I ignored his question, because I couldn't get past the fact that I'd been out for a whole hour. "LeBron," I said. "We have to do the Location Spell...now!"

"Already done," Ray said.

I looked at Moira, and she nodded. "You won't believe where he is," she said.

"I think August knows where he is already," Ray said, before blowing out a long stream of smoke.

"Blackham," I said without hesitation.

"You must have made some impression on the man for him to want to detonate his bomb in your home town," Ray said.

I shook my head. "Motherfucking psychopath...I have to go, *right now*." I spotted my trench coat draped over one of the chairs, and I went and put it on, as if I was a soldier gearing up for battle. A quick check told me that my magic reserves were at maximum thanks to Ray's rejuvenation methods. "I'll be needing Max back as well."

"With pleasure," Ray said as he stood up, tensing for a second as Max's spirit left his body and jumped into mine.

"Hello again, Creed," Max said. "Feeling better, I see."

"Yeah," I said. "No thanks to you. This is just temporary. Don't get too comfortable in there."

"I have no intentions of sticking around after I take you to where you need to go. I'm curious though, why don't you teleport yourself? Anyone would think you like me being in you."

I tutted in disgust. "As if. I'm just conserving my magic."

Max laughed. "I will miss you, Creed."

"I'll miss you too, Max...like a fucking hole in the head," I said. "Now take me to LeBron."

"Wait," Ray said, as if he'd heard my conversation with Max. "I'm coming with you."

I shook my head. "This isn't your fight, Ray."

"Bollocks it isn't my fight," he said. "I live on this planet as well, don't I, along with the billions of other people this asshole LeBron is planning on blowing up. Not my fight..." He shook his head again in annoyance.

"All right, fine," I said. "I don't have time to argue with you."

"No, you don't."

"Can we just go now?" Max said. "I'm becoming bored by all these heroics."

"You should be sticking around to help, Max," I said. "This is your playground, is it not? How would you get your fun if there's no one here to...do what you do with?"

"There are other worlds in the multiverse. Earth is not the only fruit. Far from it."

"Fine, whatever," I said. "Take us where we need to go, then you can fuck off forever."

"No need to be so tetchy, Creed. You humans, so easily offended, so..."

"Whatever, Max," I said aloud, then looked at Ray. "Let's go, Ray."

Ray had his battered brown trench coat on now. He also held his centuries old Druidic staff. "Ready," he said as he grabbed my arm.

"What about me?" Moira asked from across the room. "Am I supposed to just hang around here?"

"Make yourself at home," Ray said. "Just stay out of the East wing."

"What's in the East wing?"

We had already teleported before Ray could answer.

# PLAYING FIELDS

e landed in Gadsden Park, which was situated across the river in Bankhurst. According to Ray, this is where LeBron is supposed to be. We stood just outside the front entrance of the Zoo, memories of my recent protest here coming back to me; memories that would probably have brought a smile to my face if current circumstances were not so dire. "This park is massive," I said. "LeBron could be anywhere."

"Don't worry," Ray said holding up his staff. "He won't be hard to find."

"Time for me to leave now, Creed," Max said. "I'd like to satisfy a few urges before there is no one left on this planet to kill."

"Thanks for the vote of confidence there, Max," I said.

"Well, I'll say this for you, Creed. If anyone can stop LeBron, it's you, and your...uncle. You know your uncle has a very weird inner life?"

"Isn't everybody's inner life weird?"

"Where humans are concerned, I suppose you are right."

"Thanks for the lift, Max," I said as I looked around the park for signs of LeBron, and seeing nothing but darkness and shadows. "Sure you don't want to stick around? Your power could prove useful."

"No, thanks," Max said. "I'm sure you can handle it, Creed."

"Fine. Just don't blame me when there's no one left to play with."

"You'll be the first person I'll blame."

"I'm sure of that."

Max laughed. "Well, Creed, it's been real, as you humans say. Try not to get everybody killed."

"Fuck off."

He exited my body in a rush at that point, his spirit moving invisibly through the night to God knows where. Probably into the body of some other chump, who most certainly wouldn't survive the experience the way I did. If anyone survived this night, that is.

"I have a lock on LeBron," Ray said as he pointed his staff toward Cedar Lake and the playing fields beyond. "He's that way."

"Are you sure?" I asked him. "We only get one chance at this."

Ray threw me a look. "Who do you think you are talking to, some apprentice?"

I shook my head. "Of course not. I'm just..."

"I know." Ray held his hand out. "Come. I'll teleport us over there."

When we landed near the playing fields, I looked around and couldn't see anyone, and then Ray pointed with his staff to the center of the field. Squinting in the darkness, I saw a hunched figure, the half moon barely providing enough light to create an outline around it. "That's him," I said with certainty, my anger beginning to rise once more as I thought about my family, and what LeBron had done to them.

"We should call for backup," Ray said. "Just to be on the safe side."

I shook my head as I focused on the figure in the middle of the field. "There's no time, and who would we call anyway?"

"I've already tried to contact Tetsuo...again."

"And?"

"He may be off world. I got no response."

"Then it's just us."

"It would seem that way," Ray said. "Let's go and get this bastard."

Just as we started to move toward LeBron, the sky above his head seemed to tear as a small portal of reddish energy began to form, glowing against the dark backdrop. "Fuck," I said halting mid-step. "That can't be good."

"He's opened a bloody portal!" Ray said.

My hand slipped inside my trench coat and pulled out the Druidic knife from its sheath. "Not for long."

My focus was on LeBron as I started running toward him, my boots thumping loudly on the wet grass, which LeBron obviously heard, because he turned around. A smile came over his face as he saw me running at him, my arm up as I held the knife behind my head.

LeBron waited, still smiling at me as the portal continued to open.

When I got to within six feet of him, I threw the knife as hard as I could, with a shout of rage-filled aggression. I had practiced the same throwing technique thousands of times at the Sanctum, so there was no doubt in my mind that the knife would find its target in LeBron's chest.

And it would have done, had LeBron not been standing inside a protection circle that completely shielded him from outside forces. The knife seemed to halt in mid-air as it came into contact with the virtual forcefield LeBron was standing behind. The forcefield sparked slightly as the knife hit it, and then the knife itself fell harmlessly to the ground. "Motherfucker!" I cursed as LeBron laughed and shook his head.

*Time to try a different tact*, I thought, as I concentrated on welding my magic. I tried the brute force option first, to see if I could simply tear a hole in LeBron's forcefield, but it resisted the violence of my magic. Sparks of energy shot out all around LeBron, as I continued to batter at the forcefield to no avail.

"You'll never break through, Creed," LeBron goaded. "Your magic isn't strong enough."

"Maybe not," Ray said, now standing beside me. "But mine is."

LeBron didn't seem overly concerned by Ray's threat. "Do your worst, old man. My money is on the shield."

Ray's face set into a serious scowl as he pointed his staff in LeBron's direction, sending bolts of blue energy from out of the staff, to try and blast right through the forcefield. He even brought down a blast of lightning from the sky, but to no effect. After several more high-powered blasts, it was clear that he wasn't making a dent. "Brute force isn't working," Ray said.

"No shit," I said, barely able to contain my frustration, not to mention my ever growing hatred for the smug bastard currently grinning at us like the cat who got the fucking cream.

Ray and I spent the next five minutes throwing every spell we could think of at LeBron and his protective shield, but we got nowhere. In the end, I was reduced to walking right up to it, and battering on the invisible wall with my fist, like some pathetic drunk who'd been locked out of the house by his wife. "I'm going to fucking kill you, LeBron!" I screamed.

"I think that should be the other way around," the smug bastard hit back. "I'm the one who is going to kill *you*...and everyone else."

I let out another scream of frustration as Ray came up next to me, his concerned face not exactly filling me with confidence that we we're going to stop this crazy bastard.

"I must say, Creed," LeBron said, putting his face right next to mine. "I'm surprised to even see you here. I didn't think you'd have the balls to leave your family to die...for good that is," he finished with a chuckle.

My anger wanted to boil up again, but I managed to keep it under control. All the energy I had expended in trying to break the forcefield had left me feeling a little calmer. I still hated LeBron with every fibre of my being; I just didn't show it as much. Thus, LeBron got the dead-eyed stare, instead of the rage-filled glare. "Tell me again that you weren't bluffing about that," I said.

"I wasn't bluffing," he said straight away. "Your family is no more. Is that clear enough for you?"

"Crystal," I said nodding, even though it was gut wrenching to see that he was obviously telling the truth.

"Good." He stepped back into the center of his protection circle. "Now if you don't mind, I have souls to harvest."

"Where's the bomb, LeBron?" I asked.

LeBron laughed hard, and did so to the point where I felt like screaming. "The bomb? Please tell me you are not that stupid, Creed."

Just then, a torrent of bluish-white energy burst out of the portal above LeBron's head, and all the energy began to pour into him as he rapturously received it with open arms.

Then I understood.

There was no physical bomb, no contraption with wires and a detonator button.

LeBron was the fucking bomb.

## 3 3

# STRANGLEHOLD

$\mathcal{R}$ ay and I could only watch as the soul energy kept pouring from the portal and into LeBron. "Can he even hold that much energy without..."

"Exploding?" Ray said. "We'll soon see, although I think exploding is the point."

"Yeah, but not until he has enough to..."

"Blow up the whole damn world?"

"Exactly."

Ray looked grimly on as megaton after megaton of magical energy somehow managed to enter LeBron's body and stay there without imploding within him. "What the hell are we going to do, August?"

My head turned slowly to look at Ray, as if he had just told me he had slept with my mother. "You're asking me? You're the master wizard here..."

"So what the fuck are you, son? Some second year apprentice? Think!"

I'd never seen Ray so rattled, not even when we stood up against Gordon Grayson, which already seemed like a lifetime ago. I'll be honest, him being so rattled, it rattled me as well.

But he was also right. It was my show. Mine and LeBron's. It was up to me to finish it. The question was how, though. LeBron was too powerful, as all these power hungry bastards seem to be in the end.

*Though that hasn't stopped me before.*

It was an empowering thought, and one which got me to thinking: how did I manage to beat the other psychopathic assholes I stood up against in recent times? How did I ultimately beat my father, Baal, Gordon Grayson and all the rest over the years? They all had one weakness: their ego. These guys were so arrogant they thought they couldn't be beat, and that always tripped them up in the end, because they inevitably ended up underestimating me.

I just needed LeBron to do the same.

Walking to the forcefield, I stopped just in front of it as LeBron soaked up the last of the soul energy coming through the portal. He practically glowed with all the energy he had contained inside of him. Hard to believe the man standing in front of me held the explosive capacity of a thousand nuclear bombs, but with a far greater reach than any ordinary bomb. A reach that would stretch around the whole planet.

"Can you feel it, Creed?" LeBron boasted, so fucking high he looked like he had just snorted a whole kilo of cocaine in one huge line. "Can you feel the power coming off me. It's...glorious!"

"I'm sure it is," I said. "Maybe if you stopped hiding behind this forcefield and step out of that circle, I might be able to feel it. I mean, it's not like I can stop you now, is it? I doubt anyone can."

LeBron smiled widely. "You are right, no one can stop me now...and no one will."

"At least let me feel all that power before you blow us all to hell."

"You want to feel my power?" He chuckled to himself. "Are you coming on to me, Creed?"

"Not likely. I just want to know what all that soul energy feels like."

LeBron cocked his head to one side. "I see what you are doing, Creed. You are trying to lure me out, aren't you?" He shook his head. "You still think you have a chance at stopping me, don't you?"

"Of course not, I—"

"Don't lie!" He took a few steps forward, and I realized with almost nervous excitement that he had finally dropped his forcefield. "The hero in you thinks he can still save the day. Well, come on, Creed." He beckoned me toward him. "Come on! Try to stop me, Creed!"

For the first time, LeBron was now vulnerable, though it was questionable just how vulnerable a man of his current power could actually be, even without protection around him.

*Let's fucking see then.*

In an instant, I conjured the strongest energy ball that I could, and hurled it at LeBron with all my might. The power of the blast would have been enough to take down whoever stood in its path, or at least knock them on their ass.

But not LeBron, who merely splayed his arms as if he welcomed the energy I threw at him, absorbing it into himself as if it was just more grist for the mill. Then he laughed. "Is that all you've got?" he asked. "This isn't going to be a very fair fight at all."

"Who said anything about fair?" Ray said, who had slyly positioned himself to the side of LeBron. Then, before LeBron knew what was happening, Ray used his staff to cast an Encasement Spell, which effectively trapped LeBron in a bubble of yellowish energy. As LeBron shook his head and began to push against the energy surrounding him, Ray looked at me. "It won't last long. Drain him, August!"

I didn't need to be told twice. It took me just a few seconds to work up the magic needed to begin draining LeBron of the soul energy he had within him. Both my hands were out facing LeBron as I directed my magic toward him. When I had connected with his stolen energy, I started to pull it out of him, and then send it back through the portal from whence it came.

LeBron flew into a rage at that point, and needless to say resisted me all the way. But by the time he was able to free himself, I had siphoned off at least half of the soul energy that was in him.

But it still wasn't enough. LeBron still had more power than either me or Ray could contend with. He was so angry now that his skin began to glow a hot reddish color, as if the energy left in him was heating up, the atoms becoming agitated along with his emotions. He then shot out a hand toward Ray and hit him with a blast of energy that lifted Ray off his feet, shooting him back into the air as surely as if he had been hit by a cannon ball. I could only watch in horror as Ray's body was flung several hundred yards, eventually disappearing into the darkness and landing at the far end of the playing fields.

"No!" I shouted, feeling sure that there was no way Ray could survive such a great fall intact. In my anger, I went to attack LeBron again, but before I could, he held me in an invisible grip that was as strong as any vice.

"I suppose you think that little stunt was clever," LeBron said as he came toward me. "All you've done is delay the inevitable. I'll get every drop of that energy back, but not before I kill you, Creed, which I should have done long before now."

I struggled against the power he was using on me, trying to break it with my own. But even with half his power gone, LeBron was still much stronger than me. "Come on then, motherfucker!" I screamed in frustration, knowing in my gut that the game was up. It was over, and LeBron had won. "Fucking kill me then! Come on!"

He ran at me, and slammed his fist into my face, shattering my nose and knocking me to the ground where I lay choking on my own blood. "With pleasure," he said as he sat on top of me, like a cage fighter about to finish his opponent with a burst of ground and pound.

"Fuck you!" I said, spitting blood at him.

Wiping the blood from his face, LeBron stared down at me. "You know what? With all this magic around, sometimes I forget about the unique satisfaction that comes from using your bare hands to do a job. In this case, that job would be beating you to death, Creed."

His fist came down on my face again, smashing my already busted nose. Then another fist swung down into my jaw, and then another and another until I felt my mandible crack.

"Oh yes!" LeBron said. "That feels good..."

The hits kept coming as his fists pounded at my face, each punch coming with a roar of effort as he put everything he had into every punch. In no time, my face and neck were wet with blood, and I lay half conscious, totally unable to fight back. It's hard to think about defensive magic when you're getting the face pounded off you.

Then I felt LeBron's large hands wrap themselves around my throat, and begin to squeeze.

"Once upon a time," he said, breathing hard, having tired himself out throwing all those punches. "I used to kill people exactly like I'm about to kill you now. I would wrap my hands around their throat, and then I would squeeze until all the life was squeezed out of them, like air from an old tire..."

I tried to say, "Fuck you," as I lay looking up at him through eyes that stung with blood, but nothing came out because of the pressure he was putting on my throat, his thumbs sinking deep as they pressed on my windpipe.

"Don't worry, Creed," LeBron said as the world started to fade around me, the blackness of death swallowing it up slowly but surely. "I'll see you on the other side, where I'll subject you to more pain and punishment than you could ever dream of..."

# FUCKING DIE YOU CUNT

*I* was on the verge of slipping away into oblivion when I felt the pressure on my neck suddenly stop, and the weight of LeBron no longer on me. I was still basically unconscious though, so I couldn't really figure out what was going on. All I could do was lie there as my lungs took in oxygen again, and my mouth filled up with blood. It wasn't until I heard a voice that my mind started thinking straight again.

"All right, Creed, time to get up now. Let's go!"

It was Max's voice inside me. "What...why..." I barely said back to him.

"I just saved your life. You can thank me later. Now get the hell up before he's on you again!"

I felt a jolt of pain in my chest, as if someone had just zapped me with forty volts. I couldn't help but gasp and sit bolt upright, the world suddenly spinning into dizzying view again. "What the..."

"I put him down for you," Max said. "He won't stay down for long, though. In fact..."

As I looked straight ahead, I saw LeBron pick himself up from off the ground and shake his head, as if someone had clocked him on the jaw. Our eyes met for a second. "I see your stinking demon has come to your rescue," he said as he stood up. "For all the good it will do you."

Almost in slow motion, I saw him raise his palm, as a sphere of swirling red energy formed in it. Then he drew his arm back slightly as he prepared to send the destruction magic my way. My instincts took over at that point, thank God...if I'd been waiting on my mind to protect me, I'd be dead.

As the blast magic came speeding towards me, I raised one arm and formed a magic shield in front of myself, formed from a thin layer of bluish magical energy. The blast magic hit the shield and got absorbed into it, the impact almost knocking me back.

A surge of adrenaline went through me then, enough for me to get to my feet and face LeBron. My focus was laser sighted. The only thing I could see in front of me was LeBron and his grinning face as he realized I wasn't ready to go down yet. Not by a fucking long shot, and certainly not because of him.

"You looking for round two now?" he asked me, then shook his head as if he couldn't be bothered. "You've wasted enough of my time, Creed. I think I'll just go ahead and set the world on fire now, if that's all right with you."

"Aren't you forgetting something? You only have half the energy you need. You'll have to siphon it out of the portal again. You think I'm going to let you do that?" I focused hard on him as the rage built up inside me once more. "You'll have to fucking kill me first, asshole."

LeBron made a snarling sound as he realized I was right. "You can be most fucking infuriating, you know that?"

"I do."

"So be it." He conjured another ball of blast magic in his hand and threw it at me, which I blocked with my shield. Then, before he could get another blast off, I conjured my own and fired it at him, catching him on the head and knocking him back on his ass.

He looked surprised for a second that I was able to knock him over, but his surprise soon turned to anger and aggression as he brought up his own shield, and then used his other hand to direct a continuous steam of blast magic at me. My shield absorbed most of the blast, but I could begin to feel it weaken under the strain, especially because I now had to counter with my own stream of blast magic, which LeBron's shield also absorbed.

As LeBron jumped to his feet, and we continued to blast each other with our respective magic, I realized it had now come down to a battle of wills...and power.

It was just a question of whose power would give out first, and after a few moments, I soon realized it would most likely be mine.

As did LeBron.

"You are not strong enough to defeat me!" he shouted as he started to push me back, further weakening my shield and the stream of blast magic.

I screamed in effort as I tried to turn the tables and force him back, but after straining massively, I had to concede that I was getting nowhere. All the while, LeBron kept getting closer.

Then suddenly my shield gave in completely, and the blast magic it had been protecting me against got through and hit me square on the chest, slamming me into the ground as surely as a ten ton hammer would.

"Where has your heroics gotten you now, Creed?" LeBron said as he stood over me. "I'll tell you where...soon to be dead like everyone else on this planet."

"Did I save you just so you could die?" Max asked bluntly.

It was a fair question, and one which stuck in my craw. "*No*," I said aloud.

"No what?" LeBron asked.

I focused on his face, noticing with satisfaction the glimmer of shocked fear in his eyes when he looked into mine. "No one is dying tonight...except you."

As LeBron shook his head in mock boredom, I gathered within myself every ounce of magic I had left, which wasn't much at all by that point...which is why I had to try a different tact.

"What...what are you doing, Creed?" Max asked.

The truth is, I wasn't even sure what I was doing. I didn't have enough magic left to attack LeBron with, so I borrowed some of Max's power instead. Don't ask me how I did it. All I know is, I couldn't die without avenging my family. In my mind, I had already failed them when I didn't get them safely out of the Realm of the Dead. I wasn't going to fail them again by letting the man who wiped them out of existence go on living.

No fucking way.

So in the process of digging deep to scrape up my remaining magic, Max got pulled into the fray, and I was able to tap into his considerable power, despite his protestations.

"Creed, I don't like this," Max said, for the first time ever sounding afraid of something. "You're stealing my power...invading me..."

"Now you know how it feels, Max," I said as a massive surge of power traveled around my body, which I then focused into a single sphere of blast magic.

"Again?" LeBron said. "Really? If it didn't work the first time, it's not going to—"

I fired the bowling ball sized sphere of blast magic at his chest as hard as I could. When it hit, he was knocked right off his feet, as he then went sailing back several yards before landing with a hard thump.

As I clambered back to my feet, so did he.

"Time to end this," he said. "I think I'll just take half the planet, and come back for the other half later, when you are good and dead, Creed."

A smug smile came over his face, and I realized what he was about to do.

"No!" I shouted.

Reality seemed to slow down at that point. Suddenly all of my rage, hatred, sorrow and grief focused into a single stream of emotion that seemed to empower me more than the magic did.

LeBron was about to detonate himself.

Without thinking, I ran at him, as hard and as fast as I could, because it seemed like the only thing to do. I thought that if I could get to him, I could stop him. That was the only thought going through my mind as I charged at him, and he continued to stand there with a maniacal grin on his face.

There was logic in my actions too, underneath all the aggression and raw emotion, a logic I didn't comprehend, but which was there nonetheless: magic of any kind takes concentration, and if a person can't concentrate, they can't wield magic. It's that simple. Blowing himself up with soul energy would be an act of magic. I just had to make sure he couldn't focus long enough to complete that act.

So I charged into the cunt like a raging bull, knocking him hard to the ground, hearing his lungs empty of air as I fell on top of him.

*I can't let him finish...I won't let him finish...*

Before LeBron could recover, I straddled him. Then I began to beat his head and face with my fists.

*He can't focus, he can't blow us up...*

With each successive punch, the rage and hatred I was feeling intensified as the punches got harder, and more numerous.

*If he can't think...*

I kept punching, screaming now like a mad man. "FUCKING... DIE...YOU...CUNT..."

777

With every punch thrown, I saw the faces of my family, my mother, my brother...my dear sister.

"AAAAHHHHHHHH..."

I felt my knuckles crack as I broke the bones in his face, pulverizing the soft tissue, smashing his eye sockets, destroying his nose; teeth and blood flying everywhere after every blow.

The punches only slowed down when I became physically incapable of swinging them anymore, due to exhaustion. Raising myself up, I hit him one final time, and then nearly collapsed on top of him.

"FUCK YOU!" I screamed at him, and I realized that tears were streaming from my eyes now, making it difficult for me to see the pulverized lump of meat that used to be LeBron's head.

When I rolled off him, I lay on the cool grass crying and shaking, the pain of loss like a knife in my belly, and seeming greater than it ever did before.

# TOO OLD FOR THIS SHIT

"*I* always knew there was a killer in you, Creed," Max said as he stood over me.

I didn't answer him at first as I looked over at LeBron, who lay motionless on the grass, his bloody face misshapen and unrecognizable after the beating I gave him. I was calm but exhausted, my grief having turned to cold disregard for the man I just beat to death. "Fuck him," I said.

Max smiled. "His soul still lingers. I can see it. Perhaps I can drag his butt back to the Underworld with me..."

A small laugh escaped me. "His ass," I said. "You'll drag his *ass* to the Underworld."

"That's what I said."

"You said butt."

"Whatever..."

I soon managed to drag myself to my feet as I stood to face Max. "I don't understand, Max."

"Don't understand what, Creed?"

"Why did you come back?"

Max smiled and remained silent for a moment, before finally answering, "I knew you would only get yourself killed if I didn't."

I shook my head. "I didn't think that would bother you. You going soft, Max? Maybe you're spending too much time with us humans."

"A strange feeling came over me, that's all."

"What feeling?"

"Something I've never felt before. Well, I have, but only in humans. I felt torn."

"Torn?"

"Yes."

I smiled. "It's called doing the right thing."

"Do you think you did the right thing in killing him?"

I looked down at LeBron's stiffening body. "Absofuckinglutely."

"I'm pleased to hear it. Maybe one day I could teach you some of my tricks. I know ways of killing humans you could never even imagine..."

I held a hand up. "I don't think so. I didn't kill the son of a bitch for pleasure, you know."

"You don't know what you're missing."

"I think I'll be fine."

A brief silence ensued as I stared at my bloody knuckles. I'd killed men before, but never with my bare hands. Never in so animalistic a fashion.

"Afraid it felt good, Creed?" Max asked.

I shook my head. "Shouldn't you be getting back now, before LeBron's soul escapes?"

"Deny your instincts if you want. You forget I know you better than you know yourself. I know what's inside you, Creed..."

"Jesus," I said. "You never stop, do you? You're like a fucking recruiter for Murder Inc."

Max laughed. "We'll part ways then...for now."

When Max's spirit finally left me, and he had taken himself and the soul of LeBron away to the Underworld, I muttered, "Don't hurry back..."

I let out a deep breath then, as it was just me and LeBron's corpse left behind.

"And Ray..." I suddenly said. "Oh Jesus...Ray!"

I sprinted off across the playing fields in search of Ray, hoping that my uncle was all right. The blast magic he was hit with, and the massive fall he would've taken, didn't fill me with confidence that I would find him in good shape...or alive even.

Dawn was beginning to break, giving me just enough light to see by as I searched the playing fields for signs of Ray, calling his name as I went.

Then I found him lying unconscious on the grass. "Oh fuck..." I breathed as I went to him, praying he wasn't dead. I couldn't lose another family member.

He was all I had left.

Relief washed over me as I noticed he was still breathing at least, and I gently shook him a few times. "Ray...it's me, August...wake up, Ray, please..."

Ray's eyes suddenly opened, and he started coughing and spluttering as he clutched at his chest. "Bloody hell," he said. "That hurts..."

I couldn't keep the smile off my face, despite the obvious pain he was in. "You're okay, Ray."

Ray continued to lie on the grass for another moment while he got his bearings. "I'm sure I've said this before," he said wincing. "But I bloody mean it this time: I'm getting too old for this shit."

"You could be right."

He shook his head. "Smartass. What about LeBron? As we're still here, I take it you dealt with him."

I nodded. "Yes."

Ray stared at me a moment, seeing something in my eyes that made his face soften. "Come on," he said. "Help an old man to his feet, will you?"

After helping him up, I then had to search for his staff, which he said he wouldn't be leaving without. I handed it to him once I'd located it nearby. "There you go, old man," I said with a smile. "There's your walking stick."

"You can mock, son. One day you'll be as old as I am, and then..."

"I'll still be doing the same shit."

Ray smiled and put a hand on my cheek. "I hope so, son," he said. "I hope so..."

# WHEN PEOPLE MAKE PLANS...

$\mathcal{R}$ ay decided his old bones needed some resuscitating (his words, not mine), so he said he was heading off to Sanaka's Sanctum so he could bathe in the Resuscitation Bath. Apparently getting tossed across a field like a football wasn't good for the back. When I pointed out that Sanaka wasn't home, Ray said he wouldn't mind him using the place, and that they "had an arrangement".

Once Ray had teleported away, I called Brentwood and told him about the corpse in the park, telling him only as much as he needed to know so he could send his people to pick up LeBron's body and dispose of it. He still sounded a little off with me, which was unsurprising, given recent events. But he would get over it, he always did, if only because he knew he needed my skillset more than he cared to admit. And hell, if he wasn't used to my brand of crazy yet, he never would be.

I used the little magic reserve I had left to teleport into my Sanctum. The living room to be precise. I froze slightly when I noticed Blaze lying on the floor a few feet away. He immediately jumped to his feet and eyed me with cold suspicion. "Take it easy, buddy," I said raising my hands. "It's me this time. The demon is gone. I promise."

Blaze raised his thick snout as if to sniff the air for a few seconds, and then his yellow eyes softened somewhat. A second later, he padded over to me, and I bent down to greet him, pulling him in so I could hug the big bastard. "Sorry about before, buddy. It couldn't be helped. You been looking after Leona for me? Is she here?"

"She's right here."

Slightly startled by the voice, I looked to see Leona standing in the doorway, wearing just a black T-shirt. She must have came down the stairs from bed.

I smiled at her as I stood up. Blaze made a few small mewling noises before heading off to the kitchen like he wanted to give us privacy. I didn't know what else to do except stand and stare at Leona. I didn't know what to say to her.

A frown of concern came over her face as she noticed the state of my face, and she came toward me and gently touched my face with her hand. "Jesus, Creed, what happened?"

My smile widened for a second as tears stung my eyes. All I could do was shrug, as if I didn't know where to start.

"Creed?" she said, her voice gentle for once.

I puffed my cheeks out as if I didn't know what to say. "I..."

Leona waited a second before speaking. "Tell me."

"My family..." I couldn't say anymore, as I was afraid if I did I would break down completely.

Leona gave a small sigh as she came and put her arms around me, pulling me in tight. "Oh, Creed," she said in a small voice. "I'm sorry..."

There wasn't much else to say.

I just held her and cried.

* * *

LATER, AFTER I'D FINISHED TELLING LEONA ABOUT EVERYTHING THAT HAPPENED in the Realm of the Dead, and about my confrontation with LeBron—and after a good half a bottle of Glenfiddich—Leona fell into contemplative silence for a few moments, and I was happy to let her. I was tired of talking anyway, though not as tired as I was of the pain and loss that seemed to be such a constant in my life these days. I couldn't even save my family, and they were dead already. Who was going to be next? Ray? Leona? It was something I didn't want to think about as I poured myself another drink. When Leona spoke again, I was glad of the distraction.

"I've come to the conclusion that this will always be our lives," she said as we sat together on the sofa. "There will always be this...chaos."

"Chaos? Isn't everybody's life just a state of chaos?"

"Maybe, but not quite like yours."

"Don't you mean ours? Our life?"

"I guess they're one in the same now."

"Does that scare you?"

"Does it scare *you*?"

I shook my head. "Not at all. Do you think you're making a mistake?"

"I think it's more like I'm taking a leap of faith," she said. "There's no training for this."

I broke into a smile. "No, soldier, there definitely isn't. You just gotta take each day as it comes."

"As you do?"

"Sure."

"You make it sound so easy. I'm used to planning, order, neither of which are a big factor in your life."

I leaned over and kissed her. "I know it's scary, but you couldn't be in better hands."

She shook her head. "That's what scares me."

I was about to come back at her with a witty rebuttal when I heard the front door being knocked. Throwing my head back, I sighed. "Who the hell is that?"

"Probably a potential client," Leona said. "I've been discretely advertising our services."

I looked at her in surprise. "Wait, what?"

"I asked a few of the people I helped out to spread the word, that's all. It would surprise you how many people have troubles of the supernatural kind in this city, especially now that it's all out in the open. There's no more bogeymen. When people see a monster, or experience something supernatural, they know exactly what it is now. They don't run scared, they get help. From us."

I nodded, impressed. "Glad to see you're taking this partnership so seriously."

"I am, I just need you to take it seriously as well."

The door knocked again, but I ignored it. "I couldn't take it any more seriously than I already do."

"I know. I just mean you need to be more organized about things, instead of— that's the door again. You better go answer it."

"They'll leave in a minute."

Another long knock sounded, louder than the last one, and I set my glass on the table. "Fuck's sake...don't they know what time it is?"

"It's nearly six in the evening."

"Exactly," I said getting up. "At least wait until after dinner."

"Where you taking me, by the way?" Leona said as I walked to the hallway. "Somewhere expensive, I hope."

"Actually." I paused in the doorway. "I was thinking the cabin for a few days. I need the peace and quiet."

She raised her eyebrows. "The cabin? Even better. Can I bring my bow?"

"What for?"

"To hunt us some rabbits, obviously. I make a mean rabbit stew. Old family recipe."

"Sounds awesome," I said with slight sarcasm, before walking to the front door.

"It is awesome, I'll have you know..."

The door started banging again before I got to it. "Jesus," I said loudly enough for the person on the other side to hear. "I'm coming..."

When I opened the door, I was surprised to see Jennifer standing there. I didn't even need to see the tears of blood running down her face to know that something was wrong. I felt it immediately.

Jennifer said nothing for a moment as she just stood there staring at me, as if she expected me to intuit what the problem was.

"Jennifer," I said. "What's wrong?"

"It's...it's..." She started shaking her head. "I shouldn't even be here..."

She was starting to scare me, I'll tell you the truth. Jennifer doesn't usually exhibit such frightened behavior. If she was scared, something was badly wrong.

"Come inside," I told her.

She seemed reluctant for a second, but stepped inside.

Then Leona appeared in the hallway. "Creed?" she said. "What's going on?"

"This is Jennifer," I said. "Angela Crow's daughter."

Leona just nodded warily. It was her first time seeing Jennifer in the flesh.

"Come into the living room," I said to Jennifer, and she nodded and followed me in, before I directed her to take a seat as I sat down next to her. Leona remained standing.

"I didn't know where else to go," Jennifer said in a small voice.

"That's okay," I said. "You're always welcome here, you know that."

"Did something bad happen to you?" Leona asked, and I threw her a look for her bluntness.

Jennifer nodded. "You could say that..."

"What exactly?" Leona said.

Jennifer turned her head and looked at me then, her eyes filled with blood. "They killed her, Creed," she said.

"Killed who?" I asked, although I already knew who she was talking about. I just didn't want to believe it.

"My mother," she said. "My mother is...dead."

I let out a long breath as I shook my head in disbelief. The grief and sorrow that was already in me in abundance came to the fore again, and I closed my eyes for a second. Then the questions inevitably started running through my mind: who killed Angela, and why? How the fuck did they kill her, and why did Jennifer, or Angela's legion of vamps, not stop it from happening?

Leona and I exchanged glances, and she raised her eyebrows slightly as if to reference our earlier conversation.

*Well*, I thought. *It looks like we'd have to postpone that rabbit stew...*

# NOTE TO READER

It is with some sadness that I must inform you that I will not be continuing with the *Wizard's Creed* series. The decision is a purely business one. Just like TV networks cancel a show when it doesn't pull in the ratings, I've had to cancel this series because it simply was not pulling in the sales. As disappointing as this, please bear in mind that as a full time author my main priority is to feed my family by putting bread on the table, and to do that I have to make sales of my books. Spending another four or five months writing more books for a series that isn't pulling its weight in terms of earning me a living would not be the best use of my time, and as reader, I hope you can respect that. As an author, my time would be better spent writing a new series that likely will bring in more sales to enable me to keep writing and providing people with stories.

I have grown rather fond of Creed since I conceived him, and I will miss going on his adventures. I realize the last book ended on something of a cliffhanger, so if it helps:

Angela Crow was killed by the corporation that Jennifer Crow worked for on Babylon. Jennifer stole the blueprints for tech that would allow the corporation to gain mass control over Earth's citizens. Creed went after the corporation and its leader, eventually forcing them to vacate Earth altogether. Jennifer then took her place at the head of the Council that oversees all supernatural activity throughout the world. As for Sanaka's mysterious disappearance, it turns out he was abducted by an old foe from many years ago who wanted revenge over something that Sanaka did. Creed managed to track Sanaka down and helped him defeat his abductor.

As for Creed and Leona, they finally got their vacation in the cabin in the woods, where they managed to conceive a child. Nine months later, a little girl named October Creed was born...

Once again, I hope you enjoyed the series. I also hope you will check out my other series and join my mailing list for news about future series as well.

*Slainte!*

# THANKS FOR READING

Thank you for reading the book. I know there are a lot of great books out there vying for your attention, so I'm privileged that you chose mine.

Be sure to sign up to my Reader Group and be the first to hear about new releases, cover reveals and special promos. Plus get access to my private fans only Facebook group:
http://www.npmartin.com/n-p-martin-reader-group/
Thanks once again for reading!

Neal

# CORVIN CHANCE SERIES

They knew I was back. I don't know how, but they did. *Who?* you might ask. Well, I'll tell you who, once I figure out who's following me and then do something about it, of course. At this point, as I walked along the Lower Ormond Quay with the River Liffey flowing to the right of me, I was more inclined to avoid whoever was following me. I'd only just arrived back in Dublin after a stay in London, and I was in no mood for confrontation.

I was picking up on goblin vibes, though I couldn't be sure until I laid eyes on the cretin. I did, however, know that Iolas employed goblins to do his dirty work for him, as the wiry little bastards were sneaky and good at blending in unseen.

As I moved down a deserted side street, hoping my pursuer would follow me, I weighed up my options. There were a number of spells I could use: I could create a doorway in one of the walls next to me and disappear into the building; or I could turn myself to vapor and disappear that way; or I could even levitate up to the roof of one of the nearby buildings and escape. Truthfully though, I didn't like using magic in broad daylight, even if there was no one around. Hell, I hardly used magic at all, despite being gifted with a connection to the Void—the source of all magic —just like every other Touched being in the world. Despite my abilities, though, I was no wizard. I was just a musician who preferred to make magic through playing the guitar, real magic that touched the soul of the listener, and not the often destructive magic generated by the Void.

Still, Void magic could come in handy sometimes, like now as I spun around suddenly and said the word, "*Impedio!*" I felt the power of the Void flow through me as I said the word loudly, and as I looked down the street there appeared to be no one there.

Only I knew there was someone there. I walked quickly back down the street and then stopped by a dumpster on the side of the road. Crouched behind the dumpster was a small, wiry individual with dark hair and pinched features. He appeared frozen as he glared up at me thanks to the spell I had used to stop him in his tracks, preventing him from moving even a muscle until I decided to release him.

"Let me guess," I said. "Iolas got wind I was coming back, so he sent you to what... follow me? Maybe kill me, like he had me ma killed?"

Anger threatened to rise up in me as blue magic sparked across my hand. Eight words, that's all it would've taken to kill the frozen goblin in front of me, to shut down his life support system and render him dead in an instant. It would've been so easy to do, but I wasn't a killer... at least not yet. If I was going to kill, it had to be the right person, and this creature before me was not the right person.

The goblin was straining against the spell I still held him in, hardly able to bat an eyelash. To an ordinary eye, the goblin appeared mundane, just a smallish, weasel-like man in his thirties with thinning hair and dark eyes that appeared to be too big for his face. To my Touched eye, however, I could see the goblin creature for what he really was underneath the glamor he used to conceal his true form, which to be honest, wasn't that far away from the mundane form he presented to the world. His eyes were bigger and darker, his mouth wider and full of thin pointed teeth that jutted out at all angles, barely concealed by thick lips like two strips of rubber. His skin was also paler and his ears large and pointed.

"I don't know what you're talking about," the goblin said when I released him from the spell. He stood up straight, his head barely level with my chest. "I'm just out for a stroll on this fine summer evening, or at least I was before you accosted me like you did..."

I shook my head in disgust. What did I expect anyway, a full run down of his orders from Iolas? Of course he was going to play dumb, because he *was* dumb. He knew nothing, except that he had to follow me and probably report on my whereabouts afterward. Iolas, being the paranoid wanker that he was, would want eyes on me the whole time now that I was back in town. Or at least until he could decide what to do with me, as he probably saw it.

"All right, asshole," I said as magic crackled in my hand, making the cocky goblin rather nervous, his huge eyes constantly flitting from my face to the magic in my hand. "Before you fuck of out of it, make sure Iolas gets this message, will you? Tell that stuck up elf... tell him..."

The goblin frowned, his dark eyes staring into me. "Go on, tell Iolas what?" He was goading me, the sneaky little shit. "That you're coming for him? That you're going to kill him for supposedly snuffing out your witch-bitch mother—"

Rage erupted in me then, and before the goblin could say another filthy word, I conjured me magic, thrusting my light-filled hand toward him while shouting the words, "*Ignem exquiris!*"

In an instant, a fireball about the size of a baseball exploded from my hand and hit the goblin square in the chest, the force of it slamming him back against the wall, the flames setting his clothes alight.

"*Dholec maach!*" the goblin screamed as he frantically slapped at his clothes in an effort to put the flames out.

"What were you saying again?" I cocked my head mockingly at him as if waiting for an answer.

"*Dhon ogaach!*" The goblin tore off his burning jacket and tossed it to the ground, then managed to put out the remaining flames still licking at his linen shirt. The smell of burnt fabric and roasted goblin skin now hung in the air between us.

"Yeah? You go screw yourself as well, after you've apologized for insulting my mother."

The goblin snarled at me as he stood quivering with rage and shock. "You won't last a day here, Wizard! Iolas will have you fed to the vamps!"

I shot forward and grabbed the goblin by the throat, thrusting him against the wall. "Firstly, I'm a musician, not a wizard, and secondly—" I had to turn my head away for a second, as the stench of burnt goblin flesh was atrocious to my nostrils. "Secondly, I'm not afraid of your elfin boss, or his vampire mates for that matter."

Struggling to speak with my hand still around his throat, the goblin said in a strangled voice, "Is that why... you ran away... like a... little bitch?"

I glared at the goblin for another second and then let him go, taking a step back as he slid down the wall slightly. His black eyes were still full of defiance. He was tenacious, I'd give him that.

"I've listened to enough of your shit, goblin," I said, forcing my anger down. "Turn on your heels and get the hell out of here, before I incinerate you altogether." I held my hand up to show him the flames that danced in my palm, eliciting a fearful look from him. "Go!"

The goblin didn't need to be told twice. He pushed off the wall and stumbled quickly down the street, turning around after ten yards as he kept walking backward. "You've written your own death warrant coming back here, Chance," he shouted. "Iolas will have your head mounted above his fireplace!" His lips peeled back as he formed a rictus grin, then he turned around and ran, disappearing around the corner a moment later.

"Son of a bitch," I muttered as I stood shaking my head. *Maybe it was a mistake coming back here*, I thought. I should've stayed in London, played gigs every night, maybe headed to Europe or the States, Japan even. Instead, I came back to Ireland to tear open old wounds... and unavoidably, no doubt, to make new ones.

Shaking my head once more at the way things were going already, I grabbed my guitar and luggage bag, and headed toward where I used to live, before my life was turned upside down two months ago, that is.

As I walked up the Quay alongside the turgid river, I took a moment to take in my surroundings. It was a balmy summer evening and the city appeared to be in a laid back mood as people walked around in their flimsy summer clothes, enjoying the weather, knowing it could revert back to dull and overcast at any time, as the Irish weather is want to do. Despite my earlier reservations, it felt good to be back. While I enjoyed London—as much as I could while mourning the death of my mother—Dublin was my home and always had been. I felt a connection to the land here that I felt nowhere else, and I'd been plenty of other places around the world.

Still, I hadn't expected Iolas to be on me so soon. He had all but banished me from the city when I had accused him of orchestrating my mother's murder. He was no doubt pissed when he heard I was coming back.

*Fuck him*, I thought as I neared my destination. *If he thinks I'm going to allow him to get away with murder, he's mistaken.*

Just ahead of me was *Chance's Bookstore*, the shop my mother opened over three decades ago, and which now belonged to me, along with the apartment above it. It was a medium-sized store with dark green wood paneling and a quaint sort of feel to it. It was also one of the oldest remaining independent book stores in the city, and the only one that dealt in rare occult books. Because of this, the store attracted a lot of Untouched with an interest in all things occult and magical. It also attracted its fair share of Touched, who knew the store as the place to go if you wanted to get a hard-to-find book on magic or some aspect of the occult. My mother, before she was killed, had managed to form contacts all over the world, and there was hardly a book she wasn't able to get her hands on if someone requested it—for a price of course—and that price was often high, not just in terms of money, but in favors owed.

As I stood a moment in front of the shop, my mind awash with painful memories, I glanced at my reflection in the window, seeing a disheveled imposter standing there in need of a shave and a haircut and probably also a change of clothes, my favorite dark jeans and waistcoat having hardly been off me in two months.

Looking away from my reflection, I opened the door to the shop and stepped inside, locking it behind me again. The smell of old paper and leather surrounded me immediately, soliciting more painful memories and a sense of deep sorrow as images of my mother flashed through my mind. After closing my eyes for a second, I moved into the shop, every square inch of the place deeply familiar to me, connected to memories that threatened to come at me all at once.

Until they were interrupted, that is, by a mass of swirling darkness near the back of the shop, out of which an equally dark figure emerged with two slightly glowing eyes glaring at me.

Then, before I could muster any magic or even say a word of surprise, the darkness surrounding the figure lashed out, hitting me so hard across the face I thought my jaw was broken, and I went reeling back, cursing the gods for clearly having it in for me today.

*Welcome home, Corvin,* I thought as I stood seeing stars. *Welcome bloody home...*

# THE NEPHILIM RISING SERIES

Nephilim Rising is my first urban fantasy series, and there are a total of six books in the series. The series tells of Leia and her struggles against demons and her troubled past. These struggles take her all the way to Hell, in which two of the books are set. If you've ever wondered what Hell might be like, these books will give you some idea. It's a fun but brutal adventure series packed with action, humor and a little bit of romance. Below you can read a sample chapter from the first book, *Hunter's Legacy*.

*  *  *

For a few seconds, I stood frozen to the spot, staring at Frank as he fired off two more rounds, each shot making me flinch. Then Frank turned and yelled, "Get to the bedroom and stay there! GO NOW!"

My mouth was opening and closing like a fish out of water, opening and closing without any words coming out. Then I heard a sound that was halfway between a screech and a snarl, sounding like it came from the mouth of some foul creature. What the hell kind of demon made a sound like that?

Whatever it was, Frank started advancing down the stairs toward it, rapidly firing shot after shot as he did so, filling the landing with clouds of smoke. My heart was hammering so hard in my chest, I thought it was going to burst. There was so much fear-fueled adrenaline bursting at the seams of my system, that I hadn't even the first clue as to how to handle it.

My mind obviously did, though, as I found myself backing away into the closest bedroom, which happened to be Diane's.

Downstairs, I heard a roar coming from Frank that chilled me almost as much as the sound of the demon he seemed to still be fighting with.

In the bedroom, I stood by the dressing table, catching sight of myself in the mirror. My face was covered in sweat, and I was white as a sheet. I couldn't look any more terrified if I'd tried. At least in the alley that night with Kasey, it looked like a man standing in front of me, despite the demon inside, which made the situation easier to deal with. Now, though, I was trapped in the house with demons who sounded like real monsters, and probably fucking looked like monsters as well.

Downstairs, the sounds of struggle between Frank and the demon increased. As Frank had stopped shooting, I assumed he was now going hand to hand with whatever demon was attacking him.

*You have to help him.*

I don't know where the thought came from. It was like someone put it there. I looked at my face in the mirror again, and said to myself, "You can do this. You were *born* to do this."

Somehow, just saying those words helped me cut through my fear, allowing my power—my grace—to spread throughout my body, until it felt like my every nerve ending contained a tiny electric current that combined to create one hell of a jolt.

A calmness washed over me, followed by a Zen-like state that made my fears seem like a distant memory. Suddenly, the whole room came into focus, and I became intensely aware of every detail, every micro movement, every sound. This awareness fanned out as far as downstairs, where Frank was still fighting the demon. Frank's breath was heavy, and I could almost sense his movements just by the way he was breathing. Same for the demon trying to kill him. I could sense it's total malevolence.

*Hang on, Frank...*

I went to rush out of the room so I could help Frank, and hopefully not die in the process (which strangely wasn't a primary concern at that moment), when a loud crashing sound from behind me caused me to spin around.

Something had just jumped through the bedroom window, landing near the bed, surrounded by broken glass. At first glance, I thought the creature looked human, as it remained crouched, its head down. But then I noticed the pitch black skin that seemed as thick as leather, and the long pointed ears jutting out of its bullet-shaped head.

When the creature slowly stood to its full height, I got a proper measure of it. There was no doubt it was a demon, but it was unlike any I'd ever seen before. So far, all I had seen were faces, as monstrous as some of them were. The demon in front of me, though, was the full package. It stood over six feet tall, and was densely muscled. It's basic anatomy appeared to be human, except for the lack of genitals, and the strange spikes that covered most of its body. The demon's face was also vaguely human, although its eyes were huge and black, and its mouth was filled with shiny, pointed teeth that were as obsidian black as the rest of it.

The demon suddenly dropped down to all fours and roared at me, making a sound so awful it hurt my ears and chilled my blood. The rest of the world seemed to disappear at that point, until it felt like there was just me and the demon, facing each other in some kind of void that only one of us could walk away from. I knew there would be no use in running. The second I turned my back, that fucking thing would be on me. The only choice I had was to stand and fight. The grace flowing through me was the only thing keeping me from turning tail...or falling to pieces in the face of such a terrible threat.

I had no idea what I was doing as the demon suddenly leaped toward me like a wild animal, and yet I was still able to instinctively jump aside to avoid the attack. I then lashed out unthinkingly, swinging my fist at the demon's head just as it landed. When my knuckles made contact with the demon's thick skull, I heard a cracking sound, and then a burst of pain shot up my arm. If it wasn't for the massive amount of adrenaline pumping through me, I might've been incapacitated by the pain. As it was, I just shouted, "Fuck!"

The demon turned to face me, its ugly mouth seeming to smile at me.

*This fucker is going to kill me.*

Under other circumstances, such a thought might've been enough to render me incapacitated with fear.

But not now.

Now I had genetics on my side. Now I had the certain knowledge that I was meant to be a soldier, someone who kept the monsters of the world at bay.

I had all the confidence at that point, but unfortunately none of the skill.

Perhaps prematurely, I went on the attack, and tried to strike the demon again, this time doing my best to load the strike with grace. I did manage to hit the demon on the jaw with my undamaged hand, but I didn't manage to channel much power into the punch. Worse, I lost my balance after landing the punch, and practically fell into the demon's waiting arms.

The demon lifted me and slammed me down hard onto the floor. Then it straddled my waist, it's weight making sure I couldn't move. After slapping me twice in the face with barbed-skinned hands, the demon grabbed my wrists, causing the pain in my injured hand to flare terribly again. It then leaned over me as it kept me pinned to the floor, its snarling face only inches from my own. Thick saliva dripped from the demon's sharp teeth, causing me to squirm uncontrollably as it landed on my face.

Its black eyes portrayed nothing but cold malevolence.

As strong as I was with my grace flowing through me (to some extent anyhow), the demon was stronger, and easily resisted my attempts to get out from under it. Panic wasn't far behind as I realized I was trapped, and probably about to die.

The demon opened its mouth wider, until it seemed like a gaping chasm getting ever closer to my face, about to engulf me. Turning my face to one side, I couldn't help but close my eyes.

*This is it, it's all over...*

But a second later, I felt the creature tense on top of me. I opened my eyes, and was faced with what appeared to be the tip of a knife no more than an inch from my face. The knife was sticking out of the demon's mouth, a silent scream frozen continuously upon its face. Its eyes were wide open, registering its shock. Then I noticed the hand that was gripping the demon's head, pushing it sideways as the knife was retracted, causing the demon to fall off me at last.

"Frank?" I said in equal parts shock and relief.

"I suggest you move," he said, just as the floor beneath started to get hot. I quickly got to my feet and looked down to see something like searing hot energy forming around the demon on the floor. Within seconds, the demon's body had fallen from sight into the now gaping hole in the floor, a hole which seemed close up as quickly as it had formed, leaving nothing but a large black scorch mark behind.

"What the fuck?" I said, wondering how much more craziness my mind could take in one day. "What just happened?"

Frank looked at me like he'd seen it all a thousand times. "A portal to Hell just opened up, and the demon fell into it. Can we go now, please, before more of these bastards show up, if they haven't already?"

I nodded. "I'm fine, Frank, thanks for asking."

Frank wiped the blade of his large knife on his jeans, then slid the knife into a sheath inside his jacket. 'Let's go."

Shaking my head, I followed behind him as he led us down the stairs. "Were they demons?" I asked as I stepped around a large scorch mark in the hallway, the remnants of the demon Frank had been fighting with.

"Lower demons, yeah," Frank said as we went through the front door. "Like attack dogs. They're called Pit Demons."

Attack dogs. Seemed like a good comparison to me. "Who controls them, though?"

Frank stopped suddenly as he neared his car, and whipped his gun out, aiming it down the street. "I'd say that guy there."

When I looked, I saw the rotund figure of a man about thirty yards away, standing in the middle of the street. At first glance, the man seemed normal enough, dressed as he was in a dark suit. But then that weird flickering thing happened, and the man suddenly became something much more demonic. He resembled a huge toad that stood on two legs, with the biggest mouth I'd ever seen. "Jesus Christ," I breathed.

"Go!" Frank shouted as he started firing shots at the advancing demon, none of which appeared to effect it much. "Take the Mustang and meet me on Clear Mountain Road."

"What? What about you?"

"It's you they want." Frank fired another burst of bullets. "Go now!"

I glanced once more at the demon in the street. It's blubbery body was oozing dark blood from Frank's bullet wounds, but it still kept advancing at an unhurried pace, as if it knew Frank couldn't hurt it.

*I hope you know what you're doing, Frank.*

As if to prove that he did, Frank shot down a Pit Demon that had been hiding in the bushes of Diane's house along with a number of others, their eyes glaring through the brush as they awaited unspoken instructions from the bigger demon. After shooting the first one, Frank pumped several bullets into the next Pit Demon to show itself. The rest stayed in hiding after that.

Turning, I ran to the Mustang and got in. As Frank continued to shoot at the demon, I frantically searched my jacket for the keys. When I finally found them, I started the ignition, then looked in the rearview mirror to see Frank reloading his gun, and the demon much closer to him than I would've liked. Once again, I hoped he knew what he was doing, though I was nonetheless in awe as I watched his fighting form in the Mustang's rearview mirror whilst still pulling away from the curb. He pivoted and turned, shot left and right, high and low, his body seeming to follow his head with the slightest of gaps, time enough to shoot and eventually reload; his ready mag clicking in at astonishing pace, his free hand whilst still free, stabbing and slicing with commensurate speed as he took on the demon. It was hard not to be impressed by such a show of fearless skill.

I drove off up the street, gunning the Mustang much too fast through the narrow city streets, on my way to the location Frank had given me. I was jacked up on so much adrenaline, I couldn't even hold a thought. The only thing I was focused on was getting to Clear Mountain Road, just outside the city.

By the time I got there, I realized I couldn't remember barely any of the journey. The first rest stop I saw, I pulled in and cut the engine. Silence then enveloped me in its claustrophobic grip. For long moments, I just sat there, staring out the window into the dark, completely numbed by everything that had happened.

Then I thought of Josh and Diane, and I started to shake uncontrollably. As soon as I said Josh's name out loud, I broke down completely and slumped against the steering wheel, where I stayed crying for a very long time.

* * *

**The Nephilim Rising Series is available from all good book stores.**

# BOOKS BY N. P. MARTIN

**The Corvin Chance Chronicles**

SERPENT SON
DEATH'S HAND
DEADLANDS
BLACK FAITH
WILD CARD
BOOK 6 (MAR 2019)

**The Wizard's Creed Series**

CRIMSON CROW
BLOOD MAGIC
BLOOD DEBT
BLOOD CULT
BLOOD DEMON

**The Nephilim Rising Series**

HUNTER'S LEGACY
DEMON'S LEGACY
HELL'S LEGACY
DEVIL'S LEGACY
BAD GRACE
LUCAS

# ABOUT THE AUTHOR

I'm N. P. Martin and I'm a lover of dark fantasy and horror. Writing stories about magic, the occult, monsters and kickass characters has always been my idea of a dream job, and these days, I get to live that dream. I have tried many things in my life (professional martial arts instructor, bouncer, plasterer, salesman...to name a few), but only the writing hat seems to fit. When I'm not writing, I'm spending time with my wife and daughters at our home in Northern Ireland.

Be sure to sign up to my mailing list:

http://www.npmartin.com/creed-mailing-list

And connect with me on Facebook:
http://www.facebook.com/npmartinauthor/

16865541R00430

Printed in Great Britain
by Amazon